F ZHA
Gold mountain blues /
Zhang, Ling, 1957-
908737

P9-DUM-174

eu NOV 12

LU NOV 2013

HD APR 2014

LC AUG 2014

NS SEP 2016

HD DEC 2018

GOLD MOUNTAIN BLUES

GOLD MOUNTAIN BLUES

LING ZHANG

translation by
NICKY HARMAN

VIKING
CANADA

VIKING CANADA

Published by the Penguin Group

Penguin Group (Canada), 90 Eglinton Avenue East, Suite 700,
Toronto, Ontario, Canada M4P 2Y3 (a division of Pearson Canada Inc.)

Penguin Group (USA) Inc., 375 Hudson Street, New York, New York 10014, U.S.A.
Penguin Books Ltd, 80 Strand, London WC2R 0RL, England
Penguin Ireland, 25 St Stephen's Green, Dublin 2, Ireland (a division of Penguin Books Ltd)
Penguin Group (Australia), 250 Camberwell Road, Camberwell, Victoria 3124, Australia
(a division of Pearson Australia Group Pty Ltd)
Penguin Books India Pvt Ltd, 11 Community Centre, Panchsheel Park, New Delhi – 110 017, India
Penguin Group (NZ), 67 Apollo Drive, Rosedale, Auckland 0632, New Zealand
(a division of Pearson New Zealand Ltd)
Penguin Books (South Africa) (Pty) Ltd, 24 Sturdee Avenue, Rosebank,
Johannesburg 2196, South Africa

Penguin Books Ltd, Registered Offices: 80 Strand, London WC2R 0RL, England

First published in China by Beijing October Literature and Arts Publishing House, 2009
Published in Viking Canada hardcover by Penguin Group (Canada),
a division of Pearson Canada Inc., 2011

1 2 3 4 5 6 7 8 9 10 (RRD)

Copyright © Ling Zhang, 2009
Translation copyright © Nicky Harman, 2011

All rights reserved. Without limiting the rights under copyright reserved above,
no part of this publication may be reproduced, stored in or introduced into a retrieval
system, or transmitted in any form or by any means (electronic, mechanical,
photocopying, recording or otherwise), without the prior written permission
of both the copyright owner and the above publisher of this book.

*Publisher's note: This book is a work of fiction. Names, characters, places and incidents either are the
product of the author's imagination or are used fictitiously, and any resemblance to actual persons living
or dead, events, or locales is entirely coincidental.*

Manufactured in the U.S.A.

Library and Archives Canada Cataloguing in Publication data
available upon request to the publisher.

ISBN: 978-0-670-06513-4

Visit the Penguin Group (Canada) website at **www.penguin.ca**

Special and corporate bulk purchase rates available; please see
www.penguin.ca/corporatesales or call 1-800-810-3104, ext. 2477

This book is dedicated to the ONE who sheds perpetual light on my path when darkness seems to prevail and engulf me; to a man whose shoulders and arms are a safe harbour for my restless soul; and to a mother and a father who have taught me, through means I may not have understood in my youth, how to labour, to achieve, and to wait.

Ling Zhang

PREFACE

꿍껳껳꿍

The idea did not occur to me last year. Nor the year before.

The idea came to me in my very first fall in Canada, when I arrived in Calgary from Beijing, China, in September 1986.

It was a sunny afternoon. Leaves were turning a prism of colours for a final desperate show of life before winter killed them. We, my friends and I, were driving around the outskirts of the city to catch a last glimpse of autumn, when we had a flat tire. While waiting for assistance, I started to explore the surroundings. It was then that I noticed them, the tombstones, scattered among the knee-high grass and covered by moss and bird droppings. Most of them had Chinese names carved on them, some with fading pictures revealing the young but weathered faces with harsh cheek-bones and hardly any smiles. Dates on the stones ranged from the second part of nineteenth century to the first part of twentieth century. These people died very young, possibly of unnatural causes. It didn't take long for me to realize that they were early Chinese settlers, or coolies, as they had once been called.

What kind of lives did they lead in their villages in southern China? Whom did they leave behind when they decided to come to the "Gold Mountain," a term they used to describe the wilderness of North America where gold deposits were discovered? What kind of dreams did they hold when they embarked on the harsh journey across the Pacific, not knowing whether they would ever return? What did they think when they first set eyes on the Rockies?

These questions started to form in my mind, dense and heavy. Of course I did not know that they would haunt me for many years to come.

A book. I could write a book about these people. I should, I told myself on the way home that day.

For the next seventeen years I flirted with the idea of such a book, but I was too busy. There were too many things needing my immediate attention: two academic degrees, a career as an audiologist, the right man to marry, a house I could call my own, a comfortable life in Canada. The idea of a Gold Mountain book got pushed down to the bottom of my to-do list. Every now and then, it would resurface, especially when I read in the news about the anniversary of the Vancouver riot, or the "Head Tax" compensation debate in the parliament, but I suppressed it as quickly as it appeared.

Then, in the fall of 2003, an unexpected opportunity presented itself to me. I was invited, together with a group of Chinese writers residing overseas, to tour one of the villages in Kaiping Canton, China, known for its unique residential dwellings called *diulau*, literally translated as "fortress homes." These houses were built with the money the coolies sent home, to protect the women and children they left behind, since this area was susceptible to flooding and bandits roamed the countryside. Since the coolies were scattered all around the world, the style of the fortress homes bore clear marks of the country where the money came from. One could easily detect baroque, Roman and Victorian characteristics weirdly moulded into southern Chinese architectural expression, not exactly a piece of eye candy.

Through the help of a smart local resident, we were able to slip into a fortress home abandoned for decades, and not yet remodelled for public display. On the third floor of the house, we found an old wooden closet. To my great surprise, I found a woman's dress. It was pink, embroidered with faded golden peonies and full of moth holes. I uncovered yet another surprise—a pair of pantyhose was hidden in the sleeve. They looked thread thin from repeated washing, with a huge run spreading from the heel all the way up to where the legs part. While my fingers were tracing the run, I was struck with a sudden surge of energy, like an electrical current. I could hear my heart pumping in my chest, loud as thunder, as I stood there, quivering with awe.

What kind of woman was she who owned this pair of pantyhose almost a century ago? Had she been the mistress of the household? On what occasion would she wear this elaborate dress? Was she lonely, with her husband away toiling in the Gold Mountain trying to make enough money so that she could afford such expensive things?

Once again I felt the urge to find out the answers to my questions.

Another two years would pass before I finally committed myself to writing this Gold Mountain book, an interval allowing me to complete my third novel, *Mail-Order Bride*, and several novellas.

It was an all-consuming journey, digging into the rock-hard crust of history. I travelled to Victoria, Vancouver, and villages in Kaiping, China, trying to find people with knowledge, direct or indirect, of the era of my book. I frequented archives at all levels, both in person and through the internet, as well as university and public libraries. I found myself shaking with anticipation whenever I spotted a special collection on this subject, or heard a friend mention someone who was the offspring of a Pacific Railway builder. I spent many a sleepless night thinking about a better way to find the answers to my questions haunting me for so long. However, I never really found the answers. Instead, I found stories. From endless pages of books and many a conversation with descendants of Chinese coolies, stories started to surface of people who braved the ocean to come to a wild land called British Columbia, leaving their aging parents, newlywed wives or young children behind, to pursue dreams of wealth and prosperity that always eluded them: stories of champagne parties celebrating the last railroad spike, while the builders of the railroad, the Chinese coolies, were not even mentioned; stories of husbands and wives separated by the head tax, the Chinese Exclusion Act, and the great vast ocean, who kept their marriages alive for decades with a strong will to build a future for their children. I heard stories of a lengthy and profound journey of two races finally becoming reconciled after a century of distrust and rejection.

The actual writing was not any easier. My train of thought was constantly interrupted and distracted by my addiction to accuracy: accuracy of historical fact and accuracy of detail. To find out a particular style of camera used in 1910s, for example, I would surf the net night after night to find a detail that would yield just a few sentences in my book. For information about pistols popular at the turn of century, I would engage my friends with military background in endless discussions until they absolutely dreaded my phone calls. I finally came to the realization that I was a hopeless perfectionist, something my friends had told me long before.

It was a cold December afternoon in 2008, a week before Christmas, when I stood up from my computer desk, stretching out my fatigued body with a sigh of relief; I finally had completed the draft of a novel entitled *Gold Mountain Blues*. Snow started falling. With Christmas music permeating the air, and juicy white snowflakes kissing my windowpanes with a gentle laziness, I felt the kind of peace that I had not known for a long while. I knew that I had accomplished a mission; I had given voice to a group of people buried in the dark abyss of history for more than a century, silent and forgotten.

I would like to take this opportunity to thank professor David Lai of University of Victoria, a member of Order of Canada, for his outstanding achievements in investigative work on the history of Chinatowns, who generously let me share his research on early Chinese immigrants in Canada; Dr. James Kwan, whose fascinating childhood tales in Kaiping village have given my inquisitive mind great pleasure—I hope I did not bore him to death with my endless questions; professor Xueqing Xu at York University and Dr. Helen Wu at University of Toronto for letting me share their access to university libraries, which helped to build the framework of my research; professor Lieyao Wang at Jinan University and his lovely graduate students for taking me to tour the villages in Kaiping and arranging for my accommodation there; my writer friend Shao Jun for accompanying me, like a true gentleman, on the tour; professors Guoxiong

Zhang and Selia Tan of Wuyi University for sharing with me their in-depth knowledge of the contents of the Museum of Overseas Chinese; my dear friend Yan Zhang and her well-known newspaper *The Global Chinese Press* as well as the Chinese Canadian Writers' Association for facilitating my research in Vancouver and Victoria; professor Henry Yu of University of British Columbia for sharing his knowledge in native Indian subjects; Mr. Ian Zeng and Mrs. Jinghua Huang for proofreading my first draft; Ms. Lily Liu, a well-published author herself, for sharing with me stories of her coolie ancestors; and many other friends who kindly offered me photos and information on related subjects. Last but definitely not least, I'd like to thank my family for constant emotional support without which I could not have endured the difficult and sometimes despairing journey of writing such an expansive book.

God bless you all!

P.S. Two years after the publication of *Gold Mountain Blues* in Chinese, I am very pleased to see the launch of its English edition in both Canada and Great Britain. I'd like to express my gratitude to my agent, Mr. Gray Tan, and the people he works with for placing their faith in me as an artist; to my translator, Ms. Nicky Harman, for her tireless explorations of the exciting but sometimes treacherous space between the two great languages in the world; to Ms. Adrienne Kerr for helping me through every step of the way with her in-depth knowledge as a seasoned editor; and many friends whom I can't possible name in such a limited space for their unfailing emotional support during some of the darkest moments in my life as the book was being born.

NOTE ON NAMES

Surnames come first: Fong or Tse or Au or Auyung.

Given names have two parts: a generation name (the same for each member of the same generation of a family) and a personal name, which comes last. People are known familiarly either by their nickname or by a diminutive formed by adding Ah- to the personal part of their given name. So, Kwan Suk Yin (surname Kwan) is known by her nickname, "Six Fingers," or Ah-Yin (by her husband) or, later in life, Mrs. Kwan.

Cantonese and Mandarin (pinyin romanization)

We have used a Cantonese spelling for all names of people who spoke Cantonese to each other, and local places in South China. For national figures (for instance, Li Hongzhang) and names of provinces, we have used Mandarin pinyin romanization. The exception is the Chinese Revolutionary commonly known in the West as Sun Yat-sen (Mandarin pinyin: Sun Zhongshan).

TABLE OF MAIN CHARACTERS

[m. = married to]

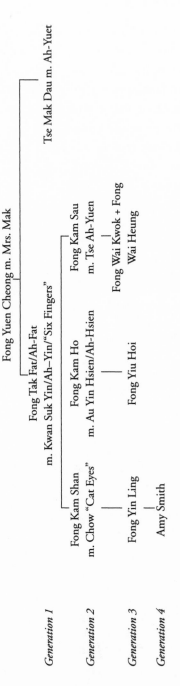

Generation 1 Fong Yuen Cheong m. Mrs. Mak

Generation 2 Fong Tak Fat/Ah-Fat m. Kwan Suk Yin/Ah-Yin/"Six Fingers" · Tse Mak Dau m. Ah-Yuet

Fong Kam Shan m. Chow "Cat Eyes" · Fong Kam Ho m. Au Yin Hsien/Ah-Hsien · Fong Kam Sau m. Tse Ah-Yuen

Generation 3 Fong Yin Ling · Fong Yiu Hoi · Fong Wai Kwok + Fong Wai Heung

Generation 4 Amy Smith

THE AUYUNGS

Generation 1 Auyung Ming
Generation 2 Auyung Yuk Shan
Generation 4 Auyung Wan On

GOLD MOUNTAIN BLUES

PROLOGUE

⟡⟡⟡

Guangdong Province, China, in the year 2004

Amy elbowed her way through the bustling throng in the arrivals lounge at Guangzhou Baiyun International Airport and stopped in front of two gentlemen holding a sign which read "Ms Fong Yin Ling." They stared at her, dumbstruck. What on earth was this foreigner with her chestnut hair and brown eyes doing here?

The Office for Overseas Chinese Affairs had sent two men to pick her up: Ng the young driver, and an older one, the head of the local O.O.C.A., Auyung Wan On. "You, you, you're...." Ng began, stuttering in flustered astonishment. He found he was speaking to her in English.

"That's me," Amy said in decent Chinese, indicating the sign. It was enough to reassure Ng and Auyung and together they escorted her out to the airport carpark.

Although it was only May, the weather was blisteringly hot. To Amy, accustomed to the lukewarm sunshine of Vancouver, the sun in Canton seemed to be full of tiny hooks which pricked her painfully all over. She got quickly into the black Audi and waited for the chill of the air-conditioning, wiping her sticky forehead with a tissue.

"How far is it?" she asked Auyung.

"Not far. The car can easily do it in a couple of hours."

"Are all the documents ready? I'll sign them as soon as we arrive. Can you get me back to Canton this evening?"

"Won't you stay one night? That way you can check over the antiques you've inherited tomorrow morning."

"I can't see the point. Get someone else to box them up and ship them to me."

Auyung looked taken aback for a moment. Then he said: "No one's been in the building for decades. There's a lot of stuff which dates from the time it was built. You need to make an inventory because they're antiques. Apart from what is strictly personal and private, we hope everything will be left for display. Of course, you can take photographs to keep as mementoes—that's clearly stated in the contract."

Amy sighed. "Looks like I'll have to stay one night then. Have you booked me into a hotel?"

"Yes, that's all fixed," said Ng from the front seat. "It's the best one in town. Of course it's not up to Canton standards, but it's very clean, there are hot springs and it's got internet." Amy said nothing, and just sat fanning her sweaty face with a book.

It was quiet in the car. Auyung broke the silence: "Mr. Wong, our director, has been expecting you since last spring. He had plans to entertain you himself. Then we heard you were ill and the trip was postponed a few times. Now you've arrived, but Mr. Wong has just gone to Russia on business. He left a message asking you to wait until he returns. You're the only one left out of all Fong Tak Fat's descendants. It wasn't easy tracking you down."

Amy gave a laugh. "I'm not the Fong Yin Ling your director was expecting. She's my mother. She's still ill, so she sent me instead." She got a business card out of her handbag and handed it to Auyung. It was in English, but he could read it:

Amy Smith
Professor in Sociology
University of British Columbia

Auyung tapped Amy's card lightly against the palm of his hand. "Now I understand," he said, "no wonder...."

"Do I really look that old?" asked Amy.

Auyung laughed. "It's not that. I just couldn't understand why Fong Yin Ling didn't want to go and pay her respects at her grandmother's grave."

Amy looked blank for a moment, then remembered the bag her mother had pushed into her hands before she left.

Amy's mother had been getting letters from an office in Hoi Ping for over a year. They were official letters stamped with the municipal red seal and were about her family's home. The Fongs' was one of the oldest *diulau,* or fortress homes, in the area, they said. It was currently being registered as a World Heritage Site, and was to be renovated and turned into a tourist attraction. The letters requested the Fong descendants to return and sign an agreement assigning trusteeship to the regional government.

As a small child, Yin Ling had been brought home by her parents on a visit and had lived in the *diulau* for two years. She was too young for it to make much of an impression on her, and the passage of some eighty years had almost completely effaced the memories. The Fong family had not lived there for many years, and besides, the use of the word "trusteeship" sounded too much like compulsory repossession. So Yin Ling had simply thrown every letter into the wastepaper bin without saying a word to anyone about them.

To her surprise, the authorities in Hoi Ping had been persistent, sending more letters and even making several international phone calls—though she had no idea how they had found her number.

"This is a heritage site, nearly a hundred years old. How can you bear to see it crumble to dust like this? If it's taken into public trusteeship, it will be restored to the way it was, and will be a fitting monument to the Fongs. You won't need to spend a cent, or put in an ounce of effort, but you retain all the rights. It's the perfect outcome."

The words, constantly repeated, gradually wore down Yin Ling's resistance. However, just as she was warming to the idea, she fell ill. She had been confined to bed for over a year now.

Up to age seventy-nine, Yin Ling had been as unmarked by age as a tree luxuriantly covered in pristine foliage. But then overnight, it was as if she had suddenly been felled by a hurricane.

It happened on her seventy-ninth birthday. She had invited some of her usual mahjong friends to eat at an Italian cafeteria, and then back to her house for a game of mahjong. When Yin Ling was young, she used to get annoyed watching her mum playing mahjong with her cronies, but in old age her own few friends were all mahjong players. Amy had not been there that day and, without her daughter present, Yin Ling really let her hair down, chain-smoking and knocking back the booze until she was uproariously drunk. The party did not break up until midnight. Yin Ling went to bed that night but did not get up in the morning. Overnight she suffered a stroke.

After the stroke, Yin Ling could not speak English any more. As a child she had attended the city school, and all her boyfriends had been White Canadians, so whether at home or at work, she rattled away in English. Now, bizarrely, it was as if some tiny perverse hand had meddled in her brain, erasing it all. When she woke up in the hospital and heard the doctors and nurses talking to her, she looked completely blank. And her speech, when it came, was so garbled it was incomprehensible. At first, they thought the speech centre in her brain had been affected. It took several days for Amy to solve the mystery: Yin Ling's squawks were actually Cantonese—the Cantonese her granddad had spoken at home when she was a child.

Yin Ling was a different woman after her illness. She left hospital for a convalescent home and then, a few months later, was transferred to a nursing home. Every time she arrived at a new place, there were furious rows. Amy pulled out all the stops and eventually got her mother into a Chinese nursing home. Here she could make herself understood, and things seemed to calm down.

One day, Amy was in the middle of teaching a class when she received an urgent phone call from the home. She dropped everything and rushed there—to see the old lady strapped into a wheelchair with a leather belt, her face streaming with tears. Her mother got up that morning, Amy was told, and suddenly started yelling that it would be too late, too late! When the nurse asked what would be too late, she made whooping sounds and, when this was not understood, Yin Ling picked up her walking stick and bashed the nurse in the face with it.

"We can't cope with a patient like this—it's not safe for the nurses or the other patients," the director told Amy.

Seeing her elderly mother in the wheelchair, straining to break free of the belt and foaming at the mouth like a fish tied in twine and gasping for breath, Amy fell to her knees beside her and wailed. "Oh God, whatever do you want me to do with you!"

Yin Ling had never seen her daughter cry like this before. The shock seemed to calm her down. Then, after a moment, she put out her hand and said to Amy: "You go."

In Yin Ling's palm was a letter, crumpled and damp, and stamped with a Chinese red seal.

Amy had to read it through a number of times before she understood what it meant. "OK," she sighed, "I'll go, but you have to promise not to get into fights with the nurses." Her mother grinned, showing tobacco-stained teeth.

"And don't ever think kicking up a fuss will make me take you home. I'll just take you straight to a mental hospital. If I can't keep you under control, then they will," Amy finished fiercely.

"Could you move her into a single room—keep her away from other patients and give her a nurse of her own?" she begged the director. "I'll take care of the costs. Assess the situation in a month when I'm back from China and then come to a decision, OK?" She put on a brazen smile.

Amy left the nursing home that day cursing under her breath. Spring had come to Vancouver in full force. The grass was lush after showers of rain, the climbing roses against the white walls of the home were touched with splodges of vivid scarlet and birds sang shrilly in the trees. But Amy paid absolutely no attention. Her mother, Fong Yin Ling, had looked so small and shrunken in her wheelchair that she might have been a wizened nut blown down from a tree by a gust of wind.

The journey took much longer than Auyung said. They bumped along the potholed road, past building sites and roadworks until finally, towards evening, they arrived at the village. Amy felt as if all the bones in her body had been jolted around in the car.

Every wall in the village was plastered with gaudy bank advertisements offering the best rates for overseas remittances. "Are they trying to hijack each other's customers?" asked Amy.

"When the oil flows like this, who's not going to take advantage of it?" said Auyung. "Every dog in town has a relative overseas. In the old days it was the seabirds and the town horses with their shoulder poles who delivered the 'dollar letters' to the villages. Nowadays the money is wired back home. It travels in a different way but it's the same thing."

Amy knitted her brows: "Is that supposed to be Chinese? I can't make head or tail of what you're saying. What seabirds? What horses?"

"The seabirds were the people who carried dollar letters back by boat, the horses were the men who delivered the letters to the villagers." Auyung glanced at her. "So you're beginning to get interested...." "I'm interested in any sociological phenomena," replied Amy tartly, "whether it's over here or back home, there's no difference."

The Fongs' *diulau* was some way off the road. The car set them down and they had to walk the last stretch.

The track ran alongside an abandoned factory and was so overgrown it looked as if no one had walked it for years. The banana trees had been left to fend for themselves, and their dead leaves were strewn on the ground in a thick layer. Although the sun was still bright, the grass was full of whining mosquitoes. They bit Amy through her clothes, and she felt lumps coming up all over her.

Auyung gave her some mosquito repellent to rub on and shouted angrily at the village cadre coming to greet them: "I told you ages ago someone was coming to visit. Why didn't you clear the track? You're so busy making money that you can't spare a minute for anything else!"

The man bit back an angry retort and gave a loud laugh instead. Then he turned and bellowed at the crowd of women with babies in arms looking on curiously from a safe distance: "What do you think you're gawping at? Haven't you been taught how to behave in front of foreigners?" The women giggled nervously but continued to tag along behind them.

"It's been so many years since Deng Xiaoping's economic reforms. How come your grandfather and your mother didn't want to come back for a visit?" Auyung asked Amy.

"Mum said that Granddad died just as China and Canada re-established diplomatic relations. Granddad had a few friends who made inquiries about getting a visa to go back but he and Mum decided they couldn't go."

"Why?"

Amy stood still and looked at Auyung levelly. "I was hoping you would tell me that."

After a moment's silence, Auyung said: "Everything was crazy back then. Not just the people, even the river in the village went crazy—there was torrential rain and it rose to levels not seen in a hundred years and flooded the entire village."

"Haven't you got a better explanation than that? I am a sociologist, in case you've forgotten," Amy replied coolly.

"Of course. But now isn't the moment to talk about it. By the way, I've done studies of overseas Chinese too so we have quite a lot in common."

"Mr. Auyung's a professor too, Ms. Smith," Ng the driver chipped in. "He's made a special study of these *diulau* homes. That's why the Office for Overseas Chinese Affairs contracted his service so he can deal with the preservation of these homes."

Amy concealed her surprise. "So then you'll know why in a place where every inch of land is worth its weight in gold, this place is so desolate, won't you?"

Auyung gave a slight smile. "Do you want the textbook answer or the local tales?"

Amy smiled back. "Both please, I'd like to hear both."

"The textbooks will tell you that this land suffered heavy industrial pollution, and was abandoned because crops can't be grown on it."

"And the other version?"

"The locals say that things happened here, back in the past, and there have been supernatural phenomena, so no one wants to build here. "

"You mean it's haunted?"

Auyung shook his head. "No, that's not what I said. Of course, you've every right to interpret local tales just how you wish."

Amy burst out laughing. This old boy was certainly interesting. It might not be such a bad idea to stay a couple of nights.

They stumbled down the track and arrived at the building. In fact, it had been clearly visible from a distance, but it was only now that they were right in front of it that it revealed its age. It was a five-storey Western-style concrete building, south-facing, with overhanging Chinese-style eaves on all sides. There were numerous windows, all very narrow and so weather-beaten that they had lost their original shape. They looked more like cannonball holes than windows. The iron bars fitted to every window and door were heavily rusted. There were Roman-style mini-columns under the eaves, and the columns and windows were all covered in carvings now scarcely visible.

Auyung brought a large stone over and stood on it. Extracting some sheets of newspaper from his briefcase, he began rubbing the lichen and bird droppings from the door. Eventually, a name appeared: "Tak Yin House." The characters were carved in the Slender Gold style of the Song dynasty, and in the deeper parts traces of pink could be seen. Originally, no doubt, they would have been painted vermilion red.

The door was narrow and covered with an iron grille with locks at the top, middle and bottom, called "heaven, earth and middle" locks, as Auyung explained. The heaven and earth locks were operated from the inside and, if not bolted, the door could simply be pushed open. Only the middle one was a real lock. Originally, it had been around four inches across but had expanded considerably with the rust. "Do you have a key?" Auyung asked the cadre.

"No one's been in here for years. Of course we haven't got a key" was the reply. "Anyway now the owner's turned up, she can break the lock herself."

Ng went back to the track, picked up a sharp stone and handed it to Amy. The lock was very old and broke after a couple of blows, but the door was sturdier and juddered before finally opening a crack. With a grating cry, a sooty-black bird flew out, its wings nearly grazing Amy's head. Amy's knees gave way and she sat down on the ground, clasping her hands tightly over her chest, her heart thudding.

The village cadre looked uneasy. "The rites ... has she performed the ancestral rites yet?" he whispered to Auyung.

"Whatever's the matter?" Auyung said. "Her ancestors have had a long wait for her to get here. They've scarcely had time to rejoice, let alone be offended. The rites can wait until tomorrow, she hasn't been to the graves yet."

"I'm off outside for a smoke," said the cadre, clearly alarmed. And he waited at the entrance as Auyung led the way into the house.

As she stepped over the threshold, Amy heard the scrunching of dirt under her feet. The glass in the windows was broken and the evening sunshine streamed in, turning the dust particles to gold. Amy stood still. Gradually she began to make out the interior; it contained no furniture except a water barrel with a large crack down the side.

"The kitchen and the servants' rooms were on this level," explained Auyung, "the Fongs' rooms and bedrooms were all on the floors above."

They made their way over to the stairs.

Its treads had collapsed in so many places that the staircase looked like a ribcage with the intestines rotted away. Auyung and Amy cautiously made their way up, testing each step as they went, until they finally arrived at the second floor. Against the wall facing them was a long wooden table, its paintwork faded. Two round objects stood on it. Amy took a closer look and realized they were copper incense burners, their elegant shapes ravaged by the thick layers of verdigris which covered them. In a small alcove in the wall stood a statue of Guan Yam, the Buddhist goddess of mercy. Her head and shoulders had been lopped off, and only the fingers holding the lotus flower remained as a reminder of her compassion. The paint had worn off the characters engraved above the statue and only a few could be made out:

Candle … create … flower
… incense … out … peaceful home

Under the statue there was a wooden memorial tablet with no paint left on it at all. Rainwater had leaked in and most of the tablet had disintegrated. Only at the far right side were a couple of lines of characters still legible:

illustrious twentieth generation … ancestors
father, head of the family, Mr. Fong Dik Coi
mother, Mrs. Wen, mistress of the house

"This was where your family used to worship the spirits of the ancestors," said Auyung.

What looked like broken sticks of furniture lay in a heap on the floor. Amy turned them over with her foot, raising a cloud of dust which caught in her throat and made her cough. Auyung pulled out a stick and passed it to her. It looked something like a flute, but thicker and longer. A fine chain was attached to the body of the pipe and in the middle was a raised bowl with an opening. Amy blew away the dust and saw underneath a yellowish pattern, rather like vines twisting around a tree branch. She flicked it with her finger and it made a pinging sound. It was not made of bamboo.

"This is an opium pipe. It's carved from elephant ivory, and it's worth a fortune," said Auyung.

1

Gold Mountain Dream

꿍꿍

Year eleven of the reign of Tongzhi to year five of the reign
of Guangxu (1872–1879)
Spur-On Village, Hoi Ping County, Guangdong Province, China

The village lay within the boundaries of the township of Wo On in Hoi
Ping County. Newfangled as its name sounds, the village was actually a
couple of hundred years old. Legend has it that in the reign of the Qing
emperor Qianlong, two brothers fled from famine-stricken Annam and
settled here with their families. They cleared the land, tilled the soil, raised
cattle and pigs and within a decade or so were firmly established. As he lay
dying, the elder brother issued an exhortation to the whole family—they
were to spur themselves on to ever-great efforts. Thus the village acquired
the name Tsz Min, or Spur-On Village.

By the reign of Tongzhi, Spur-On Village had grown into a sizeable
place, with over a hundred families. There were two clans: the Fongs, the
dominant family and descendants of the Annamese brothers, and the Aus,
outsiders who had come from Fujian. They were almost all farmers, with

the difference that the Fongs owned large, contiguous fields while the Au clan, who had arrived later, cultivated scraps of land which they cleared at the edges of the Fongs' fields. Later the two families began to intermarry, the daughters of one with the sons of the other. As the families merged, so, gradually, did the fields, and the differences in status between the Fongs and the Aus blurred too. This did not last: events took place which sharpened edges previously blunted ... but that was not until much later.

One boundary of the village was marked by a small river, while at the other end was a low hill. The fields lay in a depression between the two landmarks; after years of intensive cultivation, they were fertile and productive and, in good years, their produce was enough to support the entire village. In times of drought and flooding, however, sons and daughters were still sometimes sold as servants.

Apart from growing crops, the people of Spur-On Village also reared pigs, grew vegetables, and did embroidery and weaving. They ate a little of their own produce, but most was taken to market and the cash used to buy household goods. Almost all Spur-On families had pigs and cattle, but there was only one slaughterman among them: Fong Tak Fat's father, Fong Yuen Cheong.

Three generations of Fong Yuen Cheong's family had been slaughtermen. As soon he was weaned and able to toddle without falling over, Fong Tak Fat would squat bare-bottomed next to his father and watch him butcher pigs. The knife went in white and came out red but he was not the least bit scared. "The furthest I've been to butcher pigs is ten or twenty *li*," his father boasted to the other villagers, "but our Ah-Fat will travel thousands of *li* to butcher pigs." Only half of this boast was correct, the bit about thousands of *li*.[1] He was wrong about the butchering because before the time had come for him to hand his son the knife, Fong Yuen Cheong died.

Yuen Cheong's branch of the Fong family had been getting poorer with every generation. His father had still owned a few *mu*[2] of poor land, but by Yuen Cheong's time, they were reduced to renting a few patches here and

---

[1] One *li* is approximately one-third of a mile.

[2] One *mu* is approximately 0.16 of an acre.

there. After the rent on the land had been paid, the yield was only enough to fill half the family rice bowl. They relied on Yuen Cheong's butchering work for the other half. If he killed his own clan's pigs in Spur-On Village, he received only the offal. It was when he worked for families who were not related, like the Aus, or who were from other villages, that he could earn a few coppers. So the family rice bowl sometimes stayed half-empty. It depended on the weather, the number of animals to be killed, the agricultural almanac and the cultural calendar—at propitious times when there were more weddings and more houses being built, more animals were killed.

Beginning in year ten of the reign of Tongzhi, there were two successive years of drought. The river which ran past the village dried to a strip of ooze over which clouds of insects swarmed as the evening sun went down. The fish and shrimps were nowhere to be seen. The parched earth, like an infant mewling for the breast, longed for rain which never came. The harvests were poor and few pigs were killed. It got harder and harder for Fong Yuen Cheong to feed his family.

But then Yuen Cheong's fortunes changed. It happened one market day in Tongzhi year eleven.

He got up at the crack of dawn that day and killed a yearling pig. He had wanted to keep it until the end of the year and cure its meat but he could not wait. The family *wok* had seen not even a drop of lard for too long. The pig could not wait either—by now it was hardly more than skin and bones. When he had killed it, he set the head, tail and offal to one side and cut the body and legs up into several pieces to take to market. He hoped he could buy a few lotus seed paste cakes with the money; his younger son, Tak Sin, would be a year old the day after tomorrow. They could not afford a birthday banquet but at least they could share the pastries among the neighbours.

Before he set off, his wife, Mrs. Mak, laid a few lotus leaves lightly over the meat to stop the flies getting at it. Then she lit an incense stick before the statue of the *bodhisattva* and prayed that the sun would not get hot too quickly; fresh pork could not stand too much sitting in the hot sun. As Yuen Cheong went to the doorway, he heard her grumbling: "It's Red Hair's mum's sixtieth birthday and we're invited to the dinner but my skirt's full of moth holes." She wanted him to buy her a piece of material with the pig money, and suddenly he felt a rush of anger. Putting down the shoulder pole, he rounded on his wife:

"They've got family in Gold Mountain, but we haven't, have we? All you do all day is try and keep up with the neighbours!"

With a wail, Mrs. Mak slumped to the ground. Fong Tak Fat went to the door, grabbed the shoulder pole and thrust it firmly into his father's hand. His father was still glowering but he put the pole back on his shoulder and walked out, sweat beading his forehead. Ah-Fat, as everyone called his older son, was a shrimp of a nine-year-old, a child whose body had not begun to fill out. He said little but he gazed at the world with piercing eyes. His father was secretly a little afraid of him.

Shooing away some half-starved dogs, Yuen Cheong padded barefoot along the mud track out of the village. When he reached the river, he went down to the dried-up bed, where he could see that a puddle of water had collected in the crack between the rocks. Scooping up a handful, he washed his face. The little eddies distorted his reflection so that his eyes and nose appeared to jump off his face. He pursed up his thick, heavy lips as if he were going to smile, but then did not. The water ran down his forehead and gradually cooled him. His heart felt lighter. He knew why he had hit out at his wife, and it had nothing to do with her skirt. It was all to do with Red Hair.

Red Hair was a distant cousin. He got his nickname because, with his high nose and deep-set eyes, he looked a bit like one of those White foreigners who were supposed to have reddish hair on their heads. By now, few people remembered his real name. As children, the pair of them used to catch fish and shrimps in the ponds, grope for loaches in the paddy fields and steal melons from other people's melon patches. Red Hair was older by a few years, but he was a bit of an oaf. Yuen Cheong was the smarter of the two and bossed Red Hair around. That only changed when, a few years ago, Red Hair married an Au girl in the village who had a cousin in Gold Mountain. Then, somehow, he stumbled onto the boat and off he went too.

There were lots of stories in the village about Red Hair in Gold Mountain. One went like this: he had gone to some remote mountains to pan for gold. The water he collected in a wooden bucket dried up under the fierce sun and he found solidified gold dust left. According to another story there was a plague in Gold Mountain a few years back. Red Hair stuffed his mouth with a thick cloth, carried corpses for the *yeung fan*[3] and got a dollar a corpse. He also used to deliver gruel to the leprosy hospital for three coppers a bowl. People asked his mother whether these stories were true, but she just gave a smile and would not say yes or no. No one really knew what it was that Red Hair did in Gold Mountain, but they did know that he had made a lot of money and sent dollar letters home every month. In fact, every time his mother got one of these letters, she was on cloud nine. No one else cared one way or the other, but Yuen Cheong was furious. He knew Red Hair inside out. He was too stupid even to wipe his own arse properly.

But Red Hair had become a rich man while Yuen Cheong still slaved away at that half-a-rice-bowl work.

As Yuen Cheong carried the pork meat to market that day he had no idea of the extraordinary turn his life was going to take. Fate had something completely different in store for the simple, impecunious slaughterman— and his family were to find themselves transported from a life of abject poverty to the heights of riches along with him.

Yuen Cheong meandered on his way and finally arrived in town—to find all quiet and hardly anyone around. This being a market day, the streets should have been jammed with people so tightly packed that they stepped on each other's toes. He eventually came upon a couple of hawkers, and discovered that the town had been attacked by bandits the night before. They had swept through the house of one of the richest families like a hurricane, plundering and killing two people. Government troops were now patrolling the town but its inhabitants were too frightened to stir out of doors.

Yuen Cheong had come all this way and could not turn back now, so he put down his shoulder pole and sat down at the roadside to try his luck. By midday he had sold only one trotter and one piece of tenderloin. The sun rose high above his head and the shrilling of the cicadas drilled holes in his

---

[3] White Canadian

eardrums. In the wicker baskets, the meat gradually turned pale and sweaty. Yuen Cheong cursed furiously at the lousy hand fate had dealt him. If only he had known, he would have salted down the pig meat. That way, the meat and the lard could have flavoured their meals for a few more months.

A moment later a couple of swarthy fellows dressed in short jackets appeared. They ran frantically down the street and thrust a bag into his hands. "Look after this carefully, brother, and don't move from this spot," said one in low tones. "We'll be back for it in a few hours—and we'll make it worth your while." Yuen Cheong had sharp eyes and he could see the weapons bulging at their waists. He said nothing but began to tremble like a leaf. As he watched them dart into a nearby alleyway, he felt something warm trickling down his thighs—he had wet his trousers.

Yuen Cheong hugged the heavy bag to himself and waited at the roadside until the sun dipped down towards the horizon, the night wind got up and the few market-goers dispersed. Still those fellows did not come back. He looked carefully around, then surreptitiously pulled a corner of the bag loose and peeked inside. What he saw made him go weak at the knees and his eyes glaze over.

The bag was neatly stacked with gold ingots.

He chucked the bag into his basket and covered it with the meat wrapped in lotus leaves. He put the heavy carrying pole on his shoulder, pulled his bamboo hat down low over his eyes and crept away into a side street.

It was almost midnight by the time he got home. The three children were asleep and only his wife waited up for him. She sat on a stool by the stove airing her feet. Since water was now so scarce, she could only wash her feet every couple of weeks. This was quite a business—just unwinding the wrapping cloths took a long time. The women of Spur-On Village always worked alongside their menfolk in the fields, so most of them had feet of a natural size. But Mrs. Mak was from San Wui Village and her feet had been bound from the age of five. As she aired her feet, she embroidered the edging for a woman's hat which she would sell in the market. It was black with tiny pink oleanders around the brim. To save on oil, Mrs. Mak had trimmed the lamp till the flame was pea-sized. She frowned over her work but could hardly see the needle in her hand. Hearing the dog bark, she threw the embroidery down and hobbled on the tips of her bare feet to open the door.

Yuen Cheong came in pouring with sweat. His wife's foot bindings lay curled on the stool like a sloughed snakeskin and the air was thick with a fetid smell. He held his nose before giving an almighty sneeze. Then he put down the carrying pole and slumped to the floor, staring straight ahead of him. His wife looked searchingly at him, but he said nothing.

She could see that little of the meat had been sold, and guessed that Yuen Cheong was tired and angry. She ought to offer some words of comfort but did not dare open her mouth. Finally, she went into their room and brought out a towel for her husband to wipe the sweat from his face.

"Tomorrow, I'll send my younger brother to Canton to buy a skirt for you," Yuen Cheong said feebly, rolling his eyes.

It took only half a day for Yuen Cheong to go from being a poverty-stricken nobody to a stupendously wealthy member of the Fong clan. Then it took his family another half-dozen years to slide back into poverty again.

With the money which had dropped into his hands, Yuen Cheong bought up neighbouring fields and built a residential compound with three entrance courtyards on one of them. He had a low opinion of the village bricklayer, so instead sent for a master bricklayer from Fujian, and paid through the nose for it. The walls were of pure red brick, the tiles were glazed green, and the ground was covered with large grey-black flagstones. Each courtyard was laid out in exactly the same way, with an open paved area, main hall, side hall, east chamber and west chamber. Guests were received and offered tea in the main hall, while the side hall was the study. Fong Yuen Cheong could hardly read, but he knew the value of literacy and wanted his sons to be well read. The second and third courtyards were to be used by his sons when they grew up and married. For this reason, they each had a side entrance so that if by any chance the wives did not get along, they could use their own gates. Yuen Cheong had it all worked out.

Spur-On villagers had seen little of the world and had never seen a courtyard residence like this before. Compared with the houses built by the Gold Mountain workers for their families, this was rather more stylish.

When the Fongs moved in, the villagers gathered in droves to watch as Yuen Cheong and his children set off firecrackers, sending the village chickens and dogs into a frenzy. Red Hair's mother was among the bystanders, standing silently on the far edge of the crowd.

The Fongs' land was rented out to tenant farmers, but Yuen Cheong continued to butcher pigs and cows—not for the offal or for cash, but to keep his hand in. He found that if he stayed at home for days on end, he would wake up in the night to a swishing noise coming from his knives hanging on the wall. He would get up the next morning and go house to house asking if anyone needed butchering done. He looked so restless that the villagers would even give him their chickens and ducks for slaughter, and he was happy to oblige them.

The Fongs' compound now housed half a dozen farm labourers, manservants and maids, and Mrs. Mak did not have to worry herself about either the heavy work in the fields or the housework. But Mrs. Mak had spent a lifetime working too and could not rest now. So every day she taught her daughter Ah-Tou how to sew and embroider, in preparation for the time when she would make a good marriage. Her younger son, Ah-Sin, was a toddler and spent his days chasing the chickens and scrapping with dogs in the courtyards. Her oldest son, Ah-Fat, went to a tutor school every day.

There was a teacher named Mr. Ding, in Spur-On Village itself. He was from neither of the two village clans, but had moved in with his Au family in-laws on marriage (only the most indigent men did that). He knew the classics, and spent his time writing letters for the villagers, and painting couplets for them to hang beside their doors at the Chinese New Year or when there was a death in the family. He also taught a few of the village children to read and write. But Yuen Cheong felt the pedantic old stick was not worthy to teach his son, and asked around for a suitable teacher in the township. Mr. Auyung Ming was found. He was an erudite young man who was well versed in the classics. He had also studied Western subjects with a Christian priest in the city of Canton, and taught both kinds of learning at the tutor school he set up in the township. In fact, he was only interested in teaching the exceptional students and rejected any child who might be a bit slow. To reinforce this message, the school fees were set very high. This was just what Yuen Cheong wanted for his son, and he got a friend to take the boy along for an interview. Mr. Auyung looked him up and down, and said simply: "What a shame." After that, every day, come rain or shine, Ah-Fat walked the dozen or so *li* to attend Mr. Auyung's lessons.

Life burned brightly for Yuen Cheong in those days—the way a pile of brushwood thrown together goes up with a whoosh when a favourable wind happens along. But the fire burned hotly, and extinguished itself too soon.

The reason was Yuen Cheong's addiction to opium.

Fong Yuen Cheong smoked his opium in the most refined way. The main hall in the first courtyard of his residence was turned into his smoking room. It had a four-panelled screen covered with embroidered animals, birds, fish and flowers in the Suzhou style. All the furnishings—couch, chest and table—were of carved rosewood. Yuen Cheong's pipe was made of Burmese ivory and he smoked the highest-grade raw opium exported by the East India Company.

Mrs. Mak became expert in attending to her husband when he smoked. Just before the craving came on, she would prepare the pipe so that the opium bubbled up ready for her to put it into his hand. She had learned just the right height for the pillow, the right angle for the footstool, and the choice and arrangement of the snacks. As soon as he lay down on the couch, five little dishes would be artfully laid out on the table ready for him. Jerky strips, *char siu* pork buns, and various cakes made of green beans, sesame or lotus paste were the usual fare, together with a cup of milk. His smoking implements were rubbed until they glistened and were laid out neatly in the chest until the time came for them to be used.

Mrs. Mak was distressed to see the family fortune dissipate in the smoke from the opium pipe, but she had her own way of calculating the losses and gains. Her husband had been a vigorous and energetic man who would not stay put at home, and who spent his time eating and drinking and getting into fights. It was far better that he should be tied to the house by an opium pipe. She knew too that if she did not attend to his needs, he might go and buy himself a concubine and get her to attend to him instead. That was what men did when they had enough money.

Once his urge for a smoke was satisfied, Yuen Cheong became the mildest of men. He was not yet thirty years old, but when he smiled, there was a touch of an old man's benevolence in his expression. He spoke gently and even with a touch of wit. He liked his wife to parade around in front of him in the clothes and finery he bought her in Canton. Sometimes this was in front of the servants, in the opium-smoking room. At other times, it was when they were in their bedroom; then he would shut the doors and windows and would use more than his eyes. Mrs. Mak minced around in an attempt to evade his groping hands, her face flushed just like in the heady days when they were young.

Not only were the jagged edges of Yuen Cheong's once-fiery temper rubbed smooth by the opium—so too were the rough edges of the wide world. He was at ease with the world and it with him. As his twinkling gaze swept over everyone around him, he had no idea that, thousands of *li* away, the Empress Dowager in Beijing's Forbidden City was desperately shoring up what remained of the Qing Empire after the onslaught by Western armies. He also had no idea that, much closer to home, his tenant farmers and household servants were stealthily nibbling away at his family's property like so many hungry mice.

When he had had his fill of opium, Yuen Cheong would make his eldest son sit beside him and, breaking off a piece of sesame or green bean cake, put it into Ah-Fat's hand. "And what did Mr. Auyung teach you today, son? Did you practise your calligraphy?" He had seen straightaway that his eldest was a quick learner. Maybe one day his son might pass the Imperial examinations. He racked his brains to see if he could remember any Cantonese operas in which a slaughterman's son passed the Imperial examinations creditably enough to achieve an audience with the Son of Heaven in the Golden Carriage Palace—but could not think of any.

Looking at the smoking equipment scattered around the opium couch, Ah-Fat said nothing but his eyebrows drew together in a worried frown. His father was used to this expression on his son's face; since the moment he was born, the boy had seemed grown up. Yuen Cheong soaked a piece of beef jerky in the milk to soften it and stuffed it into Ah-Fat's mouth, saying gently: "Isn't Daddy good to you then, son?"

Ah-Fat swallowed the morsel before it choked him: "Mr. Auyung says foreigners sell us opium to break our spirit," he said. "If the spirit of the people is broken, then the country is broken too." Now it was his father who could think of nothing to say. After a few minutes, he ruffled his son's head. "How many years has your old dad got left then? After that, it'll be you the family depends on. So long as you don't smoke, you can save the family. I'll be passing the responsibility on to you sooner or later."

Ah-Fat sighed: "Mr. Auyung says, if the young Emperor can break free of the Dowager and ascend the throne, he can use his knowledge of the West and work out a way to contain the Western powers...." but his father quickly put his hand over his son's mouth. "Isn't he afraid of losing his head, saying things like that?" he cried. "Us ordinary folk shouldn't meddle in politics. I just want you to look after your family."

But circumstances put a premature end to all Fong Yuen Cheong's plans for his son's future. Six years after he so unexpectedly came into his fortune, he overdosed on opium and died on his couch. In retrospect, he was lucky to die when he did. Even if he had not, it might still have been his last smoke. By the time he died, almost all the Fongs' land had been sold, and the family's remaining valuable jewellery had been pawned. All that was left was his stone-flagged residence—and the queues of creditors waiting at the gates.

That was how Fong Tak Fat, aged fifteen, became head of the household in the space of a night.

Most of the Fong compound was sold and Ah-Fat lived with his family in the first courtyard. They rented back some of the land they had sold, and Ah-Fat was the main labourer. With her bound feet Mrs. Mak could not do farm work, but she did have one special skill. Her brocaded cloth was the finest in the township. She sewed beads onto the cloth and worked it with flower designs in gold and silver thread. She made aprons, shoe uppers, hats and belts which she could sometimes sell on market day for a few cents. She was in demand in the village too, to embroider garments for weddings, funerals, births and longevity birthday parties. She did not charge a fee, but in exchange for her work the family would send a strong, young farmhand to help Ah-Fat in the fields at sowing and harvest times.

The winter that Yuen Cheong died, his youngest son, Ah-Sin, had an epileptic fit. While eating his dinner he suddenly fell from the stool and bit off a piece of his tongue. When he came to, he seemed only half there. From that day on, he had fits everywhere—in the fields, on the ground, in bed, at the table, in the toilet—all completely without warning.

Mrs. Mak wove and embroidered from morning till night. Eventually eyestrain, together with her worries about Ah-Sin's epilepsy, led to severe conjunctivitis. Her eyelids swelled up and the rims of her eyes were thickly smeared with pus. She could not sew any more and the entire responsibility for the Fong family now fell on Ah-Fat's shoulders.

To raise money to treat Ah-Sin's illness Mrs. Mak was forced to sell off her daughter, Ah-Tou, to a family who lived twenty *li* away.

Witnessed by the elders of the clan, she put her thumbprint on an irrevocable title deed. It read as follows:

> Through this deed, Mrs. Fong-Mak gives her daughter, Ah-Tou, to Chan Ah Yim of Sai Village as a maid and has today received fifty silver dollars in recompense for this gift. From the day on which her daughter is given over, she shall have nothing more to do with the Fongs. Each side shall be satisfied with this agreement and there shall be no dissenting voices on either side, the signing and witnessing of this deed being the written guarantee thereof.

> Signed the fifth day of the eleventh month of year four of the reign of Guangxu (1878)

Ah-Tou was sold to a family that had a small dyers business. The head of the family was fifty-eight years old, and had a wife and two concubines, but none of them had borne him a son and heir. He had a bit of money but the family was not especially well off, and he could not afford more concubines. His solution was to buy in girls from poor families, to use partly as maids, partly as concubines. All the time and effort Mrs. Mak spent teaching her daughter elaborate needlework was wasted. Ah-Tou would only be doing rough work from now on.

Ah-Tou was only thirteen when she left home. Mrs. Mak arranged to meet the Chans in town to hand her over, but fearing her daughter would refuse to go, lied to her. Ah-Tou thought they were going to market. Just before they left, Mrs. Mak put two hard-boiled eggs into Ah-Tou's handkerchief. It was a long time since Ah-Tou had had an egg to eat. "Have Ah-Fat and Ah-Sin had any?" she asked. "No, only you," said her mother. Ah-Tou peeled one and ate it so fast that it stuck in her throat. Eventually she managed to summon enough saliva to swallow it, after choking and sputtering till purple veins stood out on her forehead. When it came to the second egg, she cracked the shell but then gave it back: "Let's leave it for Ah-Sin," she said, "he's just a little kid." Mrs. Mak quietly took out a silver dollar from inside her jacket: "Keep it safe," she said, giving it to her daughter. "Don't let anyone see it." Ah-Tou gripped the dollar tightly in her sweaty palm and was silent. Finally she asked: "What shall I buy in the market with so much money?" "Whatever you like." Ah-Tou thought for a moment. "I'll go to the Christian priest's pharmacy in town, Mum," she said finally, "and get a bottle of eyewash for you. With what's left, I'll get four walnut cookies, one for Ah-Fat, one for me, and two for Ah-Sin." Ah-Tou was the in-between child, two years younger than Ah-Fat and six years older than Ah-Sin. She had carried Ah-Sin around on her back ever since he was a baby, so she was as much a mother to him as an elder sister. Mrs. Mak turned away: "Eat it all, child, it's all for you. Don't leave any for anyone else," she said, the tears running down her face.

When they reached the market, Mrs. Mak saw the Chans and gave her daughter a little push. "Go for a walk with Auntie Chan," she said. "I'm going to the toilet." She walked away a few steps, and then hid around the corner of a wall. She watched as Ah-Tou, dragging her feet behind the Chan woman and looking around for her mother, receded into the distance. Mrs. Mak felt as if a piece of her heart had been cut out.

She made her way home in a daze. It was nearly nightfall. She did not light the fire or get dinner ready, just sat staring blankly at the stove. Ah-Fat came in from the fields. "Where's Ah-Tou?" he asked. "I haven't seen her all day." There was no answer. He persisted and she finally said through gritted teeth: "I've cut out my own flesh to feed to the dogs." When Ah-Fat finally realized he would never see his sister in this life again, he threw down the bowl of water, ran out and squatted by the roadside. It was many years before the Spur-On villagers forgot the sounds of his sobbing. He did not cry loudly, in fact he choked the tears back until they sounded like the broken whimpers of a dying dog. Life had been terribly hard these last years and the Spur-On villagers had seen and heard enough weeping to turn their hearts to stone. But Ah-Fat's grief still brought tears to their eyes.

The next day, Ah-Fat went to say goodbye to his teacher. Mr. Auyung was stretched over the table doing calligraphy. When he heard Ah-Fat's news, he threw down his weasel-hair brush, spattering the table with ink. "There's no cure," he said, "it's terminal." Ah-Fat knew he was not referring to himself.

Before Ah-Fat left, Mr. Auyung chose a few books for him to take home. "Even if I can't teach you," he said, "you should still read your books." Ah-Fat shook his head. "If you have any books on farming and keeping livestock, you can give me a couple of those." His teacher was silent.

Ah-Fat did not eat his dinner when he got home. In the middle of the night, Mrs. Mak was woken by a rustling, a noise like a rat nibbling at rice straw. She pulled her clothing around her shoulders and got up. By the light of the lamp's tiny flame, her son was ripping up sheets of paper. She was illiterate but she knew these were the copybooks and textbooks he used at Mr. Auyung's school. Over the years he had stored a stack of them carefully away. She nearly seized them from him, but what was the use? They had already been reduced to confetti. Mrs. Mak felt comforted too, for she could see that Ah-Fat had accepted his fate.

From that day on, Ah-Fat threw himself into farming.

Six months after Yuen Cheong died, Red Hair came home from Gold Mountain.

Ah-Fat heard about Red Hair when he was transplanting rice seedlings, with a farmhand whose help his mother's needlework had secured for him. The other villagers had finished theirs, but he had had to wait a few days for the man to arrive. The paddy water was cold in early spring, and his feet, planted in the mud, soon went numb. He was not good at farm work. Years spent at home and at school had distanced him from the land. The land knew he was an outsider and bullied him. He felt like his calves and back were bound together with wire. Every time he bent down, the wire pulled taut and cut into his flesh, giving him sharp jabbing pains. The farmhand walked in front of him, working swiftly and planting neat rows of evenly spaced seedlings, compared to his own, which were messy and crooked. When he thought of his mother's infected eyes and his epileptic brother, his skin crawled and terror gripped him. Above him the lowering sky pressed down on him like cotton wadding.

Even though it was overcast today, he knew that sunset was a long way off. When will it all end? he wondered, with a sigh that stirred eddies in the paddy field.

"The Gold Mountain uncle! He's arrived!" the children's cries went up. Ah-Fat spotted them racing excitedly along the dyke.

Behind the children came a dozen porters, each pair carrying a trunk between them. The trunks were of camphor wood, two to three feet high, and reinforced at each corner with gleaming metal bands. They hung low from the carrying poles which rested on the porters' shoulders and creaked as they went along.

"It's Red Hair, Ah-Sing's relative. He's come back to get married," said the farmhand.

Red Hair was a widower, and this would be his second marriage.

The first was ten years ago. When his wife was three months' pregnant, he left for Gold Mountain, but she died in childbirth, and the baby too.

His new bride came from the Kwan family. She was only fourteen, and a good-looking young woman. Red Hair had been away in Gold Mountain for a long time and his views about women were different from those of the other villagers. He did not like women with bound feet, and he wanted someone tall and buxom. He hoped she could read and write a bit too. He put all his requirements down in a letter to his mother and she listed them to the matchmaker, who did not look encouraging. There were certainly girls without bound feet, but southern girls were generally short. Tall, well-built girls were hard to find, especially ones who could read and write. Luckily the matchmaker had found the Kwans.

Mr. Kwan was a scholar who had failed the county-level Imperial examinations, and made his living as tutor to a wealthy family. The Kwans were poor but his children were literate in the classics. Not only did the pair's horoscopes match, but the girl fulfilled Red Hair's requirements in every other way too. Red Hair was delighted and decided to invite all the villagers to the wedding banquet.

The day of the wedding feast, Ah-Fat was in the fields thinning the rice seedlings. By the time he had finished, it was getting dark. He went to wash his muddy feet. From where he sat on the riverbank, he could see a hazy red glow, looking a bit like a forest fire, over the village far in the distance. These were the lights from the banquet, he knew. He rolled his trouser legs down, brushed the mud off himself and headed straight to the village without bothering to go home.

The wedding feast was in the open air. Ah-Fat counted the tables carefully—thirty altogether. There were dishes of chicken, duck and fish, and half a gleaming suckling pig on every table. Ah-Fat sat with the other youngsters, all of them ravenously hungry. Grabbing at the suckling pig, they wolfed it all down, but Ah-Fat was quick and sneaked a piece for his little brother. Ah-Sin gripped the meat and nibbled at it, savouring every mouthful. The fat ran down his wrist and he stuck out his tongue and licked it clean. Ah-Fat thought he looked like a beggar on a street corner but did not admonish him. Since their dad died, none of the family had tasted even a morsel of meat.

They drank rice wine brewed a few months before by Red Hair's mother in preparation for his arrival. As soon as the jars were opened, the fumes from the wine threatened to knock them out. Red Hair staggered drunkenly from table to table, clutching a big bowl of wine and encouraging his guests to drink toasts. He wore a long, sapphire blue brocade gown embroidered all over with gold *ruyi* designs and, tied across his shoulders, a length of red silk with a big bow. His skullcap was adorned with a glittering piece of translucent jade carved with a dragon and a phoenix. That evening Red Hair's cheeks were flushed red too, and the sweat formed shallow pools in his deep-set eye sockets. His tongue thickened till it seemed about to drop out of his mouth and the muscles of his face jerked spasmodically as he beamed lopsided grins in every direction.

Red Hair reached the table where the youngsters were sitting. It fell to Ah-Fat, as their senior, to offer formal congratulations, but his elders at nearby tables put a stop to that. "He's the bridegroom, so even a stray dog can tease him today. No need to go bowing and scraping to him." Someone pointed to Ah-Fat and Ah-Sin: "These are Yuen Cheong's kids." Red Hair ruffled Ah-Sin's hair: "Your poor dad," he said. "Such a good head on his shoulders. Who would have thought it, eh?" And he got two small boxes out of his pocket and put one into each boy's hand.

Ah-Fat opened the box and peered at its contents. It held things that looked like black beans, but bigger and rounder. He put one in his mouth and chewed. It crunched between his teeth, and for a moment he was scared a tooth had come out. When he looked closer, he realized there was an almond hidden inside the bean. The dark coating was sweet, with a peculiar kind of fatty sweetness he could not put into words.

It was only much later, when he was in Gold Mountain, that Ah-Fat learned that these black beans were called chocolate.

Ah-Fat quickly grew drunk at the wedding feast and it was his own doing— no one forced him to drink toasts. It was his first taste of alcohol, and it slid smoothly over his tongue, burning its way down his throat and into his belly. It did not stay there long, but soon crept up to his head. Now it was several times more powerful, and exploded in a great fireball in his brain. Ah-Fat felt his body shrinking away like a jellyfish. Crawling out of the crater left by the fireball, he floated gently in some distant place in mid-air. From his vantage point far above the earth, he peered mistily down at the banqueting tables and the village scattered beneath him.

Suddenly he felt the black beans grappling with the rice wine in his belly. His guts knotted up, and he hurriedly shoved his way through the diners and made for some waste ground by the road. He pulled his shirt up and his trousers down just in time to release a stream of liquid shit so foul-smelling it almost knocked him down. He grabbed a banana leaf, cleaned himself up and kicked some dirt over the mess. This, at least, had sobered him up; he was down from mid-air and had both feet planted solidly on the ground.

The noise of the revellers had faded far into the distance. Around him the only sound was the night wind rustling the leaves in the treetops. The frogs in the pond croaked loudly and got on his nerves. He threw a stone into the water and the splash shut the frogs up but disturbed the birds roosting at the water's edge so that they flapped up and away, their wings etched against the night sky. The clouds cleared, revealing a mass of stars right down to the horizon.

Was that where Gold Mountain was? he wondered. What kind of a place was it that could turn Red Hair into such a fine figure of a man? Were the six huge, heavy trunks he had brought back laden with Gold Mountain gold?

Ah-Fat sat down at the roadside and fell into an uneasy doze.

Some time later, he felt movement around him and awoke. A half-starved dog come to lick up the shit, he thought, but then he turned his head and saw a little girl about two years old looking at him with a foolish smile on her face. She was wearing a long red brocade gown and a red hat embroidered with clusters of peonies on each side. It was certainly an eye-catching outfit. Ah-Fat remembered the ghost stories told by the villagers. He broke out in a chill sweat and the hairs stood up on the back of his neck. Then he got to his feet and saw behind the girl the vague outline of a shadow. Reassured, because he knew that ghosts did not have shadows, he asked: "And who are you?"

The girl did not answer. Instead she stuffed her fists in her mouth and a dribble of saliva ran down her chin on each side. Ah-Fat felt in his pocket for Red Hair's black beans and put one in her mouth. She did not have enough teeth to chew it, but she sucked it noisily and the dribbles gradually turned brown. When she had swallowed it, she held out her hand for more. There was something odd about her hand and, looking carefully, Ah-Fat saw something growing out at an angle next to her thumb—a sixth finger.

Just then there was a shout and a woman with a lantern hurried over to them. It was Auntie Huang, one of the servants from Red Hair's household. She grabbed the child, crying frantically: "Oh my God, Six Fingers! Where have you been? You're so quick on your feet, you were gone in the blink of an eye. Whatever would I say to the bridegroom if I lost you even before the wedding feast was over?" "Is she a relative of Red Hair's?" asked Ah-Fat. "How come I've never seen her before?" "She wasn't, but she is now," Auntie Huang smiled. "This child is the bride's little sister. She was born with six fingers. Her mum and dad were afraid they couldn't marry her off and couldn't afford to keep her so they sent her off with the bride to Red Hair's family." Ah-Fat smiled. "Red Hair is a rich man," he said. "It's nothing for him to take in Six Fingers."

As Auntie Huang led the child away, Six Fingers dragged behind. She kept turning to look back at Ah-Fat, fixing her luminous dark eyes on him.

She's going to be quite a girl when she grows up, thought Ah-Fat to himself.

This time Red Hair stayed home more than a year, long enough to see his bride safely delivered of a son. Only then did he make preparations to go back to Gold Mountain.

And this time he took with him a companion—Fong Yuen Cheong's son, Fong Tak Fat.

The idea of going to Gold Mountain first occurred to Ah-Fat the day he saw Red Hair's porters arriving in the village with those weighty Gold Mountain trunks slung from their shoulder poles. In the beginning, the idea was only a vague one but he kept it tucked away in his breast and would not give it up. It had no shape but it grew on him till he felt like he was going to explode. Eventually, he sought out his old teacher, Mr. Auyung.

"Do you have any idea what life is like in Gold Mountain?" asked the teacher. Ah-Fat shook his head. "Uncle Red Hair doesn't want to talk about it." After a moment's hesitation, he went on: "I don't know what it's like there but I do know what it's like here—a tunnel with no light at the end." Mr. Auyung struck the table with his fist. "That was what I was hoping you'd say. There's nothing for you here. Over in Gold Mountain you can at least fight for your life." Suddenly Ah-Fat's vague idea took form and substance. He had got the advice he wanted.

He still needed the money for the journey so he mortgaged the family's remaining quarters in the compound for a hundred silver dollars. When he ran over to Red Hair's home with the dollars bundled in a handkerchief, Red Hair sighed. "If I say I don't want you coming along, your mum will say I'm refusing to take care of Yuen Cheong's son." After a pause he said: "OK, OK, if you're not afraid of hardship, then you can come."

Ah-Fat was up early on the day of their departure. He had a cloth bundle packed and ready: it held just one new suit of clothes, three pairs of cloth shoes, five pairs of thick cotton socks and a few ordinary items of clothing. He also took a few tins of salt fish to eat on the ship. His mother had spent night after night painstakingly sewing the shoes for him. By now she was almost blind and the stitching was all over the place. "Don't waste your time," Red Hair told her. "Cloth shoes won't see Ah-Fat through a Gold Mountain winter, it's far too cold. He'll need to buy leather shoes." But Mrs. Mak made the shoes very loose-fitting so Ah-Fat could wear three pairs of socks inside them. She could not imagine there was anywhere on earth where three pairs of thick cotton socks would not be warm enough.

Awake before dawn, Ah-Fat kicked out at his little brother who was curled up fast asleep at his feet. Since the epilepsy, Ah-Sin slept almost round the clock. Ah-Fat kicked out again, this time with more force. Ah-Sin grunted, then turned over and went back to sleep again. His brother gave up and got quietly out of bed, pulling the thin blue-patterned quilt over the child. Ah-Fat could not know that this would be the last time he would see Ah-Sin. Even before his ship arrived in Gold Mountain, Ah-Sin was dead. As he cut grass for the pig, he was taken with a fit and fell down the grassy slope to his death. For years after, Ah-Fat regretted not having woken Ah-Sin up that morning. He would like to have said a few kind words to him.

Ah-Fat felt at the top of the bed for the cloth bundle, then groped his way to the door. There he tripped over something soft. It stirred and he heard a snuffling sound. By the faint light of the stove, he saw it was his mother, wiping tears from her eyes. She had already heated up the green bean porridge for him to eat before he left.

She blew her nose and, in a muffled voice, told him to light the oil lamp.

Ah-Fat did not move. "It's getting light, I can see without it."

He did not want to see his mother's face. It was hard to believe that her eyes, reduced now to two tiny holes, had so many tears left. Sometimes he felt as though her tears were tentacles dragging him down, and that he would be devoured by her grief. But he also knew that today he had only to lift his foot over the threshold and he would be out of reach of her tears in a place where her grief could not touch him any more.

"Ah-Fat, light the lamp." Her voice was suddenly harsh.

He did as he was told. His mother gripped the door jamb and pulled herself to her feet. She pointed her finger in his face and ordered him: "Kneel down. Kneel before your dad."

Ah-Fat knelt before his father's portrait. The flagstones felt hard and cold through the thin cotton of his trousers. His father's face wore a weary, even sleepy expression in the faint glow of the lamp. His father could not look after him now.

Ah-Fat felt the tears well up. He twisted the end of his sleeve into a lump and stuffed it into his mouth. By swallowing hard a few times, he got himself under control.

"Dad, my uncle's going to till our fields, with your blessing and protection," he said.

Then he went on: "Dad, I'm going to Gold Mountain. But I'll be back, rich or poor, dead or alive. I'll never let the incense go out at your tomb."

His mother knelt by his side. Her nose was stuffed up from crying and he could feel her laboured breaths fanning his cheeks. Her bound feet in their pointed slippers looked like upturned conical bamboo shoots as they trembled gently under her long loose cotton jacket.

"Ah-Fat's dad, please let him die rather than touch opium. If he ever gets addicted to opium, ever, he'll be stripped of your family name, and then he'd better not think of ever crossing this threshold again."

By the time Ah-Fat walked out of the courtyard, the sky was turning pale. The neighbours' chickens had been cooped up all night and now scurried impatiently along the field verges hunting for scarcely wakened worms. Two belligerent young cockerels fought over a large black worm, flapping their wings fiercely. Ah-Fat threw a clod of earth at them to break up the fight, and they flew off with loud squawks, scattering feathers in the air. In the distance he could hear the squealing of the water wheel as it began to turn. Many villagers started their work before the sun was up.

Ah-Fat picked a stalk of bristle grass from the verge. It was heavy with dewdrops. These were God's tears, he remembered his mother saying. He twisted the strands together and pushed it up his nose. The thunderous sneeze he gave seemed to shake every bit of his body loose—bones, muscles, veins. All the accumulated mess and muddle which had weighed on him for all of his sixteen years was sneezed out through his nostrils and he felt cleansed and fresh.

He found Red Hair's family and the porter he had hired waiting outside their house. Red Hair was a man of the world, and his baggage was different from Ah-Fat's small bundle. At each end of the carrying pole hung a brightly gleaming rattan box. Red Hair's mother shielded her eyes and peered at the sun to reckon the time. It was a month since Red Hair's wife had given birth and she was no longer confined to the house. With her forehead wrapped in a scarf against the morning chill, she stood cradling her infant and holding Six Fingers by the hand. She talked to Red Hair in low tones. Then she placed the baby's palms together. "Daddy's going to Gold Mountain. Say a nice bye-bye to Daddy," she said, her voice breaking before she had finished the sentence. The baby stared fixedly at his father and suddenly began to bawl so loudly the veins stood out purple on his forehead. Red Hair's wife rocked him and shushed him, and finally pacified him by letting him suck on her finger.

Then she used her leg to give Six Fingers a hard shove forwards. "What did I teach you last night? What do you say?" Even though she had grown a lot this year, Six Fingers was a skinny child with sticklike arms and legs, who looked as if a gust of wind would blow her over. After a good many pushes of encouragement, she finally bowed her head and whispered: "My two elder brothers are off to Gold Mountain. Come back soon and send us lots of money."

Those standing around her burst out laughing. "You're letting that kid Ah-Fat off too lightly. He's not your elder brother! He may be a big lad, but he's still your nephew!" Overcome with shyness, Six Fingers fled into the house, refusing to come out again.

The three men set off.

The porter was heavily laden but he still set a good pace and left Ah-Fat and Red Hair far behind. The sun gradually rose high into the sky, the dew dried up and fine dust covered the road. Sharp-pointed lotus buds stuck up from the pond surface. At some point, the water wheel had stopped turning and the cicadas had not yet started chirping. Apart from the sound of their footsteps, all was quiet around them.

"Uncle Red Hair," began Ah-Fat, "is there really gold everywhere in Gold Mountain?"

2

Gold Mountain Perils

❦

Years five to seven of the reign of Guangxu (1879–1881)
Province of British Columbia, Canada

Yesterday afternoon, citizens of Victoria, gathered at the docks, enjoyed an extraordinary spectacle: the steamship Madeley *put into port at approximately 3:15 p.m., with three hundred and seventy-eight people from the Empire of the Great Qing on board. The steamship had started her journey in Hong Kong, but because cases of smallpox were suspected, she was run aground in Honolulu for more than a month before finally making her way to Victoria. This is the biggest ever wave of Chinese to arrive on these shores. The provincial legislature has on several occasions proposed levying a head tax on Chinese workers and placing restrictions on the places which employ them, and yet an ever-increasing tide of Yellow labourers continues to pour in. The journey has lasted many months for these coolies (known as "piglets" in their language). In a ship which has been described as a floating hell, they have had to endure the torments of fetid air, appalling food and storms at sea, and appear anaemic, filthy and ragged to a man. There is not a single woman or child to be seen within their ranks. However, although they are uniformly male, they have very long pigtails, some hanging straight down their backs, others worn coiled up on their heads. They all carry a flat shoulder pole made of bamboo with a basket hung from each end, into which are packed all their bundles. They look apathetic, walk unsteadily and have none of the noble bearing of "celestials." Indeed, their weird garb is in forceful contrast to their surroundings. Amongst the crowds who came to watch the goings on, there were some children who threw stones at them, but law enforcement officers quickly put a stop to that.*

Victoria Colonial News, *5 July 1879*

When Fong Tak Fat emerged from the hold, a dazzling whiteness met his eyes. He had never experienced sunshine like this, sharp as a newly ground knife and stabbing him right in the eyes. Even when he closed them, he could still feel the sun's keen edge against his eyelids. He and Red Hair had both made do with steerage tickets on the steamship. Steerage was below the water line, and day and night had been the same for a very long time. Now the sun seemed like a bullying stranger to him.

Ah-Fat guessed it must be summer by now. When he left home, the sun had still been soft and gentle—not nearly as powerful as the sun here. He was not sure how many days he'd spent at sea. Without an almanac, the only way he could mark the days was to make a scratch on his shoulder pole every night before going to sleep. As the ship came in to dock, he carefully counted the scratches. There were ninety-seven altogether. But it had actually been between one hundred and one hundred and two days since he left home. The ship had no sooner put to sea than he grew seasick. He lay prone on the cabin floor, feeling as weak as a soft-shelled crab and unable to stir. Then he was struck down with malaria which burned and chilled him by turns, and he lay comatose for days. None of the passengers reckoned he would live. Red Hair even dressed him in his new clothes to "send him on his way." The rule on ship was that anyone who died on board had to be buried at sea. But against all odds, he pulled through. After he woke, he asked how many days he had been asleep; some said three days, some four and some five. The exact length of his passage to Gold Mountain would always be a matter of conjecture.

Before he went on shore, Ah-Fat donned the clean suit of clothes that Red Hair had dressed him in when he was so ill with malaria. His mother had got Fatty the tailor at the entrance to the village to make them for him before he left. The tailor had used homespun blue cloth with five or six layers of patches sewn into the wristbands and knees, all ready for when he needed them. Mrs. Mak was preparing clothes that he could wear for a long time, right up to the day he came home. The patches were stiff and heavy, so that the clothes banged against him when he wore them, rather like a suit of armour. He cursed Fatty for wasting cloth and making the trouser legs so wide and long, but Red Hair patted him on the shoulder: "You've just been to the gates of hell and back, so don't blame the tailor." It was only then that Ah-Fat realized how thin he had become.

The ship had been docked for hours, but still they could not disembark. A rumour circulated that they were waiting for someone. Eventually, three people turned up. They were dressed in white garments, with white gloves, and wore squares of white cloth over their mouths. The masks covered more than half of their faces. Only their eyes were visible, sunk deeply into their sockets. Ah-Fat had seen Christian missionaries with eyes like these men in his hometown so their appearance did not strike him as particularly strange.

The three men divided up the crowd on the deck into two rows and ordered them all to stand straight, side by side, with their hands palm up, face to face and eye to eye with the man opposite. Red Hair shot a meaningful glance at Ah-Fat, which he knew meant that he must remember to say he was eighteen years old to anyone who asked him a question. But no one asked him any questions. Instead, the shortest of the three made straight for Ah-Fat and, opening a small leather bag, took out a variety of shiny bright metal objects. His eyes were of an intense grey-blue, like a "goose egg" pebble on a stream bed worn smooth over time by the waters. Shorty gripped Ah-Fat's ear and thrust a long, icy-cold implement into it. He twizzled it around a few times as if he was stirring up night soil, then took it out. It tickled and shivers ran through Ah-Fat. Then the man pulled his eyelids up and leaned in close to peer into his eyes. They were eye to eye, and Ah-Fat could see his irises glimmering blue like two will-o'-the-wisps. He finally let go but forgot to pull the lids down, and Ah-Fat had to force himself to blink a few times. They still prickled, as if a grain of sand had stuck inside, and the tears began to run.

Shorty pried open his mouth, and pressed down on the root of his tongue with a stick. Ah-Fat retched and his mouth flooded with brownish saliva. He spat it out, but his mouth still tasted foul.

The man pulled out a piece of cotton cloth and rubbed at the droplets of saliva which flecked his sleeve. Then he pulled off Ah-Fat's jacket and pinched and tapped his chest and stomach. Ah-Fat had always been ticklish. When he was little and fought with Ah-Sin, his younger brother only had to get up close and puff a few breaths at him to reduce Ah-Fat to weak, helpless laughter. This time, of course, Ah-Fat did not dare to laugh; he just kept shrinking backward, until he had gone as stiff as a turtle. The man put his snowy-white head right in the middle of Ah-Fat's chest. His hair was very sparse and he had a pink bald patch on the crown of his head with a black mole in the middle of it, like a woman's nipple. Ah-Fat tried so hard not to laugh that he began to quiver violently all over.

When Shorty had finished tapping his belly, he turned Ah-Fat around, made him stand against the wall and undid Ah-Fat's trouser string. Ah-Fat did not resist and his trousers slipped down onto the deck, revealing bare legs as skinny as sticks. Shorty pulled his buttocks apart and peered between them, and then he loosely pulled the trousers up and gave them back. Before Ah-Fat could tighten his belt, the man turned him around to face him and, reaching inside, fished out the wrinkly thing which hung between his legs. He laid it in the palm of his hand and turned it this way and that, inspecting it. The skin of Shorty's hand was silky smooth and Ah-Fat felt his thing gradually swell like a toad, until it hardened into an iron cudgel. Ah-Fat had never seen it grow so big; he felt everyone's eyes riveted on him until his whole body seemed to burn painfully. He was so mortified he felt close to tears.

Finally it was over, but Shorty did not tell Ah-Fat he could get dressed; he simply nodded towards a tall man at the stern of the ship. The tall man picked up a long snakelike thing from the deck and came over to Ah-Fat. Before Ah-Fat could get out of the way, a jet of icy-cold water hit him right in the middle of his torso, numbing him to the core. Ah-Fat had seen water in rivers, ponds and wells but he had certainly never seen a snake that could hold so much water in its belly. He was so astonished it did not occur to him to be afraid. Then Red Hair shouted over to him: "It's disinfectant, to kill the bugs on you!" Ah-Fat picked up his clothes, damp as they were, and put them back on. He must remember to ask Red Hair what "disinfectant" actually meant.

A wave of passengers flowed ashore and, led by those who had come to meet them, gradually dispersed into the nearby streets and alleyways. The onlookers dispersed too. Only a few children were left, and these followed behind the new arrivals, keeping a cautious distance, with shouts of "Chink, chink, China monkey." Ah-Fat did not understand the foreign words, but he guessed that they were rude. He staggered along at Red Hair's heels, baskets balanced on his shoulder pole, concentrating on the road and looking straight ahead. After months at sea, he felt like he was still on the ocean waves, and he was unable to walk steadily.

The sun gradually sank and clouds like splotches of blood flecked the sky. The evening wind got up and there were hints of a chill in the air. Ah-Fat crouched down and bound the cuffs of his trousers tightly. The wind back home was not like this. The wind back home was rounded and soft, brushing gently and leaving no trace. The Gold Mountain wind had edges and corners, and if you were not careful it would take a layer of skin off as it passed.

Suddenly, a bell clanged. Ah-Fat looked up, to see a horse-drawn carriage coming towards them. The horse was a great big animal with a gleaming jet-black coat and big, sturdy hooves clopping along the road. Its saddle was dark red and embroidered with gold flowers. An old man wearing a black suit with a black top hat on his head drove the carriage, and two young women sat inside. Their gowns—one was red, the other, blue— were tight-fitting and pinched in at their slender waists; the skirts were so long and wide they looked like two half-opened umbrellas. The women wore hats, with a few feathers stuck into the brims of each. Ah-Fat could not help turning back to stare after the carriage. The plumes looked like pheasants' tail feathers, he thought to himself. Back home, if people killed a pheasant, they did not bother to keep the feathers after plucking it. Only

37

Mr. Auyung, his teacher, would collect them and put them in a pen pot as a decoration. Actually, the feathers stuck in the Gold Mountain ladies' hats looked quite pretty.

He turned back again, saw Red Hair in the far distance waiting for him at the roadside, and hurried to catch up. Red Hair glanced at him. "Pretty, aren't they, Gold Mountain ladies?" But Ah-Fat was still angry because of Shorty on the boat, and refused to answer. Red Hair laughed and said: "You just get an eyeful of all the marvellous things in this town. In a couple of days' time you might be up the mountain working, and then there'll be fuck-all to see."

Red Hair referred to the place where they got off the ship as "the town," and Ah-Fat did the same. It was only a long time afterwards that he learned its proper name, which was almost unpronounceable: Victoria, named for the Queen of England.

That day, Ah-Fat, Red Hair and a dozen other men from neighbouring villages headed off to a lodging house run by a man from Hoi Ping. The Chinese in Gold Mountain went to such lodgings to relax, eat, and exchange news. Red Hair went there to find out about earning money in town or in the mountains. But that was not why Ah-Fat was going. Finding a way of earning money was Red Hair's business, and all Ah-Fat needed to do was just stick close behind him. Ah-Fat was going for a very simple reason: he wanted to drink hot water, eat his fill, and then find someone to shave the whiskers on his face. He had spent three months on board ship; when he went on board, he was just a smooth-cheeked kid. But by the time he disembarked, he had become a man, with a face covered in black whiskers. He had missed out on a whole season, the one in which the gradual, orderly process of becoming an adult should have happened.

In no time at all, the weather cooled down. Victoria was on the coast so the days cooled gradually, starting from either end: morning and evening. At first, the middle of the day was as warm as before, but slowly, the middle was swallowed up as the cool of morning, and evening lasted longer and longer, until the days turned really cold.

Ah-Fat had brought only unlined trousers with him and when he went outside into the wind, they felt as thin as paper. It was only by reaching down and pinching the material that he knew he was wearing trousers at all. Red Hair hunted out a ragged cotton jacket full of holes, tore it into strips and, with a thick needle, sewed the pieces into lengths. He showed Ah-Fat how to wrap them round his legs and feet, starting from the tips of his toes right up to his knees. When he got up in the morning, he wound the cloths round and round his legs, and when he went to bed at night, he unwound them. They smelt foul, like the cloths his mother, Mrs. Mak, used to bind her feet, but at least they kept him warm.

Although the days were unbearably cold, Ah-Fat longed for them to get even colder. During the summer, he and Red Hair, together with a score of fellow villagers, had spent a few months clearing a patch of land for the owner. It was several dozen acres of wasteland and they chopped down the trees, cleared the undergrowth and levelled it, in preparation for the following year when a factory would be built on it. There was a mountainous pile of chopped-down timber which the owner could not be bothered to move off the site. He gave it all to the labourers, who made it into charcoal, bundled it up into sacks and went door-to-door selling it. No one wanted to buy it when the weather was hot, so they waited until it grew cold and they could get a good price for it. Ah-Fat sent home every cent of his earnings from this job, keeping back only money for his rent and food. His mother was waiting for the money to redeem their home. The mortgage term was one year, and Ah-Fat's money would have to grow legs and race back to make the deadline. Much later, when that was done, he wanted them to buy a field, but just now Ah-Fat did not dare to think of it. Just now, all he wanted was for his mother to have a roof over her head.

By day Ah-Fat went out to sell charcoal, and in the evening he returned to sleep at the Tsun Sing General Store on Cormorant Street. The people who lived on Cormorant Street were all Chinese, and the store was owned by a man called Kwan Tsun Sing from Chek Ham. Ah-Sing, as everyone called him, had two shacks, one behind the other. In the front one, he sold general goods, and in the rear, he had erected two long bed planks which he rented out to twelve people. Each bed plank was five feet wide, and would just fit six sleepers if they pulled their legs in and slept one against the other crossways. If one slept too soundly and stretched out straight in his sleep, his feet would dangle over the edge. If two people stretched out at the same time, then all hell would break loose. One morning, Ah-Fat awoke to find himself sleeping on the floor, squeezed off the bed by the others.

Ah-Fat and Red Hair had now been living at Ah-Sing's store for six months. The rent, which included bed and board, was ten dollars a month. Ah-Fat only earned twenty dollars a month, and hated to spend so much. After asking around discreetly, he discovered this was the lowest rent in Chinatown, so he had to put up with it.

That evening, Ah-Fat sold all his charcoal and limped back in through the door later than usual. The cloth shoes he had brought with him had long since worn through. He stuffed them with two layers of oilcloth and bound his feet with the strips. This made the shoes tight so that they rubbed his feet sore. Everyone had already eaten; a bowl of rice gruel, a strip of salted fish and two chicken claws were left in the pan for him. Ah-Fat pulled off his shoes, sat down on the bed plank, got the gruel and drank it down. Then he started to unwind the foot cloths, but the sores had formed scabs which stuck to them. He jerked them free and found his feet covered in blood.

Ah-Sing came over with a basin of warm water and told Ah-Fat to wash his feet. He immersed them in the water, frowning with a sharp intake of breath as he did so. Ah-Sing said the leather shoes made by the Redskins were really good. "They're lighter than a fart, with a helluva nice fur lining, warm as a charcoal burner, and they won't wear out in a hundred years. You should barter a bag of charcoal for a pair. Otherwise, your feet won't last a Gold Mountain winter." Ah-Fat started to work out in his head how much a bag of charcoal would sell for, but did not say anything.

A dark mass of men were crammed onto the bed planks, some picking their teeth, some rubbing at the skin of their feet, others smoking. Only Red Hair lay in a corner, head pillowed on a broken Chinese fiddle, gazing vacantly at the ceiling. In the summer, after their arrival in port, Red Hair had been to the North to find out about gold panning. He was told that even in the North, the gold was exhausted. The sandy debris had been panned two or three times too. In the end, he turned round and returned to Victoria. On the way, he found the Chinese fiddle, which became a treasured possession. Every now and then he would pick out some Cantonese melodies to relieve the boredom.

The men began to tease him: "You know they say you were gold panning with a man in Cariboo when you found a gold nugget as big as a man's fist. You hid it in the crotch of your trousers, and made off with it the same night. Is that true?" "Mother-fuckers!" Red Hair swore at them. "Do you think I'd still be living in this damned room of Ah-Sing's if I had a nugget as big as a fist?" "Then how did you pay for such a fancy wedding feast?" they asked him. "You had over a hundred chickens slaughtered, and that was just for starters, so we heard." "I scrimped and saved for ten years and more," said Red Hair. "Why shouldn't I kill a few chickens?" But no one believed him. They crowded around and tried to pull his trousers off, shouting: "Lets see if there's a gold nugget in your crotch!" Red Hair flailed and shoved until he finally fought his way out. He stood up, holding his trousers up and said: "Ah-Fat, write a letter for me to my old woman. She'll run off with another man if I don't write."

The oil lamp was hurriedly twiddled so it gave more light. Someone ground ink in the ink stone, spread out the paper, chose a quill and handed it to Ah-Fat. Of all the men in the room, only Ah-Fat had done a year or two in a tutor school and could write a few characters, so writing everyone's letters home fell to him. Ah-Fat took the pen, smoothed the tip to a point on the ink stone and waited for Red Hair to speak. Red Hair clutched his head and scratched his cheeks for a long time, and finally said: "Are Mum and young Loon both well?" There was an uproar in the room, and shouts of "Rubbish! You should ask your old lady if she's all right! We all know she's the one you miss." But Red Hair just told Ah-Fat to get on and write, and ignored them.

"Did you get the bank draft for twenty dollars I sent with Uncle Kwan Kow from Bak Chuen village?" he continued. But before Ah-Fat had put pen to paper, Red Hair started to swear: "Fuck it, you received it and you didn't write me a word in reply. You're so lazy, you've got maggots growing under your feet." "Is that what you want me to write?" asked Ah-Fat. "Yes! That's what I want you to write!" Ah-Fat smiled: "You finish talking, and then I'll write it all down at once, so you don't change it later."

Red Hair thought a bit more and finally continued: "'I'm still living at Ah-Sing's house, and I haven't been ill. Next time I send a dollar draft back to you, look after it carefully. The streets of Gold Mountain are full of "piglets." There are too many people and too little work, and when the winter snows come, there's fuck-all to do. You look after Mum and young Loon at home. And don't let your sister Six Fingers slack off. Send her out to do lots of work.'"

Ah-Fat laughed at this. "How big's Six Fingers then? You're not telling me a child of three can do real work!" "Pah!" Red Hair snorted: "When I was three, I used to go with my dad to catch loaches. Write this for me too, 'Before I left, Wet Eyes from Bak Chuen village came and borrowed three measures of rice grain. Get a move on and press him to repay it. But he's a loser with fuck-all to his name, so if you really press him and he doesn't repay, then wait a bit. That way he won't go throwing himself in the river or hanging himself. And for Mum's back pain, there's a good decoction that's made in Gold Mountain. Next time someone goes home, they can take some. Brew it up for Mum.'"

"Finished?" asked Ah-Fat. "Yes, yes, I've finished!" So Ah-Fat wrote out the letter:

Dear Suk Dak:

I hope that you have no worries at home, and that all the family are at peace. I think of you a great deal. I assume you received the twenty silver dollars which Uncle Kwan Kow from Bak Chuen village took with him for you the last time he returned. I am still living at the same address as before, at ease in body and soul, so do not worry about me. The weather is gradually getting colder and it is not easy to find work, so I hope you are making careful plans for the dollars I send and spending as little as possible. Please take all possible care to look after Mum, our son Loon and Six Fingers. You do not need to press for repayment of the three measures of rice grain owed by Wet Eyes' family in Bak Chuen village. I have found an excellent prescription for Mum's back pain and will send some with someone in a few days. I send you my best wishes for a peaceful winter,

Your husband, Red Hair, the nineteenth day of the first month, 1880, Victoria, Canada

Ah-Fat finished writing, sealed the letter and threw down the pen. He put his hand to his mouth and gave an enormous yawn. The storekeeper, Ah-Sing, brought him some tea. "Drink a nice bowl of tea, Ah-Fat," he said. "And use the rest of the ink to write a letter for me too. It's been two months since I got my old mum's letter, and I haven't replied." But Ah-Fat flung himself dejectedly down on the bed board without taking off his clothes. "Ask me another day," he said. "I'm sleepy." Red Hair swore at the boy as he gathered up the ink stone, quill and paper. "You think you can put on airs just because you know a few characters!" But before the words were out of his mouth, Ah-Fat was asleep and snoring. They all sighed. They were not surprised he was tired: he had left at five o'clock in the morning and had only just got back. He had not yet bought a pair of shoes and the sores on his feet were so deep, you could see the bone through them.

The oil lamp was extinguished and the men lay down. But they could not sleep, and a desultory conversation started up. Someone said that a few days ago a *kwai mui*, a young White woman, had gone into the opium den at one end of Fan Tan Alley, the street of gambling dens. She was dressed in black, with a black hat and black skirt, and was such a fine-looking woman that she gave the owner a real scare. He had no idea how to address her and could scarcely get a word out. To his surprise, she knew exactly what she was doing. She lay down on the smokers' couch and, without waiting for anyone to attend her, faced the opium lamp, held the pipe in the palm of one hand and the bodkin in the other, let the opium bubble up, scooped it into a wad, plunged it into the eyehole in the pipe bowl and, when she had finished smoking, rose and left. She came again the next day too. It went on day after day: she came at the same time, smoked a pipe and left. Apparently, a reporter went with her and wrote an article as big as a window and published it in a Gold Mountain English-language newspaper. The men tutted in astonishment: "Find out what time she goes and we'll go and watch how this *kwai mui* does it." Then someone else said Ah-Chow from the lodging house had told him that young Chung's case had come to court. He had been sentenced to a month in jail and fined thirty dollars. Any Chinese who went to jail had their pigtails cut off but Chung had clung to the pillars outside the courtroom and refused to go at any price.

One of his teeth had even been knocked out. Young Chung was from San Wui, and sold tobacco, candies and melon seeds in front of the tea house in Fan Tan Alley. One day, he let off a firecracker and a horse belonging to a *yeung fan* reared and went down in the street. Chung was taken to court.

They all sighed. "Does the Emperor of China know how badly we're being treated?" said one. "What the hell use would it be if he did know?" someone else responded. "Chinese law has nothing to do with Gold Mountain law. Besides, even if he did know, and leapt on his horse and took a ship, it would take him months to get to Gold Mountain. And young Chung will have had his pigtails cut off long before that. He can't wait till the Emperor arrives, can he?" "I heard from Ah-Chow," said Red Hair, "that Imperial Minister Li Hongzhang asked some smartass to make something called a telegram, which only took a few hours to get from the Empire of China to Gold Mountain." "Did it have long legs or long wings? How did it fly faster than a bird?" they asked. "You dickheads," said Red Hair. "A telegram goes faster than dozens of birds added together." There was a chuckle from Ah-Fat in the darkness. "Hey, Ah-Fat, weren't you asleep?" the men shouted. "What are you laughing at?" Ah-Fat fell silent.

Red Hair sighed: "If only my old lady could ride over on a telegram." Of all the men in the room, only Red Hair was newly married. The men began to tease him. "So you're thinking about that, are you? Last time you went home, how many times a day did you do it with your old lady?" Red Hair just laughed loudly. When they pressed him, he said he never counted, he just did it when he felt like it. "I go all these years without it, why shouldn't I make up for it?" The men grew more interested. "Is she bony or plump and fleshy?" they asked. "Fuck," said Red Hair, "she doesn't have much bone or flesh, but there's plenty of juice!" There were shouts of laughter. Suddenly, Ah-Lam, who was lying next to Ah-Fat, shouted: "Hey, Ah-Fat, you little shit! You're sticking me so hard up the back, it hurts!" There was more uproarious laughter.

Red Hair banged the bed plank and shouted, "Go to sleep! It looks like there'll be snow tomorrow morning. If we get up early, we can sell a lot of charcoal." The men gradually grew quiet. Some time later, Red Hair could be heard turning over. "We'll all contribute to one bag of charcoal," he said, "and exchange it with the Redskins for a pair of shoes for Ah-Fat. We always used to give eggs and sesame pancakes to the man who taught our kids and wrote the Chinese New Year couplets for us, didn't we?"

There was silent agreement.

Ah-Fat opened his eyes wide and stared into the darkness. After a long time, he could make out breaks in the gloom. Actually, he already knew these breaks well. For instance, in one corner there was a yellow glow, where a rat had gnawed its way in to steal rice. The pale area at the window was where there was a hole in the sheet which they used to block out the light. From the cracks of light he guessed there must be a full moon and he had a good idea just how cold it was too. It was his first winter in Gold Mountain and he did not know how long it would last. He only knew that the river had frozen over and the road to the mountains was impassable. There was no fishing to be done, crops to be planted or goods to be carried. That mountainous pile of charcoal had gone down considerably and if the weather went on like this for another couple of weeks, it would all be sold. How would they get work after that?

He had asked Red Hair. "You young devil, you're a worrywart. All you have to do is tag along with me. There's always a way to make a living." But Ah-Fat knew that this time even Red Hair was stumped. That morning he had seen him take something out of the bottom of his shoe. It was a fifteen-dollar draft that he was about to send home, but then he put it back again. Red Hair was leaving himself a way out.

Ah-Fat had no way out. Behind Ah-Fat stood his mother, with her swollen, inflamed eyes. Those eyes gnawed away, wolf-like, at Ah-Fat's calves. Ah-Fat just had to shut his eyes, gather his strength and run forward.

Ah-Fat was running for his life.

Gradually, over recent years, Vancouver's Chinatown had shown signs of growing, across Cormorant Street, and over Douglas Street and Store Street. These were now lined with Chinese-owned stores and lodgings. There was even a scattering of Chinese living in Fisgard Street, a little to the north. Streets only in name, they were actually dirt roads with no sidewalks or gutters. In fact, even calling them dirt roads was doing them a favour because they were very narrow. In the narrowest places, the storekeepers displayed their goods in baskets which they pushed six inches or a foot into the street. Then they sat on a stool at the front of their stall. If someone living on the other side of the street happened to come out of their house, the storekeeper could stretch out an arm and grasp a cigarette passed to him by the other. They could exchange all the gossip of Chinatown across the "street" without ever needing to raise their voices.

Chinatown was in the low-lying part of Victoria. If you thought of the city as a giant bowl, then Chinatown was the hollow at the bottom. Whenever it rained, all of the city's water collected and ran into it. Even clean water went black as it swept down into the muddy bottom.

The dirt roads were flanked by densely packed houses made of thin boards nailed together. Most were of one storey, although here and there were two-storey buildings, but they all looked like workmen's huts, with gaps of varying widths between the wooden boards. The muddy rainwater leaked in through the doors and wall cracks, adding a layer of black grime to the inner walls and the bed legs, so the men inside had to take off their shoes, roll up their trousers and go barefoot. In just a few steps their legs would be black too. When the sun shone outside and the water retreated, a layer of silt remained in the houses. Of course, this was not pure mud. It was usually mixed with vegetable leaves, fishbones, eggshells, old shoe uppers and sometimes dead rats. This rich mixture stuck to the bottom of the men's shoes, and was trodden from one room to another and from one street to another, until the whole of Chinatown was impregnated with its rich colour and smell.

Not all of Chinatown was so dilapidated, however. There was one brick-built house on Fisgard Street, which, although it was a low, single-storey affair, was built of good honest bricks, and tiled with real tiles. When the sun shone down, the brightness glared off it. And on Store Street there was another building, so square and flat it looked like a box of Pirate-brand cigarettes lying on its side. Most of the time, its door was closed, as if closely guarding a secret. There were no stalls in the street in front of the door, and there were never any men resting and sunning themselves in the corner against the wall. Its door did not bear even a shop sign. It was a pity that the only two remotely presentable-looking buildings in the whole of Chinatown were not lived in, at least not by the living.

The low, single-storey building on Fisgard Street was the temple of Tam Kung, who was worshipped by the people from Guangdong Province. Chinatown belonged to the people from Guangdong's Four Counties. Tam Kung's birthday was celebrated every year at the beginning of the fourth month of the lunar calendar, and on that day, Chinatown was as noisy and bustling as on market day. In the temple, offerings were made and incense burned. In front of the temple, there were lion and dragon dances, staged operas and vendors selling snacks. Even the *yeung fan* came to Chinatown. They were there not to pay their respects to Tam Kung, but because the noise and excitement was irresistible. The real reason for the hustle and bustle lay thousands of miles away and was not the slightest concern of theirs.

The square, flat building on Store Street was the morgue, though it did not contain any coffins. Instead it was piled high with small wooden caskets, each of which contained one complete set of bones. Each skeleton belonged to someone who had been dead seven years: their bones were brought from all over Gold Mountain and collected here to wait for the boat back to Hong Kong. On each casket, the following details were meticulously noted: full name, place and date of birth and date of decease, and also the number under which the death was registered. The souls of the registered lay quietly in the pitch darkness of their caskets, yearning for fair wind from the Four Counties to start the sail home. Unlike Tam Kung Temple, the morgue was a well-kept secret within Chinatown, a secret as tightly sealed from the outside world as a pearl within an oyster shell. If it had not been for a fire a few years back which bore Chinatown's secret on the winds to the rest of the city, no one would ever have guessed at the "spirit goods" inside.

Today was a half-day holiday in Chinatown so all the shops were shut. Not because of the Chinese New Year or for Tam Kung's birthday, but because today the steamship had arrived from Hong Kong. The many hundreds of souls that had waited so long in their caskets could finally begin the journey back to the Four Counties, and everyone in Chinatown would go and see them off.

This farewell was a solemn occasion because the Chinatown folk felt grief for the dead. But their grief was mixed with other, more complex feelings too. The contents of these number-registered caskets had started out as flesh-and-blood human beings, who had disembarked at these docks and dispersed into the streets around. Chinatown had not looked after them properly and had abandoned them in these caskets. There was also a feeling that they would all share the same fate eventually. These flesh-and-blood beings had brought many stories with them and now they were going back with even more. But once the lid of each casket was shut, those stories were chopped cleanly in half—one-half in the world of the living, the other in the box. The living tales that had been passed from one person to another were eventually changed beyond recognition, while the half which lay in the casket would never be known by anyone ever again. The living who came to bid farewell to the dead grieved for these untold tales. They did not know when their own stories would be chopped in half by the shutting of the casket lid.

Ah-Fat was on holiday today. He was now helping out in the San Yuen Wash-House across from the Tsun Sing General Store. Every day he went to meet the steamship as it docked and collected the seamen's dirty clothing. He stuffed it into big sacks which he loaded onto the carrying pole and took back to the laundry. The next day, he delivered the washed and ironed clothes. Sometimes he made this trip several times a day. None of the three helpers at the laundry knew any English, but Ah-Fat could count in English so he was the one who dealt with the seamen. The sacks were stuffed so full it was like carrying two iron balls, and the pole bowed under their weight. Ah-Fat crept along all day long, bent low to the ground like a praying mantis with a rock on its back. The laundry was open seven days a week, which meant no days off. Ah-Fat's shoulders had been yearning for a rest for a very long time.

Ah-Fat was no stranger to the caskets. Ah-Sing, the owner of the Tsun Sing General Store and Ah-Fat's landlord, had a cousin who had died several years before and was buried in an out-of-town cemetery. On the day of the steamship's arrival, Ah-Sing summoned Red Hair and Ah-Fat, and asked them to go with him to the cemetery to dig up the bones. This had to be done seven years after the burial, to give time for the flesh to rot away from the skeleton. They poured cooking wine onto cloths and covered their noses and mouths. The bones, when they dug them up, were a yellowish-brown like aged elephant ivory, but they whitened up once they had been carefully rubbed clean with the cloths dipped in the wine. Ah-Sing and Red Hair laid the cleaned bones out on the ground to make sure that they were complete, and then called Ah-Fat over to pack them one by one into the wooden casket. The big bones went at the bottom, the smaller ones on top, then finally on the very top, the pigtail, as desiccated as year-old raw-silk threads. Not a scrap of flesh clung to the bones.

As Ah-Fat was collecting the bones together, he discovered that one shin bone was thicker on one side than on the other, and on the thick side there was a black mark. Thinking he had not cleaned it properly, he scratched it with his fingernail. But however hard he scratched, he could not get the mark off. Ah-Sing told him his cousin had broken his leg and had not been able to get up for three months. "Who broke it?" asked Ah-Fat. Red Hair shot him a meaningful glance but Ah-Fat did not notice. He kept on pestering Ah-Sing with his questions until eventually Ah-Sing lost his temper: "Quit asking so many fucking questions!" Then he gulped down the last of the wine and hurled the bottle as far away from him as he could. It hit the ground and rolled off down the hill until it finally hit a rocky outcrop and shattered with a dull thud. Ah-Fat was quiet then, and nailed the casket down. He covered it with gold paint and recorded on it the details as Ah-Sing dictated: full name, place of birth, and birth and death dates. It was only when he had finished writing that he realized that the cousin had just had his twenty-second birthday when he died.

"Are you scared?" asked Red Hair. "No," said Ah-Fat. Red Hair went on, "These bones have rotted away so clean there's fuck-all on them. Even a starving mongrel wouldn't bother licking them." Ah-Sing sighed. "It'll be up to you to collect my bones," he said to Red Hair. Ah-Sing, at forty-three years old, was older than the rest. "You can't tell who'll be collecting whose bones," said Red Hair. Then he gave Ah-Fat a shove: "You can send my bones back, you little shit. I brought you out here, you send me home, then we're quits."

"Uh-huh," said Ah-Fat indistinctly. It sounded like he was agreeing, but it was an automatic response, one which did not come from his heart. He could not know then just how important that "uh-huh" was to be. He was very young, after all, just starting out in Gold Mountain. All this talk of death made no more impression on him than a flat stone skimming across the surface of a pond. At the moment, all he thought about day and night was earning money. He wanted nothing more than to have three pairs of eyes and four hands so he could learn every detail about how to run a laundry. Sooner or later, he would open a laundry of his own. It would have six men to do the fetching and carrying, two horses and carts, each with a driver, and would run twenty-four hours a day. A pair of lanterns would hang from the eaves, and its name would be painted in big red letters on the doors. He had already thought of the name, Whispering Bamboos Laundry, taken from the beautiful lines by the famous classic poet Wang Wei: "Bamboos whisper of washer-girls returning home/Lotus-leaves yield before the fishing boat." He had learned this classical poem at school with Mr. Auyung. None of the *yeung fan* customers would understand the allusion, nor would the other workers, but it was enough that he did.

That day, there was an incense table with offerings arranged in front of every lodging house and store in Chinatown. There was a big table right in the middle of Chinatown too, piled high with offerings of cakes and fruit of every sort, and chickens and ducks and roasted suckling pigs which gleamed golden. At each end of the table were two burners for the "spirit money." From a distance, the whole street seemed to be wreathed in smoke. At midday, a propitious time chosen according to the lunar calendar, the consul gave a great shout and the orchestra struck up. There were ten master players of the Chinese fiddle, dressed in white gowns, with their instruments swathed in white cloth too. The strings trembled and an almighty wailing issued forth, the high notes ear-splitting and the low notes like dull hammer blows, overwhelming the listeners with waves of melancholy. When the first piece had finished, there was a sudden change in the weather: a chill blast of wind swept the ashes of the paper money in the burners into the air, where they spiralled upward, the column of ash getting thinner as it blew higher, until the very top formed a sharp point which lingered high in the air.

There was consternation among the watching crowds. The consul, a man of mature years and experience, threw himself on his knees in front of the burners and cried loudly: "Great Buddha, our countrymen have died in foreign parts. They suffered numerous injustices, yet today, finally, they can begin the journey home. There they will pay their respects to their ancestors, and will be reunited with their earthly sons and daughters. We beg you to bless them with a fair wind and a smooth sailing. When one spirit is safely home, ten thousand spirits will rejoice." As he finished speaking and raised his head, the ash plume dispersed and the wind dropped.

In front of the mortuary, eight horses stood harnessed to four open carriages covered in white mourning drapes. The order was given and the horses slowly set off towards the docks, heavily laden with several hundred wooden caskets. As the sound of the horses' hooves gradually faded into the distance, and nothing remained but a faint puff of dust, some of the spectators could be seen wiping their eyes with their sleeves.

"He bartered some tea for a pair of boots from the Redskins, and gave them short measures. The Redskins beat him up," Red Hair told Ah-Fat on the way home.

"Who?" asked Ah-Fat.

"Ah-Sing's cousin."

Years seven to thirteen of the reign of Guangxu (1881–1887) Province of British Columbia, Canada

This afternoon, five hundred Chinese navvies from Victoria and New Westminster boarded a steamship bound for Port Moody. They are part of the work force which will build the Pacific Railroad. After ten years of intense negotiations within the Canadian Federal Government, work can now begin on the railroad project. In order to cut costs to the minimum, Chief Engineer Andrew Onderdonk has overseen the recruitment of over five thousand navvies from Canton and California. Several thousand more will arrive over the next few months. These figures do not include a significant number of Chinese already living in Victoria who have joined the work teams.

The Pacific Railroad will extend through the precipitous Rocky Mountains of the Fraser Valley region. Here the rocks are of solid granite and all the railroad foundations will have to be hacked out by hand.

Between the towns of Yale and Lytton alone, a mere seventeen miles, it will be necessary to hack out thirteen tunnels. In one mile-and-a-half section, four tunnels will be built in quick succession. The coolies will undertake the most dangerous work, pitting human flesh against hard rock.

Within these construction teams, those who blast the rock earn the highest wages, estimated to be four dollars a day. Metal-grinders earn three dollars fifty a day, bridge-building carpenters earn three dollars a day and brick-layers, two dollars fifty to three dollars a day. Wood cutters earn two dollars a day. The least skilled of the workers earn one dollar seventy five per day. Although some among them are hefty and strong, most of the workers are quite diminutive. Some appear like pre-pubescent boys, though all workers are required to show documentation stating they are at least eighteen years of age. When the navvies arrive on site, they are divided into groups of thirty men, each headed by a foreman appointed by the railroad company. Each work group includes a cook and a record keeper.

The record-keeper logs the hours of work completed and liaises between the workers and the foreman. Most of the Chinese workers understand almost no English, and the authorities are concerned about whether they can properly understand work instructions. Another safety concern is the peculiar long pigtails they wear. A representative from the railroad company explained that the Chinese regard their pigtails as sacred because they are bestowed by the Emperor and their parents. Indeed, to the Chinese, they are more important than life itself. According to the English Constitution, which enshrines the protection of basic human rights, no one can force a Chinese to cut off his absurd pigtail. And so thousands will set out on this unknown road with their pigtails and their bags of rice.

The British Columbian, *New Westminster, 7 April 1881*

They lived in rudimentary tents, each made of seven tree branches and covered by two tarpaulins. The trees used were either fir or silver birch. These were felled and the branches stripped off, leaving only the trunk. They were erected in two rows of three on each side, interlocking at the top, and along the three forks was laid the seventh, thicker trunk, forming the roof pole. Over this went the tarpaulins and these were sewn together with the coarse thread used for making fishing nets, by means of a needle made from an animal bone. All of this was learned from the Redskins.

Fires were kept burning all night on either side of the tent; anyone who got up for a piss in the night would add a bit more firewood to them. At daybreak, when the cook got up to make breakfast, he only needed to rake the remaining fire and add some sticks and he could make their porridge. As soon as the sleepers in the tent opened their eyes, the porridge would be ready. Making fires in the mountains served several purposes: they kept the men warm, gave light, cooked food and gave them courage. Before these men arrived, the mountains were the domain of wild beasts.

The tents were simple because the men struck camp and moved on every couple of weeks. As the building of the railroad proceeded the men moved with it, keeping pace with the construction. Striking camp meant rolling up the tents and sleeping mats, loading the rice sacks and water buckets onto the pack horses and then walking to the next camp. They did not take the branches with them. One thing the mountains had in plenty was trees, so they could fell them as they needed. Every time they struck camp, Ah-Fat sewed a cross on the corner of one of the tarpaulins. There were six crosses now.

Ah-Fat was awakened by the screeching of Red Hair's fiddle, which seemed to be sawing right into his skull. He kicked away the leg which Ah-Lam, a fellow navvy in his team, had flung across him in his sleep, crawled out of the tent and chucked a stone at Red Hair. The fiddle screeched to a halt and Red Hair swore: "That's a bridal tune. If you stop me playing, you'll never get yourself a bride, ever!"

It had rained in the night and leaked into the tent, wetting Ah-Fat's trouser bottoms. As he wrung them dry, the sun burst through. The sunlight was cut into fine-ribboned rays by the dense stands of trees, which cast damp shadows underfoot. Overnight a layer of white mushrooms had sprung up among the trees, some as small as buttons, others as big as plates. On the top of one mushroom perched a spotted squirrel, quite a young one, only a few inches long. It had a thin covering of fur and beady black eyes. Ah-Fat picked up a stick to tease it and the little creature was not afraid, it just whiffled its nose and sniffed. Ah-Fat pulled up his jacket and relieved himself with a long piss in the direction of the mushroom. Startled, the squirrel raised its tail in the air and scurried away, rustling through the undergrowth. Ah-Fat could not help laughing out loud.

Ginger woke up too, stretched lazily and emerged from behind a tree, cocking his hind leg and pissing against the tree trunk. Then he raked the ground with his claws, filling the forest with a dense musky odour.

Ginger was a stray dog that had attached himself to them when they got off the boat at Port Moody. They had tried to shake him off several times but he stuck with them. Then someone said a dog would give them courage in the mountains, and they kept him.

After she pissed, Ginger wagged his tail and, placing his wet paws firmly against Ah-Fat's leg, licked him till the warm drool ran all over his hand. Ginger was a wolf-dog cross and stood so tall that if he stretched, he could almost reach Ah-Fat's shoulder. Ah-Fat had to shove the dog away a few times before he finally got rid of him.

He asked the cook what was for breakfast. "Boiled potatoes, rice porridge and salt fish."

"It's potatoes every day," complained Ah-Fat, "potatoes every meal. We piss potatoes ... can't we have something different?" "You don't know how lucky you are," said the cook. "If we ever get snowed in, there won't be a fucking crumb to eat." "If there's no fucking crumb to eat, then at least there won't be potatoes," said Ah-Fat. The cook's expression tightened: "Potatoes are all the supply team ever bring into the mountains. Even if you killed me off, you wouldn't get anything different to eat."

When they had finished breakfast, the record-keeper relayed the foreman's instructions: "You're breaking up stones all day today." The stones which had been blasted out the previous two days all had to be carried up the mountainside basket by basket and tipped down into the canyon. The thirty-strong team would be divided into groups of ten, one to do the stone-breaking, another to load the baskets and the third to carry them up the mountain. Red Hair and Ah-Fat were stone-breakers; Ah-Lam was in the carrying team. "Mind your step," said Red Hair to him as he set off. "If you miss your footing, you'll be over that damned cliff quicker than an eagle can squawk." "I know my way well enough," said Ah-Lam. "Don't go wishing bad luck on me."

The stone-breakers had to break the stones small enough to fit into the baskets. Some of the stones could be broken up just using a sledgehammer but the bigger ones had to be split with a rock drill first, and then each piece had to be broken into smaller pieces. Red Hair and Ah-Fat worked as a team then: the boy held the drill and the older man swung the sledgehammer. The constant jarring soon made the skin between Ah-Fat's thumb and forefinger crack and bleed. He had to rip the lining of his cotton jacket into pieces and make a bandage. The blood leaked through and formed a hard scab. He soaked his bandage in water every evening when they got back to camp, then dried it over the bonfire, ready for work again the next day. The cracks would begin to heal overnight, only to split again the next day. Gradually the cracks got bigger and would not heal over. Rock dust got in and they began to look like dirty black gullies.

Red Hair told Ah-Fat to go and buy a pair of deerskin gloves with a good thick lining of animal pelt inside them, from the Redskins. When Ah-Fat heard they cost three dollars a pair, he refused. Red Hair sighed: "That's two whole days' wages if you don't spend a cent on food or drink, or shell out on a woman," he said. "Those thieving motherfuckers have hiked the price sky-high."

Ah-Fat said nothing but he suddenly realized that he was not capable of being a carpenter, a bricklayer or a grinder. Back home, all he could do was farm work (and he had never done more than muddle along at that). If he worked himself to the bone all day breaking and carrying stones, the most he could earn was one dollar and seventy-five cents a day. But as soon as work started on the railroad, prices shot up and all his wages went on daily necessities. At this rate, how long would it take him to save up enough to buy fields and property? His mother might not last that long.

The break that Ah-Fat was hoping for came just five days later.

The group had set up camp in a new spot, but after two whole days, there was still a blank next to their names in the record-keeper's work log. Several attempts to blast the rocks had failed, so none of the follow-up work could proceed.

The proper name for the explosive they used was nitroglycerine, but no one ever called it that. They just called it Yellow Water. When put into bottles, it looked about as harmless and innocent as lemonade, pretty even. No one could have imagined it capable of razing mountaintops. It was hotheaded stuff too, and had to be handled with the greatest care. If, by some mishap, a drop escaped and landed on hard rock, and it happened to be a hot day, the whole lot would go up in smoke in the blink of an eye.

The tunnel to be built was through a cliff face, and could only be reached by crawling across loose scree. The first man to go up was hand-picked by the foreman because he had the most blasting experience. As he crossed the last bit of scree, he trod upon an overhanging rock, lost his footing and fell. There was a deafening, muffled roar—not of detonated explosives but of cascading rock which rolled with him down the mountain. Man and Yellow Water bottle alike hit the surface of the water, floated for a moment, then disappeared from sight.

The second navvy got up the steep slope without incident, but near the entrance to the tunnel twisted his ankle on a loose stone. All that could be seen was his blue cotton jacket fluttering in mid-air like a sparrow hawk with a broken wing, and then the whole cliff face shook. When the dust cleared, the men's mouths opened and shut ludicrously, but no sound came out. They had been deafened by the blast.

The *yeung fan* foreman kicked angrily at a pile of loose stones by his foot. There was no need for an interpreter; the navvies knew he was swearing. But there were no more takers, no third man ready to give up his life on the mountainside.

Not that day.

Not the day after, either.

On the third day, the men awoke to find they had an extra egg with their breakfast. They gathered together afterwards, to find the foreman smoking gloomily. He sat on a low rock and the men formed a circle around him. The foreman smoked on and on, lighting the next cigarette from the butt of the one before. The pile of half-finished cigarette ends grew around him. The men were surprised to see that their young foreman's hair was thinning on top—and he suddenly seemed vulnerable to them. This foreman was their boss, but there were still others above him. He had to answer to the foremen's foreman. Progress had been nil the first day, nil the second day. If there was still no progress today, then he would have to figure out a way to complete four days' work by end of day tomorrow. The men gradually began to feel that they did not want to be in his shoes.

Finally the foreman threw his cigarette away, stood up and pointing at the record-keeper said: "You tell 'em."

The men opened a crack in their ranks and the record-keeper walked into the centre. He stared at his toecaps and, stammering slightly, said: "He … he says anyone who's successful in getting the explosives into the hole and detonating them, can, can apply to, to get his wife over to Gold Mountain. One ticket will be paid for."

There was a silence so absolute you could hear the wind rustling in the trees and the moths flapping their wings on the underside of the leaves. Ah-Fat's fingertip gave a tiny quiver. He was not aware of it—but Red Hair was. Red Hair grabbed hold of his hand in a grip that was as sharp, savage and unrelenting as a crab's pincers. Ah-Fat could hear the bones crack. "I've got a wife, you haven't," Red Hair whispered in his ear.

To the record-keeper, Red Hair said: "You tell that *kwai lo* (white devil) that if he doesn't keep his word, I'll kill his mother."

The record-keeper relayed most, though not all, of the message. He was adept in sandpapering away the roughest edges of the words he had to translate. The frown lines on the foreman's face gradually relaxed into something akin to a genial smile.

Red Hair set off up the mountain carrying the bottle of Yellow Water and the tin tube with the gunpowder packed in it. Ah-Lam started after him: "Mind your step, Red Hair," he called. Red Hair turned and smiled: "Don't pull such an ugly face," he said. "Just you wait till my wife's here to serve you porridge with preserved eggs." Ah-Fat tried to say something too, but the words stuck in his throat. His eyes smarted as he watched Red Hair proceed up the slope.

Red Hair was walking very strangely, like a lame antelope, with one leg long and the other short. The short leg was clamped firmly to the ground while he stretched out the long one and made a circle. Ah-Fat realized he was testing the firmness of the terrain. Stepping slowly but surely, he made his way to the hole in the cliff face. His blue cotton jacket fluttered for a moment at the entrance and then disappeared. Ah-Fat began counting to himself.

One, two, three, four, five. He should have put the bottle of Yellow Water down by now.

Six, seven, eight, nine, ten. He should have stuck the tin tube into the bottle.

Eleven, twelve, thirteen, fourteen, fifteen. He should have set the tube in position inside the hole in the mountain.

Ah-Fat counted to fifty but still there was no sign of Red Hair. Some of the men began to panic. "Send the dog into the hole to look." The words were hardly out of their mouths when there was a muffled thud, like a miserable fart, and something shot out of the hole in the cliff face. The explosives had not ignited properly.

When the dust settled, Ah-Fat and Ah-Lam raced up the mountainside and brought Red Hair back. Half of Red Hair's face had been burned black, and there was something else odd about it too—he had lost an ear. Blood gushed out of a hole the size of a copper coin on the side of his head. Ah-Fat tore off his jacket and pressed it to the wound. In a little while, the cotton cloth was soaked through. Red Hair's body was as limp as a rag doll.

"Get the foreman to ride for a doctor! Quick!" Ah-Fat yelled at the record-keeper. The foreman was the only one who had a horse, apart from the supply team.

The record-keeper went and spoke to the foreman. His words were brief—just one sentence. The foreman launched into a long preamble. The men grew impatient. "What the hell's up? This is a matter of life and death!" The record-keeper came over and mumbled: "He says there's no doctor for a hundred miles. Besides, it was arranged with the contractor that in case of illness or injury, you look after yourself, the company's not responsible. It's clearly laid down in the contract that...."

The record-keeper did not finish what he was saying. He swallowed it back because Ah-Fat got to his feet and walked over to him. Ah-Fat walked up close and the record-keeper could see the axe in the boy's hand. This was the axe Ah-Fat used for felling saplings for their tent. The axe blade had been nicked in a few places but was still an excellent tool for chopping trees.

"Down in the valley there's a Redskin tribe with a medicine man," said Ah-Fat. There was a gleam in his eyes which made the record-keeper tremble. The last time he had seen that kind of a look was one early spring. A brown bear had come down from the mountain after a winter of starvation—it had eyes like that.

The record-keeper went back and told the foreman what Ah-Fat had said. The foreman gave Ah-Fat a sidelong glance and launched into another long, incomprehensible speech. This the record-keeper did not translate. He knew the best he could do was take the rough edges off the man's words, but there was no way he could blunt the knife blade. And now there were knife blades on both sides. He went back to Ah-Fat: "You do what you want. It's none of my concern."

Ah-Fat shoved the record-keeper aside and went up to the foreman. Gently he raised the axe, until it almost rested against the foreman's nose. It still bore the fresh resin smell from the branches he had cut that morning. The foreman started to retreat, but too late. The crowd of men seethed around the pair, squeezing them into the centre of a circle which grew smaller and smaller. It was getting hard to breathe. The foreman's temples began to throb and his eyes looked like they were about to pop out of their sockets.

"Doctor. Right now. You." Ah-Fat enunciated the words one by one.

It took a few moments for the foreman to realize Ah-Fat was speaking English, albeit of a rudimentary kind.

"You're wasting your breath, Ah-Fat," a voice shouted from the crowd, "just cut him down. Our lives are cheap. Two and a half of ours for one of his. Fair's fair."

The foreman suddenly bent down and swiftly pulled something out of his boot, and put it against Ah-Fat's middle. It felt blunt and rather heavy, not like a sharp weapon. Ah-Fat suddenly realized it was a pistol. They had no idea the foreman carried a gun. Ah-Fat dropped his axe with a thud. The atmosphere became as brittle as if it were a sheet of glass of which everyone held a corner in his hand, and dared not make a false move in case it shattered.

The foreman muttered something. Then, pushing Ah-Fat in front of him, he walked him slowly away. The ranks of men parted like water to let them through and came together again behind them. Harsh breathing could be heard but no one said a word.

It was only when the pair had gone some way off that the men found the ashen-faced record-keeper standing among some low bushes. The crotch of his trousers was wet, and urine still dripped from the bottom of one trouser leg.

"He—he said he'd go with Ah-Fat and, and get a doctor." The record-keeper's lips trembled so much he could hardly get the words out.

Half an hour later, the medicine man from the Redskin tribe rode up, bringing herbals to stop the bleeding and inflammation.

Ah-Fat tugged at the record-keeper's sleeve: "Tell him to bring me the stuff."

"What stuff?"

"The bottle of Yellow Water."

The record-keeper looked astonished. "You mean—you're going up?"

"Tell him I don't want a boat ticket, I want a bank draft."

The record-keeper went over and relayed the message. This time the record-keeper spoke fluently and at length while the foreman's answer was brief. In fact, it was a single word, which everyone understood without the need of a translation.

"Yes."

Ah-Fat tied the Yellow Water bottle to his waist, looped the tin tube over his shoulder and then set off. As he walked past the men, he heard sighs but no one tried to stop him.

"If someone's got to die, better for it to be someone without a wife and kids," one man said.

As he climbed the slope, Ah-Fat copied the way Red Hair had gone up—one leg long, the other short, one in a fixed position, the other testing the ground ahead. The difference was that Ah-Fat was younger so his steps were lighter and faster. The half-moon of the cliff face had suffered repeated injuries that day and the newly exposed rock had the terrifying whiteness of a woman's naked breast. Ah-Fat's black shadow fluttered moth-like back and forth across the crevices between the rocks. When he reached the entrance to the hole, he turned around and waved—perhaps in greeting, perhaps in farewell.

A short while later, Ah-Fat emerged from the hole. Forgetting the measured steps he had taken on his ascent, he came down fast. There was no testing of the ground this time. Ah-Fat's legs seemed to have left his body in their frantic flight. But he was not fast enough to outpace the gunpowder in the tin tube. He had not run more than a few steps when the cliff face collapsed.

"That's done it," said the foreman quietly. He did not sound as satisfied as one might have expected. Three and a half lives for one tunnel. Even when he made the usual calculations, he was still not sure the formula made sense.

Besides, he had actually started to like this shy yet rough Chinese kid.

In the middle of that night, the whole camp was woken up by frantic barking. The cook got up for a piss and shouted at Ginger, then tossed a bit of left-over rice cake in the dog's direction. Ginger ignored it, sunk his teeth into the cook's trouser leg and would not let go. The cook grabbed a stick and shoved him off but the dog still howled mournfully. The cook walked over to see what was out there and came across a black bundle on the ground, seven or eight paces from the tent.

He gave it a kick and the thing moaned—it was a man.

The cook lit a lantern and by its light saw a lump of blackened flesh. The flesh moved, revealing two rows of pink gums.

"The bank ... the bank draft," Ah-Fat mumbled.

When the railroad reached the town of Emory the cook's worst fears came true.

It was almost unheard of for the Fraser River to freeze over, but that winter it was covered with a thick layer of ice. The boats of the supply teams could not get through, the camp was cut off and the rice rapidly ran out. Work on the railroad halted and several hundred navvies were trapped in their camps.

Preparing the rice each day became a time-consuming business. First a few spoonfuls of rice grain were boiled to a thin porridge. The *wok* with the porridge in it was put outside the tent to freeze solid, then three or four times the quantity of water was added. The porridge was boiled up and then put out to freeze again. This was repeated three times until the few spoons of rice grain had turned into a *wok*-ful of porridge, enough for a big bowl each. The trouble was this food would not stay put in their bellies. At first they felt full enough to burst, but as soon as they had walked a couple of paces, they farted and then felt ravenously hungry again.

The potatoes had long since been eaten up. The first two days after supplies dried up, there were a couple of slivers of salt fish to add to the rice, then there was just half a spoonful of salt. By the fourth day, that was finished too, and all that was left was one meal a day of watery rice gruel. Eventually, the cook washed out the *wok*, giving each man a little of the rice water. Then he threw down the ladle and said: "You'll have to look after yourselves from now on."

They all knew this was the last mouthful of food but no one said anything. For the starving, even a sigh is a waste of effort. They did not measure their energy in pounds and ounces any more, but in tenths of an ounce. They scrimped and saved every tiny scrap of energy they possessed for the time when the overland supply team would arrive. On the overland route, it would take the pack horses at least three days to arrive from the nearest small town. And that was their speed in summertime. When there was snow and ice on the trail, it might take four days, or five, or forever.

Ah-Fat still kept the one-hundred-dollar bank draft in the pocket of his under-jacket. He had not had a chance to send it to his mother. When he first got it, he was afraid that if he slept too soundly, someone might pull his jacket off him while he slept. So he took the jacket off, folded it very small and used it as a pillow under his head. With the constant folding and re-folding, the bank draft gradually lost its crispness, and the edges became tattered with moisture. As Ah-Fat pillowed his head on the bank draft, he dreamed over and over again that this small piece of paper turned itself into *mu* after *mu* of land, expanses of glossy black earth that would grow anything planted.

But gradually Ah-Fat's dreams changed. He stopped dreaming about land. Now his dreams were full of banquets, with tables laid out from one end of the village to the other. When he woke up, every detail of every dish was still clear in his memory, its colour, its form, its taste, even what dish it was served in and the patterns on it. Then he stopped dreaming. He could not be bothered to keep his eye on the bank draft and just left it by his pillow. He knew perfectly well that the piece of paper which had nearly cost him his life was worthless if he starved to death. It was not even big enough to wipe his arse with.

After drinking the last of the rice water, Ah-Fat fell into a doze, but soon after he was woken by pangs of hunger, gnawing away at his belly like tiny flesh-eating creatures. He could actually hear the rustling as they scrabbled around inside his belly. If someone cut him open right then, he was sure that they would find his belly riddled with tiny holes. His whole body felt as rigid as if it was bound in a straitjacket, and every fibre of his being seemed to have shrunk several inches. He knew he was suffering the effects of the bitter cold.

He slowly crawled out of the tent. Outside it was a dull day, the sun so weak you could only tell where it was by looking at the shade. Before the snow on the trees had had time to melt, it froze again, forming icicles on the branches that swayed in the wind. They had exhausted the supply of firewood and the charcoal fire sputtered into extinction. No one had the energy to go and cut more fuel.

Ah-Fat felt something nudge the small of his back and, turning round, he saw Ginger. The dog walked soundlessly, making as little disturbance as a puff of wind. Ah-Fat reached out and felt his belly. Ginger wearily raised a hind leg, pissed a few drops of urine, then stopped. When Ah-Fat had been at work in the camp, it was so unbearably cold he used to put his hands in the urine whenever Ginger pissed, to warm them up. The dog came to understand what Ah-Fat was doing and would hold back until Ah-Fat reached out his hands. But Ginger had not eaten for many days. The dog's belly was empty and he hardly had any urine left. There were deep cracks all over Ah-Fat's hands and the urine hurt like hell. Ah-Fat shook his hands dry and kicked the dog away with his foot. Ginger whimpered and shook the snow off his coat. Then he crept back to Ah-Fat and pushed his head against his chest.

By now Ginger was nothing but skin and bones, and his sagging belly hung down to the ground like a wrung-out cloth bag. His ribs showed. Ah-Fat stroked her head, flattening a few stray hairs. Then his heart skipped a beat. He had an idea.

He stood up and fetched the axe he used for chopping down trees.

"Ginger, you're gonna die anyway," he said quietly, "you might as well save us."

As he raised the axe to strike, he saw a flicker of fear in Ginger's eyes. But the dog made no move to run away. Instead, he made a slight movement and sank down on the ground, as if to sleep off a good dinner.

Ah-Fat checked the axe for a moment, then struck the dog's neck. The blood spurted out, spattering a line of drops over the snow. The dog's eyes opened wide. In them Ah-Fat saw the mountains, the trees, the sky. He knelt down and pushed the lids down. The dog's tongue quivered and he licked Ah-Fat's hand one last time. The dog's eyes had opened again but the image of the mountains, the trees and the sky gradually faded. Ah-Fat felt something prickling his face. He rubbed it with the back of his hand and was surprised to find it wet with tears.

A couple of hours later, the forest was filled with the smell of cooked meat. Ah-Fat ladled out a bowlful of soup with two slices of lean meat floating on top and carried it to Red Hair. Red Hair's wounds had not healed and still wept blood and pus. The flesh had begun to smell. Ah-Fat propped him up and helped him eat the soup. Unsalted and without any oil in it, it tasted rank. Red Hair forced himself to swallow a mouthful but, like a hydra-headed snake, it fought its way back up and spurted out of his nose, mouth and throat. He was shaken by a violent cough which pulled at the wound on the side of his face. The excruciating pain made him howl in agony. "Ah-Fat!" he shouted suddenly. "Why's it got dark so quickly? Light the lamp!" "It's broad daylight! What d'you want a lamp for?" The chopsticks fell from Red Hair's hand. "It's got dark. I can't see anything…" Red Hair's eyes had a glassy stare. Ah-Fat realized that he had just gone blind.

Ah-Fat hurriedly helped Red Hair to lie back down again.

Red Hair tried to cough but was so weak that the breath caught in his throat and he seemed about to choke. Ah-Fat thumped his chest hard a few times, and his breathing eased a little.

Suddenly, Red Hair gripped Ah-Fat's hand. "When my kid Loon gets married, will you see to the wedding as his uncle?" "You're woozy with sleep, Uncle Red Hair," said Ah-Fat with a smile. "Loon's like my younger brother, he's the same generation as me. He needs a real uncle to marry him off. Besides, he's a little kid, just out of his nappies. Why are you worrying about getting him married?" Red Hair gave a sigh but said nothing. Ah-Fat freed his hand and noticed that all Red Hair's fingers were swollen and club-like. He knew the reason why—the lack of fresh vegetables. What he did not know was whether Red Hair would make it through the winter.

During the night, Ah-Fat awoke to find Red Hair sitting up holding on to one of the tent struts, his eyes glittering brightly. "What's up?" he asked in surprise. "Do you want to take a piss? Do you want me to help you outside?" Red Hair shook his head. He turned towards Ah-Fat and said something into his ear. His voice was so weak that Ah-Fat did not understand at first. Red Hair said it again: "Fiddle." "What do you want the fiddle for?" asked Ah-Fat. "It's the middle of the night." "I'm giving it to you, the fiddle…" Red Hair started coughing weakly again and said nothing more.

Red Hair died that night. When they woke up the next morning, the tent stank. Red Hair had pissed on his mat. When they tried to shake him awake, they found his body was stiff.

They hurriedly wrapped Red Hair in one of the sleeping mats and carried him outside. It was snowing so heavily the sky seemed to be falling on them. Great, fat snowflakes hit them silently in their faces, almost blinding them so that they could not make out each other's features. It was impossible to dig a hole to bury Red Hair, so they tied the bundle up with twine and laid it down under a tree, weighted down with stones.

They stumbled back to the tent. "It's cold enough to freeze your piss today," said someone. "Red Hair won't start to rot in this weather for a couple of weeks or more." Ah-Lam gathered up Red Hair's soiled clothes. "Who knows how many of us'll live," he said with a sigh. "Better wait a few days and bury all the bodies together. It'll save digging a hole for each one." This possibility had occurred to all of them but only vaguely. By speaking the thought out loud, Ah-Lam gave it a terrible clarity. It faced them squarely, and there was no getting away from it. When they lay down again, the tent felt strangely roomy. The space Red Hair's body had been crammed into was tiny, but now that he was gone, it seemed like a yawning gap. As they listened to the thunderous drumming noise from the trees above the tent, they trembled in fear.

Their hunger had numbed them. But the dog meat soup they had gulped down yesterday aroused the hunger pangs again, acute and fierce. When they lay down to sleep, they felt terrible gnawing pains. They did not dare close their eyes for fear they would never wake up again, like Red Hair. The cook, who had lain down for a moment suddenly sat up again. "I'm going to eat snow!" he said. "I've heard just drinking water can keep you alive for two weeks."

There were desperate shouts and they all sat up and crawled outside. They scraped up the snow with their bare hands and ate it. They stuffed themselves with it until they felt they would burst, stood up to piss and ate again. After three rounds of eating snow and pissing, they staggered back to the tent and lay down again, still hungry but this time with full bellies.

Finally they could not stay awake any longer and drifted into a lethargic sleep.

Ah-Fat was the first to hear it—he was awakened by a strange noise from neighbouring tents. It was a little like the wind rustling in bamboos or a rope dancing in mid-air. It was the sound of someone whistling, he realized.

"The pack horses! The pack horses!" someone screamed.

When the snow stopped, Ah-Fat took them to bury Red Hair.

When they scraped away the snow, they discovered that the twine had been gnawed through. The mat had come undone and Red Hair was missing two fingers. Another finger was broken at the joint but still attached by the skin.

Ah-Fat re-wrapped the body, bound it up tightly and told the others to start digging the grave. The ground was frozen hard as iron and their pickaxes pinged against it. The men dug until they were covered with sweat, but all they made was a shallow hole. They tipped the matting bundle in and covered it with a few clods of earth. Suddenly Ah-Fat dug the body out again and rearranged it. He pointed it in a different direction and started burying it again. The men were puzzled but Ah-Lam could see what he was doing: "It points East now, towards Tang Mountain."

To stop wild animals digging up the body, they piled stones on top of the earthen mound and stuck a tree branch in as a marker. Ah-Fat thought the branch would blow down at the first gust of wind, so decided to carve Red Hair's name on the trunk of a nearby fir.

He took the axe to the tree but then realized that he only knew Red Hair's surname—Fong—but not his formal given names. No one else knew either. Finally he just carved "Red Hair Fong" in crooked characters on the tree trunk.

Ah-Fat stood looking at his handiwork in a daze. After a while he said: "Uncle Red Hair, wait seven years and I'll be back to collect your bones." He suddenly remembered what Red Hair had said that day when they helped Ah-Sing collect his cousin's bones in Victoria: "I brought you out here, you send me home, then we're quits." Red Hair's words had been prophetic.

"I'm sorry you're missing a bone or two, Uncle Red Hair," said Ah-Fat as he knelt with all the ceremony he could muster before the makeshift grave.

The Pacific Railroad wound first northward, then eastward, snaking its way along the Fraser Valley and biting a great hole in the belly of the Rocky Mountains. As this great dark snake crept forwards, inch by inch, the camps kept pace, moving along in its trail until, before Ah-Fat knew it, he had sewn more than sixty crosses in the corner of the tarpaulin.

One day, just as Ah-Fat had sewn the sixty-eighth cross, he saw the record-keeper hurrying over. "The foreman's called a meeting," he said. The men were squatting on the ground, slurping at their bowls of porridge. They did not move. "Could be the Lord in Heaven above, but you gotta fill your belly first," said one. The record-keeper glanced at them. "He doesn't want any of you, he wants him," he said, indicating Ah-Fat. "So he wants you to make another trip with the Yellow Water bottle, does he?" said someone. "A hundred-dollar bank draft won't be enough this time. Times have changed…" "You dickhead, there'll be no carrying Yellow Water anywhere," Ah-Lam retorted. "All the tunnels are finished and they're waiting for the tracks to be joined up. There's fuck-all blasting to do now." "Oh, but the boss thinks Ah-Fat carried the bottle so nicely, maybe he's going to let him enjoy his wife as a reward," put in another man. "You're still a virgin, Ah-Fat, aren't you? Lucky you to have a hell of a woman for your first time around!"

Ah-Fat walked away with the men's mocking laughter ringing in his ears, prickling him like a sticky burr clinging to his back.

The foremen's tent was about a hundred paces away up the slope. As he looked up, Ah-Fat could see horses, already saddled and bridled, tied to trees far in the distance. He watched the horses, heads lowered, drinking from the water buckets as the record-keeper went in and reported his arrival. He recognized his foreman's horse, a skittish black pony two to three years old, kicking out and swishing its tail. It snorted playfully as it drank from its bucket. Ah-Fat walked over to it and began making plaits all the way down its mane. The pony looked round at him. It seemed to enjoy the attention, and rubbed its neck against Ah-Fat's hand, whinnying softly.

The record-keeper called Ah-Fat inside.

The tent was exactly the same as the one Ah-Fat lived in, except that his was shared between ten men, and this one housed only three. They were all foremen, each in charge of their own horses and men. The lamp had been turned up to its brightest and the men were playing cards in intense silence. They had no table, so two bedrolls, one on top of the other, served as a card table. The floor was littered with empty liquor bottles. Back when he lived at Ah-Sing's store, Ah-Sing had told him that the *yeung fan* drank something with a strange name, "wee-skee," and a peculiar smell. Now that Ah-Fat could smell it for himself, he thought it had a smell like mouldy cloth shoes. It tickled right inside his nostrils and nearly made him sneeze. It was still early in the morning, and the sun had only just started to brighten the tops of the trees. But the foremen had already drunk enough to turn the tips of their noses bulbous and red, and the sleeping mats were not rolled out. Ah-Fat guessed they had been up all night drinking. He knew that camp rules prohibited alcohol, so it was odd that they were flouting them today. Then his foreman brought the fanned cards in his hand together with a swish and waved at the record-keeper to get out. The record-keeper and Ah-Fat were both startled—the foreman normally communicated through the record-keeper and had never spoken directly to a navvy before.

The record-keeper made a respectful bow and exited through the tent flap, leaving Ah-Fat alone. The three foremen finished their card game. Ah-Fat's boss appeared to have lost—he grimaced and frowned grimly. Then he stood up, brought a sack out from a corner of the tent and said something. His face formed complicated creases as he spoke and Ah-Fat was puzzled. Were they an expression of annoyance or of sadness? But he had worked for almost five years with this foreman and, if the man spoke slowly, Ah-Fat could understand about half of what he said without needing the record-keeper's help.

"This is for you."

Ah-Fat undid the twine tied around the sack and opened it. It held crispy rice cakes. Ever since the time when the team nearly died from starvation, food supplies consisted mostly of rice sheets imported from Hong Kong, with only small amounts of loose rice. The rice was cooked in a dry *wok* till crispy on the bottom, then compressed and cut into sheets a foot square. Once they were dried out, they were much lighter than rice so the supply teams could bring more supplies in one trip. Plus the rice in the rice sheets was already cooked and, at a pinch, could be eaten without further cooking. Once the men had pitched camp, the sheets could also be soaked in water and boiled up into rice or rice porridge.

Ah-Fat reckoned at a rough glance that the sack held about a hundred sheets. Generally, the supply teams would hand over supplies to the cook in each work team. They had never given them directly to the navvies. Ah-Fat thought he must have heard wrong. He pointed to the sack and then to himself. "Give ... me?"

The foreman nodded. "The railroad's soon going to be finished. We're letting you all go. Understand? Let go. I mean…" The foreman flapped his hands dismissively and Ah-Fat suddenly understood.

"What time?"

"Now."

The saddled horses, the card table, the liquor. Ah-Fat's head was spinning but all these disparate fragments gradually began to make up a complete picture. Like a thunderbolt, the realization came to him that all the men in the camp were being abandoned in the wilderness.

"This ... each person?" he asked, pointing at the sack.

"No, just you." The foreman pointed at Ah-Fat's chest.

"Contract, contract…" Ah-Fat was trying to say, "What about the compensation stipulated in the contract?" but his English was not up to it. All he could do was repeat the word "contract."

The foreman understood anyway. He started to speak, but the only words that came out were a repeated "Sorry, sorry."

Ah-Fat ran out of the tent and said to the record-keeper, who was standing at the entrance: "Call the men, all of them, quick!"

The record-keeper looked at the foreman who had followed Ah-Fat out and dared not move.

"You afraid of that dickhead? They're trying to dismiss us on the spot! If you don't go, the whole camp will starve. Quick!" Ah-Fat gave the record-keeper a savage kick and the man stumbled off down the mountain.

A fierce argument broke out among the three foremen and although Ah-Fat could not understand, he hazarded a guess that the other two were pinning the blame for this new trouble on his foreman. After the shouting had continued for a bit, the three men went into the tent, rolled up the bed mats and slung them across the horses' backs. They were about to mount, when Ah-Fat pulled a bottle from his pocket and blocked their way. "You dare make one move," he said, "and I'll smash this. I'll take your three lives with my one life. Fair's fair."

The foremen could not understand a word Ah-Fat said, but they did not need to. Their eyes were drawn to the bottle in Ah-Fat's hand and the yellow liquid that glinted in the early morning sunlight. They suddenly looked ashen, as if a receding tide had sucked all the blood from their faces, exposing a network of livid lines and wrinkles.

A dense black cloud started to roll up the mountainside. It was a black cloud of men, several hundred Chinese men, all from the dozen or so tents that made up the camp. They came brandishing shovels, hammers, pickaxes, rock drills, axes and sticks. They brought the brazier shovels and the ladles too. Anything that could be moved, they brought with them. The black cloud coalesced from scattered puffs of vapour, gathering speed and momentum as it surged up the slope and arrived at the foremen's tent.

Ah-Lam was first on the scene. He was holding a knife which he had grabbed from the cook—one used for peeling potatoes and cutting up cabbage. He had torn his trousers running here and the tatters flapped in the wind like the wings of a sparrow hawk.

"You motherfucker," he raged at the foreman. "We gave years of our lives for you, and now you think you can get rid of us just like that."

Ah-Lam grabbed hold of the foreman's jacket and lunged at him with the knife. The foreman dodged and Ah-Lam deflected, missed his footing and tumbled down the slope, coming to rest against a sapling. The tears in Ah-Lam's trousers caught on the branches and he had to make several attempts to stand upright. A trouser leg ripped off in the process, leaving him with one bare leg. His hair stood up like wire bristles and, his eyes blazing and almost starting from his head, he launched himself into a new attack.

Just as he was raising his knife to bring it down on the foreman's head, he glimpsed, out of the corner of his eye, something which leapt, panther-like, from the crowd of men. It seized his arm. Ah-Lam saw it was Ah-Fat, and his aim faltered—but too late to stop the knife on its ferocious plunge downwards.

Ah-Fat felt a smack on the face and shut his eyes involuntarily. When he opened them again, it was to see a bright red duck egg suspended over his head. After a few moments, he realized it was the sun. Gradually his vision cleared and he looked at the trees and the men standing around him. They seemed to be slowly spinning, each branch and leaf and face coloured in a single hue—the vermilion red of the print in his school books.

There were shouts of "Ah-Fat, Ah-Fat!" Some of the men rushed to pull Ah-Fat to his feet, others made to grab the foremen.

"Don't move! Or I'll blast you with this!" Ah-Fat leaned against a tree trunk, holding the bottle of Yellow Water in his hand. The men froze, and the shouts died in their throats, reduced to astonished gasps.

"It's the Pacific Railroad Company who took this decision. What's the point of killing these three? It'll take us a month or more to walk back to the city, and if we don't get supplies, we'll all starve. We'll keep two of them here and send the third down the mountain to cable for supplies. If no supplies turn up, then we'll keep them pri—"

Ah-Fat crumpled to the ground before he finished talking.

Three days later, the supply team arrived in the camp heavily laden with sacks. There were eighty rice sheets for every navvy. Carrying the food sacks and tools over their shoulders, the motley crowd of men trailed like yellow ants down through the autumnal forests, at the start of the long trek through the wilderness to the city.

Ah-Fat dozed fitfully on the back of the foreman's horse. His wound was long and deep—it stretched from his left temple to the right side of his mouth. He was capable of walking but the foreman insisted that he ride pillion on his horse—at least as far as the major road.

"You nearly took my life, but you nearly lost your life to save me, so that makes things even and we're quits," said the foreman and asked the record-keeper to translate.

"What's his name?" Ah-Fat asked the record-keeper. He could only speak through one side of his mouth and his words came out faint and fuzzy.

"Rick Henderson."

When they parted, the foreman took a walking stick out of his baggage and gave it to Ah-Fat. It had been made by a Redskin and was of hardwood, with a grinning eagle carved at the top. The foreman patted Ah-Fat's shoulder. "Maybe we'll meet again, kid." Ah-Fat got down, holding the walking stick, and felt the weakness in his legs.

I hope I never set eyes on you again, was what he thought to himself. But he did not say it. Instead he said: "Maybe, Rick, maybe."

Ah-Fat began to walk but he had not gone far when he heard the clopping of hooves behind him. The foreman was back again.

"Nitroglycerine is kept under lock and key. How did you get hold of it?" he asked.

Ah-Fat laughed. His lips were thickly swollen and the laugh twisted his features into a savage grin.

"That was horse piss. Your horse."

As Ah-Fat made his way through the almost uninhabited forests towards the city, carrying on his back one long cloth bag and a smaller round one, he had no idea that the last spike had been driven into the railroad sleepers in a little town called Craigellachie. At long last, the Pacific Railroad had joined up with the Central and Eastern Railroads, creating a great artery snaking across the chest of the country. Lavish celebratory banquets were taking place, to the popping of champagne corks, and gentlemen in black tuxedos shouted and laughed in between clinking wineglasses. Newspapers and magazines flew off the printing presses, carrying photographs and news reports on their front pages.

But not a single photograph or news report made mention of the Chinese navvies who built the railroad.

That was something else Ah-Fat did not know.

Ah-Sing got up early in the morning and, before opening up the store, shouted to the boy to come and hang up the lanterns. They had been hung up last New Year and then been put away in the attic in the intervening months. They were dusty and the boy took off his apron and gave them a rub, revealing gold lettering underneath: "Years of Plenty" on one, and "Everlasting Peace" on the other. He was too short to hang them on the nails on the wall even when he stood on a stool, so he fetched a bamboo cane and lifted them up onto the nails. A tenuous air of good cheer filtered grudgingly through the door and windows and into the street outside.

The boy shook out his apron and the air filled with clouds of grey dust.

"Uncle Ah-Sing, how much New Year stuff do you want me to get today?"

The boy was referring to gift boxes of snacks such as sesame and green bean cakes and lotus crisp, with a festive red paper cover stuck on top. Ah-Sing bought these in from the cake shop. He did not stock them or make them himself.

Ah-Sing counted up on his fingers. "Five boxes," he said. "Just five, each kind."

The boy was startled. "Five?" he queried. "Will that be enough for the New Year festival?" "If we sell 'em all, then you can go and light incense before your mother's picture!" said his boss. "Haven't you seen the railroad navvies are back and the streets are full of them? They haven't even got rice to eat. How can they afford cakes?"

Ah-Sing watched the boy clopping off down the street, two large baskets slung from the ends of his carrying pole. Then he went back inside and opened the shop, laying the goods out on display. He looked up at the sky. A thick cloud pressed down so low, it was almost as if he could put up his hand and tweak one corner. Leaden skies like this meant snow, he knew, and it would come down with a whoosh just as soon as the wind blew an opening in the cloud. The snow might tip down for the duration of a day, or a season. You never knew.

On a cold day like this, no one would get up at such an early hour to come to his store. There was no hurry.

The truth was that it was a long time since he had had any fresh food. By the last month of the old year, fruit and vegetables were long gone, except for a few apples he had stored since the autumn, now so dried up, they were smaller than tangerines and as wrinkly as an old woman's face. There were a few South China delicacies like dried bamboo shoots which he got in last autumn too, but they had not sold either. Even the cigarettes and tea which always sold well had gradually stopped moving off the shelves. At least the tea leaves were packed in foil in wooden boxes and would keep for a year or so. To prevent the tobacco from going mouldy Ah-Sing wrapped it in cloth bags and put it in sacks of rice which absorbed any moisture.

Business was going from bad to worse.

The Pacific Railroad had taken five years to build, stretching farther and farther into the interior. Before it had time to begin carrying goods and people, the trash it created began to surge towards the city—an army of unemployed for which absolutely no preparations had been made. They appeared overnight on the streets of Victoria's Chinatown and scurried hither and thither like rats hunting for a corner to take shelter, searching for food and warmth in the chinks left between one man and the next.

Things were constantly being pilfered from Ah-Sing's shop: an egg, a cucumber, a bag of rice, a potato, even a pack of needles and thread. So Ah-Sing moved all the goods displayed at the entrance back inside the shop. Then he locked the side door and back door and kept just one side of the double front door open. That way, everyone who came into the shop had to pass in front of his eyes. Even so, things kept disappearing. He simply did not see how these pilferers could use such seamless sleight-of-hand tricks. What he did not understand was that a hungry man could learn tricks in one day that someone with a full belly would never learn in a lifetime.

In recent years, the city had found itself with more and more mouths to feed, and less and less to feed them with. If you had had a full plate of food before, now you only had half. If you had only had half a plate before, now you only had a few crumbs. If you had had a few crumbs before, now you did not have a single one. The city's inhabitants believed that it was the Chinamen with the pigtails hanging down from the back of their heads that had brought this bad luck upon them. The newspapers explained that it was the fault of the Chinamen that everyone only had half the amount of food on their plates, so a campaign was launched to prohibit doing business with them. A few young hotheads even noted the names of people who continued to buy from the Chinamen and scrawled a sign on their walls with whitewash during the night. Anyone marked with such a sign met scowls in the street or suddenly found themselves being elbowed out in business deals with other White men. Little by little, Ah-Sing's *yeung fan* customers dropped off.

Today, Ah-Sing had scarcely finished arranging the baskets of produce when the first customer came in.

He was squatting down at his work and at first only saw a pair of feet. He could tell straightaway that this was a navvy from the railroad. He had on a pair of boots so worn that the uppers were coming away from the soles but the toecaps looked almost new because metal strips had been nailed over them. The trouser legs were covered in burn holes, where sparks from a fire had scorched the material. Ah-Sing gradually raised his eyes to the man's body. He was wearing a heavily patched, double-fronted jacket. The stitches around the patches were so crude that they looked like crawling maggots. He had a bag slung over each shoulder, a long one and a smaller round one of the sort used to carry foodstuffs on long journeys. This one looked saggy. The long sack had something solid packed into it but it was impossible to tell exactly what. Then he saw the man's face. He dropped the rice wine bottle he was holding and it shattered on the floor.

The man had a scar that stretched from his left eyebrow to the right side of his mouth. Although the scar no longer wept pus, it had not healed over either. The winter wind had dried it to a desiccated gash which looked like the furrow of a newly ploughed field.

"Give me a sup of porridge," said the man. "I haven't eaten for a day." He spoke gently, even with a slight smile. But the scar refused to cooperate with the expression on his face. The smile and the scar kept falling out, and the scar turned his gentle smile into a sombre grimace.

The hand which Ah-Sing was using to collect the fragments of glass began to tremble. "You want porridge?! You can kiss my arse! " was what he wanted to say. He had seen too many beggars in Chinatown. But this one was different and he did not dare give him the brush-off. Instead he stammered out: "Fi ... Fisgard Street, at the Chi ... Chinese Benevolent Association, they'll see to you. Have you, have you paid your dues?" Ah-Sing knew that every Chinese who stepped ashore at Victoria paid two dollars towards the Association fees.

The man burst into a laugh so loud it set the window frame shaking.

"You wouldn't know your own granddad, would you, Ah-Sing? What kind of a song-and-dance routine is this you're giving me?"

Ah-Sing was startled. He looked up again and scrutinized the man's face carefully. It looked vaguely familiar. "Are you that ... are you that...?" he began.

The man put down the bags and with his toecap hooked out a stool from under the counter with complete familiarity. Sitting down, he said: "I'm that ... that Ah-Fat."

Ah-Sing's mouth dropped open and stayed open.

"You were just a snot-nosed kid, Ah-Fat," he finally managed to say. "You've grown so tall. And who did that gash on your face?"

"What gash? If a railroad navvy comes back alive, that's divine protection enough, isn't it?" "Red Hair and Ah-Lam went with you, didn't they? What happened to them?" asked Ah-Sing. "Red Hair's gone." "What do you mean 'gone'?" "How many ways of 'going' are there? If you didn't fall to your death or get killed in an explosion, you got sick or starved to death. Red Hair's luck ran out, he was killed off by all of those." "What about Ah-Lam, is he 'gone' too?" "I don't know if he's dead or alive. We walked together from Savona to Port Moody, then we got separated. We only had a few rice sheets left. But we'd already agreed that whatever happened, we'd meet up again at Ah-Sing's store."

"You walked all the way from Savona?" said Ah-Sing in astonishment. "How long did that take you?" "We started out last autumn. There were one hundred and fifty-six of us. By the time we got to Port Moody, only ninety or so were left. We'd worn out three pairs of shoes. Do you rent out places to sleep still?" "Yes I do, but not at the same prices as back then. Board and lodging is four dollars a week now." "You're a bastard, Ah-Sing!" "Hey, prices have skyrocketed these last years, you must know that! We're just clawless crabs—we don't have any other skills to sell. Keeping the shop and renting out sleeping space is the only way I've got of earning a living!"

Ah-Fat offloaded the long bag he carried on one shoulder and handed it to Ah-Sing. "This is Red Hair's fiddle," he said. "You keep it here for now and I'll take it back to China sometime. I'm going to move in here. Give me a few days to get the week's rent together. Give me a bit of porridge and I'll go and get work today."

Ah-Sing scraped some rice from the bottom of the pot and heated it up in some hot water. Then he got a few pieces of pickled vegetables out of a jar. As he handed Ah-Fat the bowl, his expression tightened.

"Ah-Fat, it's not that I don't want to look after folks from back home," he said, "but too many men come to me with the same story every day. Get work? What work? Just walk around and see how many out-of-work people there are. Haven't you seen the announcements put out by the Association telling folks from the Four Counties not to come to Gold Mountain to look for work any more? The railroad is finished and there's nothing else for 'piglets' to do. I can't let you stay here. If I let you stay, we'll just starve quicker together."

Ah-Fat just kept eating and did not answer. He ate slowly, as if he were counting every grain of rice in the bowl. He had lived off hard rice sheets for months and had almost forgotten what porridge tasted like. He wanted the gentle warmth of the rice to last forever—but eventually the last mouthful went down. He tucked the last piece of pickled vegetable under his tongue. Its rank, salty flavour permeated his saliva and coated his tongue from root to tip. In the end, the saliva almost made him dribble and he reluctantly swallowed it.

He put down the bowl, picked up the long bag and the small one, made a deep bow to Ah-Sing and went out into the street.

The wind had got up. It whipped round every corner and gathered in the middle of the street. It penetrated every hair of Ah-Fat's head and every bone in his body. The clouds parted, but what came down was not sunlight but snow. Fat, wet snowflakes turned into grey slush where they landed. Ah-Fat looked up. The whole sky was a dirty grey.

As he got out into the street, he heard a squelching sound as someone laboured through the slush behind him. He looked around, to see Ah-Sing running after him. When Ah-Sing caught up with him, he pulled out of his inside pocket a yellow paper packet with a red label fixed to it. "Put this into your food bag," he said. "I sent the boy to get some in today. After all, it is the end of the old year and you should have something for the New Year. There's no work here in Chinatown. Try your luck where the *yeung fan* live. When you get work, come back and I'll let you have a place to sleep—three dollars fifty a week for you."

Ah-Fat never imagined that this would be the way he acquired his knowledge of the city of Victoria.

Up till now, Chinatown was all he knew. It had been his whole life, providing him with a place to sleep, eat, piss and shit. While in this Gold Mountain city, he had never gone beyond Chinatown—either physically or in his imagination. He had no idea that anywhere else outside Chinatown even existed.

Now he discovered that Chinatown was only one corner of Victoria. In the time he had been away building the railroad, this Canadian town had suddenly grown from a little kid into a hale and hearty youth. In every street and alley radiating out from the steamship docks, new houses had sprung up like mushrooms after spring rain. Their walls were built of neat red or grey-black bricks. The roof tiles were more varied—terracotta red, grey, grey-green, buff, even black. There were always steps leading up to the door, at the foot of which were lawns and flowers. Once, Ah-Fat had a serious look at these gardens and came to the conclusion that they were nothing like any that he had seen before—but he knew there was an amazing variety of things on this earth. At the top of the steps were the door and windows. A wreath often hung on the door; at the windows, the linen curtains were usually drawn, revealing only shadowy figures behind them. When the lamps were lit on dark evenings, their faces shone more brightly through the curtains than in full daylight. Despite Ah-Fat's very limited knowledge, he could see that these homes were very different from the ones in Chinatown. He wanted to describe them with words like "warmth," "plenty" and "sweet dreams."

Gradually Ah-Fat learned about the people who lived behind these linen-curtained windows. Every day at the time when the sun rose to the level of the forks in the tree branches, the mistress of the house would make an appearance. She came to the door to see her husband off to work and her children off to school. He watched as she came out of the front door onto the driveway. Before the horse and carriage clip-clopped away, she would bend forward from a waist nipped in so tightly that it seemed about to snap in two, and peck at the cheeks of her man and her children, in rather the same way that a hen pecks at rice grains. He learned that this pecking motion was called a "kiss." When the sun rose to the top of the tree, it was time for lunch. This was a simple meal for the mistress of the house since her husband and children did not return: usually a slice of bread, a doughnut and a cup of tea. Things only really got busy behind the curtains when the sun started to go down—that was when the cook prepared the evening meal. Ah-Fat could guess pretty accurately by now what they would be eating and how many guests would be there.

He guessed that from the contents of their trash.

After dinner the servants threw out the household waste, and these provided rich pickings: potatoes which had sprouted, rotting tomatoes, the dirt-ingrained outer leaves of cabbage, fish heads, tails and gills, meat bones which had not been gnawed clean, a tin of caviar which still had something left at the bottom. Sometimes there would be mouldy bread. If there were guests at dinner, Ah-Fat might even find a half-empty bottle of wine.

Ah-Fat stuffed it all in the smaller of his two bags. By the time he got back to Chinatown, all the shops were shut. He would scurry through the familiar, narrow, dark streets until he got to the back door of Ah-Sing's store. There was an overhanging roof which warded off the rain and he sat down under it, pulled out the contents of the bag and heated it all up on the stove. In all Chinatown, only Ah-Sing left his stove outdoors once he had finished cooking. The stove, once extinguished, was not hot enough for Ah-Fat to cook the food but just enough to warm it up. In any case, he never waited until it heated through to swallow it down. Nowadays, he had a cast-iron stomach which could withstand anything—hot, cold, cooked or raw.

Finishing his meal, he took off his cotton jacket, used it to cover himself, leaned against the wall and went to sleep. He could sleep through any amount of wind or rain but was instantly alert and awake at the first cock-crow. Before anyone in Chinatown was properly up, he would slink away without leaving the smallest trace that he had been there.

One night, however, Ah-Fat never made it back to Chinatown.

He had made a new discovery during his wanderings through the city, a discovery so closely connected to his belly that it was hard to say which was cause and which was effect.

He was wandering aimlessly down a small street to the west of the docks one day when he heard a slight sound. The street was stirring after its midday rest, but the slight sound which Ah-Fat suddenly caught was something different, something which he had been familiar with as a child, something which had seared itself into his childhood memories so deeply that nothing in the intervening years could efface it.

It was the sound of a hen scurrying around in search of food.

With its constant diet of rotten vegetables, Ah-Fat's belly had grown ascetic. But the sound awoke in him fierce longings for meat. And those fierce longings wriggled, as lively as hordes of worms, through his scarred and pitted guts, until every fibre of his being was seized with an uncontrollable trembling. He had always been able to keep his desires at the trembling stage. On any other day except this, he would have shouldered his bag full of rotten vegetables and made his way back to Ah-Sing's unlit back entrance, with its stinking puddles of filth, to fall asleep and dream, perhaps, of chicken meat. But today something completely unexpected occurred to upset his normal routine.

He saw a fine, fat tawny hen squeeze through a hole in its pen and skip away in the direction of the street.

Ah-Fat's hand seemed to function independently of his brain. His hand deftly grasped the hen and folded its wings back. The hen went limp and he stuffed it into his bag. He had used this neat trick as a child to persuade his mother's chickens back into their coops. He was surprised that he could remember so well how to do it.

As he shouldered his bag, he suddenly saw two eyes watching him from behind the pen. A pair of eyes thickly fringed with lashes the colour of clear blue lake water. The eyes watched him for a few moments, then they fluttered and the lake water darkened.

"Mummy! Thief!"

Ah-Fat heard the child's shrill cry, and the door flew open. A man and a woman rushed out.

He could have made a run for it. His years of climbing the wilderness trails had given him the sure-footedness of a deer. But he stood rooted to the spot, as helpless as the captured hen that was struggling in his bag, because he had seen the long metal thing, glinting black in the sunlight, which the man held in his hand.

A bear hunter's gun.

The couple came closer and he could clearly hear them talking. He did not understand everything they were saying but he caught the gist. The woman said something about "police." The man replied, "No, no need … lesson…." The man waved the woman back into the house. She reappeared after a few moments holding a water jug in one hand and a basket in the other.

The couple marched him along the street, which had begun to fill with afternoon shoppers. He did not need to look around to know that an ever-growing crowd was tailing him. "Yellow monkey! Yellow monkey!" That was the children; their elders did not join in but did not stop them either. The adults remained silent but it was an oppressive silence, which seemed to conceal many different feelings.

They came to a halt by a wooden pole, from the top of which hung a gaslight. The man put down his gun and took the rope which the woman had been carrying in the basket. He pushed Ah-Fat to the ground and bound him to the pole—or rather, bound his pigtail to the pole. He fastened the rope tightly with a secure running knot, then felt around in the basket.

The basket was full of bits and pieces and it took some time for him to find what he was looking for—a tin containing nails. He spat in his palm and began to hammer a nail through the rope into the pole. He used all of his strength, and the rope and the pole began to complain under the force of the hammer blows. Then he tugged on Ah-Fat's pigtail. It did not budge. At that point, he picked up his gun and nodded to the woman.

The woman came up and got an old wooden bowl out of the basket. She put it in front of Ah-Fat and filled it to the brim with water. Then, paying no attention to the crowd of onlookers, the pair walked away. They had not gone more than a couple of paces when the woman ran back and threw down a pair of scissors.

After a moment, Ah-Fat and the onlookers realized what was happening.

What stood between Ah-Fat and his liberty was nothing more, nothing less, than his pigtail. There was only one way for him to escape, and that was to use the scissors to cut it off.

The water in the bowl only offered a temporary respite.

A sigh rose up from the crowd. It was a sigh which expressed many things, and astonishment was only one of them.

The night, like a wolf-hair brush laden with ink, slowly daubed the trees, streets and houses until they faded from sight. The air was heavy with moisture—you could almost wring the water from it. The rain, when it came, fell first as a fine drizzle, then as spattering drops, then in steady columns, then finally as sheets which slashed the ground like a knife leaving great gashes everywhere.

The rain fell on Ah-Fat, but, at first, he did not find it painful. That came later. In fact, he longed for it to come down harder—and harder still—because it put the crowd to flight like startled birds. The street filled with the pattering of retreating footsteps. Ah-Fat sat on the ground and, screened by the rainfall, relieved himself with a long piss. He had wanted to hang on until he got back to Chinatown. When he was captured, his first thought was to wonder how he was going to deal with his bursting need to piss.

Now the rain had unexpectedly come to his rescue.

The warm urine leaked from his trousers and formed a rank-smelling puddle. His body was relaxed now and, since he had been tied up for some time, he began to feel hungry. During the whole of the previous day, he had only eaten a couple of rotting potatoes the size of hens' eggs. He was racked by almost overwhelming hunger pangs. Even if he had eaten that fine, fat hen, he thought, it would only have filled a small corner of his belly. He could not think of anything which was capable of filling up that yawning cavity.

The rain poured down now. The whole of his body felt as if it was covered with nothing more than a thin membrane into which the rain drilled little holes. Every time he took a slight breath, each of the holes hissed with pain.

When he could not stand the pain any more he kneeled and faced east. He wanted to kowtow but his pigtail was tightly bound to the post and threatened to pull his scalp off. So he just placed his palms together and raised his face to the heavens.

"Oh, my emperor, my ancestors," he muttered, "I, Fong Tak Fat, am forced to live in degradation...."

Then he reached for the scissors.

A long howl echoed down the street.

The sound startled even those men of the neighbourhood who were seasoned hunters; they had only ever heard a starving wolf make such a sound. It was so ear-splitting the city streets vibrated. The rain abruptly ceased, and the clouds cleared away to reveal a firmament full of stars.

Ah-Fat threw down the scissors and got to his feet. Far in the distance, he could hear a pitter-pattering noise brought to him by the wind. When there was a strong gust, it was as sharp and clear as corn popping; when the wind dropped, the sound was muffled, like toads blowing bubbles under water.

It was the sound of firecrackers welcoming in the Chinese New Year.

Ah-Fat slunk quietly off to the back door of the Tsun Sing General Store and sat down under the overhanging roof. His jacket ran with so much water it hung on him like a stiff board. He took it off, wrung it out and put it back on again. He trembled like a leaf in the wind. It was a good thing Ah-Sing's stove was still giving out a few miserable dregs of heat. He huddled close to it. It was at that point he discovered that he had dropped the small bag. He still had the long bag, though the fiddle inside was wet through. The snakeskin had blown up and split open with the soaking, and the sound box was full of water.

Ah-Fat upended the fiddle to empty the water out and heard a clunk, as if something had fallen out of it. He felt around and picked it up. It was a stone.

Ah-Fat's heart gave a wild leap and began to hammer so hard the whole street could have heard it.

As soon as he felt the veins which streaked the stone, he knew exactly what it was.

It was a nugget of gold.

It was the nugget which Red Hair had hidden when he was panning for gold.

No wonder Red Hair had not let the fiddle out of his sight. That was how he had kept it hidden all those years. In fact, he had told Ah-Fat about it that evening in the camp, but Ah-Fat had not been paying attention.

That morning the sleepers in the Tsun Sing General Store were awoken by a strange noise. Ah-Sing pulled on some clothes, got out of bed, lit the lamp and went to open the back door. There he found a man, his clothes soaked through and his head covered with a cloth bag, sitting on his woodpile, sawing away at a broken fiddle and making blood-curdling screeching sounds.

"It's New Year's Day, so you won't refuse me a bowl of rice porridge, will you? And I'd like it hot." Ah-Fat gave Ah-Sing a broad grin although his teeth chattered audibly.

In year thirteen of the reign of Guangxu (1887), on Dragon Boat Festival Day, a new laundry opened up in the city of Victoria. It was right on the edge of Chinatown, with one foot on *yeung fan* turf.

It was a lot different from the city's other laundries.

It had a different sort of name, for starters. The city's laundries were usually named after the owner. For instance there was "Ah-Hung's Wash House" and "Wong Ah-Yuen's Laundry" and "Loon Yee's Washing and

Ironing." But this laundry had a strange name. It was called the "Whispering Bamboos Laundry Company."

It was furnished and decorated differently too. Outside, there hung from the wall two hexagonal lanterns, each face of which was covered in delicate flower and bird designs. Unlit, the lanterns were an unassuming, restrained shade of red. But lit up, that red illuminated the whole street with an intense glow of colour. If you pushed open the door and went inside, scrolls hung to the left and right. On the west wall, there was a watercolour of the beautiful Xi-Shi washing gauze. On the east wall, there was a calligraphy scroll with a poem written in a flowing cursive hand:

> Bamboos whisper of washer-girls returning home,
> Lotus-leaves yield before the fishing boat.

If it were not for the mountainous pile of clothes on the counter and the coal-fired iron on the wooden ironing board, the customers might have thought they were entering a tutor school or a shop selling paintings.

The laundry was registered under the name of Frank Fong.

A month before the laundry opened, Mrs. Mak, of Spur-On Village, Hoi Ping County in Guangdong Province, China, received a long-awaited dollar letter from one of the "town horse" couriers. In the envelope, there was a cheque for three hundred dollars. The letter was short and was full of smudges. Mrs. Mak was illiterate so she took it to Mr. Ding, who ran the village tutor school, and he read it out loud to her:

My most esteemed mother,

Your son had a very hard year in Gold Mountain last year and had no money to send home. My hard-working mother must have been anxiously waiting. But this year, I came into a bit of money and am sending you three hundred American dollars. Please write to me as soon as you receive them so that I do not worry. One hundred and fifty dollars belong to Uncle Red Hair's wife and I hope you will immediately give it to her so that she can use it to send his boy Loon to school. The rest is for you to spend. Your son in Gold Mountain is fine, please do not worry yourself.

This was the largest amount of money Ah-Fat had ever sent Mrs. Mak. She used it to redeem the parts of their courtyard residence which had been pawned for Ah-Fat's passage to Gold Mountain. Then she got Ah-Fat's uncle to buy a few *mu* of land and hire labourers to cultivate it.

3

Gold Mountain Promise

2004
Hoi Ping County, Guangdong Province, China

"Tak Yin House *diulau* was built in 1913. It's one of the earliest fortress homes in the area," Auyung told Amy. "Everything needed to build it was shipped in all the way from Vancouver via Hong Kong by your maternal great-grandfather, Fong Tak Fat—the cement, the marble, the glass, the kitchen and toilet fittings. The workmen were hired locally, but they had to follow his plans to the letter. He even chose the designs for the carvings on the windowsills, doors and eaves.

"He sent over extremely detailed plans," Auyung continued. "It took nearly two years to build and he spent fifteen thousand Hong Kong dollars on it, which was a fortune in those days. Because he ran up such huge debts building it, he couldn't afford the boat fare back home to supervise the work. So he didn't come back until after it was finished."

Amy shook her head. "What a shame," she said. "If you ask me, it's a terrible mishmash of a building. The fact that it's airy is one of its few good points."

"The purpose of a building like this was to protect its inhabitants primarily against bandits, and secondly, against flooding. Spur-On Village was in a low-lying area. One rainstorm and all the villagers' chickens and dogs might be washed away. All other considerations were secondary. In fact, the decision to build it was forced on your great-grandfather by a very serious event which happened to the family. As for its architectural style, you can't ask too much of a peasant who hardly had any proper schooling."

"What serious event?"

"Did your grandfather never talk about it?"

"I never saw much of him. My mother left home when she was very young. She couldn't say more than a few words without getting into a fight with him, and one of those would be a four-letter word."

"And what about you? Did the same apply to you and your mum?"

Amy looked startled. "How did you know?" Auyung gave a loud, toothy laugh: "Well, otherwise, how would you know so little about your family history?"

Amy laughed too. "Mr. Auyung," she said, "under your excellent guidance, my interest in my family history is growing."

Auyung showed Amy into the second-floor bedroom.

"This building has five floors. The locals had never seen buildings with several floors and apparently one of the builders, when he got four floors up, refused to build any farther. He said if he went any higher, he'd be able to touch the Thunder God's family jewels!"

Amy looked puzzled. "What family jewels?" "I'm sorry," said Auyung. "I should mind my language when I'm with a lady." Amy suddenly understood, and could not help laughing.

"Apart from the balcony under the eaves, where the weapons were kept, all five floors were lived in. There was a courtyard in the centre with rooms arranged on all four sides. Every floor was the same: two passageways, a reception room, two bedrooms and a storeroom.

"On the ground floor were the kitchen and the servants' rooms. Your great-grandfather's mother and your great-aunt had their rooms on this floor. The shrine to Guan Yam, the Buddhist goddess of mercy, and the spirit tablets to the ancestors, were here too. That was to save the old lady from having to climb the stairs. When your great-grandfather came back from Canada for a while, he lived here too.

"Your great-grandfather's uncle lived with his family on the third floor. Your great-grandfather's daughter lived on the fourth floor—that was your grandfather's younger sister. She was nearly twenty years younger than him, and was the only one of Fong Tak Fat's three children who was born in this house. The fifth floor was originally empty but then when your grandfather's younger brother came back and married, his wife and son lived there."

Amy covered her mouth and gave a long yawn.

"I'm sorry, I've been talking too much," Auyung said. "Let's take you to the hotel. We can come back tomorrow." "No, no, let's get it over with as quick as we can. I've got a ton of things to do when I get back home."

Amy walked into the bedroom. It held a bed and a wardrobe. The bed was of old-fashioned red rosewood, its four posts carved with designs. The original colour had long since faded—only in the deepest parts of the carving were there traces of yellowish-brown. Amy perched cautiously on the edge of the bed, running her fingers up the dragon and phoenix designs on the bedposts until she got to the wooden pearl in the dragon's mouth. Even this light touch left her fingertips covered in a layer of dust. She examined them carefully. Could you talk about dust being old?

"Did my great-grandfather get married here?" asked Amy.

"Of course not. By the time Tak Yin House was finished, your great-grandfather's eldest son—your grandfather—had already left for Gold Mountain. Even your great-uncle was thirteen years old."

The bed was covered with a fine-woven mat which was riddled with moth holes. The cord which bound it together had come unravelled, so that it flopped over the bed base like a boned fish. Amy carefully lifted one corner, and found underneath a slender length of bamboo. She took it out—it was a silk fan. The silk was yellowed with age. On top of this background colour, there were areas of yellow which shaded darker at the edges, perhaps from water stains. On the fan was painted a landscape and a pavilion, but it was hard to make out the details. Some characters were still just about visible but Amy found them almost impossible to read.

Auyung took off his reading glasses and held them over the fan. With the characters enlarged, they could just about make out two lines:

... this brush to write ... words of love
And send them to ... in Gold Mountain

"Your great-grandmother's handwriting!" Auyung exclaimed with a cry of delight.

"Was she a painter?" asked Amy.

"She wasn't just a painter. There was no one like her around here. You'd call her a 'liberated woman' if you were writing a thesis. Of course, that's if there were liberated women a hundred or so years ago...."

"Hmmm," said Amy, and lapsed into silence. Then she went on: "Finally you're really getting me interested, Auyung."

She got up and went to open the wardrobe.

The wardrobe was made of the same red rosewood as the bed. A mirror was mounted on the door, and the mirror frame was carved in the same dragon-and-phoenix designs as the bedposts. But the mirror glass was covered with a sort of mottling, so that things were reflected dimly as if from a distance. Amy opened the door. It was empty except for a woman's jacket decorated with a wide border around the edges, and flowers embroidered at the neck under the collar. The flowers were big and showy, probably peonies, but their colour was a dull yellow. Amy could not help sighing. Nothing could withstand the ravages of time. No matter how vivid the original colours, it reduced everything to this muddy hue.

Amy opened out the garment and discovered a pair of sheer silk stockings folded inside. She took them out and saw a tiny hole in the calf of one. It started out as small as a sesame seed, but had burst into a hole as big as her hand farther up the leg. Amy imagined her great-grandmother walking down the narrow village lanes in a pair of sheer stockings like this, and smiled in spite of herself. She put the jacket around her shoulders. It amply hid all her curves, and she guessed that her great-grandmother must have been a woman of generous proportions. How did she carry herself then, in this village of short people tanned dark by the tropical sunshine? Was she demure and self-effacing or did she walk tall and proud?

Amy stuffed the stockings back inside the jacket and began to button it up. These were traditional Chinese knot buttons, intricately made of fine strips of satin coiled into tight circles and sewn securely—although the stitching had long since come loose. Frowning intently, her thumb and forefinger joined at the tips, Amy carefully pressed the buttons against the front of the jacket,

Suddenly she stopped; her fingers froze, forming a circle in mid-air. She looked up to see a pair of eyes reflected in the mottled mirror.

Just eyes, two faceless eyes. Deep black in colour. Melancholy. Flickering. Staring out at her.

Amy felt a cold draught of air starting at her fingertips that crawled up her spine until the hairs on the back of her neck stood on end.

She shoved the jacket back into the wardrobe and hurried Auyung down the stairs. "Take me to the hotel to check in. We can come back tomorrow."

Outside, Amy got quickly into the car, and curled up with her chin resting on her knees. Her hands would not stop shaking. "I expect the jet lag is catching up with you," said Auyung. "You look like you need a rest." Amy shook her head. "I don't need a rest, I need a stiff drink." "Well, as it happens, the O.O.C.A. is hosting a dinner for you tonight, and it'll be awash with drink."

They had booked Amy into the best hotel in town. She took a shower, then followed Auyung. The banquet was taking place in the hotel dining room and was, naturally, an ostentatious affair. She was given a glass of wine and her hosts started in on lengthy words of welcome. Amy interrupted almost immediately: "I don't want this wine. I want something with a real kick—a whisky on the rocks." There was general puzzlement at her request, until Auyung explained to the wine waitress: "She wants a glass of whisky with ice cubes in it." She was given her drink and, without waiting to clink glasses with anyone, tossed it back.

It was a splendid meal. Abalone, sea snails, grouper fish, suckling pig, pigeon breast and other seasonal delicacies. But Amy ate little. She gulped at her whisky and, after two glasses, relaxed and found herself becoming quite garrulous.

She tugged at Auyung's sleeve. "My mother told me that all of Great-Grandmother's family died in Tak Yin House. Is that right?" Auyung nodded. "How did they die?" Auyung made an effort to distract her by raising his glass to hers. But Amy was not to be put off: "You think it's inappropriate to talk about it here, is that it? Don't try and fob me off just because we're in company!" Auyung looked at their hosts, visibly embarrassed. Just then, the restaurant hostess came over and said: "There's someone in the lobby asking for Ms Fong Yin Ling from Canada." Amy scraped her chair back and stood up: "Who's asking for my mother? I'll go and see." And without waiting for her hosts' reaction, she stomped out of the room, Auyung trotting along behind her.

An elderly man seated in a wheelchair was waiting for them in the lobby. He was completely bald, and his face was seamed with wrinkles. His eyes were clouded milky-white and the rheum had dried into shiny yellow crusts at the corners. He turned when he heard their voices and tried unsuccessfully to struggle to his feet. Then he banged on his armrest and shouted in a cracked voice: "Fifty years! I can't believe it's really taken fifty years for just one of you Fongs to come back!" His assistant, a dark-skinned man, looked on indifferently, making no attempt to calm him down.

"Grandpa Ah-Yuen, this isn't Fong Yin Ling. Fong family business has nothing to do with her," said Auyung. But the old man was deaf to his words. Instead, he reached out and gripped Amy's sleeve: "You Fongs didn't keep your word, did you? You abandoned Kam Sau and her mum. Give me back Kam Sau and Wai Heung," and he began to weep loudly, his tears wetting Amy's sleeve. Auyung hastily called the security men, who dragged the old man off. He was forcibly pushed back into his wheelchair and wheeled away.

Amy was rattled. The whisky she had drunk all of a sudden got to her. She sat down on the ground and was violently sick. Finally, when there was nothing more to come up, she wiped her runny nose and streaming eyes and got trembling to her feet. "Who is Kam Sau?" she asked. "Your great-aunt. Your grandfather's little sister." "Who was that old man?" "That was Kam Sau's husband."

Amy gave a sigh. "Auyung, how many people are we going to upset doing this?"

Auyung sighed too. "If your great-grandfather had married someone else, then perhaps the Fongs would not have left so many stories. Actually, Fong Tak Fat was supposed to marry a different woman, not your great-grandmother at all."

Years twenty to year twenty-one of the reign of Guangxu (1894–1895)
Spur-On Village, Hoi Ping County, Guangdong Province, China

At Ah-Fat's command, the sedan chair halted at the entrance to the village. Ah-Fat wanted to do the last part on foot.

Ah-Fat could have done that walk blindfolded. To the right of the spot where the sedan had set him down, there was an ancient banyan tree. At the foot of the tree, there were the steps which led down to the river—three steps altogether. The river had no name. When the water was high, only half a step was visible. When all three steps were visible, it meant there was a drought. When he was a boy coming home from herding the cows or cutting grass, Ah-Fat would go down those steps to the river to wash off the mud and grass before going back home.

To get home, Ah-Fat did not go down to the water's edge but walked straight along the riverbank. The path to the house was flanked by fields on one side and water on the other. The scenery on the river side was unchanging, while the fields looked different every day. The main crop planted in the two growing seasons was paddy rice, interplanted with a few green vegetables and squashes. If it rained, the paddy rice would be noticeably taller when he went home in the evening than it had been in the morning. Chickens and dogs often scratched around for things to eat among the great clumps of banana palms by the side of the road. Ah-Fat and his brother, Ah-Sin, knew every chicken along the road. The village dogs were a scatterbrained bunch and barked at every strange person or animal they saw. If the dogs at the roadside all barked in unison, then you knew that a stranger was approaching or new cattle were being herded into the village.

Ah-Fat went straight along the road, past the grey stone well that dated from the reign of the emperor Kangxi, and turned right again. The three-courtyard residence that his father had built and squandered, had been restored by his mother. It had taken her seven and a half years to reassemble all the different parts into a single residence where she and his uncle and the family now lived. It was exactly sixteen paces from the road to the front gate. That is, it was sixteen paces fifteen years ago—though probably not so many now. Ah-Fat knew every bump and every pebble on this path—in fact, he had often felt them under the soles of his feet in his dreams.

And now Fong Tak Fat was thirty-one years old. As he trod the path to his front door in the warm spring sunshine, he had the odd sensation that he had gone back in time.

His luggage would come later.

Twenty Gold Mountain suitcases, their corners reinforced with metal strips, all made of the same wood, painted dark red, and fastened with a two-leaf lock in the shape of the lips of a lion. When the lips were closed, the secrets of each case were locked inside. The cases contained all manner of things—from food to clothing and household items. There was Canadian honey, chocolate, olive oil and corn candy; there were clothes, hats and shoes for adults and children, all of course in the Western style, as well as all kinds of Canadian-produced fabrics; for the home, there was foreign soap, matches for lighting the stove, clocks which chimed the hour, and foreign-style knives for cutting cakes and vegetables, china tea sets and dinner sets. And so on and so forth. All these goods were packed into the first nineteen cases and would be given to his mother, uncle and aunt, nephews and nieces, as well their neighbours in the village and even the servants and hired hands.

The last case, however, held things which were purely decorative: ladies' lipsticks and nail varnish, perfume, embroidered brassieres and other underwear, linen tablecloths from Victoria in all shapes and sizes, English and French silver, gold rings and earrings. He was not going to share round the contents of this case; in fact, he would not even open the lion's-head lock. He would give the entire case, just as it was, with all its secrets, to a woman upon whom he had never set eyes. He had only a fuzzy, thumbnail-size photograph of her, although her image often haunted his dreams.

This was the woman to whom his mother had betrothed him six months previously, and he had made this long sea trip back home in order to marry her. He did not know much about her, only that she was the eldest daughter of a family called Sito from the town of Cek Ham. She was fifteen years old. The family ran a tailoring business. The horoscopes of Ah-Fat and the girl had been cast and matched perfectly. The fortune teller said that the girl was destined to make her husband rich, and any family she married into prosper. The fortune teller also said that the girl was destined to have nine and a half sons (the half, of course, being a son-in-law). It was not only these reasons that had persuaded Ah-Fat's mother though—she had her own as well. She knew that the parents had taught the girl to sew and she had become an excellent seamstress. Even though Mrs. Mak could no longer sew, she still stubbornly believed that a woman who could not sew and embroider was not a proper woman.

In the eyes of the villagers, these reasons for choosing a bride were perfectly acceptable. But Ah-Fat wanted to know a bit more than that. Was this girl literate? He had asked his mother this when he wrote to her. She had had the village letter-writer write back but she had not answered his question. Instead, she had simply asked, what was the point of having a wife who could read and write? The proper duties of a wife were to serve her in-laws and her husband, produce children, and feed and clothe them. From this letter, Ah-Fat inferred that the girl probably could neither read nor write.

He knew there was not one in a hundred among these country girls who could read and write. Or, if they could, they could only write their own names and read a few numbers. It was the same with all the country folks. They all walked a road which others had made for them; they had only to follow in those ancient footsteps. Because it was such an old, well-trodden road, it saved them a lot of trouble. The new road that Ah-Fat had taken, however, had to be hacked out by Ah-Fat alone, and it had been a gruelling process. He had left his youthful vigour behind on the railroad in Canada. At thirty-one years old, he bore the scars of his ordeal all over his body, and he was halfway to being an old man. At his age, the village men were grandfathers, while he was not yet even a father. He had lived a tough life and what he needed now was a woman who would nestle close to him and lick his wounds. Any woman could do that, no matter whether she could read or write—and that was the reason why he had finally agreed to his mother's choice of wife for him.

He just wanted an honest wife who could endure hardship and who would serve his mother as a dutiful daughter-in-law should.

Or so he repeatedly tried to persuade himself. But he still had lingering regrets. They niggled like a tiny muscle in his back which every now and then gave him a twinge, but which did not stop him working or walking.

Ah-Fat had seen not a soul in the village. The only sound was the scuffing of his footsteps on the stony surface of the lane. The sun gradually rose higher and the wind got up, making his long gown flap around his legs. The earth felt as hard under his feet as it always did at the end of winter yet he also had the feeling that under that solid surface, there was a world of creatures marshalling themselves for spring. As he passed the old well, he spotted a child squatting on the ground having a crap. "Where's everyone got to?" said Ah-Fat. The child looked scared. After a long pause, he said: "Market ... it's market day, isn't it?" Of course, it suddenly dawned on him that today was the eighteenth of the first lunar month—a big market day. Everyone would have gone there.

Half a dozen hungry strays snarled around him and snapped at his trouser cuffs. From the front opening of his jacket, he got out a lotus-leaf dumpling stuffed with sausage and rice, left over from his journey, and threw it down. The dogs forgot him straightaway and scrambled for the dumpling. Ah-Fat laughed: "Sonofabitch, Ginger!" He suddenly realized that he had shouted the name of another dog—one he had never forgotten in all these years, the one who had saved all of them in the tent, who had actually licked his hand with his last breath. After Ginger, he had never beaten a dog that came begging for food.

It took him only thirteen paces today to get from the road to their house. He must have grown in the years since he left. The old stone lions still stood by the door. His father had bought them from a Fujian stone-mason at the time he had the house built. Carved on the back of the lions' ears were the mason's name and the year the work was finished. When he and Ah-Sin were children, they often used to ride these lions as if they were horses, eventually making a shiny patch on the back of each beast. When their father smoked his opium, and was in a good mood, he would call for a boy to bring out a reclining chair so he could lie in the entrance, sunning himself as he watched his sons riding the lions and shooting sparrows in the trees with their toy bows and arrows.

Ah-Fat gave the lions a rub. They seemed smaller and somehow less fierce. There was a fine crack along the back of one.

The stones have got old too, thought Ah-Fat.

The main entrance was shut tight. The brass rings of the door knockers seemed like two eyes peering shyly at him. The door was still painted in vermilion red, although it was not the same vermilion he remembered. The old red had known his father, his brother, Ah-Sin, and his sister, Ah-Tou, and had seen many things happen to the family. But this fresh red had wilfully covered everything up. It knew nothing of tears and death and was utterly superficial. Heartlessly ignoring the family's past, it prepared to celebrate the long-awaited homecoming of the master of the house.

There were couplets pasted to the pillars on either side of the door. The one on the right said, *"Pairs of swallows on the wing greet the newcomer,"* and the one on the left: *"With a rat-a-tat-tat, firecrackers chase out the old year."* The horizontal one across the top read: *"Good fortune comes with spring."* It was only the first month of the new year, and although the corners had curled up a little with the wind, they were still bright and new. The four dots at the bottom of the character for "swallow" had been done as thick blobs and looked as if the ink might drip at any minute. Ah-Fat touched them with his finger, but they were quite dry. He looked at the calligraphy of the couplets, which was elegant and spare, rather like the Slender Gold style of the Song dynasty. Old Mr. Ding, who used to write couplets for the villagers in the old days, must surely be long dead. Who was the author of this fine calligraphy? he wondered to himself.

Ah-Fat banged the door knocker but no one answered. The door was not locked and opened with a gentle push. He went in. The courtyard was completely empty. The sun had risen to the forks in the tree branches and their shadows bobbed about on the ground. Although it was a windy day, the courtyard was warm. In the corner, beside the bamboo drying poles, stood a crudely made pottery vase. Someone had picked a great bunch of all-spice blossoms and stuck them into the vase, and their gorgeous colour seemed to set the whole wall on fire. Ah-Fat took the flowers in his hand and sniffed—they gave out a lingering perfume. He sat down heavily in the bamboo chair by the drying poles and it gave a loud creak. He settled into it cautiously, and then pulled a newspaper out from the folds of his jacket and opened it.

It was the *China-West Daily*; he had bought it when he disembarked in Canton but this was the first opportunity he had had to read it. When he had left home for Canada, he did not even know what a newspaper was. He had only discovered them when the overseas Chinese from Malaya brought newspapers from back home to Victoria's Chinatown. He opened it wide. The first page had a large half-page advertisement for a Dutch toilet spray made by Tai Luk Wo Pharmaceuticals: *"Long lasting, aromatic and invigorating!"*

The next page had a Watsons Drugstore advertisement for Scott's Emulsion Cod Liver Oil: *"Tastes like milk, very palatable, more than three times as effective as pure cod liver oil. The best cure for consumptive diseases. Works every time."* On other pages there were advertisements for sugar, wine, kerosene, handkerchiefs and sweatshirts. On and on—there were more than a dozen of them. Ah-Fat was astonished. Nothing was the same as before he left. How was it possible for Western goods to be causing such a stir all the way up the Pearl River? He wondered about the towns and villages of Hoi Ping. Were they still as cut off as before, a different world from Canton?

Among the advertisements, there was a column about the world of sing-song girls. The first item was a news report about a fire on the Guk Fau sing-song girls brothel boat, in which twelve prostitutes and six of their clients were burned alive. The second was about a *pipa* player called Bin Yuk, who excelled at Cantonese opera. The article read: *" When Bin Yuk, 'the oriole,' begins to sing, she is exquisitely melodious, equal to our finest actresses. Few of her listeners are left unmoved."* The article then described at some length how she collected her fee from members of the audience: *"She adopts a very severe mien when it comes to money. If someone gives her coins, she throws them to the ground—the sound they make tells her what their metal content is. If they give her copper coins or unusable tender, she gives it right back to them and demands silver. She will not take no for an answer. No matter how many times in an evening they ask her to sing, it is the same every time."* The article made Ah-Fat smile in spite of himself.

Looking through the paper, he discovered it was all local gossip of this sort. There was very little about national politics. There was one small news item at the bottom of one page saying that Japanese "pirates" were defying the Imperial government in northeast coastal waters. General Li Hongzhang had reviewed the Beiyang fleet, and ordered that they should maintain calm and bide their time. Ah-Fat felt that nowadays the Peking of the Empress Dowager amounted to no more than a bit of windblown fluff. Even lowly Japanese pirates dared to lay their hands on it. And when news of these tumultuous events in the capital city of China finally arrived in South China, they merited no more than a brief exclamatory note following the advertising and tidbits on sing-song girls. He put down the paper, lost in thought, then quoted bitterly to himself two lines from the ancient poet Du Mu: "Singing girls care nothing if national calamity looms/As, on the far bank, they sing the lament *Courtyard Blooms.*"

He suddenly thought of his childhood tutor Mr. Auyung, who would get into passionate arguments about national affairs, thumping the table until his writing brush jumped. He was never afraid to speak his mind. After Ah-Fat went to Gold Mountain, he kept up a correspondence with Mr. Auyung, and learned about his old teacher's wanderings around China and beyond—from Canton to Shanghai, and south to Annam. Quite recently he had come home and reopened his tutor school in the town. In one of Ah-Fat's twenty trunks there was a gift for Mr. Auyung—a map of the world. Mr. Auyung took a lively interest in Western sciences. Once he had recovered from the journey, he would go and pay his respects to Mr. Auyung.

He got up from the chair and went into the reception room.

The room was darker than the courtyard outside and it took a few moments for Ah-Fat's eyes to become accustomed to the gloom.

There was a young woman in the room. She was dressed in a long blue cotton gown with piping round the edges, and stood on a stool hanging a picture. Her hair was braided into a long, thick plait fastened with a red felt flower. She was holding a scroll painting depicting bright green bamboos tipped with fresh shoots, and guava trees. The reds, greens and blues were vivid and festive without being vulgar. The calligraphy on the painting read

"What joy that the guava is about to set seed and the bamboo to give birth to grandchildren!"

After she had finished hanging the painting, she stepped down from the stool and took a few steps back to see if she had hung it straight. In her haste, she trod on the hem of Ah-Fat's gown, almost falling over. She turned and then leapt back as if she had seen a ghost. Her eyes grew round as saucers and she clasped her hands over her heart.

It was the scar which had startled her, Ah-Fat knew. Over the years, far from fading, it had grown more prominent and more twisted. Now it looked rather like a centipede. Ah-Fat put his hands over his face and laughed. "Don't be afraid," he said. "I'm not a ghost. Look at my shadow. Ghosts don't have shadows, do they? I'm Fong Ah-Fat."

"Oh!" she exclaimed. She relaxed her hands and rubbed them against the front of her gown. "So you're young Master Fong! How did you get here so quickly? The steamship company said you wouldn't be arriving until next market day. So your mum and your uncle and the family have all gone to the Tam Kung Temple in town to light incense and pray you have a safe trip." Ah-Fat guessed the woman must be a servant. "Why didn't you go along with the mistress?" he asked. "The mistress wanted me to stay and get all the calligraphy and painting scrolls properly hung so they'd be ready when you arrived, but you got here before I'd finished."

"Who wrote the couplets?" asked Ah-Fat. "He got it wrong. I'm obviously not a newcomer, I've just been away a long time." She gave a slight smile. "The newcomer is not you, it refers to your ... your ... intended." And two vivid spots, as bright as the red in the painting, rose up her cheeks. It suddenly dawned on Ah-Fat that the room had been hung with the scrolls for his wedding. He looked at her again. She was not bad-looking and seemed bright too. Perhaps she was the daughter of a good family who had been forced into service when her family fell on hard times. He was reminded of his little sister, Ah-Tou, sold all those years ago, and he made a special effort to speak kindly to her.

"Would you show me to a room where I can rest and wait for the mistress to come home?"

The girl did as he asked.

The room she led him to was actually Ah-Fat and Ah-Sin's old room. The bed was the very same bed they used to share. The bedding looked as if it had been freshly sewn. The cotton wadding inside the quilt was thick and soft and the quilt cover was stiffly starched. Ah-Fat pulled back the quilt and saw that the old pillow was still there. It had been filled with dried chrysanthemum flowers because his mother maintained that they regulated the body's temperature and could cure Ah-Sin's epilepsy. Ah-Fat felt the pillow—there was a slight indentation in it. Could this still be the mark made by Ah-Sin's head? He lay with his head in this hollow and his nostrils were invaded by the smell of chrysanthemums freshly dried in the sunshine. He fell into the sleep of his childhood.

Suddenly the heavens darkened and it clouded over. It began to rain very hard, and there was no shelter. He was getting soaking wet. He remembered his mother had given him brand new bedding and shouted for a servant to come and close the window. He shouted so hard he finally woke himself up. He knew it had just been a dream, but when he touched his face, it was wet. He opened his eyes to see a little old woman sitting at his bedside. She wore her hair in a sleek bun, with a white felt flower tucked into one side. She had a handkerchief tucked in the front of her grey cotton gown, and was just pulling it out to wipe her eyes.

"Mum!" Ah-Fat gave a cry and, leaping out of bed, he straightened his gown, threw himself to his knees in front of her and kowtowed.

"I haven't been a dutiful son. I've been away in Gold Mountain all these years and you've suffered so much hardship."

The woman said nothing, but bent to take Ah-Fat's hand. Her own hand inscribed circles for some moments in the air before finally gripping his. Ah-Fat realized that his mother was now completely blind.

He felt a surge of emotion. There was a lump in his throat which he could neither swallow nor spit out. It stuck there until it forced tears from his eyes. He kowtowed twice more, knocking his head hard on the grey flagstones. His mother could not see, but at least she could hear what he was doing, which was what he most wanted.

He was going to kowtow again but was firmly prevented from doing so. The room was full of people kneeling—younger cousins, nephews and nieces on his uncle's side. Someone passed him a small towel. Ah-Fat wiped his face, and saw red stains on the towel. He had made his head bleed knocking it on the floor.

The only person not present from the household was the girl who had been hanging the pictures in the reception room.

The market-goers did not return to the village until nightfall, and they had not eaten all day. They hurried home the dozen or so *li* to the village with rumbling bellies, and the women were in such a hurry to light the cooking fires and cook the soup and rice that they did not even take a moment to go and piss. They had just got the fires lit when they heard the dogs bark.

Most of the time, the village dogs barked in a desultory, sporadic sort of way for no particular reason. But today they seemed to have come to an agreement. One after another, they took up the cry, echoing each other's barks and seemingly prepared to go on all evening. It was the way dogs barked when they were presented with something wholly unfamiliar, something which had come in from the big, wide world; they were hysterical with excitement and fear.

The women threw down the dried grass and twigs with which they had been feeding the cooking fires and ran outside. They were met by the sight of dozens of porters, all dressed in black livery, laden with heavy cases suspended from carrying poles. They were filing along the narrow village street like an undulating black centipede so long that you could not see its head or its tail, enveloped in clouds of the dust which they were kicking up beneath their feet.

The villagers trailing behind the dust cloud saw them put down their burdens in the Fong family courtyard. Blind old Mrs. Mak sat on a low stool feeling the lion's-head lock in the centre of each case as it was put down. One. Two. Three. Three cases were piled on top of each other and there were seven piles, the last of which only contained two cases.

So there were twenty trunks, Mrs. Mak muttered to herself, and her wizened lips parted in a gap-toothed smile.

"Off you go and cook your dinners," she ordered the crowd of onlookers. "Ah-Fat will fix a day when every one of you, young and old, will be invited over for a banquet to celebrate his homecoming."

She kept waving her handkerchief, but her attempts to send them away were futile. An ever-increasing number of people anxious to see Ah-Fat pressed in, as impossible to brush off as stove ashes stuck to a bean cake.

She tried again: "Ah-Fat's been on the boat home for weeks and he hasn't had a single good night's sleep. He fell asleep as soon as he got here, without even waiting for dinner. He needs a good rest in the comfort of his own bed. Leave him be and come back tomorrow and you can greet him properly."

The crowd finally began to disperse.

Mrs. Mak went into the house, elbowed the bedroom door open and felt her way over to the bed. Knocking the tip of her walking stick on the floor a few times, she said: "Ah-Fat, what are you frightened of? You still count as a Gold Mountain man, even if you're a scar-face. Those twenty cases prove what a man you are. How many people have been able to do what you've done? Tomorrow we'll go out of the house together. Everyone's got to see you sooner or later."

There was no movement from the bed. After a few moments, Ah-Fat gave a chuckle. "Mum, how did you know I'm a scar-face?"

Mrs. Mak smiled too. "I pushed you out of my belly and you can't lift a leg without me knowing what kind of fart's coming out. From the moment you came into this house, you haven't looked at me when you spoke."

Ah-Fat sat up with an exclamation of surprise. "Mum, you may be blind but your eyes are still sharper than everyone else's. I can see all the servants are neat and tidy and the way they speak and behave, it's obvious they've been well taught." "Your aunt takes care of all that," said his mother. "I can't see anything and I can't be bothered with overseeing the servants." "That young woman you got to hang the scrolls up, she's prettier than all the others, and smarter too." "Huh," said his mother. "Leave her out of it. She's not a servant. That's Six Fingers, Red Hair's wife's little sister. All the calligraphy and the paintings in the house were done by her."

Ah-Fat's eyes filled with astonishment at her words. Now he had so many questions on the tip of his tongue, he just had to find a way to ask them. Finally, he thought of a way to begin:

"She's quite grown-up now! Who taught her to write and paint?"

His mum sighed. "She's had a hard life. Writing and painting is the only thing that keeps her alive."

Six Fingers had come to live in Red Hair's house along with his bride, Mrs. Kwan. She was much younger than her sister—only three when their son, Loon, was born. Before Red Hair went back to Gold Mountain for the second time, he impressed on his wife that she must get a private tutor to come and teach Loon to read and write when he was old enough. It was several years before the news of Red Hair's death reached his wife's ears. She was not unduly worried because, although there were no letters from him, every now and then bank drafts would arrive. It was only much later that she found out that it was Ah-Fat who had been sending them.

When Loon was six or seven years old, his mother duly found a tutor for the boy. Six Fingers was always around and she picked up a smattering of learning too. Her elder sister had learned to read and write from her father and did not object when she saw how much effort Six Fingers was putting into her studies. The tutor was keen on calligraphy and painting and liked nothing better than to divert himself with a little painting practice. It was a quirk of his that he would do it only when he had Six Fingers in attendance—the boy was too much of a fidget. So Six Fingers was constantly being called on to light the incense, grind the ink and lay out the paper. When the tutor had finished painting, she would wash his brushes and the ink stone and bring him tea and cakes.

One day, the tutor took his refreshments and went for a siesta. Six Fingers picked up the brush and, with the leftover ink and paper, did a quick sketch of some pine trees and bamboos, as she had seen her teacher do. When he awoke, came out of his room and saw the painting, he stood twiddling his beard thoughtfully in his fingers. Finally he sighed: "Such a pity you weren't born in the body of a boy." After that, if he was in the right mood, he would teach Six Fingers a thing or two about composition, about making a painting appealing and even about mounting techniques. Neither of them realized that the day would come when Six Fingers would be in dire straits, and that what she learned from this idle chit-chat would be the saving of her.

In the spring of the year in which Six Fingers turned twelve years old dysentery plagued the village. It was only many years later that the survivors learned that its proper name was cholera, and that the cause was contamination of the waters farther upstream. The first afflicted with it in Red Hair's family was his son, Loon. He succumbed after three days without so much as uttering a word. He gave it to Red Hair's mother who, after getting better and then relapsing, sank into unconsciousness and died after a couple of weeks.

Mrs. Kwan was already ill by the time her mother-in-law died. She had it mildly and could have recovered but she did not want to live any more. Six Fingers prepared rice gruel for her elder sister, but when she tried to feed it to her, Mrs. Kwan shut her mouth firmly and twisted away. "What do I have to live for? My husband and son are both dead." (The news of Red Hair's death had reached her by then.) "If you care for me, let me die. It's a lot less bother than living." Six Fingers burst into tears: "What about me? Don't I mean anything to you?" Mrs. Kwan's eyes were as dried up as well holes. She looked dully at her younger sister and did not shed a tear.

"Dad gave you to me to rear, and at least I let you learn to read and write a bit. You might be able to use that to get along in life—depends what fate has in store for you."

These were her parting words to Six Fingers.

Within one month, three of Red Hair's family had died, and there was not a cent to bury them. Finally, the village elders took the business in hand. They mortgaged the family's three-room house and used the money to get the rites performed, to set aside the burial plot, buy coffins and bury the bodies.

After Mrs. Kwan died, the villagers sent word to her family that they should come and fetch Six Fingers. But there was no word from her parents and they never came to claim her. It was Mrs. Kwan's parting words to her sister which threw the girl a lifeline.

Old Mr. Ding, who used to write letters and do couplets on scrolls for the villagers, was too old by now to hold a brush. The villagers knew that Six Fingers could write and they felt sorry for her, so they asked her to do the work instead. They discovered that she was better at it than the old man— her calligraphy was steady and full of vigour. She also had a skill Mr. Ding did not have—she could paint. They would call her in for all sorts of jobs, from ordinary letters and New Year couplets, to calligraphy and paintings to celebrate births, deaths, weddings and old folks' birthdays. The motifs she painted of course varied according to the occasion: for a wedding, it would be a dragon and phoenix in harmony, and a guava tree setting seed. For a funeral, it would be cranes flying west towards the setting sun. To celebrate the birthday of an elderly person, it would be celestial ladies or a lucky bird offering a longevity peach in its beak. For the one-month celebration of the birth of a son, she would illustrate a fairy story like Noh Tsa playing in the sea, or paint a unicorn bringing good luck. She adapted her calligraphy and painting to the circumstances and tastes of her customers.

Six Fingers enjoyed the work and would go wherever she was wanted. But she did not get paid for it in cash. Instead, they would give her a few eggs, a pound or two of rice, a piece of fabric, some fuel for her stove, or whatever the master of the house decided. She did not get rich from her work, but it was enough to feed one person three meals a day.

However, she only had a shed to live in, by the pigpen. It had been used by Red Hair's family for storage and then fell into disrepair. It was leaky and draughty and smelt mouldy. The second summer after her sister died and she was left alone, a typhoon destroyed it completely, leaving her without any shelter from the elements.

One of the village women took pity on her and took her in. Auntie Cheung Tai's husband had gone to Gold Mountain and she had not heard from him for many years. She had no sons or daughters so when she died the family line would run out. Six Fingers moved in with her and paid for her bed and board by splitting her earnings two ways. At least it gave her a roof over her head.

As Ah-Fat listened to Six Fingers' story, he felt pangs of grief, as if a cord was being drawn tight around his heart. He thought back to when he and Red Hair set off for Gold Mountain. Red Hair had left behind a flourishing family of young and old, but nothing remained now but a pile of rubble. Six Fingers, however, was as tenacious as a weed that had crept out from under the rubble in search of light and managed to put forth a leaf. She was a survivor, that girl.

He told his mother that he had made several trips over the years to the camp where Red Hair was buried, but the virgin forest was now a city and he had searched in vain for the pile of stones. "But you must have a few of

Red Hair's belongings, haven't you?" said his mother. "I brought back an old fiddle which he used to carry around with him in Gold Mountain." "Then wrap it up and take it to Red Hair's family grave in a day or two, and bury it next to Mrs. Kwan. The grave is still open, you should get someone to come and seal it. Then the family won't need to wait for his bones any longer." "I'll take Six Fingers with me," said Ah-Fat. "After all, it was her sister and brother-in-law."

"After dinner, I'll get the maid Ah-Choi to heat the water nice and hot, and you can wash and shave. Tomorrow, the brothers are coming. They heard you're back and they want to meet you."

"Whose brothers?"

"Don't be such a dope! The brothers of your betrothed!"

After breakfast the next morning, Ah-Fat went out. He walked west through the village. He heard some knocking noises before he got near the old wooden shack and, through the open door, saw Auntie Cheung Tai at her loom.

She was a scrawny little woman, only just able to work the loom by perching atop pieces of wood to raise the level of her stool. Her two hands gripped the shuttle like a bow pulled taut but still could not push it to the end of the frame. She was weaving a rough country cloth, greyish-yellow in colour so when the end of the yarn fell on the floor and got mixed up with the dirt, it took her some time to find it. This kind of cloth was for clothes the men wore when they were ploughing or harvesting. It was unattractive but would withstand a couple of seasons out in the wind and rain. Unfortunately Auntie Cheung Tai had let the tension go slack because her arms were too puny and short to hold the yarn. Her workmanship fell far short of Mrs. Mak's.

Busy at her weaving, she suddenly saw a big black smudge on the cloth. She rubbed away at it unsuccessfully—until she realized it was someone's shadow. Looking up, she saw a man had come into the room. He was well-built and wore a skullcap and a lined grey satin gown, which must have been brand new since it still had sharp creases from being folded in the trunk. The man gave her a smile, and a worm seemed to crawl slowly up one side of his face. Auntie Cheung Tai's small bound feet slipped off the stool and she pitched forward so her nose nearly banged against the loom.

The man helped her back up and greeted her politely with hands pressed together. "Your husband was my father's cousin, Auntie," he said. "He was like an uncle to me." From the front opening of his gown, he extracted two small paper packets and gave them to her. "Something foreign for you, Auntie, from Gold Mountain."

Auntie Cheung Tai wiped the corners of her gummy eyes with her sleeve, making it wet. "Ah-Fat, are you really back? Oh, look at your face.… Well, at least you're alive. Do you have any news of your uncle Cheung Tai?" Ah-Fat shook his head. "No. I went to the Chinese Benevolent Association, but they didn't have anyone of that name on their lists. He went to Gold Mountain so long ago, maybe they didn't have lists back then." "The year before last, two men from Sai Village came home," she said. "They said they'd seen someone the spitting image of uncle Cheung Tai in Fan Tan Alley, with a Redskin woman." "They must have been mistaken," said Ah-Fat. "If he was still alive in Gold Mountain, surely he would have been in touch with you, Auntie." She clamped her mouth shut and was silent. Finally, she said icily: "It makes no difference who he was with. The marriage documents were exchanged with me."

Her lower jaw trembled so hard that her teeth chattered. Ah-Fat could think of nothing to say to comfort her. Uncle Cheung Tai must have gone a long time ago. If he was still alive, he would at least have come back to pay his respects to his ancestors. But Ah-Fat could not think which was worse—the old man dying or marrying another woman. So he bit back the platitudes that had been about to trip off his tongue.

Auntie Cheung Tai held the two packets to her nose and sniffed, then sneezed. "Whatever's that strange smell?" she asked. "How do I get my teeth into that?" Ah-Fat burst out laughing. "It's not to eat. It's soap to wash your face with. Once you've washed, you'll smell nice all day." She laughed too: "Who's going to smell this old woman's fragrance? This is for a young woman." Ah-Fat hesitated then said: "Auntie, if you really think it has an odd smell, why not give it to Six Fingers? If you can smell it on her, that's as good as if you were using it yourself."

Auntie Cheung Tai shouted for Six Fingers to bring some tea for the guest. Ah-Fat heard an indistinct murmur of response but there was no movement. He glanced towards the back door and saw Six Fingers standing under the overhanging eaves, feeding the pigs. There were three of them, two white and one spotted. They were still young, and pressed around Six Fingers' trouser legs eagerly, squealing for food. Six Fingers splashed some pig swill into the trough with a ladle, but it was too thin for the piglets' liking. They nuzzled the liquid and then left it. Six Fingers got a bunch of dried grass and mixed it into the feed with a piece of wood, then whacked the piglets on their rumps by way of encouragement. The squeals quietened and turned into chomping sounds. Six Fingers had on a cotton tunic today, loose-fitting with wide sleeves, buttoned slantwise across the front, and decorated with piping round the edges. It had faded almost white probably through repeated washing. It also concealed all her curves, until she bent over—then the hem at the back rode up, revealing sturdy round buttocks under her trousers.

When Six Fingers finished feeding the piglets, she went into the kitchen. They could hear her applying the bellows to the stove. The tea was ready almost before the smell of burning grass and twigs reached their nostrils, and Six Fingers brought in a tray with a bowl for Auntie Cheung Tai and one for Ah-Fat. Ah-Fat took the bowl in both hands and saw that it was not tea but an infusion of popped rice grains. The layer of grains looked like maggots swimming in water and a few osmanthus flowers floated on the surface. Auntie Cheung Tai took a sip and smacked her lips: "How much sugar did you put in, you little wretch?"

A grain of rice stuck between her teeth and she extracted it with her thumbnail, exclaiming as she did so: "Six Fingers! Why's your face all spotty?" The girl rubbed her face and her finger came away covered in black ink. She looked down and smiled: "I was doing some couplets for Ah-Yuen's family." "What sort of couplets?" asked Ah-Fat. "For the birthday of his old dad. He's sixty." "Let me see what you did," said Ah-Fat.

Six Fingers led him into the room at the back which served as a kitchen. There was a stove with two holes for the pots—one large, one small, a table for eating at and a large earthenware crock. The rest of the floor space was taken up with piles of grass and twigs for the stove, dried grass for the pigs and skeins for the loom. Six Fingers used the table for her calligraphy, and the paper was spread out on it waiting for the ink to dry. The room only had one small window and was darker than the front room. Six Fingers had trimmed the lamp to its lowest, to save on oil, and the flame was no bigger than a pea. Ah-Fat had to screw up his eyes to make out the characters.

The right-hand couplet read: *"Long-lived as the southern mountains, your every move spreads love."* The left-hand one read: *"Good fortune as great as the eastern seas, you bring good luck to all."* The strip that went across the top read: *"Fortunate old age without end."*

She had used gold-flecked red paper and although it was not many characters, the verticals and horizontals were neatly aligned and the brush-work was firm. Ah-Fat looked the work over from every angle and then turned to Six Fingers. Under his steady gaze, her head shrunk turkey-like into her neck, which was flushed as red as her face. She works like a man, thought Ah-Fat to himself, and her calligraphy is masculine too. But to look at, she's just a lovely girl. "Where did you get the couplets from?" he asked her. *"The Compendium of New Year Couplets Old and New"*? She shook her head. *"Couplets and Characters for Farmers"*? he asked again. Again she shook her head. "Mr. Ding only ever used those two," he persisted. "Surely you haven't got other books as well?" Six Fingers shook her head once more and twisted her hands in the folds of her jacket. Finally, she said: "I don't have any books at all."

Ah-Fat was astonished. "You mean you made them up yourself?" The blood surged again into Six Fingers' cheeks. "They don't make a neat pair, do they?" she whispered. "I think they make a fine pair," said Ah-Fat. "Perhaps if you changed 'your every move spreads love' to 'you spread love all around,' it would contrast better with 'you bring good luck to all'." "That's true! That sounds much better!" She was about to tear it up and rewrite the couplet when Ah-Fat, suddenly interested, offered: "I'll do it." Six Fingers ground and prepared more ink, laid out the paper, wetted and smoothed the brush and gave it to Ah-Fat.

Ah-Fat loaded the brush with ink and, after a long moment of contemplation, began to write. He wrote the whole thing without pausing, except to load more ink onto the brush halfway through. Then he threw the brush into the water and paid no further attention to it. Six Fingers tidied away the brush and ink. "Master Ah-Fat, your calligraphy has become more vigorous as the years go by. Did you get a chance to practise in Gold Mountain?"

"How do you know my calligraphy?" Ah-Fat was startled. Six Fingers gave a little laugh. "Every time you wrote home, your mum called me over to read it to her." "So every letter I've had back from her was written by you?" Six Fingers nodded. Ah-Fat had to laugh. "No wonder!" "No wonder what?" "I couldn't understand how that old turtle Ding had got so good at writing!" said Ah-Fat.

Six Fingers wrung out a towel in hot water and gave it to Ah-Fat to wipe his hands. Ah-Fat protested it was a shame to dirty such a clean white towel and instead grabbed a dirty rag from the table and gave his inky fingers a quick rub. Six Fingers saw him to the door. In the glaring sunlight, the tree branches seemed to have grown fatter—if you looked closely you could see that many of the leaf buds had burst open. Ah-Fat's blue cotton shoes left faint marks on the bare earth but did not raise any dust. Instead, the earth had begun to give out a gentle dampness.

As Ah-Fat walked into his house, he smelled grass burning fragrantly in the stove. A servant was busy preparing the midday meal. Mrs. Mak sat in the front room, podding peas. She may have been blind but she had "eyes" in her fingers which unerringly saw the two ridges running down the length of the pod. With her thumb she pressed at one end, and the pod split down its length, dropping plump peas in a steady stream into her bamboo basket.

Mrs. Mak had extra eyes not only in her fingers but in her ears too. These "eyes" gave a light blink and saw the hem of Ah-Fat's new gown brush the door sill, a moist hen dropping sticking to it, and float across to where she sat.

"Mum, take a break and sit in the sun for a bit. Ah-Choi can do that."

Mrs. Mak continued to bend her head to her work. However, a crease at each corner of her mouth trembled slightly.

Ah-Fat knew that meant she was struggling with two conflicting feelings—indignation working its way up from her heart and resignation, which crept down from her head. The two conflicting feelings came to blows at the corners of her mouth; Ah-Fat had been familiar with this expression of his mother's ever since he was a child. He saw it every time his father got into a fight or smoked opium or he or Ah-Sin failed to collect enough grass for the pigs.

"All morning they waited for you," she said.

Ah-Fat suddenly remembered that today was the day he was supposed to meet the family of his betrothed.

"What a dope I am. When I got up this morning, it went clean out of my head!" He clapped his forehead in exasperation.

"It's nearly twenty *li* so they had to set off while it was still dark. Then they just turned around and went straight home, and refused even a bite to eat."

Ah-Fat fetched a stool and sat down beside his mother to help her with the peas. They were small and he had big hands. Without the advantage of Mrs. Mak's deft fingertips, he groped blindly at the pod and felt the peas squeeze through the cracks between his fingers and shoot off in all directions.

The creases at the corners of his mother's mouth gradually began to soften.

Ah-Fat's hands suddenly slowed and she heard a sigh—or rather, to put it more accurately, she saw the sigh. The "eyes" in her ears strained to see where, in her son's heart, this sigh had emanated from. Then it gradually rose to his eyebrows where a tiny knot formed at the spot where the eyebrows met. Finally, it fell heavily into the basket, scattering the peas.

"Such a pity," sighed Ah-Fat.

Mrs. Mak suppressed a smile—her son might have been away in Gold Mountain living with those devils of White people for all those years, but he was still as good-hearted as ever.

"It's not the end of the world. Get Ha Kau to take you over tomorrow. You can go and see them and say sorry, and that'll be the end of it. They're reasonable people."

She had misunderstood but Ah-Fat did nothing to enlighten her. He carried on podding the peas in a desultory fashion. After a moment, he said: "That sister-in-law of Uncle Red Hair, she's such a talented girl. Too bad she's had such a hard life."

Mrs. Mak shook her head. "Six Fingers certainly is talented," she agreed. "But respectable families don't care two hoots whether their daughters are talented or not, since they're going to marry out, come what may. The only girls who get taught properly how to read and write are the *pipa* players in Guk Fau." (She was referring to the child prostitutes in a high-class brothel.)

"But Mum, in Gold Mountain, boys and girls all go to school," Ah-Fat protested. "If girls are literate, they can't be tricked so easily, and when they get married, they can teach their own children."

"Huh!" said his mother. "I can't read a word but I've never been tricked. Didn't you and your brother go to tutor school? What did you need your mother to teach you for?"

Ah-Fat laughed. "If you could read and write, then you wouldn't have to get someone to write your letters to me, and you'd save all those eggs, and all that tea, and cash. You don't even know what your letter-writer actually wrote. When I sent you a cheque, you didn't know how much it was for, so you could have been cheated, and you'd never know."

Mrs. Mak laughed too, showing all her chipped teeth. "Yes, you're right. So long as she doesn't cost too much in school fees or slack off around the house. Then when you have a daughter, it's up to you whether you educate her."

They fell silent. Mrs. Mak looked up. She could see a fuzzy brightness, so she knew the sun had risen to its zenith and the shadows cast by the trees in the paved courtyard would be at their shortest. There was a vibration in the "eyes" within her ears, and she "saw" hosts of worms rustling through the soil under the roots of the banyan tree in the courtyard. It was nearly the end of the first month of the new year. As soon as the earth changed, it would be time for ploughing and sowing. Ah-Fat's wedding had to take place before that started. Tomorrow, a day would have to be fixed.

"Ah-Fat, you little fool!" Mrs. Mak exclaimed, feeling in the basket. "Why are you throwing in all the pods?"

Ah-Fat roused himself hurriedly, to find he had thrown all the peas away and put the pods in the basket. He scrabbled around picking up the peas, and rinsed the dirt off them in a bowl of water.

"Is Six Fingers betrothed to anyone, Mum?" he asked.

"At the end of last year some people from Sai Village came here visiting relatives and saw the scrolls hung in their house. When they found out Six Finger had done them, they got the matchmaker to propose the son of the family to her. But Six Fingers refused. Her mum and dad are still alive but they didn't want to take her back. That makes her really an orphan with no one to decide things for her. So she's her own mistress now. But it's not proper, putting a girl's calligraphy and paintings on show to strangers."

"Why did she say no?"

"She said the boy was illiterate."

Ah-Fat pushed the basket aside and fell on his knees, on top of all the pea pods.

"Mum," he begged. "Let me be my own master! I want to marry Six Fingers...."

To Mrs. Mak, it was as if the sun had exploded at her feet, scattering a myriad sparks which peppered her eardrums, making them hum like a hive full of honeybees. When finally the bees flew away, she could hear the sound of her own voice, but now it was a thin, thread-like sound. Her words shredded and were scattered on the wind:

"Wretched boy! Have you forgotten? You're already betrothed!"

"Of course I haven't forgotten, Mum. But I don't know her, and I do know Six Fingers. You know what a good girl she is and I really like her. When I was in Gold Mountain and about to starve to death, Mum," he went on, "it was only the gold nugget Red Hair left behind that saved me. He was my benefactor. Now all his family are dead and there's only Six Fingers left. If I marry Six Fingers, that'll be my way of repaying Red Hair."

"Have you got maggots in your brain? Red Hair was your uncle, so he was senior to you. He married Six Fingers' elder sister so that puts Six Fingers in the generation above you too."

"Yes, but I've thought about that too, Mum. Six Fingers is not related to us by blood even if you go back five generations. She and Auntie Cheung Tai are like mother and daughter now, and if Auntie has made Six Fingers her daughter, then that makes Six Fingers the same generation as me."

"And what about your betrothed and her family, and the three mule-loads of betrothal gifts we're giving them? It's all arranged. What's the poor girl done to deserve having her engagement broken off?"

"Mum, if we let them down, it's our fault. Of course, we can't claim the gifts back, and we'll give them two hundred dollars as well, to show we're sincerely sorry. With that kind of money, they'll even be able to find a son-in-law to come and live with them."

"And what about my reputation? I arranged this betrothal for you, and it was witnessed by your ancestors. If you turn it down for no good reason, how will I ever hold up my head in the village?"

"Mum, I left for Gold Mountain when I was sixteen years old and I went through hell there. If it hadn't been for you, I would have become a beggar and begged my way back home. I'm back now, who knows for how long, maybe a year, maybe a few months, but sooner or later I have to go back to Gold Mountain. I'm not afraid of hard work. I just want to marry a girl I get on with, who can make me happy and who'll look after you properly when I'm gone. We don't know what that girl's like. But the whole village knows Six Fingers is a good and virtuous girl. Her needlework may not be up to yours but it's quite decent and she'll be a great help to you. Please, Mum, let me have what I desire!"

"The reason why her parents gave her to Red Hair and his family was they thought her sixth finger would bring bad luck and they wouldn't be able to marry her off. Doesn't that scare you off her?"

"Her parents are just ignorant. Magistrate Huang has a sixth finger too, and he's in charge of a whole county of five-fingered people. Maybe Six Fingers is destined to become rich and powerful! Besides, she does all the villagers' scrolls for their family events, doesn't she? I've never heard that she's brought them bad luck."

His mum gripped the pods in hands which trembled slightly. The juice ran out between the fingers and trickled across the wrinkled skin of the back of her hand.

"You can't back out of that betrothal, I'd lose too much face. You can marry Six Fingers, but as a second wife. Go and see your future father-in-law tomorrow with Ha Kau, and see if he'll agree to you marrying his daughter first, and then marrying Six Fingers."

Ah-Fat was about to say something more but his mother was already on her feet and hobbling off towards the kitchen without the aid of her stick.

"We'll have to get her horoscope done first. That's just as important for a second wife as for the first. Our family has only been at peace for a few years. We can't have a woman bring calamity on us."

When Auntie Cheung Tai had seen off her guest and went into the back room of the house, she found Six Fingers sewing. She was altering a lined jacket which had been left to her by her elder sister. It was made of a silk weave, not the most expensive kind but almost new, and had been kept in a trunk for a few years. By the time Six Fingers remembered it, there were a couple of moth holes, but fortunately they were in the sleeve under the armpit and with a small mend would not show. The material was a sapphire blue colour embroidered with dark blue flowers—something an older woman might wear but still fashionable: it had wide decorative edging, a stand-up collar and big sleeves, rather like the Manchu-style jackets worn in North China. It would suit Six Fingers' tall figure.

Six Fingers had finished her mending and was pulling the sleeves through. When she was sewing, she used her thumb and forefinger but the extra stump of a finger which grew next to her thumb wobbled as if it was putting in a big effort too. In fact, its efforts were just a distraction and it got in the way. Unlike the care she gave to the rest of her fingers and toes, Six Fingers paid no attention at all to this extraneous finger—it might as well have belonged to someone else and just have been planted on her. This contrary stub had nothing to do with her.

She might have had a completely different life, she thought to herself, if this finger had not butted in so unreasonably, changing it into what it was today. Was it a good life? She could not answer that question. She had nothing to compare it with. However, she did secretly wonder if, without this extra stub of a finger, fate might have offered her another kind of life.

Auntie Cheung Tai put down a packet in her hand and sat beside the girl. The packet was wrapped in thick yellow paper with a strip of festive red paper stuck on top. Even though it was sealed, it was obvious from the grease which had seeped through that it contained cakes bought in a shop in town.

"Walnut cookies. Third Granny gave them to me. Have a bit." Third Granny was the matchmaker in their village.

Six Fingers shook her head. "No thank you, I'm not hungry." This was only partly true. She was not hungry because she had just had a large bowl of sweet potato porridge and felt completely full up. But she would have liked a bit of cookie. Since her elder sister died, she had rarely tasted fatty food, in fact she had not even seen much of it. Just seeing the grease mark on the packaging made her think of the shape, flavour, colour and texture of the delicacy inside it, and made her mouth water.

Auntie Cheung Tai stroked the jacket lying on the table and tut-tutted. "Silk from Three Gold Circles.... No one else in the village has anything like it. Your sister certainly knew how to shop. Why are these sleeves so short? They'll only reach your elbows." But Six Fingers picked the jacket up and held it up against the older woman. "They're not short, they're just right." "That can't be for me!" Auntie Cheung Tai exclaimed, flapping her hands in agitation. "It's not the right style for an old woman like me!"

Even as she shook her head in protest, the corners of her lips curled in a moist little smile which told Six Fingers that she really liked the style. A few days before, she had been boiling up the piglets' food and sparks from the fire had burned several large holes in her old lined jacket. She could not mend it—the jacket was too heavily patched for that.

"Did you hear what Third Granny said?" she asked as she snipped the ends of the threads for Six Fingers.

Six Fingers neither nodded nor shook her head but stayed silent.

"He's a decent man—you've met him, he's spoken to you. He's a good man and fine-looking. It's just a pity he has that scar on his face. Well, you've seen that too. Not like when I got married. My head was covered with the wedding veil so I could hardly see anything of my new home and husband. It was only when the veil came off that I saw his face was covered in pockmarks."

Still Six Fingers said nothing. There was no sound in the room apart from the hiss of the needle and thread being pulled through the material.

"You've lived with me for years," Auntie Cheung Tai went on. "And even though I'm not your birth mother, I'm almost a mother to you. I can take care of this for you. Being junior wife to a Gold Mountain man isn't the same as with other families. There you'd have to put up with the mother-in-law and the first wife's bad temper. But ten to one, this Gold

Mountain man would take you back with him and you could be happy together in Gold Mountain, and leave the first wife to look after the family back here. That's what all Gold Mountain men do.

"He'll marry his first wife at the end of the first month, then two months later, he'll marry you. After he's spent a year or so in the village, if you both get pregnant, then he might be holding two 'Gold Mountain babies'."

Six Fingers' sewing came to a halt and her fingers froze in mid-air. Only her extra finger continued to tremble like a startled dragonfly.

"They've prepared the betrothal gifts and they've been very considerate. They didn't want to offend you so you'll get almost the same amount as the first wife. I can see he's really taken a fancy to you. If he hadn't already been betrothed, you might have been his first wife. First wife, junior wife, it really doesn't mean anything. He likes you so he'll naturally treat you better. It's just like with the emperors of old: whomever they really loved became the favourite concubines, and never mind the empress."

Six Fingers put the jacket down, got up and went towards the stove. When the fire was out, it was a dark corner and the gloom swallowed her up as if she had been enveloped in a dark cloth. She had disappeared but Auntie Cheung Tai heard a rustle as she reached for something.

"Mother Cheung Tai, I don't want to go to that family." Her soft voice came through the mantle of darkness.

"Why? You usually get on with Auntie Mak, and Ah-Fat is certainly good to you. Is it the scar that bothers you?"

Six Fingers said nothing. There was a heavy silence, thick as a blob of lumpy ink. After a long pause, it dissolved a little and a trembling voice floated out:

"They're all good people."

Auntie Cheung Tai heaved a sigh. "Then how can you not agree, you silly girl?"

"Mother Cheung Tai, I ... I won't be a junior wife."

The older woman sighed. "Six Fingers, you were eighteen this New Year. At that age, a girl's more than ripe for marriage. You'll end up an old maid if you don't. Last year you could have married that man, and been his first wife too. But you refused, and I was with you there. He really wasn't right for you. But Ah-Fat's exactly the kind of man you need. It's just your fate to be a junior wife. If you won't accept that, you'll end up getting old with me, won't you?"

Six Fingers suddenly burst out of the darkness, bent over as if she had a heavy bundle of faggots on her back. She was panting as she said:

"I'm not going to be a junior wife, Mother Cheung Tai."

The older woman's patience was wearing thin and seemed as if it might break at any moment.

"If you miss out on this one, Six Fingers," she said, "where do you think you'll find another man that doesn't care about your six fingers? Of course everyone wants to be a senior wife. It's just not going to happen to you. You should give thanks to the Buddha that this family has sent this many betrothal gifts to someone who's going to be a junior wife."

Six Fingers had something heavy at her waist which she took out. She gripped it in her hand so hard that she seemed to be trying to squeeze water from it. It gave her courage and her words were brusque:

"I'm not going to be a junior wife, Mother Cheung Tai."

Auntie Cheung Tai had her back to Six Fingers and was tidying up the sewing things. Her reply was just as brusque.

"This time it's not up to you. I've already given our reply to Third Granny. The twenty-fifth day of this month is propitious. The gifts are all arranged."

Six Fingers did not answer. Auntie Cheung Tai heard a dull thud, and looked around to see Six Fingers on the floor. Something dark red oozed over the back of her hand and blossomed wetly on her jacket front. The girl must have spilt the red ink she used in her paintings, Auntie Cheung Tai thought. Then she saw that a stub of a finger had fallen on the floor and lay shrivelled and slug-like in a sea of blood.

Six Fingers had used the pigs' fodder knife to chop off her sixth finger.

Six Fingers hovered between life and death for three days. The village herbalist came, looked at the wound and took her pulse. His verdict was that the knife blade was contaminated and she had blood poisoning. He did not hold out much hope for her recovery.

When the news reached the Fongs, Ah-Fat was busy practising his calligraphy, copying out a famous poem by a Southern Song dynasty poet. He had chosen the best and most absorbent paper and wrote rapidly, in a free, cursive style. When he heard the matchmaker talking to his mother, his writing hand froze in mid-air and a blob of black ink fell from the wolf-hair brush, spoiling the paper.

When Ah-Fat emerged, the matchmaker had gone. A hen in the yard had just laid an egg and was flapping and clucking around Mrs. Mak hoping for some grains of rice as a reward. Ah-Fat threw a stone at it. There was pandemonium as squawking hens took refuge on the fence, filling the yard with a flurry of wings. Mrs. Mak brushed off a chicken feather which had stuck to her face. "The pot of sticky rice is still hot," she said. "Shall I get Ah-Choi to bring you some?"

Ah-Fat did not answer. Although his mother could not see him, she could tell his face had grown as dark as a thundercloud. His heavy silences were more and more oppressive to her. She felt as if her whole body was being crushed flat under their weight. Her son's heart had turned to stone and she felt incapable of making any impression on it. She racked her brains for something to say. Her voice came out weedy and etiolated.

"I'll send a message with Ah-Choi to Auntie Cheung Tai. We'll pay for three days of Daoist ceremonies, to expiate the soul of the dead girl."

Her words seemed to fall like a pebble into ancient still waters. It was some time before the ripples gradually appeared on the surface.

"Six Fingers isn't dead yet, Mum."

"The herbalist said to prepare for the funeral."

Ah-Fat made no sound. She strained to stare with the "eyes" in her ears, but they suddenly seemed to have grown opaque. Now she knew she was completely blind. Never again would she see into her son's heart.

"I'm going to find out when the next boat for Gold Mountain leaves, Mum."

Her son had changed his clothes and put on his shoes and was off to inquire about the boat—when it suddenly dawned on Mrs. Mak that she was being very foolish. Every brick and tile of their house, every field and every beast they owned, every grain of rice in the bowls of everyone from mistress to minions, had come to them thanks to Ah-Fat's bank drafts. She had been under the impression that she commanded her son, but now she realized that actually it was her son who commanded the whole family. He was master of all their fates; the whole family's continued existence depended on his loyalty to her. If she lost his heart, then they were all lost. She was filled with terror and muddy yellow tears gathered at the corner of her eyes.

It also occurred to her that Six Fingers had quite a few merits. She was capable, upright and had a mind of her own. When it came to important family affairs, there was no way that blind old Mrs. Mak or her weak and helpless sister-in-law could cope. What they needed, when her son was not there, was someone like Six Fingers to be the mainstay of the family. She had not permitted Ah-Fat to marry Six Fingers as his senior wife because she was afraid of losing face in the village. Yet face was only a veneer on the surface of their lives. Face without life was no face at all.

Besides, Six Fingers did not have six fingers any more. With the stroke of a knife, Six Fingers had altered her fate.

"Ah-Fat, tell Ah-Choi to get Third Granny here. I want Third Granny to say to Auntie Cheung Tai that providing Six Fingers pulls through, we'll scrap the other betrothal, and you'll make Six Fingers your first wife," she said. "All this trouble can only be sorted out by the person who caused it. And she was born tough, that girl. Who knows, when she hears the news, it may bring her back to life."

Mrs. Mak heard her son's footsteps slow down.

"Right," he said. "But I'm not calling Ah-Choi. I'll take you to see Third Granny."

Mother and son hastily left the house, Mrs. Mak hobbling so fast that Ah-Fat could scarcely keep up with her.

Third Granny went into Auntie Cheung Tai's house and Ah-Fat and his mother waited outside. Mrs. Mak was gripping a handkerchief, which had been brand new and crisply starched but was now wringing wet. She could hear Ah-Fat's big feet pacing up and down on the tamped mud pavement in front of the house and the sound not only grated on her ears but seemed to grate slivers of flesh from her heart too. She was as anxious as her son.

A long time later Third Granny came out. She seemed downcast and instead of her usual glib manner, she spoke awkwardly.

"She didn't say a word, didn't even give a flicker of her eyelids."

"Did you ask Auntie Cheung Tai to tell her, or did you tell her yourself?" asked Mrs. Mak.

"Of course I told her myself. I spoke right into her ear. Too bad it doesn't look like I'll be enjoying your matchmaking gifts. The herbalist says it'll be tonight."

On the way home, Mrs. Mak could not keep up with her son. She felt as if the heavens above had caved in on her. She could hardly drag her little "lotus" bound feet along and the walking stick in her hand seemed to groan mournfully under her weight.

"Ah-Fat, if you really want to leave, I can't stop you, but at least wait until Six Fingers is buried," she shouted hoarsely after him.

In the middle of the night, Auntie Cheung Tai went to relieve herself in the backyard and heard a strange sound. It was something like a draught whistling through cracks in the wall or the earth drinking in a fine drizzle. She looked up at the frangipani tree but it was not moving; she felt its trunk but it was not wet. It was a dry, still night. Holding up her trousers, she groped her way to where the sound was coming from—and arrived at Six Fingers' bed.

"Porridge ... porridge...." the girl mumbled.

2004

Hoi Ping County, Guangdong Province

In the morning, Amy was woken by the phone. Confused about where she was, she sat up and opened her eyes. White spots like flowers or butterflies seemed to be dancing on the walls. She finally realized it was the sun's rays filtering in through the curtains.

She had a splitting headache, and the relentless ringing of the telephone seemed to hammer away at the cracks in her skull, pounding tiny sparks from it.

"How's the hangover?" asked a man's voice.

Amy had no idea who it was.

"This is Auyung from the Office for Overseas Chinese Affairs. We met yesterday," he said.

Amy began dimly to recall the previous evening.

"Did I have a lot to drink?" she asked.

"You could say that! Not to put too fine a point on it, you got blind drunk."

Amy jumped out of bed. "Impossible!" she exclaimed. "I never drink with strangers."

"Then maybe you don't regard me as a stranger," said Auyung with a chuckle.

"Maybe not. But how are you going to make me believe that I got really drunk?"

"You sang a song. In English. Over and over again."

"No!" yelled Amy. "Impossible! I never sing. Certainly not in public."

"It's a wonderful thing, alcohol," said Auyung. "*In vino veritas*, as they say. The song was 'Moonlight on the River Colorado.' In English. Shall I sing a bit?"

Amy said nothing. She used to sing that song a lot when she was a student at Berkeley. She had not done a lot of studying in those days. In fact, she had spent most of her time on sit-ins in City Hall Square with her friends. All kinds of sit-ins, pro or anti one thing or another: anti-war, anti-discrimination, anti-exploitation. Pro-women's rights, pro-draft dodgers, pro-gays. Sometimes, after a day sitting in the town square, she had forgotten why she was there. When she and her fellow students got bored, someone would strum a few chords on the guitar and they would all sing. The most popular song was "Moonlight on the River Colorado."

That was all such a long time ago. How strange that a bottle of liquor should unlock those long-repressed memories.

"I must have made a horrible noise. When I was a kid, I only had to open my mouth and my mother would yell at me for singing out of tune."

"It depends what you're comparing it with. Compared to me, it was music to the ears."

"What other embarrassing things did I do? Better have it all out in one go. It's less scary than finding out in bits and pieces."

"Actually I think you should have it in instalments. Otherwise, seeing me might send you right over the edge."

Amy burst out laughing. Under that droopy exterior, Auyung was quite a character, she thought.

"So, Mr. Auyung, did you get drunk too?"

"I certainly felt like drinking, if I hadn't had today's duties ahead of me...."

"What duties? Surely not another evening's drinking with your bosses?"

"That's only one duty. There are lots of others, for instance clearing all the remaining antiques out of the Fongs' *diulau* with you, and persuading you to put your signature on the trusteeship document. Of course, the most urgent problem facing me right now is getting you up and dressed so we can go and have breakfast. The hotel stops serving breakfast in half an hour."

"Ten minutes ... give me ten minutes."

Amy hurriedly showered—then discovered there was no hair dryer. No iron either. She rifled through her suitcase looking for the painkillers, but in vain. In the end she dug out a T-shirt that was not too crumpled, and a pair of jeans. She pulled a rubber band off her wrist and tied her wet hair roughly in a ponytail and flew down the stairs.

From a distance she saw Auyung sitting on a sofa in the hotel lobby, his eyes narrowed and with a foolish grin on his face. She waved at him but there was no reaction. It was only when she was up close that she realized he was asleep. Amy had never seen someone look so silly in sleep. She could not resist pulling out her camera and taking a close-up shot. At the flash, he woke up with a start. Wiping a drop of saliva from the corner of his mouth he put his head on one side and looked at Amy. "Yesterday you were a prof. Today you look like a student," he said. "I prefer the student."

Amy cocked her head and looked back at him. "Now you're awake, you look like an old man. When you were asleep, you looked like a kid. I like you better asleep."

Auyung put his finger to his lips. "Shhh. Best not to say things like that in a public place. People might get the wrong idea."

They both roared with laughter.

"How come you're sleepy at this time in the morning?" asked Amy. "One person's morning is another's midday," he said. "I've already done two hours' work." He looked at his watch. "Right. We're too late for the hotel breakfast. Let's go straight to the *diulau* and then I'll get the driver to go and buy some soy milk and a sticky rice cake for you."

They got into the car. "What was my great-grandmother's name?" asked Amy. "Her full name was Kwan Suk Yin," he replied. "But when she was young, everyone called her Six Fingers, and when she was old, it was Granny Kwan. Hardly anyone knew her proper name."

Amy thought for a moment. Suddenly, light dawned. "My great-grandfather was Fong Tak Fat and my great-grandmother was Kwan Suk Yin. The name of the *diulau* is Tak Yin House—they must have put the two names together."

"Nowadays it's no big deal to call a house after a woman," said Auyung. "But in the countryside of Guangdong in 1913, it was considered very avant-garde. In those days, no one outside the family knew the names of unmarried girls. When a girl reached marrying age, the full name would be written out properly on a piece of paper, sealed inside a red envelope, laid on a gold-painted tray together with her horoscope and given to the matchmaker to take to the boy's family. That's why asking for a girl's hand in marriage was also called 'asking the girl's name'."

"Was she pretty, my great-grandmother?" asked Amy, remembering the eyes she had seen in the wardrobe mirror the day before.

"There should be a photo of her in Tak Yin House. You can see for yourself."

Years twenty to twenty-one of the reign of Guangxu (1894–1895)
Spur-On Village, Hoi Ping County, Guangdong, China

The wedding took place at the end of the first month of year twenty of the reign of Guangxu. For many years after, the elders of Spur-On Village still remembered that day, even though they had only been children then.

The banquet began when the sun had just risen to the tops of the trees and continued till midnight with guests dropping in and partaking as they pleased … a "running water" banquet, it was called. The chef and his assistants had been commandeered from the famous Tin Yat Tin Restaurant in Canton city. There were six of them and they were on their feet the whole time, alternately preparing and chopping the vegetables and cooking the food. As time went on, some of the children began to make a racket. Their mothers beat them over the head with their chopsticks, berating them: "This is Uncle Ah-Fat's big day. Don't you go spoiling it! Get a bowl of food and take it home to eat." The children were quick to catch on: obediently they filled their bowls to overflowing with something from every dish. They did not eat at home, of course. Instead, they ran off to play on the muddy banks of the village river, before going back to the banquet again. When their foreheads felt the blow of their mothers' chopsticks once more, the whole performance was repeated. For many days after the wedding, no smoke rose from the chimneys of Spur-On Village as every family continued to enjoy the bounty of Ah-Fat's wedding banquet.

The longer the banquet went on outside, the more the bride suffered torments in her bridal chamber.

In the small hours of the morning, Auntie Cheung Tai woke Six Fingers with the news that the helpers had arrived. They washed her, trimmed the fine hairs on her face and neck, dressed her and applied her makeup. A dazed Six Fingers found herself gripped and kneaded from head to toe by a dozen hands. She had still not fully recovered from her illness but the face powder covered her sickly pallor. Half a dozen women worked for several hours to get her ready. Then someone gave her a square mirror. In its reflection, she saw a stranger, one with a pearly-white complexion, pink-blushed cheeks and lustrous bright eyes. She smiled. The stranger smiled back and the jewelled headdress jiggled gently.

At midday, the palanquin came to take her to the Fongs' house, though the distance was no more than fifty yards or so. The heavy mantle over her head left her in complete darkness, but this only made her other senses more acute. She could tell who the bearers were, which route their black cotton shoes were taking, whose dog was barking furiously as the sedan passed, how hot the sun's rays were on the palanquin roof. She could smell the scorching heat of the gaze of the bystanders as their eyes burned through the curtains of her palanquin, and she could even distinguish a fiddle in the welcoming band whose timid notes were slightly out of tune. She had not imagined that the road from girlhood to her new life as a married woman would feel so simple, so trouble free and so familiar.

It was the first month of the new year and, although it was still cool, the icy chill that had held them in its grip in winter was gone. Her forehead and the palms of her hands perspired slightly. She knew she had a scarlet handkerchief tucked into her waistband and could perfectly well have used it to wipe her face and hands. She tugged at it gently—then put it back. It was a gift which the matchmaker had brought her from Ah-Fat when she delivered his written marriage proposal, and she could not bear to use it. Ah-Fat had also given her two bracelets, one gold and one silver, an eight-panelled, embroidered skirt in silk gauze, four pieces of satin and two pairs of embroidered shoes. All these gifts had come from Canton city. "Everything he bought in Gold Mountain for the first girl has gone to her and her family," the matchmaker informed them. The woman had passed on Ah-Fat's message but not what it meant, since she did not know, but Six Fingers had understood immediately. Ah-Fat wanted to start their lives with a clean slate, putting new wine into a new bottle and leaving the old bottle for the past. So when Auntie Cheung Tai grumbled that the Fongs had been hasty and mean with their wedding gifts, Six Fingers merely looked down and smiled slightly.

In return, Six Fingers had given to her new husband the traditional gifts a bride gives the bridegroom: a figure of a boy on a lotus leaf, modelled in flour paste (symbolizing a succession of precious sons), ten guava fruits also made from flour paste (symbols of plenty), a pair of shoes and ten bags of salt. Everything was put together by Auntie Cheung Tai except for the shoes—a personal gift which she had made entirely herself, from gluing the cloth and stitching the soles to cutting out the uppers and sewing them together. She had not let Auntie Cheung Tai help her in any way, not even by finding out what his shoe size was. The day that he and she had written the scroll together in the back room, she had found out his shoe size. She had measured it at a glance.

Six Fingers used two kinds of stitches for the soles: chain stitch on one side, cross-stitch on the other. Of all the women in Spur-On Village, only her future mother-in-law had worked the stitches this way, when she was a young woman. On the uppers, she embroidered two clouds, each in a different colour of blue-grey, one light, one dark, one half-concealed behind the other with just a slender "tail" showing. It took Six Fingers three nights to complete these shoes. At cock crow on the third day, the matchmaker was waiting at the door for them. The shoes were still moist from her fingers as Auntie Cheung Tai wrapped them in red paper and gave the package together with the marriage proposal to the matchmaker. Six Fingers suddenly felt as if her heart had emptied, as if those shoes had taken her body and soul away with them.

Bridal firecrackers welcomed her as she stepped out of Auntie Cheung Tai's house, and they continued to pop and sparkle until the palanquin arrived. When she felt it tilt slightly, she knew the bearers were about to take her up the steps of the Fongs' house. One, two, three, four, five. As they reached the fifth step, she suddenly remembered the couplets which hung on either side of the door, the ones Mrs. Mak had asked her to do. Neither of them had had any inkling that she was writing the scrolls to celebrate her own wedding.

Life was a strange thing, she thought, unable to suppress a small sigh.

The palanquin halted and she heard the light tap-tap of a bamboo fan against the door—a signal for her to alight. She knew who had tapped, and she heard its urgency. Under the thick veil, she felt her face flame as hot as a well-stoked fire. The beads of sweat seemed almost to sizzle. The curtain was drawn back and someone pushed something into her hand. She ran her finger over it—it was a key.

I mustn't let it drop, she thought.

She gritted her teeth and clenched her fists until the key scored sharp teeth marks on her palm. She knew that what she was gripping was not just a key but her future—indeed, the future of the entire Fong family. From this day on, her life did not belong to her alone. It would be chopped into little pieces and mixed in with their lives. There would be no more "mine," "yours" and "his." The thought made her hands tremble a little, and feelings of both terror and warmth crept over her. Terror because she had lost herself—from today, she would be made up of fragments which did not form a whole. Warmth because although she was leaving her old self behind, she would gain what she had never had before—companionship, support and courage.

As she got out of the palanquin, someone handed her one end of the "wedding stick" and, holding it, she was led into the Fongs' house. She could not see where she was going. She only saw scarlet flowers—on the hem of her skirt—dancing lightly along as they brushed the dark grey flagstones. She felt sure-footed. She knew who it was that held the other end of the stick. He would not let her stumble and fall.

With the customary bow to heaven and earth and the parents, she entered the bridal chamber. Outside, the wedding feast was about to begin. She heard the man tell Ah-Choi in a low voice: "Take her a bowl of lotus seed soup. She must be hungry." The man's shoes scuffed on the floor and she heard his footsteps retreating. She did not know if the man was wearing the shoes she had made for today. Ah-Choi came in with the soup. "For the young mistress!" she said. It took Six Fingers a moment to realize that that was her. The servant put the bowl down and went out, leaving Six Fingers sitting motionless in the chamber. The noise of the banquet outside came at her like the roar of waves in a typhoon. But her ears passed over the clamour and alighted on an almost inaudible sound—the sizzling of the lotus seeds and jujubes in the boiling-hot soup. Her belly rumbled in answer. It felt like hordes of rice weevils were gnawing at her. Not a drop of water or a crumb of food had passed her lips since getting up in the early hours of the morning. She knew the bowl was on the low table next to her. The sweet scent of osmanthus flowers rose from it and filled her nostrils. She only had to make a small movement with her hand to touch it. But she must not touch it. The bride could not go out to use the toilet until the guests had gone. She would have to bear her hunger.

The desire to relieve herself grew gradually. It started as an obscure, dull need which invaded her body. Then it became an insistent, acute jabbing in her gut, desperately seeking a way out. She felt as bloated as an inflated paper lantern, which the slightest movement might cause to split open. So she sat straight, absolutely motionless. She even slowed her breathing, smoothing the gap between her breaths in and out.

But her body rebelled. Her nostrils, beaded with sweat, began to tickle. Hold it in. You've got to hold it in.

She was still thinking the thought to herself when her body shook and she was overwhelmed by an enormous sneeze. A warm gush of liquid coursed down her thighs, leaving a dark streak on her silk skirt.

She shot to her feet, hoisting up the skirt, and squatted by the bed. The warm urine spurted onto the floor, forming a dark puddle. She must not soil the bridal bed, whatever happened.

She pulled off her veil and bolted the bedroom door. On the bookshelf she found a pile of good-quality absorbent rice paper. She made a thick wad of the paper and, squatting down again, mopped up the urine, then threw the sodden paper under the bed. Fortunately there was only one wet patch on the skirt—her body heat would dry it. She picked up the bowl of soup and drank it all down. The liquid and the lotus seeds and jujubes made only a small dent in her hunger, but they at least served to boost her courage. She unbolted the door, veiled herself again and took up her position, seated upright on the bed. Even before the pounding of her heart had eased, she was suddenly overcome by an overpowering urge to sleep.

She was awakened by a fierce light; two glowing orbs seemed to shine right through her.

Ah-Fat's eyes.

"Ah-Yin, I never gave you any of the nice things I brought back from Gold Mountain," he said.

Suk Yin was the name she had been given at birth, but no one knew it outside her immediate family. For her whole life, she had been called Six Fingers, until the day the matchmaker had given the big red marriage proposal, with her name written in it, to Ah-Fat. Now it was their secret. And he had released the secret from its red packaging and given it back to her. A violent tremor shook her.

"Next time. Bring me something next time," she stammered.

"There won't be a next time. I'm taking you with me to Gold Mountain and you can choose whatever you like for yourself."

Ah-Fat blew out the red candle and pulled down the silk curtain behind him. He said no more but his hands began to speak as he felt for the buttons which fastened the front of her jacket. The fabric was a soft satin but it was heavily embroidered with peony blossoms, leaves and branches and was as stiff as armour plating. The buttons were made from fine strips of satin coiled into elaborate knots in a cloud pattern, and it was with some difficulty that Ah-Fat finally managed to undo them.

He took off her jacket and was unprepared for the infinite softness of her body. His own hands felt like rough sandpaper that would snag the threads of its satiny surface no matter how careful he was. Thank God, he thought secretly, her body remained unspoiled—soft and smooth—despite her years of hard work. His hands hesitated, as if unsure how to go on. Then he heard a moan. It was so faint it seemed like a grain of dust brushing against his eardrums, but he also heard the pleasure contained in it. His hands took up their movements with new vigour.

Ah-Fat was in fact no stranger to women's bodies. His knowledge had mostly been picked up in the brothels and tea houses of Gold Mountain, where he had learned how to go into those women's bodies. He had gone into them countless times although his knowledge of how to explore the scenery within remained sketchy. He had always thought that these explorations stopped at the threshold itself—until Six Fingers made him aware that the threshold was only the beginning of the exploration.

Afterwards, the two of them lay soaked in sweat, catching their breath.

Six Fingers lay with her head pillowed on Ah-Fat's shoulder. "Is Gold Mountain really good?"

Ah-Fat made coil after coil of the damp hair which clung to Six Fingers' forehead with his finger but said nothing. When she asked again, he gave a slight smile. "Good ... and not so good," he said. "If it was all good, why would we all come home? If it was all bad, then there wouldn't be so many Gold Mountain men, would there? Anyway, you'll be coming. Then you can see for yourself whether it's good or bad."

Six Fingers sat up abruptly and propped herself against the head of the bed. It was bright moonlight outside, and the moon's rays streamed through a crack in the curtains, pooling in her luminous eyes.

"Do you really want to take me to Gold Mountain, Ah-Fat? You won't be like Auntie Cheung Tai's husband ... go over there and forget your family?"

Ah-Fat sat up too and crushed her in such a tight embrace that Six Fingers heard her bones crack.

"Six Fingers, I promise solemnly before Buddha that we will make a life together in Gold Mountain."

Six Fingers freed one arm and put her hand against Ah-Fat's cheek. Her hand had not yet completely healed and was still bandaged, which made her movements somewhat clumsy. With one purple swollen finger she gently traced the scar on Ah-Fat's face, feeling a jolting in her heart as she followed its ridges and furrows.

"Ah-Fat, is it true what they say ... that you got your scar in a fight in Gold Mountain?"

Ah-Fat retrieved her fingers and pressed them against his chest. After a pause, he shook his head.

"I fell. I was on a mountain track," he said.

When Auntie Cheung Tai awoke the next morning, it was already light. She had feasted at the wedding banquet until midnight and had fallen asleep sprawled on her bed. When she sat up, she discovered she had not even undressed—she still wore the sapphire blue jacket embroidered with dark blue flowers. Her hair was a mess. She sprinkled water on it, used her ox-bone comb to smooth it down and coiled it into a bun. Then she sat in the front room to await her visitors.

She waited and waited but no one came. The paper which covered the window slowly changed from grey to white. She heard a chorus of barking dogs and crowing cocks. One after another, the neighbours banged open their shutters and she heard the splash of potties full of urine being emptied into the street. The children crying, their parents berating them, the footsteps of people going to market—every sound jabbed her until her heart seemed to hum with anxiety. Finally she could stay still no longer.

She got up and opened the door to the street, and found to her astonishment that her visitors had been and gone while she was still in bed.

In front of the door sat a large iron pot tied with red string. She took off the lid, to find a whole roasted suckling pig inside, shining brown and succulent. She examined it carefully. It was all there: head, tail, tongue, limbs. The piglet lay belly-side down on a white cloth. She pulled out the cloth and looked at the red streaks on it, evidence of the bride's virginity.

"Merciful Buddha!" she cried, giving her chest a thump with her fist.

Then she murmured: "Six Fingers, you've really landed on your feet. Buddha's brought you this far. What happens from now on depends on whether you're destined to be lucky."

In the spring of year twenty-one of the reign of Guangxu, candidates came from all eighteen provinces to take the Imperial examinations. When the examinations were finished, they waited in the capital for the list of successful candidates to be announced. It was an eventful springtime, the Imperial examinations being only one of the causes of excitement. The candidates swarmed into restaurants and tea houses and the frantic buzz of their debates filtered out through the cracks in the doors, walls and windows, down the streets and into the smallest back alleys, to be chewed over, in turn, by ordinary folk sitting in their courtyards after dinner or over their wine.

The candidates' topic of conversation had nothing to do with the outcome of the exams and everything to do with a war and a treaty. The war cost the Empire of the Great Qing its entire Beiyang fleet. The treaty cost two hundred million ounces of silver in war reparations and the peninsulas of Shandong and Liaoning, as well as the island of Taiwan and the Penghu Archipelago.

This was the First Sino-Japanese War, and the Treaty of Shimonoseki.

Gradually, the candidates calmed down and they drew up a petition ten thousand characters long. Several thousands of them congregated before the Office of the Superintendent and requested permission to present their petition to His Imperial Majesty. Their demands: the treaty should be rejected, the capital should be relocated, a new army should be trained and constitutional reform should be implemented.

The tumult in Peking reached Ah-Fat's ears through Mr. Auyung Ming.

Since Ah-Fat's return from Gold Mountain, he had become firm friends with his old teacher. Mr. Auyung had been left a small family inheritance which was enough to support all the members of his household and he did not need to bother much with his tutor school. He only had a very few students, but his house was filled from morning till night with visiting friends and acquaintances. They were a motley crew: private tutors like himself, petty officials, rickshaw-pullers and Cantonese opera singers, as well as hangers-on around local government offices. They did not come empty-handed to eat and drink at Mr. Auyung's table—they brought the latest news and gossip which they had picked up in the streets and markets. Most of it was about events at the Imperial Court in Peking, and this was precisely the kind of news that their host was most interested in.

Inevitably they were introduced to Ah-Fat during these dinners, and when they heard he was from Gold Mountain and was literate, they plied him with questions: What kind of constitution did Gold Mountain have? Did the common people live decently and in peace? There was a queen, Ah-Fat told them, but she did not govern. The country was governed by Parliament, whose members did not depend on passing the Imperial examinations, or on the Queen's favour. They were elected by the common people. A member of Parliament had to curry favour with the common people so that they would vote for him. "You're one of the common people," said the other guests. "Do they try and curry favour with you?" Ah-Fat sighed: "The likes of us are just coolies. The Gold Mountain government doesn't give us the right to vote."

Mr. Auyung thumped the table with his fist so hard that the rice grains jumped out of the bowls onto the floor. "Our emperor has studied Western sciences, and he knows what's good about the West. If it wasn't for that person who gets in his way, we'd have had a new government like a Western government long ago."

Everyone knew who he was referring to, and they lowered their voices. The rickshaw-puller got up to shut the door firmly before saying quietly into Mr. Auyung's ear: "Over in Sanwui, they've just set up a new party and they're armed with weapons. They say they're going to raise money and send hired assassins to Peking to kill that old woman and clear the way for the young emperor."

Ah-Fat was horrified when he heard this. He pulled at Mr. Auyung's sleeve: "Aren't you afraid of being killed yourself, if you allow this kind of wild talk?" But his friend just roared with laughter: "Her days are numbered, can't you see? Who knows who'll die first?"

Just as Ah-Fat was seeing off Mr. Auyung, who had come to visit him that day, Six Fingers went into labour.

The midwife hung a large red curtain over the door. No one was allowed in except Ah-Choi, the servant. Behind the curtain, Six Fingers moaned and groaned. Her moans at first sound stifled as if she had stopped her mouth with cotton wool. Later they turned into hoarse, pitiful wails. Ah-Choi came out of the room carrying a wooden bowl and emptied it into the gutter. The water in the bowl was red with blood. A vision of his father butchering pigs suddenly came into Ah-Fat's mind and he made a dash for the bedroom door. His way was blocked by his mother.

"It's what every woman goes through in childbirth. She's just got to put up with it. It'll soon be over. And if you get sight of her blood, it'll bring disaster on all of us. There's no way you're going in there."

Mrs. Mak told the servants to light incense, knelt down in front of her late husband's portrait and made a trembling kowtow. Ah-Fat could not stay in the house any longer. He rushed out of the courtyard and over the road, and sat down with his back propped against a tree and his hands clamped over his ears.

After he had been sitting there an hour or so, Ah-Choi came running out of the courtyard gasping for breath. Her jacket was spattered with blood, and her lips trembled as she tried to speak. Finally, she stammered out the momentous news: "It's a boy. A boy...."

Ah-Fat got to his feet. It felt as if all the suns in the heavens were bathing him with light from all directions, leaving not a shadow in sight. He hurried indoors, his legs so weak he was afraid they might give way under him.

In the bedroom, Six Fingers lay in the bed, her sweaty head askew on the pillow and her lips covered in purple teeth marks. Beside her lay a cloth bundle, tightly bound, with just a head showing at the top. The face looked just like an old yam left out in the fields to get wrinkly and frosted. It was not a pretty sight, but it made his heart melt all the same. Ah-Fat picked up the bundle in his arms, carefully, awkwardly, as if he was holding delicate china that might shatter.

The baby suddenly opened his eyes, squirmed vigorously and let out a wail so ear-splitting it set the roof beams trembling and the motes of dust dancing.

Six Fingers' eyelids were so heavy they might have been weighed down under pools of sludge. Her lips formed the question "What shall we call him?" but no sound came out.

All siblings and cousins of the same generation in the family shared a first given name. For this generation, it was Kam. Ah-Fat had been thinking about names for a few months and had settled on one name for a boy, and another for a girl.

But when he saw the teardrops rolling down his baby's face, he suddenly changed his mind. He remembered that examination candidate from Taiwan kneeling with the petition before the Office of the Superintendent in Peking, sobbing: "Give us back our rivers and mountains!" They would call him "shan" meaning "mountains."

"Kam Shan, that's his name," Ah-Fat said to Six Fingers.

Perhaps by the time Kam Shan had grown up, the rivers and mountains of the Empire of the Great Qing would no longer be in the sorry state they were in now, he thought.

When Kam Shan was a month old, Ah-Fat left for Gold Mountain again. But before he went, he took Six Fingers and the baby to pay respects to the tomb of Red Hair and Mrs. Kwan. The space for Red Hair was no longer empty—in it had been buried the Chinese fiddle and a suit of old clothes. The tomb had been sealed. After all those years, it was during this eventful springtime that the spirits of Red Hair and his wife were finally reunited.

"From now on, so long as my first-born son is alive to burn incense to me, there will always be someone to light incense at your tomb too," said Ah-Fat, making a deep kowtow to the tombstone.

4

Gold Mountain Turmoil

✦

2004
Hoi Ping County, Guangdong Province, China

By the time she found the shoes, Amy was almost in despair. She and
Auyung had spent almost two whole days in the *diulau* by then.

By the afternoon of the second day, they were familiar with the complicated layout of the building, and had a rough idea what room or staircase
lay behind every door and at the end of every corridor.

But they found disappointingly little.

From a distance, the building looked as if it harboured countless fusty
old secrets. But once inside they very soon discovered that no secrets lay
hidden beneath the dust at all, at least not the kind which they had so
eagerly anticipated. Apart from the garment inside Six Fingers' wardrobe,
there was nothing else worth mentioning throughout the entire five floors.
The years, like a giant hand, had laid down layer upon layer of dust, filling
and levelling smooth every crack which had marked the traces of human
existence. It was as if no one and nothing had ever been here.

Of course, the building was not completely empty. On the balcony under the roof, they found a child's tricycle, although its three wheels had rotted away. Auyung opened the little paring knife which hung from his key ring, and scratched away a patch of rust on the frame until a maker's mark was dimly visible. They both studied it carefully and were finally able to make out the words in English: "Made in Manchester, England, 1906."

They also found a silver teapot in the corner of a room on the third floor, its metal tarnished with the passage of many years. The body of the pot was engraved with an exuberant creeper design and words in English were entwined like flowers on the base. This was a Western teapot, probably once part of a set, now separated from its brothers and sisters and living out its days in this long-forgotten corner. Amy took off the lid and found black specks like mouse droppings stuck to the bottom of the pot. She found it odd that a mouse should have been able to get inside a teapot with the lid on but Auyung said thoughtfully: "These are tea leaves left behind after the tea was brewed—they must be decades old." Amy was struck by the sudden thought that Six Fingers might have been the last person to drink tea from the pot. Did she put it down and leave, never to come back again? Could those crumbs of tea come back to life if you poured hot water on them, unfurling to reveal their veins after all this time?

The teapot was mute, as were the tea leaves.

On the wall of a room on the third floor they discovered strange wallpaper. Saturated by decades of humidity, the paper was covered in mould and a latticework of moth holes. The mould and the holes covered the entire surface so almost nothing of the original pattern and colours was visible. Auyung ran his magnifying glass over the wall, and discovered the number "20" written in the outermost corner. He called to Amy, who took a good look and exclaimed: "They're American dollars! The wall has been papered with dollar bills! There's writing up there ... the words 'God ... trust.' It must say 'In God we trust,' which appears on the back of every American banknote."

"During the Republican period, Chinese currency lost value on a daily basis, so Gold Mountain families around here only recognized American and Hong Kong currency. They called dollars 'top bills.' Your family actually papered their walls with them!"

"Only someone who really loved, or really hated, U.S. dollars, could have done that with them," Amy mused aloud.

Auyung was silent for a moment, then said: "There's a third possibility, Amy. Maybe the person who did this neither loved nor hated dollars, but was simply indifferent to them."

Amy looked startled for a moment and then burst out laughing. She put her arms round him and planted a kiss on his cheek. "You're such a smartass!"

Auyung froze. His face assumed a wooden expression. Then his wrinkles began to make random jerks, and finally resolved themselves into something resembling a smile. Auyung looked strange, Amy thought—then she realized he was going red! The colour surged upward, and then drained away again. Amy stared so intently she seemed to be pinning him to the wall.

"I never knew that a man of your age could blush."

"You mean, how could a pathetic old man like me have such a thin skin?"

"No, that's not what I meant." Amy shook her head. Suddenly she nodded. "Yes, you're right, that is what I meant. You've surely been hugged and kissed by a woman before ... I mean, what about your wife?"

There was a long silence. Finally Auyung said: "My wife passed away in 1981. Back then, hugging and kissing existed only as words in foreign-language dictionaries."

"I'm sorry," Amy said hesitantly, suddenly abashed at her uninhibited behaviour.

They sat on the ground in silence, looking around at the empty room.

Why, in a household which had once been abundantly wealthy, had only a few knick-knacks remained? It was as if Six Fingers had known that her end was coming and had quietly picked up and put away every vestige of her existence. Yet she also seemed to have been taken by surprise, because her last mouthful of tea had remained undrunk at the bottom of that foreign teapot.

The objects they found in their search revealed only the hazy beginnings of a story. It was as if they had taken the first steps into a deep cave and were blanketed in dense, unfathomable darkness. What they had found might be of some interest to folklorists but Amy needed something more than that.

What she wanted was history. A sentence. A piece of paper. A letter which could nail their conjectures by providing incontrovertible proof. A photograph that could quell doubts and turn them into solid reality.

But there was nothing … not the smallest clue.

They picked up the briefcase and camera and prepared to go downstairs.

"Those few old things in the house we found, leave them on display," Amy told Auyung. "I've photographed them for myself. And the place must be restored to its original condition. You can have gaps in history, but you can't have substitutes. Add that clause to the contract, otherwise I won't sign it. You can bring me the modified contract to sign at the hotel this evening."

Auyung did not reply. After a little while, he said with a smile: "It was a marvellous feeling."

"What feeling?" "That hug." They both laughed.

They went down the stairs. As they turned a corner where one of the treads had collapsed, Amy missed her step and twisted her ankle. She took off her shoe and sat on the stairs to give it a rub. As she bent her head, she found herself looking at a pair of shoes. They were lying upside down in the recess at the back of the stair and she hooked them out. They were a man's cloth shoes with hand-sewn layered soles. They seemed never to have been worn—there were no traces of mud on the soles—but the fabric on the uppers had lost the sturdiness once provided by the interlocking rows of stitching. The shoes were stuffed with cloth bags. As Amy touched the bags they fell open, to reveal a thick pile of papers rolled up inside.

They were letters.

Letters densely covered with lines of Chinese characters written with a brush.

Carefully, Amy pulled the yellowing sheets out of their envelopes and spread them out on the floor.

"Hold the magnifying glass over them," she ordered.

"Good heavens above!" exclaimed Auyung in delight. "These haven't been written with a fountain pen. Otherwise, the writing would have completely faded."

Amy's eyes lit up. "My great-grandmother? But why would she have hidden these letters back there?"

"Your great-grandmother spent her whole life waiting. First for a boat ticket to Gold Mountain, then for someone to come and collect these letters. She's waited all these years for you to come. Don't you believe in spirits?"

Amy suddenly recalled the pair of eyes she had seen floating in the wardrobe mirror two days before. A strange feeling crept over her and seemed to flood her heart.

It was pain, she realized finally. What she was feeling was pain.

"Auyung, I'd like to be alone with my great-grandmother for a while," she said.

Years twenty-one to twenty-two of the reign of Guangxu
(1895–1896)
Vancouver, British Columbia

My dear Ah-Yin,

Many months have passed since I left and much has happened. My address has changed several times and things have not gone smoothly so I have not been able to send dollar letters home regularly. The day you saw me off on my journey with Kam Shan in your arms, he was too small to understand but you were plunged into such deep sorrow that I can never forget it. If it were not for the weakness of the Great Qing Empire and the impossibility of making a living, people like me would never have left our homes and families. You have so many responsibilities now that I am gone—my mother, our child and the management of the fields. For my mother's eyes, you should consult a doctor in Canton. There is an Englishman called Dr. Wallace who specializes in eye diseases. Kam Shan must be made to work, even when he is little, so that he develops a healthy mind in a healthy body. Do not let him become spoilt. When he is old enough, you should approach Mr. Auyung and ask if he would be good enough to accept Kam Shan as a pupil. He is a teacher of inestimable worth, whom I have always greatly admired. This year Vancouver is flourishing, and most of the Chinese have moved here from Victoria to find work. I have done the same. Not long ago, I ran into a man I worked with when we built the railroad, Ah-Lam. It was a great pleasure to see him again and we discussed working together. As soon as I have got the laundry going, I will send dollar letters home to support the family. My last trip home exhausted all my Gold Mountain savings, and I have had to start all over again. The government is very hard on us Chinese and heaps exorbitant taxes on us. As soon as I have saved enough money to pay the head tax and your passage, I will bring you and Kam Shan over to join me.

Your husband, Tak Fat, the third day of the ninth month, 1896, Vancouver

A city is born in the same manner that a seed comes to life buried deep in the ground. The germination period is long, dark and quiet, and fraught with unforeseen difficulties. Conditions have to be just right: soil, sun, humidity, fertility, winds. Yet these very same factors can also prevent a seed germinating. A seed can lie dormant for a very long time—for a whole season or even longer—waiting for a fortuitous combination of the elements. Only then can its first green shoots spring from the soil.

Victoria burst forth like a green leaf, in just this way. Before the age of the railroad, water stimulated Victoria's growth. The ocean breezes brought ships from every country and all corners of the earth to make landfall on the island. Waves of people surged ashore, blown by these favourable winds and currents, and along with them came opportunities for wealth. In this way, these long-desolate shores gave birth almost overnight to a flourishing green tree of a city.

But the train changed all of that.

First the train snaked westwards from the East Coast until it met the impenetrable barrier of the Rocky Mountains. Then, desperate hordes of men came to gouge a great hole in the belly of those mountains with their bare fists. Finally the train penetrated the tunnel made by these men and huffed and puffed its way to a spot on the West Coast across the water from

Victoria. This spot faced the ocean with the mountains at its back. The mountains brought the railroad, the ocean brought the sails. The mountains formed the feet of the ocean, which, in turn, gave wings to the mountains. And so, the door of opportunity opened wide. Here, where sea and land came together, enormous wealth accumulated, multiplied and dispersed; accumulated, multiplied and dispersed again. Blessed by its natural advantages, this spot where mountain and sea converged quietly developed the power to transform itself. Victoria, surrounded by water, did not benefit from the expansion of the railway. Gradually, people began to see the city's limitations. Suddenly one day, a thought struck them like a thunderclap: Why not cross the water and live on the other side, in the new coastal city?

Almost overnight, the new city on the other side of the water was on everyone's mind.

At first, the Chinese in Gold Mountain could not get their tongues around the surname of the English captain. To them it sounded like a snack, or perhaps a disease. It did not sound anything like a place name. So they chose their own name instead, "Salt Water Port." Many years passed before their children learned how to utter the syllables of its proper name.

"Van-cou-ver."

After Ah-Fat arrived back in Gold Mountain from Hoi Ping that summer, he moved from Victoria to Vancouver. Borrowing a bit of money from fellow Cantonese, he set up a laundry. It was called Whispering Bamboos, like the first one, but this one was in the *yeung fan* part of town. In the year that Ah-Fat had been away, rents had shot up and so had other costs. Although it looked the same from the outside, his new laundry was smaller than the first. There was a front room and a back room. The back room was for drying and airing the clothes, and it had two large wooden tubs in it and a cobweb of clotheslines overhead. If you were not careful, you could bark your shins on the tubs or get water down your neck from the wet clothes. The front room was for greeting customers and for doing the ironing. It was even smaller than the back room: just big enough to hold a counter and two ironing boards.

Ah-Fat hired a boy to help. It was his job to do the heavy work, washing and hanging up the clothes, while Ah-Fat did the ironing and mending, which required more skill and care. Every day at midday, the boy would load the tubs full of dirty washing onto the cart and drive the horse a few *li* to the river. Here he would fill the tubs with water and wash the clothes. By the time he had finished it would be dinnertime. If the clothes were not needed urgently, they could be left to dry slowly in the back room, after which they would be folded in neat piles. If it was a rush job, Ah-Fat would light the charcoal in the iron straightaway and iron them dry. If he had a lot of rush jobs, he might spend the whole night ironing.

One day, he did not finish the ironing till dawn. It was too much bother to go home so he stretched out on the ironing board and had a nap. He was awakened by cries of "Saw-lee, saw-lee, saw-lee....!" He opened his eyes to see a *yeung fan* customer arguing with the boy. A spark from the charcoal in the iron had singed a hole in one of the garments the man had come to collect. The boy only knew the odd word of English so all the customer got was a stream of apologetic "saw-lee, saw-lees." Ah-Fat could see the hole was at the bottom, and so small it hardly showed, so he got out his sewing kit and gestured to a stool. "I'll fix it," he said. "Just wait a moment." When Ah-Fat was at home, Six Fingers had taught him some of her darning skills, though he never imagined they would come in useful so soon.

The *yeung fan* did not sit down, however. Instead, he stared intently at Ah-Fat. Ah-Fat knew it was the scar that had drawn his attention. He was used to that now, after all these years, but at the beginning when the scar was fresh, those looks felt like a teasel prickling his skin.

"Didn't you work on the railroad?" the man asked hesitantly.

Ah-Fat looked up and scrutinized his customer. Although he had got to know some Whites during his years in Gold Mountain, he still found it hard to tell them apart. This one was much the same as all the others he encountered in the street: he was tall with a ruddy complexion and slicked-back hair separated into strands by his comb; he wore a dark grey, three-piece suit and a fob watch in the pocket of his waistcoat. Ah-Fat made a quick mental check of all the *yeung fan* men he knew, but none of them cut as respectable a figure as this one. He could not place him.

"Twenty-nine. Aren't you twenty-nine?" asked the man.

Ah-Fat was startled. Twenty-nine was his work number in the railroad construction team. They had been divided into a large number of groups of thirty men each. He was number twenty-nine in his group. The *yeung fan* foreman did not know his name, and did not need to. To his foreman, he was just a number on the worksheet and the payroll. His number was like a string bag which could wrap itself around him; the foreman held the drawstring and only had to tweak it with his finger for Ah-Fat's whole life to be caught inside the bag.

During his years on the railroad, Ah-Fat used to write his name on the trees in the clearing outside their tent, over and over, in all the calligraphy styles he knew, because he was afraid of forgetting how to write his own name. But he could not help looking up now and answering to the number twenty-nine, even long after the railroad work was finished.

The *yeung fan* leaned over the ironing board and gripped Ah-Fat in a bear hug.

"I'm Rick Henderson. Don't tell me you've forgotten me. That goddamn railroad!"

Ah-Fat looked blank. Then he suddenly realized. This man was his old camp foreman. His first thought was, how the hell had a railroad turned that roughneck into such a respectable-looking man? Unfortunately his English was not up to phrasing the question. What he actually asked, after the thought had rolled around in his head a few times, was something quite different.

"Mr. Henderson! What ... what are you doing here?"

The *yeung fan* released him and laughed: "What's all this 'Mister' talk! Call me Rick. You saved my life and I've done something with it since then. I've opened a guesthouse here with a friend, so employees of the Pacific Railroad Company and their families have a place to stay."

Ah-Fat looked at the immaculately knotted tie at Rick's shirt collar and suddenly thought of Red Hair and Ah-Lam. Red Hair had been number twenty-eight and Ah-Lam, number thirty. Their numbers had spent many years squeezed together on the record-keeper's work log, just like they had squeezed together onto sleeping mats in the tents. Red Hair in front, Ah-Lam behind, and Ah-Fat in the middle. They were packed in so tight that the only way to sleep was to curl up one behind the other like prawns. Half-suffocated by Red Hair's farts, and with Ah-Lam's snores rattling against his neck, Ah-Fat sometimes woke up in the night itching to throttle one with each hand. But he was squeezed in so tight he could not even sit up. Then one day Red Hair's space was empty and Ah-Fat's arms and legs finally had space to move. Later still, Ah-Lam's space was empty too. That was when he learned that he much preferred to be squeezed. If he should fall, there was someone to catch him. Being squeezed meant being supported.

Ah-Fat sighed. "That railroad...." he said. "It made so many men rich, and took the lives of so many others." Ah-Fat might speak with a heavy accent, but Rick heard the cutting edge in those words and embarrassment showed in his face. After a pause, he echoed Ah-Fat: "That railroad, huh! Last year I took the train to Montreal, and the ghosts flew around outside the train window as we went along. Actually, I was unemployed for a couple of years after it was completed. I was stuck in a small town by the rail track without work. It was only when I met an old acquaintance from the Pacific Railroad Company that this opportunity came up.

"What about you, number twenty-nine?" Rick asked, and then exclaimed: "You know, after all this time, I still don't know your name. You Chinese have such strange names!"

"Even if I tell you, you won't be able to say it. Forget it!" But Rick gripped his arm and insisted: "No, come on, let me hear you say it. Who says I can't learn it? After all, I can blow up mountains!"

Ah-Fat enunciated the sounds one by one, and Rick repeated them after him as best he could, until Ah-Fat could not help laughing. "Please! Spare me!" he said. "Just say it in the English way and call me Frank. As you can see, I run this laundry, been running it for the past few years. I started in Victoria and moved here just a couple of months ago. Everyone says business is booming here, but there are laundries everywhere and business is going from bad to worse."

Rick looked around him. He thought to himself for a moment and then said: "I've got a few dozen rooms in my guesthouse. I can send all the bedding and tablecloths to you to wash. I've got a few other friends with guesthouses too, and I can send them along to you, but you'll have to smarten this place up, and hire some more boys to help you. And whatever you do, don't scorch the cloth next time."

Ah-Fat pulled out a thread from inside the shirt and darned the hole. It did not take him long and he gave the shirt back to Rick. The mend was flawless. Ah-Fat smiled. "You caught us out today. Usually I would have mended it before you saw it and you would never have known. It would just have been between me and the Lord above."

Rick shook his head in wonder. "God must have just woken up the day he created you, Frank. He made you devilishly skilful. They're saying the Pacific Railroad Company is going to build a huge guesthouse here. Of course it'll be called a 'hotel,' not a 'guesthouse.' It'll be like a palace, with several hundred rooms. Imagine how many sheets and table cloths and napkins that'll be. When the time comes, I'll get hold of someone I know and we'll see if we can find a way to give the work to you. Then you'll really need to hire another dozen boys."

After Rick left, Ah-Fat told the boy to mind the shop and went off for a big meal in Chinatown. By the time he got there, the sun was up as high as the forks in the trees. The air was mellow and the wind had filled the street with a mass of soft pink blossoms. Ah-Fat hummed a little tune as he went along. It was, he remembered, the bridal tune which Red Hair used to saw away at on his battered old fiddle. He kicked at pebbles and the flower petals and thought to himself that that bastard Rick was not such a bad sort after all. At least he had not forgotten that he owed his life to someone else. He could not help imagining the new business Rick's guesthouse would bring him. He could almost feel the bank drafts clasped in his hand, and the softness of his wife's body as she lay curled up in his arms.

"It won't be long, Ah-Yin. Good times will be here soon," he muttered.

He went into the Wong Kee Congee Cafe on Dupont Street, and sat down at his usual table by the window. He used his sleeve to wipe a small patch of greasy tabletop and leaned his elbow on it. "A bowl of rice porridge with lean meat and preserved egg," he told the boy. "And two silver thread rolls, a plate of prawn rice rolls, and a dish of chicken feet and one of snails." The boy taking the order was surprised. "Tripped over a pile of dollars on your way here, did you?" he asked. Ah-Fat laughed but said nothing.

He looked around him as he waited for his food. Most people had already had their breakfast and gone and the place was almost deserted.

Apart from him, there was only one other customer. The man had his head down, slurping a bowl of plain rice porridge. A bluebottle was climbing up the edge of his bowl and had almost reached the tip of his nose. When Ah-Fat noticed, he reached across and rapped on the man's table. "Hey, mate, do you eat flies too?" The man looked up at Ah-Fat. His bowl dropped from his hand and crashed to the ground.

"Ah-Fat, you motherfucker! You're not dead! How many years have I spent looking for you?"

Ah-Fat stared at him in shock. "Ah-Lam? Or is it your ghost?"

Ah-Lam sighed. "I wish it was. My ghost wouldn't be having such a hard time." He stretched out his left leg for Ah-Fat to see. "When we got separated in Port Moody, I took a tumble down the mountainside and broke a leg. I couldn't walk so I had to stop where I was. I lived in a Redskin village, stayed there some eight years and only got back to Victoria last year. I came over here to Vancouver at the beginning of this year with everyone else."

"What are you doing in Vancouver?" Ah-Fat asked.

"There's not a lot I can do, dragging this leg around. I heard there was work at the canning factory cleaning fish so I thought I'd go and try it out. But that's only summer work. As soon as it gets cold, that'll stop too."

It was still warm, but Ah-Lam had on a lined jacket. It was shiny with grease and fraying at the collar and cuffs, and his hair was grimy and tangled. Ah-Fat could see that he was struggling. He called the boy over: "Bring a portion of prawn dumplings and some mixed seafood *ho-fen* noodles for my friend here." He turned to Ah-Lam: "Do you want to come and work for me at my laundry? It's ironing and mending. It's not difficult to pick up, you just have to take care with it." And he told him what Rick had said that morning.

It was uncanny the way the three of them—brought together ten years before by a railroad, and then scattered because of the same railroad—had all bumped into each other today. They both felt it had to be more than just coincidence.

They talked of old times. "Have you heard anything of Ah-Sing?" asked Ah-Fat. "When I got back to Victoria earlier this year, I went to the Tsun

Sing General Store but it was shut. I knocked but no one answered."
"Didn't you know he's doing time?" said Ah-Lam.

"Doing time for what?" asked Ah-Fat in surprise. "He was as honest as
the day!" "Over the years, he saved up a bit of money, enough to pay the
head tax and boat fares, and then he went back home and got married. The
next year, the wife joined him in Victoria. She was practically the only
Chinese woman there who wasn't working as a whore in Fan Tan Alley or
the tea-shacks, and she was good-looking too. Ah-Sing was worried and
kept her locked up all day in the back of the shop. But he couldn't keep the
letches away from her. When he wasn't home, they'd be up at the window
peering in at her. And she was lonely; she couldn't stand being cooped up
all day every day. In the end she fell for one of them and one night she was
off. Ah-Sing went after them on horseback and caught up with them. Then
he went crazy. He slashed at them with a knife. He got the woman on the
face, but she wasn't badly injured. But he killed the man on the spot. He's
been in jail for over a year now."

There was a moment's silence, then Ah-Fat said: "He was a good man,
Ah-Sing was." "Last year when I saw him," said Ah-Lam, "he talked about
when the railroad work finished and you came back to Victoria. You'd been
through really bad times, and had nowhere to live and nothing to eat. So
he used to leave the stove outside the door for you every day."

Ah-Fat was speechless.

That stove, with the flicker of warmth it provided, outside the back
door of the Tsun Sing General Store had warmed his hands, and the food
he had scavenged too. Ah-Sing had left it there to save his life.

Ah-Sing had known that he was spending every night outside the back
door of his house. He had known all along. But he never let on.

"What jail is he in?" Ah-Fat asked.

*Thousands upon thousands of Chinese gathered today at the Canadian
Pacific Railroad steamship docks to welcome the famous Li Hongzhang
from the Empire of the Great Qing to Canada. This gentleman holds a
number of official positions, including Imperial Viceroy and
Superintendent of Trade for the Northern Ports, although he has been
stripped of some of them following China's defeat two years ago in the*

Sino-Japanese War. China lost its entire fleet in that war, and has had to pay two hundred million ounces of silver in war reparations—a sum equivalent to the gross national product of Japan for seven years. Viceroy Li has now been on his sea voyage for seven months. After visiting Russia, Germany, Holland, Belgium, France and England, he arrived in America at the end of last month. He is making this journey on the Imperial edict in order to foster relations between all these nations and China. Vancouver is Viceroy Li's last port of call; from here he will return to China via Japan. His visit to Vancouver was unexpected. We understand that he was due to visit Seattle but that rumours of angry crowds of Chinese emigrants awaiting his arrival there forced a change of plan (although Li himself has denied this adamantly). The reason for their anger is the Chinese Exclusion Act that has just been passed in America. The last-minute nature of his visit here has in no way dampened the excitement of Vancouver's Chinese.

Today the entire length of Howe Street is bedecked with lanterns and coloured pennants. A gigantic ceremonial arch which, we understand, took large numbers of Chinese emigrants several nights to erect, has appeared at the dock. It is formed of one main arch and two side arches. Above them, three pointed roofs are formed of swags of drapery. At the apex of the drapery over the main arch hangs a ball in which has been mounted a Union Jack. The Chinese and Canadian flags hang from each of the side arches. Four welcome banners hang from the tops of the arches and several exquisite "palace lanterns" are hung underneath. The one beneath the main arch is especially eye-catching, as it is two feet in diameter, and its frame is swathed in silk fabric painted with flowers and Chinese designs and lettering. Multicoloured tassels hang from the bottom of the lantern, and the effect is extraordinarily beautiful. Today the dock was crowded with people, many of them Whites who had come to see the pageantry. A brawl even broke out at the end of Howe Street. There is speculation that the affray may have deliberately been caused by thieves hoping to steal onlookers' wallets. Two monks stood among the crowds doing a roaring business hawking the incense used at temple ceremonies, which they said was to welcome Viceroy Li .

Viceroy Li was conveyed from the docks in a special horse-drawn carriage accompanied by Mayor Collins, Mr. Abbott, the General Superintendent of the Canadian Pacific Railroad in British Columbia, and Chief Constable Ward. Li's entourage (which included his son and a nephew) followed, riding in an ordinary carriage with all the party's baggage. It is understood that the most important item that Viceroy Li carries with him is a coffin made from superior quality nanmu *wood. At seventy-four years of age, the Viceroy anticipates that he may die on his voyage. As the carriage brought him close to the ceremonial arch, the patiently waiting crowds of "celestials" performed their customary welcoming ceremonies. First there was the crackle of firecrackers, followed by the explosions of huge fireworks, thunderous drumming, and the noise of many hundreds of people shouting in unison. This was accompanied by musicians playing their peculiarly fascinating music, and some people sang Qing Imperial songs.*

Viceroy Li's eyes sparkle with intelligence. He sports old-fashioned steel-rimmed spectacles, has high cheekbones in a fleshy, dark-skinned face, and appears to be in good health. He stoops, which makes his six-foot frame visibly shorter. Today he wore an over-jacket of the famous Imperial yellow, shaped rather like a cape and of no obvious practical use. Under this he had on an outer garment of dark blue brocaded silk and, under that, a dark red robe printed with darker flower designs. He wore a pair of boots with thick, white soles and a Manchu official hat, with a deep, swept-back brim, set back to reveal a gleaming pate. Long pigtails tied with silk ribbons hung from under the back of the hat, reaching down to his knees. The brim of the hat was black edged with gold. Velvet ribbons cascaded from the peak of the hat, which was decorated with a huge gem, and a plume of peacock feathers sporting three "eyes." A diamond ring sparkled brilliantly on the little finger of his right hand.

There were obvious differences in social rank among the crowds who had come to meet the Viceroy. About a dozen Chinese businessmen were permitted inside the roped-off area to meet him. It was clear that these were of the upper classes from the expensive quality of their attire. Indeed, their elaborate garments were a far cry from what we are used to seeing on the Chinese in Chinatown. The ordinary labourers standing

151

some distance away, were dressed in cotton jackets and wide trousers gathered and tied at the ankle. Many of them had closed their laundries and shops for the day and had made the trip here from neighbouring towns and villages, in order to welcome Viceroy Li. All these sons of the Great Qing emperor—wealthy merchants and ordinary labourers alike—continue to wear the long pigtails to which age-old custom has given symbolic value, even though many have lived in Canada for a number of years.

Vancouver World, *14 September 1896*

Ah-Fat stood far back in the crowd, squinting up at the flags which hung from the ceremonial arch. They flapped in the brisk autumn breeze, furling and unfurling. The red sun on the Qing flag was the colour of the glistening yolk of a duck egg, and the slender black dragon seemed to writhe madly in a frantic attempt to catch the egg yolk in its mouth. Ah-Fat had seen a flag like this before, in the Chinese Benevolent Association, but he had never seen it displayed on such a fine day. The weather was beautiful, and when the yellow flag completely unfurled flat against a bright blue sky, Ah-Fat had the sudden feeling it was a Chinese New Year picture, hung on a blue backcloth.

Ah-Fat had flattened himself so that he could squeeze into a narrow crack between one person and the next. All his bulk was in his shoulders, while the lower part of his body was feather-light. Still, every now and then, he caught muttered curses from his neighbours as he trod on their toes. In the bright sunshine the horizontal banner across the ceremonial arch was clearly visible to him: "Welcome to Your Excellency Li Hongzhang," but the characters on the four vertical banners were much smaller, and Ah-Fat had to force his way halfway along the street until he was close enough make them out.

The Great Li Hongzhang bestows honour on all the places he deigns to visit

The Great Li Hongzhang has journeyed far at the Emperor's orders, to establish friendly relations with neighbouring nations

The Great Li Hongzhang, in speeding across the Pacific Ocean, shows us the loving concern he feels for the Emperor's subjects who live in foreign lands

When Your Excellency returns home, we hope His Majesty will suitably reward his loyal elderly minister

He read them several times over from start to finish, until he had a rough idea what they meant. Then he heard the sound of stringed instruments, and people singing: *With a golden palace towering over, and the grand Purple Pavilion....* It sounded like nothing he had ever heard before, something you might chant to the ancestors or in a temple, with a serene and solemn tune. Much later he found out it was called "Li Hongzhang's Anthem." Li commissioned lyrics for the music, and it made do as a Great Qing National Anthem, so they had something to sing to the foreigners.

The carriage came through the arch and drew near them. It was drawn by two fine Mongolian ponies with red harnesses, looking from a distance as if they had been painted gleaming black. Their sturdy hooves kicked up dust and pebbles as they trotted along. They set off sporadic bursts of cheering as they passed by, too. But the ponies had been well trained; they were used to ceremonies like this and took no notice.

Ah-Fat could now see the occupants of the carriage more clearly. There were four of them, two facing forward and two backward. Three of the four were *yeung fan*, so the Imperial official at the back on the left was, without any doubt, Viceroy Li. The hat on his head seemed to be very heavy and he leaned slightly forward under its weight, propping his arm on the side of the carriage. He had bags under his eyes so droopy they might have contained two walnuts. His chin trembled continuously as if he was trying to master a cough which might burst out at any moment. He held a silver cup in one hand which he used as a spittoon. In the other hand he held a pipe. Ah-Fat had heard somewhere that the Viceroy was a heavy smoker. But the Viceroy did not smoke Chinese-produced tobacco; instead, his pipe was filled with the tobacco used in American cigars.

If you stripped him of his gorgeous attire and took off his ornate feathered hat, Viceroy Li was just a man who had reached an advanced age. The process of aging was gradual—a wrinkle here, a white hair there—and it was impossible to tell on which morning, or after which evening meal, a particular wrinkle or white hair had appeared. But when observed together, all of the details of aging suddenly made a person old. After the sea battles of the Sino-Japanese War, Viceroy Li had aged into a truly old man.

Old people like this could be found all over the place in Hoi Ping, sprawled dozing with their heads resting on the customary "stone pillow" in summer or sitting in a cane chair enjoying the sunshine when the weather got colder. Grimy sweat lodged in the multiple folds of their necks, grains of rice and drops of soup from past meals stuck to their chins, and they hissed through the gaps in their teeth as they talked.

But Viceroy Li was different. Court dress and an official hat meant that getting old was regarded as acquiring dignity, slowness of mind was regarded as profoundness and sloth as solemnity. A peacock feather created a gulf between the nobility and the marketplace which could not be breached. Viceroy Li stood on the other side of the gulf, and even in old age, he was separated by thousands of *li* from the marketplace.

His train of thought scared Ah-Fat.

There was a ripple among the people crowded around Ah-Fat, and he saw the wheels of the Viceroy's carriage rolling past.

"Peace to Your Excellency!"

Around the carriage, the crowds dipped low like a rice paddy blown by the wind. Some bowed, others lifted the hems of their jackets and knelt on the bare ground. Suddenly the view opened up before Ah-Fat and he saw, or rather felt, the Viceroy's eyes from behind those thick lenses, boring painfully into his cheek. Out of the thousands of people milling around, Li Hongzhang's gaze had fastened on this swarthy scar-face who was still standing.

Ah-Fat made a low bow.

"Please, will Viceroy Li convey our best wishes to the Emperor, and wish His Majesty good health. May the Great Qing rise again," he shouted at the carriage.

His words had scarcely left his mouth when they were swallowed up by the general clamour. Perhaps the Viceroy heard, perhaps he did not. In any case, he signalled to his driver and the carriage slowly came to a halt. A wave of people surged towards it but was stopped by policemen who rushed up and linked arms to form a protective human wall. The water lapped at the foot of the wall but did not break through. Gradually calm was restored and the wave of people rested where it was, peering through the stalwart shoulders of the police at the carriage which had halted so close to them, and the elderly man who sat in it.

"Do you live well here?" the old man asked with a languid gesture towards Ah-Fat and the men standing around him.

They all looked at each other, wondering how to answer and not daring to speak. Eventually someone mumbled: "We're fine." "That's rubbish," said someone else, pulling at the speaker's sleeve. Ah-Fat glanced at the Mayor, then said: "Your Excellency, times are hard for us here. We can't get decent government jobs. We can only do dirty jobs the Whites don't want to do, and we earn half of what they do. If we open up a small business, we have to pay high taxes so there's precious little profit left at the end of the year."

As Ah-Fat spoke out, the men plucked up courage. A young man pushed himself through until he stood right in front of the carriage. "The Canadian government is discussing a bill to raise the head tax. We won't be able to afford it even if we save every cent for years. We'll have to spend our whole lives as bachelors and never have a wife and family."

An older man interrupted: "I'm married but what good has it done me? I can't raise enough for the head tax so my wife can't join me. I might as well be single. When do I ever get a leg-over?" Some of the men sniggered at the coarse language. The expression on Viceroy Li's face tightened. "I see," he said. Then he shut his eyes and fell silent.

The carriage wheels creaked and the ponies set off, their hooves stirring up little eddies of dust which filled the air with a haze.

In the blink of an eye, the autumn day had grown old.

Ah-Fat watched as the carriage receded into the distance, and gave a little sigh.

Year twenty-six of the teign of Guangxu (1900)
Spur-On Village, Hoi Ping County, Guangdong Province, China

Six Fingers got up and dressed, and pulled back the bamboo curtains. She startled at the sunshine which streamed into the room. They had had five continuous days of rain that seeped into their houses and through their clothes until it felt as if everything was coated in layers of slime. Yet now, without warning, the weather had suddenly cleared, revealing a perfectly cloudless sky. There was not a breath of wind. The sun shone on the raindrops so that the banyan tree in the courtyard appeared to be covered with glistening golden gems. Autumn had roared in like a lion this year, but in weather like this the cicadas still filled the trees with their full-throated calls.

Her mother-in-law, Mrs. Mak, had been up for hours, and sat neatly dressed in the courtyard, fanning herself with a cattail fan. "Have you bought the moon cakes for tonight?" she asked Ah-Choi. The servant had just finished the washing and was giving the drying poles a wipe before hanging out the clothes. "The young mistress got them in yesterday," she said. "There are four kinds: double-yolk lotus cakes, milk cakes with coconut flakes, walnut and apricot cakes, and jujube paste and osmanthus cakes."

Kam Shan had been squatting by the tree, pouring a big bowl of water into an ants' nest. When he heard the word "cake" he dropped his bowl with a clang and flung himself at Ah-Choi. Grabbing the front of her jacket, he begged loudly for cakes. "These are cakes for the Moon Festival," she told him. "I don't give them out. You'd better ask your granny." He pushed her away and threw his arms around Mrs. Mak's knees. "I want a cake, Granny!" he shouted. She wiped the sweat from her five-year-old grandson's forehead with her jacket and shook her head. "These are Mid-Autumn Festival mooncakes. You can't have them till this evening when Old Lady Moon comes up." "How long will that take?" Kam Shan asked. "The time it takes to have two more meals," said Mrs. Mak. Kam Shan opened his mouth and wailed, the tears running down his face like two rows of peas. The sound of his crying grated painfully on a tender spot in Mrs. Mak's heart. She grasped her walking stick and stood up. Holding the little boy's hand, she felt her way to the kitchen.

"You can have a piece of double-yolk cake, and that'll fill you to bursting. You won't need any lunch or dinner."

Kam Shan immediately stopped crying and his face lit up in a radiant smile.

Six Fingers tried to keep a straight face. Mrs. Mak normally had a flinty exterior, she thought to herself. It was only that naughty Kam Shan who knew how to worm his way into her heart.

Six Fingers sat down on the bed and leaned over to look at Kam Ho who was sleeping sweetly. The evening before, he had puked up his milk, and she had not got him to sleep till after midnight. When Kam Ho was asleep, he frowned so that a small pink knot formed between his eyebrows. A knot like a skein so tangled you could not find the end of the thread. Six Fingers went to smooth it out gently with her finger, but withdrew her hand hurriedly when the baby jerked awake. Kam Ho gave a few quavering cries of protest and gradually quietened again until his little snores filled the room like the buzzing of a fly.

Kam Ho was so different from his elder brother, Kam Shan, they were night and day. He was just over a month old, but he seemed to be brooding about something all the time.

Six Fingers sat at her dressing table and began to brush her hair.

It was long and thick and spilled in an untidy dark mass over her shoulders and down her back. Not that anyone else ever saw her hair like this— only Ah-Fat. Six Fingers always wore it combed into a bun. She took a bone comb, dipped it in hair oil and began slowly to pull it through her hair. Then she plaited it tightly and wound it into a thick bun at the nape of her neck. The village women usually used water in which tung-tree wood shavings had been steeped to dress their hair, but Six Fingers had Luk Mui brand hair oil which Ah-Fat bought her in Hong Kong. It was made by a Dutch company and had a faint flowery fragrance. She fastened a red felt flower onto one side of the bun and looked in the mirror. Her face shone back at her in the silvered glass. She put the mirror away, opened a small drawer in the dressing table and took out a finely carved sandalwood box. It had a brass ring fastening the two halves together and looked like the sort of box a wealthy lady might keep her jewellery in.

Six Fingers gave the ring a little twist and opened it to reveal a stack of closely written sheets of paper. In the box she carefully hoarded all the letters Ah-Fat had ever written to her. The one on top dated from more than a year ago. Ah-Fat had written it just before boarding the steamship to come home. He had stayed a whole year this time and had gone back last market day. He would still be on his way back to Gold Mountain and she could not expect another letter from him for another two or three months. She opened his last letter and read it again. She had folded and refolded it so many times that it had begun to fray at the folds. She could recite by heart what it said. When she got to the words "after so many years apart, my heart flies back like an arrow, and all I desire is to rest in the arms of my beloved," her face grew hot. She was secretly thankful that her mother-in-law could not read. Every letter from Ah-Fat had parts meant only for her. She skipped over them when she read the letters aloud to Mrs. Mak.

On his return this time, Ah-Fat had raised enough money to pay the head tax and his original intention had been to take Six Fingers and Kam Shan back with him. He went to ask his mother's permission. What Mrs. Mak's response was, Ah-Fat never said. Six Fingers saw Ah-Fat coming out of his mother's room with a face like a thundercloud. He never mentioned his plan again.

So Six Fingers thought she would write and ask Ah-Fat what he was going to do. If the post was fast, the letter might even get to Gold Mountain before Ah-Fat himself. She laid out a sheet of writing paper, carefully ground the ink in the ink stone, smoothed the wolf-hair brush and had just written the words "My dear husband" when she felt a gush of milk soak the front of her jacket. Kam Ho's birth had been quite different from Kam Shan's. He had popped out with hardly any effort at all on her part, as easy as a hen laying an egg. In fact, he was already halfway into the world by the time Ah-Choi got back with the midwife. Ah-Fat had hired an old woman whose sole job was to attend to her during the month after the birth. Three meals a day, with generous helpings of chicken, duck and fish had given her a plentiful supply of milk, enough to feed three Kam Hos and still have some left over.

Six Fingers undid the buttons and wiped herself dry with a towel. She wore a thin silk jacket fastened slantwise across the front, over a fine linen corset that Ah-Fat had brought back from Gold Mountain for her. According to Ah-Fat, Gold Mountain ladies wore hooped petticoats too, but Six Fingers laughed at that. "If I wear both, the stripes will make me look like a bee!" After much persuasion from Ah-Fat, she consented to wear the corset. At first, she felt so tightly squeezed inside the tube of fabric that it made her short of breath. But she got used to it, and now if she went out without it on, her breasts bounced uncomfortably up and down and she could not walk with her usual energy. But she was adamant that she would not wear the hooped petticoat. She could not get any work done in it. Ah-Fat had to give in on that one.

Once Six Fingers had dried herself and changed her jacket, she sat down again and continued with her letter.

Kam Shan and Kam Ho have both been fine since you left. Mum's eyes have not got any better, but they have not got worse either.

Having got this far, Six Fingers felt that this was not at all what she wanted to say. She crumpled up the paper, threw it into the wastepaper basket and began again with a fresh sheet of paper.

My dear husband,

All the family has been fine since you left. Mr. Auyung has been here once and gave us a children's story and copying books. Kam Shan can start school sometime next spring. The crops have been good this year and the first season's rents have all been collected. Next market day, Mum is going to buy two more plough oxen for the spring. She has also arranged a match between Ah-Choi and Ha Kau, and they will marry in the first month of the new year. They have lived with us for a long time, Ha Kau working the land and Ah-Choi in the house, so it will be a harmonious match.

By now Six Fingers' hand was aching. She had not lifted a brush once during the month after Kam Ho was born, and had got out of the habit. She felt she had covered most of the family news, but there was still something else that she had not said. What she had written seemed to float to the surface of her heart like millet husks, which, at the merest puff, could be blown to the paper, light and easy. But what remained unwritten was like damp flour sticking to the deepest recess of her heart, difficult to bring to the surface and put into a letter. Even if she could bring it up, it would have gathered dust in the process, losing much of its original clarity. Six Fingers sat deep in thought, then finally added the last sentences:

> *When the moon is full, that is when I miss you most. Who knows when our Gold Mountain promise can be carried out? The mountains and rivers stay the same, but I'm afraid I won't stay beautiful forever. All I can do is use this brush to write you words of love and send them to the man of my dreams in Gold Mountain.*

Your wife, Ah-Yin, Spur-On Village, the Mid-Autumn Festival, 1900

She put down her pen to the sound of whispering behind her. When she looked round she saw the faces of her female neighbours at the window. Six Fingers opened the door and the women clattered in. "Six Fingers, your Ah-Fat's only just gone. Are you missing him already?" Their husbands had also gone to Gold Mountain. Some had come back but others had not, and from time to time the women would beg Six Fingers to write letters for them.

"Huh!" retorted Six Fingers. "Missing him? It's my mother-in-law who asked me to write." But the women knew how much Ah-Fat and Six Fingers missed each other. "Right then, we'll ask Auntie Mak what's so urgent she needs to tell her son, shall we?" they teased her. Six Fingers was flustered. "Do you want me to write letters for you or not?" she asked, going scarlet in the face. There was raucous laughter.

As they chattered, their hands were busy at their stitching, embroidering the brim of a hat or sewing cloth shoes. The room was filled with the clack and hiss of needles and thread.

"Will you write to that man of mine and ask why no dollar letters have arrived for the last two months?" asked a woman called Ah-Lin.

Ah-Lin's husband was the oldest of the Gold Mountain men, at fifty-six years of age. He had chronic asthma and could not do heavy work. A few years previously he had saved up a bit of money and bought himself a concubine at one of the tea-shacks. He had two children with her and, since then, had not been back home. He just sent the necessary dollar letter every couple of months, to maintain his first family. In fact, for both families, it was the woman's earnings in the tea-shack which kept body and soul together.

"What's the point of asking him?" said someone. "Isn't that woman in charge?"

This was a sore point, and Ah-Lin said fiercely: "I've had all the rotten luck, while she's out in Gold Mountain enjoying life with him."

Several women piped up at once. "She's a tea-shack girl. What do you expect? She's the rotten apple at the bottom of the barrel. Anyway, it was your man who made her his fancy woman."

Ah-Lin bit her lips until deep teeth marks showed. "Huh!" she said. "I'm the one Ah-Kyun married officially. That worthless bit of baggage!"

Six Fingers could not help herself. She jabbed her finger in Ah-Lin's face: "And what about your nice tiled house and your silk clothes? That girl has slaved away to pay for them, hasn't she? You only eat if she has food. If she doesn't have food, you'll all just starve to death. Why don't you just write a nice letter and ask what's going on? What's the use of whining?"

That silenced Ah-Lin.

One young woman, just married, was a bit of a tease. She grabbed the letter Six Fingers had not had time to put away and began to read it through. There was general laughter and cries of "Since when did you learn to read, Ah-Chu? Haven't you got it upside down?" Ah-Chu paid no attention. She frowned and peered at the letter, tracing each character with her finger. Finally, she shouted in triumph: "'Field,' there's the character for 'field' here, Sister Six Fingers! I know that one! And 'ox,' I know 'ox' too! And there's a 'four' here. I've got it! You're going to buy four plough oxen, right?"

Six Fingers did not know whether to laugh or cry. She took the letter back, saying: "A little knowledge is a dangerous thing, isn't it? The worry's not someone who's illiterate or literate, it's someone who's semi-literate."

Ah-Chu was young. Her husband had gone to Gold Mountain straight after their wedding. She was now five months' pregnant with her first child so, unlike the village women with children in tow, she was free to please herself and enjoyed coming over to Six Fingers' house for a bit of fun. Six Fingers sometimes taught her a few characters.

"You mean even a dumb-bunny like Ah-Chu can learn to read?" the others exclaimed. "It's not difficult," said Six Fingers. "If you learn one character a day, you'll know three hundred and sixty-five by the end of the year, and in a couple of years you'll be able to write your own letters. Then if you've got something private to say, no one else needs to know."

There were nods of agreement. "That's true," said someone. "Six Fingers knows all our innermost thoughts. And we have to give her presents of eggs and cakes into the bargain!"

Amid the general chatter and laughter, Kam Ho suddenly woke up and gave an ear-splitting wail. Six Fingers hurriedly pointed towards the back room and the women lowered their voices. But it was too late. They heard the tap-tapping of a walking stick and Mrs. Mak came into the room.

She waved her stick in the air, then pointed it right at Six Fingers' forehead—the "eyes" in her ears were as acute as ever. "You should have fed that baby ages ago. What have you been doing since you got out of bed?" Six Fingers hurriedly picked up Kam Ho, undid her buttons and pressed a nipple into his mouth. Kam Ho whimpered and then settled down to feed.

Mrs. Mak's walking stick made another circle in the air. "And you lot, haven't you got any work to do at home? It's the fifteenth of the eighth month. You should be helping your parents-in-law get things ready for the Mid-Autumn Festival." The women exchanged glances, not daring to speak, and then crept away like mice fleeing a cat.

Six Fingers knew that her mother-in-law did not like her mixing with the wives of Gold Mountain men, in case they led her into bad ways and she became uppity at home. Cradling Kam Ho in one arm, she helped Mrs. Mak to a chair. "Mum, it would really help if I can teach them to read and write a bit. It'll stop them pestering me to write their letters for them, and that'll save our family a lot of trouble." "Huh!" the old woman responded. "It's better if a woman can't write, then there's nothing to distract her from attending to her in-laws."

Six Fingers heard the sting in that remark and saw the black look. She redoubled her attentions to her mother-in-law. "Mum, did you not sleep well last night?" she asked. "Huh!" Mrs. Mak said again. "How do you expect me to sleep well? I miss my Ah-Fat. He was nothing but skin and bone this time back. He has such a hard life. The whole family depends on the dollar letters he sends. He slaves away day and night in Gold Mountain, and never gets a hot dinner. And if his clothes need mending, there's no one to mend them for him. That husband of Ah-Lin, he can't hold a candle to my Ah-Fat, but he's doing all right. He's got his first wife looking after the family here and a second wife to look after him there."

Six Fingers was aghast. Her mother-in-law seemed to be saying she wanted Ah-Fat to take a concubine in Gold Mountain. Before she married, she had been adamant that she would make her own match and would never become a second wife. But now that she was married to Ah-Fat, there was no way she could stop him taking a second wife. Was that what he had been discussing with his mother before he left? No wonder he had not talked to her about taking her to Gold Mountain.

She took a deep breath but there was still a tremor in her voice as she asked: "And does Ah-Fat have anyone suitable in mind?"

Mrs. Mak sighed. "He doesn't want a second wife. He won't listen to his mum. Now that he's married, he only listens to his wife. Everyone knows you're the only one he listens to. If you really want the best for him, you'll write and suggest that he spend a bit of money on a concubine here to take back with him to Gold Mountain. Gold Mountain women, you don't know where they've come from. You can't trust them."

Six Fingers found herself unable to answer either yes or no. Myriad ants seemed to be crawling over her skin. She was torn between being happy at Ah-Fat's fidelity, and worried about how Ah-Fat was coping in the face of such hardship. She could not bear the feeling of Mrs. Mak's blind gaze, or rather the eyes behind her blind eyes, boring into her. She finally muttered: "Yes, Mum."

Mrs. Mak got up and went out. When she got to the door, she turned and said: "Six Fingers, I know what you're thinking. Every wife finds it hard to accept her man taking a second wife. When Ah-Fat's dad was alive, I was dead against him having a concubine too. But Ah-Fat can't go on year after year without someone to look after him. Unless of course you're thinking of leaving your old mum-in-law here all alone and going off to Gold Mountain to be with him."

This last statement had a distinct rise at the end of it, so that it sounded more like a question. Mrs. Mak finished speaking but did not move. Leaning on the door frame, she seemed to be waiting for an answer. Six Fingers knew that if she did not give it, her mother-in-law could stand there forever.

"I'd rather stay here, Mum, and attend to you for a hundred years," Six Fingers said. She did not look at her, dared not look at her. Mrs. Mak's blind eyes could see through her all too clearly.

Mrs. Mak's stick tapped away into the distance, then halted.

"Ah-Choi, put eight of the best moon cakes, two of each kind, in a nice decorated box and take them to Auntie Cheung Tai. She deserves them, for taking in the young mistress when she was little. It can't have been easy."

The old woman's words echoed sibilantly around the courtyard.

Year twenty-nine of the reign of Guangxu (1903)
Vancouver, British Columbia

"Name?"

"Ah-Lam."

"Surname?"

"Chu."

"So Ah is your first name, and Lam is your middle name. Is that right, Mr. Chu?"

Ah-Lam looked at the interpreter. "Are you talking Chinese? I can't understand a word you're saying."

Ah-Fat clenched his teeth together, and bit back the laugh which threatened to escape like a fart.

The public seating area was of moderate size, just ten rows of seats with a gangway down the middle. Ah-Fat was seated on one side, and there was a *yeung fan* on the other. The *yeung fan* held a *Provincial News*, and had already leafed through it a number of times. Now he was perusing the advertisements, in particular a small one outlined in red ink:

The Whispering Bamboos Laundry announces the opening of a new branch, situated opposite the Vancouver Hotel in Georgia Street. The Whispering Bamboos Laundry has over a decade of experience in washing, starching, ironing and mending, and has more than twenty employees. We are at the service of hotels and individual customers. Prices are reasonable and your satisfaction is guaranteed.

The interpreter was a short man dressed in a neatly pressed three-piece suit. Holding his hat in his hand, he stood ramrod straight, reminding Ah-Fat of the clothes prop in the back room of his laundry.

"Yes, Your Honour. Chu Ah-Lam says that is the case."

Bald-headed traitor, Ah-Lam swore silently to himself, disrespecting your ancestors, cutting off your pigtail and eating out of the White man's hand.

"The case of Hunter v. Chu is hereby convened. Mr. Hunter, will you swear in God's name that today you will tell the truth, the whole truth and nothing but the truth?"

Mr. Hunter was the plaintiff in the case against Ah-Lam. He took a thick, black, leather-bound book from the judge, raised his right hand and rattled something off. When he had finished, the interpreter took the book and passed it to Ah-Lam.

"I'm not swearing on any black book. I don't believe in that Long Beard god of yours."

"What does he say?" the judge asked the interpreter.

"Mr. Chu doesn't believe in God so he can't take the oath on the Bible."

"Well, what does he believe in, apart from money?"

"You motherfucker" was Ah-Lam's response when the interpreter translated the judge's question. The interpreter was aghast. After a pause, he said to the judge with some embarrassment: "Mr. Chu hopes your mother is well."

This time, a snort of laughter escaped Ah-Fat.

"Thank you. But you still have not told me in the name of which god you would like to take the oath. Do you want to do what you did before?"

This was not the first time Ah-Lam had been in court. He had been accused of pilfering clothes three months previously. His accusers were different but the offence was the same. Each man had given Ah-Lam clothes to wash and had collected them from him after washing. But each man claimed afterwards that Ah-Lam had not returned their clothes. Ah-Lam could talk the hind legs off a donkey but had not been able to argue his way out of it and the judge had fined him thirty dollars. On the last occasion, Ah-Lam had taken the oath before the portrait of Lord Kwan, but Lord Kwan had not looked after him, and Ah-Lam was damned if he was going to pay his respects to Lord Kwan once again.

Ah-Lam scratched his head, and finally said: "Chicken's blood."

The judge raised his eyebrows. His glasses dropped off the bridge of his nose and onto the table in front of him.

"Your Honour," said the interpreter, "solemnizing an oath with the blood of a chicken is an ancient custom among the people of the Qing Empire, and it is both commonly used and accepted. The defendant is not making fun of the court."

The judge ordered the court adjourned, and when it re-assembled a short while later, a burly police officer, at least six foot three inches in height, strode in carrying a pure white leghorn hen. The hen's wings were tightly bound to its body with a cord but it was surprisingly vigorous. When set down in the aisle, it scrabbled madly with its feet, squawking loudly and filling the courtroom with a cloud of snowy-white feathers.

Ah-Lam stuck three sticks of incense into the table in front of the judge and lit them with a taper. He slumped to his knees and bowed three times. Then from behind his ear he extracted a piece of paper rolled up tightly till it resembled a cigarette, unrolled it and began to read it aloud to the judge. Ah-Fat had written his statement out for him but Ah-Lam could not read, so with Ah-Fat's help he had learned it off by heart, word for word.

I, Chu Ah-Lam, born in Dung Ning Lai Village, Ng Wing Town, Hoi Ping County, Guangdong Province, China, have worked as a washerman at the Whispering Bamboos Laundry at 732 Georgia Street (originally of 963 Main Street) for eight years. At the beginning of this month, Mr. Hunter brought in three garments for washing—a sweater and two pairs of trousers. The sweater was to be washed and the trousers were to be washed and mended. The lighter-coloured pair had frayed trouser cuffs and the darker pair had a cigarette burn in the pocket. The washing and mending was done by the next day. Mr. Hunter's maid came to collect them at about ten o'clock. I wrapped them in tissue paper and gave them to her. That motherfucking baldie Hunter has stitched me up. If he's really lost his clothes he should ask his maid. She's the one who should be taken to court. She probably nicked the clothes and gave them to her fancy man. It's fucking bad luck on me. I, Chu Ah-Lam, swear this on this chicken's blood before God in heaven and my venerable ancestors and if I've spoken one word of a lie, may I be eaten by rats in my house and run over by a horse and cart outside it. May I choke to death on my phlegm when I lie down, may I die of purulent boils on my arse when I sit down, and when I stand, may I be struck dead by five bolts of lightning.

Ah-Lam had begun his recitation according to Ah-Fat's script, but he soon felt that the language was too high-flown. It sounded to him as pulpy as a frosted eggplant, so he dropped the paper and proceeded to improvise the rest. As the interpreter got near the end, he broke out in a sweat and could not go on. He mopped his face with a handkerchief, and said to the judge: "In summary, Mr. Chu Ah-Lam has enumerated many different ways in which he is prepared to die if he has told a lie."

The hen, which had squawked itself into a state of exhaustion, was laid on a tile. The court officer cut its head off with a heavy axe. The hen's blood spurted onto the floor where it formed a sticky puddle. The head flopped onto the tile but the body of the hen shot upright and rushed away with great strides, leaving a trail of crimson claw prints on the floor. By the time the court officer had pulled himself together, the hen was out the door.

Passersby were treated to a rare spectacle that day: a headless hen, its wings bound tightly to its body, racing across the lawn in front of the courthouse, its neck sticking up like a wine bottle from which gurgled bloody bubbles. A man in police uniform gave chase. He reached down clumsily to grasp it, but the hen, though headless, easily evaded his outstretched hands. The fact was, the court officer was too well-built for the job and it cost him a good deal of effort to keep bending down and straightening up. After a few attempts, he was clearly out of breath. He planted his hands on his knees, and watched as the bloody hen collided with the iron grille surrounding the fountain in the middle of the lawn, left one last grass-green dropping on the white granite steps, finally fell to the ground and died.

The court officer returned the headless runaway to the courtroom where Ah-Lam still knelt. By now, he was growing impatient, and as soon as the hen came within reach, he stretched out his finger, scooped up a blob of congealing blood from its neck and smeared it on the paper on which his statement was written. Then he set the paper alight with the incense stick and sat back down in his seat.

"You say Mr. Hunter sent his servant to collect the clothes. What was the servant's name?" the judge asked Ah-Lam.

"You'll have to ask him that," said Ah-Lam, pointing to the man who sat at the plaintiff's table. "How do I know what his servants are called?"

"Can you tell us if the servant had any special characteristics? Even if you don't know her name, you can tell us what she looked like, can't you?"

Ah-Lam chewed his fingertip and thought for a while. Eventually he said to the interpreter: "These *yeung fan* all look the same. How the fuck should I remember?"

The interpreter was translating for the judge when Ah-Lam suddenly piped up in a loud voice: "She had big tits. That woman had tits which hung down to her belly."

Ah-Fat wanted to laugh but did not dare. But when he had heard the translation, the plaintiff, Mr. Hunter, guffawed. The judge banged twice with his gavel, and pointed with a face like thunder to Ah-Lam. "This is contempt of a court of the British Empire. You're fined ten dollars." Ah-Lam pointed to Mr. Hunter: "He's the one who laughed. What kind of a law is it that says you should fine me and not him?" The judge banged his gavel once more. "I'm adding five dollars to the fine." Ah-Lam was about to protest but was quelled by a warning cough from Ah-Fat.

The judge turned to Hunter. "What evidence do you have that Mr. Chu stole your clothes?" "Your Honour," replied Hunter, "I only know that I sent five garments to the laundry and did not get one garment back.

Isn't that enough proof? Do you think I have nothing better to do than take this bunch of 'celestials' to court?"

Ah-Lam clenched his two fists together until they cracked. In the blink of an eye, three garments had become five. He was about to start cursing, when he heard the interpreter ask him: "You say you did not steal Mr. Hunter's clothes. What proof have you got? A signature, perhaps?"

"You don't sign a contract for three items of clothing! It's not like selling your wife or your fields!"

The judge closed his eyes for a long moment. Then he opened them and said: "The plaintiff accuses the defendant of stealing his clothes; the defendant swears that he did not. The plaintiff has insufficient evidence and so does the defendant. I do not entirely believe either of you. Therefore you will bear the costs equally. Five garments, somewhat worn, divide the value in half, that's five dollars. Add the courts costs, that makes a total of twelve dollars. Mr. Chu pays Mr. Hunter twelve dollars. The loss of the other half of this sum must be borne by you, Mr. Hunter. Let that be a lesson to you not to bring a case with insufficient evidence."

Ah-Lam stamped up and down in rage. "What kind of a dumb judge is he? Any blind magistrate from way out in the sticks would give a more sensible judgment than that!" The judge did not wait for a translation of what he knew was a rude comment, but tugged his black robe around him and made to leave the court. Suddenly the *yeung fan* in the public seats stood up. "Your Honour, would you wait a moment? I have important evidence." The man had been seated for the whole case without opening his mouth. Seeing that he was dressed like a respectable member of the community, the judge put on a slight show of civility and asked: "Who are you?"

The man bowed. "I am Rick Henderson, deputy general manager of the Vancouver Hotel, owned by the Canadian Pacific Railroad." The judge grunted. "The Duke of Wales and Cornwall stayed in your hotel with his wife when they came to visit and I got an invitation to the cocktail party they gave." "Not only the Duke of Wales and Cornwall," said Rick, "every member of royalty stays with us when they visit the West Coast. If you want to enjoy afternoon tea, British style, in the very dining room where royalty have dined, you have to book two weeks in advance. At afternoon tea on Victoria Day in May, the Royal Philharmonic Orchestra will be coming from London to play chamber music. They include two violinists who played for Queen Victoria at her Golden Jubilee. Of course, all the seats have long since sold out." Rick took a gold-monogrammed envelope out of the pocket of his lightweight wool suit and handed it to the judge. "Perhaps Your Honour would like to verify that I am who I say I am."

The judge opened the envelope and took out a sheet of paper with the same gold monogram on it. He turned it over and looked at the back and gradually a faint smile appeared on his lips. He carefully put the letter away in an inner pocket of his black gown and asked: "Mr. Henderson, you have come as a witness for Mr. Hunter?" Rick shook his head. "Quite the contrary," he said, "I have come as a witness for Mr. Chu—although he didn't invite me.

"Mr. Chu Ah-Lam is an employee of the Whispering Bamboos Laundry, whose proprietor, Mr. Fong Tak Fat, is also present today. In the last eight years, the Whispering Bamboos Laundry has provided laundry services for the Vancouver Hotel. For the first five years, they washed and ironed the bed and table linen, just for the ordinary guests, of course. We have specialist launderers for the rooms of our most exclusive guests. For the last three years, the Whispering Bamboos Laundry has also undertaken personal laundry and mending for our ordinary guests.

"The Whispering Bamboos Laundry has now, I know, opened another branch in Vancouver with around twenty employees. This branch provides services for hotels and guest houses, and has very few private customers. In the last eight years, the Vancouver Hotel has not lost a single bedsheet or tablecloth. Nor have our guests made a single complaint of this nature. Of course, they have made other complaints, for example, that it's hard to make the laundry workers understand English and so on. As I understand it, there are several hundred dialects of Chinese within the Empire of the Great Qing alone, so it's a bit like the Tower of Babel, with everyone speaking their own language. We surely cannot expect them to completely understand the language of the British Empire, just like that, can we? But Your Honour only has to give it one serious thought, and it will become immediately apparent that a laundry business which has serviced the Vancouver Hotel for eight years is hardly likely to bother pilfering some trifling item of clothing from an individual customer. I hope that you will give due weight to my testimony, Your Honour."

The judge shook his head and grumbled: "Are you having a joke at my expense? Why didn't you bring all this up when the court was in session? It would have saved everyone a great deal of trouble. That poor hen might have been spared to lay a few more eggs." And he banged the gavel hard on the table: "The case of Hunter v. Chu is hereby concluded. The evidence of the plaintiff does not stand up in court. Mr. Chu does not need to pay any compensation to Mr. Hunter. Mr. Hunter will bear all the legal costs. The court is dismissed."

Rick bowed to the judge. "Your Honour, I hope that my witness statement can be kept permanently on file. It's hard enough for these poor Chinese to run their small businesses without these people who constantly make trouble for them. If the Whispering Bamboos Laundry is ever taken to court again in a case like this, the judge can refer to my testimony, or call me as a witness."

Once outside, Ah-Fat could not resist asking Rick: "What the hell was written in that letter?"

Rick looked around to check no one was listening and then muttered: "An invitation as an honoured guest to the Royal Afternoon Tea on Victoria Day. The seats closest to the orchestra."

If Ah-Fat's English was rudimentary, Ah-Lam's was even more so, and he was unable to say anything much to Rick. However, he tugged at Ah-Fat's sleeve and said: "You did the right thing, kid, when you saved that *kuai lo's* life on the railroad." "That's all very well for you to say. The scar's not on your face, is it?" Ah-Fat retorted.

Rick snapped his fingers at a carriage on the other side of the street and the driver brought it slowly over. Rick jumped in, and then turned back to Ah-Fat: "Next time customers come to pick up their clothes, get them to sign for them. It'll save you a lot of bother." "Right," said Ah-Fat, with a nod. The carriage creaked away but after a few paces stopped again at Rick's command. Rick came back to say to Ah-Fat:

"That eminent Chinese scholar of yours, Mr. Liang, is staying at the hotel. From what I hear, he's been promoting his reform movement and planning to overthrow the Empress Dowager. He's giving a lecture this evening. Are you coming?"

Even though Rick broke his sentences into short sections and spoke very slowly, Ah-Lam still did not understand. "What bullshit's he talking now?" he asked Ah-Fat. "We'll put up the shutters early today and we're going to the hotel." "But Ah-Yee's already delivered the washed and ironed linen we got yesterday. What's the point in going back there again?" "Mr. Liang's here and he's staying at the hotel." "What Mr. Liang?" "Liang Qichao, the one who plotted constitutional reform with the Emperor, and the Empress Dowager put a price on his head of a hundred thousand ounces of silver. He's lecturing tonight." "If you get involved with the Monarchists, and they get wind of it back home, your whole family will be killed." "A lot of Chinese here in Vancouver have joined the Monarchists. If we don't go shooting our mouths off, they won't get wind of it." "You go if you want. Me and Ah-Yee, we're off to the Fan Tan gambling dens. Whatever party's in power, the rich are still rich and the poor are still poor. So what if Mr. Liang's here? I still have to wash clothes to earn a living."

"Bullshit," said Ah-Fat. "If China was just a little bit stronger, would you and me have to leave our parents, wives and kids and come and work over here, and have the *yeung fan* make trouble for us all the time? We've got a young, promising emperor. He's had a Western education, and if he can take power, he can use that knowledge to contain the Westerners and revitalize our country. Then you and I can get back home and live with our families." Ah-Lam had married a few years before, but had not managed to raise the money for the head tax or the boat passage home, and had not seen his son since his birth. Ah-Fat had touched a raw nerve, and Ah-Lam fell silent.

When they had put the shutters up, Ah-Fat and Ah-Lam spruced themselves up and changed into the long gowns and mandarin jackets that normally only came out for New Year. They walked to the Vancouver Hotel through the darkening streets, their blue cloth shoes kicking up fine dust which bore the faint smell of new grass, feeling an excitement which gradually rose to fever pitch.

They arrived in good time at the hotel. At the door, Ah-Fat saw a familiar face—familiar yet strange, as if the man had changed out of his usual clothes and did not look like himself any more. Ah-Fat stared for a moment. Then the man smiled at him and a black mole at the corner of his lips migrated up his face. Suddenly he knew who it was.

Ah-Fat lifted the folds of his gown and knelt down in a respectful bow: "Mr. Auyung! When did you come to Gold Mountain? No wonder Ah-Yin wrote and told me she couldn't get in touch with you. We wanted our son Kam Shan to become your pupil last year."

Mr. Auyung pulled him to his feet. "Two years ago, I wrote some articles on constitutional reform and the government put a price on my head. I had to leave my home. I first went to Japan, but then I heard that Mr. Kang Youwei and Mr. Liang Qichao were in North America so I came here too."

Auyung pulled the two men to one side and they talked for a long time. When they finally went into the hotel lecture hall, there were no seats left and the aisles were full of people standing, both Whites and Chinese. By the time Ah-Fat and Ah-Lam had squeezed themselves into a small corner, they realized they had missed the beginning of the speech. In any case, the tenor of Mr. Liang's speech was high-flown in the extreme; these grand, distant phrases seemed to fall like boulders in a disorderly heap. Even for a man who had some education like Ah-Fat, negotiating this boulder-strewn road cost him a good deal of effort. Fortunately, Auyung had smoothed the way for them beforehand and, having heard his simplified version, it was easier to make sense of what Liang Qichao had to say.

It was midnight before they got home from Liang Qichao's lecture. Neither of them could sleep, so they sat on the bed smoking one cigarette after another. The laundry boys were already asleep, and rhythmic sounds of snoring filled the room like a chorus of cicadas. In the darkness, all that could be seen was the glinting light from two pipe bowls. Ah-Lam kicked off his shoes and sat on the bed picking out the grime from between his toes. "A woman's made herself the boss of the Emperor and the boss of our whole country. Mr. What's-it Liang—what the hell was he going on about? I say we should simply hire someone to stick a knife into her. I've never heard such a boring lot of shit." Ah-Fat did not answer. There was more swearing from Ah-Lam but then he got tired of it, and grabbing his pillow, he lay down. Immediately, his breathing became heavy.

Sometime in the early hours, Ah-Lam was woken by the need to piss. Opening his eyes, he was astonished to see a will-o'-the-wisp glinting by the bed. "Ah-Fat! You still not asleep, you little sod? It's almost dawn!" The light shifted position and he heard a low, muffled voice:

"I'm sorry, Ah-Lam. I'm going to have to do you out of your rice bowl. I've decided to sell the laundries, both of them. The Qing Empire can't be saved without educated men like Kang and Liang," Ah-Fat went on. "We can only help by giving money; we don't have enough education to help any other way."

A gasp caught in Ah-Lam's throat. But, astonished though he was, he knew that once Ah-Fat had made up his mind, nothing would make him budge.

"Once I've sold them, you and I will go and get work in the fish cannery. You won't starve while I've still got a mouthful to eat."

"I won't starve but what about your wife and kids? Their eyes are going to pop out of their heads, waiting for your dollar letters."

Ah-Fat was silent. Then he said: "I won't be able to go home for a while. Ah-Yin'll just have to wait."

Two months later, Ah-Fat sold his laundry business to a greengrocer who hailed from Toi Shan for eight hundred and ninety-five dollars. He divided the money into three. The largest part he sent to the North American headquarters of the Monarchist Reform Party. The middling portion he sent to Six Fingers with one of his friends who was going home to Hoi Ping. The bit of cash that remained he kept for himself.

After that, Ah-Fat completely lost touch with Mr. Auyung. In the years that followed, every now and then, a rumour of his whereabouts might come his way: Auyung had joined a plot to assassinate the Empress and had been betrayed to the police and beheaded at the entrance to the vegetable market in Beijing; he had secretly gone back to Guangdong and organized a militia to go to the rescue of the Emperor in Beijing but had died of a chill he caught en route; or he had gone to Japan, taken a Japanese woman as a second wife and abandoned politics, immersing himself in the study of the sages.

Whatever the truth of it, Mr. Auyung glittered briefly in Ah-Fat's life like a star and then vanished forever.

Year thirty-one of the reign of Guangxu (1905)
Vancouver, British Columbia

It was only when he came within sight of the two lanterns hanging outside the gambling den that Ah-Fat felt tired. It usually took him an hour and ten minutes to get from the factory to Chinatown but today he had quickened his pace, almost breaking into a jog, and did it in three-quarters of an hour. Ah-Lam had given up trying to keep up with him after a while and let him go ahead.

Hawkers swarmed around him like flies, carrying baskets on their arms or slung over their shoulders and offering their wares: sesame crisp, *char siu* dumplings, green bean cakes, sticky rice balls, chickens' feet in briny gravy, and strips of cold, cooked pigs' ears. He had a ten-dollar note tucked away in an inner pocket—the wages he'd just been paid. He reached inside and fingered the note, its former crispness sodden from his sweat. Tonight he could afford anything from the baskets, and not only from the baskets. He could take a very small corner of his note upstairs to a room above the gambling den screened off by a roughly nailed curtain, where a woman was desperately eager to take it off him. In the last few years, the head tax for Chinese immigrants had soared to five hundred dollars—a sum so huge that it was almost impossible to save up even if you scrimped and saved for years. Very few Chinese women came to Gold Mountain, so their prices had naturally gone up. A whole night of tenderness was beyond his means, but every now and then he could afford fifteen minutes.

Ah-Lam was a regular customer here. There was no way Ah-Lam could raise five hundred dollars, so Ah-Lam's wife was still stuck in her home village. But Ah-Lam did not neglect his own needs. He regularly told stories about what went on in that dark room. Ah-Lam's descriptions set Ah-Fat on fire, and when he could not stand this fevered state any more, he went too. He did not think of Six Fingers when he entered, only when he left. Every time he pulled aside the old curtain and went in, his whole body was ablaze; then, when he let the curtain fall behind him and left, he felt a desolate chill.

There was no getting away from the pain this fire and chill caused him. They both had to be borne; one could not take the place of the other.

Ah-Fat's eyes only gave a cursory glance at each of the baskets but his belly rebelled, crying out in shrill tones its urgent need for food. He had only had half a bowl of rice and drunk some boiled water at lunchtime. He had walked a long way since then, and now his hunger seemed to be gnawing painfully at his innards. But before he could satisfy it, he needed to find a place where he could have a piss.

There were plenty of unlit walls around the gambling den, and passersby who needed to relieve themselves would normally pull up their jackets, undo their trousers and piss there. In the past, Ah-Fat had done that too, but today he did not want to. Holding it in, he walked a few steps through the alleyway, bright with painted signs and warmed by shop lanterns, until he finally came to a large maple tree where he stopped. Its shade enveloped him like a black cloak. Underfoot lay a pile of ancient refuse the stench from which almost knocked him backwards. Ah-Fat pulled up the front of his jacket, undid his trousers and pissed. The stream of urine hissed as it fell on the trash, raising a cloud of flies in the darkness, the buzz of their unseen wings breaking the quiet around him.

Having relieved the pressure on his bladder, his mind was free to think of other things and he became aware of the rank smell coming from his jacket. He and Ah-Lam had started work at six o'clock in the morning and had spent the whole day washing and gutting fish. Of course they wore aprons but his knee-length jacket still got spattered in fish scales and blood. Since selling his laundry business two years previously, he had worked at the fish cannery. The workers were all Chinese and Redskins, the former all men, the latter all women. The men washed the fish and cut them up, while the women packed the cooked fish into cans of various sizes. The men's work was very dirty, the women's a little less so. When Ah-Fat and Ah-Lam started there, they used to wash the fishy smell off their clothes every night when they got back home. You felt like a different person once you had poured a basin of water and washed your hands and face with carbolic. But the smell of fish gradually impregnated their clothing, the pores of their skin, even seeped into their veins. Nothing could wash it off. Ah-Fat thought that even his phlegm smelt like fish.

Still under the tree, he took off his jacket and shook it out vigorously. There was a rustling as the fish scales fell to the ground. It was midsummer and the evening breeze still held some of the warmth of the day. Ah-Fat wore a thin white cotton undergarment next to his skin. It was buttoned down the front and Six Fingers had tied a piece of red string to the button over his solar plexus. She had done the same for all his undergarments, to ward off evil. He turned the jacket inside out and folded it into a square, then tucked it under his arm and walked back to the gambling den. The light from the lanterns grew closer and the darkness of the night was left behind. Now that he had his jacket off, his arms bulged visibly, the muscles as prominent as ridges in a freshly ploughed field. He pinched his biceps between thumb and forefinger but there was no superfluous flesh. He may have been forty-two years old, he thought, but he was still in his prime.

He bought two green bean cakes and a cup of cold tea from a peddler and wolfed it all down sitting on the steps of the gambling den.

"Has the performance begun?" he asked the man.

"No, the troupe has only just gone in, and they haven't got their costumes on yet."

Ah-Fat relaxed.

His belly had been empty for so long that the cakes dropped into it like pebbles into an expanse of water—they did not even ripple the surface and he could not tell when they reached the bottom. He took out a few more coins and bought a dish of chicken feet in briny gravy. With the first bite, he realized he had made a mistake. Chicken feet were for people to nibble as they sipped liquor on a full belly. Hungry as he was, he lacked the patience for such tidbits. He bought half a roast duck and two *char siu* dumplings, and after downing these, finally began to feel himself once more.

He pushed open the gambling den door and was immediately engulfed in a wave of noise. Today was payday and the place was full. A sea of dark heads crowded three deep around each of the dozen or so tables where games of mahjong and *pai kao* were played. Players and spectators alike were absorbed in the game. Hawkers with small baskets hung from their necks squeezed themselves through the mass of bodies with hoarse cries of "Tobacco! Candies! Pumpkin seeds! Olives!"

Ah-Fat squirmed his way through the solid mass of bodies, making straight for the stage in the back room. A troupe had been invited to perform—though to call them a "troupe" was overstating it since there were only seven of them. One played the Chinese fiddle, another the flute and the remaining five were actors: three men and two women from San Francisco. They may have been few, and their performances scrappy, but the ticket prices were dirt cheap at fifteen cents. Even a seat so close to the stage you could see the performers' toecaps was only twenty cents. Added to that, no players had been here for a very long time, and the troupe included women too, which explained why the audience had turned up so early.

When Ah-Fat's father was alive, he had taken Ah-Fat and Ah-Sin to opera performances in all the small towns surrounding their village. In those days there were no female actors. When his father had told Ah-Fat that the women onstage making graceful "orchid" gestures with their fingers and coyly hiding their faces behind long white silk "water sleeves" were actually men, he was struck dumb with astonishment. Those men playing women were more feminine than women themselves. Months before he died, his father had taken him to Shun Tak to see the Cantonese opera *Testing the Wife in the Mulberry Garden* at New Year. It was the first time that Ah-Fat had seen male and female actors on the same stage. The roles of Chau Wu and his wife were played by actors who were actually husband and wife. Their amorous glances and uninhibited acting enraged an army officer in the audience. There were shouts of "Shameless! Shameless!" and soldiers leapt onto the stage, tied the actors up and carried them off. They heard afterwards that the pair were condemned for outraging public morals and beheaded the same night. The incident put a stop to mixed performances, and until now Ah-Fat had not seen women on the stage.

But tonight there was a mixed cast. And the gamblers, all single men, had only half their minds on the gambling table. They all waited for the strings to start playing to call them into the back room. The truth was that they were here to see the women rather than the play. You only had to look at the streets of Chinatown to see that they were packed with men—and only men. Every month or so, the steamship would bring a handful of Chinese women but if they were decent, they would marry and be kept at home, so they were never seen in public. If they were the sort who "sold smiles," they would soon find themselves bundled into the back alleys behind the tea-shacks by madams. Theatrical performances offered another option. There were two female members of the opera troupe and the patrons of the gambling den would be able to ogle them to their hearts' content. They waited in feverish excitement.

Ah-Fat went through into the temporary theatre. A decorative gas lamp glared from each corner of the stage, and a sheet of paper was stuck on the wall to the side of the stage, bearing the hastily scribbled words:

> *The Clear Spring Opera Troupe will this evening give a complete showing of* The Fairy Wife Returns Her Son to Earth.
>
> *Gold Mountain Cloud—brilliant in the male role of Tung Wan*
>
> *Gold Mountain Shadow—extraordinarily dainty as the Fairy Wife.*

A tour in Gold Mountain increased an actor's fame back home, so they added the tag "Gold Mountain" to their names as a reminder to their audiences. Ah-Fat was happy to see that Gold Mountain Cloud still had top billing. Ah-Fat had seen Cloud and Shadow on the first evening and felt they were not bad … perhaps not absolutely heart-stopping in their performances, but original in their way. He had decided to come again.

Ah-Fat had seen *The Fairy Wife* several times with his father. It was a short play, about the Seventh Fairy who is forced by her father, the Jade Emperor, to return to the celestial palace, leaving her husband, Tung Wan, behind in the human world. The next year, she fulfils her promise to send her son back to Tung Wan. This opera was often used as a curtain raiser for performances. But this evening's version followed the Anhui Opera tradition: it began with the Seventh Fairy dreaming of the earthly world and recounted how she married Tung Wan, and how the Jade Emperor forced them apart, and how she then returned to the human world to give her son to her husband. It was a full evening's performance.

Ah-Fat had only seen it performed with an all-male cast but tonight there would be male and female actors. In fact, they would cross-dress and play a role of the opposite gender, with the Fairy Wife played by a man, and Tung Wan by a woman. Ah-Fat had seen a man play the part of the

Fairy Wife but never a woman cast as her earthly husband. He was eagerly looking forward to it.

He flung a few coins down on the ticket table, and found himself a seat right in the middle at the front. The old man on the door came after him: "This is fifty cents. It's enough for four to five tickets. I'll get you the change." "Use it to buy cups of tea for the troupe," said Ah-Fat.

The fiddler struck up a tune to call the audience to their seats. The gamblers duly threw down their dominoes and dice and began to stream into the "auditorium."

When the fiddler saw all the seats filled and people gathered in the aisle and around the door, he winked at the flute player, who blew his first note and the performance began.

It was a new production and had obviously been put together in a hurry. The singing, supported as it was by the fiddle and the flute, was smooth. But during the dialogue, the players kept making mistakes. Apart from Tung Wan, the other roles were new and unfamiliar to the players. The attention of the audience wandered and bursts of laughter disrupted the performance.

Ah-Fat had been told that the members of the troupe were of the same family. The man playing the Jade Emperor was the father. The fairy, Tung Wan, and the umbrella maid were played by his children. The musicians and the acrobat were his nephews. They had all originally been in other troupes, playing bit parts on tour in Gold Mountain and South-East Asia. Cloud was the eldest daughter. She had a broad and dignified face and a velvety voice. She had started by playing minor female roles, to no great acclaim. Then it occurred to her to try the male lead role and, quite unexpectedly, she began to make a name for herself. She changed her name to Gold Mountain Cloud, formed her own troupe entirely from family members, and began to tour from town to town all over Gold Mountain.

It was only when the Seventh Fairy was abducted by the Jade Emperor and taken back to his palace—with her husband, Tung Wan, in hot pursuit—that everyone sat up and listened.

Oh, my wife, your departure will kill us both with pain unspeakable
While you, like snowflakes blown by wind,

Fly to your celestial destination unreachable
I pine hopelessly for your return, like pining to recover the lost moon in
ocean unfathomable

At this point Gold Mountain Cloud switched to singing in her natural voice. Ah-Fat had never before heard such tone. Chinese opera was characterized by a falsetto style, but Gold Mountain Cloud's voice was sonorous, as if emanating from a bell fissured with cracks, each one permeated with sadness. Ah-Fat's eyes were riveted. She seemed to him not wholly masculine but not wholly feminine either. Gold Mountain Cloud had smoothed the rough edges of a man's body like a whetstone yet she had also brushed away the powdery softness of the female body as if with a feather duster. When she stood onstage, she was more gently refined than a man, yet more heroic than a woman. She positioned herself somewhere between the male and female, and he found the effect disturbing.

When the performance was over, the stools were cleared away and the floor was swept clean of pumpkin seed shells, cigarette ends and olive pits, raising clouds of dust. The acrobat shinnied up the columns to take the gas lamps down, one by one, and the room gradually darkened. Ah-Fat stood rooted to the spot in front of the stage. Suddenly he heard a voice behind him: "It's late. Shouldn't you be off home?" He looked round, to see a youth standing in the shadows. The youth wore a deep blue soft brocade coat with a gown of navy blue silk underneath and a Chinese round cap. Beneath it were thick eyebrows and rosy cheeks in a large face. It was Gold Mountain Cloud with only half of her stage makeup removed.

Ah-Fat knew that opera singers liked to indulge in this or that new fashion but did not expect to see Gold Mountain Cloud in male costume when she was offstage. She looked strikingly handsome in it. His astonishment was audible when he managed to speak:

"Your natural voice, troupe leader, is truly big-hearted."

Gold Mountain Cloud said nothing, but just stared fixedly at Ah-Fat. Ah-Fat rubbed the scar on his face. "I got it years ago, when I worked on the railroad," he said. "Don't worry, I haven't robbed or murdered anyone." Gold Mountain Cloud chuckled: "I'm an opera singer. There's nothing I haven't seen. What I'm interested in is the fact that you came yesterday too and sat in the same place."

Ah-Fat laughed, and then asked: "Did you study martial arts? In the scene when the Seventh Fairy weaves a length of cloth for Tung Wan, your moves were so skilfully executed." The actress was clearly delighted that Ah-Fat knew what he was talking about. "When I studied opera as a child," she said, "the master made everyone, no matter what role they played, learn martial arts for a year and a half. He taught us that everything was in the footwork, and that opera only carried force if you got the footwork right. He made us do somersaults every day and if you didn't get them right, you went to bed without any dinner."

Ah-Fat gave a sigh. "There's no profession that isn't hard to learn, is there? The dialogue could have done with a bit of polishing though." Gold Mountain Cloud sighed too. "We've put on ten plays in a month, there isn't time to rehearse properly. This one is completely new and some scenes we've improvised. That makes it interesting. We'll be more familiar with it by the time we get to Victoria." "Is that where you're stopping next, Victoria?" "New Westminster first, then Victoria. Then we'll take the train east to Toronto and Montreal."

"Do all the places you go in your travels have theatres, troupe leader?" asked Ah-Fat. There was another laugh. "Don't keep calling me troupe leader. Cloud will do fine. South-East Asia is not bad, there are big stages. But in some places in Gold Mountain there aren't even any stages, let alone theatres. We heard the Monarchist Reform Party is going to build a theatre in San Francisco, which will at least be a base for travelling players." Ah-Fat checked there was no one within hearing. He lowered his voice and asked: "Are you in with the Monarchists, Cloud?" "We sing opera, we don't belong to any party or faction. But having a proper theatre would be better than nothing. What about you?"

Ah-Fat was tempted to say: "No, I'm not. But I sold everything I had to help the Emperor, and look what a miserable state I'm in now." But remembering Ah-Lam's warning he swallowed his words and merely replied: "Lots of Chinese in Vancouver have joined the Monarchist Reform Party. How long are you staying in Vancouver, Cloud?" he went on. "Ten more performances." Ah-Fat hesitated. "Then I'll come every day."

In the flickering light of the last gas lamp they talked on. Suddenly Ah-Fat said: "Wait just a minute, I'll be right back." He hurried away, then returned holding lotus-leaf dumplings in his hand. "You've been singing all evening, you must be hungry. It's late and all the shops are shut now. I just got a few sausage and rice dumplings. Have some. I'm afraid they'll have gone cold." Cloud took them from him. A scrap of warmth came from them, probably from the man's hand, she thought. Almost all the men in the audience were there to stare at the girls. This was the only one who had seemed to appreciate the opera, too.

The acrobat took down the last lamp. All at once, the illumination was reduced to a single small circle, spotlighting Gold Mountain Cloud and giving her a ghastly pallor. The boy got down off the stage and came their way. "Big sister, Mr. Wen's been waiting ages for you at the door." "I see," said Gold Mountain Cloud and gave the dumplings to him. "Share these between everyone, one each." Then she pointed her finger at Ah-Fat. "You make sure you come tomorrow, I won't sing until I see you." The finger which had performed the graceful orchid gesture was now right in Ah-Fat's face. It gave off a slight smell of jasmine powder which wafted up his nostrils, almost making him sneeze.

She left, casting a slender shadow which stretched long and thin in the remaining light, seeming to waver like bamboo leaves. He found himself following. From a distance, he saw a carriage waiting at the entrance to the alley. Through the glass windows, he could see the shadowy figure of a man in a suit. He opened the door and helped Gold Mountain Cloud in. The driver shouted to the horse and they drew away, the horse's hooves clip-clopping away into the darkness of the night. Ah-Fat stood there, suddenly feeling disconsolate.

When he got back to his lodgings, Ah-Lam and the others were not home yet. Everyone stayed out late on payday. If they were not gambling or smoking opium they would be in a girl's arms. Ah-Fat lit a cigarette and smoked for a while but still could not sleep. He turned up the oil lamp, got out paper and brush and prepared some ink. His hand trembled slightly and he had trouble grinding the lumps out of the ink. He smoothed some paper flat and began to write to Six Fingers. The characters seemed as distracted as he was, and lacked their usual dignified firmness.

Dear Ah-Yin,

An opera troupe has come to Vancouver and New Westminster. When I was a kid, I used to go with my dad, but I haven't been for years. There was a woman playing the lead male role. She was not as heroic as the male usually is, nor as delicate and gentle as the female role, yet she was more appealing than both. Is there anything which comes halfway between a man and woman? If there is, then that third gender must surely embody the essence and the energy of both man and woman because they are not constrained by either. There is something wonderful and fantastic about that. You're probably thinking I've gone crazy. Ah-Yin

Ah-Fat went to all ten remaining performances, but did not have a chance to talk to Gold Mountain Cloud again. Every night after the play was finished, she changed into her everyday clothes and was picked up straightaway by the carriage waiting at the stage door. Every evening as she came onstage, her gaze swept over the audience. Ah-Fat felt her eyes boring into him and the scar on his face burned. He could almost hear her heartbeat returning to normal, just before the performance began. He remembered her words on the other night, "I won't sing till I see you." Perhaps they had not been entirely empty words.

The last opera they put on was *Giving a Warm Coat at Night*. It was a very long and rather subtle piece and Ah-Fat found his attention wandering. He felt torn that evening, between longing for the play to be over, and wanting it to go on forever. When it ended, he could speak with Gold Mountain Cloud again. He could be, for another moment, in her presence. But with the last performance completed, she would move on to a new town and disappear from his life forever. He needed to catch hold of this spirit that was half-man and half-woman. But he did not know how, nor what he should do with her once he had her in his grasp. He was full of vague longings.

Finally the performance ended. Gold Mountain Cloud bowed deeply at each curtain call. Her looks and smiles included everyone, and Ah-Fat got his fair share too. Yet somehow that made him feel that he had been left with nothing at all. Gold Mountain Cloud finally disappeared behind the curtain and was gone. Ah-Fat derided himself for imagining that a rising opera star would remember a fish cannery worker like himself who understood so little about Cantonese opera. He meant nothing to her. To believe otherwise was wishful thinking; the feeling was all on his side. As he stood there lost in thought, the acrobat came over to him carrying something wrapped in cloth. "For you, from Gold Mountain Cloud," he said. Inside the cloth was a large disk, black in colour, covered with fine circular grooves, like waves, around a small central hole. Around the hole was pasted a label illustrated with a big horn and a brown dog with the words "Victor Talking Machine Co., 1905." Ah-Fat inspected it on both sides but was none the wiser.

The next day Ah-Fat took the disk to Rick, who told him it was a record. The brown dog listening to a big horn was a well-known company logo. "What's a record?" asked Ah-Fat. "The music and singing of the opera is sealed on the disk," explained Rick. "When you want to listen to it, you just get it out and listen. Like covering a cup of water with a lid, and opening it every time you want to drink. Except that in the end you drink the water up, but you can go on listening to the record forever." "Is the sound still on the record when the singer dies?" "It's still there ten years, or a hundred years afterwards." Ah-Fat held his record in both hands and contemplated it in silence.

Much later, when Ah-Fat went back to his *diulau* home in Spur-On Village, he took the record with him. Then, Gold Mountain Cloud's singing would fill Tak Yin House to the rafters, striking every stone and every board with its piercing, rending tones.

The singer left Vancouver, and Ah-Fat heard no more of her, until one day about two years after Kam Shan arrived in Gold Mountain. They had a visitor from back home, a restaurant owner in San Francisco. He mentioned that a new theatre, the Grand Stage Theatre, had just been built in the city. An opera singer called Gold Mountain Cloud leading a troupe of twenty members had made the theatre her home base. She had quite a reputation as a singer. Ah-Fat smiled to himself when he heard this. That piercing, rending voice would echo in his ears for years to come, but the longing which the singer had created in his heart had long since died away.

More time passed, and Ah-Fat saw a small item in the Overseas Chinese newspaper, *The Daily News*. The famous Cantonese opera singer Gold Mountain Cloud was engaged to be married to a Mr. William Huang and a very grand wedding would soon be held in Honolulu. Ah-Fat had never heard of this Huang fellow, though he later found out he was the younger son of a Honolulu property magnate.

That was not the last that Ah-Fat would see of Gold Mountain Cloud, although he did not know it. Much later, the dormant buds of their friendship were to put forth unexpected new shoots.

Year thirty-three of the reign of Guangxu (1907) Vancouver, British Columbia

My dear Ah-Yin,

Thank you for the letter and school photographs of Kam Shan and Kam Ho which you sent at New Year. When I last saw them, Shan was just a naughty kid and Ho was still in swaddling clothes. Time flies by—who would have thought I would be gone seven years? My sons are so grown up now. Ah-Yin, do you still remember your Gold Mountain man after all these years? You, of course, are often in my dreams. How could I forget my wife's face? I have made plans to come home several times during these years, but every time something unexpected has happened. I have not managed to raise enough for the boat passage. My dreams of us living together as husband and wife are constantly shattered. Business has been slack at the fish cannery since last autumn, and on top of that, the boss bought an American machine that can de-scale, wash and split the fish automatically, around thirty times faster than a man. The yeung fan make a mockery of us Chinese and call it the "Iron Chink." Since the machine arrived, many of the cannery men, including me and Ah-Lam, have lost their jobs. Life has been hard, but not long ago I borrowed a bit of money from a countryman, rented a couple of rooms facing the street and opened a laundry. I hired a boy from San Wui to help out. He is a good tailor and can make Chinese- and Western-style clothes, so we can do tailoring and mending as well as laundry. I have kept the old name, Whispering Bamboos Laundry. This is my third and I hope this time round it will do better and last longer than the other two. I will probably be able to buy a passage home at the end of this year. Mum will be sixty years old next year, and it is my fervent wish to be there to host the longevity party for her. I hope that you are looking after yourself, and are doing your utmost to attend to Mum and take good care of Kam Shan and Kam Ho, so that I do not need to worry about you.

Your husband, Tak Fat, sixteenth of the fourth month, 1907, Vancouver

It was dark by the time Ah-Fat left his shop. As he secured the shutters, he glanced casually at the calendar hanging on the wall. It was September the seventh by the Western calendar, or the first day of the eighth month according to the Chinese lunar calendar. He took a bit of tailoring chalk and drew a circle round the date—a date which, unbeknownst to him, would find itself constantly popping up in the history books in the years to come. Ah-Fat simply marked the calendar because this day had seen him finally clear the loan he had taken out on the shop. Business was brisker now that he had hired the tailor. It had not been an easy ride but Whispering Bamboos Laundry, third time round, was now finally on a sound footing. He could almost feel the dimes in his pocket gradually coming together in the form of a boat ticket to China.

He was in a good mood and in no hurry to go home. Once he had fastened the shutters and locked the door, he said to Ah-Lam and the tailor boy: "Let's go to the Loong Kee for some snacks. It's on me." What he really had his mind on was drink. He had been thinking about that drink since early morning, before even a grain of rice or a drop of water had passed his lips. The signed and witnessed document stating that the debt had been paid off lay neatly folded in his pocket, banging against him with every step he took and urging him to get a move on and get that drink down.

It was pitch dark when they started off down the street, and lanterns lit up the shops that opened late. Their hazy glow pierced the darkness with eyes of varying sizes, the biggest of them concealing the gambling and opium dens. "Fuck," said Ah-Lam, "I'm so damn fed up with the same old faces in the tea-shacks." "Who has time to look at a girl's face?" said the tailor. "There's always a long queue waiting to get in." "If they got here last year, they're fat old hags by now," said Ah-Lam. "They've had so many men queuing up to handle them, of course they're fat," said the tailor. Ah-Fat aimed a kick at him. "And how come you've learned so fast? You're no more than a snot-nosed kid." Ah-Lam screwed up his eyes and looked at Ah-Fat. "And what are we supposed to think of, kicking our heels here without our women, year after year?" "Come on, let's have a drink first. When we've had a skinful, then we'll see."

That "We'll see" concealed within it ideas which startled even Ah-Fat himself. He did not just want to drink tonight, he wanted to do something more. The document in his pocket had set him free, but he did not know what to do with his new-found freedom. His head raced ahead of his body and, like a snake without a lair, pushed its way into all the darkest nooks and crannies of Chinatown, sliding through the cracks between windows, doors and walls and prying into whatever was hidden there. That evening, head and body ran a mad race.

The three of them went into the Loong Kee and the waiter came over. "What would you like to eat?" he asked. Ah-Fat jerked his thumb at the other two. "Ask them," he said. He lit a cigarette and began a leisurely smoke. When they had ordered food, he said: "Bring two bottles of wine, one red, one white." The wine came and the waiter filled three small cups to the brim. Ah-Fat promptly emptied his, and then had another and another. The wine went straight to his head and the colour gradually drained from his face. Only his scar stood out crimson against the bloodless skin, looking like a worm wriggling up his cheek.

The young boy was alarmed at the sight. He picked up a piece of the crispy-roasted pig chitterlings with his chopsticks and put it in Ah-Fat's bowl. "Eat something, before you drink any more, mister." Ah-Fat laughed. "You're good with your hands, you little sod," he said thickly, his breath coming in heavy snorts. "When I open another branch next year, you can be in charge of it." "Let him be," Ah-Lam told the boy. "He's happy today. After all, he's finally said goodbye to all those debts."

They drank and drank, went out the back to piss streams of yellow urine, and came back to drink some more. Ah-Lam and the boy were scarlet in the face by this time. "You two have been in Gold Mountain all these years," the boy said. "Not like us who've just got here and don't have anyone to help us out. Why's it taken till today to pay off the debts?" "Ask him," Ah-Lam said recklessly, jerking a thumb at Ah-Fat. "Your boss here donated everything he had, lock, stock and barrel, to the Monarchist Reform Party. That left both of us with fuck-all. We've been through hell. And after he gave them that huge bank draft, do you think we've heard shit from them?"

Ah-Fat flushed red and hurled his cup to the ground. He jabbed his finger in Ah-Lam's face and shouted: "No wonder the Qing Empire is practically on its last legs with sonofabitch citizens like you who don't give a shit about our country being humiliated." Ah-Lam lost his temper and seized Ah-Fat by the front of his jacket: "You puffed-up little jerk! So I'm a sonofabitch? And you're a high mandarin, are you? You may think you're a Monarchist but the Emperor doesn't even know who you are!"

The boy tried to pull Ah-Lam off. "Don't go saying things like that, mister! If word gets back, they'll murder your whole family." Ah-Lam was too drunk to care and flung off the boy's hand. "The world's a big place and the Emperor's a long way off. By the time they get to hear of it, there'll have been a change of dynasty." The boy went pale in terror at this. Grabbing Ah-Fat's sleeve he pulled him towards the door, whispering in a trembling voice: "Mister Ah-Fat, let's go home. It's late." But Ah-Fat was in no mood for caution. "Home? What d'you want to go home for?" They scuffled and the sleeve of Ah-Fat's jacket ripped at the shoulder. Ah-Fat looked at the tear and slapped the boy's face, furious: "How dare you, little snot-nosed kid!" The boy put his hand to his cheek and said nothing. Ah-Lam threw down his cup and joined the fray: "Ah-Fat, you're a big man, why are you taking it out on the kid?"

They were interrupted by the sound of shouting in the street and a loud crack like a gunshot. Before they had time to recover from the shock, there was another, even louder, crack. The restaurant owner ran in bleeding heavily from the head and covered in shards of glass. "Ah-Fat, you know a bit of English, go and see what's happening outside, will you? The street's full of *yeung fan.*" Ah-Fat, who had sobered up at the noise, ran outside. There were two holes as big as a wash basin in the glass windows of the

Loong Kee Café and the wind was whistling through. A dark mass of people streamed along the road, fists in the air, carrying banners, flags and sticks. There were too many of them to hear what it was they were shouting, but Ah-Fat finally made out words like "Chinaman … out.…" The *yeung fan* were here to make trouble.

They had come before, but never so many. The restaurant owner suddenly remembered his two children playing in the street and rushed out, to find them knocked to the ground by the marchers. He put one under each arm and ran back inside. Ah-Fat shouted to the waiter to bolt the door and put out the lights, then herded everyone towards the kitchen. Behind it was a small storeroom piled with sacks of rice. Ah-Fat made them take shelter there.

The young son of the restaurant owner had a lump the size of an egg on his forehead where he had been hit by a stone. He wailed loudly for his mum to come and rub it. Ah-Fat put his hand over the boy's mouth. "If you keep crying, the foreign devils will get in here and kill you all," he said in a low voice. The terrified child choked back his sobs and gave a little whimper.

Ah-Fat squatted behind the rice sacks, listening to what sounded like muffled peals of thunder—the sound of thousands of marching feet. The ground trembled, making the hairs stand up on the back of his neck. Someone thumped a few times on the restaurant door, but it held firm. The restaurant owner's wife squatted next to Ah-Fat, her teeth chattering audibly. The room filled with the rank smell of urine. Glass shattered pane by pane from one end of the street to the other, starting as gigantic, muffled explosions which turned into sharp tinkling and then died away as a sibilant echo. In the intervals they heard a couple of sharp barks. But before other dogs could take up the refrain, the barks were drowned out by the shouting. The roar of thousands of voices was like silk threads woven into a great fat plait, but suddenly, Ah-Fat was able to separate the strands.

"Give me back a White Canada!"

The words started feebly, seeming tentative, lacking in conviction, but as they travelled through the throats of the marchers, they gathered strength and momentum. In no time, the words had become a roar so terrifying that both shouters and listeners were stunned into temporary silence.

Ah-Fat's legs, folded under him, went numb. He shifted his position and pins and needles shot up from the soles of his feet to his middle.

The uniforms. Oh God, the uniforms.

He suddenly remembered that Rick had given him three hundred uniforms to wash and iron. They were of the best quality, red fabric meticulously edged with gold braid, and were worn by top-level employees who staffed the staterooms and dining rooms. All three hundred had been laundered and left folded and stacked against the wall. Six tall piles, fifty to each pile. They were right by the window, and even a glimmer of light would reveal the thick gold braiding. If the window was broken, you would only have to reach in to take them. Rick had told him that only the Vancouver Hotel could afford such luxury uniforms and that they cost fifty dollars each. How much were three hundred worth?

Ah-Fat's head felt as if it was going to burst.

Whispering Bamboos. Maybe it was the name. Maybe he should never have picked a name like that. It had nothing to do with laundries. Time and again that name had raised his hopes to the skies, and time and again, those hopes had been dashed. Three times, actually. He decided then and there that he would never, ever, fall into that trap again.

Suddenly he heard the clatter of horses' hooves. Then, the shrill sound of a whistle. "In the name of King Edward the Seventh," cried a loud voice, "I order you to disperse immediately!" Cautiously, Ah-Fat crawled out from behind the rice sacks and went to the door. Outside, a group of Mounties on huge horses charged. The crowd scattered in all directions under the horses' hooves, like a receding mud flow. Then it re-formed and ran back to the centre. This was repeated again and again. Gradually, however, the flow lost momentum, broke up into ever-smaller patches of mud and then vanished.

After the sound of shouting and hooves receded into the distance, there was absolute silence in the street. Ah-Fat unbolted the restaurant door and went out into a world he no longer recognized. Every lantern outside every shop had been torn down and lay broken on the ground, flattened by marching feet. The street had had all its eyes plucked out. Every shopfront had lost both windowpanes and frames, and the dark openings gaped wide. Not a single person, or dog, was to be seen on the dark street. They were there somewhere, he knew, hiding in those pockets of darkness. There was no moon, only a handful of pearly stars to brighten the night sky. The ground was covered in heaps of glass shards, which twinkled like a thick layer of autumnal frost. Ah-Fat walked down the street and tripped over something soft. A cat. It mewed pitifully; Ah-Fat felt the animal and his hands came away sticky with blood.

He groped his way through the streets until he got to his shop. It had no door. The plank of wood had been ripped off and lay on its side across the doorway. A shop without a door was like a person without a face, so changed it was unrecognizable. He trod on the door plank and walked in. It was very dark inside and his eyes took some time to adjust. When he could make out shapes, the room looked oddly crowded. He realized that every piece of furniture had been smashed into several pieces.

The clothes. The three hundred uniforms from the Vancouver Hotel. He felt along the windowsill. Backwards, forwards, left, right. There was nothing. Those six piles, so tall they had almost reached the ceiling, had vanished from his shop as if they had never existed.

Ah-Fat rushed out into the street. "You motherfucking scum!" he howled, his face upturned to the skies in a frenzy. "You scum of the earth!" He wanted to go on but the words would not come. He felt as if the tendons at his temples and neck had burst and molten liquid was pouring from them down his body. His cries, echoing in the air above him, somehow reminded him of the beasts slaughtered by his father's hand.

Suddenly a large hand clamped over his mouth.

"Don't shout. They've gone to Japan Town, but they may be back any moment."

Ah-Fat froze. The man was speaking English. He realized it was Rick.

"I've been waiting ages for you," said Rick.

At Ah-Fat's cries, the people hiding in the dark recesses of their shops began to emerge in ones and twos. They stood gazing blankly at the ruins of the street. They looked at one another, seeing desolate expressions in each other's eyes. They no longer knew their street, or each other. They did not even know themselves.

The owner of the Loong Kee was the first to pull himself together. Without a sound, he walked up behind Rick and threw a savage punch at the back of his head. Rick was taken by surprise. His body sagged, then straightened again.

"Kill the *yeung fan*, kill him!"

The onlookers shook themselves awake and surrounded Rick, hemming him in.

"Don't ... don't hit him, he's ... he's not...." Ah-Fat tried to explain but found himself suddenly incapable of speech. All he could do was put his arms tightly round Rick. The blows rained down on his body although it was his mouth which took the full force of them. Ah-Fat tasted blood. By the time the crowd realized that they were beating up one of their own, Ah-Fat had lost one of his front teeth.

Ah-Fat helped Rick to his shop and stood in front of him like the god of gateways, blocking the way. The men glared at the pair of them, their eyes shining green and wolf-like in the dark.

"You idiots, he's with us," Ah-Fat said, spitting out bloody saliva.

Then they heard two dull thuds in the distance.

"It's guns. The *yeung fan* are firing," someone said. A tremor ran through the crowd, and shadowy figures surged back towards the dark door openings.

"They're Japanese guns," Rick said to Ah-Fat. "The Japanese sector has its own armed militia but Chinatown has no protection at all. The mob won't hang around there. They'll be back here any minute.

"How many women and children are there here?" he asked. Ah-Fat made a quick calculation. "There can't be more than twenty or so, we're almost all single men around here," he said.

"Get them together. The secretary of the Japanese Chamber of Commerce is my friend. They can take shelter there, I'll take them. You men go back indoors and hide. Don't light the lanterns and don't go out before daybreak. More Mounties should be here soon. They may seal the district off to keep all non-Chinese out. You'll be safe then."

Rick took something wrapped in cloth out of his pocket and gave it to Ah-Fat. "Be careful. This is the real thing." Ah-Fat fingered it lightly—a pistol.

At that moment, thunder rumbled in the distance and the ground began to tremble again.

Ah-Fat knew what that meant. The *yeung fan* rabble had come back.

Dear Ah-Yin,

At the end of last year, I received a little over nine hundred dollars from the Canadian government. Mr. Henderson engaged a lawyer who got me compensation for the destruction of my laundry business the year before last, by a yeung fan *mob who came to Chinatown. I was hoping to use this money to get a boat passage home, but then I heard that some of our fellow countrymen have been buying land in New Westminster, about twenty kilometres from Vancouver. They cleared it and planted fruit trees and vegetables and now they do good business selling their produce all over the place. Ah-Lam and I followed their example and moved to New Westminster this New Year. I have used the compensation to buy land to farm. Who knows whether Heaven will favour me with a good harvest. I have opened three laundry businesses here and none of them made good, for all sorts of reasons which could not have been foreseen. So I decided not to do that again. I still have around five hundred dollars left over, which is enough to bring one person to Canada. If Mum insists that she does not want you to come, could Kam Shan join me? Clearing and farming this land is back-breaking work. Ah-Lam is in his fifties, and I'm catching up to him. We really need someone younger to help. I am sure that Mum will be unhappy about Kam Shan leaving, but I hope you will make her see reason. When you receive this letter, will you ask my uncle and Ha Kau to go to Canton and find out the time of the boats, so he can come as soon as possible?*

Your husband, Tak Fat, twenty-ninth day of the third month, 1909, New Westminster

Springtime, year two of the reign of Xuan Tong (1910)
Spur-On Village, Hoi Ping County, Guangdong Province, China

Mak Dau crossed No-Name River with Kam Ho on his back. The sun was up and warm enough to bead his forehead with sweat. The women following behind giggled at the dark sweat marks which appeared on the back of his jacket. "Your Mak Dau's like a leaky sieve, Six Fingers," one said. "Hot, cold, whatever the weather, he always pours with sweat." Six Fingers took a small towel from the basket on her arm, caught up with Mak Dau and gave it to him. Mak Dau hoisted the boy higher up his back, but refused the towel. He gave a little smile and Six Fingers understood he did not want to dirty it. When Mak Dau smiled, Six Fingers suddenly felt the day brighten. He had the whitest teeth in the whole of Spur-On Village. The other men's teeth were a dirty yellow from the tobacco they smoked. Only Mak Dau's teeth were like a row of pearls, a dazzling, almost bluish-white.

Mak Dau was a younger cousin of Ha Kau on his mother's side. Since he and Ah-Choi had married, Ha Kau had been promoted to steward in charge of the entire property. The Fongs owned scores of *mu* and a large residence with three courtyards, housing two families and a dozen or so labourers and servants. It was too much for Ha Kau to manage alone and he brought Mak Dau to help out. Mak Dau became the odd-job man and anyone in the house could call upon him at any time.

"Mak Dau, Ah-Wong's twisted his ankle. Go and finish planting out the rice seedlings in the riverbank field."

"Mak Dau, the pigs have made a hole in the door of the piggery, go and fix it, quick."

"Mak Dau, I'm out of fuel, go up the hillside and get an armful, and hurry, I've got cooking to do."

"Mak Dau, the water barrel's got a crack in it. Get Wet-Eyes Loong to come and mend it."

Mak Dau's name came naturally to everyone's lips. It was handy to have him around, and calling upon him became a household habit. Mak Dau could plug any gap, round or square, small or large. If the household was a cart, Mak Dau was neither the axle nor the rim, still less was he the spokes. But he was the layer of oil on the wheels. He was invisible, yet he was everywhere. Without Mak Dau, the wheels would still turn, but not smoothly.

The two brothers, Kam Shan and Kam Ho, were the first to discover just how useful Mak Dau was.

Mak Dau knew the names of all the birds in the woods. Mak Dau need only hear a cricket chirp once, and he knew exactly which leaf it was hiding under. Mak Dau could jump into No-Name River and stay under water (without a single bubble breaking the surface) until Kam Ho grew so frightened he shouted for help. Mak Dau picked banana leaves, soaked them in salt water till they softened, and stripped the thick green layer off the leaves, leaving behind a network of fine veins. Then, he would roll them up into a tight coil and put them to his mouth like a cigar. When he blew through them, out came extraordinary sounds, like the wind in the trees and raindrops on water. Mak Dau only had to glance at a cockerel by the roadside to know whether it could beat another cockerel in a fight.

But there was one thing that Mak Dau could not do, and that was read.

Poor Mak Dau. His name meant "writing ink" but he could not read his own name. Once he plucked up the courage to ask Kam Shan how his name was written. Kam Shan thought for a while, then went to his mother's room and fetched some paper. He wrote out "Shit Heap Tse," Tse being Mak Dau's family name, and got Mak Dau to paste it on his back with rice glue and walk around the village. When Six Fingers saw him, she took one of the bamboo poles from the drying frame and thrashed Kam Shan till he howled. She decided that from that day on, Mak Dau should study alongside the boys.

When Mrs. Mak found out, she was tight-lipped. "What's the point in teaching a servant to read and write? It's a waste of time and energy." But Six Fingers said: "Mum, this servant spends all day with your grandsons. If he doesn't study a bit and learn a few characters, I'm afraid he might have a bad influence on them." Mrs. Mak said nothing more. If Six Fingers wanted her mother-in-law's consent to do something, she had only to drop in the names of the two boys, and all obstacles would be smoothed out of the way. Though Ah-Fat had written several letters about Kam Shan going to Gold Mountain, Mrs. Mak could not be persuaded to let him go. The boat trip was postponed again and again, and so Kam Shan remained at home with Six Fingers and Mrs. Mak.

The boys' school was in Yuen Kai, a few *li* from Spur-On Village. Gold Mountain emigrants from the surrounding villages raised money for it, so most of the pupils (all boys) were from Gold Mountain families. The school was run by Protestant missionaries. The teachers were recruited by the Church; some were locals, others had come from North China. The lay teachers taught traditional Chinese classics, while the missionaries taught mathematics and Bible studies. They also taught singing and, at the New Year and other festivals, they staged plays and invited all the mums, grannies and granddads to the school to see the performance. Kam Shan had been given a part in the Easter play and Six Fingers organized a joint outing for the Gold Mountain wives of Spur-On Village. Kam Ho had run a fever during the night and overslept. His brother left for the school play without him, so he had to go with his mother.

They got everything ready the night before, including a bamboo basket filled half with eggs and half with sesame cakes and layer cakes. The eggs were a present for the teachers, and the cakes were to eat on the way. Six Fingers went into the courtyard, the basket on her arm, to find her mother-in-law holding a broken egg between finger and thumb, berating Ah-Choi. "This would never have happened if you'd got out of bed earlier. You pay no attention to me these days. No one in this house does what I say." "What happened?" Six Fingers asked Ah-Choi. "One of the hens must have laid an egg with a soft shell, and it got trampled and broken in the coop."

"Next time, check the nest first thing each morning so this doesn't happen again," said Six Fingers with a wink in Ah-Choi's direction. "Now go and light the hand-warmer for Mrs. Mak, the weather's still cold." "Really? The sun's hot enough to make you sweat!" Another wink from Six Fingers. "If I tell you to go, then go. No wonder the Missus says you don't pay her any attention. You're so lazy, you'll have maggots growing under your feet." Ah-Choi finally took the hint and went to the kitchen.

After she had gone, Six Fingers called Kam Ho: "Come and say good morning to Granny." Mrs. Mak took the little boy's hand and the vertical frown lines at the corners of her mouth and between her brows resolved themselves into horizontal ones. "Kam Ho, you've still got a temperature. You shouldn't go to school. Stay here and keep Granny company." "But I want to go and see Kam Shan in the school play!" "I'd forgotten! What a bad memory Granny's got!" she said, slapping her forehead. "What part's your big brother going to play?" "A donkey. He's going to be a donkey. Jesus is going to enter the city riding on his back." "That teacher needs a good beating," exclaimed Mrs. Mak. "Fancy making your big brother a beast of burden!" "Kam Shan laughed all the way through the rehearsals, Granny, so the teacher made him be the donkey as a punishment." Mrs. Mak gave a gap-toothed laugh at this. "And so he should! He's a naughty boy, your brother, not like my little Kam Ho, who's so honest, and good to his old granny."

Six Fingers took the boy by the hand. "We have to be off, Mum, otherwise we'll be late for the play. Ah-Chu and Ah-Lin are waiting at the entrance to the village." Mrs. Mak's eyebrows drew together again. "Are you going too? To where those hairy foreigners are? I wonder you young women aren't scared of them!" Six Fingers knew her mother-in-law was referring to the Protestant missionaries. She smiled: "They all dress like us and wear their hair in a pigtail, Mum. You'd never know they were *yeung fan* to look at them. They speak our language too, and they're friendlier than the Chinese teachers from the North." "Huh! If the *yeung fan* look like us, then a wolf looks like a sheep," Mrs. Mak retorted. And she turned towards the kitchen and shouted for Mak Dau.

Mak Dau was sharpening knives for Ah-Choi. Machetes, meat cleavers, vegetable knives, potato peelers, knives for scraping the bristle from the pigs' hides, all were laid out on the floor. Mak Dau was finishing with the potato peeler. He had been at it for a while and the blade was covered with a layer of swarf. Mak Dau wiped the knife clean with an oily cloth and held it up to his eyes. He blew gently on the blade and it made a humming noise. Hearing Mrs. Mak's call, he stuck the knife in his belt and ran to the courtyard.

"Go with Kam Ho and the young Missus to the school. It'll be mayhem there so you take good care of them and when the play's finished, come straight home."

"Yes, Missus." Mak Dau nodded. He was the sort of young man who did not waste words. The corners of his eyes and the spot between his brows expressed what he was thinking. It took a good hour to get from the house to the school on foot, without stopping on the way. If you took a break to have a drink or eat snacks, then it was two hours. He took the boys to school every day, but he had never made the trip with the young Missus before.

Mak Dau could hold his own with any of the dozen or so residents of the household, except the young Missus. With her, he could hardly get a word out. She was perfectly friendly to him, not severe like the old Missus. But Mak Dau was more afraid of the young Missus's friendliness than the old lady's severity. Severity was straightforward, and straightforward silence was an adequate response. The friendliness of the young Missus was much more nuanced, so his answering silences had to be nuanced too. All the same, Mak Dau was happy to be accompanying her today.

He looked up now and saw that Six Fingers had exchanged her cotton-padded jacket for a new lined one. It reached to the knees and the mauve fabric was embroidered all over with a design of dark green asparagus ferns. The jacket buttoned slantwise with traditional knot buttons and a light green handkerchief hung from the opening. Now that she was no longer wearing the thick winter jacket, you could see her full figure. The ferns trembled lightly as her jacket rose and fell. She wore a jade hairpin in the bun at the nape of her neck, and an agate pendant hung from one end of it. The pendant tinkled next to her ear every time the young Missus moved. Every tinkle made Mak Dau's heart skip a beat, and his breathing became a little ragged.

"Shall I carry it for you, Missus?" he asked, indicating Six Fingers' basket. "There's no need for that. You look after Kam Ho. He's not over his cold yet."

Six Fingers, Kam Ho and Mak Dau joined the others on the riverbank and the party set out. The man and the boy walked in front and the half-dozen women followed, leaving behind footprints of all shapes and sizes in the soft surface of the track.

The talk among the women was of their menfolk. "When's your Ah-Kyun arriving?" Six Fingers asked Ah-Lin. "Soon. We heard he's got to

Hong Kong. We're waiting for a letter from the hospital and then someone'll go and get him." They were talking about Ah-Kyun's remains. He had died of consumption in Gold Mountain. That was more than seven years ago so Ah-Lin had been a widow for all that time. The first year she wore a white felt flower of mourning stuck into her bun, but had changed this for a black one in the second year. The black flower of widowhood had remained there ever since and she never went without it.

The truth, however, was that Ah-Lin had been a widow long before she put the white flower in her hair. Ah-Kyun had taken a concubine in Gold Mountain and had only been home once in more than a decade. When he left again, he took his eldest son with him. Ah-Kyun had been ill for quite a few years, and for all those years the concubine had supported his two families through her work in the tea-shack. After he died, she had gone to live with another man, again as his concubine, and after that it was Ah-Kyun's son who sent dollar letters home. Ah-Lin said that her husband knew he was going to die and that was why he had taken his son to Gold Mountain, to take over responsibility for supporting the family back home. She also said that Ah-Kyun was a kind-hearted man and that was why he would not abandon his family in China. And that he had made it clear to his son that he wanted to be buried at home. And that being a lawfully wedded wife was quite different from being someone's fancy woman. As Ah-Lin said all these things, the colour rose in her face, so that she looked like a peachy-cheeked bride in a wedding sedan.

"Huh!" said Ah-Chu. "It depends on the man whether he comes back or not. Auntie Cheung Tai exchanged marriage contracts with Uncle Cheung Tai, and even when she died, he never came home for her funeral." Auntie Cheung Tai had died the year before and it was Six Fingers, as her adopted daughter, who had buried her. Her husband had not shown up. There was a reason for Ah-Chu's remark: her husband had come home last year and got himself a second wife from Tung Koon. Within four months, he was gone, in a hurry to save enough for the head tax and a boat passage. But he still had not told them which wife he was going to take to Gold Mountain.

"Your Ah-Fat hasn't been back for years. Has he got a woman over there?" asked someone.

When Ah-Fat last saw Kam Ho, he was only a month old. Now he was going to school and Ah-Fat was still not back. He had been short of money in recent years and though he sent dollar letters every couple of months, they were for much smaller amounts. What had gone wrong? asked Six Fingers in one of her letters. Ah-Fat's reply had been brief. I'll tell you more when I come home, he had said. She knew then that there had been some trouble. She imagined all sorts of things, and these imaginings weighed heavily on her. But still she smiled at the women's questions: "It's fine if he's found a woman. At least I don't have to worry about him."

Halfway to the school, the women grew tired. They looked for a shady spot to sit down, and took out the cakes. Kam Ho had been asleep on Mak Dau's back and had dribbled on his shoulders. Mak Dau set him down and gave him to Six Fingers. He found a spot to sit some distance away, took off his jacket and sat down on a stone to let the sweat dry in the sun. Next to him a big yellow butterfly with black markings rested on the leaf of a shrub. The black and the yellow reminded him of the border of a paper window covering, standing out so clearly they could have been cut out with a knife. In the bright sunshine, the butterfly's wings fanned gently.

Pity I didn't bring a cricket cage, Mak Dau thought. It's so pretty; I could have caught it and given it to the young Missus to hang from her bed curtain.

The wind got up but the warmth of the sun mellowed it, and smoothed its sharp edges. The wind blew the smell of Mak Dau's sweat over to where the women were sitting. He was wearing a rough cotton vest under his jacket. It had shrunk through much washing and now his muscles threatened to burst out of it. "How many head of cattle are you buying this year?" Ah-Chu asked Six Fingers. "None," she replied. "We bought them all last year and the year before." Ah-Chu pursed her lips and nodded towards Mak Dau. "But haven't you just bought a bull? Look at those muscles. He'd plough a fine furrow!" There was much ribald laughter at this. At a safe distance from their in-laws, the women's talk got quite smutty.

Kam Ho pulled at his mother's sleeve. "I need a poo, Mum." Six Fingers was strict with her children, and they were not allowed to piss and crap wherever they wanted outdoors. Now she looked around her at the land, which was open and flat, and she could not see anywhere for him to go. But there were a couple of trees not too far off which, at a pinch, afforded some sort of cover. Next to them were the ruins of a wall a couple of feet high. Six Fingers took Kam Ho by the hand and they walked over to the wall.

Kam Ho went behind the wall, pulled his jacket up and his trousers down and squatted. Suddenly, there was a gust of wind in his ears and darkness covered him. First, he thought he must have dropped into a deep pit, but then he felt his body moving, even though his feet were not touching the ground. He seemed to have grown wings and to be soaring like a bird. "Quick, someone's coming," he heard a gruff voice say in an accent which was not local. He realized he had fallen into the hands of bandits.

Six Fingers heard a movement and turned around. Her cry of alarm was cut short and her mouth flooded with a salty taste. She tried to scream but the sound died in her throat as if muffled in cotton wool. Someone had gagged her with a smelly sock. Much later, when she thought back to that day, she realized that what she had shouted was "Mak Dau!"

Ah-Chu was the first to realize that Six Fingers and Kam Ho had disappeared. She looked around to see where they had got to, and saw three burly black-clad figures running away with two bundles on their backs. They looked like three giant bats flitting away along the field bank, but from the bottom of one bundle an embroidered shoe could be seen, twisting and kicking.

"They've been kid ... kidnapped!" Ah-Chu's lips trembled so much she could scarcely get the words out.

Mak Dau, who had been snoozing on the rock in his vest and trousers, was on his feet in an instant and streaking after them. When she recounted the story afterwards, Ah-Chu would swear that Mak Dau's legs took leave of his body that day and simply took off after the bandits on their own. Mak Dau had almost caught up with them when he suddenly remembered the freshly sharpened knife that he had hastily stuck into his waistband that morning. He touched it to the jacket of the black-clad figure next to him and the man sagged like a half-full sack of potatoes. As he fell, he grasped Mak Dau tightly round the ankle. Dragging this heavy sack of potatoes, Mak Dau ran on but more slowly than before and could only stare after the two figures as they disappeared into the distance with Six Fingers and Kam Ho.

Mak Dau dragged the injured bandit back to the house. He tortured the bandit's name out of him: Kam Mo Keung. He was a stooge for the outlaw Chu Sei. Chu Sei and his band had gone into hiding in the area, and were making forays out to kidnap and rob, especially from the families of Gold Mountain men. His ransoms were high and he did not negotiate. He was a cruel man.

When Mrs. Mak heard this her eyes darkened and she fainted. Ah-Choi managed to bring her round with a glass of pepper water, but she could not stand. "We should tell the local officials," said Ha Kau. "At least we've got Kam Mo Keung in our hands." "Kam Mo Keung's just small fry," said Mak Dau. "Chu Sei doesn't give a shit about him. He could die a hundred times but he still wouldn't be worth what Chu Sei can get for the Missus and the young master. We've got to be quick and get the ransom together."

"How much?" asked Mrs. Mak. "Anything less than five hundred dollars and you won't see your young master again," said Kam Mo Keung. "Chu Sei's never accepted anything less than that. He doesn't normally bother to kidnap women. Women are worth nothing, because most families won't bother to buy them back. Six Fingers only got bundled away with her son because she cried for help."

Mrs. Mak ground her teeth and fainted again. They carried her into her room and Ha Kau went to speak with Ah-Fat's uncle and aunt. But the pair hummed and hawed so indecisively that Ha Kau had no option but to turn to Mak Dau. Between them they arranged to sell off the family fields.

Forced to sell in haste, they had to accept the derisory amounts they were offered. It was not enough. They made Ah-Fat's uncle and aunt sell some jewellery, and finally bundled up all the money and prepared to ransom Six Fingers and Kam Ho.

Mak Dau went with Kam Mo Keung. "You'll have to leave any weapons behind when you see Chu Sei," said Kam. "Before they let you into the stockade, they'll search you from the hairs on your head to the soles of your feet. If they find anything, they'll have your head off on the spot." Mak Dau squatted down without a word and smoked half a pipe. After a few moments, he pulled Ha Kau to one side. "Go and buy some firecrackers from the village store, the more the merrier," he said. "Are you mad? The sky's falling in and you want to mess around with firecrackers?" "You listen to me, Ha Kau. Wrap them up good and tight and put them in the pigpen. And whatever you do, don't let anyone see you."

Ha Kau did as he was told and threw the bundle into the pigpen. Mak Dau went into the pen. "Watch the door and don't let anyone in," he told Ha Kau. A little while later, he came out with his pipe in his hand. Ha Kau went in behind him to have a look. The ground was littered with scraps of red paper, but he had not heard any firecrackers go off. "What kind of a prank is this?" he said. Mak Dau held up the pipe. "They're all in here, all your firecrackers," he said. "I can't be sure of blowing up the whole stockade and everyone in it, but I can guarantee I'll get one or two." Ha Kau went pale. "You … you … you trying to get yourself killed?" he stuttered. "Your mum gave you to me to look after and I've got to give you back to her in one piece." Mak Dau laughed. "Don't worry, Uncle, I'm going to bring the Missus and the young master home. If I die, how'll they get back?"

Mak Dau set off at dusk. No one dared go to sleep. They lit a votary lamp and waited. In the dead of night one day later, a bedraggled Mak Dau came into the courtyard carrying a dark bundle on his back. They peered at it; it was the Missus. Her hair had come loose and dark masses of it cascaded down her back, enshrouding her body. Mak Dau put her down and she sagged to the ground. Kam Shan threw himself on her, grabbed the front of her jacket and shook her. The distraught family burst into sobs.

After a while, a dusty ball of a figure tumbled in—it was Kam Ho. Mrs. Mak enfolded him so tightly in her arms that her long pale fingernails gouged deep dents in his flesh. Ah-Choi brought out a bowl of rice gruel; only when Six Fingers and Kam Ho had both drunk a little did she allow herself a little sigh of relief. Six Fingers got to her feet and stumbled a few paces to Mrs. Mak. Kneeling before her, she cried, "Mum!" Mrs. Mak's eyes stared sightlessly at her but the old woman said nothing. Six Fingers kowtowed three times before her. "I've been an undutiful daughter-in-law. I've caused you such a lot of distress."

Mrs. Mak grunted. "Would I make so bold as to fret about you? Since the day you married into the Fong family, have I had any control over where you went or what you felt? You go where you want; you do what you want to do. Ah-Fat spoils you and you just run rings around me. If you'd listened to me that day, if you hadn't insisted on going to see that devil-play at that school run by foreign devils, none of this would have happened. Every cent Ah-Fat's worked so hard to earn these last twenty years in Gold Mountain, all the land we've bought with that money, it's all gone because of you. You've cost my son dear, you have."

Six Fingers had nothing to say to that. The iron had entered Mrs. Mak's soul all those years ago, when Ah-Fat had broken off his engagement to his betrothed and married Six Fingers instead. She now knew the bitterness still festered. Mak Dau felt for his pipe and went to light it. "You want to die?" shouted Ha Kau, grabbing it from him. Mak Dau froze for an instant, then smiled. "This is another pipe," he said, lighting it and taking a couple of leisurely puffs. Then he said: "Don't get angry, old Missus. You know, Chu Sei has had his eye on our family for a long time. Even if the young Missus had stayed at home every day to look after both the young masters, he would have come knocking."

Mak Dau's teeth lit up the whole room, but sadly Mrs. Mak could not see it. She shouted furiously: "And who might you be? Who gave you the right to speak in the Fong family?" And she hurled her walking stick blindly at him. Mak Dau easily dodged the stick, which hit one of the pillars and snapped in two. There was dead silence, not a cheep or a rustle to be heard. Even the banyan leaves were still. Everyone knew that Mrs. Mak was strict, but they had never seen her humiliate the young Missus in public or beat a servant with a stick.

After a moment, Kam Shan knelt down in front of his grandmother: "Please don't be angry, Granny. Mum and Kam Ho are back safe and sound now. When I'm big, I'll buy back the fields for you, and we'll have even more than before."

Mrs. Mak allowed his words to touch her heart. Her eyes moistened and, wiping them with the front of her jacket, she sighed. "Take Six Fingers and Kam Ho to their rooms," she told Ah-Choi. "Wipe them down and give them some lotus-seed soup. They shouldn't eat till they've had the soup. People who've gone without food for a long time mustn't eat solids straightaway."

When everyone had left, Mrs. Mak called to Ah-Choi. "From now on, you keep an eye on her for me. You report to me if she wants to go out." Then she added: "That Mak Dau, he's more use than your husband. You keep a good lookout for a suitable woman servant. They can marry and then he can stay with the family." "Yes, Missus," said Ah-Choi. She was about to go, when Mrs. Mak coughed, and said a few words in a low voice into her ear: "I want you to take a good look and see if she's got *any* injuries." Ah-Choi looked blankly at her, and then finally caught on. "Yes, Missus."

For a couple of weeks afterwards, Mrs. Mak kept to her room, burned incense and prayed to the Buddha. Every corner of every courtyard echoed to the rhythmic striking of the wooden fish as Mrs. Mak intoned her prayers.

One morning, Ah-Choi came into the room just as Mrs. Mak was kneeling to kowtow before the yellowing portrait of her husband on the wall. "She … she...." she began. Ah-Choi was a woman who flustered easily, and when that happened, she stammered. Mrs. Mak straightened up. "What is it? Spit it out if you've got something to say." Ah-Choi hesitated, then started again: "The young Missus, she … her … her period's come."

Mrs. Mak clasped her hands over her heart and her body went as limp as a boned fish.

"Merciful Buddha," she muttered to herself.

It was several months before Ah-Fat found out that Six Fingers had been kidnapped. He heard it from some of the men who had gone to visit their folks back home. He wrote to his wife straightaway:

My dear Ah-Yin,

I suppose you did not tell me about this grave family event because you did not want to worry me. I have now decided to build a fortified diulau for you to live in so you will be protected from bandits. I have got an architect to draw up plans based on the instructions I gave him. I will buy all the materials here in Vancouver and in a few days will dispatch them home via Hong Kong. The Sincere Company from Canton will contract the builders to do the work. They have agents here and have worked with Canadian firms for some years, so I know they are completely honest. I will manage the funding myself. However I cannot afford the passage home to oversee the work so Mak Dau and Ha Kau must supervise it very carefully. Please tell Mum that I am sorry not to be able to come home for her sixtieth birthday as a dutiful son should. Have you any definite news on when Kam Shan's boat sails? I await his arrival eagerly. Do not send Kam Ho to school any more, in case any further accidents should befall him. Look for a suitable teacher who can teach him at home. Ask Mak Dau to find servants who can handle weapons, buy some Western and Chinese arms and keep the front gate guarded. Please take very good care, wife, and do not go out without taking men as bodyguards. I mean this most seriously.

Your husband, Tak Fat, the twenty-seventh day of the seventh month, 1910, Vancouver, Canada

Year one of the Republic (1912)
Spur-On Village, Hoi Ping County, Guangdong Province, China

As she dressed, Six Fingers realized she had put on weight. She had had her jacket made the previous autumn and now she could hardly get the buttons done up. The fabric cut into the flesh under her armpits and over her belly when she bent down. She knew it was because she had taken little exercise lately. Mrs. Mak had kept a close eye on her since the kidnapping two years before. Even though they had hired half a dozen strapping bodyguards to protect Six Fingers and Kam Ho round the clock, Mrs. Mak would not allow Six Fingers to take a step out of the house. Since she could not go out, Six Fingers shut herself in her room and practised her calligraphy and painting. Both, she felt, had markedly improved.

Six Fingers opened the window and heard Kam Ho reciting his morning lessons in the reception hall. A new teacher had just been engaged.

As for the way autumn takes shape, in colour it is bleak, the fog lifts and clouds begin to dissipate; the atmosphere is fresh and clear, with the sky high above and sunlight crystalline. The weather becomes cool, chilling men to the bone; it conveys desolation, amidst deserted mountains and rivers. Thus as it produces sound it is chilly and cutting, crying out in great anger. When luxuriant grasses are bright green they struggle to stand out; when the beautiful trees are lush it is easy to enjoy them. But as the grasses meet autumn their colour changes, and as the trees meet autumn they shed their leaves. The reason for this destruction and falling is the excess harshness of all its breath.

Six Fingers leaned against the window listening quietly. It sounded familiar. Maybe as a child she had learned the text in class with her nephew, young Loong. Wasn't it from the "Rhapsody on Autumn Sounds" by the Song dynasty poet Ouyang Xiu? She should ask Kam Ho when he finished his class.

Kam Ho sounded so unlike Kam Shan, she thought to herself. Kam Shan had been gone two years now. Even before he left, Mrs. Mak was so sad she could not say his name without heaving a sigh that filled the reception hall like a draught. If Six Fingers tried to comfort her, Mrs. Mak would say she did not miss her men, not even her own flesh and blood. But if Six Fingers said nothing, Mrs. Mak would accuse her of wanting to take the whole family to Gold Mountain—leaving her, a lonely old woman behind, just waiting to die. So no matter what she said, she could not get it right. Mrs. Mak's grief was so great, Six Fingers almost forgot that it was she who should be weeping and grieving over her son's departure.

The year that Kam Shan left, he grew as fast as a moulting silkworm. His voice suddenly became gruff, and he croaked like a drake. When Ah-Choi washed his hair for him, she said: "The young master's growing a beard!" At fifteen, the boy was already as tall as Mak Dau. Last New Year, in the gown and jacket he put on for the ancestral rites, he looked like a proper adult, although he still behaved like a headstrong kid. Kam Shan had never suffered a day's illness in his life. He was as sturdy as a giant bamboo, as unyielding, and as impervious to blows. When the two brothers stood side by side, there was not the slightest likeness. Ever since birth, Kam Ho had been a sickly and accident-prone child. He had not yet begun to fill out but remained small, like a stunted shoot. He was so slender that he looked as if you could snap him in two. Even the voice in which he recited his lessons sounded like the whine of a mosquito; it had nothing of Kam Shan's forcefulness.

When Six Fingers had heard enough of Kam Ho's lessons, she leaned out of the window, and saw that the clump of bamboo which grew against the wall in the corner of the courtyard had changed colour. It was no longer green and yellow but was speckled with white. When she went out to look, she realized it was covered with a fine layer of flowers. Her heart skipped a beat.

Bamboos lived from a few decades to as much as a hundred years, she knew. They were evergreen and vigorous growers. But once they flowered, they died within a short time, so country folk regarded them as a portent of disaster, like the fall of a dynasty. The Qing dynasty had indeed fallen, the Emperor had stepped down and they now had a Republic. Was this "state of the people" really of the people? In regions remote from the capital, nothing had changed—they were as bandit-ridden as ever. Last market day in Chek Ham, dozens of college students and their teachers had been kidnapped by bandits in broad daylight. If the Emperor had been unable to keep control of the regions, then neither could the Republican government. The old dynasty had gone, yet the bamboo was in flower. What did it portend? Had an accident befallen Ah-Fat or Kam Shan? Feeling alarmed, she went back into her room to write them a letter.

She spread the paper flat but the words would not come and her brush remained poised in the air. There was much on her mind yet she could not tease out the end of the thread in the tangled skein of her thoughts. Ah-Fat, Kam Shan and Kam Ho, Mrs. Mak—they were all there in her thoughts. So too was the *diulau*. She could write and tell him family news, skimming the surface of things like a bamboo ladle collecting duckweed from the surface of a pond. But there were other thoughts too, lying like stones at the bottom, which she could not get a grip on.

Since the day two years ago when Mak Dau had rescued her from the bandit Chu Sei, not a single member of the household had asked what happened to her during her captivity. Although they did not ask, their suspicions were writ large on their faces. Mrs. Mak spoke less and less, but she sighed more and more. She had different kinds of sighs: there was one which came from her nostrils as a kind of snort, which Six Fingers knew was meant for her ears. There was one which slid off her tongue, which was meant for the rest of the household; then there was one which lay quiescent in her heart before finally slipping between her lips, and that sigh was for Mrs. Mak's own ears only.

Whenever Six Fingers walked in the courtyard, she felt the servants' eyes on her back. Every corner and every room of the Fong residence seemed to be filled with chatter. But as soon as she walked into a room, the noise would cease abruptly and the world would be plunged into silence.

Taken all together, these silences were nothing compared to Ah-Fat's. True, he had written more frequently in the last two years, but his letters were all about the petty details of the construction. From the Roman-style columns under the roof to the decorative carving at the front entrance, Ah-Fat was tireless in explaining exactly what material should be used, down to the last detail. What he never mentioned was Six Fingers' abduction. He never even came near to touching on it in his letters. His silence on the matter was impenetrable. Six Fingers could handle the others. She would use her own steadiness to fend off their suspicions. But Ah-Fat's silence she found far more alarming. She did not know where its edges were, and she felt suddenly out of her depth.

Just then, Mak Dau come running in, his face gleaming with sweat. "Missus, I've carried out your instructions." He did not look at Six Fingers as he spoke but kept his eyes fixed on the tops of his blue cloth shoes. He was referring to the position of the shrine for the ancestral tablets; in the original plans, these had been positioned under the roof so that their protection would extend to the entire building. However, Six Fingers, knowing that her blind, elderly mother-in-law would never manage all those stairs when she wanted to light incense and worship the ancestors, had ordered the builders to move it down to the second floor. The builders had not been very happy about having to go back down and make changes.

"Did you see Mr. Lau from the Sincere Company?" asked Six Fingers. "Yes." "Did you talk about the alteration?" "Yes." "Did Mr. Lau agree to it?" "Yes." "Did Mr. Lau say when the work would be finished?" "He said, as soon as possible." "Keep an eye on it, will you? The completion date is fixed. It's the last market day of the first month next year—that's the twenty-second. It's an auspicious day for moving home, and it was fixed when the groundwork was started on the building last year. The Daoist monk has been paid the retainer to sacrifice to the ancestors and drive out evil spirits that day."

Mak Dau said nothing.

Six Fingers laughed shortly. "Has the cat got your tongue? Normally you can't stop talking." Mak Dau carried on staring silently at his toecaps. After a moment, Six Fingers went on: "Is there anyone who trusts me in this house? You're just the same as the rest." Mak Dau reluctantly looked up, and saw a film of tears in Six Fingers' eyes. A wave of tenderness flooded over him and his tone softened. "Has she given in about moving to the *diulau?*" he asked. Six Fingers knew he was talking about Mrs. Mak who, even though the fortress home was her son's initiative, was refusing to budge.

She was quite clear about her reasons. She said she had lived in this house for decades and this was where she had waited on her in-laws and cared for her children. She was used to it, and she had no intention of moving. Besides, the *diulau* was too high, how would a blind old woman with bound feet climb all those stairs? Six Fingers said she would hire someone specially to carry her up and down on her back. There was a moment's silence, and then Mrs. Mak retorted: "I'm not like you. I don't let just anyone carry me around." Six Fingers' heart sank. She realized that her mother-in-law had other, hidden reasons for not wanting to move.

Since the groundwork started the previous year, Mrs. Mak had not been well. Hers was a strange illness: she had no vomiting or diarrhea, no fever, no ague or pain. But she had no appetite and spent all day dozing. She grew thinner and thinner. They had called in a number of herbalists and she had drunk dozens of decoctions, but nothing made her better. As she got worse, she was alternately lucid and confused. When she was lucid, she would stare silently at the ceiling; when she was confused, she talked on and on. Two days ago, she had eaten breakfast and then sat up, her hair in disarray, and thumped the bed, swearing at Ah-Fat. "I'm going to take you before the county magistrate, you disobedient, undutiful son of mine, you black-hearted wolf! You never came home for my sixtieth birthday!"

Six Fingers hurriedly helped the old woman back onto her pillows. "Mum, Ah-Fat's money's all gone on the new house, but he's built it to make you happy." Mrs. Mak gripped Six Fingers' palm, digging her pointed fingernails in. "He built that house for you, not me," she said, "and that's why he has no money to come home. If you hadn't been kidnapped, he would have spent the money on buying land. Why would he want to build a *diulau*?" "Mum, once the family's moved, we can sell the old house and buy fields with the money," said Six Fingers.

Mrs. Mak opened her sightless eyes wide and stared dully at Six Fingers. Finally, she said fiercely: "Pah! And who is your family? Do you dare call yourself a Fong after coming back from Chu Sei?" Six Fingers flung off the old woman's hand. She felt as if a crevasse had opened up beneath her feet, and she was being drawn deeper and deeper down into it. Mrs. Mak was not in the least confused; she was just acting that way to speak her mind freely.

A drop of Mrs. Mak's saliva had fallen on Six Finger's cheek. She wiped it with the front of her jacket and walked unsteadily from the room. Some of the servants were outside but no one looked at her. They simply carried on with what they were doing, but Six Fingers knew they must have heard. Among them she spotted Mak Dau; he was mending a hole in a woven basket used for rice. He looked wild-eyed and, throwing down the strips of bamboo, he knocked his head against a pillar in frustration: "Missus, please let me tell them! Why won't you let me tell them?"

"Are you getting sick in the head just because the old Missus is?" snapped Six Fingers. "Don't talk such rubbish! Get on with your work, all of you!" The servants scattered.

From that day on, Mak Dau would stiffen like a fighting cock every time he saw Six Fingers, but he kept his thoughts to himself.

Finished with her letter writing, Six Fingers put the writing materials away and posed a question to Mak Dau: "How old are you this year? Is it twenty-five or twenty-six?" "My birthday's at the end of the year, Missus, so you can call me either." "You should be getting married by now, shouldn't you?" Mak Dau said nothing. "What do you think about Ah-Yuet?" Ah-Yuet was Ah-Fat's aunt's servant. She was eighteen this year so she was of marriageable age too. Mak Dau still said nothing. When Six Fingers pressed him, he said reluctantly: "She waddles like a hen." "She's hard-working and honest. Not bad-looking either. You don't have to look at her from behind. Look at her front." Mak Dau had to laugh, and his teeth lit up the room. "Even if I'm trying not to look at her, I can't avoid her if she's walking in front of me." "I think she'll suit you," said Six Fingers. "If you marry someone in the family, you'll be in the same position as Ha Kau—you'll be able to live here for the rest of your life."

Mak Dau stood there looking blank. After a long silence, he said: "If you think it's right, young Missus, then I'll do it." "Good. In a couple of days, I'll get Third Granny to bring you the proposal."

Mak Dau turned to leave, his head down. Then he turned back and said hesitantly: "Why won't you let me speak, Missus? I feel bad that you've been wronged. When the Master comes home from Gold Mountain, he'll believe all that gossip, and then what will you do?" Six Fingers smiled: "If he wants to believe it, then telling him a hundred times won't make any difference. The truth will be out in any case, whatever you say." Mak Dau said nothing and went out. Six Fingers leaned out of the window and ordered: "Go and see if it's time for the teacher to have his tea. If it isn't, don't disturb him. If it is, tell Kam Ho I want him."

A few minutes later, Kam Ho trotted in. "Your father's spent all this time and money building us a fortress home and Mak Dau's overseen all the work. I've never set eyes on it and it'll be finished at the beginning of next year. Let's go and take a look." Kam Ho looked doubtful. "What about Granny? We're not allowed out."

Six Fingers smiled dryly. "Chu Sei couldn't keep me locked up and neither can anyone else. Don't worry, my time hasn't come yet. When the Grim Reaper comes for me, it doesn't matter whether I'm at home or out, there's no avoiding him. But if it's not my time, then even a knife at my throat won't harm me." Kam Ho was as fed up as his mother with being confined to the house and had been trying to find an excuse for an outing. Her words gave him courage.

They were on their way out when they bumped into Ah-Choi. The servant stammered: "The old Missus...." but Six Fingers fixed her with a look and Ah-Choi hurriedly fell back. All she could do was to look meaningfully at some of the bodyguards, indicating that they should stick close by Six Fingers and Kam Ho.

Six Fingers walked down the steps of the house and reached the sandy roadway at the bottom. It had just rained and the sky had not completely cleared. A few rays of sunshine filtered through the clouds. The road was wet and the moisture seeped through the soles of her embroidered cloth shoes. When Six Fingers looked up, the sun's rays hurt her eyes. The wild banana trees at the roadside were covered in fat white blossoms. The flowers and leaves stirred in the breeze, looking almost ghostly. Six Fingers thought she would like to go closer, but although her head willed it, her legs felt weak. She had not gone out for nearly two years. The road, the sun, the breeze all seemed to be ganging up on her.

She walked unsteadily for a few more paces and then caught sight of the new building. The position originally chosen for it by the *fengshui* master was a piece of high ground at the entrance to the village, a propitious place for the dragon to show off its pearl, but there were protests that building such a tall house there would block the good fortune of the other villagers. They were forced to choose a piece of wasteland at the other end of the village next to a stand of wild banana trees. To reach it they needed to walk farther, but they could see their new house from where they stood. "House" was how Six Fingers referred to it to herself, but all she could actually see at this stage was bamboo fencing. This was to prevent others from seeing it before it was finished and to give shelter to the builders if it was wet or windy.

She could at least see how tall the building was. She knew they had only reached the fourth floor but its height still frightened her. She had never seen such a tall building. It made everything else nearby dwindle by comparison. The few feeble rays of sunlight that had broken through the clouds seemed to shine right down onto the roof of their new house. Six Fingers put her hands to her heart and gasped in astonishment. "Oh, Ah-Fat!" She could think of nothing more to say.

"This must be the tallest building in the whole township area, mustn't it?" she said to her son.

"Mum," said Kam Ho, "we've never been inside the Emperor's palace but this is definitely the tallest building in the township. Even the church in Yuen Kai has only two storeys."

Gradually Six Fingers' eyes brightened as if lit by the sun's rays. She gave a small sigh. "Kam Ho, when you grow up, you must go to Gold Mountain like your big brother and help your father. Life's been so tough for your dad." "When's Dad coming to get me?" asked Kam Ho. "When you're a big boy. Will you miss your mum when you leave?" Kam Ho did not answer. He was only twelve, and did not understand what separation meant. His mind was on something else. After a pause, he asked Six Fingers: "Mum, is Gold Mountain really paved with gold?" "Of course not. Your father scraped together enough to build this by saving every cent, and it's taken him decades." "But people who live here save up every cent too, so why don't they build a *diulau* like this?"

Six Fingers had no answer to that.

"Missus! Missus!" Ah-Choi shouted, running towards them.

"The old ... old Missus!" she stammered, out of breath.

Six Fingers stood rooted to the spot as Ah-Choi panted like an ox. There was no point in pressing her when she was flustered. You had to give her time to calm down before she could get the words out.

"The old Missus, she's spitting blood!"

By the time Six Fingers and Kam Ho got back to the house, the herbalist had finished taking the patient's pulse and was putting his medicine chest in order. Mrs. Mak lay in the bed, her face deadly pale, with just a crimson spot on her lips where the blood had not been wiped off. Her breathing was very faint. Ah-Fat's uncle and aunt were there, wailing as if she had already died.

"How is her pulse?" asked Six Fingers. "You should prepare for the funeral," said the herbalist. "She has been ill for a very long time and there is little hope that she'll recover now." "Can't you give her another decoction?" The herbalist shook his head. "All you can do is pray now."

Six Fingers showed him out. The eyes of everyone in the room were on her. She knew they expected her to cry, but her eyes were dry. Try as she might, she could not muster a single tear. They waited expectantly, then began to look at her askance.

Six Fingers cleared her throat. "Don't cry. Mum needs peace and quiet." They sniffed back their tears. "She has had such a hard life, how can we not cry?" said Ah-Fat's aunt. She was a woman who never had an opinion of her own, in fact hardly ever spoke or did anything. Now that she did speak up, her words, though few, seemed to fall like lead weights and gouge craters in the ground. Six Fingers walked unsteadily among the craters, scarcely able to keep her balance. She forced herself to stand still. "Wait outside," she commanded Kam Ho. Then she addressed the others: "Go back to your rooms and rest. I have things I want to say to Mum." Ah-Fat's aunt led them out, sobbing inconsolably: "It's too late for talking now!" Six Fingers ignored them and simply shut the door.

She went to Mrs. Mak's bedside, seeing how frail she looked; she seemed to have shrunk to the size of a child. Her sightless eyes, sunken into their dark cavities, were like deep wells of sadness. Her mother-in-law's life hung by a thread. She knelt and grasped the gaunt, claw-like hands.

"I know you're waiting for Ah-Fat, Mum. I know you don't like me because Ah-Fat loves me too much. But believe me, he hasn't wasted his love for me—I can be here for both Ah-Fat and me. I can show you how much we love and honour you. Don't go, Mum, stay with me."

She quivered as something sharp—Mrs. Mak's talon-like fingernails— jabbed the palm of her hand.

Six Fingers freed herself from the old woman's grip, pulled up the front of her jacket and got out the knife that she carried in her waistband. It was a small knife, about six inches long, in an ornamented silver sheath. Mak Dau had bought it several years before from one of the *yamen* guards, for a considerable amount of money.

Nowadays Six Fingers carried it with her all the time, supposedly for self-defence. She had no idea how to use it but it gave her a sort of Dutch courage. In reality, she had never so much as killed a chicken. As a child she used to stop her ears and hide in the farthest corner of the room when the neighbours' pigs and cattle were slaughtered. She could not even bear to hear live fish thrashing in the hot oil of the frying pan, let alone the squeals and bellows of dying beasts. She had only once in her life used a knife on a living creature—herself. When she was seventeen, she had used Auntie Cheung Tai's fodder knife to cut off her sixth finger.

It had never, ever occurred to her that she might have to use a knife on herself a second time.

Six Fingers took the knife out of its sheath. Its blade shone with a cold gleam. Even though she never used it, Mak Dau took it back every couple of weeks and sharpened it for her. She held it close to her eyes and blew some hairs across the blade—the blade sliced them noiselessly in two. It was a trick Mak Dau had taught her for testing how keen the blade was.

She rolled up her trouser leg. She had put on wide trousers today for their trip out to the new house, and once she had folded them loosely a couple of times, she could see her thigh. Her flesh gleamed too, soft and white. She grasped the handle of the knife and began to tremble. She suddenly felt her age. She was thirty-five now, not a fearless seventeen-year-old any more.

Back then she had had no one else to worry about. She had determined on one course of action and nothing was going to get in her way. Things were different now; her heart belonged to many people ... her husband had a piece, so did her sons, and her mother-in-law. Only the smallest piece of her heart could be claimed as her own and that single-minded courage was gone.

She raised the knife, then let it fall, raised it again, lowered it again. She put her left hand over her right, to force her right hand to do it. Cut, commanded the left hand; I'm afraid, whimpered the right hand. Torn between obeying the left and the right hand, she hesitated, and hesitated again. Just then, Mrs. Mak gave a groan. It was this sound which spurred Six Fingers into action and, without any further thought, she sliced downwards. She felt a sharp pain which ran up to her heart and seemed to take a piece out of it. She gave an agonized gasp. But when she dared to look down, she saw that she had only cut a thin layer of skin from her thigh.

She did not have the courage to try again.

"Mother!" she cried, throwing away the knife. But then remembered she had no mother. She found herself overcome by a fit of weeping. The tears came now not in drops but in torrents, surging down her face. Six Fingers wept uncontrollably.

Picking up the knife, she jabbed it fiercely into the quilt next to where Mrs. Mak lay. Again and again she stabbed, in a rising frenzy, until cotton wadding filled the air like snowflakes. Mrs. Mak's frail body pitched and tossed as Six Fingers pounded the bed.

The old woman groaned again, and this time it was a long-drawn-out sound. She was calling for Ah-Fat.

Six Fingers raised the knife again and, with her eyes shut, sliced down into her thigh. At first she felt no pain, just a creeping numbness. She tried to move her leg but it seemed not to belong to her body any more and her muscles would not obey her. She opened her eyes and saw on the tip of her knife a red lump the size of a pigeon's egg, one end of which was attached by a flap of skin to her thigh. Her flesh. It was her own flesh.

The pain was like thousands of fine wires pulling so tight around her heart that they shredded it into tiny pieces. She tugged hard at the red lump and it came away in her hand. It was warm and sticky, and seemed to be pulsating. "Oh Buddha!" she tried to shout, but the sound died in her throat.

Mak Dau was the first into the room. Six Fingers was sitting in a pool of blood. She thrust the thing in her hand at him. "Tell Ah-Choi, boil it up and give the soup to the Missus, quick." Then she fell backwards onto the floor.[4]

A short while later, Ah-Choi came in with the soup for Mrs. Mak. The bedding had been changed and the floor swept clean of cotton wadding, but a faint, rank smell of blood still lingered in the air. Ah-Choi felt a soft lump in her gut pulsing upward as if at any moment it might burst from her mouth. Mrs. Mak clenched her teeth and Ah-Choi had to force them open with the spoon. Finally, the bowl of soup went down.

The old lady slept deeply for the entire afternoon. Towards evening, she awoke suddenly, opened her eyes wide and called for her servant. These were the first words she had spoken for two days. Ah-Choi hurried in. Mrs. Mak had thrown back the covers and was sitting upright, her withered hands scrabbling wildly in the air.

"Soup ... soup!" she was saying.

Ah-Choi shouted to the cook to bring a bowl of lotus-seed soup.

---

[4] There is an old Chinese story about a good son who, in a desperate attempt to save his dying mother, decided to cut a piece of flesh from his own thigh to feed her, as a form of sacrifice. His filial piety moved Heaven and as a result, his mother was miraculously healed.

Mrs. Mak drank a spoonful—and spat it out. "Soup … that soup!" she repeated emphatically, the black holes of her sightless eyes directed intently at Ah-Choi.

Ah-Choi suddenly understood that she meant the soup she had had at midday.

"No, no, you can't have any more of that," Ah-Choi said into her ear. "The young Missus cut off her own flesh so we could make that soup for you. So you'd better hurry up and get better."

Mrs. Mak said nothing. She sat motionless, leaning against the bedhead. A long time passed. Ah-Choi was alarmed and tried to help the old woman lie down, but Mrs. Mak gripped her arm.

"Tung-tree water. Comb."

"You're not going out. What do you want to dress your hair for?"

"Carry me … to see … the *diulau*," commanded Mrs. Mak.

Year two of the Republic (1913)
Spur-On Village, Hoi Ping County, Guangdong Province, China

Kam Ho saw them coming as he rode his tricycle towards the stand of wild banana trees.

His dad had sent the tricycle from Gold Mountain when he was six years old. No one had ever seen such a thing back then, and hordes of village children pursued him madly as he rode it from one end of the village to the other and back again. When he had had enough of riding it, they wanted to borrow it. There were so many of them that he did not know who to lend it to. "Get them to bring you something in exchange," advised Kam Shan. The children queued up in droves, some holding grasshoppers, others with sparrows or glass marbles or cakes made of green beans or sesame seeds. Kam Ho still could not make up his mind and was happy to take his elder brother's advice. So, for a while, the brothers were cocks of the walk and a magnet for trouble in the village. But it did not last; children from other Gold Mountain families were sent tricycles too and Kam Ho's was no longer a rarity.

Kam Ho had outgrown it years ago: his thirteen-year-old legs were bent double over the tiny wheels and looked quite comical. He wanted his mother to write and ask his father to send a bicycle, a big one like the missionary teachers at the school in Yuen Kai rode, but she refused. He was saving his money for a boat passage home, she told him, and she would not ask him to spend it on anything else. Kam Ho's father had left when he was barely a month old and he had no memories of him. He was eager to see his dad, but he also badly wanted a bicycle. He'd just have to wait until his dad saved up the money and came home. Then he could ask him.

It was midday and all the men were taking their noon meal in the fields, eating the sweet potato and rice, and radish soup that their women had brought them in pottery containers. As the women waited for them to finish, they brought out their needlework and sat on the field embankments, their fingers flying deftly back and forth. There were no children to be seen in the village at this time of day—they were down at the No-Name River, splashing naked in the water. This year the spring rains had gone on and on. But then quite suddenly they had ceased and it was summertime. The children had waited a long time for this moment, and as soon as the first rays of sunshine broke through, they were impatient to get into the river. So the village was quite quiet. Even the dogs could not be bothered to bark.

Two men walked on the road beside the river, one in front and one in back. The first wore a grey silk gown, clearly brand new from its sharp folds. He had a felt hat on his head and a yellow oiled-paper umbrella in his hand. Every aspect of his appearance seemed out of place: after all, it was too warm for felt hats, and there was no need for an umbrella. Behind him came the porter; he wore a bamboo hat, a short patched jacket and rolled-up trousers which revealed legs covered in mud. He was weighed down by his carrying pole and the loads at each end almost brushed the ground.

The pair made slow progress, the porter because of his load but the other because he seemed distracted. He looked all around him as he walked along, and Kam Ho at first thought he was unsure of the way. Then he saw that his feet nimbly avoided every rut and stone without the need for eyes—they knew every inch of the road.

Kam-Ho wanted to approach them but could not—his granny told him never to wander beyond the stand of wild banana trees. Farther than this, he needed a servant with him. His granny had kept a close eye on all the members of the household since the time when he and his mother had been kidnapped by Chu Sei. So he sat on the tricycle seat, watching closely as they came nearer.

The men craned their necks to get a good look at the *diulau*. It was a square building, with the roof resting on circular pillars all the way round. The pillars were thick at each end and slender in the middle. They appeared to be made of stone, or perhaps jade—they were a brighter white than stone but duller than jade. In fact, they were made of marble, in the style of a Roman colonnade. The building had numerous windows, though these were so narrow that they were not especially eye-catching. Alongside some of them there were round dark gun-holes, for use in case of attack. Deep eaves projected over each window at each end of which hung a large ball, so that from a distance, each window looked as if it had eyes.

As the pair came close, they saw that the *diulau*'s great iron gate was surmounted with a stone tablet at least twenty feet long. This was elaborately carved in relief with layer upon layer of exuberant foliage. The flowers were unusual—they did not look Chinese. The entire carved area was painted: gold background, green leaves, ochre-coloured entwined stems and magenta flowers. But in the centre, where the name should have been, there was a blank space. The house as yet had no name.

When they were a few paces from Kam Ho, the men halted. The man in front told the porter to put down his burden and take a break. He took off his felt hat and fanned his face with it as he looked the boy over. His eyes roved over him so intently that Kam Ho began to shrink under his scrutiny. Then the man's gaze came to rest on the tricycle. He burst into laughter which made crinkles at the corners of his eyes.

"That trike's too small for you, Kam Ho! Why are you still riding it?"

The man squatted down and gripped the handlebars.

Kam Ho was startled. How did the man know his name? he wondered. Suddenly he saw the livid centipede wavering slightly on the man's cheek as he laughed. Kam Ho flung the tricycle down and fled. He ran like the wind, kicking up a cloud of dust behind him, and arrived back at the steps of his home with one shoe missing.

"Mum … Mum!" Kam Ho stumbled into the house and flung himself at his mother, his heart thudding as if it was going to leap out onto the front of her jacket.

The man could easily have caught up with Kam Ho but he did not. He put the abandoned tricycle over one shoulder and followed slowly behind him. After a few paces he came across the lost shoe. He picked it up, brushed the chicken droppings and dust off the sole, hung it from the handlebar and walked on.

Six Fingers was in the kitchen, stitching the sole of a shoe as she watched the cook make steamed osmanthus rice cakes. The shoe was for Mak Dau. She was making his wedding gift on behalf of the bride, Ah-Yuet. The day of the marriage had been fixed for the tenth day of the tenth month. Mak Dau's family had already presented wedding gifts to Ah-Yuet. Ah-Yuet's birth family had given her up when they sold her to the Fongs as a maidservant, so the Fongs gave presents to Mak Dau on her behalf. The only thing not yet completed was the traditional pair of cloth shoes for the bridegroom. And since Ah-Yuet was all thumbs, Six Fingers was making them for her.

Kam Ho huddled into his mother's chest like a piglet rooting for milk, his face hot and sweaty, his breath coming in gasps. Six Fingers wondered how it was possible that two such different boys could have been born from the same belly. She loved them both but in different ways. The elder came from her guts, the younger from her heart. Those guts had given birth to a masculine courage, and the heart, to a feminine gentleness. The one with the guts was far away, though she could depend on him. The son of her heart still had a hold on every fibre of her being.

Six Fingers wiped Kam Ho's face with the front of her jacket. "What's up? Someone set fire to your tail?"

"It's Dad. He's … he's back," said Kam Ho, pointing to the door.

"Rubbish. He said in his letter he'd be here the middle of the eighth month at the earliest."

"It's true. Dad's back."

Six Fingers burst out laughing: "You don't know what your dad looks like! How do you know it's him?"

"The scar." Kam Ho traced a line down his cheek with his finger.

Six Fingers pulled up the backs of her embroidered slippers and ran for the front door. She peered through the peephole, and the shoe sole she had been sewing dropped to the ground.

"Bolt the door. No one is to open it until I say so," she ordered.

She flew up the stairs. As she turned the corner, she saw her mother-in-law on her knees, burning incense before the portrait of her late husband. "Mum!" she shouted. "Ah-Fat's back." Without waiting for a response, she ran into her room and banged the door behind her.

She sat down at her dressing table, her heart racing. She had not used her mirror for a long time, and the glass was covered in a fine layer of dust. She wiped a small window on it with her sleeve and saw a sallow face, dotted with a few freckles. The glimpse of her own face after so long alarmed her. She pulled open the drawer and felt around for the rouge. Eventually she extracted the box from one corner and opened it, to find that the years had turned the rouge into a rock-hard lump. She scraped off a little with a fingernail, put it in her palm and moistened it with saliva. Then she smeared it on her cheeks and lips. At least she would not look so pale.

Her hair was bare of ornaments. It had been many months since she had even stuck a flower in her bun. She thought of the jade hairpin which she had been so fond of. Ah-Fat had bought it for her on his last visit home, paying as much as a *mu* of land for it. She kept it wrapped in a piece of red cloth in the secret drawer behind her mirror. One end of the pin had broken, but the agate pendant which hung from the other end was still as good as new. She put the mirror down and took out the jade hairpin. The broken end was sharp and snagged her hair painfully, but she finally managed to push it firmly into place, hiding the broken end beneath her hair. The agate pendant tinkled against her ear, and she suddenly felt her spirits lift.

Six Fingers would have liked to change her clothes but there was no time. She could hear knocking at the door downstairs. She stood up, with a sharp intake of breath, and nearly knocked over the stool. The wound on her thigh had healed but the scar tissue was puckered and tight, and pulled painfully whenever she made an awkward movement.

There's no makeup that can cover up my lame leg, she thought.

She opened the door to her room. Someone stood in the gloom on the other side and almost fell into Six Fingers' arms. It was Mrs. Mak. At first Six Fingers could only make out a dark shadow but as her eyes got accustomed to the darkness, she saw Mrs. Mak was holding something bundled up in her hand. She thrust it at Six Fingers. It was a strip of cloth: Mrs. Mak's freshly washed and dried foot-binding cloth.

"Stuff this into your shoe, then it won't look as if one leg's longer than the other."

Six Fingers felt a rush of warmth; tears filled her eyes and trembled there for a moment. She swallowed them back, and there was a salty taste at the back of her mouth. She knelt down on all fours in front of the old woman, as if she were a beast of burden.

"I'll carry you downstairs, Mum, so Ah-Fat can pay his respects to you."

When Ah-Fat had seen the last guest off and went into the bedroom, Six Fingers was sitting at the mirror, removing her makeup. The jade hairpin with its broken end lay on the dressing table, catching the light with a cold gleam. In the lamplight, Six Fingers looked a little tired. Thirteen years of separation had left crow's feet at the corners of her eyes and on her forehead.

Ah-Fat picked up the hairpin and ran his hands over it. The edge of the broken end was rough and scratched his skin.

Ah-Fat let her mass of loose hair run over his hand. With one finger he traced a line around her neck until he reached the dip just below her right ear. There was a round scar there, the size of a pea.

Six Fingers stiffened. His finger ran over the scar, backwards, forwards, as if he were gradually smoothing its rough surface with fine sandpaper. The scar was a reminder of her kidnapping by Chu Sei. When the bandit tried to rape her, she had stabbed herself in the throat with her hairpin. Chu Sei had let her alone then, because he urgently needed the ransom money.

"Does it still hurt here?"

Six Fingers was startled. "Who told you?" she asked. Ah-Fat laughed. "How many people around here have you taught to write? Even the Fong family's dogs are literate these days. You can't hide any family business from me."

It must have been Mak Dau who had written to Ah-Fat, she realized. No one else knew except him.

"Ah-Yin, stop using this hairpin," said Ah-Fat. "In a couple of days, I'll go to Canton and get you a silver one. Fashionable women don't wear jade any more, they wear silver ornaments." "Just get a jade carver to grind the broken edge smooth, then I can wear it," said Six Fingers. "It was so dear, how can I just get rid of it?" "Nothing is dearer to me than the honour of my family," said Ah-Fat. "I'd buy you a house of gold if I had the money."

Six Fingers gave a little laugh. "You might have had. Is it true you gave it all to the Monarchist Reform Party?" "Who told you that?" asked Ah-Fat. "You may have your sources but so have I," said Six Fingers. "Do you regret it? How much land and property could you have bought with all that money? And after all that you couldn't keep the Emperor on his throne." Ah-Fat sighed. "Who can foresee what's going to happen in the world? If the emperor Guangxu was still alive, then the Great Qing Empire could have been saved. But once our country passed into the hands of the young emperor, there was no hope for it."

Six Fingers looked at the ever-deepening lines on Ah-Fat's face, and took his hand between her own. "It doesn't matter whether it's the empire or a republic, there's nothing we common people can do to rescue it. You just look after your own family."

Six Fingers' hands were soft. They had not dug soil or shovelled manure or been soaked in soap or brine for many a year. They were plump and white, with five dimples on the backs of each one. Ah-Fat's gaze stumbled from one dimple to the next and his hands, trapped between hers, began to get ideas. He freed them and reached inside her jacket. He felt an obstruction. "Are you wearing the corset?" he asked.

Six Fingers gave another laugh. "Of course I am. You bought it for me, didn't you?" Ah-Fat's fingers began clumsily to wrestle with the complicated fastenings, but it took him several attempts before they surrendered. Finally his hands roved unimpeded all over her body. Like frozen earth warmed by the sun, her body slumped soft and shapeless against him. Then before Ah-Fat could stop her, she blew out the candle and the room was plunged into darkness.

Ah-Fat groped his way to the bed, Six Fingers in his arms. She had grown much plumper than before, something that Ah-Fat's hands told him before his eyes had explored her carefully. His hands told him of another change in Six Fingers too—her body was on fire and the flames licked around him, enveloping him and singeing his own body and fingers until they sizzled. Ah-Fat felt a frenzy in Six Fingers which he had never felt before.

Afterwards, Ah-Fat stroked her damp hair. "Ah-Yin, don't turn out the light next time, OK? Every scar on your body you got because of me. Let me look at them, then I can remember." Six Fingers was silent. She did not want Ah-Fat to see the tears on her cheeks.

By the time her tears had dried, snores were coming from Ah-Fat. Six Fingers did not remember him snoring on his last visit home. His snores vibrated like rumbles of thunder in her ears. She could not sleep, and shook him awake.

At first Ah-Fat did not know where he was. "Leave me alone, Ah-Lam!" he mumbled. Six Fingers was seized with a sudden fear. "Ah-Chu's old man came home last year and gave her syphilis. Do you go off with women when you're out there too?" she asked quietly after a moment. Ah-Fat was wide awake now but did not answer. When Six Fingers asked again, he said: "Ah-Yin, I'm only staying four months this time. I want to get back to pay off the money I borrowed to build the *diulau*. Then when I've saved up the head tax, I'm taking you out with me."

Her question remained unanswered, thought Six Fingers, but she felt she could not ask again.

"What will happen to Mum when I've gone?" she asked. "I'll borrow more money and bring you both over together." Six Fingers sighed. "But Mum's getting old, she won't want to be uprooted and go to Gold Mountain. Just getting her to move from the old house to here...." Ah-Fat ran his hand over the dent in Six Fingers' thigh where the scar tissue had formed, and could think of nothing to say. On one side there was his mother, on the other, his wife. He could not do without either of them. He knew the only hope was to wait till his mother passed away. But how long would that be? It could be a year, or five, or ten, or even twenty. Maybe he would die before his mother. Or maybe by the time she died, Six Fingers would have become a silver-haired old woman. The two of them seemed destined to steal happiness from the brief time allotted them between the death of one and the death of another.

"Take Kam Ho. Take him with you. When he's bigger, he should be able to help out," said Six Fingers.

Ah-Fat grunted. "Not much hope there," he said. "Can't expect much from either boy." With the tip of her finger, Six Fingers smoothed the knot which had formed between Ah-Fat's eyebrows. Cautiously, she asked: "Has Kam Shan done something to make you angry?" She was aware that since his arrival, Ah-Fat had not said a word about his eldest son.

Ah-Fat did not answer. Instead he turned over and went to sleep.

They were still in bed the next morning when the cook sent up two bowls of jujube and lotus-seed soup. As Six Fingers bent over the soup, ready to drink it, she saw the shadow of a magpie in the liquid. She knew then that Ah-Fat had planted a seed in her belly.

Ah-Fat did not drink the soup. His digestion had accustomed itself to coarse fare during his time in Gold Mountain, and he needed time to get used to refined home cooking. He gazed absently at Six Fingers as she drank.

"Ah-Yin, we haven't given the house a proper name. I think we should call it 'Tak Yin House.' I, Fong Tak Fat married you, Kwan Suk Yin, and that has brought the family great good luck. And there's something else: if you get pregnant and give me another boy, call him Kam Tsuen. If it's a girl, she should have the generation name Kam, and you can choose her other name."

Nine months later, Six Fingers gave birth in Tak Yin House.

While she was still resting after the birth, she got Kam Ho to write to Ah-Fat, who had returned to Gold Mountain, to tell him that he had a baby daughter, named Kam Sau.

5

Gold Mountain Tracks

⚜

Year two of the reign of Xuan Tong to year two of the
Republic (1910–1913)
British Columbia

"How many siblings does your grandfather have?"
"He only has one younger brother."
"How many children does his younger brother have?"
"My great-uncle has one son and two daughters."
"What is the son called?"
"Fong Tak Hin."
"Where does your great-uncle live?"
"He lives with us."
"Does he live upstairs or downstairs?"
"He lives in the second courtyard."
"How many steps are there to the courtyard?"
"Two."
"Wrong. Last time you said five."

"There are five steps up to the main entrance. But from the first to the second courtyard, there are only two steps."

"Is there a river in your village?"

"There's a little river. All the village kids swim in it in summer."

"What's the name of the river?"

"It hasn't got a name, so it's called No-Name River."

"Whose houses do you pass if you walk from the river to your home?"

"Once you've gone up the steps from the river, you get to old Missus Cheung Tai's house first, then Pigmy Fong's house, then Au Syun Pun's. Pigmy Fong's house and Au Syun Pun's houses are back to back. Then there's the village well, and then it's us."

"Which way does your woodshed face?"

This question stumped Kam Shan. It was new, not one of the many his dad had prepared him for. He knew where the woodshed was—he and Kam Ho used to play hide and seek in it when they were little. And he knew that its doorway faced neither the kitchen nor the courtyard but a point somewhere in between. So did that count as north facing or west facing? He hesitated, then said doubtfully: "North, it faces north." His interrogator and the interpreter exchanged glances and both men wrote a question mark in their notebooks. Kam Shan's heart sank.

Kam Shan was taken back to his cell.

It was a small room, lined with upper and lower bunks on three sides. He had four roommates, two adults and two children. Only a boy of about ten was in the cell when he returned. He was from Toi Shan and had arrived a couple of days previously. He lay on his bunk bed looking utterly bored, picking at the frayed ends of his jacket cuffs. The moment Kam Shan came through the door, he vaulted to his feet in a rising handspring. "Have they finished with you? That was really quick. What did they ask?" Kam Shan sat down looking glum and said nothing.

Kam Shan had come on the same boat as Ah-Lam's wife and they had been in Gold Mountain for five days. They had been heading for Vancouver but, just before arriving, the boat changed course and berthed at Victoria instead. Half of the several dozen Chinese passengers on board had been brought straight to detention; Kam Shan and Ah-Lam's wife were among them.

His dad and Ah-Lam had visited once. His dad stood outside the building, with the interpreter keeping a close eye on him, shouting up at Kam Shan's window. It was blowing a gale and Ah-Fat's words scattered in all directions, so that his son only caught a few of them.

"Are … they … feeding you?"

"Are … you … warm enough … at night?"

Looking down from above, Kam Shan saw his father through the grille covering the window. His dad's head looked like a melon cut in two: the front half was white with some dark bits showing through (that was the shaven bit) and the back half was dark with some white showing through (that was because his dad was going grey).

He had not seen his dad for ten years, and did not remember seeing any grey hairs, although that may have been because he had not had such a commanding view from above back then. Today Ah-Fat had on a grey cotton jacket, loose black trousers tied tightly at the ankles and a pair of round-toed cotton shoes. His clothes were shabby and patched at the cuffs and knees, and made him look like an old peasant who had never left the confines of Spur-On Village.

Kam Shan knew his dad had come over from New Westminster to see him. That explained his appearance; he had been working in the fields when he got the news of his arrival and had come straight here without bothering to change or wipe the mud from his shoes. Still, he looked completely different from his last visit home, when he had worn a brand-new gown with creases still crisp from the suitcase. He had strolled confidently along, holding a folding fan in his hand for show, apparently unconcerned as to whether the day was warm or not. Back there, his dad drawled his words instead of yelling the way he did now. Now he was getting on a bit, not much to look at, a real backwoods man. Which one was his real father—this one or the one who came home to Spur-On Village? Kam Shan shouted down: "Write to Mum and tell her.…" but the last half of his sentence was blown back into his throat by the wind and he bent over in a fit of coughing. Afterwards, he realized that he had not called to him: "Dad!"

On the day that Kam Shan's date of departure to Gold Mountain was fixed, Six Fingers cried. She never let him or anyone else see, but he could tell from her reddened, puffy eyes when she got up in the morning that she had cried every day since the news. The day she saw him off at the entrance to the village, she wept openly. "Kam Shan, the house will be empty now that you and your dad have gone," she cried. Kam Shan replied, "But you've got Kam Ho, haven't you?" The tears coursed down his mother's face: "He'll go too, sooner or later. Every son of mine will go. Maybe if I have a daughter, I might be able to keep her."

"We'll bring you to Gold Mountain one day," was what Kam Shan wanted to say. But he knew this was an empty promise. As long as his granny was alive, his mum could not budge. Kam Shan may have been only fifteen but he already knew that certain things were better left unsaid. "When I get to Gold Mountain, I'll write," were his only words.

"The women are making a racket today," the boy from Toi Shan said. He had been alone for hours, and wanted to talk. "Someone went into the women's cells to do medical inspections but they refused to strip. They fought like wildcats to keep their clothes on."

Kam Shan had no desire to chat and pretended to be asleep. He had said a lot in the interrogation today, enough for a whole lifetime. Before he left, his dad got someone to sketch a map of Spur-On Village, showing how it was laid out and which family lived where. He said the head tax had been going up and up over the years until now it was five hundred dollars, but that had not stopped the Chinese. When the Gold Mountain men went back home, they went for a year or maybe two. Some had children while they were there, some did not. But all of them, when they returned to Gold Mountain, made sure to register a birth with the local government. According to the register, they had all had sons, and some had had twins. In an attempt to stem the flow of Chinese immigrants, the government had built this detention centre, where they kept the new arrivals for a couple of days to several months. They gave them medical exams and compared the statements of the fathers and the sons. At the slightest discrepancy, the detainee would be ordered back to Hong Kong on the next boat. Only the fit and healthy, whose testimonies were corroborated, were permitted to make the payment of five hundred dollars in head tax.

His dad had insisted that Kam Shan learn every detail of that map. He wrote out pages of questions so that Kam Shan could memorize them and get the answers right under cross-examination. The questions were about every detail of the construction of their home, and the age of every family member. Kam Shan had been questioned several times in the last few days, and no question had tripped him up. But still his dad's preparations had not been exhaustive enough. His dad had overlooked the woodshed. Which way does the woodshed face? Kam Shan knew every brick and tile and every corner of his home but he did not know the answer to that question.

North facing, Dad, you've absolutely got to say north facing, Kam Shan mouthed silently.

The boy from Toi Shan had given up his efforts at conversation, and Kam Shan stopped pretending to be asleep and opened his eyes. He was in the bottom bunk and the view was limited to a few square feet of the bed board of the upper bunk. The board was smeared with spots that looked suspiciously like snot. Kam Shan's imagination made them into the clumps of wild bananas at the front of their house in Spur-On Village. Then they morphed into the water wheel in the fields, then the storm clouds that presaged rain. Then he got bored and stopped thinking about them.

The weather was good today and the sunlight glared on the wall beside his bunk. Someone had scratched some lines in Chinese with a knife, in tiny, cramped writing. When Kam Shan bent down and peered at them closely the day he arrived, he could only make out the characters: "Inscribed by Mr. No-name of San Wui." Now, with the sunlight on the wall, he could begin to make sense of them. He sat and scrutinized the writing close up. The rest of it said: "The black devil is absolutely unreasonable, making me sleep on the floor. And I'm starving; they only give us two meals a day...."

The room suddenly went dark. The kid from Toi Shan was standing in front of the window, blocking the light. He had been here two days but he had been neither visited nor interrogated. He was bored stiff and spent his time pestering the others to talk to him. Now he was counting the number of bars in the window: one, two, three, four, five, six. And backwards: six, five, four, three, two, one. Then from one to six again. Then again from six to one. Kam Shan began to feel sorry for him. "Does your dad know you're here?" he asked. "He's in Montreal. He can't come, so he asked my big brother to come and get me." "Why hasn't he come?" The boy did not answer. He just said: "In the village, they said it was a good sign if the *yeung fan* put you in the cell. In the end you always get out of it. If they really don't want you in Gold Mountain, they won't let you off the boat."

Kam Shan was annoyed. "Get out of my light!" he yelled. The boy snickered. "It's gonna rain soon, that's why it's getting dark. It doesn't make any difference whether I'm in your light or not." "Huh!" said Kam Shan. "And you're the Jade Emperor, are you, deciding whether it's going to rain or not? You won't get far, seeing as it's such a nice day." The boy pointed to the bars on the window. "If you don't believe me, come and look." Kam Shan crawled out of the bunk bed and went to look. The window bars were coated in a mass of ants, one piled on another so thickly that each bar had more than doubled in size. It gave him goosebumps to look at them. "Bring over the stool by the door." "What for?" "Do what I tell you." So the kid got the stool and put it down in front of the window.

Kam Shan stood on the stool, hitched up his jacket and put his hand down his trousers. He pulled out his penis. It grew thick in his hand, and its colour changed from brown to pink. He directed it at the window and began to squirt a stream of hot, yellow urine up and down the window bars. The ants scrambled over each other to escape. The liquid turned a muddy black from the ants, and the window bars thinned down again. The boy was taken aback at first, then burst out laughing.

They were still hooting with laughter when they heard a cry in the corridor.

It was a terrible scream, so razor sharp that it seemed to slash the heavens, drain the sunlight away and plunge everything into gloom. There was a confused patter of footsteps from the courtyard and half a dozen white-coated *yeung fan* rushed past their door carrying a stretcher. A body lay on it, covered from head to foot in a white sheet stained crimson. It was wrapped tightly around the body but not tightly enough, and Kam Shan saw the pointed toe of a very small shoe poking out.

It was a cloth shoe, with a pink lotus flower on the toe. Women in Spur-On Village often embroidered this sort of lotus flower on the shoes they wore for visiting.

But Kam Shan knew this particular lotus flower: it had a yellow dragonfly resting on it.

It belonged to Ah-Lam's wife.

"She must have cut her throat," commented the kid from Toi Shan.

But it was another two weeks, when his father finally came to get Kam Shan out of the detention centre, before he found out how she died.

She had not cut her throat. She had rammed a pair of chopsticks into her ears and bled to death. Earlier that morning, they had taken her clothes off and groped her all over. They told her it was a medical examination, but Ah-Lam's wife had never had a medical examination like this, and after it, she no longer wanted to live.

That evening, Kam Shan shone the light at the wall by the bed and scratched four words on it. He did them with his thumbnail, big and clear enough that they could be read without the need for sunlight.

"I fuck your mother," he wrote.

After the Whispering Bamboos Laundry was looted, forcing the business to close for the third time, Ah-Fat decided to try a new tack. He had bought a piece of wasteland on the outskirts of New Westminster, about twelve miles from Vancouver, and he and Ah-Lam cleared it and went into business as market gardeners. They hired two labourers, and kept several dozen chickens and ducks, a dozen sheep and a dozen pigs. The manure fertilized the fields; they could sell the eggs and meat at the farmers' market in town and keep back a small quantity for their own needs. They even bought a cart to carry the goods.

Ah-Lam's family had been market gardeners in Hoi Ping and, although the varieties of vegetables in Gold Mountain were a bit different, he knew all about growing them. Ah-Fat had grown up watching his father slaughter pigs and sheep, so that part came easy too. And so Fong Yuen Cheong's prediction that his son would "travel thousands of *li* to butcher pigs" came to pass, after all these years.

The two men left Vancouver's Chinatown and began a new life. Under Ah-Fat's management, the piece of wasteland eventually turned into a big farm, famous for miles around. But that, of course, was later. Just now Ah-Fat was thinking of turning those eggs, vegetables, fruit and meat into money, and that money into more land. After thirty years in Gold Mountain, Ah-Fat had developed a yearning for Gold Mountain land.

The day that Ah-Fat fetched Kam Shan from the detention cell at Customs and Immigration, Kam Shan had no time to become acquainted with the marvels of Vancouver. They headed straight home. It was well into autumn by then and the fruit trees had lost their leaves. All the vegetables had been harvested and the land lay bare and bleak. A small, flimsy shack stood at the edge of the field, with a rough fence erected around it. Along the fence were a number of large, upended baskets, the "pens" for a hundred or so chickens and ducks that squawked and quacked frantically. It had just rained and, at the edge of the track, piglets rootled through the muddy puddles, flicking their tails and leaving behind piles of smelly dung on the ground. The field, the hut, the track—the entire scene was bleak and desolate in a way that Spur-On Village never was.

It was not that Kam Shan knew nothing of Gold Mountain. But his expectations had been gleaned from his father's Gold Mountain suitcases, Gold Mountain clothing and Gold Mountain habits. That was the far-distant Gold Mountain. He had not the faintest idea that the real Gold Mountain would not live up to his dreams. The truth left him dumbstruck.

Kam Shan followed Ah-Fat to the hut without speaking. They pushed open the door. An old man sat inside, lighting a pipe. There were stools in the hut but the old man was squatting on the floor, making slurping sounds—not from sucking his pipe but from the trails of snot which ran in and out of his nostrils with each breath. It was a warm day but he wore an old padded jacket, the front of which was encrusted with bits of dried rice and sauce.

"Kneel and kowtow to your uncle Ah-Lam," said Ah-Fat to his son. Kam Shan was taken aback; he scarcely recognized the old man. It was only two weeks since Ah-Fat and Ah-Lam had come to the detention centre to visit Ah-Lam's wife and Kam Shan. But the death of his wife had reduced him to a feeble and senile state. A man really could not live without a wife.

Ah-Fat got Kam Shan's bundle down from the cart, then wrung out a wet towel and gave it to his son to wipe his face and neck. "Kam Shan," he said, "I've been thinking I really want to send you to school before you start working. There's a school here on the way to the farmers' market. I can drop you off on my way." Kam Shan shook his head. "But Mum sent me to help you. Mum said you were only a year older than me when you got here, and the moment you got off the boat you were working to support the family."

Ah-Fat was momentarily lost for words. He could not help remembering his arrival with Red Hair all those years ago—it was like another life. Red Hair's bones must have turned to dust by now. He sighed: "I had no choice back then. It's different now. The children of Gold Mountain men all go to school when they get here. And you've got to learn some English, haven't you? I'm hoping you'll soon be able to do business with the *yeung fan.*" "I've studied all I need to study," said Kam Shan. "And I know a bit of English, the missionaries taught me. I'm not going to any school."

Ah-Lam sniffed noisily. "And if you don't go to school, what'll you do?" he asked. "Work the land? Look after the pigs? Slaughter the chickens? Hardly any Gold Mountain children do that kind of heavy work. Their parents mollycoddle them." Kam Shan was silent for a minute. Then he said: "Dad, I can go to town with you and sell the vegetables. I mean, I do speak a bit of English...."

Ah-Fat had often heard Six Fingers say how pigheaded their son was, and decided to drop the subject for now. There would be time enough to work on changing his mind. He stifled his reservations and said: "If you don't want to go to school, I won't force you, son. But there's a Protestant church about fifteen minutes from here. The old pastor comes around almost every day to collect the hired hands and take them to church. You can go there and learn a bit more English."

Kam Shan looked more cheerful at this. "I know about Protestant missionaries," he said. "They're nice. The ones in Yuen Kai town dressed just like Chinese, in gowns and jackets, and they wore false pigtails too. Twice a month, they prepared three big woks of rice porridge and gave it out for free in front of the church. People lined up down the street for it."

Ah-Fat frowned unhappily at Kam Shan's enthusiasm. "You're not having anything to do with that religion, you're just going there to learn English." "What's wrong with following their religion?" objected Kam Shan. "Everyone does in England, France, Germany and America. They've abolished the emperor, and poor and rich are equal."

Ah-Fat was overcome with a rush of uncontrollable anger. He hurled Kam Shan's bundle to the floor and shouted: "If you want to be like the foreign devils, with no emperor to rule the country, no patriarch to rule the family, then you just go ahead!" He was rigid with fury and thick, livid veins bulged from his forehead. But Ah-Lam pushed him onto a stool. "Heaven's high and the Emperor's far away," he said. "What's the point in getting on your high horse because your son's said something against the Emperor? The porridge and pickled eggs is ready in the pot. Eat it while it's hot. Kam Shan'll be hungry after that long journey even if you're not."

Then winter was on them, and there were no vegetables to sell at the market. The eggs kept well enough, so there was no need to go to town every day. Kam Shan went to church to learn English in the evenings, but by day he had nothing to do except listen to the two men telling him everything they had picked up about farming, to which he paid little attention.

For the first few months, Kam Shan hung around on his father's patch of land, until it came time to sow the new crops. The climate on the West Coast was so mild and humid that almost anything would grow. Ah-Fat planted all sorts of things—cucumbers, tomatoes, aubergines, broccoli, green peppers, mint and a variety of cabbages, and more besides. Some of the seeds were imported from Guangdong and these too flourished, in spite of the different soil and climate. He had fruit trees too, apples, peaches, pears and cherries he had grafted himself. Even though the fruit was not ripe for harvesting yet, they had cucumber pickles and jam left over from the previous year, and freshly killed poultry and pork and lamb and eggs to take to market. Every few days, Ah-Fat would load up the cart with their produce, go and sell it in Vancouver, or sometimes New Westminster, and bring back any household items they needed. And Ah-Fat discovered that the son who took no interest in farming had something in his favour after all—he had a very useful face.

Ah-Fat drove the cart to the farmers' market first, and then put anything that was left over in baskets and hawked them door to door in the neighbouring streets and lanes. So long as he had his son with him, he could get rid of all the remaining produce quickly, and at a good price too.

Kam Shan would not allow anyone to knock him down on prices.

The way he stood up to people who wanted a bargain was both original and simple. He wreathed his face in a big smile. He was nothing like the other Chinese children who had just arrived in Gold Mountain, his father thought to himself with surprise. They were shy and timid, and, when in company, would huddle in the shadow of their elders. They hung their heads mutely and would not look you in the eye. They were rather expressionless—no great emotion ever crossed their faces. Everything about them recoiled from extremes so that they looked almost wooden.

Kam Shan bore no resemblance to these children.

On his first visit to the farmers' market with Ah-Fat, a *yeung fan* woman twice his size tried to knock him down on a price. He beamed a smile at her that stretched from ear to ear. He could have bargained but he did not. He simply looked quietly at his customer again. His gaze needled her, but those needles were wrapped safely in the softness of his smile. Before they began to hurt, she was suddenly overcome by shame. None of the shoppers had even seen a smile like this, especially not in a young Chinese. There was no more quibbling about prices.

Every market day, when one of the hired hands began to load up the cart, Ah-Fat would see his son's face transform. It started in his eyes, where a watery pearl would moisten each eyeball. This pearl of moisture would expand until it filled his eyes and flowed into the corners, up to the eyebrows and down to the mouth. By the time Ah-Fat twitched the horse's reins and the first muffled clop-clop of its hooves sounded on the narrow lane outside their door, Kam Shan's smile had fully bloomed.

Kam Shan's smile, however, could ebb just as quickly as it surged up his face. After their produce had sold, and the hired hand started piling the empty baskets onto the cart, that smile shrank to nothing, like a puddle under the noonday sun. The horse plodded home through the gathering dusk and at the door of their hut, Ah-Fat could see that his son's face had become as parched as a dried-up creek. It remained that way until the next market day.

His son belonged in crowds. His element was the hustle and bustle and the bright lights of the city. The farm was too dull, too small and too quiet. Ah-Fat wondered how he would ever anchor him there.

"Is Vancouver a big, noisy city, Dad?" Kam Shan suddenly asked Ah-Fat one day as they were sweeping the cart out ready for the journey home.

Kam Shan was not like the other Gold Mountain children who used the name "Salt Water City" as their elders did. He called the city by its proper Canadian name. Ah-Fat realized that he had never shown his son around the city which had been his home for so many years.

So one day, when they had sold all their produce, instead of setting off for the farm, Ah-Fat took his son to the newly built theatre in Vancouver's Chinatown. The full version of *The Fairy Wife Returns Her Son to Earth* was showing that evening. Ah-Fat scrutinized the playbill carefully but could not see Gold Mountain Cloud's name anywhere. He mocked himself for imagining that Gold Mountain Cloud, no doubt at the height of her fame now, would remember him.

A few weeks later, Ah-Fat took Kam Shan to have afternoon tea with some of his old friends. After, they went to look at the crowds thronging the *yeung fan* department store, and finally Ah-Fat showed him the house where he had lived and where he used to keep shop.

"This is the place the *yeung fan* destroyed. It's been rebuilt.

"This is where me and your uncle Ah-Lam first lived. They've added another storey to it now.

"Italians lived here originally. In those days, no one wanted to rent to Chinese, except this old Italian. Too bad he died last year. He wasn't even sixty."

Kam Shan only half-listened to Ah-Fat. He was too young to feel nostalgic about the past. Instead his eyes were drawn to the newspaper stand pasted with Chinese broadsheets. Watching his son standing on tiptoe, craning to see past the mass of bodies in front of him and read the news of the overseas Chinese community, suddenly reminded Ah-Fat what it was like being sixteen. He felt close to tears.

"Any news?" he asked. His eyesight was not as good as it had been and he had trouble reading the newsprint.

"Cockfighting. That's in the *Daily News* here. Over there it's the *The Chinese Times*. The Monarchist Reform Party and the Revolutionary Party are at each other's throats."

"Rabble," said Ah-Fat, pressing his lips together disdainfully, and Kam Shan knew he meant the Revolutionary Party.

"There's someone called Freedom Fung who rants away and he's quite right. Why should we Chinese be ruled over by the barbarian Manchu for centuries?"

Ah-Fat could not be bothered to argue. He pulled Kam Shan away, thinking to himself, ten or twenty years ago, I wouldn't let you get away with talking crap like that. But Ah-Fat was no longer the hotheaded youngster he had once been.

Ah-Fat showed his son all over Chinatown though he was careful to give a wide berth to the gambling den and the dingy room above it. They were the heart of Chinatown, but only grown men went there. One day his son would find his own way, and his experiences there would make him a man. It was not time yet to introduce Kam Shan to what went on in these shadowy nooks and crannies.

Kam Shan felt completely at home in the farmers' market of Vancouver. When the farm work got busy, he said to his father: "Let me and Loong Am go and sell the produce. You and Uncle Ah-Lam can carry on with the farm work." Loong Am was the hired hand. Ah-Fat was not keen at first, but it soon became clear that Ah-Lam was deteriorating by the day and could not be left in charge. Kam Shan got his way.

For the first few trips, Kam Shan was up before dawn to load the cart and back by dusk to eat dinner with them. He always came back with an empty cart and a careful record of all their sales. Ah-Fat, reassured, left him to his own devices.

Later, however, things started to change. Kam Shan arrived back later and later, first by half an hour, then by one hour, then by two. One night, he didn't get home till midnight. He said it was because there were more people keeping poultry and it was getting harder to sell the eggs. When he could not sell them in the market, he had to go house to house to get rid of the rest and it took longer. Ah-Fat was only half convinced and took Loong Am to one side. The hired hand was an honest soul. He admitted that when Kam Shan had sold the vegetables, he bought Loong Am a theatre ticket and arranged to meet him at the entrance after the performance. What Kam Shan did in the meantime, he had no idea.

Ah-Fat said nothing to this, but resolved to make a careful check of the accounts each day. The losses mounted up gradually—one day ten cents, the next, fifty cents—until finally receipts were down one or two dollars per trip compared to the earliest accounts. Those one or two dollars per trip added up to quite a considerable sum over time.

One day Kam Shan got back from Vancouver after the evening meal. He was surprised to see no lights in the shack. Usually his father waited outside for him, holding the lantern to light his arrival. Not tonight. He unloaded the empty baskets, then groped his way to the door, carrying the whip. As he opened the door, he bumped into something hard. He rubbed his sore knee, and saw a small, winking red dot before his eyes. His father stood smoking a cigarette.

He turned to run but it was too late. He felt a kick from a hobnailed boot at the back of his knee and he slumped to the ground. It struck him then that he was in the light and his father was in the shadows. His father could see him perfectly clearly, in fact had been waiting in the shadows for him for some time.

He dropped the whip, and before he could retrieve it Ah-Fat snatched it up and thrashed him ferociously. The lashes fell upon his back and shoulders, again and again, though not on his head. He felt a stinging heat, as if he had rubbed pepper in his eyes. The real pain came later.

When Kam Shan was little, his mother had beaten him for all kinds of misdemeanours. She thrashed him with the bamboo canes they dried clothes on until he rolled around on the ground in pain. Although his mother had inflicted many such punishments on him, he never feared her. His mother's wrath had boundaries which were set by his grandmother. The current of his mother's anger might run strong and swift, but it would always be contained within the riverbed of his blind grandmother's authority.

The punishment inflicted by his father was a different matter. He had never experienced it before and he did not know how far his father's anger would take him.

Kam Shan made no sound. He knew that he was kneeling at the threshold of adulthood. If he cried out, he would be denied entry. If he could endure this whipping, he might become a man.

"How dare you steal from the mouths of your mother and grandmother," Ah-Fat yelled.

"Did you go to the gambling den?

"Did you? Tell me!"

Ah-Fat had not intended to whip his son so viciously. Kam Shan had worked hard since his arrival in Gold Mountain. Even though he had no particular aptitude for farm work, he ploughed, planted, collected eggs, cut up the meat, loaded up the cart and sold the goods at the market, just like the hired hands. The only difference was that he, unlike the others, received no wages, not a single cent.

The money Ah-Fat made, he carefully divided into two parts, sending one to Six Fingers and keeping the other for himself. He could not stint by a single cent on the portion he sent home because he knew that a dozen or more people waited, mouths agape, for the food he dropped into them. Their lives depended on those dollar letters. And he tried as hard as he could to limit the amount he kept for himself. This money had to stretch far, and in many directions.

He had borrowed from several people to build the *diulau* fortress home and the debt had to be paid back. His mother was over sixty and in poor health. When she passed on, then Six Fingers could come and join him in Gold Mountain. So he had starting saving to pay the head tax for Six Fingers.

He had something else in mind too: Kam Shan's marriage. The boy was nearly sixteen. Back in Spur-On Village, all boys of that age would be betrothed. It'd be too late to wait until the matchmaker knocked on your door to save up for wedding presents.

He had not told anyone of these plans, not even his wife or his son. He just kept a tighter and tighter grip on the money he kept back. Every time he paid the hired hands their wages, he would turn away and try not to look at Kam Shan. His son's eyes had a naked yearning in them. Ah-Fat could only pretend not to notice.

Ah-Fat knew that the small change his son filched from the accounts was insignificant compared with the wages he had denied him. Besides, they lived in a remote place, with no neighbours apart from a few *yeung fan*. Kam Shan, like any kid of that age, was filled with lively curiosity, yet he had not a single companion to amuse himself with. It was normal that he should go looking for a bit of fun in Vancouver. When Ah-Fat was Kam

Shan's age, Red Hair had taken him to explore all of Chinatown's darkest corners.

As he whipped his son, he waited and prayed for Kam Sham to say something: a denial, an excuse, a protest, even an accusation. More than anything, he wanted Kam Shan to speak so that the beating could cease, so that he could accept his son's plea or apology and save face. Then he would fetch the sausage-and-chicken rice he had kept warm all evening, and eat a late dinner with his son. He had had nothing to eat while he waited for Kam Shan's return.

But Kam Shan said nothing. He did not make a single sound. The boy gave in to the gathering tide of rage which rose in his father. Kam Shan did not try to put even the smallest barrier in its way, and now that rage threatened to sweep away all before it.

"Is it daylight already? Why haven't the cocks crowed?"

Ah-Lam emerged sleepy-eyed from inside the house carrying a small oil lamp. He was wearing a tattered old jacket which exposed his bare legs in the dim lamplight. His flaccid penis drooped between them, looking like a brown pipe begrimed by years of use.

Ah-Fat threw down the whip and frantically pushed him back into the house. Grabbing the lamp from him, he pulled a pair of trousers from the bed and threw them at him. "What's all this nonsense? It's still evening. You should be ashamed of yourself, parading around like that in front of Kam Shan." Ah-Lam looked at him in a daze: "If your son's here, why hasn't Ah-Tak got here?"

Ah-Tak was Ah-Lam's son. He was still in a village in Hoi Ping County. Ah-Lam had planned to scratch together the money for the head tax on Ah-Tak after his wife arrived, only he never expected his wife to die before she left the detention centre. Ah-Fat was alarmed at the dazed look in Ah-Lam's eyes and attempted to calm him: "Put these trousers on and get a good night's sleep. Tomorrow, I'll write to Ah-Tak for you and tell him to buy passage on the next boat."

Ah-Lam bent over the trousers, trying unsuccessfully to get one leg in. Finally he sighed: "It's too late for that. And if Ah-Tak doesn't come, who'll take my bones back home?" His lucid words saddened Ah-Fat more than his confusion. He helped the old man back to bed. "Don't worry. If Ah-Tak doesn't come, Kam Shan'll take your bones and mine back home, just you see if he won't." It occurred to him that Kam Shan was still kneeling outside. He was dismayed by the thought that if Ah-Lam had not blundered out when he did, his wrath might have caused injury that no amount of remorse could heal. Ah-Lam was, perhaps, sent by Buddha to save his son.

Ah-Fat carried the lamp outside to where his son still knelt on the ground. The back of his jacket was shredded by the whip lashes; he could not see if he had drawn blood. Kam Shan stiffened when he heard Ah-Fat's footsteps and did not look round. In the oppressive silence, Ah-Fat felt himself shrinking. The atmosphere was as prickly as a ball of thistles and thorns capable of stabbing you painfully wherever you touched it. He knew that he and his son were within a hair's breadth of straining each other's forbearance to the breaking point.

Ah-Fat turned and went into the kitchen. He got two bowls and two pairs of chopsticks and laid them on the table, then brought out the iron pot filled with the sausage-flavoured rice. He could not make up his mind whether to fill two bowls or one. His hand quivered in indecision. He served only himself and sat down.

He was ravenous and the smell of the sausage made his belly shriek with hunger. But he could not eat. The grains of rice seemed to turn to sand in his throat. He felt his son's eyes boring into his back, needling him just enough to make it impossible for him to settle in his chair.

He slammed the bowl down on the table.

"Do you want me to spoon-feed you?" he snarled.

There was a rustling behind him as Kam Shan got up. It sounded as if the boy tottered for a moment before finding his feet. Then he came over, filled a bowl for himself and sat down silently to eat. Ah-Fat looked up and suddenly saw a thread of congealing blood in his son's nostrils. The blood was inky-dark in colour. Ah-Fat almost retched, and felt the rice grains which had stuck in his throat wriggle upwards like maggots. He made as if to give his handkerchief to his son; his hand was already in his pocket, his thumb and forefinger had hold of the fabric. But his hand suddenly flagged. The handkerchief felt like a lead weight and he could not move it.

Oh, Ah-Yin, he groaned silently, feeling close to tears. He and Kam Shan were like two ancient, flint-hard rocks pressed together under the weight of a mountain. Six Fingers could have kept them apart, he thought, prying open a tiny crack. That little space would be life-giving; without it, he and his son would be condemned forever to a stalemate.

He suddenly missed Six Fingers terribly.

From that day on, Ah-Fat sent Loong Am with Kam Shan when he went to market and impressed on him that he was to stick with Kam Shan every step of the way. Kam Shan got up early and came home early, and the money he brought back more or less added up. Ah-Fat secretly felt that he could do with a few thrashings, it made him a man. He gradually relaxed.

He was soon to discover how wrong he was.

The patch of land he had bought two years before, through the crops it grew and the beasts it pastured, had brought him several surprisingly fat bank drafts. And when, in spring, his Italian neighbours decided to sell their property and to live with their son in the Prairie region, he was able to buy them out at the kind of knock-down price he had only dreamed of. His new purchase gave him a property several times bigger than before. He could stand at the field edge and not see the far boundary. Today he stood looking across the land; it had just rained and the leaves of the crops drooped low, covering the ground in an unbroken carpet of green. This was not last year's green, it was the fresh green of the new year. Ah-Fat sighed comfortably. What a vast place Gold Mountain was. A piece of land this big could have fed many people back in Hoi Ping. Even the biggest landlord there did not have this much.

And there was the house too, of course. The Italians had done a good job building it. The upper floor was of wood, but the ground floor was solidly constructed of red brick. It would have been hard to find even one sturdy, well-built house like this in the whole of Chinatown. It would not stay empty for long. He would write to Six Fingers, reminding her to get the matchmaker to find a bride for Kam Shan. In the not-too-distant future, this would be Kam Shan's new home.

But just for once, Ah-Fat did not send the money left over from buying the house and land back to Six Fingers. He put it aside for Ah-Lam, who was now a broken old man. Only the husk of the man remained; he was rotting away on the inside like a worm-infested apple. Who knew how much longer he might last? He did not want Ah-Lam to die in Gold

Mountain so he planned to take him home after the coming harvest, and to get Kam Shan betrothed at the same time. He would use the leftover money for Ah-Lam's passage and pocket money. Without it, Ah-Lam would lose the respect of his son and grandchildren forever. Ah-Lam had not had an easy life, and if he could, he would ensure that Ah-Lam died in peace and dignity.

Then, just as Ah-Fat had carefully constructed his plans, a whirlwind reduced them to a heap of sand. There was absolutely nothing Ah-Fat could do to gather them up—no matter how big his hands.

It happened a week later.

Ah-Fat went to the farmers' market in Vancouver that day, taking a pig and a sheep and some eggs. Selling his goods was not his sole intention. He planned to take Kam Shan on a trip to Vancouver. When he was not at the market, or eating or sleeping, his son sat by the stove in their shack, scooping handfuls of pumpkin seeds into his mouth. He already had little nicks in his front teeth from cracking them. He said little to his father, and sometimes went for days at a time without uttering a single complete sentence. Ah-Fat was beginning to worry that he might be growing ill. Today's trip was intended to give Kam Shan a day out.

Ah-Fat had planned the day carefully. They would sell what they could in the morning market, and then leave. The weather was not so hot that the meat and eggs would spoil. Any leftover meat could be salted down and the eggs pickled for them to eat at home. The market was not far from the city centre and they could be there in under half an hour. He would not bother with Chinatown; they would go and look around the *yeung fan* part of town instead. They were meeting Rick for lunch at a fish and chips restaurant near the Vancouver Hotel.

He had not seen Rick since he left Vancouver. According to Rick, the restaurant was run by Irish people and the food was not bad. Ah-Fat did not have much faith in this recommendation because *yeung fan* and Chinese tastes in food were a million miles apart. He guessed the fish would probably have cheese and onions in it, as this was the sort of rank-tasting stuff that was added to all *yeung fan* food, and that they would get two tiny slices of fish reposing on a thick layer of greens, only enough to fill a bird's belly. All the same, Ah-Fat was willing to eat it, however disgusting it was, because Kam Shan had not yet tried foreign food. Nor had he met Rick. Ah-Fat packed two pork ribs with a nice mixture of fat and lean, and a basket of eggs as a gift for his friend.

It did not matter if they did not get enough fish to eat. Ah-Fat was going prepared—with a bottle of tea wrapped in a thick cloth to keep it warm, and some green bean cakes, so that his son would not go hungry. After lunch, he planned to take Kam Shan to the Hudson's Bay Company Department Store. If a couple of things took Kam Shan's fancy, so long as they were not wildly expensive, Ah-Fat could buy them for him.

The pig and the sheep had been butchered the night before. The piteous squeals of the pig and the bleating of the sheep grated on Kam Shan's ears as painfully as a nicked and rusty knife and he could not get back to sleep. Father and son could not have been more different: Ah-Fat, as a boy, would sit without moving a muscle, his eyes glued to the knife as his father did his butchering, but Kam Shan always refused the meat from the animals his father slaughtered.

Kam Shan smelt the reek of blood the minute he dressed and stepped outside that morning. It was no longer fresh but just as pungent, and there were suspicious patches of a dark brownish colour under the walnut tree outside the door. Kam Shan gave an almighty sneeze. Acid came up from his empty belly, and he squatted at the edge of the path, retching violently.

"If you don't get going right now, we'll be selling salted meat instead of fresh!" Ah-Fat shouted at him.

Ah-Fat was appalled at his own words. He had intended to say something like "Let's go. When we've sold the meat, I'm taking you for a treat." But those words died in this throat. Off his tongue rolled something completely different—strange, icy and wounding. He wanted to take it back the moment he said it. He did not know why his mouth fought his mind every time he talked to his son.

Kam Shan said nothing. He went into the house, brought out an old quilt, and threw it into the cart. Spring nights were still cold hereabouts and if by any chance a cart wheel broke on the way home, the quilt could save their lives. Kam Shan leaned against the rolled-up quilt and handed the whip to his father—every time father and son went out together,

Ah-Fat took the reins. He was convinced Kam Shan was hot-headed and drove the horse too hard. It was an old horse, no longer as sure-footed as it had been, and Ah-Fat felt sorry for it.

The road was lined with silver birch, the dark trunks blurring into one another against the glazed blue of the sky, as they passed. A great flock of crows flew up, darkening the sky with their wings and cawing loudly. "The Cantonese call people who say unlucky things 'crows'," commented Ah-Fat. "And back home the caw of a crow is considered a bad omen. In Gold Mountain, the cities are full of crows and no one gives a shit when they caw."

Kam Shan grunted but said nothing.

"I'll take you to the department store after lunch, shall I? What would you like me to get you?" said Ah-Fat, keen to get the conversation going. Kam Shan was making a paper bird, a sparrow hawk, out of some scrap and, without looking up, said: "Whatever you say, Dad." "What about if I get you a pair of leather shoes?" Ah-Fat tried again. Kam Shan had been wearing the cotton shoes Six Fingers made for him ever since he arrived. But fashionable young Chinese in Gold Mountain wore *yeung fan* leather shoes.

Kam Shan finished folding the bird but its wings were floppy and it would not fly. He pulled it apart and folded it again. "Whatever you want, Dad" was his only reply.

"Would you like to buy Pastor Andrew a box of chocolates?" asked Ah-Fat. "He's taught you English but you've never converted, have you?"

Kam Shan finally finished folding his paper bird and opened it out gently with two fingers. Its wings flapped up and down.

"Whatever you like, Dad."

Looking at Kam Shan's apathetic expression, Ah-Fat found his patience wearing thin. With difficulty he bit back an angry retort. He knew that if he spoke he would give his son a thorough tongue-lashing, and he was not going to quarrel today. So he swallowed the bitter words—and felt them turn to gall inside him.

Kam Shan tired of the paper bird and, with a wave of his hand, let it go. It was a fine day and the bird glided easily for some distance on the breeze.

"Dad, can we buy Mum a ring? A 'grandmother green' emerald one? Pastor Andrew's wife has one. Her mother left it to her," he said.

Ah-Fat was taken aback. The bitterness that filled him dissolved like water. His son had been apart from his mother for months. Fathers give sons courage; mothers give sons love, thought Ah-Fat. A life without motherly love was a comfortless one. Poor Kam Shan missed the old days, his home and his mum. And if he missed his mother, then he was not a lost cause. Six Fingers would come to Gold Mountain one day, and Kam Shan would have both courage and love. And he would no longer feel like a stranger to Ah-Fat.

Ah-Fat could not bring himself to say that the money he had in his pocket was not enough to buy even one corner of an emerald ring. So he just laughed and said: "One day, we will, one day...." He suddenly felt much more cheerful. Nine suns seemed to be shining down on him, making the roadway glint and sparkle. As the cart rolled on, he found himself humming a little song. He had forgotten some of the words and sang out of tune, but his happiness gave it a rollicking rhythm.

You say words of love, but love must be sincere
Do not spread your love all around
The snares of love have fallen ... ta-ta, ta-ta
You've got to ... ta-rum, ta-rum ... wake up

They arrived at the market to find business unusually brisk. Within an hour or so, they sold all their produce. They still had some time before they were due to meet Rick, so Ah-Fat took his son to Chinatown, where they could buy some pastries to take home. Ah-Fat went into the cake shop to choose. "Dad," said Kam Shan, "I want to go and read the papers at the stand." Ah-Fat let him go, knowing how much his son loved the newspapers. "Just don't be long. I'll wait for you here."

But Kam Shan did not come back.

Kam Shan had not been to Chinatown on his own for a while. There were some new broadsheets on display on the stand. His eyes raked over every item—art and culture, wars, home and overseas news—looking for a particular name, Freedom Fung. It was not there.

Two long articles took up almost all of the politics pages—the Monarchists and the Revolutionaries were waging a rhetorical war. The article from the Revolutionaries' perspective was by a supporter he did not know; he read it cursorily but thought little of it. It was disjointed and crudely expressed. The only person who could write a decent piece of this sort was Mr. Fung, thought Kam Shan; his articles were lucidly argued, and no matter whether he was expressing indignation or sarcasm, they were all powerful stuff.

He left the newspaper stand to return to the cake shop to meet his father. Halfway there, he passed a sign for the offices of the *The Chinese Times*, and found himself stepping inside. An old man who did odd jobs around the office shouted over to him: "Kam Shan! We haven't seen you for ages! Been making your fortune, have you?" Kam Shan did not answer the question, but asked instead: "Where's Mr. Fung?" "He's not here today. He's got guests." "They must be very important guests if he's not writing for the paper any more!" exclaimed Kam Shan. "Without his articles, the paper's no good for anything except wiping your arse with!" The old man burst out laughing. "Don't let the boss catch you talking like that or he'll wallop you," he said. Then he pulled the boy aside and whispered: "The Cudgel's here from the States, he's raising money for some big plan of his, and he's taken Mr. Fung around with him on his lecture tour." The Cudgel was boss of the Hung Mun, a Chinese secret society.

Kam Shan knew everyone at the *Times*. After reading Mr. Fung's articles, Kam Shan had been filled with curiosity and admiration and had gone to pay his respects to Mr. Fung at his office. Later still, when he heard the man expound his views on the political situation in East and West, he grew to believe that Mr. Fung was the only man in Gold Mountain worthy of his respect and friendship. From that moment on, every time he went into Vancouver to sell their produce, he sent Loong Am off to the theatre and took himself to the *Times* to see Mr. Fung.

Mr. Fung was not only highly educated, he was eloquent and charismatic as well. As he put it, the Manchu (Qing) dynasty took resources that properly belonged to the Chinese people and used them to appease the Western powers. The dynasty's days were numbered. According to Mr. Fung, the most important task facing them—destroying the Manchu barbarians and returning China to the Chinese—could not be accomplished without the support of overseas Chinese living all over the world. Mr. Fung's eyes blazed like two lanterns on a dark night when he spoke, and his impassioned speeches set Kam Shan on fire.

Though Kam Shan read the newspapers, he did not fully understand Chinese national politics. He did not doubt, however, that Mr. Fung's campaign was brilliantly clever. He started to filch small change from the proceeds of the produce to put in the collection box at the newspaper office. Mr. Fung always counted Kam Shan's donations carefully, wrote him out a receipt for the "loan" and told him that he would get double the amount back once the revolution succeeded. Kam Shan smiled but his thoughts were not on repayment. He gave because Mr. Fung inspired him. The revolution was a far-off, hazy prospect for Kam Shan, out of sight and out of mind. Mr. Fung made him feel as if he could reach it, but the vision dimmed as soon as he stepped out of the *Times* office and into the street. As the sweat-stained receipts filled his jacket pocket, he wondered how he could ever explain to his dad where the money had gone.

Kam Shan knew that Mr. Fung was a Hung Mun secret society member, and that the *Times* was a Hung Mun newspaper. If the head of the Hung Mun, called the Cudgel, had come to Vancouver that meant something significant was going to happen. "What's the Cudgel's name?" he asked excitedly. "Sun Yat-sen," said the old man. Kam Shan remembered having read the name frequently in Mr. Fung's articles. "Where are they now?" he asked. "Giving a lecture in the theatre in Canton Street. There are thousands of people there." All thoughts of meeting his father at the cake shop immediately went out of Kam Shan's head, and he pushed open the door and raced off down the street.

As he hitched up his gown and ran, he did not notice the dense clouds massing like cotton wool above his head. The wind blew up eddies of dust, tickling his nostrils. But Kam Shan ran on, unaware that fate was drawing him deep into an abyss, trapping him in a predicament for which he was completely unprepared.

When he got to the door of the theatre, the sky opened. All of a sudden, it poured down so intensely that not even the most agile of passersby could avoid the deluge. One of Kam Shan's feet was over the threshold of the theatre when the rain started, but the rain caught his back foot, and by the time it crossed the threshold to join the first, his gown was drenched. It was of rough blue cotton, stoutly sewn, but the dye was not fast and the rain made the colour run. As the rainwater dripped from it, Kam Shan left a river of blue water behind him. Once inside the building, Kam Shan dropped the hem of his gown and wiped the rain from his face with one hand, smearing it a ghastly indigo as he did so.

The theatre was full to bursting with people standing in the aisles, but they all fell back as this blue apparition approached. So Kam Shan squeezed his way through, and found a place to stand near a pillar. He rested against it, and suddenly felt cold. The wet gown seemed to encase him in a layer of ice which needled him all over. Very soon, he felt an urgent need to piss.

The urge impinged on his consciousness, bluntly at first, but then gradually became more and more acute until he could stand it no longer. He was overcome by a fit of shivering—and then something seemed to snap. He felt a warm dampness in the crotch of his trousers. If I go just a tiny bit, he thought to himself, then it'll let up and I'll be able to hang on.

But once unlocked, the floodgates opened; all he could do was cross his legs tightly as the warm urine ran down his legs to his ankles, and then dripped from his trouser cuffs onto the floor. The cloudy yellow of the urine mixed with the indigo dye and trickled in a zigzag down the aisle. It reeked to Kam Shan, but when he looked around, he was relieved to see that none of his neighbours, engrossed in the speeches, had noticed.

He could relax now, though he was still cold. If he stood on tiptoe, he could see the whole stage. On it stood half a dozen men, all of whom were in Western dress except for one, who wore a gown and jacket. Kam Shan recognized Mr. Fung on the stage. He had never seen the others before. The man in the middle was speaking. He was a bit older, of middling height and sported a thick, black moustache. Next to him stood a strapping figure with a gun at his waist, probably his bodyguard. He spoke in Cantonese, so that everyone understood, and was giving a fiery, rabble-rousing speech.

"The people long for Chinese rule. It is heaven's wish that the barbarians should fall and the revolution should succeed. It will happen very soon.... As we make preparations now, we urgently need to raise funds so that we can carry forward the great common enterprise of returning China to the Chinese. The survival of our country depends on this. The revolutionary army will throw itself into battle...."

With every sentence, the crowd roared in response and, as the speaker grew more and more hoarse, the crowd's responses grew more enthusiastic. Then at the climax of the speech, the man in the Chinese gown drew a pair of scissors from the front of his gown, took off his cap and pulled up his pigtail to its full extent; the scissors snipped through it. The long rope of hair fell like a headless snake, writhed a couple of times on the ground and then unravelled. Its owner brandished the scissors at the audience below and shouted: "The revolution starts here and now! Anyone who wants to follow the revolution, take these scissors from me!"

The frenzied crowd stilled all of a sudden, as if the heart had gone out of it. Until the scissors had made their appearance, revolution had sounded like a splendid adventure, one which made men's pulses race with excitement but which was, like a roll of thunder on the horizon, still a distant prospect. The scissors had cut away that distance and revolution was right before them. They had to take it up or run away—there was no middle ground.

The scissors wavered at the front of the stage, still a long way from where Kam Shan stood, chilled to the marrow. Then, as he sniffed, he was suddenly shaken by an enormous sneeze that reverberated like a thunderclap around the auditorium. The eyes of the speaker fell on him.

"You're wet through, young brother, have you come far?"

Kam Shan was startled. It was only when his neighbours gave him a shove that he realized that the man called Mr. Sun was speaking to him from the stage. All eyes in the room now fell on him, their gaze as intense as the beams of hundreds of lanterns. Kam Shan's wet gown gave off puffs of steam and his forehead beaded with drops of sweat. His lips trembled a few times but no sound came out.

"Are you in the Hung Mun?" asked Mr. Sun.

As he stammered, Mr. Fung went over to Mr. Sun and whispered something in his ear. The latter burst out laughing.

"He's not a Hung Mun man but the donations he's made to the revolution are just as generous as any member's. Brother, are you willing to join the Hung Mun now?"

Kam Shan hesitated, but then saw Mr. Fung gesturing to him from the stage. Mr. Fung was gently rapping his own chest with his fist, but Kam Shan felt the fist was falling on him, and something fiery hot surged in his heart.

"Yes, I am."

He heard himself say the words and was astonished. They seemed not to have come from inside but to have been stuffed into his mouth by someone else.

Nonetheless, they could not be taken back.

The man brandishing the scissors leapt from the stage, seized Kam Shan's pigtail and shouted: "This young brother has started the revolution. Those who enter the Hung Mun take an oath never to join the ranks of the Qing government!" Kam Shan felt his scalp tighten, then relax. His head felt suddenly so light it might have flown from his body.

There was a collective gasp, and a yell: "Revolution! Revolution!" The single shout, like a rock falling into a shallow pond, made rippling waves which spread outwards as if they would flood and crash through the auditorium walls. The scissors were passed from one head to another, and the hall filled with the sound of chopping. No one paid any more attention to Kam Shan, who was squatting on the ground.

He clutched his severed pigtail so tightly he might have been trying to wring water from it. At that moment, he remembered that his father was waiting for him at the cake shop. When he left home with him that morning, he was a whole, complete person. He had taken one step astray and, in so doing, had lost a vitally important part of his body. If he had lost a hand or a foot, even an eye, he could have gone back to his father and owned up. But he had lost his pigtail, which was nothing less than his father's heart and his pride. His father could not live without his heart and his pride.

Kam Shan pushed his way through the roaring crowds and stumbled into the street. The rain had stopped but the sky was still covered in a mass of heavy clouds. "Revolution ... revolution...." The cries found their way out of the theatre and were audible in the street, but they seemed to have nothing to do with him any more. Now that he had left Mr. Fung and the seething crowds inside, the revolution had once more become something vague and distant. The thing that came into sharp focus was his father's face: the livid centipede of the scar, and the lines that appeared on his forehead when he laughed.

"Please God, make me lame or blind but give me back my pigtail!" There was something cold and wet on Kam Shan's face. Tears, he realized. For the first time in his life, Kam Shan knew what dread was.

Duty made him want to return to his father as soon as possible, but shame took him in the opposite direction, farther and farther from the cake shop, farther and farther from Chinatown itself. The next thing he knew, he was on the riverbank.

He heard footsteps behind him at some distance, rustling as if tiptoeing across a pile of rice straw. Then they came nearer, until they almost seemed to tread on his heels. Kam Shan looked round and just had time to see a black shape, before his feet left the ground and he flew through the air.

A few days later, a short news item appeared in the local Chinese newspaper:

> *Mysterious disappearance of a Chinese youth last Sunday. A passerby saw two big men in black throwing the youth into the Fraser River. We understand that the youth was attending a Hung Mun fundraising event in the Canton Street Theatre in Chinatown and then fell victim to a plot by local Monarchists. A week has passed with no news and it is not expected that he has survived.*

> . . . .

> *We have reasons to believe, as an inferior race, the Indians must make way for a race more enlightened and better fitted to perform the task of converting what is now wilderness into productive fields and happy homes.*

British Columbia Colonial News, *9 June 1861*

Sundance awoke feeling a great weight on her eyelids. The sunlight was as heavy as honey, and it reminded her that springtime had come. She got out of bed, put on leather boots, a sturdy linen skirt and a deerskin cloak dyed ochre yellow. She could tell it was a fine day; she could hear the river burbling past outside the window and smell the faint aroma of mallard duck droppings wafting in on the breeze. The long wilderness winter was over. It had been quite a mild one; the river had not frozen over, so her father had been able to paddle his canoe into town to make purchases any time he chose.

Her dad had learned canoe-making from the ancestors, and he was famous throughout the entire region. His canoes were hollowed out of the best redwood logs, some longer than a house. They had a flat, straight body, a deep belly and two heads raised high at prow and stern. Sometimes he would carve these into an eagle's head, sometimes into a mallard's beak. Her dad never allowed anyone to watch him working on his canoes, not even her mother.

Before he began a canoe, he would perform the ram's horn dance, chant a hymn to the ancestors and give thanks to all the spirits of the heavens: the earth, the wind, the trees and the water. In tribute to his workmanship, members of the tribe would say not that he was skilful, but that he chanted well. Only he could move the spirits of his ancestors with his chanting so that the ancestors became the knife and axe in his hand. When someone wanted a canoe made, they came to him with gifts for the ancestors; game and waterfowl hung from the ceiling of their home all year round. The Chief himself would respectfully offer him three cigarettes whenever they met.

A cowhide bag hung from the tree outside their door. It was not one of theirs; her mother's stitching was much neater. Sundance opened the bag. Inside were a bright yellow cloak and a collection of necklaces, bracelets and anklets made of cowry shells and animal bone. The cloak was made of the best deerhide and little silvery bells hung from the hem. The bell in the middle had a strawberry carved on it.

Sundance held the cloak against herself tightly. It was just the kind of cloak she liked. The little bells shook themselves free and jingled cheerfully in the morning air. It was not the first time Sundance had seen gifts like these. She'd turned fourteen this New Year and since then, a series of gifts had begun to appear outside her home. She knew which family this bag had come from, and she also knew that if she accepted it, a man would turn up one evening, walk proudly into her house and sit down at the hearth. Then he would lead her by the hand to another home.

Sundance gazed longingly at the gifts. She had no intention of accepting them because she did not want to move to anyone's house just yet. She wanted to be left in peace to enjoy the pleasures of being fourteen. She sighed regretfully, then folded the cloak and put it back in the bag. Provided she did not take the bag into her house, it would be retrieved by its owner by the following morning. And when he and she bumped into each other in the future, they would smile and greet each other as if nothing had happened.

Waterfowl skimmed the surface of the river, the sounds of their beating wings echoing in the still air of the village. It was Sunday and most of the tribe were in church. Her mother and younger brothers and sisters had gone too. The priest was a White man. When he first arrived, none of the tribe members wanted to convert to the White man's religion, but after the Chief was converted, the others had followed suit. It happened like this: one day his wife became possessed by demons; she rolled around on the floor of their house, foaming at the mouth, and bit off half her tongue. The tribe's healer and the shaman tried to rid her of the demons without success. The priest then brought out a little bottle, poured a spoonful of pink liquid and forced it between her lips. Her fits stopped immediately. "What's that magic bottle that chased the demons out of her?" asked the Chief. "It's not the bottle that expelled her demons," replied the priest. "It's a spirit called Jesus." And so the Chief was converted.

Sundance was waiting for her father to come home. That was why she had not gone to church with the others. She would help him tie up the boat and unload the things he had bought. He paddled into town to barter dried salmon and reed mats for rice and charcoal. Last year, great shoals of salmon beached themselves in the shallows. Sundance and her mother spent days drying the fish on a rock at the riverbank. The fish hung in strips from the ceiling, as crowded as dancers at a powwow. Her father had gone two days ago, and was expected back today. Sundance and her mother had asked him to buy them each a little black hat with a brim, of the sort that fashionable White women wore in the city.

The priest knew perfectly well that waiting for her father was just an excuse. Sundance did not want to spend a warm, sunny Sunday listening to the priest's dry sermons about God. To Sundance, God was as free as the wind and the clouds and did not like being cooped up inside. She knew she was more likely to find God in a bird's wing than in church. When she made her excuses, the priest did not try to force her; he knew that she could trounce his arguments with a single pronouncement, ready to trip off her tongue when the need arose. So the priest treated her with some caution.

"My grandfather was baptized before your father was even born" was what she might say—but did not.

Sundance's grandfather was English. He had arrived by ship several decades before, sent by the Hudson's Bay Company to open up a trading post in the Fraser River valley. He bartered goods like matches, kerosene, bedding, needles, thread and pipe tobacco with the local Indian tribes for skins and pelts. He was not the first White man to have come to the West coast to trade with the Indians. His predecessors had had dealings with the Indians too. From these White men, the tribes had quickly learned a few business tricks like mixing good and poor-quality goods, price fixing and holding back merchandise to hike up the price. So to ensure a stable supply of goods, Sundance's grandfather allied himself with a local Indian chief by marrying his daughter, even though he already had a wife in England.

Sundance's grandfather lived in British Columbia for fifteen years and had seven children with his Indian wife. When the time came for him to retire and return to England, he told her to move to the city so that their children could go to a White school and get the best possible education. The wife did as she was bid, but before many months had passed, she returned to her tribe. She could not settle in the city; the sound of drums beat in her ears day and night and she knew that her ancestors were calling her back home. So back she went.

When Sundance's grandmother returned to her tribe, after months in the city, and years in a White marriage, she discovered a large number of children who looked very much like her own. They were the children of the White men, conceived as they passed like a whirlwind over Indian territory. The mothers often gathered together to talk about their menfolk on the other side of the ocean. On these occasions, Sundance's grandmother would say little, and would come home to impress on each of her children that they were not the same as the others. "Your father was sent by the great Hudson's Bay Company. He once had a personal audience with Queen Victoria." The marks left on her by fifteen years of marriage could not be erased; although she had returned to her own people, she found herself a stranger among them.

She never remarried. Her English husband had left her quite comfortable and she did not need to go looking for another man, unlike the other women. He never returned once he had left British Columbia. Sundance's father, the youngest of his children, was only a toddler learning to talk when he left. He had no memory of him. But it became Sundance's grandmother's mission to keep her husband present, her words like a hatchet rigorously chipping away until he was permanently carved into her children's memories.

Those memories trickled gently into the bloodstreams of her grandchildren too. She lived to a great age, and even witnessed the birth of a great-grandchild. Long before that, though, she went through the money left her by her husband, and spent the rest of her life struggling, like the rest of her tribe. Still, she wore a satisfied smile, knowing that she had fulfilled her mission: her children's children and their children would keep the memories of that man alive a hundred years.

The sun was very bright and Sundance shaded her eyes with her hand. She could see far into the distance to where the redwood trees looked no bigger than a row of nuts. There, around the riverbend at the end of the village, was where her father would emerge. She heard the sharp cry of a bird in the pine tree by her door. Though it was hidden in the gloom of the branches, Sundance knew it was a blue jay. Her father said that her hearing was sharper than an elk's.

"What are you trying to tell me? Is my dad coming?" Sundance asked, looking upward.

The bird was silent. But the branches rustled a little. Sundance could not help chuckling. Holding her hair to one side, she lay down and pinned her ear to the ground to listen. When the canoe rounded the bend, she would be able to hear the ripple of the water on the paddle. There were members of the tribe who had bought something called a motor which they put in the belly of the boat and Sundance had heard that this made the canoe grow legs and walk in the water, but her father was unimpressed. The paddle was the spirit of the canoe; without its spirit, what could the boat do?

Sundance lay listening quietly and gradually a thread of sound came to her ears, a humming noise. She knew it was the Great Earth sighing. The Earth had been asleep for too long and needed to turn over. When that happened, the grass would green, the flowers would open, the brown bear and the elk would come out of the forests and the blue jay would no longer need to skulk amid the dark branches.

But today she was not listening for the Earth's sounds.

She was about to stand up again, disappointed, when her ear caught another tiny sound, a sort of hushing noise, which brought with it a hint of warmth as it brushed her eardrum.

The sound of her father's paddle in the water.

Sundance leapt to her feet in excitement, hitched up her skirts and ran towards the riverbend. Once she reached him, they would race each other home, he in the canoe, she along the riverbank.

The blue jay suddenly flew up out of the pine tree and circled low around her head. Sundance flicked one end of her belt at the bird and it retreated a little, then came back to follow close behind. Sundance's heart gave a thud. Her father had said that the day her grandmother died, a blue jay kept circling round his head.

Sundance picked up a stone and tossed it at the jay, hitting her wing. She gave a loud squawk and flew away lopsidedly. Sundance began to run fast, but the wind was a nuisance, entangling her legs in her skirt and blowing her hair in her eyes. But she knew every tree root and every stone along the way. Even without eyes, Sundance could have found the exact place where her father would round the bend in the river.

Sundance stopped and picked a withered reed to tie back her hair. In the distance, she saw the hazy shape of her father's canoe, floating slowly towards her like a mallard duck. She cupped her hands over her mouth and shouted:

"Dad!"

The redwoods caught the sound, and sent it back in mighty echoes all around her.

She could see the canoe more clearly now. It seemed heavier than usual; the neck of the carved mallard's head sunk low in the water, so that only the bright red beak was visible.

Sundance jumped onto a rock, and could see at a glance that there were a number of large sacks in the canoe—goods which her dad had bartered for in the city. Rice, charcoal, perhaps green vegetables, even candy. There might even be two small black hats with upturned brims.

Sundance's gaze was caught by something else in the boat, and her brow furrowed in astonishment.

Among the sacks, dressed in a strange blue cotton gown, sprawled a body.

He was hot, so hot. From the soles of his feet to the hair on his head, his entire body was stuck to a burning hot sheet of iron and the fat was melting off him, just like the lard oozed from the pig when his mother cooked it at New Year.

Water, water…

Kam Shan opened his eyes, to see a red light in front of him—a firepit. Beside it floated something large and round. Gradually his eyes focused and he saw it was the face of a girl. High cheekbones, deep-set eye sockets, thick lips. A stranger. He could not think of anyone he knew who looked like that. The thought made his head ache. He groaned with a voice as reedy as the whine of a mosquito: "Porridge … is there any porridge?"

The girl stared at him uncomprehendingly. Kam Shan saw she was wearing a deerskin cloak, fringed at the neck and hem. A Redskin. She was a Redskin, though she looked a little like a Chinese. No wonder she could not understand what he said.

Oh God, he had fallen into the hands of Redskins!

He had heard stories of Redskins—how they scalped people, dug out their hearts, made necklaces of human teeth. His own experience of them in the market did not support these claims, but the beads of sweat on him instantly chilled and his hair stood on end.

He shut his eyes again. He did not want to die at the hands of these Redskins. It had never occurred to him when he and Ah-Lam's wife boarded the steamship last year that they might both wind up dead in Gold Mountain. His dad had not scraped together all that money for the head tax for him to die within the year.

There was more noise in the room now, a scuffling sound which might be leather boots on the mud floor, or a knife being pulled from its sheath. There were voices too, male and female. He could not understand a word. Kam Shan knew they were gathering around him because he could feel heavy breathing on his face.

Oh help me, my Emperor ... Kwan Kung ... Tam Gung ... merciful Kuan Yam ... Jesus ... Saint Paul ... Saint Peter. Kam Shan summoned up all the deities he could think of. If you get me out of this, I swear I'll make you a gold statue, I swear I won't make Dad angry any more, I'll write to Mum every month, I won't steal Dad's money ever again, I swear....

But it was no use. He felt the knife blade on his forehead. Strangely, it did not hurt. It felt rough and scratchy, a bit like sandpaper on his skin.

If you're going to kill me then do it with one slash, I can't stand pain, I really can't stand pain....

His prayer was silent but his eyelids fluttered like moths' wings.

"You've been asleep for a day. It's time to wake up," said a woman's voice.

Her English was broken, but he could still understand.

His eyes sprang open. The thing that lay on his forehead was not a knife blade but a cracked and calloused hand, a woman's hand. Her face was weathered a coppery colour, and the grime that marked its creases looked like verdigris. Next to her stood a man and the round-faced girl.

"Are you awake? I'll bring you some water," said the girl, not bothering to hide her excitement. When she spoke, he could see two rows of uneven, yellowed teeth, which Kam Shan somehow found calming.

She brought water and Kam Shan gulped it all down. It left a burnt, smoky taste in his mouth. He let her take the bowl back: "Is there any more?" The girl smiled. "You mustn't drink too much at once, you've been dry for days. Have something to eat, then drink some more." The girl spoke much better English than her mother, and Kam Shan had no difficulty understanding. His belly rumbled thunderously. He was so hungry he was beyond the niceties of politeness. "Is there any porridge?" was what he wanted to say, but he did not know the word in English. What he finally said was: "Can I have rice, rice with water?"

The girl looked blank but her mother gave a broad smile. "He wants porridge," she said, using the Chinese word. "Chinese people like eating porridge with black eggs in it." It's pickled eggs, not black eggs, thought Kam Shan. He looked dully at her, his lips trembling, and said: "Anything'll do." She bent down and picked up a pair of tongs, took something from the stones in the firepit and put it in his water bowl. "It's cooked," she said. "Eat it up."

Kam Shan looked at the black thing in his bowl. It smelled burnt, like roast meat. There was no salt or oil on it but he did not care. Down it went. It was fish, he realized, and it made only the smallest dent in his hunger. He remembered how his mother and grandmother impressed on him that he must never, ever, ask for second helpings when he was a guest in someone's house, but today he did not care.

He swallowed hard a few times, enough to wet his throat and form the words "a bit more" in a parched voice. But before he could get them out, the woman had gone to the fire and came back with another piece of fish, bigger than the first, which she put into his bowl. Kam Shan ate it more slowly. There were no chopsticks so he used his fingers. His fingers felt warm, and he was aware of the girl's eyes on them. Her gaze seemed to coat them in a layer of oil. Now that he was no longer so hungry, he began to feel clumsy and flustered.

He finished the fish, bones and all. He put down the bowl and burped loudly, filling the air around him with a strong fishy smell.

He looked around him at the Redskins' home. It was long and narrow, built of rough timber with a mud floor. There was a large firepit in the middle of the floor, and beds—wooden planks covered with rush matting—at each end. He was lying on a wooden plank himself, near the door. By the firepit, the head of a huge elk hung from a wall. Branches stood propped against each other in front of the fire, and his gown hung drying on them. It was a dusty grey, which meant it was nearly dry. Under the gown he could see one blue trouser leg. *His* trouser leg.

What was he wearing? Who had taken his trousers off him? Was it the woman? Or the girl?

The thought made Kam Shan flush so hotly he could have boiled a river of water. He heard giggling. He saw several pairs of eyes peering out at him from one corner, shining a wolfish green in the lamplight. When his eyes got used to the gloom, he saw three small children sitting on a wooden bed at the end of the room, barefoot and sharing a cover between them.

"Sundance!" commanded the older woman, and the girl ran over and started to dress the children.

Sundance. The Redskin girl's name was Sundance. Pretty name, Kam Shan thought to himself.

"Where do you live? How did you end up in the river?" The man had been silent, but now he suddenly broke in. He squatted on the ground, took a burning stick from the hearth and lit a cigarette. It must be some sort of local tobacco, thought Kam Shan. The cigarette was as thick as the Redskin's thumb and the tobacco smoke burned his throat. Kam Shan remembered the man pulling him into his canoe and asking the same question.

"Not far from Vancouver," Kam Shan answered vaguely.

He did not know how to answer the second question; his English was just not up to telling such a long and complicated story. About a pigtail.

But the man was not going to let him off the hook. "And how did you end up in the river?" he persisted. "You floated a long way down."

Kam Shan's lack of English effectively smothered his flustered hesitation. There was a long silence. Finally Kam Shan said: "Fight … someone pushed me … into river."

"Why?" The man looked interested.

"Woman," Kam Shan muttered.

He startled himself with this lie. As far as women were concerned, he was a blank sheet of paper. He glanced towards the shadows but could not see Sundance's face, only her hands, busy shaking out the quilt her young siblings had been wrapped in.

The man burst out laughing and clapped Kam Shan on the shoulder. "Not much of a swimmer, are you?" he said. "I thought it was a dead seal draped over that bit of wood. Good thing your girl didn't see you looking so hangdog!"

The man threw the remains of his cigarette into the fire and flicked ash from his finger. "Sundance can find him an animal-hide coat to wear and make sure he's had enough to eat. In a couple of days, when I go back to town, I'll take him along with me and give him back to his girlfriend."

Kam Shan was horrified.

It was only many years later, when he thought back to his time with the Redskin tribe, that he realized how the casual telling of one little lie had required a whole string of lies to cover it up. It was like when his mother wrote with her brush on rice paper and accidentally spattered it with ink. To erase that almost invisible blob, you had to dilute it with so much water that it eventually covered a huge area.

At the time, Kam Shan was only sixteen, too young to think that far ahead. He was cornered and his only thought was to fight his way out as quickly as he could.

And since he could not go back on the first lie, he had to go along with it.

No way could he go home to his father, at least not now. How could he explain his bad luck? What would he say? That dark abyss, which made father and son strangers to each other, remained between them. The only thing that could help him across this abyss was a pigtail. He could only go home when that pigtail grew back.

"Thing is ... I really don't want ... see that girl again," Kam Shan said now.

"Thing is ... I got no home, I just been wandering ... place to place."

The woman was feeding the fire. She brought over a pile of branches that crackled and burned fiercely in the flames, shooting sparks in all directions. The soot brought tears to her eyes, and she wiped them on the front of her jacket. "My mum told me the Chinese who built the railroad were like you. They came from so far away, but wherever the railroad ended up, they made that their home," she said.

"Can I live with you for a bit? I can, I can work...." said Kam Shan, not looking at the man. He was addressing the woman as he spoke. She had a soft heart; he could see that in her eyes.

The woman did not answer, just stared at the man. The man did not answer either but sat there absorbed in pulling at a callus on his palm. There was a sudden stillness at the end of the room as Sundance's hand paused in mid-air. Kam Shan's heart thudded so loudly he thought the whole room must have heard it.

"What can you do?" the man asked, finally looking up.

Kam Shan was stumped once more. What could he do? He could not fish, hunt, plait reeds or smoke meat. He could not do anything that the Redskin men did, or anything that the women did either. The truth was that away from his father, he could not even feed himself.

Suddenly he saw some big sacks piled against the wall. They contained the things the man had brought back from town yesterday. In the Vancouver and New Westminster farmers' markets, he had seen Redskins bartering their produce for other things they needed. Kam Shan's eyes lit up.

"Charcoal! I can make charcoal!" he exclaimed.

That was another lie. He had watched Mak Dau make charcoal back in Spur-On Village. But it was enough. Redskins were stupid: they had entire forests but they were willing to barter their excellent smoked fish for charcoal.

The woman did not wait for the man to reply. She jumped to her feet and yelled in the direction of the shadows at the end of the room: "Sundance, when the weather clears up, take him to the forest to cut wood."

An odd sort of rain fell at that time of year. It did not slant down or fall in drops, or even drizzle. Still, when you were outdoors, you only had to hold out your palm for it to fill with water. As the rain fell, the earth became saturated; the trees in the forest plumped out, and the walls and mud floors grew moss. Finally one day the sun came out and, bursting with energy after its long sleep, slurped up the moisture in the air and underfoot. When the people came outside, they found everything thick with greenery.

With the coming of spring, the missionaries got busy. (The Redskins called them God's men and God's women because though many were taught English, they could not get their tongues around the words "priests" and "lady missionaries.") With winter ended, God's men started classes again and all children under fourteen had to go to school. The Chief's children set the example, and the other children followed it. God's women were not idle either: they gathered the women of the village together and taught them spinning and knitting. "The men have ways of earning their living, and women need ways too. So when you don't have a man, you can feed yourselves."

The Redskin women did not understand. How could a woman not have a man? If you lost one, you got another. If a woman had to provide her own food, then what on earth was a man for? The Redskin women thought that God's women were pretty daft. No wonder they could never get a man. But although they looked down on God's women, they were entranced by their knitting. They had never before seen such colours and styles, felt such woolly softness and warmth. So God's women were never short of students.

Sundance did not need to go to school with her younger siblings or to knitting classes with her mother. She was too old for the school and too young for the knitting, so she was free to please herself.

Today she sat on the great rock in front of their door, sharpening hatchets.

She had two of them, one short and one long, both used for cutting wood. The long one was for cutting down branches, the short one for clearing low undergrowth. For the whole winter the hatchets had lain in their animal-hide sheaths without ever seeing the light of day. Sundance had been occupied in two quite different activities: smoking strips of salmon and making jam. She used two big bagfuls of berries harvested in the autumn for the jam. She made enough to fill an oak bucket; the family skimmed off the top for themselves and her father took the rest to sell in town. So for the whole winter, Sundance—hands, hair and all—reeked alternately of smoked fish and jam. This happened every winter and she did not object. It was just the way things were—until this year, that is. Suddenly she was sick of smelling of fish. Last night, as she lay down to sleep, she had heard the humming of her hatchets in their sheaths, and knew that both she and they were missing the woods.

While she sharpened the hatchets, her father collected his fishing rods. He'd heard the call last night too. He missed the water, just like she missed the forests. Today he would paddle to the middle of the river where the water was deepest and warmest. There the trout had slept all winter and would be eager to take the bait. The men in the tribe did not know how to plant crops or rear livestock, they could only hunt and fish. They got their rice and fresh vegetables by bartering fish and game in town.

Just before her father left the house, he put some strips of smoked venison into Sundance's leather bag. "Don't go too far today," he said, "just to the edge of the forest. A brown bear is at its most ferocious when it's hungry after its winter's sleep. If you meet one, throw it a bit of meat. If you do run, run behind it. Bears have big bellies and are too clumsy to turn round. When you're chopping down trees, keep an eye out for birds' and bees' nests. Birds are nearest to the spirits of our ancestors so you must never touch their nests. And if you see any bees' nests, keep at least fifty paces away from them too."

Sundance interrupted him, laughing: "Dad, it's not the first time I've been to the forest to cut wood." "Yes, you know, but he doesn't," said her father, meaning Kam Shan.

The wakened forest still held the dampness of winter. Kam Shan put on Sundance's father's thin hide jacket and deerskin boots, and followed Sundance. The girl cleared a way through the undergrowth chopping down branches which had died during the winter. She left the new growth alone, knowing that with a few days' sunshine, they would be covered in thick greenery. She threw the branches behind her so that Kam Shan could cut them into smaller pieces with the short axe. But Kam Shan struggled to wield it properly and very soon his palms were covered in blisters. Sundance gave him some twine so he could tie the sticks into bundles. But the twine cut into the blisters and became soaked with blood.

Sundance snickered. "You lied to my dad. You can't chop wood and make charcoal." Kam Shan threw down the hatchet and the twine and sat down on the bundles of sticks. "I can," he said lamely. "I can make charcoal, I just can't chop wood. When I was at home, I mean in China, all our firewood was chopped by the servants." "What's a servant?" asked Sundance. "People who work for you." "Oh, I know, you mean slaves. My dad says that in the old days when our tribe fought other tribes, if the other tribe lost, they left people behind to work for us." Kam Shan wanted to say no, it's not that, but his English was still halting and he could not express himself. So he just nodded vaguely and said: "Pretty much like that." "How could your mum and dad let you leave home?" asked Sundance. "Mine wouldn't let me go far away on my own."

Kam Shan did not know what to say.

Was his mother sorry to see him go? She never said. She just got the best tailor in the village, Mr. Au, to come and spend five days making clothes for him. But she did not sit idly by. She sewed cotton socks. As she worked, she kept her eye on the tailor, watching him so intently that she stabbed her finger with the needle, leaving a drop of blood as big as a pearl on the snowy-white cotton of the socks. Ah-Choi had said: "Wash it quickly. After it dries it won't come out." But his mother said: "No, I'll leave it as a memento for Kam Shan."

His mother had made the tailor cut every garment several sizes too big. "Kam Shan's still growing. And after these clothes are worn out, the next ones we make for him will be a bridegroom's clothes." As she'd said the words, her voice cracked suddenly, like a dry branch thrown on the fire. His granny had sighed: "Too bad you'll lose your son when you get a daughter-in-law," she said. Kam Shan knew this remark was directed at his mother; it was the sort of thing his granny often said to her, but his mother always turned a deaf ear.

His grandmother sat with the tailor too, staring with unseeing eyes and propped against the wall, her hand-warmer clasped in one hand, the other hand holding a box of snacks. The box held green bean cakes and sweet-potato pancakes, freshly made and gently steaming. Still, she was worried they would get cold so she held the box on top of the hand-warmer and fed them to Kam Shan in the intervals when he was not trying on clothes.

"Poor boy, poor boy," she sniffed, showing almost toothless gums every time she opened her mouth.

"You won't get anything to eat once you're in Gold Mountain," she went on. His grandmother did not cry. Recently her eyes had become as desiccated as two dried-up wells, so that she could not squeeze out a tear. Instead, her tears issued from her nostrils, like leeches sliding in and out of two sepulchres.

That had been their way of showing him that they did not want him to go. But he still had to go, whether they wanted him to or not. The responsibility for their home comforts rested on one man's shoulders, his father's. His mother hated for him to have to bear all that responsibility and had waited all these years until he, Kam Shan, was big enough to share the burden. But before he had time to help, he had abandoned him. He felt sick when he thought of his father, frantic with worry. And did his mother know?

Kam Shan suddenly missed his parents terribly.

He buried his head between his knees and pulled fiercely on the spiky tufts of his hair as if he was trying to pull his scalp off. Sundance saw his shoulders begin to shake. The hairs sticking out from between his fingers quivered as if they hid a sparrow. She could tell he was upset, but did not understand why. She threw down her hatchets and went into the forest. A little while later, she emerged holding a bunch of grasses. By now, Kam Shan had calmed down and was staring blankly at a watery blue sky. She kneaded the grasses together into a poultice which she applied to Kam Shan's palm. "This is a herbal remedy from the ancestors. It's called Squirrel's Tail and it'll stop the bleeding." Kam Shan felt as if a leech was crawling across his palm. The sensation was cool, moist and slippery and soon his palm did not hurt any more.

"Let's stop chopping," said Sundance. "We can come back tomorrow." They picked up the hatchets, bundled the firewood and balanced the thicker branches on their shoulders. They made their way home, single file, through the forest. They were not in a hurry, and Sundance stopped frequently to pick herbs and grasses and to explain their uses to Kam Shan.

"This is called Indian carpet and it cures colds and chills.

"This is mare's tail and it heals wounds and bleeding. Once the God man's husky got mauled by a brown bear. It was bleeding badly but Dad cured it with mare's tail.

"These are rosehips. Good for children when they're constipated.

"This is red clover. It cleans out your guts, and then it revives your appetite."

Kam Shan tired easily after his recent ordeal and they stopped talking. At the riverbank Sundance put down the bundle of firewood and kicked away a pebble with one foot to reveal a yellow flower growing underneath.

"This is St. John's wort. We'll take it home and I'll make a tea for you. It'll make you better."

"Better from what?"

Sundance looked Kam Shan straight in the eyes, and then said: "From going around in a trance, that's what." Kam Shan could not help laughing. He was still laughing when something yellow flashed towards him. He put up his hand to fend it off, then realized it was Sundance's cloak.

Sundance lifted the hem of her skirt and knotted it to her waistband, took off her short boots and went down to the river. The water was shallow here and only came halfway up her calves. Her legs had not seen the light of day for the whole winter and they were pallid. As she waded deeper in, they disappeared and only the top half of her body could be seen. Then he could only see her back—her head disappeared under water as she washed her hair.

Good heavens, these Redskin women were barbaric! How could she wash her hair in such frigid water and not worry about catching cold?

Sundance wore her hair in two plaits kept tucked away under a scarf. Now she undid them, and a thick mass of hair cascaded down her back. The sun was at its zenith and there was not a shadow anywhere to be seen. It was an almost windless day; the trees and stones were perfectly motionless and only the ripples on the river betrayed the slight breeze. The surface of the water seemed made of gleaming golden silk and when Sundance stood upright to shake the water from her hair, she released a shower of golden gems. Kam Shan was transfixed by the scene; he wished he had a camera, one like the missionaries had in his school in China, so that he could record it and take the photo out and look at it whenever he wanted.

When she had finished washing her hair, Sundance climbed up the bank, found a stone to sit on, undid the knot in her skirt and spread it around her. Her clothes and the rest of her would soon dry out in the sunshine.

"Come and braid my hair for me. I can't see, I haven't got a mirror," she said, beckoning Kam Shan over.

Kam Shan felt scared. He had not touched a woman's hair since the time when, as a child, he used to climb on his mother's shoulders and pull her hair free of its pins. His heart thudded and he caught his breath, reluctant to obey. But he found himself walking to her anyway, just as if Sundance had fastened a cord around his legs and pulled him to her.

Sundance passed him the ox bone comb in her leather bag but he was as ham-fisted with the comb as he had been with the hatchets and she gave a sharp intake of breath as he combed out the tangles. Finally it was done and he began clumsily to braid it.

"Your hair's really black, just like my mum's," he said.

"My mum says we Indians can never leave our native land. Why ever did you leave your mum?"

"We Chinese can't leave our native land either. Sooner or later, I'll go back and see her."

Sundance pulled a stem of sweetgrass and began chewing it. "I know. My mother's dad went home after he got rich. He went back to your country to see his mother too."

The comb dropped from Kam Shan's hand to the ground.

"What? You mean your grandfather was Chinese?"

"My mother's mother's tribe are from Barkerville. My granny opened a cake shop in town. A Chinese gold panner came in to buy cakes and they got to know each other. After that, when he came to town every couple of weeks, he used to stay at the shop. He panned for gold for four or five years and it was only in the autumn of the last year when they were about to seal off the mountain that he found an ingot. By that time, my mum had been born. My granddad divided the ingot in two and gave half to my granny. Then he sailed back to China."

No wonder Sundance's mother knew how to make rice porridge, and looked Chinese. And no wonder she had softened at the sight of him.

"And your granny let your granddad go?"

"She said that wherever your ancestors are, that's your home, and you can't stop someone going home."

Kam Shan was lost for words, but he thought to himself that some Redskins had big hearts after all. It was that Chinese who had been heartless and fickle.

They sat close together and Kam Shan could smell her body. She smelled good, a bit like water weed or wild grasses or cow's milk, and there was a hint of sweetness too. Her neck was burned tawny by the sun and a fuzz of fine hairs at the nape glinted gold in the light. As his eyes followed the drops that trickled down from her hair onto her collarbone, he saw a part of her he had never seen before.

His heart began to thump and he felt himself go hard down there, rock hard. It felt as if he would burst out of his trousers. Then his hand, seemingly of its own volition, was on her neck and sliding downwards.

Two soft, warm swellings. Quite small. He could just cup his hands over them.

Sundance sprang to her feet, startled and, at first, tried to wriggle out of his grasp, then gradually settled softly against him. Those two swellings almost melted in his hands, and from the centre of each, a little pebble jutted against his palm.

They gave him the courage of a thief. Roughly he pushed Sundance to the ground and pulled up her skirt. Her legs went as soft as a filleted salmon, and when Kam Shan prodded them slightly, they parted. Here was the way into a place he had never been before. He did not know what he was doing and she did not know how to help. Yet somehow a spark of mutual tenderness arose out of their jerky, agitated movements.

Afterwards, Kam Shan stood up. The iron rod now hung soft between his legs, his heart beat at its normal rhythm and his head was clear once more. Out of the corner of his eye, he watched Sundance wipe the blood off her legs and skirt with the back of her hand. He could not tell if she was happy or sad, and did not dare catch her eye. He wanted to ask if it hurt but the words grew barbs that caught in his throat.

After a little, Kam Shan picked up the cloak Sundance had dropped beside the track. Together they gathered the bundles of firewood and silently set off.

Sundance led and Kam Shan followed. She was limping slightly and the bloodstains on her skirt bounced like flares before his eyes until he saw stars. Kam Shan put down his bundle and said: "You walk behind me. It'll be a bit easier for you." They changed places and, with his eyes no longer full of flares, he saw more clearly. But now he was aware of her boots scuffing the stones as she followed him, her footsteps uneven. The sound grated on his ears and his heart seemed to wither inside him.

Please let her speak, just one sentence, Kam Shan begged silently.

Finally she spoke, but what she said was not at all what Kam Shan expected to hear. Her words struck him as trivial and unworthy of her, but at least they reassured him.

"Next time Dad goes to town, you go with him and buy me a present."

"As soon as I've sold this charcoal," he replied. "What would you like?"

"A round black hat with a turned-back brim, and a feather in it. I asked Dad last time he went to town but he didn't get it."

Kam Shan thought to himself that these Redskin girls were too easily pleased by fripperies. He found it almost unbearable. "I'll get you a sleeveless cowboy jacket too. They're very fashionable with city girls."

He did not look back but he knew Sundance was smiling. He felt her brilliant smile lap in waves up his spine, soaking it with warmth.

"When you bring it back, put it in a cowhide bag and hang it on the tree in front of our door. When Mum and Dad have seen it, I'll take it inside. If I don't do that, you can't make a move."

Kam Shan could not help laughing. "What a fuss about such a little present!"

Sundance laughed too. The joyous sound rose like dust in the spring sunshine, filling the air with tiny particles.

Kam Shan had just sold his first bucket of charcoal, when something happened to disrupt life in the village. The priest's camera disappeared.

At first, only one or two people knew about it. The priest told one of the missionary women and was overheard by one of the knitters standing nearby. She went home and told her daughter who happened to be in the same class as the tribal chief's son. Once he heard, it was not long before the whole tribe knew that someone had stolen the "black box that God's man shuts people up in."

When the Chief turned up at Sundance's home, her father was about to begin hollowing out a new canoe. The tree had been felled the previous autumn. It was a redwood and, although the trunk was slender, the wood was very dense and unmarked by even a single insect hole. It had been left out in all weathers for several months; now it was properly seasoned.

First, Sundance's father offered up prayers. Although he believed in the Jehovah of the White people, he was unwilling to forget the spirits of the ancestors his tribe had worshipped, so he left it vague as to which spirits his prayers were addressed.

Oh Great Spirit
I hear your voice in the wind
With every breath you take, ten thousand things multiply
I beg you to give me courage
Make my eyes keen
So that I may see the mystery of the rising and the setting sun
Make my hands skilful
So that I can discover the wonder in every thing created by you
Make my ears sharp
So that I may hear your sighs in the sound of the wind
Make my heart wise
So that I may know your true essence embodied in every stone....

When he squatted down and prepared to strike the first blow with his axe, the Chief gave a slight cough.

"Are you carving another eagle's head this time?" he asked, passing over a cigarette.

Sundance's father took the cigarette and lit it with a match, but said nothing. He was not going to divulge any details of an unfinished work to anyone, not even the Chief.

The Chief took a few puffs, then casually said: "Have you heard? The priest's camera has disappeared."

Sundance's father grunted. He was a man of few words. Though he had been baptized with the Christian name John, he was known to all in the village as Silent Wolf.

The Chief cleared his throat a few times then glanced towards the house. Lowering his voice, he said: "That guest of yours has been seen taking photographs of Sundance in the woods at the bend in the river."

The other man's eyebrows flickered. Still he said nothing, but he turned and went towards the house. At the doorway he stopped and showed the Chief in first.

"Any guest of mine is a member of my family. His reputation is my reputation. Please come and see for yourself if there's anything here which is not ours."

The Chief looked embarrassed. He clapped Silent Wolf on the shoulder: "It's your family, just ask them, all right? If you say there's nothing then there's nothing. Even if they don't believe me, they'll have to believe you."

It was quiet in the room. Sundance's mother had gone to the knitting workshop and the children were at school. It was very bright outside and silvery dust motes floated lazily in the single brilliant sunbeam that shone through the window. It took a while for the men's eyes to grow accustomed to the gloom, and then Silent Wolf saw his daughter sitting in the corner teaching Kam Shan to weave a sweetgrass basket.

Kam Shan stood up as soon as he saw the Chief. Silent Wolf's gaze swept over Kam Shan's body but his waistline looked flat as normal. He knew what the priest's black box looked like because the priest liked to stroll around the village with it slung over his shoulder, taking pictures. It was big, as big as his two hands put together, and would take up most of a cowhide bag.

"One day, you could teach me how to use a camera," he said, looking at Kam Shan.

Sundance saw Kam Shan go pale at the words, but he said nothing. The atmosphere was oppressively heavy, so that the room seemed to echo with the thuds of their hearts. Sundance felt like a stranded fish opening and shutting its mouth in desperate gasps. She could not stay there any longer and fled outside.

Silent Wolf tilted Kam Shan's chin up with one gnarled finger: "Be a man and help me clear your name with the Chief."

Kam Shan could no longer avoid the man's eyes. Coal black, they were, cold on the surface but with a fire in their depths. Kam Shan's own eyes, climbing to those cold black orbs, were blinded by the hidden fire. His mind went completely blank.

The Chief sighed: "When there was an outbreak of dysentery in the village last year, the priest rid us of the demons and saved us all. He has nothing to amuse himself with apart from that camera. He carries it around with him all day. If you took it, just give it back to him and that'll be the end of it."

Silent Wolf paid no attention to the Chief. His finger still under Kam Shan's chin, he said deliberately: "Can you or can you not?"

Kam Shan felt as if his lips had suddenly turned into two immovable stones. No matter how hard he wanted to speak, the words could not force their way through.

Silent Wolf withdrew his finger and Kam Shan's head suddenly dropped onto his chest.

"Get your stuff together."

The Chief looked at the other man. "Maybe it's not him...." he said hesitantly.

"We've never had anyone in our family who couldn't clear their name." The words were flinty, steely. There was absolutely no doubt that he meant what he said.

Kam Shan could only go to the corner where he slept and get his things together. They were few and simple: the jacket and gown that he had on when he fell into the water, a pair of cotton socks and cloth shoes. And a cowhide bag. In it there was a belt made of pheasant quills and decorated with brightly coloured feathers. He had bought it in town two days before when he went with Silent Wolf to sell charcoal, and had not had time to give it to Sundance.

The camera was not among these things. He had hidden it in a hole in a tree on the riverbank the day he passed by the children's school on his way back from chopping wood with Sundance. The priest had taken the children out for midday prayers and the classroom was empty apart from the black box on the teacher's rostrum. Kam Shan knew straightaway what it was. His heart leapt wildly in his chest. He hesitated, then picked the black box up in both hands—he would just play with it for a couple of days, then put it back again. But before he had time to return it, word got around the whole tribe that there had been a theft. That black box became a heap of shit, which he had to hang onto even though he could smell its stink. If he let go of it, then the stink would get out and everyone would smell it. He was well aware that not even a whole river could wash him clean of a smell like that.

He opened out the gown, put the trousers, socks and shoes in it, bundled it and tied it with a piece of twine. Then he opened it again and rearranged the socks and shoes. He was dilly-dallying, waiting for Sundance. He could not go without seeing her. When he opened his bundle for the third time, Silent Wolf gave a heavy cough. He stood behind him, holding two pigs' bladders tied at the neck in his hand—one with water, the other with wild rice and smoked fish. It would be something to see the boy on his way.

Kam Shan followed Silent Wolf very slowly outside. Then he stopped. Standing on tiptoe he hung the bag with the feather belt in it from the oak tree by the front door. He walked on, then turned back to check it was in a place where it would catch her eye.

At least he had left Sundance a present.

As Silent Wolf was about to launch the canoe, they heard the sound of running feet. It was Sundance, her braids flying. Trailing far behind came the fat priest, sweating profusely, clasping his bouncing belly in both hands as if to stop it from tumbling to the ground.

It was some time before the priest could catch his breath, safely release his belly and speak:

"The camera … I gave it to … this young man. I'm teaching him … to take pictures."

His words left the Chief and Silent Wolf mute with astonishment. Silent Wolf looked hesitantly from the priest to Kam Shan, but the boy did not look up or speak. Knowing he would be unable to conceal his surprise, he avoided meeting their eyes.

"Come on, young man. Tell these two gentlemen what make of camera you're using."

"Kodak Brownie, Number 2 Model B," Kam Shan muttered.

"How many pictures can it take at one time?"

"One hundred and seventeen."

"How big are the printed pictures?"

"About two inches."

The priest nodded and clapped Kam Shan on the shoulder. "I can see you're really keen on photography, young man. I did the right thing when I gave you the camera." Then he turned to Silent Wolf: "You keep this young man with you. He's got a good head on his shoulders, and he's a quick learner." Before Sundance's father could respond, the Chief said with a laugh, "It's getting late and I'm hungry. You're all invited to my house to eat. I killed an elk yesterday, and it'll take us all spring to eat it. Bring the boy too."

But Sundance was paying no attention, because she had seen the bag hanging from the oak tree by her door, swaying gently in the breeze. "Oh, Dad!" she cried in a voice choked with happiness.

By the time Kam Shan walked out of the door with his cowhide bag hung from a stick over his shoulder, he could already hear the beating of the powwow drum. He had seen the elkskin-covered drum before; it was housed in the big teepee where the ancestors were worshipped. It was huge, bigger than the banqueting table they dined on when his father was home in Spur-On Village, big enough for twelve drummers to sit around it. He felt, rather than heard, its thunderous reverberations beneath the soles of his feet.

He could hear singing too. Sundance called it singing but he thought of it more as the sounds of wild beasts—the roar of a tiger or the howl of a wolf. He did not know what the singing meant; it may have been a war chant, a song of jubilation, an invocation of the spirits of heaven and earth, or an expression of anger. When he was not with Sundance, they were just ear-piercing shrieks or earth-shattering growls.

He wondered if Sundance had started to dance. At the powwow, the men sang and drummed. The women danced, although they were only allowed outside the circle. The men sang, drummed and danced in the middle.

Sundance and her mother had been eagerly waiting for the powwow. Her mother had been sewing Sundance's dance cape for ten years, beginning the work when Sundance was just five. On her birthday every year, her mother sewed on another ten bells, making one hundred bells this year. Sundance had tried it on for the first time the evening before, filling the house with a tinkling of bells clearer than the sound of gems falling into a jade dish. Once she had her cape on, Sundance did not stop smiling all evening. Kam Shan had not slept well that night, and he knew that she had not either. He kept hearing her reed mattress creaking as she tossed and turned. When he got up to go out and piss, he found her sitting on the ground with her back against the wall, her teeth glinting in the darkness. She was still smiling.

She was happy because the cape was so beautifully made it put all the other mothers in the tribe to shame—and because this was her coming-of-age powwow. But Kam Shan knew that there was another reason why she was happy.

Yesterday evening at dinner, Sundance's father had told her mother that he would ask the Chief to preside over Sundance's wedding. Kam Shan started so violently in astonishment that the rice leapt out of his bowl.

"Sundance ... getting married?!"

He tried to catch her eye, but she bent her head to her food, and bore his gaze silently.

"When Sundance marries, she'll carry on living with us so she can help me with her younger brothers and sister," said her mother.

"You won't need to chop wood and make charcoal," said her father. "You can keep Sundance with what you earn from taking pictures."

It was some minutes before Kam Shan realized this remark was directed at him, and even more before he realized their import. His lips began to tremble: "M-me?" he stammered.

"Sundance accepted the belt you gave her, so of course it's you," laughed her mother with a glance at Silent Wolf.

Kam Shan's head seemed to explode into tiny fragments. He could not put all the bits together though he tried all evening, and all night when he was in bed. Only with the first glimmer of light in the sky did he feel that he had got his head around this whole complicated business.

Sundance was out of bed before the cock crowed a second time. She woke the little ones. Soon afterwards, her father got up. He was not normally up this early but today he had to wear his ceremonial dress as the lead dancer at the powwow. He put on a long blue gown with bears' paws sewn around the hem. On his chest he wore a decorative woven strip of yellow pheasant quills. He looked imposing, but the stateliest part of his outfit was yet to come; he donned a headdress of the finest eagle feathers, grey around the crown, white down his back. The feathers had dulled a little over the years, but Silent Wolf liked to wear feathers which had seen a bit of life. It was only young men who were seduced by freshly gathered feathers. The headdress was large and heavy and Silent Wolf needed help putting it on, so Sundance's mother rose early too.

Kam Shan was up last of all. He watched Sundance's mother paint her husband's face. Sundance had dressed the younger ones and was now changing her own clothes. She looked at him without speaking; her words were written on her clothes, in the bells which tinkled in eager expectation when she moved.

The powwow was held half a mile or so from their village, and attracted people from all the villages around. In addition to dancing and drumming, the powwow included a marketplace. Sundance's mother took charcoal and reed mats to sell and with the proceeds planned to buy a "hundred family quilt," a new set of wooden bowls, two deerskin tunics and two pairs of lightweight boots. The tunics and boots were for Sundance and Kam Shan to wear at the wedding. She also wanted to buy two big pouches of the best tobacco to give the Chief, who would preside over the wedding.

The powwow did not start until midday but no one could wait that long. "When are we leaving?" asked Sundance's father, once his face was painted. He sounded like an impatient child. "It's too early," her mother replied gravely after a moment's consideration. "The sun's not fully up yet." But she could not keep up the severity for long. "Let's go! Let's go!" she said with a laugh. "What are we waiting for?"

Then she noticed Kam Shan sitting on the edge of his bed. He was neatly dressed but in his everyday clothes. And he was holding his head in his hands as if it was so heavy it might fall off. His hands hid his expression, and he had not said a word all morning.

"What's got into you, wooden-top?" she asked.

"Don't worry. The wooden-top will dance as soon as the drumming starts," said Silent Wolf.

They set off with her father leading their pony in front. It was loaded up with two large sacks containing things they would sell at the powwow and three bladders full of food for their breakfast. Sundance's mother walked beside her father, the children followed and Sundance and Kam Shan brought up the rear.

The three young ones competed to see who could throw a stone the highest. The stones startled the birds who squawked in protest. The stocky little pony had been fed before they left, and clip-clopped along the track in a spirited manner, its head held high. Even the village dogs sensed the excitement, and set up an unbroken chorus of barking which accompanied them all the way out of the village. The sights of this powwow morning were like a scroll painting unrolling itself before Kam Shan's eyes. But he heard only one sound—the jingling of the bells on Sundance's cape.

The bells knocked against his eardrums, and his temples began to throb. In a sudden fit of irritation, he shouted: "Sundance!" His voice sounded strange—brittle like a dead twig. She looked at him: "What's wrong?" She had started to sweat and her forehead was beaded with drops of moisture. Kam Shan looked at her in a daze and saw that in the space of a few months she had become a beauty.

His lips trembled. "Sundance, I ... I...." But the words stuck and he could not go on. "What's the matter?" she asked. He shook his head. "Let's go. Your mum's waiting."

They walked on silently.

About fifteen minutes out of the village, Kam Shan suddenly slapped his forehead. "I've forgotten the camera," he said. "I can take pictures of people in the market and charge each person a few cents."

"Go back and get it and be quick," said Sundance's mother, beaming in satisfaction. "We'll wait here." She had known he was a smart boy from the first time she set eyes on him. But he replied: "Don't wait. I know the way to the powwow. We'll meet up there."

Kam Shan tossed his straw hat to Sundance. "It's hot, you'll catch the sun," he said as he started back. After a few paces, he looked back and watched as the little procession wound its way along the country track until the figures became tiny and faded into the distance. They turned a corner and disappeared from view completely, leaving only the tinkle of the bells wafting on the breeze. Kam Shan felt a great hollowness in his heart. It was only many years later, when he was middle-aged and had experienced life's ups and downs, that he was able to put a name to his feelings that day. Desolation.

He went back to the house and retrieved his cowhide bag from under his pillow. He had not opened it since the day he was almost sent packing. He took off his leather boots and put them by Silent Wolf's bed, then put on his old cloth shoes. He tied the bag shut, hung it from a stick over his shoulder and set off. The village was empty; everyone was at the powwow. The cloth of the shoes wrapped itself around his feet with such light weight that, strangely, he felt as if he were walking on puffs of air. By the time he got used to the feeling, the village was well behind him.

He had to hurry. The sun was well up by now and he needed to reach the nearest settlement before dark. He was not really worried; the bag still had the water and food in it that Silent Wolf had given him. And so long as he had the camera, he could beg a crust to eat and a place to sleep wherever he found himself. Now that the Whites had brought their cameras to the Redskins' land, the latter, after some trepidation, had come to like the strange idea of having their images shut into the black box. He did not know where the next settlement was or how far he would have to walk to reach it. His hair brushed his shoulders. In another six months, he thought, just another six months, he could face his father again.

He got to the bend in the river and stopped, rooted to the spot. His bag dropped with a thud. Someone was sitting on the stone where Silent Wolf tied his canoe. The silence was shattered with a jingling of bells.

"Get into the canoe. I'll take you," said Sundance.

She knew. She knew everything.

Emotion flooded over Kam Shan, filling his eyes with tears. He dared not look at her, or he would not be able to hold them back. He must not cry. Redskin men never cried.

"I'm not ... I'm...." he stammered, but could not finish the sentence.

She did not interrupt but when he did not say any more, she asked: "Why? Why?" She was looking upwards, as if addressing her questions to the sky.

He gave a sigh. She sighed too. The silence hung heavily between them.

"The ancestors ... won't accept you...." he began haltingly.

Sundance untied the mooring rope and gave the paddle to him. He stepped in and reached out for her hand. She got in but still he did not let go. She did not pull free but allowed their palms to rest moistly one against the other.

"That's what my granddad said when he left my granny," she said quietly.

Kam Shan had been on the road more than six months before he glimpsed, far in the distance, the pair of red lanterns that hung on either side of his father's door.

After leaving Sundance, he wandered from tribe to tribe, from town to town, for months. He took the same road his father had taken all those years before when he was building the railroad, but that he did not discover until much later. At the time, the only idea in his head was how to get to the next settlement before dark and fill his hungry belly.

As winter approached, his aimless wanderings acquired a direction—home.

The idea came to him quite suddenly. His hair was not long enough yet; in fact, he could only braid it into a stub of a pigtail. But something made him change his mind—a newspaper.

He was at a Redskin market one day when he saw a man carrying a bottle of soy sauce bought in Vancouver's Chinatown. It was a long time since he had tasted soy sauce and just the sight of the bottle made his mouth water. But what really caught his attention was the old newspaper in which the bottle was wrapped. It was so long since he had seen any Chinese characters that he paid the man a few cents for the filthy newspaper and sat down on the ground to read it.

It was several months old and had passed through many hands, each of which had left its mark on it. Kam Shan started to read it in minute detail, character by character. But then his eyes fell on one small item of news, and everything else in the newspaper receded into the background.

Chinatown's barbers have recently been doing a roaring trade. The success of the revolution means an end to pigtails and the Chinese have wasted no time in shaving their heads in preparation for the celebrations of the first New Year of the Republic.

The Chinese Times, *12 February 1912*

He put down the newspaper. His first thought was to get hold of a pair of scissors. When finally, several weeks later, he managed with some difficulty to borrow a pair from a Redskin, he hesitated. It should be his father wielding those scissors, he decided. Not him.

Dad. Oh, Dad.

The words filled Kam Shan with a sense of urgency. Home. He must go home immediately.

It was not an easy journey. It was a hard winter and the snow was deep. The cloth shoes his mother made him were soon worn through, but he had managed to buy a pair of thick deerskin boots from a Redskin. The rivers were frozen over so there were no boats; he had to make the journey on foot. Whenever he came to a market, he took photographs of people and taught the Redskins how to make charcoal. In return, he asked not for money but for food and warm clothing. His cowhide bag was sometimes stuffed to overflowing. On occasion, he could not reach a village before nightfall and had to take shelter in a hollow tree or a cave, but he kept his spirits up with the thought that every night brought him closer to home.

On the last stage of the journey, he hitched a ride on a cart going to Vancouver. When the man put him down in Chinatown, he went on impulse to the office of the *The Chinese Times*. All the staff were new, and only the old man on the door recognized him. "Where's Mr. Fung?" asked Kam Shan. "Gone back to China. Been gone a long while." "Has he got himself a job in the Republican government?" "Job? No fucking way! The Hung Mun members mortgaged their properties and gave the money to Mr. Sun to go back and seize power in China. But once the Cudgel got what he wanted, he forgot about the Hung Mun. They haven't seen hide nor hair of him."

Kam Shan said nothing. Mr. Fung was a raging torrent, and he, Kam Shan, was a mere grain of sand dragged along in its wake. In the process, Mr. Fung had let down the brethren of the Hung Mun, and he had let down his mum and dad.

He would not let his parents down ever again by going near that raging torrent. From now on, the revolution was not his business.

From now on, his parents would be his only concern.

These last two years, Dad, I haven't earned a cent to send to Mum and Granny. As he walked, Kam Shan rehearsed what he would say when he saw his father. You've had to save every cent to pay back the debt from building the *diulau*. But starting today, you just watch me. Starting today, it won't be you and Uncle Ah-Lam who do the muck-spreading, it'll be me and Loong Am who do all the heavy, dirty, stinking jobs. Except for killing pigs, that is. I can't kill pigs. You can be my helper from now on, and I'll be the roof beam that holds up the family home. I'm going to make good use of my camera from now on. The Redskins give me a couple of days' food for every photograph, and I've heard you can charge two dollars for a picture in the city.

Oh, Dad, I promise you I'm going to earn enough money to keep Mum and Granny and my brother, and us over here as well. Do you believe me, Dad?

Kam Shan got to the outskirts of New Westminster at dusk. As he went up the cracked stone steps to the front door, he felt an ocean of pent-up tears threaten to overwhelm him. He was not in Redskin territory any more and did not try to hold them back. Yet, somehow, the anguished sobs remained locked inside him, and only a few tears blurred his vision.

The red lanterns from the year of his arrival were still there, although they had grown increasingly yellowed and tatty at the edges. But the New Year couplets were different. The old ones had been worded and written by his father:

May those back home enjoy a favourable end to the old year;
May we in Gold Mountain reap bumper crops in the new year.

And across the top, *Peace to the whole family.*

The lines he saw today looked as if they had been bought ready-made from Chinatown. The paper was gold-flecked and the writing was neat, but the message was trite:

Building the family with hard work; Blessing the children with longevity.

287

And, across the top, *May the new year be auspicious.*

Why had his father not written the couplets? He had never bought New Year couplets written by anyone else before—he thought no one else wrote in a decent hand. Had something happened to him?

Kam Shan went weak at the knees at the thought. He managed to prop himself against the door jamb and knock.

Please God, let it be Dad who opens the door. Please let him be all right. If he's all right, I won't just walk in, I'll kneel down in the doorway and knock my head on the ground a hundred times to show how remorseful I am.

He had to wait a long time before someone finally came to the door.

It was the hired hand, Loong Am.

When Loong Am saw Kam Shan, he leapt back and slammed the door shut. Kam Shan was nonplussed. Then he realized that Loong Am must think he was a ghost. He thundered on the door, shouting: "I'm Kam Shan! I'm alive! Come and touch my hand. It's warm. Dead people are cold!"

There was no sound from the other side of the door.

Kam Shan tried again. "Loong Am, if I was a ghost, why would I need you to open the door for me? Come and look through the window. Can't you see my shadow? Ghosts don't have shadows."

After a long pause the door finally opened, and Loong Am cautiously emerged, his hair almost standing on end with fright. He looked Kam Shan very carefully up and down before asking: "Where have you been, Kam Shan? Your dad was frantic. He searched high and low; he practically went to the gates of hell for you. And why have you still got a pigtail? The Republic was set up a while ago."

Kam Shan did not answer. "Where's my dad?" he asked.

Loong Am sighed. "Your granny was very ill. Your dad went back to Hoi Ping. He's not been gone a month."

Kam Shan's bag dropped to the floor with a thud. He stared blankly in front of him. Loong Am, alarmed at the look on his face, hastily asked: "Have you eaten? There's some porridge in the pot. Shall I heat some for you?" Kam Shan stood rooted to the spot, still wordless. Finally, he pulled himself together and said: "Ink stone." Loong Am did not understand until Kam Shan gestured wearily: "Get me dad's ink stone." Loong Am hurriedly fetched the ink stone, paper and brushes from the other room. "Good thing you've come back," he said. "I haven't had anyone to write for me since your dad left. When you've finished writing to your dad, you can write a letter home for me."

"Where's Ah-Lam?" Kam Shan asked as he ground the ink and prepared to write.

"Dead. The month after you left. He got very confused. He used to wander off into the fields without any trousers on. The *yeung fan* were so scared they called the police. In the end, he started to piss and shit any time, any place he felt like it."

The brush poised in mid-air as Kam Shan fumbled for words which failed him.

Kam Shan pulled the curtain to one side.

The curtain was black. It was padded with cotton wadding, and was very thick, though lumpy and uneven. It was covered in marks and shiny grease stains. It had been used to wipe hands after shitting, mouths after eating, and noses after blowing. Every mark told a story and the curtain wore them all like a badge of shame.

Today he was seeing Chinatown in all its nakedness. Kam Shan's heart thudded in his chest.

He had been to Vancouver's Chinatown often since his dad fetched him from the detention centre three years before. He had got to know Mr. Fung in the newspaper office, he had been to the cake shops and the general stores, he had been to see plays at the theatre, and had eaten and drunk in all its cafés. He knew which shops had the most generous scales, which of the cafés' cooks were the most generous with the oil, and even where the snacks were likely to be stale. But although he knew all Chinatown's tricks of the trade, until the moment when he pulled aside the curtain, his knowledge of Chinatown was only skin deep.

The room upstairs from the gambling den was not marked by any hanging lanterns or signs. The men of Chinatown had no need of signs or lanterns. They could grope their way unerringly up its twisty, narrow staircase until they reached the curtain. On paydays and holidays the queue of men waiting in front of the curtain might be so long it trailed right back down to the front entrance. Impatient youngsters banged on the door frame until men emerged with their trousers still unfastened.

"What's it like?" the waiting men would ask.

"Go and see for yourself" was the invariable answer.

With such a long queue, it was not unusual to bump into someone you knew. Sometimes brothers met up, or fathers and sons. Whoever it was, you avoided their eye and kept out of the way. If you could not, you greeted them with a "You here too?"

But today was not New Year or any other holiday. It was not even payday. The weather was miserable too; the clouds were so low that if you lifted your head, you could almost touch them. Apart from the pawnbrokers who always did a brisk trade, the whole of Chinatown was almost deserted.

But Kam Shan was there.

When he got to the gambling den, he bought some Pirate brand cigarettes from a hawker. His hand shook as he tore open the packet, and it fell apart so the cigarettes dropped to the ground. He squatted down to pick them up, feeling his face grow hot. To hide his embarrassment from the hawker, he spent an inordinate amount of time retrieving the cigarettes before he stood up again and gruffly asked for a light. He pursed his lips, put a cigarette into his mouth and took a fierce drag on it. He felt as if a knife had plunged itself into his throat and he went into a fit of coughing.

Red-faced, he wiped his runny nose with the sleeve of his jacket, sidled into the doorway and began to stomp up the stairs. The hawker smirked as he watched his retreating figure. He had seen too many men going up those stairs not to know that this was a first-timer.

When Kam Shan pulled open the curtain he discovered the room was divided into two cubicles, each with its own door. He was just wondering which one to go in when the left-hand door crashed open and a swarthy figure tumbled out, clad only in underpants. The man's jacket and trousers flew out after him and landed at the bottom of the stairs. The man stumbled to his feet and tried to put on his trousers, frantically searching with his foot for the leg hole. Onlookers swarmed around him, sticking as stubbornly as soot on sticky-rice cakes.

A heavily made-up woman came out of the room. Knotting her robe around her, she bawled down the stairs to the man:

"Don't think I don't recognize you because you've cut your pigtail off. You bring me the money this time tomorrow, not a cent short, or I'll plaster your name all over the door of the gambling den for everyone to see!"

The man finally got his trousers on and, slinging his jacket over his shoulders, plunged out into the street. The crowd burst out laughing but the woman did not join them. She hawked and spat, and went back into the room, banging the door behind her. Kam Shan knew this was not the door he was supposed to go in. The madam had promised him a young girl who had not been here very long.

Kam Shan pushed open the door on the right. The cubicle's tiny, wok-sized window had a piece of cloth carelessly tacked over it, and it was as gloomy inside as the landing was on the outside. A lamp in the corner provided a small circle of hazy light. It took Kam Shan a few moments to make out the only furniture: a bed and a stool. Clearly, the bed was for after you took your clothes off, the stool was for when you put them back on again.

A quilt lay coiled across the bed. From where he stood, it looked dull green, woven with a flower design. These were the only signs of colour in the room. At the end of the bed was a bundle of dull grey clothing. The bundle moved—and he realized it was the woman he had just paid to enjoy.

Kam Shan threw down the cigarette and ground it into the floor. He sat down on the edge of the rickety bed, which squealed loudly under his weight, and pulled aside the quilt. It still held a trace of warmth in it and, right in front of his eyes, there was a large stain like the juice from a smashed watermelon. It looked so foul that he nearly retched. The quilt was too revolting so he shoved it onto the floor.

"What are you called?" he asked, tight-faced. But his voice betrayed him and even he could hear how green he sounded.

The greyish bundle pulled itself upright but remained silent.

He stood up and lit a match, holding it close. The light gave him courage and he spoke again, more roughly this time.

"Turn round. I asked you a question."

The body turned towards the light and Kam Shan was surprised to see a pair of eyes so huge they almost ran off the edge of her face. The irises were like glass beads under water, their colour changing gradually in the flickering light from dark brown to dark blue. As Kam Shan raised the match, he saw in her eyes hints of greyish-green.

"Cat Eyes?" exclaimed Kam Shan in astonishment.

The girl's irises flickered and fogged over, and the green went dark again.

"Just one, OK?"

She had stretched out her hand to beg a cigarette from him. Her fingers were wizened like sun-dried vines and there was a fuzz of fine hair on her wrists. She was so bony that her gown seemed to have nothing inside it, as if it simply hung on a bamboo frame.

She's still a child, thought Kam Shan.

He got out his packet of cigarettes, pulled one out, lit it and gave it to her. Then he did the same for himself. He turned to look at the girl, who was dragging greedily on the cigarette as if she was half-starved. She took three pulls before puffing out any smoke, holding her breath so long her neck stretched like an egret, and ropes of livid veins stood out in her neck.

"Take it easy. No one's going to grab it off you," said Kam Shan.

"I've got bad teeth. If I smoke it makes the pain better." The girl snickered and the sound, like the rustling of a snake in the grass, gave Kam Shan goose pimples.

"You know me, mister?" the girl asked.

She had finished her cigarette in a few puffs and obviously wanted another. Too timid to ask, she just smiled slyly at him.

"I heard them calling you Cat Eyes that day when—" The words stuck in Kam Shan's throat and he could not finish the sentence.

The first time he had seen her was a couple of months ago. Kam Shan and Loong Am had finished selling all of their eggs in the farmers' market, and went to Chinatown for tea. They sat down, but almost immediately Loong Am went back downstairs for a piss in the backyard toilet. When he did not come back, Kam Shan went down to look for him. There was a crowd of a dozen or more men hanging around, and a burly fellow in black guarded the entrance to the yard. Kam Shan knew the man—he was a brother of the boy whom his father had hired to do tailoring when he had the laundry—and was admitted when he said he had come to look for Loong Am.

The yard was crowded. In the middle, someone had erected a platform made of two stones and a plank of wood. A girl stood upon the plank. She was a scrawny kid and so undersized that even on her platform she was shorter than the men standing around her. She was dressed in a blue tunic and trousers, edged with a black border. The fabric was rough cotton but clean. The girl stood with her hands tucked into her sleeves, her head hanging so low that her eyes were invisible and all that could be seen was the top of her head. There was a ribbon tied to the top of her braids, which must have been bright red once, but had now gone dark and scruffy looking.

A scrawny man stood next to the girl. He was poking her with his finger and saying: "My elder brother's child. She's had a tough time—her dad died as soon as they got here. I can't afford to keep her. Just give me a bit of cash and you can take her away with you.

"Take a good look then, look at that face. Of course, I'm not comparing her to Imperial ladies of old—I couldn't do that, could I? But tell me, doesn't she outshine any opera actress you've ever seen? Have you ever seen anything like those eyes? Make her your wife or your concubine and get her to wait on you. You can't lose."

He stretched out two claw-like fingers and tipped the girl's chin up so that finally the face was visible. There was a hiss of astonishment from the onlookers.

She was just an ordinary Cantonese girl, of the sort so often seen in the paddy fields, by the fish ponds, or at her loom, dark-skinned with a broad forehead and high cheekbones. But her eyes were astonishing. They were like huge lakes so full they threatened to overflow their banks, and the irises were an unusual kind of black, overlaid with a faint greyish-green sheen.

"Cat eyes! She's got cat eyes!" the cry went up.

Scrawny pursed his lips with satisfaction and said: "You can look all over Gold Mountain—Vancouver, Victoria, New Westminster—but I guarantee you won't find another one like this. If you do, you can have this one for free."

"Is she clean?" asked a man in a short jacket, a bit older than the others.

The man cackled as if someone had poked him in the armpit: "She's only twelve! What do you think? She hasn't even been touched by a cockerel, let alone a man!"

There was general laughter. "Well, you would say that, wouldn't you? Why should I believe you?" said Short-Jacket. Scrawny spat a gob of green phlegm: "Come and feel if you don't believe me. See if she's got any pubic hair."

So Short-Jacket went up, undid the girl's trouser tie and, holding the trousers with one hand, reached into her crotch and had a good feel. The girl tried vainly to twist out of his grip, then shrank away as stiff and small as a wire-frame mannequin.

"Just a few hairs," reported Short-Jacket, nodding at the onlookers. He extracted his finger and held it up to his nose to sniff. There were gusts of laughter.

"I'll come and try," offered someone else. Scrawny's expression darkened. "You don't get a free meal every day," he said. "If you want to come and try, you've got to pay ... two dollars a go."

The crowd fell silent.

Short-Jacket laughed. "I'll give you thirty dollars," he said. "Thirty dollars and I'll take her off your hands. My wife's back home in Hoi Ping—this girl can be my second wife." Scrawny swore: "Motherfucker! My brother brought her out and paid five hundred dollars in head tax—all borrowed from my savings. I'm not trying to make a profit, but at least don't leave me out of pocket."

"Fifty dollars then? How's that?"

Scrawny said nothing, just tugged on the tie fastened around the girl's trousers and made as if to lead her away.

"Two hundred and fifty," another offer came, this time from a man standing right on the edge of the crowd, who had not spoken up till now. He was an imposing-looking figure dressed in a long, silk gown, with a big, square face.

"What about the head tax?"

"Two hundred and fifty, not a cent more."

As Silk Gown spoke, his face hardened and every crease on it went taut as a wire. Scrawny looked disgruntled and, throwing the trouser tie back at the girl, said: "All right, two-fifty then. It'll take me a year to pay back what I spent on this worthless bit of baggage."

Loong Am drove the cart home that day. Kam Shan did not say a word for the whole journey. Those huge catlike eyes pursued him. Every time he shut his eyes, they lay heavy on his lids. They flared like two sparks from a charcoal fire, until his eyes smarted and his head ached.

But by the time he reached home that day, he had forgotten about the whole affair. There was so much misery in this world. He could not take it all to heart. In the last two years, he had seen a lot of things. He had grown a thick skin too, and was no longer seriously distressed by the things he witnessed.

Still, it had never occurred to him that the silk-gowned man, having paid two hundred fifty dollars for Cat Eyes, would not take her as his own concubine. Instead, he had made her many men's concubine, allowing her to be pawed over and ground down by them. She was still Cat Eyes, but she was just not the same Cat Eyes as the first day he saw her.

"Does your uncle know you're here?" he asked her now.

Cat Eyes gave a snort of laughter. "What uncle? My uncle hasn't been born from my granny's belly yet."

"So the man who sold you wasn't your uncle?" Kam Shan asked in surprise. Cat Eyes shook her head. "I don't even know his name. I went to Canton with my elder sister to see the lights and we bumped into this man. He said he'd take us to the docks to see the foreign boats, then he tricked us and we ended up at sea."

"What about the head tax? Did he pay that for you?"

"He got me in on someone's Returning Resident Permit. The photo looked pretty much the same."

"What about your sister?"

"Someone bought her on the boat."

Cat Eyes stretched out a hand from under the quilt, covered her mouth and gave a yawn as long as a tangled thread. Her fingertips came away wet from her runny nose and she gave them a shake, so that the drops landed on the already besmeared wall. She did not sound sorrowful as she spoke, in fact she acted as if she was talking about someone else.

"Can you hurry up, mister, so I can sleep a bit? I didn't sleep at all last night, with the toothache."

She took off her top and he saw she had nothing on underneath. Her body had been covered up all winter but the traces of the field work she used to do were still visible. Scabs from sunburn had left ridges like rice weevils all over her shoulders and back. The only pallid bits of skin were those two fleshy protuberances on her chest, as small and dried up as buds withered on the branch. Kam Shan pinched them—they felt like two lumps of dough. By comparison, Sundance's breasts were so ripe that, at the slightest touch, they melted in his hands.

Cat Eyes' trousers were knotted loosely at the waist and the tie came undone with a slight tug. She had no underclothes on. Her legs were as loose as her trousers tie and at the slightest nudge they parted. Her pubes were swollen like a rotten peach, and a yellow fluid oozed from them. The stench was so overpowering that when it reached Kam Shan's nostrils, he retched and his mouth filled with the foul aftertaste from his lunchtime shrimp dumplings. Instantly, he felt himself go soft.

"Are you coming?" asked Cat Eyes.

"The hell I am!" Kam Shan swore violently. "You want to infect me so I die of the pox too?"

Cat Eyes fell silent. Kam Shan stood up and felt around for his own trousers. Something was weighing on his feet. He realized that Cat Eyes was clinging on to his trouser cuffs. "Please, mister, don't go," she begged. "You paid for half an hour. She can't kick you out before then. Stay here so I can sleep a bit, please?"

Kam Shan lifted the girl with his foot and dropped her on the bed. Her body was as light as a leaf. "Well, you better get a doctor to look at you," he said, but before he had finished speaking he heard the sound of snoring. He looked round to see Cat Eyes fast asleep on the bed, her eyes tight shut. Her lashes were as exuberant as grasses growing on the riverbank. A damp curl of hair clung to her forehead. Any coquettishness she may have had dropped from her like grains of sand. She had turned into a child before his eyes. He picked up the quilt and covered her with it. Then he sat down and took out a cigarette, the third he had smoked in his life.

It was dusk by the time Kam Shan went back out into the street. The wind had risen, rattling the branches in the trees so that they made great black silhouettes against the sky. It was dinnertime but Kam Shan was not hungry. Something was choking him up. He wanted to shout out, or vomit, but no sound came. He felt drained. He felt in his pocket for the cigarette packet. It was empty, and he remembered he had left the pack with Cat Eyes.

Mum, if you give me a baby sister this time, please never let her end up like Cat Eyes, he said to himself.

He went into a café and had a bowl of porridge with pickled egg, a cup of tea and a bottle of wine. Soon the liquids were sloshing around inside him and he made trip after trip to the outhouse. When finally he got back into the cart and started the horse for home, his tongue felt like over-risen dough bunging up his mouth. He was relieved that Loong Am had not come with him. He did not feel like talking.

He fell asleep in the cart. But the horse knew the road perfectly well—it had done the trip many times before.

When he was about three miles from home, he was woken by a fierce gust of wind. The wind caught the pile of empty baskets at his feet and they rolled to the ground. He stopped to pick them up and saw a slight movement from an upside-down basket still in the cart. Thinking it was the wind, he reached out for the basket, which reared upwards. He sobered up instantly. He had loaded the baskets himself and there was nothing in any of them. But he knew that there were unmarked graves along this road, where railroad workers had been buried.

He raised the whip and cracked it in the air. It sounded like a thunderbolt in the quiet of the night sky and gave him a little courage. His voice shaking, he shouted: "Who's there?"

Something stumbled under the basket. As it stood up, two green eyes flared in the moonlight. Cat Eyes. Kam Shan's heart returned to his chest, and the hairs standing up on the back of his neck settled back into place.

"I saw your cart on the other side of the street. When they went off to dinner, I ran out and hid in it."

"It's no use coming with me. I don't have the money to buy your freedom."

"You don't need to. You don't live in Vancouver so they won't find you."

Cat Eyes jumped down from the cart and flung herself to her knees before Kam Shan. "Mister, I saw you were a good man the minute you came in," she implored him. "I can get medicine from a doctor to cure the pox. I'm young and strong and I can do any work anywhere—farm work, fishing, embroidery, weaving.... If you've got a wife, I can be your concubine and wait on you and your wife and kids day and night. If you've already got a concubine, I'll be your servant, I swear."

Kam Shan lifted one foot and pushed her away.

"You can't come with me. If I let you, my dad would kick me out too. Forget it. I'll take you back to town."

Cat Eyes stood up, slowly pulled open her tunic and reached for the tie around her trousers. She pulled it free and the trousers slid down her stick-like legs. She stood on tiptoe, threw the tie over an overhanging branch and knotted it into a noose. Then she said hoarsely: "I'm absolutely not going back. You go. You've got your way, I've got mine. Forget me and I'll forget you."

Kam Shan pulled down the tie and flung it to the ground. "Better a live coward than a dead hero. Every cat and dog knows that, Cat Eyes. Are you stupider than a cat or a dog?"

Cat Eyes picked up the tie, made it fast around her trousers and got back in the cart. Kam Shan was silent but Cat Eyes knew that a tiny crack had opened up. She just had to keep her toe in the door and she could see the light.

For the rest of the journey, Kam Shan left Cat Eyes curled up like a sleeping cat in one of the empty baskets at the back of the cart. He did not say another word. But he kept going over things in his mind, addressing everything to his father. Ah-Fat had spent a few months back in Spur-On Village and his mother was pregnant again. His granny was much better and his dad would be booking passage and returning soon. Kam Shan dreamed up one reason after another to explain where Cat Eyes had come from. At first, each reason seemed to offer a broad and bright route but, as he pursued it, it narrowed down until he came up against a brick wall. Try as he might, he just could not find a reliable way out of his predicament.

By the time he got home, he felt as if his head was going to burst. As he jumped down, something that hung around his neck clinked against the side of the cart. It was a crucifix which Pastor Andrew had given him as a Christmas present. He was at best only half converted to the pastor's teachings, but he wore the crucifix as a kind of amulet. The clink it made comforted him, like the striking of a match in darkness.

Tomorrow. As soon as I get up tomorrow I'll go and ask Pastor Andrew. He'll know what to do, Kam Shan thought.

6

Gold Mountain Affair

⛰️

Years four to eleven of the Republic (1915–1922)
Vancouver and New Westminster, British Columbia

Dear Ah-Yin,

I have been back in Gold Mountain for more than a month but I have been worried about many things, and it is only now that I can pick up my pen to write and tell you that I am fine. During the months that I spent at home with you, I left the hired hand in charge of the farm here. There was a drought last year so the crops were poor, the livestock suffered from disease and income from the farm slumped. I have been using manure as fertilizer for years but recently my yeung fan neighbours took me to court saying it stank and contravened public hygiene regulations. This incurs heavy fines but luckily an old friend from my railroad days, Rick Henderson, was good enough to help by engaging an excellent defence lawyer for me.

But what weighs most heavily on me is Kam Shan. After he came back from the Redskin tribe at the beginning of the year, there was a big change in him. He learned all he could about farming and livestock, and threw himself into the work. It was wonderful—the prodigal son returned. But to my dismay I have just learned that he has been secretly sheltering a whorehouse girl with the connivance of a church pastor, and sneaking valuables and money out of our house to keep her. That boy has always been pigheaded and ungovernable. Finally, yesterday, I felt I had no option but to kick him out. My dearest wish is to get the farm income up again, and save enough to bring you over to Gold Mountain. Kam Shan has always been close to you and, who knows, you may be able to bring him into line. My uncle and aunt can look after my mother. I have given them a home for many years, and looking after Mum will be a small way for them to show their gratitude, and will set my mind to rest. Kam Ho is thirteen now, and when he is old enough, we can find him a suitable bride to settle down with in Hoi Ping. It won't be long before you give birth and, whether it is a boy or a girl, you can leave the baby with my uncle and aunt to look after for the time being. My most urgent task is to get you here as soon as possible. You and I have spent so little time together, and so much time apart. I miss you very much and feel guilty that I have not been able to fulfil the promise I made you all those years ago.

Your husband, Fong Tak Fat, New Westminster, the sixth day of the eighth month, 1915

Ah-Fat was up early, washed and dressed. In the southeast corner of the room, he lit a stick of incense and knelt down. The corner held a statue of Tam Kung which he had brought back on his last trip home. He had been kowtowing to the statue every day since he heard that Six Fingers was on her way. Tam Kung was the god of seafarers and Six Fingers was journeying across the ocean on her way to Gold Mountain. Ah-Fat was on tenterhooks. He had not forgotten how, five years before, Kam Shan had been put in the port detention centre on his arrival and Ah-Lam's wife had killed herself there. It was only by putting his worries in the hands of Tam Kung that he could settle to his daily work.

Six Fingers, his wife, would be finally reunited with him in Gold Mountain.

He made his decision on the very day of his departure from Hoi Ping.

Twenty-one years. He and Six Fingers had been married for twenty-one years.

For twenty-one years, he and his mother, Mrs. Mak, had been in a tug-of-war, and Six Fingers was the handkerchief tied at the midpoint. Both he and his mother wanted her. His mother's way of showing this was to nag him to get a concubine, either from Gold Mountain or Hoi Ping. She did not know the market conditions in Gold Mountain but she knew that in Hoi Ping girls would go with a Gold Mountain man for next to nothing. Ah-Fat refused and let the whole thing drag on as the days, and years, went by.

His mother knew that when Ah-Fat came back from a day's work in the fields, he cooked his own dinner, or ate cold leftovers. If ever his jacket got caught on the cart, there was no nimble-fingered woman to mend it for him. If Ah-Fat had a headache or a fever, there was no one to administer home treatments or mop his brow. When Ah-Fat was young, Mrs. Mak steeled herself to this, but he was getting on in years, and now she could not bear it.

Mrs. Mak was blind and no longer able to see his face but she could still hear her son perfectly well. He only had to call "Mum!" in a low voice as he stepped over the threshold for her to tell instantly that he had changed. His voice sounded as hollow as a worm-eaten hazelnut. He had supported a family that had as many members as a tree had branches, yet he had been reduced to a desiccated nut. Ever since her son left for Gold Mountain at sixteen, every ounce of his energy had gone into transforming his labour into dollar letters to send home.

The morning Ah-Fat left Hoi Ping, the porter carrying his suitcases led the way. Behind came blind Mrs. Mak, supported on either side by Six Fingers and Kam Ho. All three were going with him as far as the entrance to the village. Kam Ho looked at his father: "You've put on weight, Dad," he said. "Your jacket won't button up." His father smiled. "It's all the soups your mother's been giving me. She's been trying to fatten me up like a soft-shelled turtle. Don't envy me. Once I get back to Gold Mountain, all this fat'll soon be gone—there's no soup for me there." Six Fingers turned her face away and said nothing. She knew that if she opened her mouth to speak, the tears would flow. Her belly was showing now and she walked more heavily than usual. She took a few more slow steps and managed to swallow the lump in her throat. "Don't listen to your father's teasing, Kam Ho," she said. "There's plenty of fancy things to eat in Gold Mountain. How could they miss homemade soup?"

Mrs. Mak suddenly came to a halt, scowling. She thumped her walking stick so hard it dented the earth.

"Hurry up and save some money when you get back to Gold Mountain, Ah-Fat," she said.

"Yes, Mum, to buy more fields," said Ah-Fat, who had heard this injunction from his mother time and again. Fields, fields, more fields. When Six Fingers and Kam Ho were kidnapped by Chu Sei, their land had to be sold in haste to raise the ransom. Mrs. Mak had never forgotten the painful process of buying back their fields afterwards. She did not believe in money, even when she held the silver coins tight in her hand. She could only be reassured by standing atop the dykes which enclosed her family's own fields.

"No, not fields," said Mrs. Mak, waving her stick in the direction of Six Fingers. "Hurry and save enough money to take her away with you."

Ah-Fat and Six Fingers were mute with astonishment. They had waited and waited for Mrs. Mak to speak these words, and after twenty years, they seemed more improbable than a flowering sago tree.

When Six Fingers found her voice, she said: "Mum, I'll always be here to attend to you." "Huh!" came the reply. "As if I don't know where your heart lies!" The old woman had a sharp tongue and her words could pepper her listener painfully in the face. But Six Fingers had long since grown a thick skin and was inured to such wounding comments.

She merely gave a slight smile and said: "Mum, what will you do if I go?" "Huh!" Mrs. Mak said again. "I'll live with his uncle and aunt. Ah-Fat's money has made them as fat as Bodhisattvas. Ah-Fat's uncle would be a nobody without that money, so he can hardly refuse."

Ah-Fat hitched up his gown, knelt in the road and kowtowed three times before his mother. She could not see him but she could smell the dust raised by the knocking of her son's head. "I won't forget your kindness, Mother," he said. "When I get back to Gold Mountain, I'll earn masses of money so you can buy masses of land. And if I can't come home every year, then I'll get Kam Shan to come home and pay his respects to you like a good grandson."

At the mention of Kam Shan, Mrs. Mak's grim expression relaxed and a flicker of a smile appeared on her face.

"You go back and tell Kam Shan that the sugared almonds that he sent were very nice, but they were much too hard for me. Remind him Granny hasn't got too many teeth left and next time he should send something softer."

Ah-Fat grunted assent and glanced sidelong at Six Fingers. They both smiled but said nothing. They had kept Kam Shan's disappearance from Mrs. Mak but she nagged Six Fingers for news of him. In the end, Six Fingers was cornered. She penned a couple of letters "from Kam Shan" herself and read bits of them out to the old woman. Ah-Fat had brought a few curios with him and passed them off as presents from Kam Shan, and Mrs. Mak had suspected nothing. It was only now that Kam Shan had returned that Ah-Fat and Six Fingers could relax their vigilance.

So Six Fingers' journey to Gold Mountain was a hurried decision made that morning—but one that took Mrs. Mak twenty years to resign herself to.

When Ah-Fat arrived back in Gold Mountain, he burned incense and prayed every day. He was determined to save up the head tax for Six Fingers as soon as possible even if it meant postponing repayment of the debts from the *diulau*. Harvests improved and his savings grew. Within two years, he had enough for the head tax.

When Ah-Fat had finished his prayers to Tam Kung, he went to make up the bed. The cotton wadding in the quilt was not brand new but he had fluffed it up and it was nice and soft. The old quilt cover was threadbare from much washing, so Ah-Fat had bought a new one of fine linen, English-made, from the department store in Vancouver. He planned to change the quilt cover. After that, he would set off with the horse and cart to buy a few household necessities in town, and then to the barber for a shave. By then it should be just about time to go and meet the boat. It was due to dock at three o'clock.

Ah-Fat was just sewing up the quilt when the hired hand, Loong Am, put his head through the door and said: "Now that Auntie is coming, we can have soup for dinner. We won't have to eat the mouldy rice you cook up every day that even a pig would turn up its nose at." Ah-Fat spat out the end of the thread. "You've got a lot of nerve moaning that you're hard up, you young punk," he retorted, "as if you haven't done well out of me for years. And even if I give you a few extra cents it won't get you sons and grandchildren. You're better off going home to get yourself a wife, then she can cook you tasty soup whenever you want."

Loong Am gave a cackle of laughter. "You're so stingy, Uncle, you don't let a cent slip through your fingers. I'll never make any money from you. I'm lucky to get enough to eat, let alone a wife."

Ah-Fat gave Loong Am the needle and thread. He was getting long-sighted, and finding it more and more difficult to thread needles, write letters and cut his fingernails. "Uncle, my kid brother saw Kam Shan a few days ago in Kamloops," Loong Am said as he poked the thread through the needle's eye.

Ah-Fat did not answer, but the hand holding the scissors paused in mid-air.

After Kam Shan left two years ago, he wandered from place to place. He did not dare show his face in Vancouver because he had snatched the girl from the brothel. He had been heard of in Port Hope, and then Yale. At New Year, he had mailed his father a cheque for fifty dollars. There was no address on the envelope, but the postmark was Lytton. Ah-Fat had been there when he was building the railroad, though nothing now remained of it. It was hard to imagine what Kam Shan had been up to, to save such a lot of money in this ghost town. Ah-Fat's eyes flickered in agitation for days afterwards, but there had been no further news.

He regretted throwing his son out. The boy was trouble whether he was at home or not. But at least if he was home, Ah-Fat could keep an eye on him. If he was away, Ah-Fat had no idea what he was doing and never stopped worrying about him. He used to believe that what the eye did not see, the heart did not grieve over. He did not believe that any more. His son's misdeeds were a thorn in his side when he could see them. But now that Kam Shan was gone, he found himself entangled in a bramble bush from which he could not extricate himself. No sooner had he pulled one thorn out than he discovered another. It would have been better to have him close by.

The thorns hurt when they stabbed him and they hurt when he pulled them out. But Ah-Fat shared his pain with no one and, in consequence, no one mentioned Kam Shan in his presence. It was as if he had never had a son—though if he did hear Kam Shan's name on someone's lips, his eyes flickered for days afterwards.

"Kam Shan rents a corner of a shop and does a roaring trade taking people's photographs. Most of his customers are Redskins," Loong Am was saying. "They pose with boots on, with guns at their waists, like cowboys."

"Just him ... alone?" Ah-Fat asked after a moment's silence. This was the first time since Kam Shan's departure that he had asked after him.

Loong Am knew what his boss was getting at. He gave an apologetic cough, then said reluctantly: "That woman, she's there too." He looked up to see if Ah-Fat was angry, then went on: "My brother says her English is better than Kam Shan's. The White women and the Redskin women all want to talk to her."

Ah-Fat's face darkened like a storm cloud.

Loong Am pulled a knotted handkerchief out of his pocket and put it in Ah-Fat's hand. "My brother told Kam Shan that his mum was coming out to Vancouver, and Kam Shan asked when. He wanted to go and meet the boat. My brother told him not to, in case it made you angry. Kam Shan just stood there like an idiot, then he went upstairs and brought down this handkerchief and asked my brother to give it to Auntie so she could buy herself some clothes in town. Kam Shan said not to let you see."

Ah-Fat threw the bundle onto the bed without looking at it. Loong Am coughed again. "You've got a fierce temper, Uncle!" he said. "Kam Shan did nothing wrong, after all. What would you do if a girl hung onto your coattails like that? Wouldn't you take her in? Kam Shan must have got his good nature from you. Besides, why look a gift horse in the mouth? He's got a girl without you having to buy wedding gifts or pay the head tax. If you don't like her, get him another woman as his first wife and be done with it. Why get in such a temper about it?"

Ah-Fat still said nothing but his expression softened.

When Loong Am had gone, Ah-Fat shut the door and opened the handkerchief. It contained a pile of small change and a bundle of crumpled low-value notes, damp from grease or sweat. Ah-Fat counted the money: twelve dollars and eighty-six cents.

That boy! He was still his flesh-and-blood son. Ah-Fat's eyes welled up. At least now he knew that Kam Shan had settled down. Ah-Fat had sent him away and he could not call him back. But once Six Fingers arrived, perhaps she could bring them back together.

Ah-Fat drove his horse and cart to the docks, his head filled with longing for Six Fingers—and Kam Shan too. He could not bring himself to think of Kam Shan directly, only by way of Six Fingers. She was the bridge between father and son. Neither could reach the other except through her. Without her mediation, they would only ever look at each other from opposite banks.

But it was not Six Fingers who disembarked that day. It was Kam Ho.

He was the last off the boat. He staggered under the weight of a carrying pole with two enormous suitcases, inching his way along like an ant burdened with a lump of mud. Ah-Fat nearly buckled at the knees with astonishment.

"What's happened to your mother?"

"Mum said I had to come because Kam Shan's left and you need help."

"Was that your granny's idea?" asked Ah-Fat, seizing his son by the front of his jacket.

"No, it wasn't. Granny told Mum to come too but Mum said that if she came it would add to your expenses, and she wouldn't be able to pull her weight. I didn't want to come. It was Mum who insisted on buying the ticket for me."

As Kam Ho stammered out his explanation, he saw Ah-Fat's face fall. He knew then that his dad did not want him here. He had stumbled in his very first steps in Gold Mountain. How many steps did he have to take before he could stand tall and proud in his father's eyes? Kam Ho walked slower and slower, bent ever lower under his burden, as if to hide in his own shadow.

"What are you crying for? I haven't done anything to hurt you."

Ah-Fat frowned in distaste at the sight of his son's tangled, filthy hair and the dried-up puke on the front of his jacket from the long sea journey.

He wondered how on earth his two sons had turned out so different from one another.

"This is it."

Ah-Fat jumped down from the cart, handed the blue bundle to Kam Ho and walked towards to the house. It was big, two storeys, with a garden in front. Kam Ho stood outside the iron gate looking into the garden. He could not see the front door, only three porches. The midday sun beat down, bleaching everything white. The three porches stood out like black holes against the white glare. When Kam Ho thought about who lived in these black holes, a cold shiver ran down his spine in spite of the heat of the sun.

"I don't want to go, Dad! I want to stay at home and work on the farm with you" was what he wanted to say.

He had held the words back from the moment they left home. Now they had turned to stone in his mouth and he was not able to utter them.

When Ah-Fat first raised the idea, he did so gently.

"The Hendersons' maid has gone back to England to get married, and they can't find anyone to help out. Mrs. Henderson is not a well woman, and she needs a servant," he had told Kam Shan.

"Mr. Henderson is a friend I met when I was building the railroad. He's helped me and your uncle Ah-Lam a lot. If it wasn't for him, I would never have had the money to buy all this land."

It was only after Ah-Fat had talked his way around the subject of the Hendersons for some time that Kam Ho finally caught on. His father wanted him to go and be their houseboy, the way that Ah-Choi and Ah-Yuet were servants. Mr. Henderson had saved his father's skin and he could not turn him down now.

The shock of this realization stuck like grains of uncooked rice in Kam Ho's throat, making it difficult to breathe. When he could speak again, he protested: "But I've never cooked. I don't even know how to light the stove."

"Mrs. Henderson will teach you."

"But I don't understand the *yeung fans'* language!"

"You'll pick it up."

"But...."

Gradually his father's patience wore thin. His eyebrows drew together in a frown and his scar thickened. "I can't imagine why your mother sent you out here!"

Kam Ho shut his mouth then. Ah-Fat had touched a nerve, one that remained raw for years. The boat that brought him should have been carrying his mother, who could make life comfortable for his father as he got older. That comfort had been snatched away by his arrival, even though he had not wanted to come. He, Kam Ho, would never be able to redeem himself as long as he lived.

During that morning's journey, Kam Ho slumped listlessly over his bag of belongings. He was silent. He could not speak—his eyes brimmed with tears and he knew that if he opened his mouth to speak, the tears would flow. He had been in Gold Mountain for four days and had seen nothing and no one except for his father and their farm. Gold Mountain was a bottomless pit and his father was the lifeline that hung down over the edge. Without him, Kam Ho would be lost in this pitch-black hole and never see the light of day again. But today, his father demanded that he leave that one familiar face and walk through a stranger's door, to wait on a *yeung fan* woman. He had no idea if he would be able to stomach the food she ate, or sleep in the bed she provided. Worst of all, he did not know a word of her language.

"When you were at home, you had servants to wait on you. Now you're going to a *yeung fan* house to wait on them. Don't put on any 'young master' airs. Any kind of noises—farting, burping, coughing—you do them out of earshot. At mealtimes, if she doesn't ask you to eat with them, then you eat in the kitchen. Wash your feet every night before going to bed. There's a piece of salt fish in the bag, so if you don't like their cooking, you can eat this with it.

"You'll work six days a week and have one day's rest. When you've cooked the Saturday dinner, you can go. I'll come and pick you up and bring you back first thing Monday morning.

"You'll get one dollar twenty-five a day, including your day off, that's thirty-seven dollars fifty a month. All your board is covered, so you should be able to earn quite a bit in a year."

As he pushed open the iron gate and walked in through the middle porch, Ah-Fat suddenly put his arm round his son's shoulder. Kam Ho was so skinny that his bones dug into Ah-Fat's hand. Kam Ho heard his father's voice crack a little as he said: "There's a lot of money in Gold Mountain, and one dollar is equal to several dollars when you send it home. If you and I can keep this up for a few years, we can clear the debts from the *diulau*."

His father knocked on the door and a dog barked on the other side so furiously the sound made the windows and door frames rattle. The door opened a crack and a woman's face appeared. She shut the door and shouted at the dog. The dog gave an answering bark. Dog and woman continued this exchange of shout and bark until finally the dog admitted defeat and quieted down. At that, the woman opened the door.

She was tall and lanky with a pallid complexion and pale eyes. She was so colourless, in fact, she looked as though she had been steeped in water for days until all the flavour had drained out of her. She was wearing a tight-fitting top and a floor-length skirt. When she turned around, Kam Ho quickly shut his eyes in case her waist snapped.

The woman and his dad exchanged a few words but Kam Ho understood nothing. He shrank, trembling, against his father. He gripped his bag as if it were the only thing that held him together.

"Mrs. Henderson asked how old you are. I said fifteen, but she doesn't believe me. She thinks you only look about ten," Ah-Fat explained.

"Only bloody ten!" Kam Ho swore, but silently. It was the rudest utterance he was capable of.

"Mrs. Henderson asks if you have any questions."

"I'm not going to make her bed for her, no way," said Kam Ho after a long moment's thought.

His father hooted with laughter. Then turned back to the woman and said, with a straight face: "My son says he doesn't know how to make beds."

Mrs. Henderson frowned. "From what Rick says, your boy doesn't know how to do anything. Making beds is the simplest task, but of course I'll teach him."

His dad ruffled Kam Ho's hair and was gone, taking that protective shadow with him and leaving Kam Ho exposed to the woman's gaze. When Kam Ho turned to look, his father had already jumped onto the cart. "Saturday, Dad, as early as…." he said, but the words were snatched away by the wind. The horse was already clip-clopping down the street.

Kam Ho threw down his bag and leaned against the door frame, sobbing.

The tears, so long suppressed that they felt like grit in his eyes, fell heavily to the floor. His father was gone and he had no sky to shelter him or earth to hold him up. How was he going to face the world?

The woman stood in the doorway, watching him silently. The dog came out and, extending a blood-red tongue, began to lick the salty tears from his jacket.

"Just a year, Dad, that's what you said," Kam Ho said to himself.

It was something he was to repeat to himself countless times in the days to come.

Until finally, he stopped believing it.

"E … gg."

Mrs. Henderson took an egg from the basket on the table, held it up for Kam Ho and pronounced the word for him.

She put the egg back and made a circular motion with her two hands in the air, enunciating:

"Ca … ke."

Once she had done this, she pointed to a photograph of Mr. Henderson on the side table, then to her mouth to indicate eating.

Kam Ho had been at the Hendersons' for two weeks, and this was the method Mrs. Henderson had adopted for speaking to him. He did not understand in the beginning, and he did not understand now. When he first arrived, his inability to understand was like a great black cowl; now, though the cowl was still in place, glimmers of light seeped through here and there.

He understood that Mrs. Henderson wanted to make her husband a fried egg. Actually, what she really wanted was to make him a cake, a birthday cake.

Mrs. Henderson took an egg, tapped it lightly on the edge of the bowl until the yolk and the white slipped glistening out of the shell. She did the same with the second. The yolk of the third egg was broken and she threw it into the rubbish bin. She picked up the fourth egg, then suddenly changed her mind. Putting it back in the basket, she took Kam Ho's hand and pronounced slowly: "You do it."

Kam Ho guessed that she wanted him to do as she had done. He took hold of an egg and cracked it on the edge of the bowl. The contents shot into the bowl, taking with them some of the eggshell. With the second, he knew to tap it lightly. The yolk and the white slid into the bowl. When it came to the third, he tapped it lightly and threw it into the rubbish bin.

Mrs. Henderson started, then burst out laughing. She laughed so hard that her forehead came up in a bump.

Mrs. Henderson was severely arthritic, and the pain was so bad that it seemed to crawl through every artery and vein of her body. At night when she went to sleep, it was in her fingers, but when she got up in the morning, the pain had travelled to her shoulders. When she drank her coffee, the pain was down in her back and when she stood up, it was in her knees. Her face usually bore a frown of pain and she rarely smiled. But since Kam Ho had come to live with them, she had laughed several times—laughed until she cried.

The first time was the day of Kam Ho's arrival. In the afternoon, she decided to take him through the sweeping of the sitting room and the kitchen. She took a feather duster and showed him how to pass it over the tables and walls. When they got as far as the dining table, Kam Ho suddenly saw something sticking out of the wall next to it, and gave it a poke. There was a click and the room flooded with light. Kam Ho gave a shocked cry and sat down on the floor, covering his ears with his hands. She realized that the boy had never seen a high-wattage electric light before. He thought he had been struck by lightning. In Hoi Ping, they still used oil lamps and even in his New Westminster house, his father only had two ten-watt light bulbs, a bit brighter than oil lamps but still nowhere near as bright as these.

The next morning, when Mr. Henderson was in the bathroom brushing his teeth and Kam Ho was boiling water in the kitchen, there was a sudden shrieking from the living room. After much searching, Kam Ho discovered the noise was coming from a black box on the side table. Mr. Henderson came running out of the bathroom with the toothbrush sticking out of his froth-covered mouth, and gestured to the black box. Kam Ho bundled up a tablecloth and muffled the box as best he could. It rang more quietly but he could still hear it. So he fetched cushions from the sofa and pressed them on top of the box. Still it rang. Mr. Henderson related the incident to his wife at breakfast and she laughed until she shook. Poor child, she said, he's never seen a telephone. How come his father never told him about telephones?

When she finally stopped laughing, and wiped the tears from her eyes, she picked the cracked egg out of the rubbish and brought it back to the table. As she broke it into the bowl, she could not suppress a sigh. Oh Lord, how often must I explain to this Mongol boy that you don't throw every third egg away? she wondered.

Mrs. Henderson took a wooden spoon and lightly beat the eggs in the bowl, then gave the spoon to Kam Ho and made him do the same. He cut a comical figure, his shoulders hunched and his hands beating ferociously as if using a brickbat to smash a fly. It was the same every time he learned some new household skill—he learned to go through the motions but never seemed to understand why.

Mrs. Henderson watched as a tuft of hair on the back of his head bounced up and down in time with his movements. She suppressed a smile. It occurred to her that if she did not tell him to stop, this hare-brained Chinese boy would just carry on beating until he shattered the bowl. She looked for a semblance of expression on his bent face. It was as if a cloth were drawn taut over his features, masking them completely. In fact, his whole body seemed to be enveloped from top to bottom in an impenetrable suit of armour. She sometimes felt as if she wanted to pierce a hole in it, just to see what kind of blood would flow out.

But there was no need for that. On the first Saturday after his arrival, as he washed the vegetables in the kitchen, he began to look as if he was losing his wits. His ears quivered like those of a guard dog, straining to hear movement outside the front door. He was desperate for his father to turn up and take him home. Finally, she had found the chink in his armour— and it told her that he hated being at her house.

Her knees began to hurt and she had to sit down on a chair. Kam Ho's eyes were fixed on the eggs he was beating. They looked strange, these Mongols, she thought: flat, open faces, eyes that looked like two fine slits slashed in a sheet of pastry. Their clothes were peculiar too. On top, they wore what looked like long coats fastened not up the front but at the side up to the armpits. Only a short length of trouser leg was visible, the cuffs tied with string around each ankle. Their shoes and socks were made of cloth. What a performance it must be to go to the toilet wearing an outfit like that!

What they ate was as peculiar as what they wore. A few days before, she had smelled something strange, and had walked all around the house to trace its source. It was coming from Kam Ho's room. There she found Kam Ho chewing on a piece of dried fish, which he hastily stuffed into a drawer as soon as he saw her. It looked and smelled like a piece of rotting garbage. She had noticed that he ate very little at the table, and reasoned that he must have been getting hungry. His stomach was not used to the Hendersons' food. She threw away his bag of salted fish, though to touch it nearly made her vomit. She expected that he would protest. But he did not. His face remained as tightly masked as always, with not a shadow of expression showing through.

The next day at dinner, she served him a piece of fish steamed in the French way, pouring melted butter all over it. He took it to the kitchen to eat—he never sat down with them. Out of the corner of her eye, she saw him eat it all, though with difficulty and frequent pauses.

Many years ago, her husband, Rick, had worked with some Chinese railroad navvies and could still tell stories that sounded as fantastic as the tales from the *Thousand and One Nights*. Of course, that was before their marriage. She was the daughter of a Manchester cloth merchant and had come to Vancouver when she married Rick. She had had no close contact with any Chinese apart from the man who ran the Chinese grocery. When Rick suggested that they take on Kam Ho as a houseboy, she had been without her English maid for a week. This was the third maid to depart in the last few years. A properly trained maid was the greatest gift that the Lord could bestow on a British housewife. But all great gifts were hard to find and harder to keep hold of. A young maid who had crossed the

Atlantic to Canada would be sure to meet in her mistress's drawing room some decent young man desperate for a wife. Love and marriage quickly followed. It was rare to find a European maid anywhere in Vancouver nowadays. The result was that young Chinese boys were finding their way into White housewives' kitchens.

Two years ago, Rick left the Vancouver Hotel and started work at the Hudson's Bay Department Store as purchasing manager, which meant making frequent business trips to London, Paris, Munich and the Canadian East Coast. His job was tiring, and whenever she talked to him about getting a new servant, she felt his impatience. So when he suggested they employ Frank's son, although she did not agree straightaway, she did not veto the idea either. Rick's nerves were like a rope stretched thin and her ailments were the heaviest drag on it. Since she did not want the rope to snap, she had to deal with things on her own, but that was only a stopgap measure. In due course, she would find another rope to bear the weight of her problems.

This new rope was a simpleton of a Mongol boy she called "Jimmy." (She could not get her tongue around his Chinese name so she made up one of her own for him.)

"Stop, Jimmy, stop!" Mrs. Henderson said to Kam Ho.

But Kam Ho was deaf to all sounds except those of the banging of the wooden spoon against the bowl. Mrs. Henderson had to stamp her foot hard before Kam Ho heard. The spoon stopped, while his hand remained haplessly quivering—like a horse jerked to a halt by its master that carries on galloping on the spot.

Mrs. Henderson massaged her knee joints and stood up. She began the complicated process of making the cake. Flour, cinnamon, baking soda, baking powder, sugar, water, oil—she measured the proportions carefully according to the recipe. Not forgetting, of course, the vanilla custard which Rick adored. She had no idea how long it would take this Chinese boy to learn the art of baking. She hoped not too long.

Today was Rick's fifty-seventh birthday. She pretended it had slipped her mind and had not given him the slightest hint that she remembered. In fact, she had been making meticulous preparations for this evening for a few days. She had bought the wine, a fifteen-year-old red Bordeaux. They would start with a clam chowder. The appetizer was pâté de fois gras on lettuce. The main courses would be smoked salmon and shoulder of lamb. And the dessert would of course be the cake. These dishes, normally only to be found in European-style restaurants, all would be made by her. She knew that Rick was tired of the dinner parties he had to go to, preferring to slump into his own armchair to relax and then eat a simple home-cooked meal. The cake needed forty-five minutes in the oven, so it was too early to bake. Rick got home at six o'clock, so she would put it in at half past five. After Rick had come in through the door, taken off his coat and loosened his tie, the cake would appear on the cake plate, warm and spongy soft. Then she would exclaim in pretended astonishment: "Good heavens! What a nice cake. It must be somebody's birthday!"

In fact, all this preparation, although intended for his enjoyment, paled in comparison with the preparations she made for herself. She had had the best dressmaker in Vancouver make her an evening gown in the latest Paris fashion. It was of crimson satin, trimmed with lace. The first time she had met Rick in Manchester, she was wearing a long crimson dress. They had both been guests at the house of a friend. He was a balding forty-eight-year old man and she, at twenty-six, was already an old maid. They were both past the best time for marriage, but a successful man, no matter how old, could always find a mate. She held herself back that day, not making any special effort to talk to him or distinguish herself from the bevy of other young women. But he stared so intently at her outfit that she seemed to feel his gaze on her all the way home that evening. The next day she accepted his invitation to lunch. She never forgot that he liked the colour crimson. She was the daughter of a textile merchant and had grown up surrounded by bales of cloth. She knew just what fabric and colours flattered her figure and made the sparks fly. This evening, she was eager to see those sparks in the eyes of her husband.

She looked up at the wall clock. It was a quarter to three. She had plenty of time to take a short nap on a chair before going upstairs to dress for dinner. She put down the cake tin she had prepared, and suddenly felt a searing pain biting into her knees. The pain was so savage that she slumped to the ground before she even had time to cry out. Kam Ho ran over to her. Drops of moisture squeezed out from between tight frown lines on Mrs.

Henderson's face, whether tears or sweat he could not tell. Blood welled up—she had jabbed her fingernails into her temples.

Kam Ho stood frozen to the spot, then suddenly dropped to his knees, pulled her hands away from her face, and pinched the fleshy Tiger's Mouth acupressure point between her thumb and index finger. Mrs. Henderson's eyes widened in surprise as the pains in her knees gradually eased. Kam Ho pressed his lips together until they went white and his wrist trembled as if from cold. His whole circulation seemed concentrated in his pincer-like fingers, turning them into two livid sausages. Mrs. Henderson remained completely still; she was afraid that the slightest sound or movement on her part might call the pain back again.

After a while Kam Ho finally gave a sigh and released her hand. She stood up shakily, aware that the burn was still in her knees but was no longer so raw and painful. She looked up with an expression of relief to see Kam Ho's face slowly cracking into a smile—his first since coming to her house.

"My mum ... I ...," he stammered, gesturing into the far distance, then to his hand.

He was speaking in English.

She was so overcome by the pain, and then the relief, that at first she did not understand. It was only as she was limping up the stairs that she realized the boy must have been trying to tell her that his mother in faraway China had taught him how to soothe pain.

Mr. Henderson did not get home at six o'clock that day. In fact, it was a quarter to eight by the time he walked in. The dining room was in darkness, lit only by two red candles on the table. They had burned low and tears of melted wax poured down the silver candle holders. The candles formed hazy rings of light in which Mr. Henderson could make out two long-stemmed wineglasses.

"Phyllis, why are all the lights off?" he called out, flipping the switches on. In the electric light, the two candles were reduced to dim fireflies. Mr. Henderson saw that the table was laid for two: silver cutlery, gold-rimmed English bone china, monogrammed linen napkins and a lace tablecloth. His wife normally kept them in the display cabinet and rarely took them out for use; his mother-in-law had sent them from Yorkshire as wedding presents. In the corner between the kitchen and the dining room, a dark shape rustled. It was Kam Ho. He had been dozing on a footstool when the lights came on, dreaming some dream about his village and the river.

Kam Ho rubbed his eyes and stood up to take Mr. Henderson's coat and hat. A smell hung around the garments. Mr. Henderson was snorting a bit like a water buffalo and his breath was heavy with alcohol. "What's my wife got all this stuff out for?" he asked. Kam Ho did not know what to say and stood looking at his master mutely. Mr. Henderson took out his handkerchief and wiped a drop of spittle from the corner of Kam Ho's mouth. "Where's my wife?" he asked thickly. Kam Ho understood these words and he pointed upstairs.

They heard a rustling on the stairs, like the sound of locusts jumping from leaf to leaf. Mr. Henderson knew without looking round that this was the sound of his wife's skirts brushing the floorboards.

"Why are you so late, Rick?"

Mr. Henderson glanced at his wife but was overtaken by a loud belch before he had had time to say anything. It was quite clear that this was not just a single solitary belch, but the standard-bearer for a multitude of others just waiting behind. There was no time to waste. He rushed to the toilet and shut the door firmly behind him.

Mrs. Henderson stood outside the toilet door, listening to the taps running. Eventually the noise subsided. In the interval between one burp and the next, her husband spoke: "I'm sorry. I went for a drink with Mark. His wife has gone to France, and he didn't want to go home so early." Mark was Mr. Henderson's boss.

Finally Mr. Henderson opened the bathroom door and emerged. He came face to face with his magnificently dressed wife. She looked down at her toes, and her cheeks glowed a faint pink, like a girl waiting to be asked to dance by a boy at a promenade.

"Uh, very nice. The colour suits you," Mr. Henderson muttered indistinctly, patting his wife on the shoulder as he walked past her.

She stiffened momentarily, and the soft satin folds of her gown stiffened with her. She said nothing, but continued to stare down at her toes. The pink glow on her cheeks gradually receded, exposing an expanse of gaunt pallor underneath.

Kam Ho trembled. There was a soft pattering in his ears—Mrs. Henderson's tears hitting the floor.

"Have you invited guests tonight, dear?" Mr. Henderson asked his wife, leaning over the banister and wafting a scent of Lux soap down the stairs.

My dear mother,

Your letter arrived a few days ago. I was very happy to hear that Granny is in good health and my little sister can walk now. There has been fighting all over Europe in the last few years and a lot of men from Gold Mountain have joined up. With no one to work the land, Dad has been able to buy a lot of it cheaply. Mr. Henderson says the war will be over soon and then prices of land and farm products will go up. Dad says that there is a lot we can do with such good land in the future. I have been at the Hendersons' a year now and still want to go home and help Dad with the farm, but Mrs. Henderson's health has not got any better. Dad says he owes Mr. Henderson a debt of gratitude for all his help in the past and has told me to stay another year. I have learned to cook and wash and clean around the house and when I am free, Mrs. Henderson teaches me a little English. Please do not worry about me. I am making progress in everything. My brother, Kam Shan, has been here a few times. He lives in Kamloops now, quite a way from Vancouver, and has opened a photographic studio. There are a lot of Redskins living out there and they love having their pictures taken so it is easy to make money. Dad and Kam Shan are still not speaking, but now that all three of us are earning, we will be able to pay back the debts on the diulau *sooner. Then we can put money by so you and my sister can come to Gold Mountain and we can all be together.*

Most humbly, your son, Kam Ho

Year five of the Republic, the eighth day of the ninth month, Vancouver, British Columbia

According to Mrs. Henderson, this was the coldest of all the ten years she had spent in Canada.

Kam Ho had never worn a hat but this winter he did. It was an old one of Mr. Henderson's, checked, with a broad brim. Mr. Henderson had a big head, and on Kam Ho, the hat was constantly slipping right down over his eyes and nose so he had to stop and push it back.

One crisp morning, Kam Ho looked out the front door and saw long transparent sticks hanging from the eaves. The morning sunshine glinted feebly off the strange spiral shapes hidden inside them that resembled water weeds. Kam Ho had no idea what icicles were, and he knocked one down with the old broom kept in the front hall, and poked one end into his mouth. The coldness made his jaw drop open, but the ice soon melted on his tongue and the water began to trickle down his throat, stabbing his gullet as it went. He licked his numb lips and found grains of dirt stuck there. He spat the dirt out with a "pah!" and then remembered he had an urgent errand to run.

He had been taking this route once a week for a year by now and knew it well. He knew all the trees on all the corners and the cracks in all the paving stones.

After going out of the Hendersons' garden gate, it was a short walk to a middling-sized street, just big enough for pedestrians and carriages. Of course, a street this wide in Hoi Ping would only be found in town. He walked fifteen minutes along this street, turned right and came to a school. To go straight ahead, he had to walk around the school along a narrow alley, but that added an extra fifteen minutes to his journey. So Kam Ho used to take a shortcut across the school's small playing field, and in another five minutes cut through to the street on the other side. It was a short street. Kam Ho had counted carefully and there were only twenty-one houses from end to end. But he did not go right to the end. Between the eighteenth and nineteenth houses there was a narrow passage, just wide enough for a person and a dog, which brought him out at the back of Canton Alley.

He did not need to walk through to Canton Alley itself—the stuff he was looking for was not on sale there. Instead, he quietly made his way past the piles of rubbish and waste paper and pushed open the back door of a shop which went by the name of the Kwong Cheong General Store. They stocked exactly the same stuff as any other shop of this type in Chinatown—

fruit, vegetables, rice and condiments—and it was all laid out in exactly the same way, with the dry goods at the back and the fresh vegetables in the front. But this was the only place in Chinatown where Kam Ho could get what he needed today. And it would not be found displayed on the shelves.

He made his way in through the back of the shop, acting just like a regular customer, picking up a handful of yellow beans from a sack, holding them to his nose, sniffing and putting them back again. Then he picked a salted duck egg out of a basket and shook it to see if the yolk was runny. But this was just for the benefit of the shop's customers. Once they had gone, he went straight up to the counter and gave the empty bottle he was carrying to the owner, together with the money he had been carrying in his pocket. The shop owner did not bother to count it. He could tell from the weight of the coins that it was the right amount. The bottle was an old sesame oil bottle; the label was dark and transparent with grease. The owner bent down, felt around behind the counter until he found what he was looking for, then filled the bottle with the stuff and gave it back to Kam Ho. That was all there was to it. No need to talk, or even to look at each other. The owner knew that the young man would be back within the week.

Kam Ho went out the way he had come in, and started on his way home. The whole trip took him an hour or so. Usually, if the children were on a break when he came to the school, he waited until a neatly dressed woman teacher, her blouse buttoned up to the neck, rang the handbell for the children to go back into class before crossing the school playing field.

But today he could not wait. Rather, it was Mrs. Henderson who could not wait. Her shoulders had pained her all night. Kam Ho's room was at one end of the house, and Mrs. Henderson's at the other, but Kam Ho could hear her moans as she tossed and turned. No sooner had Mrs. Henderson seen her husband off to work that morning than she sent Kam Ho to get the bottle filled.

Not with sesame oil, but with opium juice.

His brother, Kam Shan, had told him that opium soothed pain. Kam Shan happened to be visiting on a day when Mrs. Henderson had an attack of arthritis. He told him to buy opium juice in Chinatown so she could try it. The Gold Mountain government had banned opium years ago, Kam

Shan said, and shut down the opium dens. Now, only the Kwong Cheong General Store sold it, but even then, only on the quiet—under the counter to known customers. He just had to mention the name Red-Eye Bat. Kam Ho stared at his brother and said nothing. Kam Shan had lived in Kamloops for years and only came to Vancouver occasionally, but he still knew the secrets of every store in Chinatown.

It was then that Mrs. Henderson started to drink opium juice. It turned out to be so effective that she would hardly let the bottle out of her sight.

As Kam Ho approached the school, he saw half a dozen children on the playing field chasing each other with sticks. They're enjoying their game so much they won't notice me, he thought to himself, I'll just cut through. He tucked the bottle inside his jacket and, making himself as inconspicuous as possible, snuck across the field.

Ching Chong Chinaman sitting on a wall,
He thinks one cent's worth twenty-four.

He heard the sharp cries as the children pinched their noses and assumed ladylike tones. Then there was a pattering of laughter behind him and he knew they were coming after him.

Chink Chink Chinaman sitting on a fence
Trying to make a dollar out of ten cents

The shrill cries were swelling into a confused clamour. They were on his heels. He clutched the bottle to his chest and sped on.

But his body suddenly flagged. Something hit him on the back. Pain flared up until his back and shoulders were on fire. They were throwing stones. The children were the same size as he was, and so they had no fear of him. He may have been seventeen but he had not grown much and still looked like a child.

A fierce pain jabbed him in his gut, as if a rope was tightening around his intestines. Tighter and tighter it pulled until his guts felt like they were trussed up. He pressed the bottle against his belly, exhaled sharply and the tension suddenly eased off. But his belly took that as an invitation to let go completely and something hot filled the crotch of his trousers. He smelled the stink.

Faster, faster, his head told his legs, but by now his head was not in charge. He heard a ping on his forehead, like the sound of a watermelon left to rot and burst open in the field, and something hot and sticky trickled down into his eyes, gluing them together. His eyes were no use any more. He had only his legs, driven on by blind instinct. They knew which way to take him without his eyes telling them.

Gradually the rabble receded into the distance.

When Mrs. Henderson came to open the door of the house, Kam Ho was standing there with blood pouring down his face. He pulled up his jacket and extracted the bottle. Pushing it into her hands, he said: "My hat ... gone," and slumped to the ground.

He was woken up by something icy cold on his chest. He was lying in a bed. Beside him stood Mrs. Henderson and a man in a black hat and glasses. The man looked familiar somehow. It was Dr. Walsh, Mrs. Henderson's doctor.

Dr. Walsh moved the cold thing around Kam Ho's chest a few times and said: "His heart rate is fine but his temperature is one hundred and five degrees. Apart from infection in the external injuries, there's still some gastric infection. How many times has he opened his bowels today?"

"I've lost count. My poor bed," said Mrs. Henderson.

"Did he eat anything unusual yesterday?"

Mrs. Henderson shook her head. "Those Mongols are like horses. They eat anything. But he eats the same as us now, and Rick and I haven't had any problems."

"Apart from medicine to settle his stomach, you need to get the fever down. Do you have any ice in the house?"

Kam Ho felt as if he were lying on a thick layer of billowing cloud. The voices of Mrs. Henderson and the doctor floated in and out. He did not understand but he knew they were talking about him.

"Henry, I've just had a thought!" he heard Mrs. Henderson exclaim. "This morning, I saw the stupid boy break off an icicle and eat it."

Kam Ho did not hear what the doctor said in reply because just at that moment, he sank into a trough in the cloud.

He just hoped it was not Mrs. Henderson who had taken off his trousers and cleaned him up.

That was the last clear thought he had before falling into a deep sleep.

It was evening when he woke up, the evening of the third day, as he discovered later. He guessed the time of day from the light coming through the curtain. The room was gloomy. The light was off, but one candle burned on the windowsill. The candle threw a flickering shadow over a blue expanse; the blue assumed a shape that was sometimes angular, sometimes round.

As Kam Ho stared at the form, it gradually turned into a woman's back, topped by two bony shoulder blades draped in a blue nightgown. The nightgown trembled. The woman was crying.

"… He eats the leftovers. I don't even know if he gets enough to eat at each meal. Last Christmas, when Rick's aunt came from Halifax, we didn't let him go home for the holiday and we didn't pay him any extra either.… Once he helped Rick into bed and Rick's shirt tore at the seams, and I called him a Mongol ass.… Oh Lord, you know everything that goes on, you know all the injustices there are in this world. Now you're punishing me, you've made him the burden I have to carry. You've made me bear the weight of my own sin. I can't bear it, Lord. I beg you to take this burden from me.… Every life is created by you, even a Mongol's life.…"

Kam Ho turned over in bed. "Ma'am," he said softly. The woman started in surprise. She had been kneeling for too long and her legs had gone numb. She struggled to her feet, tottered over and fell to her knees again at the bedside. She suddenly reached out her arms and embraced him. Two warm mounds under the thin nightgown pressed against his chest, so hard he could hardly breathe.

"You're finally awake, child," the woman murmured.

The next morning, after Mr. Henderson had left for work, Mrs. Henderson put on a thick fur coat and stood waiting in the hall. "You're coming with me," she said, pointing at Kam Ho. He wanted to ask where they were going but did not dare because her face was ugly with rage.

He followed her out the door. She walked today like a mother hen ready for battle, her claws splayed, and her feathers ruffled. Kam Ho had to trot to keep up. His legs felt like cotton wool. He was unsteady on his feet and wavered from left to right and back again. He had been in bed for some days, and although the sun was getting in his eyes now, he still felt cold.

The wind whistled down the road, cutting through his cotton jacket and whipping him painfully. He was not wearing a hat—he could not get one on because his head was topped with a thick layer of bandages. He kept his ears warm by covering them with his hands.

Mrs. Henderson crossed the playing field and marched up to the school door. She stood before the janitor, her hands on her hips, and said in a loud, clear voice:

"Go and get the principal this minute!"

Kam Ho sat on the doorstep plucking a chicken.

He had bought the chicken already plucked but it was not up to Mrs. Henderson's standards. She could not stand the black dots which showed through the skin. They made her think of bluebottle maggots and things like that. So Kam Ho had to go over the chicken once more and remove every last feather root.

The roses in the garden were in a riot of bloom, covering the garden fence in swaths of scarlet. There was a tree in the street—he did not know its name—from which hairy flowers like caterpillars fluttered down in the breeze. Jenny staggered over to where Kam Ho sat, her outstretched hands full of the flowers. "Jimmy, Jimmy!" she cried. "Look ... flowers!" Jenny was three and a half years old. She dribbled as she chattered, so she always had to wear a bib around her neck.

She was Mr. and Mrs. Henderson's adopted child and had been with them for a year. Although the couple had been married nearly twenty years, they were unable to have children. The germ of the idea to adopt a baby had been in Mr. Henderson's mind for a long time, but his wife would not agree. She was determined to prove her womb was fertile and was just waiting for the right combination of seed and weather. But as her thirty-ninth birthday came and went, she grew less confident, and finally agreed to adopt.

But it was all far too late. Mr. Henderson was learning to be a father when he was already old enough to be a grandfather. Once, all three of them were out shopping and he bumped into an old friend he had not been in touch with for years. The friend gripped him by the hand and shook it, exclaiming how well he was looking for his age: "I had no idea your daughter and granddaughter were so grown up," he said. Mr. Henderson did not enlighten him. From then on, he was reluctant to go out in the company of his wife and daughter.

Kam Ho gave Jenny's chin a wipe with the bib. "Go and watch the ants moving house," he said. He was not paying attention to the toddler, or indeed to the chicken. His mind was elsewhere. Kam Ho's ears were erect and quivering like rabbits, straining to hear a clanging sound from the street outside. It was not Saturday, and he was not waiting for his father. He was waiting for a different cart.

A vegetable cart.

The war in Europe was finally over. And now that it was done, the Gold Mountain soil had its farmers back. Almost overnight, the streets and alleyways of Gold Mountain towns teemed with vegetable and fruit sellers. They came knocking, sometimes several times a day, laden with baskets of fresh produce carried on shoulder poles or packed into horse-drawn carts.

The Hendersons' house was a stone's throw from the vegetable market which stocked everything they needed. But Kam Ho preferred to buy from the hawker who came to their own front door. It was fresh, cheap and convenient. At least, that was what he said to Mrs. Henderson, to whom he could not explain the real reason.

He had been with the Hendersons for seven years. The first two years he longed to go home but his father would not have him back. His father owed the Hendersons a debt of gratitude that could never be repaid. By the third year, Kam Ho had lost interest in moving. The job was a meal ticket after all, one which he was used to, and a lot less bother than looking for a new one. Later on, Ah-Fat's farm failed and he needed his son's wages to support the whole family, so even if Kam Ho wanted to leave, he could not.

The men came home from the battlefields, swapped their army uniforms for civvy clothes and looked around to discover that others had grown rich from their absence. Ah-Fat had used this time to secure the title deeds of neighbouring fields. Before everything went wrong, he owned the biggest farm for hundreds of miles around. He had long given up selling door to door. He had a team of nine horse-drawn carts to distribute his vegetables and fruit, meat and eggs to the markets.

Ah-Fat had paid back the debts on the *diulau* and had saved up enough to pay the head tax for his wife and daughter. But he was in no hurry to bring them over to Gold Mountain. He decided he would save up for one more season and then sell the farm and go home to live out a peaceful retirement. They would all go, and he would marry both his sons to decent girls—he still refused to acknowledge the woman Kam Shan lived with.

But that season was the ruin of Ah-Fat. His cleverness did him in.

His cleverness was like a candle which lit only the road before him. He had no idea that behind him, the skies had darkened. He had no inkling that his wealth had fanned the flames of jealousy among his competitors. He naively believed that hard work and prudent saving would be enough.

The year before, an American businessman had come to Vancouver to open a different kind of market: the produce was laid out on shelves and the customers could select for themselves, like in a department store. Ah-Fat was fired with enthusiasm and adamant that, by hook or by crook, he would sell his own produce direct to the supermarket. It would save such a lot of time and bother. And by dint of cutting his profit margins to the bare minimum, he finally succeeded in getting his produce on the supermarket shelves.

But, unbeknownst to him, someone was watching his every move.

The meat and vegetables bearing the label of Ah-Fat's farm had only been in the supermarket two weeks when disaster struck.

Ah-Fat was taken to court over allegations that his chicken meat was contaminated and had given several customers serious food poisoning.

The supermarket owner saved his own skin by dumping all Ah-Fat's produce and suing him in court.

The government blocked all Ah-Fat's bank accounts and carried out an investigation.

In the years since he set up his first laundry, Ah-Fat had been taken to court many times. He used to say he was in and out of Gold Mountain courts more frequently than his own house and knew the judges better than his own wife. Each time he had had a lucky escape, even turned it to his own advantage once or twice—but not this time. On previous occasions, he was a small man who could take it. But this time, he was a big businessman, and it broke him. No sooner had the trial begun than his creditors sprang up like mushrooms after spring rain. Banks, fertilizer merchants, the water, electricity and coal suppliers. He might get away from one but he could not avoid them all. The little cash he had left was only enough to pay off Loong Am and the other workers. Eventually, Mr. Henderson advised Ah-Fat to declare bankruptcy. Overnight, his flourishing business crumbled to dust, leaving him without a cent. The burden of supporting the family fell on Kam Ho, whose wages now went straight to his father before his own hands had time to warm the notes.

After this, Ah-Fat aged rapidly. It showed not in his face or his body but in his eyes. He had been a keen-eyed man with a sharp, crystalline gaze. Now his eyes were clouded, as if grains of sand had been dropped into them. Whenever Kam Ho went home to see his father, he would find him sitting alone in a room shrouded in smoke, a cigarette dangling from his lips. He was living on his own, and on the days when he could not be bothered to cook for himself, he got by on a mug of tea and a dry biscuit.

"Go home," said Kam Ho. "Go back to Hoi Ping and live with Mum. Mum'll feed you with good food." Ah-Fat shook his head vigorously. "I can only go when I've made money. Otherwise they'll say I've come home as a beggar." "Who would dare accuse you of being a beggar?" protested Kam Ho. "Look at all the property our family owns. Besides, I'll send you dollar letters every month and you can smoke all the tobacco you want."

Ah-Fat looked at his son and tears welled up in his eyes.

"I sent you out to work the minute you got off the boat. I never gave you the chance of an education. Your brother never wanted to study but you've had to work too hard to study. If only you had, you would understand how things work here and you could have kept all these people from hounding me."

Ah-Fat did not want to go back to Hoi Ping in the state he was in now.

He sold the only thing he still possessed—the house he had lived in for over a decade—and moved back to Vancouver. When he left the place that had caused him so much trouble, he was only a few months short of his sixtieth birthday.

Ah-Fat did not get a lot for the house in New Westminster and could only afford a very small house in Vancouver. He did his best to find work.

But his cooking skills were limited and he could not work in a kitchen. He asked in laundries but as his sight was failing, he could not do the mending or ironing. He got a job in a general store, helping to unload goods but sprained his back on the first day. In the end the only thing he could do was turn his own house into a little shop and set up in business writing letters, Spring Festival couplets, marriage announcements and purchasing contracts. However, demand for his services was negligible because, unlike in the old days, there were plenty of young people around who could read and write for themselves.

Ah-Fat realized to his consternation that at the age of sixty, he was completely useless. He could not even support himself.

One day Kam Ho said to him: "Get Kam Shan to come back and live with you, Dad." It was all so long ago since Kam Shan had run off with the girl prostitute and the Spring Gardens brothel had been closed for many years. There would not be any trouble if he came back to Vancouver. Kam Ho had made this suggestion before and his father had always been set against it. This time, however, he said nothing. Kam Ho took his silence as agreement.

Kam Ho knew why his father had given in: Kam Shan's woman was going to have a baby. This was her first. Her former profession had damaged her health and for years she was unable to conceive. Ah-Fat was getting on in years and longed to hold a grandchild in his arms, so his heart finally softened. After ten years of estrangement, Kam Shan and the woman left Kamloops and moved in with his father in Vancouver.

Jenny squatted under the tree, watching the ants. The dog sprawled next to her, watching her watch the ants. There was not a sound to be heard, not even that of a leaf tumbling from the tree. The schoolchildren had gone to school; the office workers had gone to work. The street seemed as still and lifeless as a pricked bubble. Kam Ho looked up at the sky, then down at the ground. It was nearly midday and the shadows were thin.

Why haven't they come? he wondered to himself.

It was not warm enough for the crickets to start chirping but he was beginning to sweat. He could actually have chosen a cool, shady corner in which to pluck the chicken clean but he preferred to sit where he was, with no shelter from the sun, because he got a better view of the street from one end to the other.

A faint sound reached his ears and he leapt up from his stool. It was a bell, a cart-horse bell. There were plenty of hawkers who sold their vegetables house to house but only one hung a bell around the horse's neck. Kam Ho shaded his eyes with his hand and, as he peered into the distance, a black dot came into view around the corner at the end of the street.

Kam Ho's heart began to thump so loudly anyone in the garden could have heard it. He threw down the chicken, pulled off his apron and buttoned his shirt up to the neck. He had long ago grown out of the Chinese-style tunics and trousers he had on when he arrived. Instead, Mrs. Henderson bought his clothes for him: a Western-style outfit of waistcoat, shirt, trousers and leather shoes. And at last there was solid muscle and flesh inside them too. If it had not been for the ridiculous apron, no one would have imagined that this well-dressed, good-looking, strapping young man was actually the servant in the fine house behind him.

Kam Ho flew to the gate and then felt he had been too impulsive. He was just about to go back and wait in the garden when the dog shot past him into the street and set up a furious barking. The dog was old and jowly by now but his bark was as formidable as ever and the sound bounced off the walls of the houses. Kam Ho knew that the vegetable hawker's daughter was afraid of dogs and would not get down if it was loose. He yelled at the animal but, bossy as ever, it gave an answering bark. It sounded as if man and dog were having an argument. The man finally got the upper hand and the dog skulked back into the garden with its tail between its legs.

As the cartwheels rolled nearer, Kam Ho heard a man's hoarse voice shouting in a strong Cantonese accent: "Vegs, fresh, come!" The broken English reminded him of himself when he first arrived at the Hendersons'. He suppressed a smile. This was the girl's father. Her English was a bit better than her dad's, but he knew she was too shy to shout.

A handful of women emerged from the neighbours' houses with baskets in their hands to cluster around the cart. Then Kam Ho heard her voice, thin and timid but floating clear above all the other voices. He listened as she and her father bargained, took the money and counted it, and gave back the change.

His heart hammered wildly in his chest. His money was damp from being clutched in his sweaty palm. Anxiously, he rehearsed his order as he waited his turn. Mrs. Henderson had turned all the housekeeping money over to him now and he was in sole charge of the food shopping. Kam Ho did not want to talk to the hawker's daughter in front of this scrum of women and waited his chance to catch her on her own.

The chance finally came. The women dispersed and there was quiet around the cart. The girl sat down on an empty basket, pulled out a handkerchief tucked into her front and wiped her forehead. She was wearing a blue cotton tunic, buttoned slantwise, and wide-legged trousers. Her hair was tied with a red ribbon. Her garb was typical of a country girl from Canton, and he would have found it a little unrefined on anyone else. His tastes had become more discriminating in the years he had been at the Hendersons'. On her, however, he felt it was just right.

She had come three times with her father to sell their produce, always on a Wednesday morning. He did not know her proper name, or how old she was, though he had heard her father call her Ah-Hei. He reckoned she was about seventeen or eighteen and had been in Gold Mountain a year or so. Girls who had been here a long time dressed in Western clothes and new arrivals could not speak English.

She spotted him standing on the street. She tucked her handkerchief away and grinned. After a moment Kam Ho realized she was smiling at him. He went weak at the knees. He wanted to smile back but found the muscles of his face frozen into immobility.

The few paces up to the side of the cart seemed like an endless journey. His face was red with exertion by the time he got to her.

He passed over the sweaty money and as he drew his hand back, felt something hard and angular scratch the skin on the back of his hand. It was the calluses on her palm. Like him, she had had a life of hard toil. She held the money in her hand and waited silently, looking at him. Finally she gave a little laugh and, pointing at the vegetable baskets, asked: "What do you want?" He suddenly woke up. He had not given her his order. The blood rushed so violently to his face that he thought his head was going to explode.

Keep your voice steady, his brain urged his lips, but his lips took no notice. They bounced and shook like spring rice being beaten in a mortar so his words ended up pounded to shreds.

"A handful of radishes … a head of broccoli … two hearted cabbages … just two…."

She deftly bundled them up and gave them to him. "Anything else? You always get these."

He was startled. She remembered him, and what he bought every time. He felt himself grow calmer, and the plan he had been turning over in his mind for a week began to come together.

He needed to find the right moment to speak to her father. He wanted to tell him that his father had been a fruit and vegetable hawker himself and that he knew the wholesaler who offered the best prices in Gold Mountain. Then he could casually ask where they lived … and say that he would get his father to introduce them to the wholesaler.

There was a grain of truth in what he was planning to say. He really did want his father to go to the girl's house, but not to discuss vegetable prices. He wanted his father to be quite direct and discuss Kam Ho marrying the girl.

The head tax had gone sky-high in recent years and most migrants could only afford to bring their sons. Very few brought daughters. As a result, almost no Chinese girls were to be seen on the streets of Gold Mountain. His father had said more than once that he wanted his mother to arrange a match for him back in Hoi Ping but Kam Ho was not enthusiastic, although he found it hard to explain why to his stubborn father.

"I don't want to marry like Mum and you, with me here and her over there, neither of us knowing when we can be reunited."

As soon as the words were out, he knew he had said the wrong thing. His mother and father should have had that reunion by now, only Kam Ho had taken her place on the boat and come instead. But on this occasion Ah-Fat did not lose his temper. He just sighed and said: "So you want to be a bachelor for the rest of your life?" Kam Ho felt like sighing too but he could not bear to see his father looking so glum. He put on a smile instead and said: "Wait till I've earned enough for three head taxes and I'll go back and get married and bring out Mum and my sister and my wife." His father laughed: "By the time you've earned that much, there'll be no point in bringing them out here. You might as well go back to Hoi Ping for good, and enjoy life." Kam Ho felt there was some truth in what his father was saying, but all the same, Kam Ho had been in Gold Mountain for years, and there were good things about living here. Only, he could not say that to his father.

But now, this young Cantonese woman—Ah-Hei—seemed to be God's answer to Kam Ho. They were on the same side of the ocean, which made things much easier. And he had seen her face so there would be no unpleasant surprises when he lifted the red wedding veil. She did not come to him embellished by the matchmaker's silver tongue but stood right in front of him, in the flesh. He would not have to raise the money for the head tax, he only had to gather the courage to reach out a firm hand and take hold of her.

"It's always the women who come and buy from us. Isn't there a woman in your house?" asked her father, sweeping the debris of old leaves from the floor of the cart. The girl had been brushing the mud off the front of her jacket but now she paused and he knew she wanted to hear what he would say.

"I'm in charge of the housekeeping," he said boldly after a moment's hesitation.

The first sentence was the most difficult, and after this the words came fluently.

"The master of the house is the boss of Vancouver's biggest department store, the Hudson's Bay Company. When the English emperor came on a visit, the master was invited to tea. The mistress is always going out to dinner parties with him so I'm in charge of the house."

This was the longest answer that Kam Ho had ever given in his life and when he finished he was surprised at himself. It was so much easier than he ever imagined.

The girl's father tut-tutted in astonishment. "No wonder they live in such a grand house," he said.

"Have you ever seen the English emperor?" the girl asked him as she looked up.

He found it difficult to answer. He could not bring himself to lie boldly and say, yes, he had seen the emperor. But neither did he want to say no, because he was basking in the sparkling look of admiration she gave him. Then the words slipped off his tongue. He smiled slightly: "We ordinary folk can't meet the emperor. But I've seen a photograph that the master brought home. He's quite young and handsome." Kam Ho felt satisfied with the way he had put it. It did not sound in the least boastful, but still impressive enough.

"Jimmy! Jimmy!" Mrs. Henderson was calling him.

Kam Ho was not about to answer immediately but his chain of thought had been interrupted and he found he had dried up. He picked up the vegetable basket and said: "Could you bring some beans next week?" Before the father could reply, the girl nodded her head. Kam Ho knew he would see her again next week.

"Jimmy! Jimmy!" the call came again.

Kam Ho had to go. Though he had said a lot, still he had not time to say what he really wanted to. Still, there would be next Wednesday.

As he went through the garden gate, Kam Ho suddenly stopped, put down the basket in his hand and looked for a sharp pebble. He cut the stem of a rose and ran up to the cart. Throwing the rose onto the basket where she sat, he said: "It smells nice. Have a smell." He really wanted her to put it in her hair but he did not dare suggest that. He was afraid, not of her, but of her father. The man stood between him and her and he had not yet worked out a way of sneaking past him.

When Kam Ho climbed the steps to the house, he nearly collided with Mrs. Henderson; the doorway was dark as he went in out of the sun's glare, and he did not see her.

"Mr. Henderson's coming home early today, and he's taking Jenny to Stanley Park to see the sailing boats. Go and make us a picnic lunch, and of course you're coming with us too."

Kam Ho said, "Yes, ma'am," but he had no idea what he was saying yes to, because he was not listening. He had left his eyes and ears outside. Far away down the street, he saw more women coming out of their houses and going up to her cart. He heard her timid voice like a leaf brushing his ears. "Fresh greens. Just harvested from the fields. Our own crops, no bugs in them," she said in answer to each of the women's questions.

"Was it prickly, Jimmy?" asked Mrs. Henderson.

"What?"

"The rose," said Mrs. Henderson with a slight smile.

He looked down, almost burying his head in the cleanly plucked chicken in his hand. He could not answer because he knew that as soon as he opened his mouth, he would blush. This summer, very strangely, his blood would sometimes, without any provocation, start to ripple like oil in his face.

Mrs. Henderson put the vegetables Kam Ho had bought into a basin and picked up the basket. She walked across the garden, out into the street and then along until she got to the cart. She exchanged greetings with the other housewives and then handed the basket to the Chinese girl.

As she did so, she whispered something into the girl's ear. The girl's eyes suddenly lost their shine. It was as if a film of rust covered them. The rust spread, stiffening her face, and then travelling down her neck until her whole body was rigid.

"My servant," Mrs. Henderson said, "the Chinese boy, forgot to give you back the basket. Poor lad, he's not all there. He often forgets things."

The next Wednesday, the cart did not come.

The Wednesday after, it came but the girl was not on it. Her father and brother came instead. After much stammering, Kam Ho finally asked about her.

"She's gone to Edmonton to live with her aunt, who's going to send her to school there," said her father. "Her auntie says Gold Mountain girls should go to school too."

Kam Ho paid for his vegetables but went away without them. He went in through the garden gate, up the steps and across the hall. Jenny called him, Mrs. Henderson called him, but he heard neither of them. He went straight to his room, shut the door and sat down on his bed.

Ah-Hei had gone.

Ah-Hei was a spark from a fire, momentarily lighting his way, before going out and leaving him in darkness once more. It was a different darkness than before—and he could not bear it.

He sat for a long time in his room. He heard a clattering downstairs: Mrs. Henderson was in the kitchen making coffee and toast, and preparing a salad for lunch. Getting lunch was the servant's job, he should be doing it himself. But he felt completely drained of energy, unable to move a muscle. He would sit there until the world ended and the sky fell in.

Mrs. Henderson opened the door. He heard her footsteps but he did not turn around. Ah-Hei had let him down, her father had allowed her to go; all heaven and earth were against him. He had let himself down and now he had nothing more to live for.

A pair of arms went around him from behind and held him tight. His neck melted in their soft warmth. The warmth lapped over him and he wanted to pull free but did not have the strength.

Let me drown, then, he thought to himself, and be done with it.

"Poor child. Poor, poor child," came Mrs. Henderson's whispered voice.

Kam Ho's tears began to flow.

That night, he had a dream. He dreamed his mouth was full of rose thorns. He kept trying to spit them out, and then discovered that what he was spitting was not thorns but his own teeth, handfuls of them, red and white, like persimmon seeds.

He awoke covered in sweat. Then he remembered something his mother had told him as a child.

"If you dream your teeth are falling out, it means someone in the family is to die. If it was the top teeth, then it would be an old person. If the bottom teeth, it would be someone young."

He racked his brains but could not remember which teeth he had lost.

Year eleven of the Republic (1922)
Spur-On Village, Hoi Ping County, China

In the middle of the fourth month it began to rain and did not stop until the Dragon Boat Festival at the beginning of the fifth. When it stopped, the ground was covered with a pebbly carpet of mushrooms and the banana trees had burst into luxuriant growth. Inside, the walls of the houses were covered in snail trails.

Ah-Choi, the cook and a servant were busy at the stove preparing to boil leaf-wrapped rice dumplings for the festivities. When the water boiled, the cook threw some ash into it. After the harvest, they burned the rice stalks and stored the ash. Now, sprinkled into the water through a fine sieve, the ash gave the dumplings a flavour all of their own.

They had made up the dumplings the night before. There were four kinds—sausages, sweet bean paste, salted egg and dried shrimp. Kam Sau squatted on the floor tying them up with reed, into bunches of five. Each bunch would be tied with one other so that ten were boiled together. She was in grade two at the local school and would go up into the third grade when the summer was over. The school, funded by Gold Mountain men, was in the nearest town. The children boarded there during the week and came home on Sundays, but since this was the Dragon Boat Festival, they had an extra day's holiday and Mak Dau had fetched Kam Sau and Ah-Yuen home. Ah-Yuen was Mak Dau's son and just four months younger than Kam Sau. When Kam Sau was enrolled at the school, Six Fingers enrolled Ah-Yuen too. He would be a friend and company for Kam Sau.

Six Fingers was burning sagebrush to fumigate the house. When she reached the passageway, she came upon Mak Dau cleaning a revolver he had purchased from a local militiaman a few weeks ago. He was sitting on the floor, having placed it on the stool. When Kam Ho's last dollar letter arrived, Six Fingers gave half to Mak Dau to buy it. Mak Dau said it was lightweight and convenient, and could be tucked discreetly into his waistband on long journeys. Six Fingers was a thrifty woman but she did not mind spending money on guns, since her husband and sons were away. A household without men looked weak and defenceless and a defenceless house was a target for robbers. The guns were her defence. This revolver was the third they had bought; the other two were shotguns.

"When you've bought it, wrap it in red silk and lay it on top of the box. We'll celebrate its arrival with firecrackers," ordered Six Fingers. Although she was keen to avoid attracting unwelcome attention to the family's wealth, she was perfectly happy to show off the acquisition of a new weapon.

"You put it back together exactly the way you take it apart," Mak Dau instructed his son. "Anyone can take a gun apart but you have to have a good head on your shoulders to be able to put it back together."

"Why ever are you teaching things like that to such a little kid?" Six Fingers scolded him.

Mak Dau chuckled. "It's a wicked world," he said. "Anything a boy can learn about defending himself is going to come in useful."

Six Fingers squatted down with them. "What new subjects are you going to study when you go up into the next grade?" she asked Ah-Yuen. The boy coughed and spluttered from the sagebrush smoke. He took a handkerchief from his pocket and wiped his nose before answering: "Nature, geography and music, and we'll carry on doing Chinese, math, English and history like before." Six Fingers looked at the boy approvingly. "He wipes his nose on his handkerchief," she said to Mak Dau, "not on his sleeve the way you do." "We'll be doing etiquette too," Ah-Yuen piped up. "What to wear, and how to eat and behave, and we'll get marked on it too."

Mak Dau tapped his son on the head. "An empty kettle makes the most noise," he admonished him. "You don't want the Missus laughing at you." Six Fingers threw down the brushwood. She began to comb Ah-Yuen's hair with her fingers, lost in thought.

Mak Dau knew she was missing her own sons. He checked there was no one around before lowering his voice and asking: "Have there been any letters?" She shook her head. "Not since last New Year. That's more than twelve months. Not a single one. Has something happened that they're keeping from me?"

"What about the two young masters? Why don't they write?" "You know what a temper he's got," said Six Fingers. "Both the boys are afraid of him. Neither of them would dare write and tell me if he doesn't want them to. Kam Ho has written, but just to say that Kam Shan is back in Vancouver and has moved in with his dad."

"Don't worry, Missus," said Mak Dau. "The dollar letters keep coming. I'm sure nothing's happened to the master. You must miss the boys, though … one gone twelve years, the other seven years. I miss them too."

Six Fingers bent her head and tears fell on her shoes. With sole responsibility for a substantial household, she could never let herself go in front of the servants. She knew how easy it was to appear weak before them and so buttoned her feelings up tightly. If she cried, it was only in front of Mak Dau. Mak Dau felt unsuccessfully in his pocket for a handkerchief, then pulled out Ah-Yuen's, folded it with a clean bit uppermost and gave it to Six Fingers. She wiped her eyes and said with a faint smile: "Kam Shan wrote to say his woman is pregnant and no matter if it's a boy or a girl, he's bringing the baby home to meet Granny."

"You'll be a granny in no time at all, Missus," said Mak Dau. "But to me you still look as young as a new bride." Six Fingers gave a little snort. "You'll have wasps sticking to that honeyed tongue of yours if you don't look out! And don't you dare make fun of me!" Mak Dau felt so aggrieved that the veins bulged on his forehead. "Oh no, Missus!" he exclaimed. "I'd never be so bold as to make fun of you. It's really true—you haven't changed. You look just the same as when I first entered the household." Six Fingers' eyes had a faraway look in them: "I made the bridegroom's shoes for Ah-Yuet to give you. It seems like just yesterday. But look how big the kids are now. In all this time, of course I've changed."

There was a loud knocking from the ceiling above—Mrs. Mak's walking stick, signalling to Six Fingers that she wanted to come downstairs. "I'll come and carry you down, Mum," she shouted. But as the tempting smell of dumplings wafted up the stairs, the old woman became impatient. "All that wealth my son's earned," she wailed fretfully, "and I haven't even had a bite. You'd rather feed the rats than me."

"What a way for the old Missus to talk to you, Missus," Mak Dau said disapprovingly. "It sets a bad example to the servants." Six Fingers only smiled. "She gets confused sometimes. But sometimes she's as bright as a button." "Then let me carry her," said Mak Dau. "She's too heavy for you."

"No, I can carry her. She's as light as a feather nowadays." Mak Dau sighed. "You have such a lot on your shoulders, Missus. I'm just a rough sort and I can only do heavy work, but do let me help you out in any way I can." Six Fingers was touched, and did not trust herself to speak for a few moments. Then she said: "The thing is, I'm the only one she'll let carry her." Mak Dau gave one of his dazzling smiles. "Just watch how I do it then," he said and stomped off up the stairs.

After a moment, there was more stomping, heavier this time, as he came downstairs again with Mrs. Mak on his back.

Six Fingers fetched a wicker chair for Mrs. Mak to sit on. The dumplings were ready, and the old woman sniffed: "You didn't put enough ash into the water." Six Fingers smiled: "No one's got a nose sharper than you, Mum." She got out a large dish and a small dish. "Ah-Yuet, put two of each flavour into the big dish, nice neatly made ones. And one of each flavour into the small dish." The larger portion was an offering to the ancestors, the smaller one was for Kam Sau's great-aunt upstairs. She was a widow now. The great-uncle had died a year ago and she shared her rooms with her son and his wife, as her daughters had married and left home. After the old man's death, she began to suffer from heart trouble and was too frail to come downstairs.

Ah-Yuet was ladling oil into the large bowl when her hand slipped. The bowl dropped with a crash to the floor. It was a porcelain offerings dish which Ah-Fat's father had bought in an antique shop in Canton when he became rich overnight—it had been in the family for a long time. There was an appalled silence in the room. Mak Dau smacked his wife across the face. "I've never seen a clumsier woman than you!" he raged. "You've been with the Missus all these years, and you still haven't got any better!"

Mak Dau often corrected Ah-Yuet but only behind closed doors. She had never before been disgraced like this in front of the rest of the house-hold. Mutely, she held her hand to her cheek and her lips trembled like leaves. Six Fingers frowned at Mak Dau. "It doesn't matter how clever you are, you should never hit your wife in front of the old Missus." At that, Ah-Yuet burst into noisy tears. "It's just an old dish!" shouted Six Fingers at her. "What are all these tears about? Hurry up and clear it up and bring another one."

It was obvious to them all that these words were meant for Mrs. Mak's ears; since she was blind, she could not see which dish had been broken.

Mrs. Mak smiled scornfully and beckoned Kam Sau to her side. "Yes, Granny?" Mrs. Mak took the little girl's hand in hers. "Stay away from her," she said. "She's got it in for our ancestors." There was an embarrassed silence; the "she" must surely mean Six Fingers. But to everyone's surprise, Mrs. Mak went on: "Huh! That mole's an evil omen … blood-soaked it is.…" The mole was on Ah-Yuet's chin, and indeed, it was bright red.

Six Fingers went to her. "Mum," she said shakily, "can you see Ah-Yuet's mole, really?" Mrs. Mak did not reply. Instead, she looked Six Fingers up and down. "Can't you find something nicer to put on to honour the ancestors? Hasn't Ah-Fat bought you anything?" Six Fingers had not had time to change out of her plain grey, black-trimmed cotton tunic.

When they had recovered from their astonishment, there were cries of "The old Missus can see! She can see!" Kam Sau stretched out two fingers. "How many fingers is that, Granny?" she asked. "Don't you make fun of me, you little madam! With my heavenly eye, none of you can ever hoodwink me!"

Six Fingers shot a glance at Mak Dau and they left the room. Making sure no one was following them, Six Fingers wiped the sweat from her face and said to him: "Things are not looking good for the old Missus. Get her burial shoes from the funeral shop and be quick!"

Mrs. Mak died at noon that day, still clutching a half-eaten bean paste dumpling in one hand.

She had lived for seventy-four years.

For the last twenty of them, she had been alternately lucid and confused. One last drop of oil kept the lamp of her days alight for a long time before it went out. In the end, she exhausted not only her own reserves but her daughter-in-law's as well. When Six Fingers sent Mrs. Mak on her way to the next life with the most ostentatious funeral that Spur-On Village had ever seen, she was forty-five years old.

When the wake was over, and the last of the guests had been seen out of the *diulau*, Six Fingers bolted the iron door and went upstairs. She sat on her bed and gently wiped the dust from the dressing table mirror. In a piece of clear glass the size of a palm-leaf fan, she looked at her face. She wore no powder. The fine lines at the corners of her eyes and cheekbones were puffy with tears. The white flower she wore in her bun hung crooked. She pulled it out, then put it back in again straight. She would have to wear the white flower of mourning for some time yet, but she did not mind. It made the grey hairs less obvious.

"Twenty-eight years ago, you promised that I would join you in Gold Mountain, Ah-Fat. Now, finally, you can fulfill that promise," Six Fingers murmured to herself.

Year twelve of the Republic (1923), Vancouver, British Columbia

When Mr. Henderson pushed open the garden gate, Jenny was standing on tiptoe under a tree, talking to a robin that sat in the branches.

"Do you go to sleep with your eyes shut or open?"

The bird gave a tweet, which might have meant yes or no. Jenny was annoyed and screwed up her nose: "Hasn't your mother taught you to speak properly?"

Mr. Henderson burst out laughing and went over to his daughter. He was about to give her a bear hug, but thought better of it, and instead stroked her face. Jenny had been ill almost continuously this year, with measles and a cold that led to bronchitis. She had a long-festering infection where she had fallen and hurt herself, too. Her body seemed as frail as tissue paper. Just touching it would make a hole. They had made progress though; the dribbling had stopped and she no longer wore the bib, but kept it in her apron pocket.

He took her hand and they went to the front door. It was locked and he had to use his key to open it. He almost had it open when Kam Ho came running out of the kitchen, looking flustered. Mr. Henderson sniffed: "What's that burning smell?" he asked. "Did you boil the footbath dry?" Kam Ho wiped his hands over and over again on the apron and stammered: "It could be the … the Chinese medicine the Missus takes." "Good God!" exclaimed Mr. Henderson. "My wife swigs your Chinese bilge like there's no tomorrow! Why don't you invite the witches and wizards from Chinatown over too."

Kam Ho was used to Mr. Henderson's jokes but this one he found offensive. A flush stained his face like vermilion ink spreading across rice paper. Kam Ho was a man of few words, but his face spoke his feelings in their stead. Mr. Henderson had seen him flush many times—sometimes from embarrassment, or alarm, sometimes for some unexplained reason. But this time it was anger, the kind of anger which he had to choke back.

Mr. Henderson roared with laughter and clapped Kam Ho on the shoulder. "When I first met your father, Frank," he said, "he was younger than you are now, but not nearly so thin-skinned. In fact, he was as tough as old boots." Kam Ho was still red in the face, and Mr. Henderson produced a note from his pocket and pushed it into his hand. "When you go home this weekend, take your father to the new French restaurant in the bay. Tell him it's on me."

Kam Ho took a quick look—he was holding a crisp, new twenty-dollar bill. This was more than half his monthly salary, and certainly enough to buy several excellent meals in any restaurant. Both Mr. and Mrs. Henderson would occasionally top up his monthly wages with a bit extra, but never with a note this big. It seemed to numb his hand with its weight. He would like to have said: "No, it's too much. I can't accept it." But the words refused to come. "Thank you," he mumbled. If only Mr. Henderson had not made that offensive comment about Chinese bilge, it would have felt dignified and right to thank him. As it was, he had made that comment and Kam Ho was still angry. He felt cheapened.

But he was in no position to nurse injured feelings. Immediately, he knew what he wanted to do with the money. He would not be taking his father to a French restaurant. In fact, he would not let him catch sight of the twenty-dollar bill. He would add it to the pile of small change he was saving, then he would turn it all into a letter addressed to his mother and sealed with the Gold Mountain government's official stamp. He had been putting money by for the head tax. He was going to make sure that his father got the family reunion he had been denied for so many years.

Kam Ho took Mr. Henderson's briefcase and overcoat and went to the kitchen to make coffee. A cup of strong, black coffee was the first thing he wanted when he got back home—no milk, no sugar. He liked the smell of it more than the taste, and would bring the cup, clasped in both hands, to his nose and breathe deeply as the steam curled up and misted his face. He took so long over it that, sometimes, Kam Ho thought he had fallen asleep. Once, he was on the point of taking the cup from his hands when Mr. Henderson suddenly opened his eyes and said: "Jimmy, coffee in heaven can't be any better than this."

When he had finally finished his coffee, he asked: "Where's Mrs. Henderson?" "She had a headache today, so she's just taken her medicine and gone to sleep." He would like to have said she had just drunk that "Chinese bilge." The note in his breast pocket warmed his chest and suddenly made him talkative. He was surprised to find he could tell a joke too—but in the end, he refrained.

"Well, when she wakes up, go and get my things ready. I'm going to Saskatoon tomorrow." Kam Ho knew he had a supply depot there and made frequent trips every year. "Is it nice there?" he asked. "That depends on who you ask. It's nice for cattle and horses. It's nothing but grass and more grass." Kam Ho smiled despite himself. "There's another good thing about it," Mr. Henderson went on. "The fishing's really good. Next time I make a trip, I'll take you with me and we can do some fishing." "I can fish," said Kam Ho. "When I was a kid, my brother and I used to tickle trout in the river. Will we go with the missus?"

"Huh! Go with her? If the sun's too hot, she gets a headache. If there's a wind, her knee throbs. She can't walk because her feet hurt. If it's overcast, she can't see where she's walking and if it's bright, the sun gets in her eyes. Look at Jenny. She's growing up to be just like her mother, too fragile to touch."

Kam Ho heard a slight creaking on the stairs. He had wanted to warn Mr. Henderson that his wife was on her way down but could not stem the outburst. Mrs. Henderson appeared behind her husband, and with a slight smile, she said: "I'm not really so delicate, am I, Rick? And I suppose Bridget was more robust than me?" Bridget was Mr. Henderson's first fiancée, but she had died of heart failure before they married.

Mr. Henderson looked embarrassed, then laughed and said: "Don't lock the door when Jenny's playing in the garden."

Mrs. Henderson did not reply. "Take Jenny to wash her hands," she told Kam Ho, with a meaningful look at him. "It's time to eat." The glance meant that he should prepare drinks for them. Mr. Henderson's job meant that he was often out in the evening and rarely ate with his family. When he was at home, his wife liked them to have a drink before dinner.

Kam Ho took Jenny to wash her hands and then fetched a bottle of ten-year-old port from the cellar. Mrs. Henderson's taste for port, acquired as a young woman in England, had followed her to Canada. Kam Ho put two long-stemmed glasses down in front of them. Mr. Henderson frowned and glanced at Kam Ho. He did not like wine, regarding it as a lady's drink. His tipple was whisky, sometimes on the rocks, sometimes straight. Anything else he did not dignify with the name of "a drink."

In the eight years that Kam Ho had been with the Hendersons, the greatest skill he had learned was to read their expressions. The problem was that their expressions were often at odds, and Kam Ho found himself forcibly pulled to one side. Even when he understood what they each wanted, he did not know how to act. In the beginning, he often felt bruised by the conflict. Then he learned to interpose his own energy between their conflicting energies, making three forces instead of two. This protected him from being crushed.

Kam Ho imperturbably poured a glass of port for each of them and gestured to Mr. Henderson. "Ma'am wants to drink to your health," he said, "and wish you a safe journey and a speedy return, isn't that so, ma'am?"

Mrs. Henderson downed her port in one gulp and waved her empty glass at Kam Ho. He refilled it and she gulped it down again. She had had a severe headache all day. She had taken some opium juice but before she could settle down to a nap, Mr. Henderson returned home. She was still in her night-gown, as she often was these days: a crimson Japanese silk kimono embroidered all over with butterflies in shades of blue, green and pink. It reached to the floor but was cut low at the neck, revealing a hint of snowy-white bosom.

Kam Ho did not dare raise his eyes. He found that glimpse of white flesh electrifying. Mr. Henderson must have been crazy about her before she fell sick, he thought. How sad that he no longer felt affection for her. How sad that she kept trying to revive it. Mrs. Henderson treated her husband like a god, as Kam Ho well knew, and wanted nothing more than to cling to him for shelter. But her husband did not want anyone plucking at him or doting on him. This was obvious to Kam Ho but Mrs. Henderson still could not see it. She grasped desperately at any bit of him she could reach, until there was nothing left.

"Do you enjoy being away from home, without Jenny and me bothering you, Rick?" she asked now, waving her empty glass at Kam Ho.

Kam Ho looked at Mr. Henderson, not daring to fill it up again. Mr. Henderson took his wife's glass from her. "That's enough. You'll frighten Jenny if you go on like this." At his words, the flush on Mrs. Henderson's cheeks rose upwards until even her eyes reddened.

"Just listen to you!" she said. "What a good daddy you are. Jenny, when was the last time your daddy got drunk? I think he must have forgotten that you were there."

Mr. Henderson threw the glass down and stalked up the stairs. The wine dribbled along the crease in the white tablecloth as if the table had split in two and blood was oozing from the wound. "Daddy!" cried Jenny, and burst into loud sobs.

Heavy footsteps rattled the stairs as Mr. Henderson came down again. At the door, he took his coat from the closet, put it on and bent to tie his shoelaces. Kam Ho dashed after him and blocked the way. Mr. Henderson straightened up and looked at him. "I'm going to stay the night in a hotel," he said. "Look after Jenny for me." He brushed Kam Ho off as effortlessly as if he were a leaf, and went out. Kam Ho watched as his portly figure, carrying a small grip, was swallowed up by the deepening dusk of the street. It struck him that Mr. Henderson was looking rather stooped these days.

Jenny had stopped crying and was braiding her dolly's hair. Kam Ho cleared away the wineglasses and mopped up the spilled wine. It was very quiet. The only sound came from the kitchen, where the stew bubbled away, its glug-glugs sounding like rich, oily farts. Kam Ho felt Mrs. Henderson's eyes on him, needling him painfully. It was clear she wanted to talk to him, but just now, he did not feel like it. He let the needling go on.

"Do you think a man is capable of sticking by a woman, Jimmy?" she asked.

A simple question, but one that Kam Ho could not answer. He was twenty-three years old, but so far his emotional life had been uneventful, the only ripples in its gentle onward flow caused briefly by the Cantonese girl, Ah-Hei.

Behind him, Mrs. Henderson gave a short laugh. "It's pointless to ask you, isn't it, Jimmy. I mean, you've never known a woman, have you? I mean really known...."

Kam Ho could feel drops of sweat beginning to bead his forehead and the tip of his nose. He was hot with embarrassment, the drops of sweat almost steaming. He felt the blood rushing to his face—he must have turned scarlet. Flustered, he went over to the stove and lifted the lid of the pot. It fell to the floor with a clanging noise.

"Mr. Henderson went off without any dinner," said Kam Ho.

"Of course. But he's not the only one. I'm hungry too," said Mrs. Henderson.

That night he dreamed that the Hendersons' dog had climbed in through the window and onto his bed. The dog's red tongue began to lick him, slurping at his face. The dog was a great weight on his chest, and he could hardly breathe. He pushed and pushed at it, and finally woke himself up.

He opened his eyes and saw a pair of eyes gleaming at him in the darkness. There was a full moon, and its light filtered in through cracks in the curtains and caught the gleam, making the eyes flare blue. Kam Ho's hair stood on end but a hand clamped itself over his mouth, stifling the cry of alarm he was about to utter. Another hand slithered through the opening of his pyjamas, exploring his chest then gliding down his belly until it finally reached the place between his legs.

Kam Ho felt as if his body was a fuse. The fingers played over him, setting him alight. The flames flickered back and forth. Between his legs, he grew rock hard. The flames licked at his thing and it grew fiery hot.

A groan escaped Kam Ho.

With an immense convulsion, he released a flood of hot liquid, startling them both.

The fire died down, leaving Kam Ho feeling drained, emptied of all energy. But a feeling of ineffable pleasure lingered. He had the vague sensation of being light, of floating like a cloud in the sky. Almost, but not quite. Because something was pulling him down. As his eyes became used to the semi-darkness, he saw it was a nightgown with shimmering butterflies. He was filled with a sense of doom, and his teeth chattered in terror.

Two soft, moist lips touched his cheeks. A breath, which smelled of spearmint, skittered across his ears, and he heard:

"Jimmy, it's not a sin to go looking for pleasure. Don't be afraid," she breathed.

He slept deeply after that. When he awoke, the sun was shining hot on his face. He leapt out of bed and scrambled around for his clothes.

He was too late to prepare Mrs. Henderson's breakfast.

Mrs. Henderson. The name made his heart thump, and memories of the night before came flooding back. That dream. It was just a fantasy, wasn't it? He comforted himself with the thought that he had been having very strange dreams lately. But when he threw back the covers, he found a stain about the size of a Buddha's hand. He traced its soft edges with a finger. It was still wet. He slumped down onto the bed, his heart in his mouth.

It was no dream. It had happened.

He sat on the edge of the bed. The moments passed. When he could not sit there any longer, he got to his feet and, as he did so, he saw the corner of something sticking out from under the pillow. A piece of paper. On it, the crowned head of the old English Queen.

A five-dollar bill.

It seemed to burn his hand, raising a blister on his palm.

He dressed and quickly packed his belongings. There wasn't much— three or four outfits, a pair of shoes and some letters from his mother. He still had his old bag, faded with washing. He put everything into it, tied it shut and slung it over his shoulder. How small it was.

He did not know who his next employer would be, or where his next meal would come from. He was even less certain how he was going to tell his father. But he could work that out as he went along. The most important thing was to leave without delay.

He had just stepped out of his room when he heard Jenny give a shrill wail: "Mummy!"

He threw down the bag and flew back up the stairs. Mrs. Henderson was lying on her back in the bath, her hand dangling over the edge, a fat, red worm crawling across her wrist. Kam Ho was rooted to the spot in horror. He peered at the floor. A crimson pool was spreading across it.

Mrs. Henderson's blood.

Kam Ho tore up his shirt and tied the strips tightly round Mrs. Henderson's wrist.

"Why? Why?"

Mrs. Henderson's eyes were shut as if in sleep. Her nightgown ballooned in the water; the butterflies' wings were soaked through and floated lifelessly on the surface.

"Are you trying to frighten me to death?"

Kam Ho was not aware that he was crying. But he felt something scouring his cheeks as painfully as a caustic burn.

Mrs. Henderson opened unseeing eyes, then shut them again.

"I know you want to go. You, Jenny, and him too. You'll all leave and I'll be left alone," she murmured.

He tried to get her to sit up, gripping her wrist with its improvised bandage with one hand, and holding her by the nape of her neck with the other. But she stiffened up and gave him no help at all. His clothes were soon soaked and the water slopped over the edge of the bathtub, making puddles on the floor.

"If you sit up and let me call Dr. Walsh, I swear to God I won't leave," he said.

As Kam Ho walked down the street, he admired the sky overhead—it was a beautiful blue. He had not been outdoors for a month. Since Mrs. Henderson had returned from hospital, her health had declined even further. She would not let him out of her sight. Today he had finally been granted a day off to go home. Unbeknownst to him, summer was already upon them. The lilacs had come and gone, and so had the cherry, apple and pear blossoms. All along the branches of the trees which lined the street, tiny green fruits had set, looking as if they might leak drops of acid. Crows cawed as they flew overhead, but he was used to them now. They were so common here that if they really were birds of ill omen as folks said back home, disaster would befall all the inhabitants of Gold Mountain. Disaster would not single him out. Nothing was going to dampen his spirits today.

Kam Ho had one hand in his pocket, tightly clutching a heavy cloth bag. Through the thin fabric, the banknotes seemed to stick out tiny tongues which licked his palm eagerly. He had counted and recounted them. He remembered how he acquired each one. The ten-dollar bill on which someone had scrawled an obscenity was from his first wages. The five-dollar bill with a bit of one corner missing was a present from the Hendersons on his second Christmas with them. And then there was the five-dollar bill with a tiny cigarette burn at the tip of the monarch's nose—that was the one Mrs. Henderson had stuffed under his pillow.

Over the past two years, Kam Ho had sent regular dollar letters back home to his mother, and provided his father with pocket money, but had saved every cent of what was left. His father had an inkling of what his son was doing, but had no idea that it all added up to so much. In fact, Ah-Fat often accused him of being so tight-fisted he would happily cut a cent coin in two. He also said he was cheap not to buy a present when Kam Shan's woman had her baby. But Kam Ho held his tongue. He regarded his cloth bag as a bucket which he was filling with water drop by drop. He was biding his time until the bucket was full, then he could speak out. He had had to wait a very long time for that moment to come.

When he got to the house, only his father and Yin Ling were at home. Yin Ling, Kam Shan's baby, was five months old, and lay snoring gently on the bed with a thin coverlet over her. Kam Shan's woman was a waitress at the Lychee Garden Restaurant six days a week. She left Yin Ling at home and Kam Shan took her twice a day to the restaurant to be breastfed.

Kam Ho found his father leaning over the table, grinding ink. Business was always slow between festivals, so most of the time the ink he prepared each morning went unused. By noon, if no customer had darkened his door, the ink developed a hard black crust. Ah-Fat had put up with unimaginable hardships all his life, but the one thing he could not bear was idleness. It made him as bad-tempered as a bear with a sore head.

True to form, his father greeted Kam Ho with an irascible snort: "Oh, so you've remembered you have a family!" Kam Ho laughed: "Mrs. Henderson's been ill, and Mr. Henderson wouldn't let me take a day off." "Huh!" Ah-Fat snorted again. "Why on earth would a man as capable as he is choose a wife like her? If he was in Hoi Ping, he'd have got rid of her and married again long ago." "It's Mr. Henderson who makes Mrs. Henderson ill," said Kam Ho. "If he treated her a bit better, she wouldn't be sick."

Ah-Fat threw the ink stick down, spattering the table with black drops. "And what the hell would you know about it?"

Kam Ho was imperturbable. Nothing and no one was going to wipe the smile from his face today.

"How's my brother? Is he a bit better?"

A month or so before, Kam Shan had been on his way to take portrait photographs in Port Hope when he was thrown from his horse and broke a leg. The bone-setter had attended him, but he was still hobbling.

His father scowled. "He was in pain all last night. He's gone to get some ointment from the herbalist."

Yin Ling woke up, pushed her little hands out of the blanket and broke into a wail. Babies at this age grew faster than weeds and she was much bigger now than when Kam Ho last saw her. He picked her up and, pulling a twenty-dollar bill out of his pocket, pushed it into her bib. "Don't cry, baby!" he said cheerfully. "Uncle's going to buy you candies!"

Ah-Fat turned to look at his son. "When did you get so generous? Tripped over a pile of dollars on your way here, did you?"

Kam Ho put the baby down, then unhurriedly pulled the cloth bundle out of his pocket and put it down in front of his father.

"Yes, I did. Five hundred and twenty-nine dollars, eighty-five cents to be precise. Count them."

Ah-Fat opened the bundle and looked at the heaps of coins and stack of dollar bills of different values wrapped around them. He was lost for words.

"I've saved up enough for the head tax to bring Mum here. Use that ink to write and tell her to buy the next passage."

His father seemed to shrivel up before his very eyes. Finally he slid to the floor and wrenched at his hair as if he was trying to pull it out.

"Oh Buddha of Mercy, why do you play such cruel tricks on me? What have I done to deserve it?"

Had joy driven his father crazy? Kam Ho rushed over and tried to help him up. But Ah-Fat pushed him away. Pointing to the bed, he stammered: "Go ... go and read ... the paper."

The Chinese Times lay on the bed, and someone had used a writing brush to make a big circle around an article on the front page.

The Parliament of Canada today passed a bill denying entry to people of the Chinese race or of part-Chinese descent, with the exception of consular staff, properly accredited merchants (not including owners of restaurants or laundry businesses), or university students. The family dependants of those already resident in Canada are prohibited from joining them. Current residents are required to register with the government within one year of the passing of this bill; the penalty for non-registration is deportation from Canada. Any Chinese wishing to make visits to China must return to Canada within two years. After that period, they will be denied entry. The sole permitted port of entry is Vancouver. Any boat entering Canadian waters is only allowed to carry one Chinese per two hundred and fifty tons deadweight.

When construction began in the west of Canada, the land was completely desolate. But, fearing no hardships, Chinese immigrants threw themselves valiantly into the back-breaking and dangerous work of building roads and railroads. But the government has behaved most treacherously towards the Chinese now that work has been completed, and placed numerous obstacles in our way to employment. A head tax, the first in the world, was imposed, and now this is followed by a new immigration law which, in preventing family reunions in Canada, is an insult to our country and our people. As a result, hundreds of thousands of families will be separated forever by an ocean. Our Republican government has reacted by making immediate diplomatic representations, but given its weakness internationally, these are unlikely to be effective. In the meantime, we have no option but to put up with this humiliating and bullying piece of legislation!

Kam Ho threw down the newspaper. He too, seemed to become smaller. He and his father squatted silently on the floor holding their heads despairingly in their hands, oblivious to the heart-rending wails of the baby lying on the bed. What a terribly cruel twist of fate. They had often seen such situations acted out on opera stages but they never expected to become part of the tale themselves. Kam Ho had built up his hopes, along with his savings, over eight long years and then, just as he was about to reunite his mother and father after decades of sacrifice and separation, disaster found him after all.

From deep in his lower gut, Kam Ho felt an impulse climb up to his chest and then to his throat, presaging, perhaps, a long sigh. It changed before it passed his lips—it became a little chuckle that surged and fell and surged again until Kam Ho found himself shaking with mad gusts of laughter.

He must have been driven over the edge, thought Ah-Fat in alarm, and thumped his son on the back. Kam Ho coughed up a mouthful of phlegm and finally stopped shaking. He stood up, wiped his nose and asked: "Where's the Benevolent Association in all this? They're always here when it comes time to pay our dues, but you can't see them for dust when we get clobbered."

"They're meeting to decide on a policy. Your brother goes every day," said Ah-Fat. "All the branch Associations are sending representatives to Parliament to protest. It's not just ours. Victoria, Montreal and all the rest are, too. But it's no use. Ordinary people can never defeat the government, not their own government, and certainly not a foreign one."

Kam Ho saw for the first time that the livid worm of a scar that crawled halfway up his father's face had shrunk to a hair, like a crack in a porcelain bowl. Even its colour had faded. His dad was really getting old. He would never have resigned himself to this in the old days. To the young Ah-Fat, all government officials, at home or abroad, were bastards and he would not hesitate to take a machete to them.

"If Mum can't come, Dad," said Kam Ho, "you should go back and live with her there. In two years, you can return if you want."

His father said nothing.

After a few moments, he reached out and took hold of the bag of money on the table and gripped it as tightly as if his life depended on it.

"Let me have this money, son," he said.

He spoke in his usual peremptory tones, but Kam Ho saw a hint of an entreaty in his father's eyes. His father had never begged for anything in his life. A wave of bitterness flooded over Kam Ho, that his father had been so reduced.

"Dad, you do whatever you want with the money."

His father's dull gaze suddenly came to life. "I'm going to divide it in two—the bigger portion I'll give Kam Shan so he can take you and Yin Ling back to see your mother and get his leg treated by a decent doctor at the same time. And while he's there, he can get your mother to find you a bride. The rest of the money is to keep me. You and Kam Shan stay in China for two years and I'll stay here and work for two years. I can't believe my luck's completely run out yet."

Ah-Fat's eyes reddened like a gambler's at the fan-tan table as he spoke.

"Dad, you shouldn't need to work at your age. Kam Shan and I'll look after you."

Ah-Fat stiffened. "Just give me two years.... When you and Kam Shan get back, I'll give every cent back to you. I can't go home looking like a disgraceful old tramp."

The baby, Yin Ling, had cried herself to exhaustion and only choked whimpers came from the bed. Kam Ho went to pick her up and saw a blister the size of a pebble on her forehead.

He sighed. "I can't go. Kam Shan will have to take his family without me. I promised to stay with Mrs. Henderson—it's vital for me to stay."

Year seventeen of the Republic (1928)
Vancouver, British Columbia

Opium juice was getting harder and harder to find. The police raided the Kwong Cheong General Store so often that the terror-stricken owner squirrelled his stocks away in the darkest corner he could find. Kam Ho could always be relied upon to sniff out a supply, but the price had gone sky-high. By the time Mr. Henderson discovered that astronomical sums of housekeeping were being spent on "Chinese herbals," his wife was in the throes of opium addiction. Mr. Henderson did not say anything. He just tightened his grip on his purse. Mrs. Henderson's efforts to extract money from him were fruitless.

She was forced to find other ways to subdue her pain.

This morning, she had just seen Jenny off to school when excruciating pains began to attack her knees. It felt as if they hid a nest of hungry, restless rats that gnawed at her every movement. She was defenceless against pain this acute. Kam Ho's acupressure techniques had no effect any more.

She had hardly had time to cry out before the rats were on her again, taking her breath away. She lay upon the sofa, staring at her husband as he turned away, put his brown-and-white King Charles spaniel on the leash, and went out for a walk. Although he was a senior adviser at the chamber of commerce, he went to the office only a couple of times a week—for meetings or to put his signature on a few documents. He found himself with a great deal of leisure time on his hands these days; one way of divesting himself of it was to take the dog for a walk. He took it out after every meal. His invariable habit gave him the greatest pleasure, and was postponed or interrupted only if some major event intervened. His wife's arthritis did not count as a major event.

This was the Hendersons' third dog. The first two were golden retrievers. The first died of old age, and the second was lost off leash while they were out walking. The dog had chased after a pretty feral bitch and never returned. Mr. Henderson had been inconsolable.

He had grown vague about people in the years since he retired, but he remembered everything about his dogs. They were his reference points. If he could not remember the year in which something happened, he would describe it as "the spring when Spotty arrived," or "the time when Leggy chewed up my Italian shoes," or "the time when Ruben got mange."

When Mr. Henderson left the house with Ruben, Kam Ho was in the kitchen washing up. Breakfast was simple and Kam Ho had only a few coffee cups and side plates to wash, but he was in no hurry to finish. In his pocket there was a letter from his mother, sent to him via his father. There was a photo in the envelope, a very small one, showing the round face of a young girl. She looked no different from the average village girl—high cheekbones, thick lips and an expression so wooden that it was hard to tell whether she was happy or sad.

Her name was Au Hsien Wan and she lived in Wai Yeong Village; she was distantly related to the Au family in their village. So his mother's letter had said.

His mother wrote that the girl was eighteen years old, that she had had a few years of primary school, that she could read and write and do math. Their horoscopes had been done and matched perfectly.

It was not the first time Kam Ho had looked at such a photograph. When Kam Shan came back from his visit home three years ago, his mother had sent him with half a dozen pictures for Kam Ho. The matchmaker had given her many more to choose from but she had rejected any who had not been to school; she liked women to be literate. Six Fingers had not got on with Cat Eyes for the whole two years that she spent in Hoi Ping with Kam Shan and Yin Ling because Cat Eyes could not even write her own name. Kam Ho kept the photographs his mother sent him over the years and looked at them every now and then. He would spread them out on the bed as if he had suddenly become the Yellow Emperor of old in the Forbidden City, selecting his empress and concubines from a bevy of beauties.

Kam Ho's head may have been in the clouds, but his feet were firmly on the ground. He knew he could not marry any of the girls in the photographs because anyone he chose to marry would be condemned to live life apart from him while he toiled in Gold Mountain. He did not want a marriage like that of his mother and father. He would rather be a lonely bachelor than pine for a wife he could never see.

Some Gold Mountain men felt the same as Kam Ho but were not as stoical, and shacked up with Redskin women. These unions produced children, but no marriage documents were exchanged and they did not ask for the ancestors' blessings. When well-meaning friends suggested that Ah-Fat should get his son a Redskin woman, he grimaced. "He might as well marry a sow." When he heard this, Kam Shan laughed. "Lots of Redskin women are good-looking and hard-working, and lots of Chinese women are ugly and lazy. Don't tar them all with the same brush!" "And what about when they have children, whose ancestors do they pay their respects to?" retorted Ah-Fat. "Any grandson of mine may not be royalty but he'll be every bit a Chinese and not a barbarian." Since Kam Shan's woman had been unable to give the Fongs a grandson, he had nothing to say to this.

Kam Ho had plans of his own. He was secretly saving money to take his father back to China for good. With the money he had borrowed from his son a few years back, Ah-Fat had opened a small café. Since he knew nothing about preparing restaurant food, he was dependent on a cook. The cook had slovenly habits but there was nothing Ah-Fat could do about it. The café brought in so little money that after he had paid the man's wages there was almost nothing left. The business limped along for a few years and even though his sons urged him to give it up, he insisted on keeping it going. He had borrowed money from his son and was duty bound to pay it all back. But Kam Ho knew that his father was secretly hoping that he could make enough money to put on a show of respectability when he went back home to his wife. With increasing age, Ah-Fat did not swagger as he once had, but he still had some pride. He would not let Six Fingers down.

The truth was, however, that Kam Ho was not as desperate for a woman as Chinatown's other bachelors. Kam Ho had a secret that he guarded so closely that no one could have dragged it out of him.

Working for the Hendersons had changed him. Under Mrs. Henderson's watchful eye, Kam Ho had grown from a sapling to a great tree that thrived in the dew and the sunlight. He'd matured from a skinny whippet of a kid into a strapping young man. Without her, those well-developed biceps would have hung on him like useless flesh. But Mrs. Henderson offered him forbidden fruit, fed herself to him until every fibre of his being hungered for her. Kam Ho was choosy and was loath to accept a less tasty dish.

Till now, Kam Ho had been content to disregard the letters and photographs his mother sent him, but today was different. Something his mother said needled him, not painfully, but perceptibly. It disturbed his peace of mind.

"If you don't come home and get married, your father will never live to see a Fong grandson."

It was a reminder to Kam Ho that his father would be sixty-five this year. That was the *yeung fan* way of reckoning it; they lopped off the beginning and the end of life. Back in Spur-On Village, people included both ends in their tabulation; by their reckoning, Ah-Fat was sixty-seven, only three years off an age almost unheard of in the countryside. Kam Ho shivered involuntarily. He dried his hands on his apron and took the photograph from the envelope, put it in his pocket and went to the living room.

He could not wait any longer. He had to tell her. Today.

He walked in to find Mrs. Henderson curled up on the floor, her forehead beaded with sweat. She was having an arthritic attack. He was about to help her up when she stretched out a hand and pointed to the kitchen. He knew that meant the opium juice. He had bought some last week but only the dregs remained. He could not buy more for another three days when Mr. Henderson gave him the housekeeping money. He got the bottle and rinsed it out with water, adding half a teaspoon of brown sugar to the diluted mixture. Then he poured it into a black cup to disguise its pale colour and handed it to Mrs. Henderson.

She took a mouthful. "Jimmy, you're as big a cheat as the rest of them!" she wailed, and smashed the cup down. It shattered, and the opium and water mixture trickled across the floor. Kam Ho looked at the claw-like hand that still held the handle; Mrs. Henderson's bones looked as if they had been bored by locusts. The opium juice acted as an insecticide, but no sooner had it killed one swarm than another took its place. They plagued her bones, and the opium could not kill them all.

Kam Ho squatted down to clean up the broken china. He was doing sums in his head, wondering if he ought to dig into his own savings to buy her some juice. He picked her up and carried her to her bed. He got a towel to wipe the sweat from her forehead. She reached out one hand and gripped him fiercely by the front of his shirt. He struggled to free himself and some of his buttons came off. His mind was on other matters today but Mrs. Henderson was not going to take no for an answer. Her hand followed the familiar route through the opening of his shirt, but today it was as if her hand had scales. Her touch irritated him.

Suddenly Kam Ho had had enough. He shrugged off her hand, pulled up her dress and, forcing open her legs, thrust himself into her. It was the first time he had ever taken the initiative. Now, he took her without ceremony, like a rough-mannered peasant. Mrs. Henderson was so startled that she struggled to sit up—then realized that the pains in her joints had disappeared.

It was not the first time she had felt the pain ebb away when he was with her. The locusts had not the slightest compunction in what they did to her aging body. They had no fear of her but they did fear him. His vigour swept them away like sand carried down by a stream in spate.

Kam Ho was covered in sweat, and worry tugged at him. He turned his head to look at her. Mrs. Henderson lay pink-cheeked, sweat-soaked tendrils of hair clinging to her forehead and a faint smile playing at the corners of her mouth. She was not displeased. He relaxed.

Starting from when they first became intimate, he gradually gained confidence. She hesitated about giving him money but, all the same, insistently pushed small sums under his pillow, which he accepted. Kam Ho began to enjoy what they did and missed it terribly when for a few days she did not come to him. After that, he refused the money, even crumpling up a two-dollar bill and flushing it down the toilet in front of her. From that day on, she did not give him money. Kam Ho stopped feeling that he was at her beck and call and started to feel that she should do things to please him. Every Christmas, when Mr. Henderson gave him a Christmas gift, he would clap him on the shoulder and say: "I don't know how you've managed to mellow my wife's character but she's been so much sweeter these last years. You've saved me a lot of trouble."

Kam Ho, weighing the fat envelope stuffed with notes in his hand, felt brazen but also proud.

He helped her into fresh clothes, feeling how relaxed her body was compared to its rigidity just a quarter of an hour ago. She had got thinner this summer, her breasts slacker, like a Buddha's hand fruit desiccated in the sun. It occurred to him that she had once been plump with juices; he had leached her dry. He felt a spasm of misery. But, miserable or not, there was no time to lose. He had to speak.

He pulled the photograph of the girl out of his pocket and gave it to Mrs. Henderson.

"I want to take a trip back home, ma'am, and marry this girl."

Mrs. Henderson said nothing in reply and did not look at the picture. He could almost hear her heart plummet. She stared at the wall through eyes that appeared like deep, dark, dried-up wells, with crumbling stones lying at the bottom.

Kam Ho did not dare look at Mrs. Henderson. He stared at his hands, feeling himself grow hot. Finally, he stammered:

"I can't … can't not go. My d-dad, grandson."

Still there was no reply. Then he heard the sound of stones grinding against each other in the well's arid depths. A frail, reedy voice emerged.

"Six months," Mrs. Henderson whispered. "I'll give you six months."

Dear Ah-Fat,

Kam Ho arrived home about five days ago, and because he has so little time before he has to leave, we held the wedding yesterday. The situation is very volatile here. There are bandits everywhere and we have had to be very discreet about the wedding presents. We sent all the gifts under cover of darkness to the Au family and they did the same. Fortunately, Mak Dau was able to accompany them, armed, which was reassuring. In a troubled world, it is only guns that can assure our safety, so we may buy more next year. The wedding banquet was very simple, only a dozen or so tables and family guests. Kam Ho was such a little boy when he left for Gold Mountain, only fourteen years old. He is so different now I would not recognize him in the street.

Last time you left, Kam Sau was still in my belly. Now she is sixteen and has never met her father. She has graduated from high school and is preparing to take the entrance exams for the provincial teacher-training college. The college is in the city and I am worried it is not safe for her to travel there alone, so I am thinking of betrothing her to Mak Dau's son, Ah-Yuen. Although they are not of the same rank as our family, Ah-Yuen is very bright and has done exceptionally well in his school exams. He is a young man with a promising future. Kam Sau and Ah-Yuen have been brought up together and are genuinely fond of each other. What do you think? If you agree, they could become engaged this autumn and get married when she graduates from college. You should come back and preside over the ceremonies.

Kam Ho says you are reluctant to come home because you want to earn more money. You know the Fong family properties and fields bring in enough income to sustain us for years to come. Besides, you are getting on in years and should be home with our family where you belong. I do hope you will make a decision as soon as possible. Even the tallest trees belong to their roots. The grass grows tall on your mother's grave and, although I go regularly and keep it neat, she needs her son to come and pay his respects. Has Kam Shan's leg improved? Has Yin Ling started school yet? There is a wealth of knowledge for her to learn in foreign schools but she should not forget the glories of her own language. I will finish here and hope you are in good health,

Most humbly, your wife, Ah-Yin, ninth day of the first month, eighteenth year of the Republic, Spur-On Village

Year nineteen of the Republic (1930)
Vancouver, British Columbia

Business was dismal at Ah-Fat's café that day, no more than four or five customers, ordering just small portions of sausage-flavoured rice. The cook spent all afternoon propped against the stove asleep. He woke up, crammed down a large bowlful of sausage-flavoured rice, wiped the grease from his mouth, then cut himself a fat slice of cooked pork and wrapped it in a lotus leaf to take home with him. Ah-Fat had it on the tip of his tongue to tell him to put the meat back in the fridge, that it would do for tomorrow too, but he felt that would sound too harsh. He was silent for a long moment and finally pretended he had not noticed. Instead he turned his anger on himself for being so feeble.

Ah-Fat cleared away the remaining food, then went to hang a yellow silk flower in the doorway. Tomorrow was Dominion Day in Canada. It was also the seventh anniversary of the Chinese Exclusion Act. The Benevolent Association had instructed all Chinese immigrants not to mark Dominion Day with the Canadian flag, since that would be humiliating, but had distributed badges with the character for China on it. Ah-Fat always wore the badge and made his sons do the same. But nothing ever changed, though the Association held protest meetings every year and articles appeared regularly about the exclusion of Chinese.

Ah-Fat was losing heart.

Just as he was about to put up the shutters, a woman came in and ordered roast-duck noodles. Ah-Fat pulled out the meat and noodles again and prepared her order. The woman looked around for a place to sit and eat. Ah-Fat's café was small and most customers took their orders away, so there were only two small tables and four rickety wooden chairs. She chose a clean chair, sat down and, taking a handkerchief from her pocket, wiped the table clean.

She wore a black skirt and a grey blouse, faded with much washing, and fraying at the cuffs, but still neat and clean. She appeared to be in her forties and her hair was streaked with grey. The sleek bun at the nape of her neck was adorned with a sprig of jasmine. She was extremely thin and sat perfectly straight. She wore a Benevolent Association "China" badge on her blouse. But she looked different from the usual regulars in Chinatown—and since there were very few new arrivals now, Ah-Fat knew all the women by sight. He did not recognize her.

He took the bowl of noodles and a cup of soy milk to her. "Have you just arrived in Vancouver?" he asked her politely. The woman nodded but did not speak. She wiped the chopsticks with her handkerchief and began to eat. She ate slowly, picking up the individual noodles as carefully as if she were doing embroidery. She seemed preoccupied and her ears trembled like a startled rabbit.

Ah-Fat was in a hurry to get home but it would be impolite to rush her. He brought her a second cup of soy milk when she had almost finished the first and took up his position behind her. The woman waved the milk away. "I won't charge you, you're the last customer," Ah-Fat reassured her. "I'll have to pour the rest down the drain otherwise." She accepted it and unhurriedly continued with her meal.

"Where is it from?" she asked.

Ah-Fat thought she meant the soy milk. "Ah-Wong's shop next door," he said. The woman laughed. "I meant the opera music." It occurred to Ah-Fat that she was dawdling over her meal because she wanted to listen to it. He kept a record player on the kitchen cupboard so he could put opera records on when there were no customers in the shop. The machine was old, the records extremely scratchy, and every now and then the needle would jump a groove.

"It was given to me many years ago by a friend," Ah-Fat said. "Do you like opera?"

The woman shut her eyes and began to hum along, keeping pace with the long drawn-out notes of the singer. Her voice was so sweet and true that Ah-Fat's interest was piqued and he found himself humming along with the notes. Their voices soared and dipped in time with the music from the record.

"Did you see any of Gold Mountain Cloud's performances?" she asked as they finished.

"When she came to Vancouver, I saw all twelve performances. I sat in the front row, right in the middle. It was twenty cents a ticket, really cheap."

"How did she sing?"

"She hadn't made a name for herself back then but she sung the male roles so strongly she made the rafters vibrate. She could beat a dozen male singers any day. As soon as I heard her I knew she was destined for great things."

The woman opened her eyes and extended a couple of fingers. "May I have a cigarette, please?" she asked. Ah-Fat pulled the packet from his pocket and lit one for her, then one for himself. Her teeth were stained yellow, he noticed. She must have been a heavy smoker for many years. She certainly smoked with style—legs crossed, head tipped back, her extended fingers trembling slightly. Then the smoke rings would waft gently from between her lips, floating upwards, gradually losing definition until they bumped against the walls and dissolved one by one into the air.

"You really think Gold Mountain Cloud was good?" she persisted.

Ah-Fat laughed out loud. "I was a huge fan of hers," he said. "It took me an hour to walk there every day but I was always there before they opened up. After the performance, I used to hang around in the hopes that I could get a word in. But I was just a fish-cannery worker—she had a rich gentleman waiting to take her to dinner every night. After the last performance, though, she sent me a record as a gift and that's the one I'm playing now."

The woman turned around and stared Ah-Fat in the face. "That scar on your face. It's hardly noticeable any more."

Ah-Fat was astonished. After a long pause, he asked: "Is it really you? Gold Mountain Cloud?"

She answered simply: "It was all so long ago, like another life."

After she had made a name for herself in San Francisco, she took up with one of her admirers, a rich Hawaiian Chinese called Huang. She left the stage, married him and they settled in Honolulu. For a few years, she lived the life of a wealthy lady. Then one day, Huang fell foul of a gangland dealer and was stabbed to death in an opium den. Gold Mountain Cloud was forced to return to San Francisco, where she went back on the stage, taking any singing parts she could get. In the intervening years new roles had taken the place of the old ones for which she was famous, so she could only get minor accompanying parts. Later still, she lost her voice and even those parts dried up. Once famous far beyond Gold Mountain, now she was forgotten. She was reduced to relying on handouts from her elder brother, who had given up singing long before and ran a small store in Montreal. She did not get on with her sister-in-law and when, last month, her brother died of tuberculosis, Gold Mountain Cloud came to Vancouver.

"Where are you living? What are you doing for a living now?" asked Ah-Fat.

"I look after props and costumes at the theatre. I can sleep in a corner of the wardrobe room, which saves me paying rent."

"Do they pay you?"

"Enough for a bowl of noodles."

Ah-Fat gave a long sigh. After such fame and wealth, to be reduced to such poverty. What could he say?

That Saturday evening, after serving the Hendersons their dinner Kam Ho set off for home. As he passed the gate, he saw his father waiting for him at the end of the street. Fear seized his heart and he ran down the street. "What's happened?" His father said nothing, just pulled out his cigarettes and gave him one, taking another for himself. Ah-Fat stood there without moving, smoking his cigarette, until the ash at the tip trembled and dropped to the ground. Finally he asked Kam Ho: "Have you brought any money with you?"

Kam Ho was silent. His trip back home and his marriage to Ah-Hsien had exhausted all his savings. His wife was expecting a baby soon and he was sending every cent back to Hoi Ping.

"Twenty ... or if you haven't got twenty, ten will do," his father persisted.

"What for?"

Ah-Fat remained silent but his expression said it all. He threw down the cigarette he had just lit and ground it under his feet. He hawked and spat angrily: "If your old dad asks to borrow a bit of cash, do you have to have a signed-and-sealed loan agreement?"

"I sent a dollar letter back home just yesterday," said Kam Ho, pulling a five-dollar bill out of his pocket. Ah-Fat took the note, which was moist from Kam Ho's sweaty palm.

"Dad, we've never been gamblers, the odds are stacked against us. And at your age, you really shouldn't be wasting money like this."

Blood rushed to Ah-Fat's face. He was tempted to screw up the note and fling it back into his son's face. But then he remembered Gold Mountain Cloud's jade bracelet, so flawless it glowed like a candle flame at night. This five-dollar bill, plus the five which he had saved himself, would ensure that she would not need to part with it. At least, not today.

He gritted his teeth and thrust the note into his pocket.

From then on, Ah-Fat would occasionally borrow money from Kam Ho. If not twenty, then ten. If not ten, then five. If Kam Ho could not spare him five, then he would take three or even one dollar ... or even a few cents. Finally the day came when Kam Ho refused to give him anything. "There's my son Yiu Kei's one-month-old celebration and then there's Mum's birthday to think of. The family needs more guns. Money doesn't grow on trees, you know. Dad, when was the last time you sent a dollar letter home? Who's been supporting the family all this time? Why are you taking food out of the mouths of your wife and grandchild for gambling?"

Ah-Fat stiffened and the veins on his forehead bulged. With an enormous effort, he swallowed back his anger.

"Next year. Next year, I'll sell the café and go back home. I've been making a note of every cent I borrow from you and you'll get it back with interest when I sell up," he muttered.

Kam Ho shouted with laughter. "Your café? It loses money every month. You keep the food so long the sausage is crawling with maggots. No one's going to buy the café off you even if you pay them to take it off your hands!"

Ah-Fat's face turned livid purple and he swallowed back hard words that felt like grit in his gullet. His youngest son, whom he had always slighted, called the shots now—this was something he had never expected. Kam Shan, whose leg had never properly healed, could not support himself, and the burden of supporting the families in Canada and China lay on the shoulders of just two people—Kam Ho and Cat Eyes.

It had taken Ah-Fat all these years to learn two unpalatable facts: one, that the one who sent home the dollar letters could afford to talk loud; two, that the one who begged could not stand tall. Often he was on the point of explaining to Kam Ho what he was really borrowing money for, but when it came to it, he just could not get the words out. They went round and round in his head but he could never find the way to say what he wanted to say. It somehow seemed easier to allow Kam Ho to get the wrong end of the stick.

And so he kept silent.

Just you wait, he thought. Your old dad's not got much longer to live. And if I can't earn back my self-respect and go home with my head held high, then I'll never go back, he thought fiercely to himself.

Year twenty-five of the Republic (1936)
Vancouver, British Columbia

As Jenny looked at her face in the hand mirror, she grew more and more despondent. Her face was too flat, her eyes too far apart and small at that, so she always looked half-asleep. Her cheeks were covered in freckles, but that was not the worst of it. She had none of the curves that most of her peers were developing. She was still as flat as a board.

There were three more weeks before the high school prom. Her mother had already booked the hairdresser and ordered her evening dress, and six months ago her father had booked tables for fifty at the Vancouver Hotel for a celebratory coming-out dinner. Or that was the excuse. In England, well-off families would hold dinners to launch their sons and daughters into society. Her father adopted the English custom, but his real aim was to find his daughter a rich husband. A rich husband was the furthest thing from Jenny's mind. All she hoped for was that some boy, any boy, would take her by the hand and lead her onto the dance floor.

Almost all the girls in her year had prom partners. Mary had fixed hers up in the first year of high school; Susie had had invitations from three boys and still had not made up her mind. Jennifer had accepted Billy's invitation then switched to Vincent; Billy and Vincent came to blows in the school grounds. Miss Smith, the headmistress, punished both boys by making them each clean the blackboard and carry the French teacher's dictionaries and class notes for a week.

That sort of thing only happened to other people, Jenny thought forlornly. Jenny had not yet received so much as a glance from a boy, let alone an invitation. The only other girl in the same situation was that odd Chinese girl with the slit eyes, Linda Wong. Who wanted to be lumped in with a girl whose hair and clothes stank of cooking oil? Jenny shuddered at the thought.

Jenny knelt down on the floor and joined her hands together in prayer. She had said many prayers in her life, though most of them were grace before meals or at bedtime. But the prayer she said now was an urgent entreaty:

"Merciful Father in Heaven, I beg you not to make me go to the prom without a partner, like that Chinese girl, Linda Wong. Lord, I have committed many sins in the past. The year before last, when Mummy refused to let me wear lipstick at Christmas, I made a secret curse that she would die soon. When my classmates teased me for having a Mongol houseboy, I put diarrhea medicine into Jimmy's food. When I didn't want to go to science lessons, I said I was sick and got Mummy to write a note for me. And every time I go to church with Mummy and Daddy, I sit there counting my fingers and wishing that Pastor Carter would hurry up and get his sermon over with. Lord, you have thousands of reasons for punishing me, but please, could you hold off until the prom is over? I'd rather jump into burning sulphur than walk into the prom alone, but the Sunday school teacher said that only heathens who don't believe in God get punished that way. I do believe in you, Lord, please don't let me down. There's only three weeks to go. I beg you to make me get an invitation as quickly as possible, hopefully tomorrow. Apart from Jack, who has a snotty nose, any boy will do. If you give me the boy who Susie doesn't want, even that's better than nothing. If you're listening to me, I beg you to give me a sign you've heard."

The teddy bear on the bed suddenly fell to the floor. Jenny's heart leapt. She knew that was God's answer, and that she would not be forced to walk into the prom alone. Very soon, maybe tomorrow, she would get a late invitation. No more would she have to get her school bag ready ten minutes before the end of school and rush out as soon as the bell sounded, just so she could be spared the other girls' chatter about the prom. She would be able to talk to Mary, Susie and Jennifer easily about what kind of prom dress she was going to have and what colour it would be.

Jenny felt a great weight lift from her shoulders. She was unaccustomed to that feeling of weightlessness, and clasped her hands tightly over her chest as if afraid she might suddenly take off and float up to the ceiling.

She began to inspect herself in the mirror, in minute detail. The mirror was not big enough so she had to tilt it slowly and look at herself bit by bit. She was surprised to see a faint red flush on her cheeks which somehow made her freckles less obvious. Her chest was as flat as ever but if she squeezed her chest together hard between both hands, she could see something resembling a cleavage. Her neck was too long, but that was because she wore her hair up. If she spread her hair out, or braided the ends into French-style braids, that would change things a lot. Jenny carried on inspecting herself all over and was encouraged to realize that she could remedy every shortcoming.

Jenny's hand turned sideways and the mirror grew legs and took her eyes through the half-open door to the living room. In the corner of the living room by the curtained French windows, she saw two people: her mother and Jimmy.

Jimmy was holding a jug and pouring the water from it into a cup which he held in the other hand. Jenny knew all about Jimmy giving her mother Chinese herbal medicine ("Chinese bilge," as her father called it). Her mother had been taking it for nearly twenty years to ease her pain. The price of this "Chinese bilge" climbed higher every year, and this caused increasingly bitter arguments between her parents. The older her father got, the cheaper he became; the older her mother got, the more she needed her medicine.

Jenny watched in the mirror as her mother drank the "bilge" and Jimmy gave her a towel to wipe her mouth with. But she did not take the towel. Instead, she gripped Jimmy's sleeve. Jimmy pulled his arm back, but she hung on and finally he allowed her to wipe her mouth on his sleeve. Jenny could hardly believe her eyes.

Her mother had come to rely more and more on Jimmy as the years went by. He was her walking stick, the pillow she rested on, the handkerchief on which she dried her tears. Many of Jenny's classmates lived in her street and they all knew that the Hendersons had a Chinese houseboy. Once Susie had said: "Someone saw that Chinaman scrubbing your mother's back. Is it true?" Mary joined in the fun then. "I've heard that when Chinese people get their wages, they don't put them in the bank, they stuff the money in the bottom of their shoes. Is your Jimmy like that?" Jenny flushed furiously at these stupid questions. Finally she spluttered some rude comment about Jimmy scrubbing Susie's mother's back—and did not speak to either of her friends for a week afterwards.

They did not ask Jenny any more questions about Jimmy after that, but even so, Jenny saw the suspicious looks they gave her. Their eyes were full of scorn, perhaps pity, as if they were saying to themselves: "Such a nice girl. What bad luck that she's got a Chinese houseboy." She tried to grow a thick skin and refused to let them needle her. But eventually her pride shrivelled under their relentless gaze.

In the end, it all got too much for her. One day, she was coming home from school when she met Jimmy walking to meet her along the pavement, as he usually did. She would not let him touch her school bag. She walked straight past him and up to her mother's room. She stood in front of her mother, and hesitated a moment. It suddenly seemed as difficult to broach the subject as drilling a pinhole in an iron curtain.

She looked down at her toes, and stammered: "Mummy, do we really ... really need Jimmy?"

Her mother made no attempt to probe at what lay behind the question. She simply took the words at face value. Holding Jenny's hand she said, after a pause: "Yes, we do. Your father, I, and you too, we all need Jimmy."

Jenny was annoyed at her mother's casualness. She pushed away her hand. "It's not us, it's only you," she said. Her mother was unperturbed. "If you don't believe me," she said placidly, "you go and ask your father. Who, apart from Jimmy, is willing to listen to his endlessly repeated jokes and laugh as if it was the first time he'd heard them?" Jenny felt deflated. She was quite well aware that her father depended on Jimmy as much as her mother did.

"Actually, you need Jimmy too," said her mother.

"Of course, you were too young to remember, but it was Jimmy who bathed you and changed your nappy when you were a baby. When you had diphtheria, who was it that put you to sleep by resting you on his stomach? Do you think your breakfast would fly itself to the table if we didn't have Jimmy? Would your skirt get washed and folded and put away? The dust on your desk doesn't clean itself. If Jimmy left today, you'd have to become the cook, cleaner, gardener and nurse to me, tomorrow. I'll send him away straightaway if you're ready for that."

Jenny left her mother's room without another word that day. But when she thought that Jimmy's monkey-like yellow paws had once reached into the most secret places on her body, she felt her skin crawl.

Jenny could perfectly well have turned away from the mirror or pulled the living-room door shut. Seeing that sleeve pressed against her mother's mouth had upset her and she did not want to look at herself in the mirror any more. But she kept looking at them. That was a mistake.

Her mother finished wiping her mouth but still did not let go of Jimmy's arm. Instead she gripped his hand and pressed it to her cheek. She saw her mother's hand wrapped around Jimmy's like a gaping python, slithering down her neck, in through the opening of her gown and coming to rest on her breasts.

Jenny heard an almighty crack, as if her head had exploded into myriad fragments. She had dropped the mirror, and it shattered. She was treading barefoot on shards of glass, but felt no pain.

Mrs. Henderson let go of Jimmy's hand but it was too late. Jenny whirled past, leaving a trail of bloody footprints behind her. Mrs. Henderson stood up and found that her knees, devoured by so many years of pain, were suddenly filled with renewed vigour and elasticity. Heedless of her body, they hurtled her legs forward. Down the stairs she rushed in pursuit of her daughter, and out into the street.

She caught up with Jenny at the end of the street. She glimpsed a flash of Jenny's pink dress, seized hold and flung herself on top of it. Jenny struggled but could not free herself. She elbowed her mother savagely in the chest. Mrs. Henderson felt as if she had been clubbed. She lifted her head, then saw stars.

When she came to, a group of people were standing around her. She heard a woman holding a parasol say to a man: "It's been a day for strange happenings on this street. Just now Jenny was dashing down the street and, just in front of the school gate, she was hit by a car, poor thing."

Mrs. Henderson suddenly recalled Jenny's eyes. When Jenny had looked at her, her eyes had blazed like brilliant beads.

Mrs. Henderson began to claw frantically at her cheeks, over and over, until they were covered in bloody streaks. No one knew that she was trying to dig out the glass beads buried in her face.

Dear Kam Ho,

The fifty dollars which you entrusted to Tai Sek Lou for me have arrived safely. He told me that you and your brother have finally convinced your father to close the café and are pressing him to buy his passage home for good. He has always been so stubborn and it is hard for him to face coming home in poverty. I hope you and your brother will continue to support and comfort him.

The Japanese invaders have got as far as Wai Yeong, and one market day, their planes strafed a crowd of market-goers. Three of your wife Ah-Hsien's family died and two were injured. Only your father-in-law and brother-

in-law escaped because they had taken their sows to a nearby village to be mated. Your younger brother-in-law's death was especially terrible—half his body was blown into a tree and his guts spilled all over the ground. Apart from bombing, the Japanese army commit atrocities wherever they go, raping, killing, pillaging and burning.

Given the current instability here, your father should stay where he is for now, and be in no hurry to come home. As he gets older, he hardly ever bothers to write. I have had almost no letters from him this year. I am lucky to have your frequent letters which are a great comfort to me. Your sister, Kam Sau, and your brother-in-law, Ah-Yuen, have graduated from college and returned to set up a school here. They teach boys and girls together, and the school is beginning to make a name for itself. Pupil numbers are going up. Your son, Yiu Kei, has started school. He is a bright boy and is making good progress. All the teachers are pleased with him. He and Kam Sau's son, Wai Kwok, are inseparable friends. It is sad that Yiu Kei has not yet met his father and has only the vaguest idea who you are. I too am getting older and long to have my children and grandchildren around me. I will only be happy when your father, you, Kam Shan and Yin Ling all come home after the war is over and we can be a family once more.

Your mother, eighth day of the eleventh month of the twenty-seventh year of the Republic, Spur-On Village

Year twenty-nine of the Republic (1940)
Vancouver, British Columbia

Kam Ho got up in the morning and went to make coffee. In the kitchen, he glanced out the window at the cherry tree. Almost all its leaves had fallen but he saw some small red dots and went out into the garden to look. The tree had suddenly grown a slender new branch and a few buds had sprouted. He cut the branch off, put it in a vase and carried it in and up the stairs for Mrs. Henderson.

At the foot of the stairs, he bumped into Mr. Henderson, who was on his way out to walk the dog. "Good morning!" Kam Ho greeted him. "Did ma'am sleep well?" As soon as the words were out of his mouth, he felt foolish. Mr. and Mrs. Henderson had had separate bedrooms for a number of years now.

Mr. Henderson did not reply, just peered at the vase in Kam Ho's hand. "You're not going home next weekend. I'm taking you to White Rock to do some fishing."

Kam Ho had gone fishing a few times with Mr. Henderson and had discovered that the head of the family was a poor fisherman—impatient and clumsy. Mr. Henderson's real reason for going off with a mountain of tackle was to get away from home and spend a bit of time outdoors. He reminded Kam Ho of a small boy ditching school. Kam Ho hesitated, then said: "Then there'll be no one at home. Ma'am...." Mr. Henderson shook his head resignedly: "Of course...." Kam Ho watched him walk away with the dog, and was struck by how doddery he was getting as the years went by.

By the time Kam Ho went into her room, Mrs. Henderson was awake and staring blankly at the ceiling. Kam Ho drew her hands out from under the covers and began to untie the cords which bound her wrists. All the muscle tone had gone and they were as slack as hot-water dough, which made things much more difficult for Kam Ho.

Since Jenny died, Mrs. Henderson had been alternately confused and lucid. As time passed, her moments of lucidity grew shorter and shorter; her bouts of confusion, on the other hand, lasted longer and longer. She frequently scratched her own face though she seemed to feel no pain. She explained that she was trying to dig out Jenny's eyes. Every evening before bedtime, Kam Ho tied her wrists together.

Kam Ho saw a row of red pea-sized blotches on Mrs. Henderson's wrists and guessed that she had had a restless night. He brought the vase close so that she could see the cherry blossom buds. "It looks like it's going to snow any moment, yet they're opening up. Isn't that strange?" he said.

Mrs. Henderson ignored the flowers and buried her face in Kam Ho's hair. "Jimmy, I can hear a shushing sound." "It's probably the coffee boiling," said Kam Ho. She shook her head. "No, it's not that. It's your grey hairs growing." Kam Ho smiled despite himself. "What you mean is I'm forty years old, and a Chinese man is old at forty. I should be a grandfather by now."

"But you're not a father yet." Mrs. Henderson touched his face gently. "Your son died."

The family back home had kept the news of Yiu Kei's death from Kam Ho, but in the end he had heard about it anyway, from a fellow countryman who had gone home on a visit. He had never seen his son except in photographs which his mother sent. His son had been dependent on Kam Ho for all his needs, but had no hold on his affections. By the time the news reached his ears, Yiu Kei had been dead for nearly a year and Kam Ho had felt scarcely more than a few moments' sadness. But Mrs. Henderson's caress brought it all back to him and he felt a stab of grief for which he was not prepared.

"My Jenny can be his companion," said Mrs. Henderson.

Kam Ho was startled. This was the first time for a long time that she had talked sense. He helped her to sit upright and changed her nightgown. Her whole body was slack as a filleted fish today and she kept flopping over to one side or the other until Kam Ho poured with sweat.

Finally he got angry. "If you won't help me, I'm leaving and never coming back!" he said. The threat usually made Mrs. Henderson behave, but today for some reason it had no effect at all.

Kam Ho dropped her hand and turned to go. When he reached the door, there was a cry from Mrs. Henderson: "Jenny's come!" Kam Ho felt a chill of dread. "You're off your head!" he shouted at her. "But that's a message from Jenny," said Mrs. Henderson, pointing at the cherry blossom in the vase. "Jenny's telling me to go with her."

Kam Ho gave an involuntary shiver. He suddenly remembered his granny saying that flowers which blossomed out of season were a portent of disaster. He grabbed the vase and carried it out, cutting up the branch with scissors before throwing the bits into the garbage. When he got back upstairs, Mrs. Henderson was asleep, resting against the headboard. He could not shake her awake. He fetched a wet towel, wrung it out and put it on her face. Finally, she opened her eyes slightly. There was a look of muddied confusion in them, like a pond stirred up by a rainstorm.

"Ma'am!" cried Kam Ho in a voice cracked with panic. Mrs. Henderson's mouth was opening and closing like a dying fish. No sound came out, and her eyes began to cloud over. He forced himself to call out a few times, but it was no use and he stopped. He knew he should dress her, that this was probably his last chance. He rifled through her wardrobe and picked out a dress which she had bought the Christmas before Jenny died. Frantically, he began to undo the silk ribbon tie of her nightgown.

Suddenly he felt her hand shift ever so slightly in his. He put his ear to her mouth and heard the faintest of whispers. It took him some time to make out her words: "Don't want...."

"Don't want what?" he asked, but she did not have the strength to reply.

"You don't want this dress?" he asked, but she just lay still and looked fixedly at him.

"You don't want the pastor to come?" Still she stared at him.

He slapped the bed in frustration. "Oh God, tell me what it is she doesn't want!" Then her hand gave a slight movement again. Suddenly, light dawned.

"It's him? You don't want him to come in?" he asked.

She blinked once and the hand he was holding relaxed.

When Mr. Henderson came back from walking the dog, he heard a faint noise from upstairs. It was something like bees beating their wings in the sunshine or filaments vibrating against each other in a light bulb. "Jimmy!" he shouted, but there was no answer. "Phyllis!" He stood at the bottom of the stairs straining his ears. The noise was coming from his wife's room. Going up, he knocked a couple of times, then pushed the door open and went in without waiting for an answer.

His wife lay on the bed, dressed in a bright red dress. It was such a vibrant red that it seemed to reflect off the walls. It had been a very long time since he had seen her in anything that brilliant. Jimmy was kneeling by the bed. He was wiping her face with a wet towel, in a manner that was almost comical—his arm held over her, the hand trembling slightly, his movements so gentle and careful that she might have been a priceless Ming vase.

Jimmy was crooning faint sounds through the smallest crack in his lips, the way the mature silkworm spits tangled silken strands to create its cocoon. It must be some sort of a song, Mr. Henderson guessed, but he understood nothing of it. How could he know that Kam Ho was singing a lullaby which had been sung to him by his mother in Hoi Ping when she nursed him at the breast?

A magpie sings Happy New Year
Dad's gone to Gold Mountain my dear
When he returns to bring his fortunate back here
We'll buy house and land far and near

Mr. Henderson lost patience. "Jimmy, can't you see she's off her rocker! She's in bed with high-heeled shoes on!"

Jimmy turned slowly to look at him, then pointed to the door.

"Get ... out."

The day after Mrs. Henderson's funeral, Kam Ho was summoned to her lawyer's office.

"According to her will, she's settled her entire estate of four thousand dollars on you."

Kam Ho was dumbfounded. After a pause, he said doubtfully: "But that's impossible. She was dependent on her husband. She had no money of her own."

The lawyer opened the filing cabinet and took out the will. He pointed to the already fading signature. "She made this will ten years ago," he said. "At the time, the beneficiaries were her daughter, Jenny, and you. Now that Jenny is dead, you are the sole beneficiary. The money was a personal gift from Mrs. Henderson's mother to her daughter, given to her before she married. She had the right to dispose of it as she wished."

By the time Kam Ho came out of the lawyer's, it was dark. A bone-chilling wind whistled down the street and a bird sitting on the bare branch of a tree give a loud sibilant call. He looked up—it was a balding old blue jay. Kam Ho threw a stone at it. It squawked, before flying low over his head. Kam Ho remembered Mrs. Henderson's claim that Jenny had sent her a message in the cherry blossoms after she died. He wondered if Mrs. Henderson was sending him a message now, with the bird.

Why, he thought, did you spend your whole life squeezing money out of your husband a few cents at a time, when you had a pile of money of your own? You could have bought all the opium juice you wanted! Why put yourself through hell? But there was no answer.

At last, the tears began to flow.

When he got back to the Hendersons', the house was dark, but he knew Mr. Henderson was home by the faint smell of gin lingering in the kitchen and the passageway. He made his way upstairs in the dark. He did not want to turn on the lights and risk running into Mr. Henderson. He had packed his bag the night before; he retrieved it from the bed and went back downstairs.

Suddenly the light came on in the hallway, dazzling him for a few moments.

"Jimmy, why don't you stay?" The tremulous voice was coming from the shadows.

Kam Ho did not answer. He slung his bag over his shoulder. He would open the door, go down the cracked front steps and be gone. This light, this man, this house, none of it had anything to do with him any more.

But the voice followed him and grovelled at his feet, clutching his trouser bottoms.

"I know you're angry with me because I didn't treat her well, but you know why that was?"

The voice paused a moment, then gathered strength and went on: "You. It was you."

Kam Ho dropped his bag in surprise.

"It's you I wanted, ever since the first day you arrived. But she got between us. I couldn't get to you. So I kept out of the way. Those business trips, you know.

"I never wanted her. It wasn't her fault. I just never liked women. Any women."

A rotund pink face emerged from the shadows and pressed towards Kam Ho.

Kam Ho flung himself out the door and down the steps. On the last step, he twisted his ankle. He looked round but was relieved to see that Mr. Henderson was not following him. He sat down and rubbed the bump that was coming up. He reached for his bag, but realized that he had left it behind.

He had given up twenty-five years of his life in that house. Why was he bothering about a bag?

He walked and walked in the night air. His head felt viscous like the glue his mother used to paste the soles on his shoes when he was little. Throughout his life, he had walked only one road. It had been a long and hard one but the only effort required was from his feet. There was no need for thought. When he was young, it was his mother who had told him which road to take. When she said, Go to Gold Mountain, he got on the boat and went. After that, it was his father who chose his road. His father said, Go to the Hendersons', and he went. Later still, it was Mrs. Henderson who showed him the road. She said stay, and he stayed. For twenty-five years.

The cheque in his pocket opened up countless roads before him. And now *he* would decide which one to take. He secretly admired his brother for the way he had charted his own course. Kam Shan had chosen his own road from the very day he was born. Though his parents had harsh words with Kam Shan for his rebellious streak, Kam Ho knew they liked his spirit and his guts. Now, of course, his brother was old, and had to accept being kept by his wife.

After so many years working for the Hendersons, Kam Ho had a pretty good idea of the number of uses to which he could put the cheque in his pocket. He could give some to his father for his boat passage home. He could give some to his mother to buy fields that stretched to the horizon and beyond. He could give his brother a portion so he could buy a proper house with a garden. His brother and his woman were used to life in Gold Mountain and would not easily settle back in Hoi Ping. His brother had never formally married the woman and Kam Ho still did not know how to address her. So with his brother he called her "she." When he bumped into her and could not avoid addressing her directly, he made do with "Hello!" or "You!" She never complained but he had felt awkward about it for years.

Of course, the most important reason for buying his brother a house was Yin Ling. She was a seed that had been planted in Gold Mountain soil. She would rather die than allow herself to be transplanted to the countryside of Hoi Ping. And if she would not go, then her father would not go either. And neither would his woman. Six Fingers had been talking about a big family reunion in Spur-On Village for years, but it was nothing more than a dream.

When he got to the end of the street, it occurred to him that he had not included his wife in the plans he had made for his cheque. He had lived with her for only a few months in the *diulau* after their marriage, and that was a very long time ago. She hardly ever wrote to him though she was literate. Sometimes she added a sentence at the end of a letter from his mother: "The leather shoes you sent for Yiu Kei are really nice" or "What shall I get for my father's longevity celebration later this year?" Without looking at the photograph, he could not even bring her face to mind. He had a dim memory that she had a mole on the left side of her mouth. On anyone else, a mole like this would have enlivened their features but on Ah-Hsien it just made her appear more wooden.

When he had entered the bridal chamber after their wedding banquet and taken off her veil, he was astonished to find that she was asleep, sitting upright on the bed, and drooling from the corner of her mouth. When he woke her up, she looked at him in bleary-eyed confusion as if she did not know who he was. He blew out the candle. In a few thrusts he was finished with her. She had not made a murmur, even of pain. He assumed it was because she knew nothing of what men and women did together, but as the days passed, there was no change in her. He realized that that was just the way she was. He was experienced with women, after all. Going to Ah-Hsien after Mrs. Henderson was like drinking plain water after having tasted osmanthus flower nectar. He found Ah-Hsien completely flavourless.

Which road should he take? The road back to Hoi Ping with his father, where he would live out his days with a doorpost of a wife? Or stay with his brother and do without a woman for the rest of his life? He went back and forth over the options, but could not make up his mind. The only decision he came to was to stop thinking. He would go back to where his brother and father lived, climb up to the attic room where he had a bunk bed and sleep on it. Then he would see. He could at least enjoy peace of mind. No one would expect him to get up to work for them, talk to them or feed them opium juice.

When Kam Ho arrived at the house, he found the door unlocked and pushed it open but saw no one inside. Then he heard the faint sound of opera—his father must be playing that old record of his. He bent down to take off his shoes and suddenly saw an unfamiliar pair of women's shoes. He could tell at a glance that they did not belong to Cat Eyes. Cat Eyes had been used to working in the fields as a child and had big feet. These shoes were dainty, with white soles and blue uppers with peonies embroidered on them in pink. Two small butterflies rested on the peony petals, as if about to take flight. It was rare to see dainty old-style cloth shoes like these in Chinatown nowadays.

Kam Ho went inside, and nearly fell over a pile of belongings—Yin Ling's coat and school bag. He hung the coat on the coat stand, made his way through the messy living room, down the dark passageway and into the kitchen. There he saw a man and woman standing in the kitchen by the window, singing opera. The woman seemed not to have warmed her voice up and sang hesitantly and huskily. However, she took both male and female roles while the man accompanied her.

The man was not singing but tum-te-tummed and tra-la-la'd as if he was the fiddle accompanying the woman as she sang.

The dancing butterflies have long gone
The oriole laments the shortening sun
Neither chevalier nor archer was I born
My only art is in poetry and song
To die for my fallen empire I really yearn
Rather than in shame and disgrace lingering on
But when I see the south in the grip of invaders
My people homeless and country war-torn
I'd be resigned to this life in shameful captivity
So that in peace my subjects can live on

Weeping blood and tears, your majesty
Yet with all your compromises, the new emperor shows no sign of mercy
The clouds of war hang over the southern sea
We caged birds have no hope of breaking free

Kam Ho thought he recognized the opera about Emperor Li Houzhu and the young empress Zhou. His father was humming the string accompaniment. The woman had her back to Kam Ho and all he could see was her bun at the nape of her neck. Her hair was streaked with grey, and he guessed she must be an opera friend of his father's. He knew that after he closed his café, his father had spent days in the Cantonese Opera Club in the company of other opera fans. Every now and then, he would bring one home and they would sit and smoke and sing and talk opera, until Kam Shan kicked up a fuss.

Kam Ho gave a loud cough, and the singing was neatly cut off in mid-note. "Today's not Saturday," his father exclaimed with raised eyebrows. "What are you doing here?"

Kam Ho's breath was taken away at his father's words. When he could speak again, he said: "You mean I can't come home any other day?"

The woman who had been singing turned around and the corners of her mouth twitched in a slight smile. "You must be Kam Ho," she said. "Your father says you're the most dependable son in Chinatown."

The woman was wearing a dark green silk *qipao* dress, he saw, with a jade pin at the collar. She had a pearl hairpin stuck into her bun. Her whole outfit seemed to come from another age, and even smelled a little musty. Kam Ho did not like the ingratiating tone in her voice. He smiled coldly. "I hope you're not taken in by what my father says."

The woman was taken aback at the rebuff but maintained her composure and continued to smile quietly. "Come here, Kam Ho," said his father, gesturing to her. "You're looking at Gold Mountain Cloud, a star of Cantonese opera. Twenty or so years ago, you could have asked anyone in the streets of San Francisco and they would all have known her name. She was queen of the opera in those days."

Kam Ho suddenly recalled that the singer on the old opera record his father kept playing was called Gold Mountain Cloud. He grunted, then asked: "Where's Yin Ling?" "Her Chinese class is going on a march tomorrow, to collect money for the Chinese troops, for planes to fight the Japs. Yin Ling's gone to rehearse." "And my brother?" "The Association's organizing a recruitment drive for the Chinese army, and they're having a meeting." It was on the tip of Kam Ho's tongue to say that his brother, with his injured leg, could not even support himself, so could not possibly go and fight the Japanese. But he did not want to make comments like that in front of a woman he did not know, so he simply turned round and went upstairs.

In the attic room, he lay down on the bed. It was wooden and squealed under his weight. Down below, the piercing sound of the strings and the singing started again, filtering up through the floorboards and assaulting his ears. He pulled the quilt over his head but the sound cut through as easily as if the quilt were just fish netting. He flung off the quilt and thumped on the floor but that only earned him a few moments' respite. Then there was a clattering of cooking utensils; it was his father making dinner.

It occurred to Kam Ho that he had arrived at dinnertime but his father had not asked him if he had eaten. Instead he was cooking now for this Gold Mountain Cloud woman. His father had never cooked a meal for his mother in his entire life. And his mother had brought up his three children and looked after Mrs. Mak until the day of her death.

Downstairs the clattering was interspersed with the woman's laughter. Kam Ho's heart felt as if it was leaping like frogs in a pond after rain. He felt around the pillow, the quilt and the bedside cabinet. Lucky for them, he did not find anything that could serve as a weapon. He might have rushed downstairs, knife at the ready, if he had had one.

Gold Mountain Cloud had really done nothing to offend him. And it was also true that both he and Kam Shan enjoyed Cantonese opera. Last year the Singapore Red Jade Opera troupe had come to Vancouver. He had been there three weekends in a row and bought tickets for best seats in the middle of the front row. Any other day, any other time, he would have been happy to brew a cup of tea and sit down with the woman for a good chat about Chinese opera in Canada. But today was not the right time. The unworthy way his father behaved towards this woman made him think of his mother pushing him onto the boat to Gold Mountain. Every year his father said he would go home to her; every year his mother continued to wait. It seemed as if his father's boat would never arrive, while his mother continued to grow older. And his mother was growing old alone and lonely—how could his father be enjoying himself with another woman? Especially a woman like Gold Mountain Cloud.

Kam Ho felt he could not stay at home a moment longer. He would put on his shoes and make a run for it. He fished around for his shoes under the bed with his feet, but they only brought out an old newspaper. He was flipping through it when he saw a news item under a huge headline on the middle page.

The situation of the war in the Pacific is becoming more serious every day. Overseas Chinese are buying Victory Bonds in order to raise money to provision the national army. Some hotheaded youths are even thinking of returning to China to join up, all the quicker to slaughter the Japanese bandits. Opinions differ among the Overseas Chinese on joining up. Some feel that when their country is in difficulty young men have a duty to do all they can to protect it; others that we have been in Canada for such a long time that it has become our second home. The Canadian army is now short of soldiers and our young people should join its army as a way of winning the trust of the Canadian government. However, if the provincial legislature of British Columbia persists in refusing Chinese the right to vote, our young people cannot join the army to serve the country. The Chinese have recently set up an association with the aim of persuading the federal government to allow our young people to join the army as Canadian residents, as a way to express loyalty to the country they consider to be theirs.

With a small shock, Kam Ho realized where he wanted to spend the cheque he had in his pocket.

Would it be enough to buy a plane? he wondered. He would ask his brother tonight.

7

Gold Mountain Obstacles

❦

Year thirteen of the Republic (1924)
Spur-On Village, Hoi Ping County, China

Cat Eyes made her way to No-Name River with a laundry basket on her
arm. Yin Ling was sound asleep on her back, nodding against her as she
walked. At first glance, Cat Eyes looked just like any other Spur-On Village
woman; she wore a sprig of jasmine behind her ear, her blue cotton tunic
fastened slantwise across her front, dark blue wide-legged trousers and
wooden clogs that clip-clopped along the cobbled road. Even the sling in
which she carried Yin Ling was a village-style one, made of black cotton
and heavily embroidered with peonies. Its crossed straps framed breasts
swollen with milk, pushing them out until they looked like watermelons.
Of course, only outsiders could have taken Cat Eyes for a Spur-On villager,
the same way they lumped together people from different South China
provinces. But the Spur-On villagers were sharp-eyed. They saw straight
through Cat Eyes' outward appearance to the Gold Mountain woman
underneath.

The first thing that gave her away was the underclothes she wore. The village women found out about the brassiere when Cat Eyes was breast-feeding Yin Ling. Even though she turned her back to feed the baby, they noticed that after she had undone her jacket, she opened up another layer of lacy white cotton underneath. Her panties, too, were a subject of village gossip. No one knew about them except Kam Shan until one day, one of the household servants saw them in the laundry bucket. She went out and told her friends that the woman from Gold Mountain was so stingy with cloth that she had cut down her panties until they hardly covered her buttocks.

Of course, the panties were only the beginning. Although Cat Eyes did not know it, gossip swirled around her. The villagers directed their comments to her mother-in-law, and these comments accumulated in Six Fingers' ears like earwax. Six Fingers looked glummer by the day.

Cat Eyes did not actually need to wash her own clothes. There were plenty of women servants to do the cooking, the washing and the sewing. But Cat Eyes did not want anyone to see her underwear. Besides, she found it comforting to go to No-Name River, because it reminded her of the village where she grew up. Her home village had plenty of water, just like this one, and her family had depended on its water as much as on the land for their food. She had worked in the fields alongside her mother, and when her father went fishing, she rowed the boat for him. She had had no news of her family since the day she and her elder sister were kidnapped and taken to Gold Mountain, so when she arrived in Spur-On Village with Kam Shan last year, she got him to take her back to her home village. There was no one left of her family; on the untended graves of her parents the artemisia grew tall.

It had rained continuously for some days and the waters of No-Name River had risen so high they covered all but half of the topmost stone step on the bank. Cat Eyes put the basket down, sat down on the step, rolled up her trouser legs and, with her clogs still on, stretched her feet into the water. She leaned forward until she could see her reflection. The water rippled in the breeze, elongating her face like a cucumber and stretching it as broad as a tomato. As Cat Eyes laughed, she heard the water whisper something in her ear. Softly, softly the words beseeched her: "Why not come in … come in…?"

Cat Eyes snapped out of her reverie. She remembered her father's warning to her and her sister when they were little. When it rains and the river's in spate, he had said, the water spirits lure people in. But Cat Eyes feared neither the water nor the water spirits. She stirred up the mud with her foot and retorted: "In your dreams!" And the water was silenced. Cat Eyes could not know that a dozen or so years later, another Fong would hear the waters speak and, knowing nothing of water spirits, would be lured in.

Although the water had fallen silent, Cat Eyes was still on the alert. At times like this, it would have been better to have a man with her, but Kam Shan was not the sort of man to go around with a woman. When she ran away from the brothel all those years ago and hid in his cart, he had only agreed to take her in because she threatened to kill herself. That act of kindness had estranged him from his father for many years. She knew he had done it out of pity, the way he might pity a lame horse or a dog with a broken leg. At the time, pity was enough for her. It was the lifeline that pulled her from the bog. But after she reached safety, she realized that it was not enough. She hungered for something more.

During their first two years together, Kam Shan did not touch her once. She knew that to him she was used goods, and he was afraid of catching syphilis from her. Taking her from the brothel made him guilty of abduction, so neither of them could show their faces in Vancouver's Chinatown again. They took refuge in a town so small and remote even the Thunder God would not find them. She could not find a Chinese herbalist, so, in the end, it was Pastor Andrew who managed to get hold of some Salvarsan for her, so she could treat her syphilis.

Finally, Kam Shan relented and was intimate with her. From the very first time, she knew she wanted to give him a child. He talked with fury about his father rejecting him, but she knew this anger was just a cloak he wore. Underneath it, he concealed the heart of a good son. While he was estranged from his father, he could not settle down with her and marry her properly. The only way that the two men could become reconciled was through a child. And it had to be a boy, of course.

For Kam Shan's sake, she had dosed herself with a succession of remedies—Chinese, Western and Redskin. She boiled them into broths, burned them to ashes, ground them into powder, kneaded them into pancakes and injected them through syringes. Over ten years, she had taken enough medicines to fill No-Name River, but her belly showed not the slightest tendency to swell into a bump.

Her barren womb did nothing for Cat Eyes' self-esteem and she could only watch helplessly as Kam Shan caroused with rowdy Redskin women in cowboy boots and Stetsons who sat on his knee, rolling cigarettes for him and putting them between his lips. Sometimes he stayed out all night, but when he returned, she never asked where he had been. She just lit the stove and heated up the porridge for breakfast.

Then, when she had completely despaired of getting pregnant, it finally happened. At first, as she leaned over the gutter spewing her guts out, she thought it was the medicine making her sick. But when three months had gone by without any sign of her period, she realized she had conceived. She did not tell Kam Shan until she felt the first flutter of movement in her belly. Kam Shan said nothing, but one day began to dismantle his photographic studio piece by piece. Tears coursed down Cat Eyes' face. She knew that he could go home and see his father now, and that, maybe, she could gain a foothold there too.

Though she gave birth to a girl, Cat Eyes was still pleased and proud of her accomplishment. She was still very young. Her body was a field in which paddy rice had grown and sooner or later it would produce a boy too. The fact that her firstborn was a girl meant that she would have help with all those baby boys to come. It never occurred to Cat Eyes that Yin Ling was a miracle baby whose birth was the result of the coincidence of sun, rain and soil. Her womb would remain barren for many years after.

Kam Shan had recently gone to the city of Canton and would not be back until the beginning of the ninth month. That was Yin Ling's birthday and there was to be a feast to celebrate it. Such celebrations for baby girls were rare in the village but Six Fingers had insisted. For Six Fingers, Yin Ling was life itself and the baby spent most of the time in her granny's arms. In fact, Cat Eyes hardly got a chance to look after her daughter, unless it was time to put her to the breast. In Six Fingers' words, Yin Ling was the first of the next generation. Her auspiciously round little face, fleshy earlobes and grooved upper lip were signs, according to ancient belief, that she would be welcoming many little brothers and sisters into the world.

Kam Shan had gone to Canton to get his leg treated. Even before their ship docked, Six Fingers had been making inquiries about doctors. She tracked down a highly-thought of herbalist in Canton who had once attended to the broken bones and injuries of the Imperial family. He was elderly and had retired long ago but Six Fingers, by dint of turning two *mu* of land into a large amount of silver, persuaded him to see her son.

Kam Shan's lameness meant that he could not walk much or stand for long, so he was unable to go out on photography assignments. He took pictures only occasionally, when customers came to his house. His father, Ah-Fat, was no better off: after his farm went bankrupt, creditors hounded him so mercilessly he did not dare go home. Kam Ho's monthly wages at the Hendersons' were not enough to keep two families, so Cat Eyes was forced to go out to work. A new establishment called the Lychee Garden Restaurant had just opened in Chinatown and was in need of a waitress. Cat Eyes went to see the boss and was immediately taken on.

She knew why that was.

There was a dearth of young women in Chinatown in those days, and very few of them went out to work. Those who did work out of the home were regarded as used goods. In the restaurant, Cat Eyes had to put up with every man stripping her naked with his eyes. But she didn't care. For a girl who had worked in the Spring Gardens brothel, those stares were nothing. In any case, she did not mind being a slut in their eyes so long as it meant her new family did not go hungry.

Prying eyes were not confined to the restaurant. At home Kam Shan stayed up until her shifts ended after midnight. He skulked behind the dusty old curtains, watching her fumble in her pocket for the door key, on the lookout in case some man was escorting her home. In the old days, it was she who had been worried about him messing around. Now it was the other way round—and she liked it that way. She almost hoped his leg would never heal.

Late one night, after finishing her shift at the restaurant, she returned home. Without turning the light on, she went in the door, down the dark passage and into the kitchen. Kam Shan did not speak to her, just followed her with his eyes. His eyes nibbled her all over. She gave her face a quick scrub, and was ready for bed and sleep. But Kam Shan had been at home all day with nothing to do, and now he wanted her. He pressed her down on the bed and pushed himself furiously into her. In the past, he only bothered to do it once in a blue moon, and then it was perfunctory. But now it was as if, every time he saw her, his body craved her. His eyes gleamed with a green light and she said jokingly that he should change *his* name to Cat Eyes.

It was some time before she found out why. Once, when he was drunk, he blurted out: "If other men can use you, why can't I?" He had completely forgotten he had said it, but she did not. It gnawed away at her, like a nagging pain. Though this man had never liked her, he had saved her from starvation and abuse. And it had cost him dearly; he had not seen his mother and father for ten years as a result. But his cruel words were just that—words—and nothing more, and she blocked her ears against them.

What really made her anxious was her discovery that Kam Shan had booked boat passage home to China. Kam Ho had been squirrelling away money to bring his mother over, until the Gold Mountain government passed the Chinese Exclusion Act, trapping Six Fingers on the other side of the ocean. So instead, Kam Ho used the money to buy Kam Shan's passage home to China. Six Fingers wanted to see her first granddaughter, and the baby could not travel without her mother so Cat Eyes went too. Cat Eyes was worried because she and Kam Shan had not performed the traditional marriage ceremonies; she knew how keen the local girls were to get themselves a Gold Mountain husband. If Kam Shan was planning to get himself a proper bride on their trip back home, there would be absolutely nothing Cat Eyes could do about it.

The day they arrived in Spur-On Village, she and Kam Shan completed the final stretch of their journey—from the entrance of the village to the *diulau*—on their knees, as a way of showing respect for his mother. Six Fingers received them and told Cat Eyes to get up. "What's your school name?" she asked. Cat Eyes was confused. "What's a school name?" "The name your schoolteacher gave you the day you started school," explained Six Fingers. "Mum, Cat Eyes has never even seen a school," said Kam Shan, "never mind stepped inside one."

The neighbours and family who crammed the *diulau* hall roared with laughter at Kam Shan's words. Cat Eyes knew that everyone in the Fong household, right down to the plough oxen, could read and write—they had all been taught by Six Fingers. She also knew that the Fongs would scoff at her now they knew she was illiterate. Her own man had thrown the first insult and now everyone would follow suit. Her mother-in-law gave a little laugh, but Cat Eyes did not notice. She was too busy looking for a wall against which she could knock herself. The brothel should have killed her, she thought ruefully, but instead she would be consigned to misery and humiliation in Hoi Ping.

Kam Shan took Yin Ling from her arms and gave the baby to his mother. As he did so, he whispered audibly in her ear:

"She may be illiterate but she earns good money. Half the fields you bought these last few years came from her wages."

Cat Eyes was grateful for the lifeline. Her man had exposed her short-comings, though it could just as well have been someone else. But now he extolled her worth, and that could only come from him. The trip had been overshadowed with anxiety. Now finally the sun had come out and her heart was set at rest.

Yin Ling woke up and began to thrash about restlessly in her sling. The cross-straps tightened around Cat Eyes' breasts and she felt a warm gush of milk wet her jacket front. She quickly unfastened the sling and took the baby in her arms. After several months in the village, she had finally learned how to breastfeed in broad daylight as the village women did. But unlike them, she held the baby high against her exposed breast so that Yin Ling's head concealed it like a large, round winter melon.

It was early and the cocks were still crowing in the village. The women, who got up early, were letting their chickens out and driving them onto the threshing floor. The dogs followed, wagging their tails and licking up the dew-wet chicken droppings which littered the ground. Cat Eyes breathed in the damp air through every pore of her body. It was peaceful if you got up early enough, she thought.

As she yawned lazily, the daughter and daughter-in-law of Mr. Au, the village tailor, appeared on the riverbank. As soon as Kam Shan had arrived in the village, Six Fingers got the tailor to come to the house and make them suits of clothes for summer and winter. The young women came with him to help make the buttonholes, so Cat Eyes knew them by sight. The Au clan may have been looked down on by the Fongs, but the tailor was one of its more prominent members; he and his daughters were tolerated at the *diulau* insofar as their services were required.

The daughter was just a girl of twelve. As she walked past Cat Eyes carrying the laundry basket and the baton for beating the dirty clothes, she saw the bar of soap in her basket and stopped to pick it up. Soap was a foreign curiosity to the villagers, and the girl rubbed it generously all over the clothes and her hands until she formed a rich lather. Cat Eyes was secretly annoyed; every time she came to the river and met the other women, her soap passed from hand to hand until it was reduced to a sliver. She started to cut the soap bar into smaller pieces with a knife when she went to wash clothes but the result was that by the time they had finished with it, not even a sliver remained.

"Cat Eyes, have your eyes always been like that?" asked the daughter-in-law.

"My mum told me that I woke up with them like this one morning when I was four or five."

The young woman leaned up close and peered into Cat Eyes' eyes. "Were your ancestors hairy *yeung fan?*" Cat Eyes grunted. "Not as hairy as your mother!" The other woman laughed carelessly, and the girl snickered along with her. She was still at the naughty stage, playing at washing the clothes, sinking her fingers into the soapy lather and rubbing them together.

"Gold Mountain soap is really nice. The honey locust pods we use at home for washing wouldn't make much lather even if you rubbed it till all the skin came off your hands," she said with a heartfelt sigh.

"If you like Gold Mountain so much, ask Cat Eyes if she'll let you be Kam Shan's second wife and take you to Gold Mountain with them," said the daughter-in-law.

The girl flushed bright red, and Cat Eyes went pink too. After a pause she said: "Even if you were the first wife, you wouldn't make it to Gold Mountain. The government isn't letting any new people in."

"Even so, she'd still be OK," said the daughter-in-law. "She could be the junior wife and just stay in the *diulau* eating sticky rice all day and being waited on by servants. It would be better than the way we live, sewing and sewing till we go blind from the work, scrimping and saving every cent."

Cat Eyes felt like saying that life was hard in Gold Mountain too, but she knew that would sound too much like a lie to them, and bit back the words. Instead she bent her head silently over her suckling baby.

The tailor's daughter-in-law was about to go down to the water's edge when Cat Eyes' basket caught her eye. Squatting down, she began to rifle through all the dirty clothes. When she reached the bottom of the basket, she found something long and thin and gauzy. Picking it out, she asked Cat Eyes: "What's this?"

Cat Eyes had finished feeding Yin Ling and was fastening her jacket. Glancing sideways she said: "Silk stockings." "How can they be stockings? They wouldn't keep the cold out, they're so thin. It would be like wearing nothing on your legs."

Cat Eyes smiled. "What do you know about stockings? Gold Mountain men like their women to wear stockings. They like it when it looks as if you're wearing nothing on your legs."

The other woman spread her fingers out in the stockings and, holding them up, peered through them. The sun filtered through the sheer fabric creating radiating patterns of light. Then she balled them up in her hand. "Cat Eyes, lend me them to wear for a few days so my husband can enjoy seeing them on me, please?"

"No, I can't," said Cat Eyes. "Kam Shan bought them for me. He'll be angry if you go off with them." She was about to snatch them back but the other woman gripped them so tightly in her fist that the veins stood out livid on the back of her hand.

"It's just a pair of stockings! Why are you making such a fuss about them, Cat Eyes?" And she continued spitefully: "After all, you must have seen all there is to see in the business you do in Gold Mountain."

Cat Eyes felt a great chasm opening up before her. No matter how hard she scrabbled to keep her footing, she knew she was going to slide into the void. In her mind she saw Six Fingers' face cloud over when she looked at her, and it finally dawned on her: it had little to do with the fact that she could not read or write and everything to do with her past. It would dog her wherever she went. There was no escaping the dark shadow it cast over her life.

It grew suddenly overcast, the rays of sunshine expiring in the clouds before they could even fully emerge. Cat Eyes hurriedly pushed Yin Ling back into the sling, picked up her basket, still with the unwashed garments in it, and scurried back to the *diulau*.

She could not stay here, not for a single day more.

Year nineteen of the Republic (1930)
Spur-On Village, Hoi Ping County, China

Six Fingers was awake before the cock crowed. Something on her mind had nudged her awake. It was just a trifling thing, no bigger than a mustard seed, but as the years went by, she slept more lightly and found she could indeed be woken up by something as small as a mustard seed.

It was the thought of the pigs' trotters braised with ginger that roused Six Fingers. She had started them the night before and they were nearly done. They just needed reheating and a splash of rice wine. But the final stage had to be performed with care. The boil must be not too fast or too slow, so that the meat was silky soft and almost coming off the bone. The cook prepared the meals in the Fong household, but not even the cook could make pigs' trotters braised with ginger as well as Six Fingers. Her elder sister had learned the recipe after she married into Red Hair's family, and had passed it on to her. The way she prepared it, a layer of bright red oil floated on top of the trotters, and the meat was meltingly soft. Her daughter, Kam Sau, could happily eat a whole bowlful on her own.

Kam Sau graduated from the high school for the children of Overseas Chinese and started at teacher-training college in Canton last year. At high school she had been a weekly boarder. At college, however, she could only come home every couple of months, or at harvest time, when the students were given leave to help their families. Six Fingers missed her daughter. Today was one of the rare days Kam Sau came home to visit, and she was upstairs sleeping. Six Fingers' two sons had both left for Gold Mountain as teenagers. They had been gone for many years, and each had only come home once. Kam Shan was back six years ago, bringing the woman he had never officially married and their daughter, Yin Ling. They stayed nearly two years, and Kam Shan had spent a great deal of money on treatment for his lame leg. When this proved fruitless, they returned to Gold Mountain. Six Fingers did not know when they would be back again.

Kam Ho came home last year to get married. He stayed long enough to get his wife pregnant and then hurried back, saying his Gold Mountain employers had given him a deadline.

Six Fingers felt that she had put all her energies into ensuring the men in her life grew big and strong, only to deliver them into the maw of the lion that was Gold Mountain. She fought bitterly with the Gold Mountain lion over her men, but she could never win. By the time her daughter had grown up, the Gold Mountain government had passed the Chinese Exclusion Act. The Gold Mountain men were furious about that, but Six Fingers did not share their anger. She was secretly pleased—at least she could keep one child at home.

Kam Sau attended college in Canton with Mak Dau's son, Ah-Yuen. Kam Sau had wanted to train as a teacher since she was a little girl. Her ambition was to run a school with Ah-Yuen in the village when they graduated. The school in the local town was funded by Gold Mountain men, so only their children were admitted. But Kam Sau wanted her school to be for everyone—including the children of farmers, fisherfolk and household servants. There would be no fees and the school would provide a midday meal too. Kam Sau had always shared her mother's passion for literacy. When she got home from school, she used to gather the servants' children together and teach them reading and arithmetic. When she was a young bride, Six Fingers taught all the Fongs' servants the rudiments of literacy. Now Kam Sau was teaching their children to read and count.

Although Six Fingers missed Kam Sau, she was comforted by the fact that her daughter would not be leaving home to marry as most girls did. She and Ah-Yuen would be home soon to stay. Ah-Yuen lived in the *diulau* with his father, Mak Dau, so Ah-Yuen would be the Fongs' live-in son-in-law. If Six Fingers could not count on her own two sons being around, at least Ah-Yuen, a dutiful and good-hearted boy, was as good as a son.

Six Fingers tiptoed from the bedroom, hoping to avoid waking Kam Sau. She was on the point of going down to the kitchen when she saw a crack of light under Kam Sau's bedroom door. Kam Sau had the room which had been Mrs. Mak's, right next to Six Fingers'. She pushed the door open, and found her daughter sitting up in bed reading a book.

Kam Sau was a bookworm. She stuck her nose so deep in the pages, she might have been smelling them. "Crazy girl," said Six Fingers, "have you been up all night reading?" Kam Sau grunted, then roused herself to answer: "I'm just going to sleep now." "If you carry on reading like that, you'll go cross-eyed, and then who'll marry you?" Six Fingers scolded her. Kam Sau giggled: "Isn't that what you want? Then I can stay and look after you." Six Fingers laughed too: "And then your uncle Mak Dau will be after me with a gun. He's keen to have a daughter-in-law." Kam Sau blushed.

Six Fingers sat down on Kam Sau's bed and rubbed her daughter's feet. "You don't get enough good food at the school," she said. "You're getting skinny." The truth was that Kam Sau, at seventeen, was just like a younger version of Kam Shan. She was stocky and strong, and had never had a day's sickness in her life. But Six Fingers could not help being protective.

Six Fingers flicked through the book Kam Sau was reading, *The Guide*. She looked at the page Kam Sau had marked and saw words like "imperialists … feudal comprador class … helping the warlords … suppressing the people's revolution." Six Fingers was none the wiser. The books her daughter read were nothing like the ones she had read as a child. She knew every word, but they made no sense to her. "Does 'imperialists' mean the foreigners?" she asked.

Kam Sau did not answer. Instead she said: "Mum, didn't you hear about the British and the French machine-gunning Chinese in the Shamin Concession a few years ago?" "Of course I remember," said Six Fingers. "So many were killed." "But, Mum, do you know why they died?" Six Fingers shook her head. "It started with the Japanese killing textile workers in Shanghai," said her daughter. "Then the people of Shanghai rose up in protest, and the British killed thirteen of them. The people of Hong Kong and Canton were supporting the workers from Shanghai when they got shot. The Japanese and the Westerners are all law-abiding in their own countries, but as soon as they get here, they think they can do whatever they like."

Six Fingers sighed. "Poverty is to blame—a poor country like ours doesn't stand a chance against the world powers. It's always the poor and the weak at the bottom of the heap that get kicked." "Poverty is not the problem," said Kam Sau. "It's ignorance. That's why I want to set up the school. When everyone goes to school, they'll wake up and won't let these foreigners ride roughshod over us." "But if it wasn't for the foreigners, how would your father and brothers earn enough to buy all the land we've got and build a house like this?" Six Fingers objected. Her daughter's eyebrows shot up and her voice rose in indignation: "If it wasn't for dad and his friends risking their lives building that railroad, Gold Mountain would still be a wilderness!"

Six Fingers could not help laughing ruefully. "And how did you get so much knowledge into that little head of yours?" "Mr. Auyung told me. He knows everything." Mr. Auyung Yuk Shan taught Chinese and was greatly admired and respected by Kam Sau, Ah-Yuen and the other students whom he taught. "When your father was young, he knew a Mr. Auyung Ming. He knew everything too. I wonder if it's the same family," said Six Fingers.

As they talked, it gradually grew light and the cocks started to crow. "Are you hungry?" Six Fingers asked. Kam Sau shook her head. "Just wait till I've heated the braised pigs' trotters in ginger," said her mother. "Then you'll be hungry." At the mention of pigs' trotters in ginger, Kam Sau's appetite was suddenly whetted, making her mouth water and her stomach rumble in anticipation. She got out of bed and looked out the window. In the courtyard outside, she saw an older man and a younger one seated on stools by the well cleaning the family's guns. It was Mak Dau and his son, Ah-Yuen.

Mak Dau was a gun fanatic and was always urging Six Fingers to buy more. They were expensive but Six Fingers, a thrifty woman in everything else, did not bat an eyelid when it came to guns. They had started with an antiquated rifle, then added a carbine rifle and a revolver. Two months ago, Mak Dau purchased a Browning. Now they had two long-barrelled guns and two pistols.

Mak Dau spent every spare moment cleaning and polishing them. And as soon as Ah-Yuen could walk, he had taught the boy how to take a gun to pieces and how to reassemble it. Six Fingers had reprimanded him for teaching a little boy such things, but Mak Dau said: "When I'm too old to heft a gun myself, who else will you get to protect the *diulau*?" Six Fingers had no answer to that. After that, Mak Dau was permitted to teach Ah-Yuen about guns—but only in the courtyard. They were not allowed indoors in case of an accidental discharge.

Ah-Yuen had grown tall, sprouting like new grass after a spring shower. Seated next to his father, he clearly took after him, though he was much thinner. He shared his father's love of guns and knew all the foreign and local makes. Mr. Auyung lent him books to read on armaments too. Mr. Auyung compared China to a lion with a festering boil on its body. If the boil did not heal in time then the lion would never get to its feet again. What was to be done? Mr. Auyung asked his students. Open a school and educate all the people so that they wake up, everyone answered in unison. Everyone, that is, but Ah-Yuen.

Ah-Yuen said running a school was a long-term project, like administering Chinese medicine to someone with an acute disease. If the medicine was too slow-acting then the lion might die first. A quick surgical operation, such as Western doctors performed, was what was needed in order to save the lion, according to Ah-Yuen. Military might was the only way to expel Westerners and Japanese and put China back on its feet. Ah-Yuen excelled in his studies and always came first in every subject. But when he engaged in heated discussions he was full of bravura, a quality which Kam Sau found both attractive and alarming at the same time.

Ah-Yuen's father had lived with the Fongs for many years, so many that he had carried Kam Shan and Kam Ho around on his back as babies. He used to call the boys the "young masters" until Six Fingers had finally persuaded him to address them by their given names. When the Fongs' first steward, Ha Kau, died, Mak Dau took over responsibility for the house and farm. He was, however, still a servant; he and his family ate with the other servants, and they washed their laundry in a different pool from the Fongs.

Ah-Yuen, born the son of a servant, should have remained a servant too, according to the old way of doing things. But Six Fingers had, with a slight nudge, set his life on a different course: she had sent him, as well as her daughter, to the best school for miles around. Six Fingers' decision opened the boy's eyes to the big, wide world beyond the narrow confines of their home village. Ah-Yuen was actually more mentally agile and shrewder than Kam Sau. Where she scurried along, he raced ahead, showing Kam Sau the way.

Ah-Yuen was always attentive to Kam Sau but never humble in the way that his father was. Kam Sau knew that her mother wanted Ah-Yuen as a live-in son-in-law and was smoothing the way forward for him, enabling him to walk tall, so that by the time he went in through the door of her bridal chamber he would be a respectable young gentleman. To move into the bride's house may have lowered him in the eyes of society but not in the eyes of his future mother-in-law. Six Fingers was infinitely clever. What she wanted, she made sure she got.

By the time Kam Sau got downstairs, her mother had lit the stove and was gently reheating the pigs' trotters of the night before. As the jelly softened and melted, the most delicious smell wafted through the house. While Six Fingers waited for the dish to be ready, she felt in her pocket for a bamboo comb to do her daughter's hair. She undid the braids and Kam Sau's gleaming thick hair tumbled over her knees. The sharp teeth of the comb cut through the hair as easily as butter, and the steady strokes gave Kam Sau a feeling of languorous pleasure.

She rested against her mother and asked idly: "Are you giving my sister-in-law a bowl of the trotters?" She meant her brother Kam Ho's wife. "Huh, she can come down on her own two feet, can't she? A hungry rat will find its own food." There was a giggle from Kam Sau. "You've really got it in for her, Mum," she said. "She's carrying the next Fong grandchild. Whatever happens, I'm going to treat her well," said her mother, "but have you ever seen anyone as dumb as her? The tree in the courtyard has more life in it than she does. When Kam Ho left to go back to Gold Mountain and we all took him to the entrance of the village, even Mak Dau's wife said: 'Write to us, Kam Ho, when you arrive so your mum doesn't worry.' But that dope did not even open her mouth until the very last moment, and then what she said was complete crap."

Kam Sau burst out laughing. "You never used to talk like that, Mum! You're worse than the servants now." "You know what she said?" Six Fingers continued. "She blurted out that her brother needed to fork out for a dowry at the end of the year. If that isn't crap, I don't know what is. Your brother sends home every cent he earns in Gold Mountain to support the rest of us, and she wants him to support her family as well."

"Well, dumb or not, you chose this daughter-in-law. My brother had never even seen her when he led her into the bridal chamber. You've only yourself to blame."

Out of the whole family, only Kam Sau dared to be so blunt with Six Fingers. Her mother could only sigh in response: "She looked like a steady young woman in the photo, and when we visited their house, she was polite though she didn't say much. Who would have thought that she would turn out so dumb? There was no point in her learning to read. The few characters she learned went in one ear and out the other."

"What about 'marriage for love,' like Mr. Auyung's always talking about?" said Kam Sau. "If my brother had got to know her first, he would never have settled for her." "Well, men have nothing to fear, do they?" exclaimed her mother. "If they don't like this one, they can find another one to marry. But women have to stick with what they've got, whether the man's good or bad." "That's the old way of thinking, Mum," said her daughter. "Even the Imperial concubine Wen Xiu fought for a divorce from the emperor Xuantong, so why can't other women?"

Kam Sau raised her head to begin braiding her hair and saw shadows settle on her mother's face. She smiled: "Did you and Dad really marry for love?" she asked. "My great-auntie says that Dad broke off his engagement to another girl for you, and had to pay her off with all the goods he'd brought back from Gold Mountain. Is it true?"

There was a long pause, then Six Fingers finally said reluctantly: "He paid by giving up a few Gold Mountain suitcases, but I nearly paid with my life, so we were even." "So you and Dad married for love!" said Kam Sau with a triumphant smile. "But you wouldn't let my brother marry for love. Mum, you're a tyrant!"

Six Fingers didn't understand what Kam Sau meant by "tyrant" but the rest was clear enough. "So what's so great about marrying for love?" she demanded. "I was only eighteen when I married your father. In more than thirty years, he's only visited three times. The last time he left, you were still in my belly. He's over sixty now, and he refuses to come back to me without digging out that last gold ingot. Even if he was to come back tomorrow, all the sweet nectar's gone, dried up. What's the point in that, eh?"

Kam Sau's smile faded at Six Fingers' words and she could think of nothing to say. She had never seen her father. To her, he existed only in the photos and dollar letters he sent home from Gold Mountain. But sometimes, when her mother read her father's letters home, she could see him pass like a light over her mother's face.

They heard a heavy tread on the stairs. Kam Sau did not need to look round to know it was her sister-in-law, Ah-Hsien, coming down. She was heavily pregnant and walked as if she was dragging a wooden bucket behind her. By the time she arrived in the kitchen she was sweating profusely. She came to a halt, and asked: "Are the trotters ready?" Six Fingers gave a cool smile. "I assume you're addressing the question to me? I happen to be your mother-in-law. But perhaps your mother didn't teach you any manners." "Yes, Mum," said the girl woodenly.

Ah-Hsien was a mess; her eyes were full of sleepy dust, her tunic was buttoned up wrong so that one side of it hung down, and her feet were so swollen they threatened to split her cotton shoes. "Next time, wash your face and comb your hair before you come down, will you? How could you let the servants see you like that?" Ah-Hsien fixed her eyes on the floor and said nothing.

She was puffing and panting like an ox, and Kam Sau brought her a stool to sit on. Ah-Hsien sat down heavily and one of the stool legs bent under her. Before she could stand up again, there was a crack and the leg snapped in two, dumping her on the floor like a sack of rice.

Six Fingers and Kam Sau rushed over to help her up, but Ah-Hsien sagged helplessly against them. As the deadweight of her body pulled the two of them down with her, Six Fingers shouted furiously: "Why did you choose the edge of the stool to sit on? Is there a louse waiting to bite your ass in the middle?"

Before she had finished speaking, there was an exclamation from Kam Sau. Her hand trembled like a leaf as she pointed at Ah-Hsien's trouser cuffs.

Something red was trickling down her legs and pooling on the floor beside them.

Blood.

In the early hours of the following morning, Ah-Hsien gave birth to a baby boy called Fong Yiu Kei. He was the Fong family's first grandson.

Year twenty-three of the Republic (1934)
Vancouver, British Columbia

Yin Ling was awakened by a crash. She had been dreaming of Johnny. She and Johnny were in Miss Watson's etiquette class together.

All fifth graders had to take etiquette classes. Their teacher, Miss Watson, a woman with a face permanently taut with disapproval, was meticulous in her teaching of matters of etiquette, such as how to choose the right item of cutlery at a formal dinner party or an appropriate outfit for a social occasion. She also taught them to dance the waltz, foxtrot and tango. Yin Ling had little interest in her other school work, particularly science and history, and usually managed to doze off in the first fifteen minutes. She was reprimanded so often by her teachers that she learned to fall asleep with her eyes open so as not to attract unwanted attention.

But Yin Ling was an eager pupil in etiquette class.

Actually, Yin Ling was really only interested in one part of the classes—ballroom dancing.

Miss Watson made the girls and boys dance together, and she made them change partners with every new dance. They had had several weeks of her classes and would start tango next week. Each time they exchanged partners Yin Ling ended up with some sissy boy. But she carried on hoping secretly that one day she would get her heart's desire.

Her heart's desire was Johnny.

Johnny was the tallest, most muscular boy in the class. He had corn-coloured hair with ungovernable curls, which turned into ringlets when they got wet in the rain. He hardly ever wore his school uniform properly. There was either a length of sleeve hanging down or the shirt would be open at the neck. Johnny was daring in other ways—he would sneak a quick smoke during the break when Miss Watson went to powder her nose. When he smoked, he would half close his eyes, tilt his head back and look as if he had the whole world at his feet.

And then there was his guitar. When he played, the sound was like a small hand plucking at the heartstrings. It drove all the girls crazy. Yin Ling knew quite well that every single one of them dreamed of taking his hand and dancing the tango. For her, the thought of being held in the crook of his arm while lifting one leg was worth dying for.

She did not dare think such thoughts in the daytime. She was just a skinny little slit-eyed Chinese girl, and Johnny's eyes would flit over her without pausing. But nighttime was different. Her dreams were like bulls on the rampage. For instance, that night she had been dreaming that in Miss Watson's class, her hand had been put in Johnny's. But before she had had time to look up at his hazel eyes, she had been shaken awake by that enormous crash.

She lay in bed with her hands clutched over her thudding heart, then realized it was her mother and father fighting.

Yin Ling had not had a chance to talk to her mother for a long time.

Sometimes they did not see each other from one week to the next. Her mother did not get home until after midnight from her shift at the Lychee Garden Restaurant and when Yin Ling got up to go to school in the mornings, her mother was still asleep. For months, Yin Ling had wanted her mother to take her to the department store in Dupont Street to buy a new overcoat. The coat she was wearing was a cut-down one of her mother's; the cuffs were threadbare and there was a small, black hole on the pocket where her father's cigarette had burned it. Her mother had Mondays off. So Monday evening was the only time when they could sit down together for a meal and talk.

Today was Monday.

But at tonight's dinner, both Yin Ling and her mother, Cat Eyes, had been preoccupied. Normally her mother ate all her meals at the restaurant. When she did eat at home, the atmosphere at the dinner table was so tense that Yin Ling found it next to impossible to break it with a conversation, especially one involving money.

Her father's leg was still no better. He could do no physical work at all, apart from taking the odd portrait photograph. The bits of cash he made scarcely covered his cigarettes each month. Her grandfather's café was still going, but by the time he had paid the cook and the rent, the income was only enough to buy a ticket to the Cantonese opera.

Yin Ling had often heard her mother whispering quietly in her father's ear about the café. "How come it never goes into the red?" she would say. "If it starts losing money, he'd have to shut up shop and be done with it." His father would shout at her to keep her mouth shut, but Yin Ling knew that her father hoped that her grandfather would close the business too, although for a different reason. Her father wanted him to go back to Hoi Ping and settle down with her grandmother, while her mother wanted him to help out more around the house in Gold Mountain.

The only person who earned a proper salary in the house was Cat Eyes. She was paid weekly and her cheque had to be split many different ways. One bit was set aside to be sent home to Granny. A letter would arrive from Yin Ling's granny every couple of months, and every letter would say the same: the harvest was poor, they couldn't collect the rents, there were so many mouths to feed, the cost of living had gone up. Cat Eyes could not read so Kam Shan read the letter out to his father in a loud voice which, Cat Eyes knew, was intended for her ears. Cat Eyes said nothing in front of her father-in-law but outside of his hearing, she would say to Kam Shan: "It would be cheaper to support a Buddhist monastery than your family." Kam Shan was not pleased by such talk but he had to listen. Cat Eyes' cheque fed, clothed and sheltered the whole family, an unpalatable fact which bowed Kam Shan's shoulders.

Yin Ling's mother might complain but at the end of every month, come rain or shine, she never failed to send money back to Hoi Ping. Some of what remained had to go towards paying Granddad's debts. After the collapse of his farming business, Ah-Fat was left owing substantial amounts of money and from time to time the creditors would come calling.

Basic necessities such as food and utilities also made demands on Cat Eyes' wages. By the time that cheque had been fought over, only a few cents remained. Cat Eyes hung on to them like grim death, and used them to buy a few nice bits and pieces for herself. If Yin Ling wanted a new overcoat, she would have to winkle the money out of her mother. To do that, she would have to catch her mother in an odd moment of generosity.

As soon as Cat Eyes sat down at the table, Yin Ling directed a sidelong glance at her. She was unable to make out what sort of mood her mother was in; those large, feline eyes, their irises overcast with green, moved so little they seemed to have been painted on her face. Yin Ling had only ever once in her life seen her mother laugh heartily. That was the day when her granddad had gone with her dad to Whitewater to see some old friends from his railroad-building days. Her mother happened to have a day off and had invited some of her restaurant friends over for a meal.

With no men in the house, the women let their hair down, drinking two bottles of Shaoxing rice wine between them. Cat Eyes' face was flushed deep pink. She improvised a posy of flowers for her hair out of her folded apron, and launched with gusto into the opera aria "Peach Blossom Red," making "orchid finger" gestures with her hands. Yin Ling was astonished that her mother could sing so beautifully. She never uttered a sound when Granddad put his Cantonese opera record on. Cat Eyes sang herself hoarse. Then the women sat down to play mahjong. Cat Eyes was on a winning streak that day and she swept the board. At the end, she tied her winnings into a handkerchief and sent her daughter out to buy snacks for her friends to eat. To Yin Ling, her mother had seemed like a flower squashed under a boulder, bursting irrepressibly forth as the sun's rays touched it.

But Yin Ling never saw her mother laugh like that again.

When her mother's expression relaxed, and she sat down, she was a good-looking woman. But she did not get a chance to sit down often. She was on her feet all day at the restaurant, and over the years had developed an unattractive slouch, making her look old and droopy.

Yin Ling noticed that her mother had changed into something different this evening. Normally when she was at home, she wore a grey cotton tunic buttoned down the front. She had two of these, so when she had one on, the other hung on the clothesline. But today she wore a green dress with dark-coloured flowers, and her waved hair was tucked neatly behind her ears and fastened on one side with a silver hair clip. It must mean she was going out tonight. And that could mean one of two things, either she was happy or she was depressed. Yin Ling watched her mother scooping the last grains of rice from her bowl. Finally she took the plunge.

"Mum, I want a new coat," she muttered into her bowl.

The words seemed to bounce off the sides of the bowl, scaring her with their mighty echoes.

Her mother looked as taken aback as if Yin Ling had asked her for a mountain of gold or silver. She shot her a hard look and Yin Ling felt herself shrink like a snowman in sunshine.

"And I'd like a mink coat. Are you going to give me the money?" Cat Eyes finally said coldly.

"Why not have a look in the Christmas sales?" said Kam Shan, his head buried in his bowl as well. It was not clear whether he meant Yin Ling's coat or her mother's mink.

Cat Eyes put down her bowl. "Did you hear that, Yin Ling? Come Christmastime, you just need to ask your father for the money."

Yin Ling knew there was absolutely no hope. She would have to wear that old overcoat to Miss Watson's etiquette class for the whole winter and sit in front of Johnny, who would eye her shiny worn coat cuffs and mutter: "She's just another Chink, they never change!"

Yin Ling felt her eyes burn. She had to leave the table this instant or tears of disappointment would start to roll down her face. She put down her bowl and chopsticks and flew up the stairs to her room.

She turned on the bedside light, a twelve-watt bulb which threw a tiny circle of yellow light into the darkness of the room. To save on electricity, they used these dim bulbs in every room. Yin Ling sat down. Do I really want to spend the rest of my life in a house like this? she wondered to herself. How long was a lifetime? Was it as long as the Fraser River, or ten times longer? A hundred? Would a thousand do it?

Yin Ling felt utterly dejected.

Money, money, money. Everyone in the house was busy doing sums with her mother's paycheque. Everyone kept their sums a closely guarded secret, but none of them included her in their calculations.

Yin Ling heard footsteps on the stairs. She hurriedly turned out the light, lay down and pulled the quilt over her head. She could not face anyone just now. Someone stumbled across the room, and then tripped and something crashed to the floor. She threw back the covers, turned on the lamp and saw her grandfather rubbing his knee and muttering.

He took something out of his pocket and put it on her table. "A good thing it didn't break," he said. It was a pottery pig with a big mouth and big ears and a small slit in its head, the kind of moneybox Chinese New Year lucky money was kept in.

Then he got a few dimes from his pocket, letting them drop into the belly of the pig with a tinkle. "I've given up smoking," he said. "I'm saving up to get my granddaughter an overcoat. Today I've only saved enough for a button, but in a couple of days it'll be enough for a sleeve."

Yin Ling pulled a face and did not speak. Bitter words festered inside her, and they went something like this: "It's no good. What's the point? I can't wait. By the time the piggy's full up, the etiquette class will be over."

I can't dance the tango with Johnny wearing that coat, she thought.

I'll get sick, that's it, I'll get sick. Dizziness, tummyache, a cold—any excuse will do!

She started to work out how to avoid Miss Watson's class if the teacher paired her up with Johnny for the tango.

"You know, your mum's job is hard on her," said her grandfather.

Yin Ling was thinking she ought to get up and give his leg a rub for him, but her body felt like a lead weight and she could not move. Even as she watched him hobble out of the room and downstairs, she still could not move.

Later, she heard the front door open and then click shut. Her mother must have gone out. That left just the two men in the room. They did not talk, and silence filled the house. Then gradually an acrid smell filtered from the room where they sat, through the cracks under the doors, into every room and up the stairs. She smelled it in her nostrils and it caught in her throat.

Her father and grandfather were smoking.

Give up smoking? Like hell! she said fiercely to herself.

Yin Ling tore a page from her school exercise book, sprawled on the bed and got ready to write a letter. She wrote the characters for "grandmother" in Chinese, then paused. It was not that she did not know what to say, it was that she did not know how to say it in Chinese. She spoke Cantonese at home with her family, but she still laboured under a handicap; she could neither read nor write Chinese.

In fact, when she started her third year in primary school, her grandfather had wanted to send her to classes at the Overseas Chinese School on East Pender Street. Yin Ling was always finding reasons not to go—it was too windy, it was raining, it was too hot or too cold. And of course she could always wheel out the excuse of a headache or a temperature. When she ran out of excuses and had to go, the only thing that she enjoyed was making paper cuts and dragon lanterns. Learning the strokes of Chinese characters bored her rigid. At the end of two years at the school, she could still only make out the characters in the lunar calendar.

Yin Ling wrote her first sentence.

The sentence should have had three words in it, but Yin Ling could not write the middle word. She left a big space between the "I" and the "you," because the middle word should have been huge. She racked her brains but could not think how to write the character. Eventually, she stuck in an English word.

"I HATE you."

That was just the beginning. Yin Ling had many sentences queuing up to follow the first. Like "Granny and Auntie Kam Sau, why don't you earn your own money? You're always so well-dressed in your photographs, but I don't even get a new overcoat because my mum sends all the leftover money to you every month." Like "My classmates always tell jokes about 'Chinks trying to make a dollar out of ten cents' but in our family, every single cent has to make a dollar. And it's all because of you."

Yin Ling had been storing up all these resentments for years and now they were like a river in spate, crested waves tumbling by, one after another.

But the pen point was only the thickness of a needle, and no matter how fierce her resentments, she could not force them through the eye.

Yin Ling's temples began to throb as if praying mantises were battling inside her head, and her eyes bulged from their sockets. She crumpled her letter and threw it in the wastebasket. She lay down on the bed and stared hard at a dirty brown water stain on the ceiling until its edges blurred and she eventually fell asleep.

The crash that woke her up was the sound of the door slamming. Her mother had come home and her father, who had been waiting in the passage, shut it quickly behind her. In the silence of the night when even the alley cats were asleep in doorways, the sound echoed alarmingly up and down the road, making the doors and windows shake.

Yin Ling put her slippers on, shuffled to the door of her bedroom and opened it. Then she tiptoed to the top of the stairs. She could see her mother, a small leather bag in her hand, making straight for the kitchen. She dropped her bag on top of the stove and took a towel from the clothesline. Then she bent over the basin and began to wash her face.

Her father picked up her bag and weighed it in his hand. He lowered his voice: "How much did you lose?"

Her mother snatched back the bag, hung it over her shoulder and carried on washing her face. She was scrubbing it as if it was engrained with dirt and a whole river full of water would never wash it off. Finally her father lost patience. He grabbed her by the collar of her dress and hauled her back from the sink as if he was holding a chicken by the scruff of the neck.

"You haven't got the money to buy Yin Ling a coat but you've got the money to throw away at mahjong."

Her mother flung his hand away, rubbed at her eyes with a corner of the towel and, without looking up, retorted: "Buy her a coat? What's a little squirt like that doing making eyes at the boys anyway? Are you trying to encourage her to behave like a slut? And, besides, you're happy to give all that money to that bunch of lazybones and you try and stop me spending a cent of it on myself! That's money I've earned, I'll have you know!"

The "lazybones" her mother was referring to was the Chinese Benevolent Association. Her father spent a lot of time there during the day; he had no work to go to and Ah-Lai, the secretary, was a good friend of his. He knew its business inside out—in fact, he liked to get involved, so any money he had never stayed long in his pocket. Whether the Chinese School needed renovating, they were taking the government to court, raising money for disaster relief, or building a school or a hospital, her father only had to hear about it for the small change in his pocket to make its way into the Association coffers. It made her mother furious. She nagged him endlessly about not throwing money around as if he was a lord, but it was all water off a duck's back as far as her father was concerned.

Now he retorted: "And who knows how you earn your money, eh?"

Cat Eyes' face went scarlet, then white. She flushed and paled a few more times, then she lashed out at him with the towel and said furiously: "Just you tell me, Fong Kam Shan, how I earn that money!" The wet towel hit him on the cheek, raising a red welt, and drops of water trickled down his face. It seemed to Yin Ling as if her father's hair was actually standing on end.

Kam Shan snatched the towel from Cat Eyes' hand and flung it on the ground where it lay sodden and soft like a filleted fish.

"You think I didn't see who brought you home that day?" he demanded.

Her mother sneered. "Oh, that's what this is all about, is it? There was a snowstorm that day and I wanted you to come and fetch me, but could you be bothered?"

Her mother's words stung, and her father fell silent. Fashionable folk in Vancouver all had cars nowadays and drove around town tooting their horns all the time. Not only had he no car, her father was lame and could not walk far either. It did not matter if it was blowing a blizzard, there was no way he could have fetched Cat Eyes home.

After a long pause, he opened his mouth again and the words that came out had been stored up so long, they nearly burned his throat:

"If you're so keen on cars, you'd have been better off staying in the Spring Garden instead of following me home."

Yin Ling did not know what the Spring Garden was but she saw the effect on her mother. Cat Eyes began to shrivel away like a slug from salt. Then, she suddenly reached a hand out, grabbed the tea mug from the table and hurled it at the wall. A few moments passed before Yin Ling realized that it was not the wall which had exploded, but the mug. Her mother was squatting amid the fragments, her face buried in her hands.

"I want to die, I want to die, I want to die," she wept shrilly.

This was not the first time Yin Ling had seen her mother and father fight, nor was it the first time she had seen her mother cry. But she had never seen her cry like this. The sound set her teeth on edge and gave her goose pimples all over.

"I'm not hearing this, I'm not hearing it," Yin Ling whispered to herself over and over, jamming her hands against her ears.

She knew that someone in the room just next door would have heard the quarrel too, and was also silently pressing his hands over his ears.

Her grandfather.

I'm not staying a minute longer in this house.

Despair settled on Yin Ling like darkness.

2004

Hoi Ping County, Guangdong Province, China

Around noon, Mr. Auyung Wan On took Amy Smith to the nursing home to visit Tse Ah-Yuen.

Amy had changed her travel plans twice. She had planned to stay for one day, sign the documents entrusting the *diulau* to the local government and return to Vancouver via Hong Kong.

When she arrived, places such as Canton and Hoi Ping, a *diulau* called Tak Yin House and an old man called Tse Ah-Yuen had meant little to Amy. The only reason she had come was to fulfill a promise made to her mother.

But somehow, one day had turned into two, and two into three. Before she knew it, she had been in Hoi Ping for five days. Mr. Auyung had doggedly worked away at her imagination until he had finally sparked her interest. She wondered if she should change her return ticket yet again and stay a whole week. The university term was over, so she did not need to rush back to teach classes. But she did need to talk to Mark about whether they should postpone their Alaska trip.

Mark was Amy's boyfriend, though she found it faintly comical to refer to him by that term. A boyfriend should be someone in his twenties. For a woman of nearly fifty to use the word about a man approaching sixty was as inappropriate as a wrinkly old lady donning a crotch-revealing miniskirt. But for the time being, Amy could think of no better word to use. She loathed the alternatives "lover," "partner" or "co-habitee."

Mark was a professor at the same university as Amy. She taught sociology and he taught philosophy—different departments but both within the Faculty of Liberal Arts and Humanities. There was quite a large number of professors in the faculty, however, and at first they were only on nodding terms. Then the head of the faculty retired and there was a big farewell party. Amy carried her martini over to Mark and they had their first conversation. Amy took the initiative that evening, flirting shamelessly with Mark on the pretext of being tipsy. She had just split up with her previous boyfriend and urgently needed to fill the gap in her life.

She had not picked him out at random. As she approached him, she noticed the white circular indentation at the base of the ring finger of his left hand. There had been a wedding ring there until recently. But that did not matter. The important thing was that he had taken it off.

She succeeded brilliantly in her flirting and, after three martinis, Mark was lying in the bed in her flat. He stayed all weekend. But they did not start to live together immediately. In fact, they remained weekend lovers for some time, meeting alternately at her flat and Mark's. This rigidly impartial arrangement carried on for a year until Mark suggested they move in together. Amy agreed because, after a year observing him, she realized that he had no desire to marry her. She was relieved.

They shared an antipathy for the marriage certificate, but for different reasons. Mark was making extortionate alimony payments to a previous wife, which consumed almost half his monthly salary. The remainder was only enough to allow him a simple bachelor lifestyle. If that half had to be split in half again, he would find himself sleeping on a park bench. As for Amy, she had never been married for reasons which, to use her own words, went back to the dim and distant past.

The women in Amy's family seemed destined to remain unmarried. Her mother's mother, a woman with no name, whose nickname became her only name, had lived with her man, Amy's maternal grandfather, for a lifetime without being officially married. Although the headstone on her grave read "Mrs. Chow, wife of Fong Kam Shan," these words were inscribed at the old man's whim. Amy had never met the woman they called "Cat Eyes" because her mother, Fong Yin Ling, had left home young. By the time Yin Ling made up her mind to go home, her mother had died.

Amy's mother, Yin Ling, had also never married. She just went from one man to the next. At first, she had stayed with each of them for a year or two. As time passed, each "grand amour" followed ever closer on the heels of the one before. The shortest lasted two days from start to finish. Amy happened along as a result of one of these fleeting encounters, and she still did not know who her birth father really was. Judging by the colour of her hair and eyes, the man, who never visited her mother again, must have been white. Yin Ling had no intention of giving her daughter a Chinese surname, so she chose the commonest English surname, Smith, when she registered her birth.

Maybe it's in our genes, Amy thought.

At least, that was how she explained her view of marriage to Mark.

From passive acceptance in Cat Eyes' case to active choice in Amy's, the three generations of Fong women had all stayed away from marriage, though each for a different reason.

Mark listened to Amy in silence. He put his arms around her and gave a small sigh. Amy had expected Mark to breathe a sigh of relief but it seemed to her there was almost a trace of pity in it. Amy was surprised.

Amy had arranged with Mark that they would set off for Alaska as soon as the term was over. It would be a holiday but also a chance to study Inuit culture. She had not expected to have to take a trip to China before Alaska, nor had she expected complications to arise. Alaska would have to be postponed.

When Mark took her to the airport, he had said to a sour-faced Amy: "This is your chance to find your roots." Amy gave a bleak smile: "When you're someone like me with a zero for a father and a zero-point-five of a mother"—she paused—"and the roots you've got are in half an inch of poor soil on a rock, there's nothing much to see. What's the point of looking for more roots?" But since the day she sat at the foot of the stairs in Tak Yin House with a stack of letters in her hands, she had felt something changing inside her. The photo of her grandmother smiling at the camera, holding a baby in her arms by the No-Name River, caught Amy off-guard. She did have roots, after all.

Every discovery Amy had made in Hoi Ping she wrote about in her emails to Mark. Mark was lazy when it came to writing anything other than academic research, and was even less keen on phoning for a chat. Amy wrote to Mark because she needed to get all this off her chest. She did not expect him to reply to her messages, so she was surprised when he did.

I get it.
What next?
Be patient. It takes time to get at the truth.
Unbelievable.
Dig a bit deeper.
"Why not?"

As she discovered more about the Fongs, Amy's excitement rose to fever pitch. Now she found herself moved by Mark's comments. In the three years they had lived together, this was the first time that Amy had seen a chink in his armour of nonchalance. Where she was concerned, he was obviously genuinely interested.

On the way to the nursing home Mr. Auyung reminded Amy how Tse Ah-Yuen was related to her.

"He was the husband of your great-aunt. After she died, he never married again," he said.

Amy found it hard to understand these strange words for family relationships, but this was not because her Chinese was inadequate. Her Chinese was, in fact, very good. She made the occasional mistake, but not often. For her doctorate at Berkeley, she had had to choose a foreign language. She had wavered between Swahili and Chinese, the former because her thesis was on the evolution of social communities in Africa, the latter because she had a head start which would make it that much easier to fulfill her academic requirements. She finally plumped for Chinese.

That head start in Chinese did not come from her mother, who had only ever spoken to her in English. She picked up a bit at the Chinese restaurants she worked in during the summer holidays.

The real reason why Amy did not understand the term for "husband of a great-aunt" was that the relationship section of her personal vocabulary was almost non-existent. It consisted of two words, "mother" and "maternal grandfather." She had no father, so she did not have any relatives from her father's family. And her mother was an only child, so she had almost no experience of kinship either.

Mr. Auyung got out a sheet of paper and sketched a tree with many branches. On each branch he wrote characters. "This is a simplified diagram of your family," he told her. "The ones at the top go back too far for you to have known them. We'll ignore them and begin with your maternal great-grandfather.

"Your maternal great-grandfather was the one who build Tak Yin House. He had two sons and a daughter. His eldest son was your grandfather Fong Kam Shan. He and his brother and sister are all dead. The only one left from that generation is the sister's husband, Tse Ah-Yuen. All three had children but the only one still living is your mother, and your mother had just one child, that's you. So of all the direct descendants of Fong Tak Fat, the only ones left are you, your mother and Tse Ah-Yuen. He's your mother's uncle by marriage, so you should call him 'great-uncle'."

Amy took the paper and read it through several times. "I'll take it home and print out a copy for my mother," she said. "We actually call it 'family tree' in English."

They arrived at the nursing home where the director waited at the entrance. She shook Amy's hand then, with a slight tug on Mr. Auyung's sleeve, pulled him to one side. Mr. Auyung left Amy waiting at the entrance, and followed the director into the office.

The director shut the door, looking embarrassed. "We've had several calls about this from the Office for Overseas Chinese Affairs and of course we'll do all we can to help. But Mr. Tse is refusing to see her. He said: 'When the half-breed turns up, kick her out!'"

Mr. Auyung smiled. "He's very feisty for a ninety-year-old man! Don't worry, I can handle him." "If you say so," said the director. "You're in charge, since there's an overseas Chinese involved. You should have seen him this morning. He was in such a state. But he had some tranquilizers at lunchtime and a nap, and he's quieted down now."

Mr. Auyung walked out of the office and Amy asked him immediately: "So my great-uncle doesn't want to see me, is that it?" Mr. Auyung laughed. "Well, I suppose I shouldn't be surprised you're on the ball, Professor!" "Huh!" said Amy. "The other day in the hotel, he really tried to lay into me." "Yes, well, perhaps he had reason to," said Mr. Auyung. "His whole family came to a violent end. Your great-grandfather always said he would take the family to Gold Mountain, but he never did. If he had, then things would never have happened as they did. And there's only one person he can settle old scores with, and that's you. If you're scared, we can leave now."

Goaded by his words, Amy took up a fighting posture, one foot forward and fists at the ready: "Who's talking about being scared?" she demanded jokingly. "I've got a blue belt in tae kwon do. Try me and see!" "I wouldn't dare!" said Mr. Auyung with a smile, and they set off for Ah-Yuen's room.

Ah-Yuen had woken up from his nap and lay in bed staring at the ceiling. His eyes were rheumy and as milky as a puddle after rain. Mr. Auyung sat down on the edge of the bed, wiped a few crumbs from the old man's mouth and said: "Did you have a good lunch today, Great-uncle Ah-Yuen?" Ah-Yuen's eyes flickered and he answered forcefully: "I ate a bowl of rice and crapped a bowl of stones." The old man had lost his own teeth long ago, and the false teeth he wore clattered as he spoke as if he had a mouthful of marbles.

Mr. Auyung laughed and pulled a bottle from his pocket. "Constipation's the biggest nuisance when you get old. This is foreign medicine. Mix a spoonful in a glass of cold water every day and drink it. It tastes like orange juice and it'll cure your constipation." Ah-Yuen ignored the bottle and gripped Mr. Auyung's hand: "When you talk, you sound just like your old granddad when he was young," he said. "Great-uncle Ah-Yuen, I'm over fifty!" protested Mr. Auyung. "I'm not young any more!" The old man had his hand in a viselike grip, the veins standing out purplish. "I should have gone away with your granddad all those years ago."

Mr. Auyung helped him sit upright and Ah-Yuen caught sight of Amy standing in the doorway. He pushed Mr. Auyung away. "You've brought that half-breed, haven't you?" "She's your wife's great-niece," said Mr. Auyung. "The only Fong left. She's flown all the way from Canada to see you. Don't make such a scene!"

"Huh! Don't talk to me about the Fongs. There's not a single one of them that can be trusted." The old man was so enraged that a vein started to pulse on his forehead. Mr. Auyung patted his shoulder. "Don't talk nonsense, Great-uncle Ah-Yuen. The Gold Mountain government wouldn't let any more Chinese in. What were they supposed to do? When the ban was lifted, your brother-in-law Kam Shan wrote and asked Kam Sau if she wanted to join him in Gold Mountain, didn't he? But you had your head stuffed full of revolution in those days and you refused the offer. You've only got yourself to blame."

Ah-Yuen leaned back against the headboard, gasping for breath, but eventually he became calm.

After a pause, he said dully: "You tell her to give me my Kam Sau and Wai Heung back."

Mr. Auyung gestured to Amy. "She really has brought them back." Amy took a cloth bag out of her purse and knelt down by the bed. "Great-uncle," she said respectfully, "before I left, my mother asked me to bring you this. It doesn't belong to her. My grandfather gave it to her before he died. He told her that whoever came back to Hoi Ping should bring it with them."

Amy opened the bag. It contained some photographs, yellowed with age, and a small metal box. The top of the box was decorated with the head of a beautiful woman and the words "Almond Chocolates." The manufacturer's name was written underneath. The paint had partly rubbed off and there were rust marks on the woman's face.

Amy opened the box and took out a piece of folded cloth. She opened the folds to reveal a lock of hair tied with red ribbon. She supposed it must have been red once, though now it had faded to a dun colour. A scrap of paper was tucked under the lock. Written in faded ink were the words "A memento of Wai Kwok's first birthday."

There were three photographs. One was of Ah-Yuen and Kam Sau's wedding and had a stamp on the left-hand corner which read: "Hoi Wo Photographic Studio (Canton), Year twenty-two of the Republic." There was a close-up of Wai Heung wearing an embroidered tunic, with "Wai Heung's first birthday party" written on the back. Then there was another of the whole family with Six Fingers in the centre, Kam Sau with Wai Heung in her arms on the left, and Ah-Yuen holding Wai Kwok by the hand on the right. There was no inscription either on the front or the back, but Wai Heung was still just a baby, no more than a few months old.

Ah-Yuen's hand began to shake and the photographs fluttered onto the bedsheets. He did not pick them up. He had not seen his wife's face for fifty years. Now, at the end of his life he suddenly found himself spirited back more than half a century and confronted with his younger self and his family. It was as if he had turned around while walking, to find a ghost right behind him. Overcome by memories of that terrible day, he pulled a corner of the quilt over his head and began to whimper as piteously as a whipped dog.

By the time Mr. Auyung and Amy emerged from the nursing home, it was dusk. Mr. Auyung pulled out his cell phone and was about to call their driver, when Amy asked: "Can we walk for a bit?" He put his phone away. The town streets were beginning to come to life and gaudy neon lights flared against the night sky. They walked back to the guest house in silence.

"You seem to know my great-uncle very well," said Amy, halting for a moment.

Mr. Auyung nodded.

"Our family has been teachers for generations. My great-great-grandfather taught your great-grandfather. My grandfather taught your great-uncle and great-aunt. When your great-uncle was young, he nearly went to join the army with my grandfather."

The email Amy sent that evening was very brief, just two sentences:

"I went with Mr. Auyung to see my ninety-year-old great-uncle today. I think I've killed the old man off."

Mark's email back was even shorter. A single sentence:

"There's light at the end of the tunnel, then."

Year twenty-eight of the Republic (1939)
Spur-On Village, Hoi Ping County, Guangdong Province, China

Six Fingers was sitting in the courtyard combing out her hair.

It was just past the Mid-Autumn Moon Festival and the intensity of the sun had blunted somewhat although there was still a languorous warmth in its rays. Six Fingers' hair was very long. She released it from its bun, and filled a wash basin full of water. The grey hairs were showing through but the hair was as thick and strong as ever. By the time she had finished washing it, it was thoroughly tangled. It was troublesome to comb out but still she did it herself. In the past she had tried getting her daughter-in-law to comb it for her but Ah-Hsien was clumsy and pulled so hard that Six Fingers had a sore scalp for days afterwards.

Six Fingers moved the stool to catch the breeze and waited for her hair to dry. She had her hair ornament ready, a jade hairpin with an agate pendant in the shape of a flower dangling from one end. Ah-Fat had got someone to buy it for her somewhere in South-East Asia. She had had it many years and the hair oil she used had gradually turned the agate dark red. It was a suitable colour for a woman of sixty-two, flattering but discreet.

Once she had done her hair, Six Fingers picked up a hand mirror and looked at herself. Ah-Choi had trimmed the hair around her face this morning and the skin gleamed white. Six Fingers had put on weight with the years, and the taut skin of her face plumped out her wrinkles. Today was neither New Year nor a holiday and Six Fingers had no plans to go out or receive visitors. Nevertheless, she always made sure she was nicely turned out even if she was just going to sit at home alone all day. How many times had she told her daughter-in-law that, even when her man was away, a woman should take care of her appearance? But she might as well have been talking to herself.

In the corner of the courtyard, the widow Ah-Lin sat embroidering a shoe. Ah-Lin's husband had died many years before. When he was alive, Ah-Lin used to receive a dollar letter every two or three months, but after he died the family circumstances went from bad to worse. They had sold off all their own fields and now rented a few *mu* of poor land. Six Fingers got her in to do some needlework for the household. This was partly an act of charity, but Ah-Lin, although a few years older than Six Fingers, still had excellent eyesight and nimble fingers. She was a first-class needlewoman.

Ah-Lin was embroidering a pair of children's shoes. The material of the uppers was black twilled satin. She had drawn the design and was just choosing the embroidery thread for the peonies. The shoes were for Kam Sau's daughter, Wai Heung. Six Fingers' three children had added considerably to the number of family members. Kam Shan's daughter Yin Ling was the oldest, at sixteen. Next came Kam Ho's son, Yiu Kei, aged nine. Kam Sau's two children were the youngest; Wai Kwok, her son, was five and Wai Heung, her daughter, was just a toddler.

Six Fingers now had two grandsons and two granddaughters, and considered herself lucky to have three living in the *diulau* with her. Kam Sau and Ah-Yuen lived in the school they ran in the local town and left their children at the *diulau*. Yiu Kei lived with his mother, Ah-Hsien, in her room upstairs in the *diulau*. Yiu Kei was of school age, but Six Fingers refused to let him study at his aunt and uncle's school, and got a tutor in to teach him in the *diulau* instead. She insisted the school was too far away and the journey back and forth was too dangerous. Abductions of Gold Mountain families had decreased in recent years but Six Fingers still worried.

Or so she said. Her real reason (which she did not tell anyone) was that she was used to the clatter and chatter of three children running around the *diulau*. If Yiu Kei went to board at the school, she would have nothing to listen to. The quietness would be unsettling.

Ah-Lin stuck her needle into her hair to lubricate it, and asked Six Fingers: "Mrs. Kwan, how long has it been since Kam Sau's dad last came home?" Now that she was in her sixties, Six Fingers was known respectfully as "Mrs. Kwan."

"Years ... I can't even remember how many," said Six Fingers with a faint smile. In fact, she remembered perfectly well. The last time Ah-Fat left for Gold Mountain she had been pregnant with Kam Sau, who was twenty-six this year. It was more than forty years since Six Fingers had married into the Fong family as an eighteen-year-old. It was more than forty years since that first night in the bridal chamber when Ah-Fat promised to take her to Gold Mountain.

And for all those years, Ah-Fat talked about coming home, but never said when. Every time he mentioned it, she scanned the calendar, looking for an auspicious date for his arrival. But every year the Dragon Boat Festival came and went without Ah-Fat. Six Fingers looked then to the Mid-Autumn Moon Festival. No sooner had they finished eating the moon cakes than she began to hope for his arrival in time for the new year. When the lanterns were taken down at the end of the New Year Festival, she finally admitted defeat. As each year passed her longings abated. She knew her husband was ashamed to come back bankrupt and broken and had convinced himself that his luck would change soon. This had been going on for more than ten years.

"He's been away so long. Aren't you worried he's got another woman over there?" Ah-Lin asked.

It was nothing new for Gold Mountain men to go with prostitutes, or for them to take one as a concubine. As a young woman, Six Fingers had worried that Ah-Fat would take a "second wife" either in the village or in Gold Mountain. As the decades passed, her fears had faded and that sore place in her heart had grown a thick scab. But a rim of blood could still emerge from the old wound if Ah-Lin pressed hard enough. Ah-Fat's letters home had become more and more infrequent.

Six Fingers forced a laugh. "He's over seventy-five, and he never was a womanizer like your husband. He said he was coming home for good last year, but I told him not to. It's too dangerous with the Japanese around. I told him to wait till the war's over."

Ah-Lin bit off the end of the thread and pulled her stool over to where Six Fingers sat. She looked at her and said hesitantly: "Mrs. Kwan, this is probably just someone's idea of a joke, but my nephew from Wing On—he's in Vancouver too—he came home last month. I went over to see him and he said that Ah-Fat ... Ah-Fat...."

Ah-Lin's hesitancy infuriated Six Fingers. "Spit it out, woman!" she exclaimed. "Are you saying Ah-Fat's taken a concubine and got another family over there?"

Ah-Lin gave a laugh. "Oh no, not that," she said. "But my nephew says he spends a lot of time with a woman, some has-been of an actress, and he's keeping her as well."

The heavens came crashing down on Six Fingers' head, and her heart felt as if it was splintering. She tried unsuccessfully to stab the jade hairpin into her bun. Seeing her distress, Ah-Lin threw down her shoe, flung her arms around Six Fingers' knees and rocked to and fro.

"It's just gossip, I'm sure he's got the wrong end of the stick. Don't you believe a word of it, Mrs. Kwan," she said consolingly. "You can write letters. Why don't you write and ask him what it's all about."

Six Fingers freed herself from Ah-Lin's grip and said, with a faint smile: "Well, he's mad on opera. I expect it's nothing more than that."

She got up. Her ears buzzed as if she had a wasps' nest in them. She pulled out her hairpin and poked it into her ear. A bit deeper. Deeper still. That was better. She pulled out the hairpin and wiped it on her sleeve, leaving a bright red smear.

The lame leg from which she had sliced a lump of flesh all those years ago suddenly seemed to have shortened and, try as she might, she could not put one foot in front of the other. Supporting herself on the wall, she finally managed to hobble out of the courtyard and into the house. It was deathly quiet; the only sound to be heard was the tick-tock of the chiming clock on the wall. Six Fingers stood still. When her eyes had become accustomed to the dimness, she saw Kam Ho's wife dozing on the stairs. Ah-Hsien's head was buried in her knees and rhythmic snores, like dull farts, issued from her nostrils. The white felt flower in her hair glimmered in the half-light. Ah-Hsien's mother had been killed when the Japanese bombed the market the previous year, and she was still wearing the white flower of mourning.

"Where's Yiu Kei, Ah-Hsien?" Six Fingers asked dully.

At that moment, Yiu Kei was on his way to No-Name River with little Wai Kwok.

Yui Kei was on three days' holiday from classes. His tutor had gone home to his village for the Mid-Autumn Moon Festival; normally he would have had classes at this time of day. Early this morning, Six Fingers told

Ah-Hsien to go and fetch Ah-Tsung, the village barber, and get him to cut the hair of all the men in the household. His previous visit was at the Dragon Boat Festival three months ago and the men's hair had grown long and shaggy since then. When Ah-Hsien reached the barber's, she discovered that he had overindulged in rice wine the night before and was sleeping off a hangover. Ah-Hsien got tired waiting and left without him. When she got back home, she sat down on the stairs for a snooze.

Yiu Kei saw his opportunity and snuck out of the *diulau* with Wai Kwok.

Although spring had been dry that year, autumn brought torrential downpours. On the road, the sun dried the surface to a white crust, but the mud still oozed underneath. The children sploshed through it, leaving wet footprints behind. Six Fingers rarely allowed them out on their own to play, so they found everything a novelty. Not far from the house, they came to the clump of wild banana trees. A cluster of muddy children crouched over something on the ground. Yiu Kei pushed his way through and found they were watching ants moving house.

The ants swarmed around a dead fly with a red head and a green body. The ants looked like tiny black sesame seeds as they crawled over and around their prize, but try as they might, they could not move it. Finally, a cluster of ants squeezed under the belly of the fly. The fly appeared to drift along, accompanied by the shrill cries from the children. "What's so exciting about that?" said Yiu Kei. "My teacher says that ants can move a mountain if they work together." To Yiu Kei's disappointment, the children just shouted "Sissy whitey!" at him and scattered.

Yiu Kei was left standing there feeling a bit foolish.

He had never in his life transplanted rice seedlings or harvested the rice crop, gone rowing or tickled fish in the river. His face had never been burned dark by the sun or beaten by rainstorms, so he was pale by comparison with the village children. He loathed it when anyone called him "sissy whitey." Once he asked his granny: "How can I not be white-faced?" His grandmother laughed until she shook. "It's not so difficult," she told him. "You'd just have to roll around in No-Name River and tickle fish for a couple of days. Then you wouldn't be a 'sissy whitey' any more. It takes much longer for dark-skinned people to cosset their skin back to fairness, several generations sometimes."

But Yiu Kei was not taken in by her words. He really wanted to be like the village children, barefoot and dark-skinned, turning somersaults along the dikes, diving into the water and staying under for minutes on end, then crawling out naked and calling other children names like "Sissy whitey!"

The sun was climbing higher and Wai Kwok began to feel scared. "Let's go back, Yiu Kei. We'll get into trouble with Granny." "It's not time yet. I'll take you to tickle fish," his cousin said. "Can you really tickle fish, Yiu Kei?" Yiu Kei scoffed: "Of course, any idiot can do it." They took off their shoes and walked down to the water's edge.

This early in the day, there was not a soul at the river. The sun had not yet taken the chill off the water and no swimmers would come till midday. It was so quiet they could hear the fish gulping air. Swollen by the rains, the river reached halfway up the steps. Yiu Kei felt a tug at his hand.

"Let's go home Yiu Kei," said Wai Kwok shakily.

"No," said Yiu Kei, although his voice shook a little too.

Yiu Kei wanted to go back. His "no" was just bravado. But before they could leave, a breeze blew up and the waters nodded, and suddenly came alive. Gently tickling the soles of Yiu Kei's feet, they whispered to him: "Come in, little boy, why don't you?"

Yiu Kei could not resist such a supplication. He let go of Wai Kwok's hand and went down the steps.

An hour later, Yiu Kei's body was returned to the Fongs' *diulau*. The family and servants watched as men from the village carried in a bundle caked with sludge. They laid it down on the ground and dirty water pooled around it.

Six Fingers picked up Yiu Kei in her arms and held him on her knee. She pressed her face to his, but did not cry.

Ah-Hsien wailed and ran forward to take her son from Six Fingers. Six Fingers wrenched the hairpin from her bun, and jabbed it into Ah-Hsien's face. "Why don't you just go back to sleep and never wake up," she said fiercely.

Ah-Hsien fell to the ground, holding her head in her hands and whimpering like a whipped dog. Mak Dau called some of the men and with some difficulty they carried her into the house.

Six Fingers fetched a basin of water and began to wipe Yiu Kei down. She made a little roll of a corner of the towel and cleaned his seven orifices and under his fingernails with the greatest care. Again and again, she changed the water in the basin until gradually it ran clear. But she could not clean Yiu Kei's face. It was as if the silt had seeped under the skin, giving it a dark, purplish colouring.

Six Fingers washed and washed him.

Mak Dau tried to console her. "Ah-Hsien's still young enough to give you a houseful of grandchildren. But you mustn't leave this child lying here naked. Dress him now, before he gets stiff."

Mak Dau reached for the towel in her hand. Six Fingers resisted, then finally relinquished it. Mak Dau helped her over to a tree where she could sit in the shade.

"Don't stand there like a doorpost! Get him a change of clothes, will you?" Mak Dau shouted at his wife.

Ah-Yuet brought out Yiu Kei's school uniform, dark blue with a khaki collar. He had grown so much this year, he was bursting out of his clothes and Six Fingers had asked Mr. Au, the village tailor, to make him a new uniform. It was brand new; it had never been worn.

Mak Dau and Ah-Yuet dressed Yiu Kei. Six Fingers' ministrations had made his skin as fragile as a cicada's wing and, as Ah-Yuet did up his buttons, she scratched Yiu Kei on the face with her fingernail. A trickle of blood oozed down his right cheek. "Stupid cow!" Mak Dau shouted at her. Kicking her out of the way, he finished dressing Yiu Kei himself. The uniform had not been washed and was slightly too long. Mak Dau rolled the sleeve and trouser cuffs up and combed the boy's wet hair into a middle parting. His face still had a purplish hue. He looked just like a farm boy who had spent his life outside in all weather.

It was then that Six Fingers began to weep as if her heart would break.

Years thirty to year thirty-one of the Republic (1941–1942)
Vancouver, British Columbia, and Red Deer, Alberta

As soon as Yin Ling got home from school she sensed something was different.

Her grandfather's scratchy old gramophone was on as usual, but instead of the Cantonese opera that he liked so much, he was playing a record of Guangdong folk tunes he had bought at a Fundraising for Victory meeting. Dinner was ready and the table was set. The food was freshly made, not the usual leftovers from the restaurant. Yin Ling's eyes widened when she saw the dish of tiger prawns with ginger and scallions. That was a rare treat that Yin Ling tasted only once a year. A soup was bubbling away in the saucepan. Yin Ling lifted the lid. Inside was a rich duck and bean curd broth. Her mother had the day off today, but even so, she would not normally spend it making fancy food like this. Her mother worked six days a week and could not be bothered with housework on her free day.

"There's a letter from your uncle," said her grandfather, handing over an envelope covered in stamps.

Her uncle Kam Ho had joined the army at the end of last year. At the time, the government of British Columbia would not allow foreign nationals to join up, so Kam Ho went to Manitoba. Although he had been gone for several months, this was the first letter they had received from him. Kam Shan had a foreboding about the whole business and had not dared to mention his brother to his father. But now, to their surprise, a letter had arrived.

Yin Ling opened the envelope, but before she had time to read the letter, her grandfather snatched it out of her hand. "You've hardly studied any Chinese. How d'you think you're going to understand your uncle's scribbles? Let me read it to you."

He opened the letter, put on his reading glasses and recited the words slowly. He must have learned it off by heart, because as soon as he finished one sentence he carried on without looking at the paper.

Dear Father and all the family,

I have been with the troops in France for nearly six months, and we are constantly on the move. Our operations are secret so we have not been allowed to write home, but today I am in Paris on a mission so I am able to send you this letter. Please rest assured that I am well and in good spirits. Being in France has shown me the sufferings of ordinary people under the German occupation and makes me think of the sufferings of our family in China. I wish I could be back there, fighting the Japanese devils. They say that Hong Kong has been invaded and that no letters are getting through. I do not know how my mother and Kam Sau are managing. Since I joined up, the whole burden of supporting our family has fallen on my sister-in-law, which I feel very guilty about. I do hope my brother will make allowances for her and that you will only be good to each other.

Yin Ling glanced at her mother, who was standing with her back to them, stirring the soup. She saw her shoulders twitch, and guessed that she was crying—this was the first time ever that Kam Ho had called her his "sister-in-law."

I hope my brother and sister-in-law are well. My good little niece graduates from high school this year, don't you? Are you planning on going to university? Your father and I were very young when we came to Gold Mountain, but circumstances did not allow us to go to school there. Yin Ling, you are the third generation of Fongs in Gold Mountain, and I do hope that you will go to university so the family can get ahead in life. After I send this letter, I have to go to a small town in the south of France. Again we will be on the move and I do not know when I will be able to write again. But do not worry about me, I will take good care of myself.

Most humbly, your son Kam Ho,

The tenth day of the fourth month of year thirty of the Republic, Paris, France

Kam Shan rapped Yin Ling's bowl with his chopsticks. "Did you hear what your uncle said? You study hard and get into university, then you'll understand everything and the *yeung fan* won't be able to do the dirty on us ever again!"

Her mother turned around. "Huh! What does it matter what she studies? She still has to get married and have babies. It's much more important for her to get a job and earn her living so I don't have to carry on slogging away till I die!"

Her father grimaced and began to mutter something about "a woman's ideas...." but then bit back the words, clearly trying to keep his temper under control.

Dinner passed peacefully. For the first time ever, her mother drank a glass of rice wine with her father and grandfather. When she finished the wine, she had a coughing fit. The coughs got more and more violent until she made a dash for the sink and spewed everything up. Her mother had been vomiting a lot recently, Yin Ling noticed. Her father pulled a towel down from the clothesline and gave it to her to wipe her mouth. "If you can't hold your liquor, then don't drink," he said. "No one's holding a gun to your head." Yin Ling noticed that he was speaking to her mother unusually gently today.

When Yin Ling had finished her dinner, she got up to go to her room, but her mother shouted at her.

"Can't you wash the dishes when someone's got the meal ready for you? A big girl of eighteen like you, can't you do anything but hang around boys? Such a lazybones! When I was eight years old I was getting the dinner for the whole family...."

Her mother's words buzzed in Yin Ling's ears like a persistent fly.

Yin Ling started to count. One, two, three, four. If her mother did not shut up by the time she reached ten, she would smash the plate in her hand to smithereens. But by the time she reached eight, her mother had gone to her room.

Her father and grandfather lit their cigarettes and the room filled with acrid, foul-smelling smoke.

She could hear her mother's dry coughs, which sounded as if they might turn into another bout of vomiting. Suddenly the sounds stopped. Cat Eyes came out of her room, dressed up and carrying her purse.

"Are you going out in this rain?" asked Yin Ling's father, scowling.

The only answer he got was a grunt. As Cat Eyes sat on a stool to put her shoes on, Kam Shan's face was dark with rage.

"You won't rest until you lose every last cent, is that it?" he shouted, thumping the table so hard with his fist that the tea mugs jumped and dark liquid trickled down from their lids.

"You can smoke and drink to your heart's content, but you won't let me play a few games of mahjong!" Cat Eyes retorted, and left the house without looking back.

There was a long silence in the room.

"It's not proper for a woman to go out to work to support the whole family," her grandfather finally said.

Ah-Fat had shut his café a couple of years ago. While it was open, at least he had a bit of pocket money, enough to keep him in cigarettes. After he shut it, he could not even afford a cheap ticket to the opera on Canton Street.

"Kam Shan, your studio business is going from bad to worse. No one wants photos of themselves in wartime. And if they do, they go to the big studios. Why don't you go and get yourself a job, one where you can sit down, just for a few hours each day? Wouldn't that be better than nothing?"

Kam Shan shook his head. "It's not as if I haven't looked. The only places hiring are munitions factories. You have to be on your feet from morning till night. I can't do that."

"Or we can go and buy some beans, sprout them and sell the bean sprouts in *yeung fan* shops, how about that?" his father tried again. "You don't need much cash to start a business like that, and what we don't sell we can eat at home. Ah-Tong, who lives at the end of the street, does it, and he seems to be making a bit of money.

"Not such a bad idea. When the sprouts are ready, Yin Ling can help us sell them after school. Her English is good, the *yeung fan* understand her."

Silence fell again.

"I've had rotten luck to end up getting old like this," Ah-Fat said with a sigh. "Just think of that farm I had in New Westminster, and how envious it made the *yeung fan*. I don't know how your mother's managing at home now.

"At least in the village, they've got land to sell. That must have kept them going these last couple of years," he went on. "Not like us. We just have to keep tightening our belts. That paycheque just won't stretch any further."

Yin Ling put the last plate in the dish rack, took off her apron and ran up to her room. She shut the door and bolted it, and then blew a long, loud raspberry. This house was like a sardine tin, and she was one small fish squeezed into the crowded, suffocating darkness. The thought of carrying a basket of sopping-wet bean sprouts through the vegetable market with cries of "If ten cents is too much, eight cents will do!" made her break out in a cold sweat.

Downstairs, her grandfather heaved one sigh after another. Then there was the tinkling of boiling water—her father was replenishing her grandfather's mug of tea.

"Even a dog wouldn't go out on a night like this, but she won't stay home," Yin Ling heard her father say angrily.

She knew her father was referring to her mother. Every Monday, come rain or shine, when her mother got the day off from the restaurant, she went out with her girlfriends for a few sessions of mahjong.

"Kam Shan, don't keep scolding her all the time," her grandfather said. "You know, the baby in her belly might be a boy. Maybe it's the Buddha making sure my family line will carry on after all." There was a hint of happiness in his voice.

Yin Ling was thunderstruck. It was a few moments before she could pull herself together.

Her mother, a woman old enough to be a grandmother, was pregnant.

The tiny house they shared would soon have to accommodate another. And she knew her share would not be equal to everyone else's. If the baby in her mother's belly was a boy, he would take up half the house. They'd have to split the other half between them and not into four equal parts either. Hers would be the smallest. She was not much good at math, but this calculation was not hard to figure out.

Why didn't she just die?

Yin Ling made a fist of one hand and beat her chest. She felt the card she had hidden in her breast pocket. It was her exam results for the term. She had kept it tucked into her pocket for two days and it was beginning to smell sweaty.

English	62
Mathematics	58
Science	47
History	55
Social Studies	62
P. E.	78

The principal, Mrs. Sullivan, had called her into the office and personally given the marks to her.

"We must fix a time to have a meeting with your mother and father, and discuss retaking your courses and study plan," Mrs. Sullivan said. She was a washed-out-looking woman, so pale that bluish veins showed faintly through the skin on her neck and forehead. The veins wriggled like worms as she went on "…if you want to graduate this year."

Her mother and father? A man with a lame leg, teeth yellowed from smoking, speaking pidgin English? A woman reeking of cooking oil and smoke? No way was she going to have those two marching into Mrs.Sullivan's office under everyone's gaze.

"Did you see Yin Ling's Chink Chinaman mum and dad!"

"Look at them! Do they really let men that old make their wives pregnant?"

The snide comments jumped around in her head like tenacious fleas that refused to be slapped away.

She wished the ground would open up in front of her and swallow her. That way, she would not have to listen to her mother grumbling and her father and grandfather sighing ever again. Nor would she have to see the blue veins jumping on Mrs. Sullivan's neck, or face the nightmare of selling baskets of bean sprouts in the market.

Johnny.

The name suddenly popped up from the recesses of Yin Ling's mind.

To her surprise, Miss Watson *had* paired her up with Johnny for the tango classes. Johnny seemed not to notice that her sleeve cuffs were shiny from wear, and she did not faint in the crook of his arm. After the tango classes were over, they continued to talk to each other. Yin Ling discovered that Johnny's father was a drunk who was hardly ever at home. As the middle child of three, Johnny always felt left out. By the time his mother tried to take him in hand, it was too late. During the second half of grade ten, Johnny dropped out of school. He joined a band called The Bad Boys with some other kids in a higher grade and went with them to Montreal.

After Johnny left school, quite a few lovelorn girls wrote to him, Yin Ling among them. As time went by, however, they found new boys to focus their attentions on and memories of Johnny faded. Only Yin Ling kept writing. Johnny answered sporadically.

He stayed only three months in Montreal because people there spoke French and no one listened to English songs. The band followed the St. Lawrence River west, stopping for gigs in small towns. In Thunder Bay, Johnny fell out with the others and struck out for the Prairies. In the last letter, he said he had left the Prairies and had come back West. He was in the Rocky Mountains, in a town called Red Deer in Alberta, where he was singing in a tavern.

Johnny could be Yin Ling's bolthole, her means of escape. That way she need never set eyes on her mother, father, grandfather, Mrs. Sullivan or the bean sprouts again.

To wander from one town to another, to find yourself in a new place before the streets you were in had grown familiar, to sleep under a different roof every night, to wake up to a different sky every day—that was what Johnny referred to as "skating through life." Yin Ling wanted to skate through life, too.

She made up her mind, and the fleas stopped jumping. The snide comments were silenced, and Yin Ling calmed down.

Red Deer was near Calgary. You could get an early train from Vancouver and be there by the afternoon. Her luggage was very simple, a couple of changes of clothes and a watertight pair of shoes and an umbrella. Luckily it was not winter or she would have had to take the family's suitcase, which would have attracted attention.

Money. That was what she needed.

Yin Ling took the piggybank from the table and emptied the coins from its mouth. It was all small change and took her an age to count. It came to eight dollars and ninety-seven cents. This was what her grandfather had saved up for her. He told her it was his tobacco money, but he had not given up smoking, so although he had kept this piggy for years, it had not grown fat. Still, it was enough for her train fare and anything left over could buy her a meal or two.

She would wait until next week, until her mother got paid, and take two or three more dollars from her purse. Then she would go. She knew exactly where her mother kept her money. She had thought of leaving many times, but this time she was really going to do it.

And when the money was used up, what then? Well, she would just have to cross that bridge when she came to it.

Her mother and father were still asleep when she got up the next day. She knew her grandfather was already up because she could see the flickering red dot of his cigarette down the dark passageway. She walked past him and, in the doorway, put on her shoes.

"Yin Ling, have some soy milk, it's fresh," she heard him call after her.

"No, thanks," she called back. But when she got out of the door, she stopped and turned back. Her grandfather handed her the cup and she drank the milk down.

"Thanks, Granddad," she said and felt a lump in her throat.

Red Deer was to the north and a long way from the ocean. By the time the summer sun got that far, it had almost run out of warmth.

When Yin Ling jumped down from the train with her bulky school bag, it was almost dark. Along the chilly street, the lighting was patchy and the dark gaps looked like the mouth of a toothless old woman. The wind frisked at her sleeves, making her shiver. Vancouver wind was a plump, fine-skinned hand which dipped itself into the ocean and rubbed moisture caressingly over houses and trees and people. But the wind in Red Deer was a calloused and heavy hand that felt rough on her face. Yin Ling was surprised but not frightened by it. The fear came much later. Just now, there was too much to arouse her curiosity and nothing could dampen her good spirits.

Red Deer consisted of only a few streets. Yin Ling asked a couple of passersby for directions, and made her way down three short streets to the tavern. It was at the end of a lane, and had an illuminated sign outside which read "The Goldpanner." Yin Ling sat down opposite the entrance, on a bench used by the townsfolk to rest their legs, read the paper or drink a coffee. As she sat in this strange town, on this strange bench, feeling strange eyes flicker over her, she felt every pore of her body come to life.

Through the window she saw the room was full of men wreathed in clouds of cigar smoke. The Goldpanner was an illicit drinking hole where the coal miners and farm workers came at the end of their shifts to drink and smoke and play poker. Occasionally women would go inside, but only the sort who could charm the sweat-soaked coins from these men into their own pockets. Yin Ling knew she would have to stay outside. She was prepared to wait on the bench until morning. She had never stayed out all night, but she was fired by a fierce longing and she did not feel afraid. As she waited, her longing blazed until her heart was as pleasurably hot as peanuts roasted in a *wok*.

Of all the men in the room, only one had anything to do with her. Even without looking she could hear he was there.

Go West, where there's endless gold
Go West, where there's land untold,
Where your horse stops, hey, goldpanner
That's where you stake your claim, so bold.

The guitar chords punched holes in the night sky like a handful of birdshot. He sang in a voice so raw the song sounded like it was clawing its way from his throat. The room stank of sweat and the men tapped out the rhythm with their dirt-encrusted boots on the rough pine floor. Yin Ling found her feet tapping along with them.

It was hard to believe that on the other side of the world a bloody war was being fought. She had classmates with older brothers who had joined up and were on the front line. Their families spent the time anxiously waiting for the postman to bring them news.

The music and the liquor lulled people, making them forget the war, the endless wait for news, and death.

The frenzied strumming of the guitar chords eventually made Yin Ling feel tired. She lay along the bench and went to sleep.

She was woken up by a road cleaner.

"Miss, shouldn't you be home at this time of night?"

He was a kindly looking old man, thought Yin Ling, the kind that might call the police to look after a girl like her.

"I'm waiting for my big brother. He'll be out soon, to take me home," she said.

He looked doubtful, but went away.

Yin Ling rubbed her eyes. The sky above her was an in-between confusing colour. It could be the smoky grey of dusk, or that of pre-dawn. Her clothes were damp from the dew. She looked across the street. The illuminated sign from the Goldpanner had gone out without her noticing, leaving only a dim bulb above the door while someone with a big bag on his back appeared to be locking up. Yin Ling grabbed her bag and rushed across the street, colliding with the man in the doorway.

"Johnny."

The tears began to run down her cheeks.

It was a year since she had seen him. He used to be baby-faced, but the months he had spent moving from place to place had roughened the smooth curves and given his face character. Yin Ling felt herself drawn to the new Johnny like a moth to a flame.

Johnny's face froze in a rictus of astonishment.

"Yin Ling! Whatever are you doing here?"

"Looking for you," Yin Ling said a little hesitantly.

"Do your parents know you're here?"

"Did you tell your parents when you left?"

Johnny was taken aback for a moment, then burst out laughing. The sound ricocheted off the walls, waking the slumbering street.

"You're really not like other Chinese," he said, wiping the tears from her cheeks.

Yin Ling's heart was no longer in her mouth. She had seen in those hazel eyes that he was touched and pleased.

At least for the moment.

Further than that she did not want to look.

Johnny lived in a two-storey house no more than ten minutes' walk from the tavern, where he had a room in the basement.

The house was owned and occupied by a Dutch couple. The man was a lawyer and the woman, a housewife. Their children had married and left home, except for the youngest, who had joined the army and was now fighting in Europe. When Johnny arrived in Red Deer and urgently needed somewhere to stay, they agreed to rent the basement room to him. They thought he would be company, but they hardly ever saw him. He went out every afternoon, his guitar slung over his shoulder, and only came home at dawn. When they got up, he was just settling down to sleep.

The basement room had its own entrance. When they got to the door, Johnny tucked Yin Ling under his arm as if he was carrying a cat, and quietly slipped inside with her. Yin Ling could not help laughing in the darkness, but Johnny quickly put his hand over her mouth.

"Be careful. They've got ears as sharp as hunting dogs. Good thing their bedroom's on the top floor," he whispered into her ear as he put her down.

Johnny's breath reeked of beer and cigarette smoke. It tickled her ear and neck, and Yin Ling felt a gush of wetness along her thighs. This was what her mother meant when she scolded her for being a "slut." But her mother was not here to keep her under control now. In fact, she hardly seemed able to keep herself under control. She lifted her lips to Johnny's, and he covered them with his own, slurping like a duck slurps water. Yin Ling began to tremble so violently that she could hardly breathe.

Johnny put her down on the bed. It was an old wooden cot and creaked and groaned in protest under the weight of their bodies. But Johnny paid no attention. His hands were inside Yin Ling's clothes, not bothering with the buttons, pulling up her blouse so that it covered her face. Yin Ling could not see him any more but she could feel a pair of feverishly hot hands kneading her small, scarcely formed breasts as if they were dough.

His hands left her breasts and pulled off her trousers. Yin Ling waited for the hands to knead the place between her legs too, but instead she felt something like an iron rod thrust into her body. She was unprepared for the searing pain, and for a moment, she was silenced. Whimpers of pain caught in her throat. Remembering the Dutch couple upstairs, she forced herself to choke them down again.

The rod thrust itself in and out of her body a few times more, then went soft.

"It's always like this the first time. When we do it some more, it'll be so good you won't be able to get enough of it."

Johnny pulled Yin Ling's blouse down and wiped the sweat from her forehead.

The dawn came, and light filtered in through the small basement window, rippling over Johnny's biceps. Yin Ling traced her finger down his arm and asked tentatively: "Have you done it lots of times?"

Johnny did not answer. But when Yin Ling asked again, he said: "They come to me. You know what it's like in this business, there are always women hanging around us."

Yin Ling's heart skipped a beat. She thought to herself that she was one of those women who hung around him. But they only came once or twice for the novelty of it, she assured herself. She was not like that. She wanted to stay with him for the rest of her life. She had no father, mother or grandfather any more. She had no one. Only Johnny.

She turned over and held him tight.

From now on, Johnny's home was hers too.

It would be more accurate to call it a hidey-hole than a home. Every day they slept until the afternoon. Then Johnny went to the Goldpanner to work and Yin Ling kept hunger at bay by chewing some crusts of bread Johnny brought home from the bar. She was as quiet as she could be so that the people upstairs would not hear her. Down in the basement room, the heavy tread of their footsteps was so loud it felt like they were walking on her head, and once or twice she saw the corner of a skirt brush against the basement window—it was the wife working on the garden. It all kept Yin Ling on tenterhooks.

When it got dark Yin Ling escaped from the basement room and made her way to Johnny's tavern. She walked in through the empty room, where she and Johnny greeted each other, and she went straight to the kitchen.

Johnny had got into the manager's good books, and a job was found for Yin Ling making sandwiches and washing up.

"D'you think she's pretty?" Johnny would say when he introduced her. "Her father's French and her mother's Vietnamese."

Yin Ling had had her hair cut and waved. She learned to pluck her eyebrows into a fine line, and put on dark blue eyeshadow and pink lipstick. When she looked in the mirror she began to imagine that she really did have a few drops of French blood in her veins. She had copied this style of makeup from pinups in magazines she found lying around at the tavern. "You don't look like a schoolgirl any more," said Johnny. She supposed this must be a compliment.

As time passed in Red Deer, she began to relax and was less careful about concealing her presence in the basement.

One day, she and Johnny came home in the early hours as usual, but Johnny's key would not open the door. After a moment or two of fumbling with the lock, Johnny was surprised when the door opened and the Dutch couple came out.

"How long has she been living here?" asked the landlady, pointing at Yin Ling.

Johnny started to say something in reply, but the woman interrupted:

"My son is fighting in Europe for freedom and you bring this Chinese trash into my house and do filthy things with her under my very nose!" she raged.

"Out!" shouted the man, his finger in Johnny's face. There was a thud as something flew past them. It was the bag full of Johnny's possessions.

Before Johnny could finish saying "Her father is French...." the door banged shut.

As soon as it got light, Johnny and Yin Ling started looking for somewhere to stay. They knocked on every door with a To Let sign on it. Johnny's opening gambit started as "Have you got a room to let for myself and my wife?" then changed to "Have you got a room each to let to the two of us?" and ended up as "Have you got a room to let to this young lady?" With the first approach, the householder would look meaningfully at their unadorned ring fingers. With the second and the third, the landlord's eyes would freeze on Yin Ling's face. There would be no questions to either of them, just the simple answer: No.

And no again.

Before it was time for lunch, they realized that there was nowhere in the world that would take in an unmarried couple, especially when one of them was Chinese.

Johnny looked as deflated as a punctured football as he walked along with Yin Ling following behind. His belly rumbled along with his footsteps and he finally threw his bag down on the curb, sat down on it and lit a cigarette. Yin Ling watched as he smoked it moodily, then cautiously asked: "How about I go over the road and ask?"

She pointed at a shop opposite called the Wen Ah Tsun Store. Upstairs in a tiny attic window, there was a notice scrawled in Chinese: Nice Room To Let.

Johnny did not say yes or no. He just got another cigarette out of his pocket and lit it from the butt of the first.

Yin Ling entered the store. Behind the counter stood a middle-aged Chinese woman drinking a bowl of rice porridge. Yin Ling asked abruptly: "How much is the room?" The woman looked her up and down. "Where are you from? Are you a student? I know every one of the Chinese in this town but I've never seen you before."

Yin Ling said nothing. She had learned as they went from door to door today that there was no answer good enough to get her and Johnny a door key. So she chose silence instead.

"Thirty dollars a month, not including meals."

The woman was bluffing. She did not imagine for a moment that Yin Ling would accept this inflated figure and expected her to bargain her down.

But Yin Ling did not.

She just said: "Thirty dollars it is, but if I bring a friend back, that's not your business."

The woman looked startled, and hesitated.

Yin Ling pulled some notes from her pocket and slammed them down on the counter. "I'll give you thirty-five. Half up front, half next week. You won't get anyone else in the world to take the room at that price."

The woman said nothing. She went into the back room and Yin Ling heard a muttered conversation, perhaps with her husband. After a while, she came out again and picked up the money Yin Ling had put on the counter.

"And don't complain we don't turn the heating up enough in the winter."

As Yin Ling turned to go out, she heard the woman say in a low voice: "I couldn't rent it to you if I had a daughter at home."

It was a few moments before Yin Ling understood. "If I had a daughter, I wouldn't want her to learn bad habits from you" was what the woman was really saying.

As Yin Ling walked away, she felt the woman's eyes boring into her back of her neck. The woman thought she was a prostitute.

She was not the first person to mistake Yin Ling for a prostitute, and she would not be the last. Yin Ling was well aware that wherever she went with Johnny, apart from working at the tavern, people thought she was a whore. But she did not care. Her pressing need now was for a roof over her head—a roof to shelter them both.

She could not care less that she had a reputation as a whore. In a few short weeks, she had grown the hide of a rhinoceros.

She and Johnny moved into the attic room above the Wen Ah Tsun Store. This time, however, their situation was reversed. Now it was Johnny who had to steal in, and creep out. They hardly dared breathe, in fact, because this time they were living on the floor above the landlady, not on the floor beneath.

Autumn did not last long in Red Deer. Winter and summer performed a perfunctory handover ceremony over a few rainy days. At the end of September, with the first snowfall, Yin Ling realized what the landlady had meant when she said: "Don't complain we don't turn the heating up enough." The steam heater was only turned on for two short periods every day—before bedtime and after waking. Of course, Johnny and Yin Ling were on a completely different schedule than their landlady, and they always seemed to miss out on the heat.

When Johnny and Yin Ling came home at dawn, it was to a freezing room. Without bothering to wash their faces, they would dive straight under the covers and lie, shivering, between the icy layers of quilt and mattress. Johnny would throw back the covers and sit up, then thrust frantically into Yin Ling. This was his new way of keeping warm. Yin Ling did not resist, but would try to shush him: "Remember they're downstairs!" But Johnny's cries grew louder with every thrust.

"This'll teach those Chinks to try and make a dollar out of ten cents!"

Yin Ling gave a short laugh. "Don't forget that those Chinks are the only people in the whole of Red Deer who were willing to give us a room."

Johnny suddenly went soft, and flopped onto the bed beside Yin Ling. She tried all the tricks she knew, but could not get him hard again. She pulled the covers over both of them and slid her leg over Johnny, clamping him tight to her.

"Why don't we leave, and go and try another town?"

Johnny said nothing. Yin Ling could see his eyes gleaming dully in the dawn half-light. After a long time, the light went out and she thought he had gone to sleep. But then she felt him shift against her.

"It doesn't matter where we go, we can't get away from people," he said.

December was a grim month.

The war intensified and radio broadcasts were anything but reassuring. The American fleet was almost annihilated at Pearl Harbor. Kiev was taken. Leningrad was under siege, Hong Kong had fallen. Bad news was followed by worse. Groups of men from Red Deer went off to the front, their work taken up by the women who stayed behind. If the front line was hard-pressed, the rear was equally so. Food and water were in short supply, just like electricity and coal. Prices went through the roof. Only life was cheap.

Six days before Christmas, the list of war dead arrived in Red Deer. Five families had lost their sons to the war in Europe. Christmas that year was a cheerless affair. All down the street, Christmas trees were hung with yellow silk flowers. Carols sounded like dirges for dead loved ones. Not even the Goldpanner could brazen it out and, bowing to pressure, declared that no alcohol would be served on Christmas Day in memory of the fallen.

As she walked towards the tavern, Yin Ling could see the yellow flowers hanging from the door. For some reason it reminded her of her uncle Kam Ho, serving in France. She wondered if her family had had news of him.

Her father and grandfather must have been waiting anxiously for the postman's visit every day.

For as long as she could remember, her uncle had worked for the Hendersons. He came home once a week, arriving late on Saturday evening and setting off first thing on Monday morning. Every Saturday her grandfather would urge her father to get the dinner ready early for him. Her uncle Kam Ho was a man of few words, even when he was drinking. As they ate dinner, her grandfather would ask after the Hendersons, but for every three questions he asked, he got a single perfunctory response. One Chinese New Year, Kam Ho had put Yin Ling on his shoulders and taken her to Chinatown to buy firecrackers. Her grandfather rushed after them, shouting: "Put her down, Kam Ho! If you carry a girl up near your head, it'll make your luck run out." Kam Ho just laughed: "But Yin Ling is my lucky star," he said. "And if she pees, better still. It'll wash my bad luck away."

Yin Ling followed Johnny into the Goldpanner where the rest of the staff were busy arranging the tables and sweeping the floor. Fewer and fewer customers came to drink at the tavern these days, so business was poor. Johnny took his guitar out of its bag and began to tune it. Yin Ling sat in the corridor to the kitchen putting on her work overalls. She turned her head and saw Johnny talking to the owner. The owner appeared to be smiling pleasantly, but Johnny was baring his teeth in a strange grimace. Yin Ling was trying to overhear their conversation when suddenly a small hand twisted her gut and a foul liquid flooded her mouth. Before she could bend forward, she had vomited her lunchtime shrimp noodles on her overalls. She had bought the noodles downstairs from their lodging in the Wen Ah Tsun Store. Maybe the shrimp had gone off.

Yin Ling ran to the washroom and was just cleaning up her clothes and shoes, when the little hand began churning her guts again. By this time, her stomach was empty and she had nothing left to vomit except yellow bile. She retched and retched, and finally felt better. Maybe Johnny was right when he said that you never got decent, fresh food from "Chink" shops.

She started making sandwiches in the kitchen. There were so few customers that she did not dare make many. By the time she had finished, her stomach was growling with hunger. She nibbled a corner of a sandwich but it was tasteless and she put it back. Then she heard familiar guitar chords from the front of the house and Johnny began to sing. He sang the songs he always did but today they lacked their usual gutsiness.

Before the last Chinese New Year her grandfather had looked at predictions for the coming year and said they were not propitious. Families should batten down the hatches and not make any changes. He was right. This year really had been a bumpy road full of disasters, tears and grief. It had sapped Johnny's normally ebullient spirits. Happily, there were only three more days to go till the new year. Yin Ling was excited about what the new year might bring.

When they left work to go home, a thick, wet blanket of snow was falling. The flakes blew horizontally into their faces. It was a struggle to get along in the teeth of the wind, and Yin Ling forgot to ask about Johnny's conversation with the owner. It was only when they were in bed that she gave him a shove and asked: "What was the boss saying to you this evening?" Johnny did not answer, just turned his back on her. Yin Ling climbed over him and pushed her face into his: "I asked you a question." Johnny sat up in annoyance. Pushing her off, he said: "Stop being such a nuisance!"

He had never been so rough with her before and Yin Ling was taken aback. While she was wondering what to say, Johnny, not looking at her, felt in his jacket pocket and pulled out a packet of cigarettes. The cigarettes were damp from the snow and he wasted several matches before he could get one to light. He smoked one, then lit another from the butt, and smoked that, and then another. After the third, Yin Ling said: "Are you trying to set the room on fire?" Johnny got another two cigarettes out without speaking and lit them. He put one in his mouth and gave the other to Yin Ling.

"You have a go."

She put it in her mouth like Johnny did and breathed in. The first mouthful of smoke cut a hole in her throat. The second did the same but the knife seemed less fierce. By the third breath, the blade was blunt and just tickled her throat.

Johnny looked at her. "You know, Yin Ling," he said, "you do everything with such style. Even if it's your first time you act like you've been doing it all your life." Yin Ling watched as a perfect little smoke ring issued from between her lips, grew fat and fluffy as it rose to hit the ceiling and collapsed like a soap bubble.

"Like what?"

"Like smoking. Or running away from home."

"Huh! You're making fun of me, I can tell." But Johnny turned to face her and said emphatically: "Listen to me, Yin Ling. I've never made fun of you. You are the most interesting woman I've ever met." "Because my dad's French?" she asked, and they both laughed.

Johnny gripped Yin Ling's shoulder: "I know you miss your family," he said. Yin Ling shook her head vehemently but the tears came anyway. In two days' time it would be New Year's Eve. There would be five chairs round the table for the New Year's Eve dinner, and two of them would be empty. No amount of complaining from her mother could fill them, though perhaps the new baby would make up for that.

Johnny did not want sex from Yin Ling that night. Instead, he cradled her in his arms as if she was a baby. He held her tight for so long that he began to get a cramp. Yin Ling slept soundly, dreamlessly. When she woke up, the room was dazzlingly bright; she could not tell whether from the sun or the snow. Dust motes danced in the light like a myriad of silver specks. Yin Ling stretched out an arm but Johnny's pillow was empty. Instead her hand fell on a letter.

She opened the envelope. Inside were a ten-dollar bill and a scribbled note.

> *I've been sacked by the boss because the customers say we've spoilt the "feel" of the town and they don't want us around. I've got to get on the road but I don't know where the next stop will be. Use this money to buy yourself a train ticket to Vancouver. If you're quick, you might make it home for New Year. The skating life's not for you. I'm sorry, I really am.*

After the fall of Hong Kong there were no more letters from China. There were still fearless folks in Chinatown risking their lives travelling to China to visit their families. They brought back the news that Wai Kwok had been killed in a Japanese bombardment. When he heard, Ah-Fat took to his bed and refused food and drink for two days.

On the third day, Ah-Fat got up of his own accord, helped himself to a big bowl of rice from the pot, added some pickled cucumber and scarfed it all. He put the bowl down and said to Cat Eyes: "Get out ten dollars and tell Kam Shan to take it to the Chinese Benevolent Association."

Cat Eyes pulled a face: "We donated ten dollars last time."

Ah-Fat's eyes bulged from their sockets. "Are you waiting till the Japs raze Hoi Ping to the ground before you do anything?" he shouted.

Age had made Ah-Fat apathetic, and it was a long time since they had seen him so fired up. Kam Shan tried to catch her eye, but she looked away. He tugged at her sleeve but she pulled it free.

"Even if I sold myself, I couldn't raise ten dollars. You know what we spent the last few cents on."

Cat Eyes' restaurant had opened a new branch and Cat Eyes had been transferred there as waitress. It was a long way off and Cat Eyes was too pregnant to walk. She had spent twelve dollars on an old banger of a Ford.

Ah-Fat pointed at the dishes on the table: "I'll just eat one bowl of rice a day from now on. That way we can put a bit by, can't we?"

In the last couple of years, the local Chinese had sent two contingents of young men to China to join the war effort, with some receiving training in San Francisco from Nationalist airmen sent over from China. Arms and equipment cost money, and so did food supplies. The Chinese Association had passed the hat round several times, but less and less money was raised each time. Then, articles appeared in the overseas Chinese newspapers calling on every family to have one bowl less of rice every day and send the money saved to China to help the war effort.

"You're supposed to have one bowl *less* every day, Dad," said Kam Shan, "not just one bowl a day. Who'll fight the Japanese devils if we all starve to death!" "Huh! What do singing girls care?" said his father and, folding his hands into his sleeves, went upstairs to his room.

Kam Shan had had enough schooling to recognize the lines from the old poem. He looked at Cat Eyes: "Country people can give birth even in pigsties. What makes you so precious all of a sudden?"

Cat Eyes knew this was a dig at her because she had bought a car. It was on the tip of her tongue to point out it took two to make a baby, but Kam Shan had gone out, slamming the door.

He did not come home till dinner, and Cat Eyes had gone to work by then. The house lights were blazing and his father was bent over a sheet of paper on the kitchen table, brush in hand.

It was a long time since he last got out paper and ink, and his writing hand shook badly. The ink loaded onto the wolf-hair brush meandered across the paper; in large characters, Ah-Fat had written:

Fong Yiu Mo (martial splendour)
Fong Yiu Kwok (patriotic splendour)
Fong Yiu Keung (unyielding splendour)
Fong Yiu Bon (splendour of the nation)
Fong Yiu Tung (eastern splendour)

Kam Shan realized that his father was choosing a name for Cat Eyes' son. After "Kam," the next-generation name was "Yiu." The only grandson of that generation born to the Fongs was Yiu Kei, who had drowned in the No-Name River two years ago. Ah-Fat's only remaining hope was the bump in Cat Eyes' belly.

When Kam Shan came in, Ah-Fat threw down his brush and lit a cigarette. Ash dropped from the tip as he smoked it and burned a tiny scorch hole in the paper.

"Which name do you like? I think it ought to be Yiu Mo. We need military brilliance to save the country."

"I need a piss," said Kam Shan, and hurried to the toilet. He stood holding himself over the toilet but could only squeeze out a few drops of urine. His father called him but Kam Shan turned a deaf ear. Suddenly a dark thought crept unbidden into his mind. What if his father died before Cat Eyes' baby was born? Back in their village, it was rare for a man to live past sixty. His father was seventy-eight. Surely he could not last much longer...

Cat Eyes' shift finished at midnight and she drove the juddering old Ford home. To her surprise, Kam Shan was not at his usual post by the door. He had gone to bed.

But he was not asleep. When Cat Eyes came in, he shifted over and made room for her. Cat Eyes got in under the covers and felt her body go soft as cotton batting in the warmth. In all her years with Kam Shan, he had never before warmed the bed for her.

She was just drifting into sleep when something roused her and she sat up with a jerk. Pulling Kam Shan's hand to her, she said: "Feel that! The little rascal's kicking me!"

Kam Shan put his hand on Cat Eyes' pale belly. It felt as if a puppet on invisible strings was hiding inside and kicking out its legs.

"I went to Fat Kei Herbalists yesterday and the herbalist looked at my belly and said I was carrying it so high he was ninety percent sure it would be a boy," Cat Eyes said.

Kam Shan said nothing. His hand trembled like a leaf. Cat Eyes remembered the old saying about a son in old age being the greatest happiness, and stroked the back of Kam Shan's hand: "When Yin Ling comes back home, then the family will be complete," she said.

Kam Shan tossed and turned all night but could not sleep. When he got up in the morning, he saw his reflection in the window, and was astonished to see that his thatch of hair had turned grey overnight.

Cat Eyes' shift started at midday. She was in the car and had just started the engine when Kam Shan ran out and rapped on the window. She wound down the window and could not help smiling at the sight of Kam Shan wearing a hat pulled down tightly over his ears. "You're not going out wearing a funny-looking thing like that, are you?" she said. Kam Shan stared at her but said nothing. Cat Eyes was about to drive off when Kam Shan blurted out: "Your next Monday off, can you not go out?"

Cat Eyes had heard this kind of comment for years and years, and it went in one ear and out the other. Still, this time, although the words were the same, he seemed to be saying something different. Her heart softened. "Do you want me to stay with you, is that it?" Kam Shan nodded. "And I'd like to take you to the fish and chips restaurant next to the Vancouver Hotel." Cat Eyes laughed. "Did you just trip over a bundle of dollar bills? Folks like us can't afford that kind of a place!" "I've got money," said Kam Shan. He wanted to go on. "And I've got something to say to you...." but Cat Eyes had already roared off down the road.

They never ate that meal together, because before Cat Eyes had her next day off, she miscarried.

She began to hemorrhage in the Lychee Garden Restaurant and lost consciousness. They took her to the hospital. She was only five months pregnant and the baby did not survive.

It was a boy.

When Kam Shan heard the news, he squatted on the floor and burst into floods of tears. Ah-Fat had never seen his son cry in his life. If he kept it up, Ah-Fat thought, he would cry the heavens into bits and the earth into a bottomless pit. But Ah-Fat felt that it was not wholly grief that moved his son; it was also as if a great burden had been lifted from his shoulders.

The next day, Kam Shan took himself off somewhere where he could be alone and burned a sheet of paper he had kept hidden in his pocket.

It was a deed of contract.

It read as follows:

I, Fong Kam Shan, of Spur-On Village, Hoi Ping County, Guangdong Province, China, now resident in Vancouver, British Columbia, together with my wife, Mrs. Chow, agree to sell the baby which Mrs. Chow is carrying, whether it is a girl or a boy, to Mr. and Mrs. Tseng Yiu Nam of Toi Shan, for the sum of seventy dollars, this sum to be donated to the anti-Japanese war effort fund in its entirety. This document is a permanent record of this agreement.

Third day of the eighth month of year thirty of the Republic

Up till now, Ah-Fat had never thought of himself as old.

His hair had gone grey long ago and his eyes had deteriorated, but if he wore his glasses, he could still read books and newspapers. He had lost a few teeth but was still capable of chewing his rice and peanuts. His knees were a bit crooked but could carry him along the road on his walks well enough. True, his hand shook when he held his writing brush, but he could still form the characters if he wanted to write. They all said he was an old man—Kam Shan, Kam Ho, Cat Eyes, Gold Mountain Cloud—and he accepted their comments with a smile. But although he could not be bothered to argue, in his heart of hearts he was not convinced. What other people said did not count. The only thing that counted was what he felt in himself.

When he came back from seeing Rick Henderson, he was not so sure.

Since Kam Ho had left the Hendersons, Ah-Fat had not been back to see Rick. Time went by, and one day he found himself on the street where the Hendersons lived. As he drew closer, he saw a For Sale sign stuck into the lawn in front of their house. He was surprised, and went up the steps to knock on the door. There was no answer but a neighbour came out to tell him that Rick had died.

It was about a month ago, but no one knew exactly which day it had happened. Rick had not been taking the dog out for its usual walk, the neighbour told Ah-Fat, and one day they heard the dog barking and barking. Finally the neighbour banged on the door and, when there was no answer, broke in and found Rick lying dead on the kitchen floor. He had been dead for some days and the rats had gnawed out his eyes. The dog lay dead next to him.

The next day, Ah-Fat bought a bunch of flowers and took them up the mountain to pay his respects to Rick.

It was not the first time he had been up the mountain.

There was the occasion when Jenny, Rick's daughter, had died, then another occasion when Rick's wife, Phyllis, died. This visit was his third. He put down the bunch of white chrysanthemums, a little withered from the frost, and took a packet of cigarettes from his pocket. He put one cigarette on the gravestone, lit the other and squatted on the ground to smoke it.

You had rotten luck, Rick. You bought this plot for your wife and daughter to bury you here. But you ended up burying them first and there was no one to bury you.

"You've gone, you bastard, and I'm the only one left," Ah-Fat muttered to himself.

Out of all those who built the railroad, was what he meant.

There were thirty-one of them in the team, including their foreman, Rick. Many of them died as they blasted their way through the Rockies, Red Hair among them. And many more were lost trying to get home when the work was finished and they were sacked. Some starved to death later, in Victoria, and of those who did not, some went back to Guangdong. Only four remained in Vancouver. Ah-Lam had died thirty years ago, and another died the year before last. Now Rick was dead and only Ah-Fat remained.

There were so many stories from the railroad-building days. Why had he never thought of recording them? Now, even though he could still remember, he could not write them down any more, and he would take them to his grave. Those untold tales would be trapped in his casket, waiting for weeds and moss to obscure them permanently.

As he went down the mountain, he suddenly felt as if a muscle was missing from his leg and he could not stand straight. Just like that, his whole body had suddenly shrunk.

Maybe I really am old, he thought. I suppose I must be—I'm getting close to eighty.

He hobbled down the road on his way home. From a distance, he could see the lights of Chinatown coming on, faint spots of good cheer dotted here and there in the gathering darkness. However grim life was, you had to celebrate New Year, he thought. When he got home, he would bring the festive lanterns down from the attic, dust them off and hang them up.

He thought about the family in China, in the village in Hoi Ping. There had been no letters from home for a long time, since Hong Kong fell to the Japanese. How was Six Fingers getting on? He had not seen her in more than twenty years, and if it were not for the photographs, her face would have faded from his memory.

He was trying to find his key when he stubbed his foot on a bundle lying by his front door. Why was his family so lazy they could not be bothered to take the rubbish out, he mumbled angrily. The words were scarcely out of his mouth when the bundle moved and got to its feet. "Granddad!" Ah-Fat nearly buckled at the knees in fright. He took a closer look. This was clearly no ghost; he could see the breath coming from its nostrils in the cold air. Without bothering with his key, he rapped thunderously on the door. "Yin Ling's back!" he shouted.

A moment later, Cat Eyes opened the door, Kam Shan behind her. They turned on the lights to see a figure covered in dirt and enveloped in an overcoat so impregnated with dust it was impossible to tell the original colour. In the half-light, the grey lips cracked open to reveal flesh-pink gums. "Mum, Dad!" Cat Eyes' legs gave way under her and she sat down on the ground.

"So we're still your mum and dad, are we? We spent months posting missing persons notices on the radio and in the newspapers for you. So now you've spent all the cash you took from the house, you're back, eh?"

Kam Shan pulled Cat Eyes back. "Keep your trap shut, woman. Go and heat some water so she can wash."

Yin Ling took a bath and put on some clean clothes borrowed from Cat Eyes. Glowing from the hot water, she finally looked human. Dinner was on the table. She wasn't surprised to see what she assumed was yesterday's leftovers from the Lychee Garden Restaurant. She sat down, then looked around and asked: "Where's the baby?" Her mother's belly was flat now so she was clearly not pregnant any more.

There was silence at the table.

After a moment, Ah-Fat asked: "Where did you go, Yin Ling? Your mum and dad have been tearing their hair out with worry." "Lots of places," said Yin Ling, and looked down at her bowl. She scooped the rice into her mouth but was careful not to take any of the meat and vegetables until her elders had served themselves. She's finally learned some manners, thought her grandfather.

Cat Eyes looked coldly at her daughter and noticed how thin her face was, her cheekbones sticking out knifelike above her freckly cheeks. Yin Ling got up to serve herself more rice. There was something odd in the way she walked. Cat Eyes could not ignore her growing suspicions. Without bothering to finish her food, she jumped up and dragged Yin Ling up to her room.

She shut the door behind her and gripped Yin Ling by the scruff of the neck. "When did you last come on?" she demanded. Yin Ling looked down at her shoes and said nothing. Cat Eyes asked again, this time gripping her more tightly until Yin Ling could hardly breathe. Her mouth opened and shut like a fish gasping for air, and she finally stammered: "Oct ... October."

Cat Eyes let go and stood looking at her without speaking. Her eyes sunk into their sockets as if they were two dried-up pits. "I knew it ... I knew it!" she repeated. Yin Ling was terrified. She grabbed her mother's sleeve and cried piteously: "Mum! Mum!" Cat Eyes shook her off and flew down the stairs.

The two men had just finished eating and were lighting their first after-dinner cigarette. The price of tobacco had gone sky-high but men needed to smoke so the quality of cigarettes got worse and worse. Cat Eyes cut through the cloud of smoke, grabbed the cigarette out of Kam Shan's mouth and threw it in the sink. "Have you gone completely crazy, you stupid woman?" Kam Shan fished it out but it was sodden. He tore open the paper and spread the tobacco out to dry, cursing as he did so.

Cat Eyes spat a gob of green phlegm. "That little slut you've been spoiling all her life has just gone and got herself pregnant! Three or four months now and who knows who the father is!"

Kam Shan was so taken aback, his hands convulsed and the tobacco scattered over the floor.

Cat Eyes pointed a finger in Kam Shan's face. "Did she ever listen to me? Not with a father like you, and what did you ever manage to teach her? She can go to hell, I'm having nothing to do with her."

Kam Shan grasped the finger Cat Eyes was waving at him and bent it brutally. Cat Eyes squealed like a stuck pig.

"Like daughter, like mother. It's no wonder she's a slut with a slut like you for a mother."

This was a knife in Cat Eyes' chest. She pressed her hands against it as if she wanted to pull the knife out, but her heart sucked the blade in and would not let it go. "When I was in the brothel, the whole town knew I was a slut," she said between clenched teeth. "But I didn't go running around town looking for a man, you came to me. If I'm a slut, what does that make you?"

Ah-Fat could not take any more. He thumped his fist on the table so hard the skin between thumb and finger split and bled.

"If you two want to fight, then go outside and fight, and tell the whole town about it, why don't you? Then every man in town will want Yin Ling as a wife, that's for sure."

Kam Shan and Cat Eyes fell silent.

"Go to the Fat Kei Herbalists with a bag of walnut and red bean cookies," he ordered, "and talk to the herbalist's mother. Get her to give you some medicine to get rid of it. Tell her you've fallen pregnant but you're too old to bring up a baby. The herbalist's a good son. He'll do what his mother tells him."

When Cat Eyes understood what Ah-Fat was saying, a look of embarrassment crossed her face. "What are you waiting for, woman?" Ah-Fat shouted. "There's no time to lose. If it's too late to get rid of it, who's going to marry her?"

Cat Eyes turned the house upside down before she finally found some paper to wrap the cookies.

The mixture the herbalist gave her was effective. Yin Ling began to bleed, and for weeks on end, the blood continued to trickle out.

When the bleeding finally stopped, Kam Shan tried to persuade Yin Ling to go back to school and finish her studies. But Yin Ling was adamant. "I'd rather kill myself" was her response. Kam Shan was afraid she might be as good as her word if he pushed her too hard, so instead Yin Ling started work at the Lychee Garden Restaurant as a waitress like her mother.

She did not stay long. In fact, she had scarcely had time to learn the names of the drinks on the wine list and the dishes on the menu when she was gone again. This time she went off with a *yeung fan* called John, a regular customer who had taken a fancy to her the moment he set eyes on her. It happened right under Cat Eyes' nose, but she never noticed. And so, four months after she came home, Yin Ling left again.

This time, she was gone for more than ten years. When she came back again, her grandfather and mother had both died, and only her father remained.

This time, she brought with her a daughter, whose name was Amy.

One day in early summer, 2004, a Canadian woman named Amy Smith, accompanied by a government official, Mr. Auyung, went to pay her respects at the Fong ancestral hall. In the records of the Fong Tak Fat family, she found the following text:

Fong Tak Fat's younger son, Fong Kam Ho, married a woman of the Au family, of Wai Yeung Village, in year eighteen of the Republic; they had one son, Yiu Kei, who died aged nine years. In year twenty-nine of the

Republic, Fong Kam Ho donated four thousand Canadian dollars to the Nationalist government in Guangdong to buy planes to fight the Japanese, in recognition of which he was awarded a commemorative medal for his patriotism. In the same year, Fong Kam Ho enlisted in the Canadian army and worked as a special agent in a small town in the southwest of France, gathering intelligence and training members of the Resistance. He was betrayed in year thirty-four of the Republic on the eve of the Allied victory and was killed. A bridge in the town was renamed Jimmy Fong Bridge in his honour. (Jimmy Fong was Fong Kam Ho's English name.)

8

Gold Mountain Blues

Year thirty of the Republic (1941)
Hoi Ping County, Guangdong Province, China

Six Fingers and Mak Dau noticed the plane overhead as they made their way home with Wai Kwok.

Wai Kwok had just started attending his parents' school, where he was a boarder. Yesterday, Kam Sau sent a message from the school that her son was ill. He had been treated by a Western-trained doctor but, although his temperature had gone down, he was still very tired. Could someone pick him up and take him back to the village for a few days' rest at the *diulau?*

Six Fingers carried a bag full of hot spring rolls stuffed with bean sprouts, which she had made fresh that morning. She left half with Kam Sau and Ah-Yuen to share; the other half was for them to eat on the way home.

The whole world was at war these days, and the postal system was in chaos along with everything else. Since Six Fingers could not depend on dollar letters, she had to sell off some of their land. It was a good thing she had bought some land cheaply when things were more settled a few years back. It meant she could sell it off now at a profit, one *mu* at a time, to put food on their table.

Six Fingers was keeping an ever tighter grip on the purse strings. She had dismissed all the *diulau* servants except for Mak Dau and his wife, Ah-Yuet. Even Ah-Choi, who had been with them for decades, was packed off to her home village. Ah-Fat's uncle and aunt were long dead, and their son and daughter had married and left the *diulau*. That only left Kam Sau, Ah-Yuen and their children, Mak Dau and Ah-Yuet, and Kam Ho's wife, Ah-Hsien. Six Fingers regarded Ah-Hsien as a complete fool, and left only the simplest jobs for her to do. Six Fingers did most of the cooking now.

Mak Dau walked along empty-handed. Tucked into his trouser waistband was a revolver. He took a gun wherever he went these days, even to bed. Guns protected life in these turbulent times—the lives of everyone in the *diulau*, not just his own.

The original plan was for Mak Dau to go alone to fetch Wai Kwok, but Six Fingers was so concerned about him that she insisted on going too. Mak Dau dug out an old tunic which Ah-Yuet wore for messy work, and asked Six Fingers to put it on. Then he made her take out her jade hairpin, muss her hair up and pull it back into an untidy bun. He brought a bowlful of ash from the kitchen stove and made her rub it on her face and neck. "I'm not some pretty young girl of eighteen," Six Fingers protested. "Who's going to be looking at me?" Mak Dau laughed out loud. "If you live to be a hundred, Missus, you'll never lose your looks," he said. "And if you live to be a hundred, you'll never lose that glib tongue of yours," she countered. But she was secretly pleased.

Just as they were leaving the house, Six Fingers stopped in her tracks. "I want you to promise me something, Mak Dau," she said. "What?" "Promise first, then I'll tell you." "How can I promise when I don't know what it is?" "If you don't promise, I'm not telling you." Back and forth they argued, until Six Fingers finally said: "I want you to promise that if anything happens on the trip, save me if you can. But if you can't save me, put a bullet through my head."

There was a long silence. Finally Mak Dau said: "Believe me, if I can't save you, the first shot will be for you and the second for me. I promise that

I'll always stick by you." Six Fingers was touched by Mak Dau's loyalty, and then felt a sudden pang. There was someone else who should have been looking out for her all these years: her lawful wedded husband.

When they arrived at the school to collect Wai Kwok, Six Fingers exclaimed anxiously at how thin and pale he had grown. And in fact they had only gone a short way on the road home before the boy needed a rest and they sat down to eat their spring rolls. They set off again, and Mak Dau gave Wai Kwok a piggyback. He nodded off and slumped heavily against Mak Dau, forcing him to walk along bent almost double under the weight.

"You're getting old, Mak Dau," said Six Fingers. "Well, with a grandson this big, it would be surprising if I wasn't." Mak Dau had lost two front teeth and his breath whistled through the gaps as he spoke. Six Fingers thought back to the time, all those years ago, when he had first arrived at the Fongs'. He had such strong, white teeth back then. They lit up the whole courtyard when he smiled. But everyone had to get old sometime, she supposed, even Mak Dau.

"Well, at least you've got a grandson.... I lost mine, all because of that fool," Six Fingers said bitterly.

She was referring to Yiu Kei. Every time Six Fingers thought of her grandson, she cursed her daughter-in-law, Ah-Hsien. "Haven't you gone on about this enough?" he said. "It's been nearly three years now. It's a good thing she's such a blockhead; your cursing and swearing is like water off a duck's back. It just doesn't get you anywhere. The way I look at it, Yiu Kei was never meant to be part of your family. He just visited with you for a short while on his way to another life in another place. Let him go, and he'll reward you when he returns in another life. Anyway, haven't you still got Wai Kwok? My grandson is your grandson. When the time comes, he'll be the one to look after us and bury us. If he dares to misbehave, he won't get away with it!"

Six Fingers' mood lightened at Mak Dau's blunt words.

As they walked along, a brisk wind whipped up. It was a regular market day and the road was thronged with people laden with baskets of produce hung from shoulder poles. Mak Dau and Six Fingers watched in amusement as a peddler's broad-brimmed hat blew off. He sprinted after it, but it bowled along faster just out of reach. Finally the peddler gave up the chase and sat down covered in sweat by the roadside, swearing rudely.

They were still laughing at the sight when another sound caught their ears. It was a loud humming like a giant metal fan overhead. Mak Dau looked up and saw a group of black dots on the horizon. The dots got bigger and grew wings like birds. "Planes! It's the Japs!" someone shouted. The market-goers dropped their baskets and ran frantically for cover.

It was not the first time Japanese planes had flown overhead. Years ago, they had bombed Wai Yeung Village and several members of Ah-Hsien's family were killed. That was on a market day, too. Six Fingers had never been caught in a bombing raid herself. She stood frozen in shock.

It was still early in spring and in the fields on either side of the road the crops had only just begun to put up tender shoots. There was no cover anywhere. When they looked up again, the birds were so near they could make out the red blob of the Jap flag painted on their tails. Mak Dau hastily put Wai Kwok down under a tall tree by the roadside. "Don't move!" he shouted. Then he ran to Six Fingers, flung her face down on the ground and lay beside her.

Six Fingers lay in a pile of fresh dog shit. The stink was so bad she could hardly draw breath but she was past caring. She shut her eyes very tightly and repeated over and over: "Buddha have mercy, Buddha have mercy." She counted four dull booms which seemed to come from the bowels of the earth, and the ground beneath them trembled violently. Separate sounds merged into a terrifying, continuous roar. Objects fell from the sky and hit her on the back with metallic pings—clods of earth perhaps. Her body felt increasingly heavy, as if she was being crushed under layer after layer of cotton-stuffed quilts. Everything went black. I have been buried alive, she thought.

Later, after all the noises died away, the earth stopped trembling and silence fell. Six Fingers was suffocating; her lungs felt as though they were about to burst and her eyes were popping from their sockets. She tried to call "Mak Dau!" but no sound came out. She heard a scratching. The thought came to her that a snake was trying to bore its way through the mud. But it was all too late. She knew she was going to die here.

Suddenly, light appeared and she saw a mud-covered lump with two shiny white eyes, and a pair of hands soaked red.

"Mak Dau, are you hurt...?" she croaked.

The mud-covered mouth cracked open, showing pink gums: "It's nothing. I scratched my hands digging you out."

The same thought occurred to both of them at that moment: Wai Kwok!

But where was the tree?

It still stood, but was only half as tall as before. Its top and all the branches had gone, leaving a stump a few feet high. The stump still looked like a tree on one side, but on the other, it was charred coal-black. Flames leapt from it.

Six Fingers and Mak Dau began to search frantically for Wai Kwok. They circled the tree but he was nowhere to be found. They made another circuit, but still could not find him. At the third attempt, Six Fingers found a shoe poking out from under a pile of debris.

It was of black twill, with a white sole made of layered cotton. The upper was embroidered with a tiger's head. Six Fingers recognized her own handiwork. She had made the shoes when Wai Kwok started school.

Six Fingers gave a slight tug and freed the shoe. Encased in it were a foot and half of the leg, severed at the knee. A bloody crimson froth oozed from the break, and a bone the thickness of a thumb could be seen poking out of the middle.

Six Fingers dropped to the ground in a dead faint.

Kam Sau and Ah-Yuen had built their School for All in a village called Sam Ho Lei, which was situated at the centre of a cluster of half a dozen other villages. A local scholar had lent them a piece of sloping land on which to erect the school buildings. Both were constructed of sun-baked mud bricks; one contained the classrooms, and the other the accommodation for the students and teachers. The classrooms were divided into lower and upper primary grades. Ah-Yuen was head of the school and Kam Sau was director of studies. Kam Sau taught classes in Chinese and handicrafts, and Ah-Yuen taught math and physical education. The two other teachers taught history, geography, art and literature, and natural sciences.

Fees ranged from one to five local dollars, on a sliding scale according to the family's income. Children from destitute families were completely exempted. Boarders brought their own rice rations and did not have to pay anything else for their keep. The school was especially keen to encourage girls to study and generally accepted them without payment. In addition, the girls with the best attendance records were awarded five pounds of extra rice rations every month. They had started out with a dozen or so boys, but in a few years the number had increased to over two hundred boys and thirty or so girls.

Kam Sau had sold all the jewellery and silver her mother had given her as a wedding present to set up the school. But that only went so far. Most of the money came from the old scholar who lent them the land. His son had been at college with Ah-Yuen and Kam Sau. All three of them were Mr. Auyung Yuk Shan's star pupils. The family had substantial business interests in Japan and South-East Asia and, although the son had gone on to join the military after graduating from college, he had persuaded his father to use some of his wealth to fund the school for his two friends. On opening day, Mr. Auyung attended the inauguration and wrote in his own hand the words "School for All for a Bright Future" for the tablet above the entrance.

Kam Sau and Ah-Yuen were well aware that sending sons and daughters to school full-time meant a considerable sacrifice for the villagers. It cost money and it meant the families would be short of farmhands, but they wanted to see their children succeed in life at any cost. Kam Sau and Ah-Yuen threw themselves into their teaching with a fervour which matched the families' determination. Kam Sau frequently saw the girls saving their mealtime rice rations and taking every spare grain home to their families at the end of the month. Her heart bled for them. What difficulties these girls faced! For her part, she saved as much of the food brought by her mother as she could, and divided it among a few of the girls who looked particularly pale and undernourished.

After Wai Kwok was killed in the bombing raid, Kam Sau had to take a break from teaching. Every time she stood in front of the other pupils, she was reminded of her son. The slightest thing made her break down in tears in the middle of the class. Even though she was three months' pregnant, she could not eat or sleep, and lay awake staring at the ceiling all night long until dawn touched the bedroom curtains with a pale light. When she was no more than skin and bones, Ah-Yuen took her back to her mother in Spur-On Village.

When Mr. Auyung heard, he hurried over to see what was going on. But instead of offering condolences, he said with a grim smile: "You can't have hair without a skin. When the eggs are in danger, you protect the nest. If you cried as hard for China as you have for your personal loss, you could save the whole country." "What's our school for if not for the country?" protested Kam Sau. "And I've sacrificed my son for that! If we hadn't set up this school, Wai Kwok wouldn't have been studying here. He'd be at the Overseas Chinese Children's School, and this disaster would never have happened."

Kam Sau's cheeks flamed and her voice shook with fury. Mr. Auyung glanced at Ah-Yuen: "That's better. So long as she hasn't completely lost heart, there's hope." Then he sighed and went on: "If it hadn't been Wai Kwok, it would have been someone else, and it would have happened sooner or later. The Japanese have cut a bloody swathe through our country from the very north to the far south. China is weak, and so is its army. If we can't keep the gates barred against them the people inside will die."

"I can't possibly care about everyone in this world," said Kam Sau. "It's Wai Kwok...." and her eyes filled with tears before she could finish the sentence. She swallowed hard. "I know what you're saying," she went on with an effort, "but I'm no soldier or gatekeeper, I'm just an ordinary teacher, and I'm no use to anyone."

Mr. Auyung rapped on the table with his knuckles. "Who said you're no use?" he demanded. "The students you're teaching are the gatekeepers of tomorrow, Kam Sau. When our generation is finished, China must put its hopes in the next generation. Pull yourself together and make the best job you can of your teaching. The best tribute you can pay to Wai Kwok is to turn your pupils into heroes."

Kam Sau said nothing but the flush on her cheeks gradually subsided.

Six Fingers brought Mr. Auyung a bowl of iced sweetened lotus-seed soup. He drank it with relish: "I don't know when I'll get soup as good as this again." "Are you leaving the country?" asked Ah-Yuen in surprise.

"This visit is really to say goodbye to you," the teacher said. "Where are you going?" asked Ah-Yuen. Mr. Auyung did not answer, just put down the bundle he had been carrying with him. "I've finished with these books," he said. "They're quite interesting. They're for you. I'll be in touch again as soon as things have settled down."

Ah-Yuen hesitated, then posed another question: "At teacher-training college, someone said you were a member of the Communist Party, Mr. Auyung. Are you going to join the Communists now?"

Mr. Auyung looked at him. "Whether I am or not isn't important. What matters is what you think the Communist Party stands for."

"I've read all of the *Communist Manifesto*," said Ah-Yuen. "But surely its tenets apply to Europe. Does it have any relevance to Asia?"

Mr. Auyung smiled. "Fine ideals know no frontiers," he said, "just as evil doesn't either. We can't just sit and wait for others to make a better future. Some of us have to make real sacrifices in order to realize those ideals."

Ah-Yuen accompanied Mr. Auyung out of the house and down the road. He realized that his old teacher had grown much thinner since he last saw him. Against the darkening skies, his eyes blazed from deeply sunken sockets. His hair was unkempt and locks of it bounced up and down as he talked. He had the sour breath of a man who had not slept for many nights. The hem of his blue gown flapped in the wind.

"Mr. Auyung...." he began, and then his voice cracked.

It was not just from sadness at parting with his teacher. There was something he had been mulling over for a long time but could not make up his mind to say.

It was "Take me with you."

He did not say it. He thought of Kam Sau and Wai Heung, and the baby in Kam Sau's belly. He felt torn between his family and his country. Whichever he let go, it would hurt unbearably.

There was little news of Mr. Auyung after that. When Ah-Yuen next set eyes on him, more than a dozen years had passed. Ah-Yuen was taking a group of pupils on a visit to the Guangdong Revolutionary Martyrs Museum and discovered a portrait of Mr. Auyung on horseback in full military attire.

If he had thrown in his lot with Mr. Auyung that spring night in 1941, what course would his life have taken? That was the question Ah-Yuen repeatedly asked himself over the years. So many possibilities had presented themselves to him then. But where would they have taken him? If he had chosen differently, might his family have been spared the calamity which ultimately claimed all their lives?

He did not know.

Kam Sau was busy teaching handcrafts to the younger girls when she heard a knock at the door.

The children were making decorative lanterns for different festive occasions.

Their school had more girls in the lower primary grade than in the upper one. Kam Sau knew why: it was the extra five pounds of rice per month that persuaded families to send their girls to school. The desire to have them learn the rudiments of math so that they could manage household finances when they married was secondary. Most of the girls did not go on to upper primary classes, let alone to lower middle school. Once they had completed lower primary, they would be fetched back home to do farm work. When Kam Sau planned her teaching, she had to take all these factors into account. So in "handicrafts," she taught the skills that the girls would need in their lives at home. She did not teach needlework. The girls could learn that from the older women at home. Instead she focused on making paper cuts, lanterns and gift boxes, and writing Spring Festival couplets.

They had prepared the bamboo frames for the lanterns in a previous class. Now she would teach them how to glue on the paper. She had bought a long roll of red tissue paper in town, and ordered two girls to hold it, one at each end. Kam Sau was just wielding the scissors when she heard the rapping at the door.

It was a polite knock, with a hint of hesitation between each rap. It certainly did not sound like a portent of danger. Kam Sau had reached a crucial part in the cutting. Without looking up, she asked the girl nearest the door to open it.

It was a dazzlingly sunny day outside and at first, Kam Sau could see only a white glare. The doorway was filled with a couple of jagged shapes silhouetted against the azure sky. She also saw that from each one rose something long and gleaming, but it was a few moments before she realized these were bayonets.

"Do you have any ... any food," mumbled one of the silhouettes in broken Chinese.

As her eyes grew accustomed to the glare, Kam Sau saw that the visitors were dressed in army uniforms brown with dust. Magazines hung on each side of their belts, and their bayonets had suspicious stains at the tips.

Kam Sau took all this in, her head in a whirl. The room seemed to grow dark and her terrified ears filled with a high-pitched hum.

The children. What about the children?

Outside on the slope in front of the school, other pupils were doing their exercises. It should have been Ah-Yuen's class but he had gone to town for an anti-Japanese teachers' meeting and another teacher was filling in for him.

How could she attract their attention?

"I'll go, go to the kitchen and get something for you," she stammered.

But it was too late. The dark figures were already in the room, forming an impenetrable barrier in front of Kam Sau.

"She ... go," said one of them, indicating a girl standing with Kam Sau.

"There's some leftover rice in the crockery cupboard," said Kam Sau, gripping the child's hand. She traced a message in her palm. The girl's hand twitched. She had understood.

The soldiers were Japanese and there were three of them: Sasaki, Kameta and Kobayashi. They had been separated from their unit in the Sam Ho Lei area during the march on Tan Shui Ko. They trekked through the forests and across rivers for hours until hunger had forced them to stop at the mud-brick building on the hill.

Even though they were armed to the teeth and could have slaughtered a whole village, they were well aware that hatred was a powerful weapon; a mob of unarmed Chinamen could make mincemeat of them. Their intent was to beg a meal and eat it in peace and quiet, scrounge a cigarette or two if they were in luck, and get back on the road as quickly as possible in hopes of catching up with their unit before nightfall.

But once they were inside the classroom they changed their minds.

To be precise, it was the woman they saw inside that changed their minds.

They had arrived in Hoi Ping and Toi Shan counties in early spring, under cover of a mighty bombardment. They had seen many women since then, country women with faces burned dark by the South China sun, with high cheekbones and fleshy lips, and hair full of dust and straw. In frantic haste, they stuck them with their own bodies or with bayonets. Emptying themselves into these women felt no different from relieving themselves in a toilet. These country women were not real women to them.

But the woman they saw before them now was quite different.

Her face was so fair she might never have been touched by the sun or the wind. Her skin was so velvety smooth that they were sorely tempted to reach out and touch it. Her eyes were dark and deep as the sea, with just a flicker of melancholy on the surface of the water. Her blue tunic was very plain but it was filled out by her buxom curves. Her abdomen bulged slightly, straining against her tunic and making it gape at the hem. They may have been three armed soldiers fleeing for their lives, but the sight of this woman made them aware that they were also men.

Step by step they came nearer to her. The woman said nothing, just stared fixedly at them. It was not a sharp stare—fear was written all over her face. But there was something in her gaze which hobbled their legs together like a rope.

Sasaki was in front. Her eyes met his, challenging them, and he knew that if he carried on looking he would have to declare himself beaten. So he simply averted his eyes and forced himself to stare at the wall of the classroom behind her. It was an old wall and the plaster had cracked. There were streaks of blood on the plaster from squashed mosquitoes.

Sasaki ripped the front panel of her tunic open with one downward movement, revealing a thin white vest underneath. The girl holding one end of the tissue paper roll gave a shriek of terror and Sasaki waved his finger in her face. "Shut up!" he shouted. The girl gave a shrill wail in response. Sasaki, worried that the noise might alert people outside, gestured to Kobayashi, who pulled his gun from his shoulder. A slight prick of the girl's belly with the bayonet and a gash opened. As easily as a fish spawning, coils of something white and snakelike spilled out over the floor.

Such pushovers, these Chinese, thought Kobayashi.

Kam Sau could hear her own teeth chattering violently. She addressed her pupils gravely, forcing out the words: "Shut your eyes." The girls obeyed. The only sound to be heard in the room was a trickling, as urine dripped from the thin fabric of their trousers onto the floor.

Kam Sau shut her eyes too. The door slammed shut. She could still feel the sun, the memory of light dancing on her eyelids. She felt her feet leave the ground and she was carried to the rostrum. Someone pulled her vest off, while someone else yanked on her trousers. There was a draught coming through the cracks in the walls and she felt it brush over her naked body. Hands, so many of them, felt her all over. They were cold and covered in calluses. They were as abrasive as sandpaper.

But there was worse to come. Something was hurting her back, something icy cold and hard. The scissors she had been using to cut paper were pressing into her.

Kam Sau opened her eyes. Sasaki's face was close to hers, so close she could see the soft down which would one day grow into a moustache on his upper lip, and a pus-filled pimple on the side of his nose.

He was just a boy.

Kam Sau measured the space between herself and Sasaki. She was secretly waiting for the chance to shift her right hand and get hold of the scissors under her back. She would stick them first into his windpipe and then into her own. In five seconds, perhaps ten, certainly not more than half a minute, she could put an end to two lives.

But the chance never came.

She felt a sharp pain between her legs as something thrust violently into her, pounding until she felt as if the life was being crushed out of her. Then darkness washed over her and she lost consciousness.

By the time the girl who had gone for help returned to the classroom with a crowd of men armed with knives, staves and carrying poles, the Japanese had gone. The first man through the door lost his footing, and fell over. As he got up and rubbed his knee, he realized he had slipped on a length of human gut. In the corner of the room the pupils still huddled. They could not be persuaded to open their eyes.

Their teacher, Fong Kam Sau, lay on the rostrum.

She was fully dressed and she lay perfectly straight, her face ashen as a corpse prepared for burial. A woman went to give her a shake, then pulled back her hand as if she had seen a ghost. Kam Sau was staring blankly at the ceiling, a glassy look in her eyes. When the woman had recovered from her fright, she held her hand under Kam Sau's nose and was relieved to feel a slight warmth on her fingers.

The crotch of Kam Sau's trousers was stiff with blood. Under her lay a bloody, reeking lump of flesh.

"Her baby!" the woman shrieked.

Years thirty-three to thirty-four of the Republic (1944–1945) Vancouver, British Columbia

Sundance: Thirty years ago, a Chinese man called Fong stayed at your home. He behaved like an ignorant fool, and begs you to forgive him. He has spent years searching for you. If you see this notice, you will find him any Saturday morning at the Burnaby vegetable market.

Classified Ads page of the Vancouver Sun, *5 June 1944*

Kam Shan had a dream that night.

The images were crystal clear. They appeared in colour and he could even smell them.

The bristle grass was waist high, the tips of its furry spikes gleaming silver in the sunlight. There was a rustling sound as a mangy dog crept through the brush. He was behind the dog, keeping as close as he could to someone in front. He could not see the person's face, only a pair of legs under a rawhide skirt running with the agile gait of a deer, and a head of long, tawny hair which streamed in the wind. No matter how fast he ran, he could not catch up. Once he got close enough to grasp a hank of the hair, it slithered through his fingers and was gone.

He woke up with a shout, and sat up, his face covered in sweat.

"Stop it! You're kicking like a mule!" grunted Cat Eyes. It was dawn and there was a grey light coming through the curtains. Outside, the street was waking up. This was the time when Cat Eyes most craved sleep; she would not stir from her bed till midday.

"Who the hell's Sundance?" she grumbled. Without waiting for an answer, she turned over and went back to sleep.

Did I really shout "Sundance"? Kam Shan wondered to himself.

He had been dreaming the same dream for months. The same grass, the same expanse of blue sky, the same sun, the same dog, the same woman. He even jerked awake at the same moment each time. Sometimes he woke up for a piss and afterwards would take up his dream at the point where it had been interrupted.

Were Sundance's gods calling him?

Kam Shan and his father, Ah-Fat, had been growing bean sprouts at home for some years now. Sometimes they supplied supermarkets; sometimes they sold the bean sprouts to hawkers. Many of the hawkers were Indians. The women, especially the younger ones, often attracted Kam Shan's attention. Could one of them be Sundance? He laughed at his own foolishness. She had only been a year or two younger than he, so she would be middle-aged by now. Still, he always imagined her as a young girl.

Yet in all these years, although he had had dealings with many Redskins, he had never run into Sundance, or even any member of her family. The year before the war started he had written to her, but the letter, after much forwarding, had been returned to him undelivered. He knew that many Redskins had left their reserve to work in the city, so perhaps she was in Vancouver. But even if she brushed against him in the street, she probably would not know him. How could she recognize in this puny little man hobbling along with his lame leg the fiery youth she had once known?

Kam Shan wiped the sweat from his forehead and lay down again. With Cat Eyes' snores reverberating in his ears, all thoughts of sleep vanished.

As Cat Eyes put on weight over the years, her snores grew louder. Kam Shan, on the other hand, slept more lightly. Sometimes he could not sleep at all and lay watching her. Her slack mouth hung open, and he could see her tongue moving back and forth with each snore. It was all he could do not to throttle the woman. Years ago, he could at least take refuge in Yin Ling's room and get some sleep there. After her second departure, they kept her room ready for her return. Then a couple of years slipped by without news and Cat Eyes said there was no point leaving it empty, they could get a bit of cash renting it out. An assistant cook from the restaurant moved in. After that, there was nowhere for Kam Shan to go and sleep peacefully so he just had to lie awake until daybreak.

But there was something else. And he found it much worse than her snoring.

Cat Eyes' periods had become irregular and she had a continuous discharge. Her body smelled putrid, like maggoty meat. It was not so bad during the day when she had layers of clothes on, but at night, when she took them off, the smell turned his stomach. She had been to see the herbalist in Canton Street but he just said she was overworking and was rundown. Some nourishing chicken soup would cure her. They had bought several fine hens and made soup from them but nothing had helped. Kam Shan urged her to see a Canadian doctor but she said she was not going to take off her clothes in front of a *yeung fan*. They argued and argued but she would not go.

Who would have thought that Cat Eyes would die so young? She had the most stamina of all of them, trotting back and forth all day in the restaurant, six days a week, and throwing herself into games of mahjong on her day off. And then one day she just died.

It started with her periods, then she got terrible pains in her legs. These became so bad that she had to take time off work. Kam Shan angrily accused her of laziness but Cat Eyes did not answer back. She just responded with a foolish smile. In fact, her illness made her more sweet-tempered than she had ever been. Eventually Kam Shan noticed that she could not turn over in bed without breaking out in a sweat, and realized she was seriously ill, but it was too late.

She sank into a deep sleep that lasted for several days, and then suddenly woke and asked Kam Shan to go and get her three mahjong friends. "Are you really up to playing mahjong?" asked Kam Shan disbelievingly. But his father gave him a look: "You can see she won't last much longer," he said. "Go and get them." Kam Shan set up the mahjong table at her bedside and the four women played till dawn. They knew she was dying, and let her win. That night, Cat Eyes filled a whole bag with her winnings, which pleased her immensely.

After they left that morning, she began to fail. Her face was drawn and her hands trembled. She asked Kam Shan for a cigarette. She had been smoking for some years, the cheapest brand, of course. Kam Shan took out one of his own, then put it back in the packet and went down the street to get a packet of fine-cut State Express 555. He lit one and put it in her mouth, but Cat Eyes did not have time to smoke it.

She pointed up to the attic room, and said two words: "Yin Ling...." Then she was gone.

Later Kam Shan went up to the attic. After a good deal of searching, he found a letter and a moth-eaten old handkerchief bag in one corner. The envelope was from St. Joseph's Hospital and contained some receipts and a letter with test results. The letter was in English and Kam Shan had to find someone with medical knowledge who could read it for him. It confirmed a diagnosis of late-stage cervical cancer. The letter said that the cancer had developed from chronic cervical erosion and had spread to her liver and bones. It was dated some months back.

Cat Eyes had seen a doctor and knew quite well what she was suffering from, Kam Shan realized. For all her adult life Cat Eyes had tried to put the degradation of her life as a Gold Mountain child prostitute behind her. Acknowledging this disease would have brought it all back. Rather than face that shame, she preferred to get along as best she could without treatment until death claimed her.

The bag contained a roll of mildewed banknotes, some of them nibbled by rats. She must have secretly stashed this money away for Yin Ling's wedding, Kam Shan guessed. She had slaved away for the Fong family all these years, and not one of them had honoured her for it, he thought. Even her own daughter was not there to pay her last respects.

As he held the bag in his hands, Kam Shan was overwhelmed with sadness.

The next day, Kam Shan went to the funeral home to order a gravestone for Cat Eyes. When it came to the inscription, Kam Shan realized that in all their years together, he had never asked Cat Eyes' formal given name, so he decided on "Mrs. Chow, wife of Fong Kam Shan." Cat Eyes could never have imagined that in death, she would be given the title she longed for all her life.

Ah-Fat and Kam Shan went to market to sell their bean sprouts once a week.

After their work was finished, they went to Shanghai Street or Canton Street for a bowl of jellied bean curd and pan-fried dumplings, and a browse through the Chinese newspapers, which the owner laid out on the table. They were up early on market days and there was no time for breakfast, so this meal was breakfast and lunch combined. They ate in leisurely fashion, reading the papers as they did so.

Today they were in the Lei King Restaurant. They had a bowl of soy milk each to start and then Ah-Fat ordered a portion of lotus dumplings and one of *char siu* dumplings, four spring rolls, two portions of pan-fried dumplings, a bowl of shrimp soup and finally, a bowl of trotters in ginger. "However will you eat all that, Dad?" exclaimed Kam Shan. "What we don't eat we can take away," said Ah-Fat.

Although summer was nearly over, the weather was still warm and the hot soy milk made Ah-Fat break out in a sweat. He reached into his pocket for a handkerchief to wipe his face, and felt a letter in there. It was from Six Fingers. Since the fall of Hong Kong, the mail routes had been disrupted and hardly any letters got through—only two in the last couple of years.

It was a short letter, only a few lines, addressed to Kam Shan.

My dear son,

A year has passed since your last letter. We are under constant bombardment so the rare letters which arrive are worth their weight in gold. There is tumult throughout the countryside and terrible things, too numerous to mention, have happened. I will tell you more when we meet. Fortunately, your sister Kam Sau survived the calamity that befell her, and I hope that things will be better for her in the future. Are you all right in Gold Mountain, Kam Shan? Is there any news of Kam Ho? Yin Ling must be so grown up by now that I would hardly recognize her. I burn incense and pray to the Bodhisattva every day that you are all safe and well and that we will meet again after this war is over.

Ah-Fat had had the letter in his pocket for a few days. Every day he took it out and scanned it again, and the paper was beginning to fray at the edges. There was something odd about the letter that puzzled him; it was short, but still asked for news of family members—except Cat Eyes and himself. Six Fingers never asked about Cat Eyes, as if there was no such person in the Fong family. For their part, they had not told her of Cat Eyes' death and Yin Ling's disappearance. But now, in this letter, Six Fingers had made no mention of Ah-Fat either. It struck him as odd. It occurred to him he ought to sit down one day and write her a letter to ask for an explanation, but he did not know if the letter would ever arrive.

Kam Shan was starving. He wolfed down a pan-fried dumpling, the meat juices leaving his chin shiny with oil. Ah-Fat noticed that his son's shirt cuffs were frayed and worn and he thought to himself that it certainly made a difference when there was no woman at home. They may have been poor when Cat Eyes was alive, but at least the men of the house went out looking neat and tidy. Kam Shan started to look dishevelled almost immediately following her death. Ah-Fat sighed: "Kam Shan, when things settle down and the war is over, you and me are going back to Hoi Ping so we can fix you up with another wife." Kam Shan turned one page after another until his fingers were covered in newsprint. Then he picked his nose, leaving his nostrils smudgy. Finally, he laughed. "Dad, even if I marry again, I can't bring her to Gold Mountain. I'm better off single. It saves a lot of trouble."

Ah-Fat frowned. "Aren't you going home to retire?" he asked. "I've still got family in Vancouver," Kam Shan said. "What about when Yin Ling comes back?" Ah-Fat's frown deepened. "But there's been no news of her for years," he protested. "You don't even know if she's still alive!" Kam Shan swilled his mouth out with tea and spat it on the floor. "Oh, she's alive all right," he said confidently. "Like father, like daughter. Yin Ling's as tough as old boots. When she gets fed up with messing around, she'll come home."

Ah-Fat drank his soy milk and put the bowl down. The leftover food was placed in a bag and Ah-Fat picked it up, saying he was heading home. He left Kam Shan to settle the bill.

But he did not go home. Instead, he turned the corner and headed for Canton Street in search of Gold Mountain Cloud.

She was still living in the tiny basement room of the theatre. It had a single window no more than a foot square and was so gloomy she had to keep the light on in broad daylight. Ah-Fat knew his way. He went straight down the narrow dark alley and pushed open the door of her room. Gold Mountain Cloud was working on some wool from an old sweater she had unravelled. She had washed it and steamed out the kinks in a *wok*. Now the yarn was dry and she was winding it into hanks around the back of the chair. This was pure lambswool, bought years ago when she toured Australia, and since she had not worn the sweater much, the wool was still good as new.

The dank chill made Ah-Fat's teeth chatter and the sweat on the back of his neck evaporated. "This is a rathole," he said angrily. "It's not fit for anybody to live in." "That's not a very polite way to greet someone," said Gold Mountain Cloud. Ah-Fat hurriedly turned it into a joke: "Was there ever a rat as fine-looking as you? If there was, I'd have been quite happy to marry it." "Really!" exclaimed Gold Mountain Cloud. "Just remember to repeat that in front of your son, so you have a witness." Ah-Fat looked embarrassed and fell silent.

Gold Mountain Cloud took the bag from Ah-Fat's hand, then measured his waist with a tape, doing sums in her head as she did so. "What are you doing?" asked Ah-Fat. "I'm going to knit you a new vest. The weather's getting cold, and that vest you've got on is full of holes. Not that you'd notice, since they're all on the back."

Gold Mountain Cloud was wearing a silver-grey tunic, somewhat worn, with a small darn at the collar, but clean and neat. Her hair was quite grey but still thick. She wore it coiled into a bun, low at the nape of her neck, with a sprig of jasmine stuck in it. When she talked, the fine lines which covered her face rippled outwards in a ready smile.

Ah-Fat stared at her. "What a woman you are...." he said. "What woman am I?" "You've gone from a life of luxury to dire poverty, but you're still able to make the most of it." Gold Mountain Cloud laughed. "I'm better off than many people," she said. "I've got food to eat and a roof over my head." "That's true," said Ah-Fat, "and tomorrow I'm going to buy you a coal stove. That little steam heater will never get you through the winter."

Ah-Fat took the snacks out of the bag. "Bring bowls and chopsticks, and we'll eat them while they're still warm." They had just settled down when they heard a puttering sound in the street outside. "It's gunfire," said Gold Mountain Cloud. Ah-Fat got up to look and came back saying it was firecrackers. "Firecrackers?" exclaimed Gold Mountain Cloud. "It's not a holiday!" Ah-Fat stood on tiptoe and craned his neck but all he could see through the tiny window was the corner of the street. A man passed carrying a slender bamboo cane at the top of which were tied a string of firecrackers. They exploded into the air with deafening crackles, and released a shower of red confetti which floated like moths into the sky. Crowds of people erupted into the quiet street from houses and shops.

Ah-Fat, still barefoot, leapt for the door. Gold Mountain Cloud followed and threw his shoes after him: "Such a child!" she said.

In a few moments he was back, puffing and panting, and stood leaning against the wall, unable to speak. Gold Mountain Cloud could see tears in his eyes. They spilled down over his high cheekbones and collected, glittering, in the groove of his faded old scar. Gold Mountain Cloud had never seen Ah-Fat cry. "What on earth's the matter?" she kept asking. Finally Ah-Fat got the words out: "The Japs … they've surrendered."

They sat down at the table and resumed their interrupted lunch. Ah-Fat took a bite out of a lotus dumpling, then dropped it into his bowl, took a spring roll, bit into it and threw that down too. He could not eat. Then he blurted out:

"Cloud, I can go home now. I've never seen my daughter, or my son-in-law or my grandchildren, not once. My wife probably won't even recognize me. When she writes now, she never even asks after me. She must be really angry with me."

He talked on, but Gold Mountain Cloud said nothing. With her chopsticks, she pinched a few remaining bean sprouts which had escaped from the spring roll, moving them around the bottom of her bowl but making no attempt to lift them to her mouth. It suddenly occurred to Ah-Fat that Gold Mountain Cloud had no family left in Guangdong, her elder brother having died in Montreal some years ago.

He looked at her and put the question carefully: "What if I take you back to Hoi Ping? Will you come?"

Her chopsticks came to a halt, and the scraps of bean sprouts trembled and dropped off.

"As your ... what?" she asked.

Ah-Fat felt his mouthful of spring roll turn to grit. He worked and worked at it with his tongue and finally managed to swallow it down.

"My wife's a good woman; she'll treat you with respect. So long as you don't mind."

Gold Mountain Cloud gave a short laugh. "I'd be treated as your second wife—at my age, with one foot in the grave. My reputation would be in shreds."

Ah-Fat said nothing, just lit a cigarette and inhaled. Swirls of smoke came and went across his face, but there was no disguising his uneasiness.

Then he stubbed his cigarette butt out in the bowl and abruptly got to his feet. "Cloud, you're only three years younger than my wife. She can treat you as a sister. If I decide to bring my sister home to live out her old age, who's going to make a fuss? You get your things together, and I'll get Kam Shan to find out the boat times."

And then he was gone. By the time Cloud made up her mind to go after him he had covered quite some distance. The sun was still bright and a long shadow nibbled at Ah-Fat's heels. "Wait!" she shouted. Ah-Fat turned back to see her cupping her hands around her mouth.

"Ask your wife what she thinks!"

Ah-Fat mumbled yes and hurried home to write his letter. He had not written for a long time. The materials he used for his letter-writing business had been stowed away in a corner of the attic when they cleaned up after Cat Eyes died. He brought them down and dusted off the rolls of paper. There was a crack in the ink stone, he noticed, and the paper had yellowed. But they would do.

He ground the ink, laid out the paper and wrote in shaky characters: "My dear wife." Then he stopped. He racked his brains but for the life of him he could not think what to say. Then suddenly, lines of the classical poet Du Fu came to him, from the poem "On hearing that Imperial troops have recaptured Henan and Hebei," and he wrote:

Word comes from the North of towns retaken
When I first hear the news, tears wet my gown
I turn to my wife and children, sorrowful no more
Rolling up our poem scrolls, we are wild with joy.

Once he had these lines from the poem down on the paper, it seemed to clear his head, and he wrote fluently. He reread up and down the page, time and again, well pleased. His brushwork was as bold as ever. He added a final line:

Like General Lian Po of ancient times, I may be old, but I can still chew my food. What do you think of my calligraphy, Ah-Yin?

He finished, sealed the envelope, went to the corner shop to buy a stamp and dropped the letter into the mailbox. When he got home, he shouted but there was no answer from Kam Shan. He went into his son's room but he was not there either. Ah-Fat sat down on the bed, and felt suddenly as if a great weight had been lifted from his shoulders. He lay down on the bed, feeling drained. As he took a breath, the smell of grease and dirt rushed headlong up his nostrils, making him sneeze. He quickly turned the pillow over. Men without women … it just didn't do, he thought to himself, and instantly fell into a deep sleep.

When he awoke, it was completely dark. Kam Shan was still not home and the only sound in the house was the ticking of the old wall clock. Ah-Fat turned over and felt something digging into his neck. He sat up and patted the pillow. It felt as if a piece of cardboard had been hidden somewhere inside it. He pushed his hand in and brought out a letter. The envelope was stamped with the British Union Jack at the top left and a shield on the right, set in a square. Ah-Fat recognized the Canadian flag. It was addressed to Frank Fong, and the postmark was dated a month ago. Ah-Fat was annoyed—how could Kam Shan have forgotten to give it to him?

The letter was neatly typed, in English. Ah-Fat's English was rudimentary at best and he had to read it a few times before he could understand anything. Even after reading it several more times, there were still bits which made no sense to him.

Dear Mr. Frank Fong, We deeply regret ... your son Mr. Jimmy Fong ...
fallen in battle in the Republic of France. We will always ... heroism ...
glory ... defence of liberty ...

As he read it for the fifth time, the words swam before his eyes and the page blurred.

"The light ... turn on the light," Ah-Fat mumbled to himself.

An immense darkness came down and engulfed him.

Year thirty-four of the Republic (1945)
Spur-On Village, Hoi Ping County, Guangdong Province, China

Six Fingers saw the spider on the wall when she awoke.

It progressed in stops and starts, dragging its large iridescent abdomen until it finally reached the large photograph of Ah-Fat in a white suit with a pipe in his mouth.

A lucky spider, Six Fingers thought to herself.

Ah-Fat had had the picture taken on his last visit home, in the Chu Hoi Studio in Canton. It was the year that Kam Sau was born. She was thirty-two now, which made Ah-Fat....

The morning sun seemed to cling heavily to her eyelids, forcing them shut again. Six Fingers went back to sleep before she had finished the thought.

When she woke up again, the spider was still there, perched on Ah-Fat's nose, making it look from where she lay as if there was a big hole in it.

Her heart gave an anxious leap and she felt around on the bed for Wai Heung.

Wai Heung had reached school age but Six Fingers absolutely refused to let her attend classes. She even refused to get a tutor in and insisted on teaching her to read and write herself. "At least until she's completed lower primary," Six Fingers said. "Then she can go to school." Kam Sau and Ah-Yuen argued but Six Fingers refused to budge.

Her other grandchildren, Yiu Kei and Wai Kwok, had both died young, and Yin Ling was in Gold Mountain. Kam Shan was too old to have any more children, and who knew when Kam Ho would come back home to his wife, Ah-Hsien. After she had been raped and beaten by the Japanese soldiers, Kam Sau could no longer bear children. So Wai Heung was the only grandchild at home and Six Fingers cherished and protected her in every way she knew. Wherever Wai Heung was, Six Fingers worried about her. She even shared her bed with the little girl.

Wai Heung was awake and sitting up braiding her hair. She had such a thick rope of hair that even when it was divided into two braids, they were as thick as sugar canes. She had no mirror and the results were distinctly lopsided. Smiling, Six Fingers grabbed the ox-horn comb from Wai Heung's hand: "If you can't even braid your hair, who'll marry you when you're a big girl?" Wai Heung giggled. She was a good-natured child whom it was impossible to spoil.

When the braids were finished, Six Fingers put a basket over one arm and took Wai Heung by the hand. "Come along. Granny's going to pick cucumbers, and you can pick a bunch of flowers for me," she said. These days, the Fongs' fields were all rented to tenant farmers; they had kept only a small plot for growing their own vegetables and fruit. As they went out, Six Fingers thought she heard a crow cawing harshly in the tree. She looked up, but it was actually a magpie peeking down cheekily from a branch. She felt a leap of happiness and her face relaxed into a smile.

First, the lucky spider, now the magpie. She felt sure they were signs which boded well for the day ahead.

It had rained overnight and the air was rinsed fresh and clean. The hibiscus by the roadside had exploded into bloom. Frogs in the ditches croaked loudly. Six Fingers picked a hibiscus flower, shook the dew off it and tucked it behind her granddaughter's ear. "And when's my little Wai Heung going to get married?" she asked.

Wai Heung giggled again and began to hum: "The moon shines bright on the ocean bay, my mum's marrying me to Gold Mountain far away!" Six Fingers was startled. "Who's been teaching you that nonsense?" she snapped. Wai Heung quailed at the sudden change in her Granny's mood. "Second Auntie," she mumbled, meaning Kam Ho's wife, Ah-Hsien. "That imbecile! Fancy filling your head with stuff like that! You're not going anywhere, Wai Heung. You just stick with your granny." The girl nodded obediently and the smile gradually returned to Six Fingers' face.

They arrived at the edge of the fields. The second crop of rice had been harvested and the bare earth stretched away into the distance, dotted with a few bent figures. The tenant farmers' wives and children were busy cleaning up the field. Six Fingers and her late mother-in-law, Mrs. Mak, may have differed on many points, but they shared a passion for owning land. In Six Fingers' view, having money was all well and good but it could all vanish. The only thing that could be relied on was land: no rat could nibble it, no eagle could snatch it away, no thief could steal it. Six Fingers had a mental map of every one of their fields. Those fields had a few gaps in them at the moment because she had had to sell some during the Japanese occupation. The thought of those gaps caused Six Fingers a stab of pain.

She vowed to herself that one day she would buy that land back and fill in every one of those gaps.

The cucumbers were nearly over, and only a canopy of large leaves remained. Six Fingers and Wai Heung felt between the leaves of each plant but without success. But soon they discovered that the rainfall had knocked the remaining cucumbers off their stems. Six Fingers felt in the mud and found a few decent ones, which she put in her basket. Then they heard a distant shout: "Kam Sau's mum, where are you?"

"It's my granddad," said Wai Heung.

Six Fingers straightened up, and saw Mak Dau stumbling, puffing and panting, across the fields holding something aloft in one hand.

"Letters ... from Gold Mountain!" he shouted.

"Two of them. One from Kam Sau's dad, the other from Kam Shan."

Six Fingers was startled. It was rare for Ah-Fat to write to her in recent years. If he had something to tell her, he usually got Kam Shan to write the letter.

"You open them and read them to me," she said. "My hands are covered in mud."

"Which one shall I open first?" asked Mak Dau with a wicked smile on his face.

"Don't give me that nonsense! Whichever you like."

"I know what 'whichever you like' means," said Mak Dau, still looking mischievous. He opened Ah-Fat's letter and began to read. It cost him considerable effort and the sweat stood out on his forehead. As a boy, he had attended Mr. Auyung's classes along with Kam Shan and Kam Ho, but only for a short time. He could not make much sense of the first lines of Ah-Fat's letter.

Word comes from the North of something, something...
When I first hear the news, tears wet something...
I turn to my wife and children, sorrowful no more,
Something ... scrolls, we are wild with happiness

Six Fingers clasped her basket over her belly and laughed so hard she was almost bent double. Finally, she composed herself. "Leave the weepy poem," she said. "Just read me the rest of the letter."

The remainder was much more straightforward and Mak Dau's reading speeded up:

Now that I have heard that the Japanese have surrendered, I will get the boat times by tomorrow at the latest, and buy my passage home. Then we can be together. After so many years apart, my heart speeds like an arrow to yours. There is just one thing I need to tell you: I have come to know a woman here called Gold Mountain Cloud and we have enjoyed a deep friendship over the years. Cloud has no family and I cannot bear to leave her behind alone. For this reason (Mak Dau stumbled slightly) *I am bringing her with me. I hope you will understand and will treat her as a sister, so that we can all live in ... harmony.*

When Mak Dau had finished reading, Six Fingers said nothing. Her face looked as taut as cotton stretched on an embroidery frame. Mak Dau tried, and failed, to think of something to say. Finally, he turned to Kam Shan's letter and began to read.

His hand started to tremble with the words, and the letter fluttered to the ground like a pigeon with a broken wing.

"Well? What does it say?" asked Six Fingers. Mak Dau's lips trembled but no sound came out. "Oh, spit it out, will you?" she demanded impatiently. "And do stop looking so miserable."

"Kam Sau's dad is dead," said Mak Dau. "It was a stroke. There was nothing they could do."

Six Fingers screwed up her face. Mak Dau thought she was going to cry, but she did not. Then the muscles gradually relaxed into an expression of calm as complete as water unruffled by any breeze.

Mak Dau was panic-stricken. He tugged her sleeve. "Cry," he urged her. "It'll make you feel better."

She turned to him but her eyes looked right through him and focused on somewhere far in the distance.

"He was an old man. His time had come," she finally murmured.

Year thirty-five of the Republic (1946)
Vancouver, British Columbia

As thirty-six exhausted but excited troops stepped on shore, they were met by deafening cheers and the welcoming notes of the military band. This was yet another group of soldiers returning home to their families, but with one difference; every single soldier was Chinese. These young men have returned from secret missions against the Japanese in the jungles of India, Burma and Malaya. Observe their uniforms covered in the dust of foreign soil and their faces and hands burned dark by the tropical sun. They accepted their mission with the knowledge that their chances of a safe return were slim. And although America's atomic bombs put a stop to the war before they could begin their operation, they nevertheless received a hero's welcome home today, just like any other troops returning from the battlefront in Europe. This is the first-ever occasion on which the citizens of Vancouver have accepted these young people as their own. As well they should. These Chinese soldiers volunteered to fight under the Canadian flag on the battle fronts of Europe and Asia but are still not permitted to take Canadian citizenship. These men, who have fulfilled every duty owed to their country by its citizens, will soon be in Ottawa, demanding those long-withheld rights and a repeal of the 1923 Exclusion Act.

The Vancouver Sun, *15 December 1945*

After lunch, Kam Shan began to rifle through cases and cupboards for something to wear. He owned only one Western-style suit, one he had bought thirty years ago when he was running the photographic studio in Port Hope.

He found it at the bottom of a camphorwood chest and, when he took it out, the smell of old mothballs nearly made him sneeze. He used a dampened handkerchief to smooth out the creases in the suit but they were stubborn. He rubbed so hard the dye in the fabric came off on the handkerchief and he had to give up. It was something of a battle to get his arms into the jacket sleeves after all these years; he won, but the fabric tore in the process. At least the tear was under the armpit and would not show. But, no matter how hard he tried, he could not get the buttons done up.

Looking at himself in the cloudy old mirror that hung on the wall, he could not help smiling in satisfaction. Even a suit which did not fit properly was still a suit. He needed to do something about his hair though. He went to the kitchen, poured a few drops of peanut oil into the palm of his hands, rubbed them on his hair and ran a comb through it. When he next looked in the mirror, his hair was slicked back in neatly separated strands, and now it was the suit that looked shabby.

Well, it could not be helped. He would just have to go as he was.

He looked at the old wall clock. It was only half past five. He wasn't due at the Chinese Benevolent Association until seven o'clock, and the film started at eight, but, even so, he could not wait that long. His feet itched to get going. He picked up the bag he had prepared the night before and hastily left the house.

It was early spring. As he walked through the streets of Vancouver lined with cherry trees covered in blossom, he attracted more than a few curious looks. The reason was not the ill-fitting suit, or the limping gait, or even the strange-looking bag he carried in his arms, but the fact that he was muttering to himself as he went along.

He addressed a few words to the bag at every street corner.

"At the next corner, we turn east."

"A few yards from this junction is where Yin Ling used to go to school.

"This street runs at a diagonal. When we get to the post office, we have to turn left.

"We come back the same way. If we do that, then we won't get lost."

When he approached the Association office it was still not six o'clock, but before he even crossed the street, he could see the group of young Chinese men gathered outside.

One. Two. Three ... Ten. Eleven. Counting himself, that made twelve. They had all arrived early.

These eleven men were demobbed soldiers in uniforms and peaked caps. He could not help noticing what a uniform did to a man—it made him looking dashing, taller, and straighter, it even put a glow in his face. An irrepressible pride brimmed in the eyes of every one of them.

He had never seen Kam Ho in uniform. He did not even have one photograph, he thought with regret. When Kam Ho joined up, he was already forty years old, old enough to be the father of all these men. Had the uniform imbued his brother with the same spirit? he wondered.

The soldiers who had come back safe and sound were big news in Vancouver. Every day the newspapers carried their pictures and the radio broadcast their voices. They went from talk to talk and interview to interview. From the moment they disembarked, they were borne along on clouds, and nothing had brought them down to earth yet.

All they'd fucking done was survive, Kam Shan thought bitterly.

By comparison with these fine young men, Kam Shan felt like a bedraggled, miserable specimen.

Today they were off to a film show at the Orpheum Theatre in Granville Street. Tickets cost thirty cents if you sat in the back or to the side. If he was going to the Canton Street theatre, he would not have parted with even twenty cents, but today was different. He would have happily spent three dollars on today's show if he had to. Besides, it was Kam Ho's money.

He'd divided the lump sum payout he received after Kam Ho's death into two. He sent the larger portion to Hoi Ping. He had not told them of Kam Ho's death so his mother still did not know that what she was spending was her son's blood money. With Kam Ho and Cat Eyes both dead, there were no wage earners in the family and it would be a long time before Six Fingers received any more cheques from Gold Mountain.

The smaller portion he kept for himself. He had let the room after his father died and the rent, together with the cash he earned from selling bean sprouts, was enough to keep him. So he put his share of the money aside for a rainy day. And for something else as well, though he did not dare admit it.

It was for when Yin Ling came back. She would be twenty-three this year. If she was still alive, she would be back when she had had enough of the wandering life. At her age, no matter how wild at heart she was, she would be thinking about getting married. The money would be just about enough to pay for a simple wedding.

The soldiers formed up and set off down the street, with Kam Shan bringing up the rear. They marched smartly in unison, the rhythm of their feet as regular as someone scything grass for pig fodder.

The street was the water and they were the ship. The water parted at the ship's approach. Right around the ship, it was especially turbulent. People wound down their car windows and tooted their horns, and passersby applauded as they marched.

Kam Shan was aware that the car horns and the applause were intended for the eleven men who marched in front of him. He was but a shadow following behind; his footsteps were out of kilter with their steady strides.

It was getting dark, and one by one the lights of Granville Street flickered on. There was no mistaking the neon illuminations of the Orpheum Theatre. It was a moon to the streetlights' stars and outshone them all. Tonight's film was spelled out in hundreds of bulbs: *Lady Luck*. Kam Shan had no idea what it was about, or who the lead actors were. He didn't even care. All he wanted to do this evening was go in and sit down.

The queue for the box office stretched down the street. The war had shattered the old, familiar world, but even when the planes were flying low over Hollywood producers' heads, you could not keep them quiet. They made films full of froth and fantasy to persuade people that nothing in the world had changed. Just so long as Hollywood was not bombed, the Orpheum Theatre could count on doing good business.

Kam Shan had heard all about the Orpheum Theatre from his brother, Kam Ho.

Many years ago, when Kam Ho was still a houseboy at the Hendersons', they had taken him there. It was a proper theatre in those days, putting on top-class orchestral concerts and musicals. Kam Ho could not remember what the orchestra was playing that day, what he did remember was being in a rage the whole evening.

When the three of them arrived at the entrance, they were stopped by a doorman in a maroon uniform.

"Chinese are only allowed in side seats," the man said in low tones to the Hendersons.

He did not even glance at Kam Ho.

The eleven soldiers and Kam Shan fell into place at the end of the ticket queue—but they did not stay there long. With exclamations of surprise, the people in the queue gave way before them and closed in behind. They were waved along with invitations to "Go right on in, please!" Before they realized what was happening, they were standing at the box office.

All except Kam Shan. He was spat out into the queue again like a plum-stone when the fruit has been eaten. It was, he knew, because he was not in uniform.

It was not until they were already inside the building with their tickets that they realized that Kam Shan had been left behind.

Kam Shan stood for a long time as the queue snaked forward, the big bag in his arms. Finally, he got to the front. He pulled out a dollar bill and gave it to the cashier. "Give me the best seat, in the middle," he ordered. The man shot him a look, and pushed out his ticket and thirty cents' change. Kam Shan took the ticket and left the change. "You have it. As a tip," he said. He smiled at his look of astonishment and the smile lingered on his face all the way to the auditorium.

A man in a black suit and tie stepped out from the shadows and barred Kam Shan's way. He stretched out his hand but did not touch him, merely appearing to guide him to the side door.

"This way please...."

Kam Shan felt his head spin. He searched in the recesses of his memory for words to suit the occasion. The much-used "Sorry" came to his lips but he swallowed it back. Instead he said "Never." It was a word he had not used in his life before and did not slide smoothly off his tongue. In fact, he was so unused to it, he did not know what intonation to use and it came out as a bellow which frightened them both.

He began to stammer an apology. After thirty years in the country, he still spoke broken English and in moments of stress it went completely to pieces. There was nothing for it but to pull the wooden box out of his bag. The usher could not understand his English but he immediately understood the significance of the engraved box:

Private Jimmy Fong (1900–1945)
Died on French soil in the cause of freedom

The usher looked taken aback, skeptical and hesitant by turns, but his expression finally resolved itself into a friendly smile.

"Come with me," he said.

By the time Kam Shan had settled in his seat, the lights were dimming and the film was about to begin. Before it went completely dark, he caught a glimpse of the great round dome of the auditorium above, with its host of winged cherubs and the dazzling chandelier that hung from its centre, brighter than all the stars in the sky.

"Kam Ho, you're finally in the best seats," he said to the box in his hands.

The box contained a uniform and a military cap.

Year thirty-eight of the Republic (1949)
Hoi Ping County, Guangdong Province, China

Today in Canton Ah-Yuen had come close to losing his life.

The Progressive Teachers' League had called a meeting of members from each county, to prepare to celebrate the Liberation. He and a teacher from Pak Sha had left the meeting to buy fried rice with snails for everyone's dinner. As they walked along the road by the river, they heard a deafening boom. Ah-Yuen felt as if someone had cracked him over the head with a stick. When he regained consciousness, he put his hand to his forehead. It came away sticky with blood. He looked up. Only half of Hoi Chu Bridge was still standing, the other half was submerged in the water, stained blood red by the rays of the setting sun. A cluster of wooden boats moored under the bridge had been crushed like matchsticks. Brightly coloured rags hung from the branches of the overhanging trees; as he went closer he saw they were human limbs and articles of clothing. The air was filled with the despairing cries of the wounded.

The locals reckoned that the Nationalists knew they had lost, so they blew up Hoi Chu Bridge to stop the Peoples Liberation Army troops from pursuing them.

He was excited at the news; his heart leapt and his head wound began to pulse with pain. The Peoples' Liberation Army was very close. There had been constant rumours that the PLA was soon to enter Canton, but no one thought it would happen so quickly. He forgot about getting his wound dressed or about the fried rice. He even forgot to look for his colleague from Pak Sha. He rushed back to tell the other League members the news. It was only when he arrived that he realized he was barefoot. He had no idea when or where he had lost his shoes.

It was midnight by the time his head was bandaged and he had eaten his dinner. He went to bed but he could not sleep. Then he heard on the radio that Canton was liberated. Throwing back the covers, he ran outside. PLA soldiers thronged the whole city, even down to the side streets and alleyways. They had arrived quite silently, as if they had drifted in on a sandstorm.

Ah-Yuen stood in the street staring at soldiers who lined the walls fast asleep. Their faces were thin and waxen in the glow of the street lamps, and they looked as if they had not had a decent meal or a good night's sleep for a very long time. They were equipped with an assortment of puttees and belts, some new, some old, all of different colours, as if they had collected them randomly from the battlefield. But every face bore a smile, as if they were enjoying the same sweet dream. The soldier nearest him was just a boy, smooth-cheeked and with a little drool running from the corner of his mouth. If his Wai Kwok had lived, he would have been the same age.

Ah-Yuen stood under the street lamps for a long time, unable to tear himself away. He thought back to the evening when Mr. Auyung left. If he had gone with him, he might have been among these soldiers today, sound asleep like them in the stinking gutters. They would rouse themselves in the morning, and shout in one voice to the entire city: We've brought you good times!

That night, the League took an emergency decision to send its members back to their schools. They were to travel through the night and have their teachers and students make a new national flag to be hoisted over the school for the next morning.

It was after midnight by the time Ah-Yuen arrived in Sam Ho Lei Village and felt his way through the pitch dark to the school gate. A League member had given him a ride on the back of his bicycle to the entrance to the village.

There was not a sound to be heard except for the slashing of his bamboo cane in the undergrowth. He used it to ward off snakes, which were a common hazard if you were out and about in the countryside at night. But he was also using it to beat time as he hummed out of tune:

Onward, ever onward,
To the sun we are marching forth,
Treading on our dear mother earth.
The nation's hopes to bear on our shoulders,
We are an army of undefeated strength.

Ah-Yuen had learned the new anthem this evening, one of many things he had just heard and seen and studied for the first time in his life during the League's meeting in Canton. Some of the leaders were underground Communist Party members, but Ah-Yuen did not discover this until later.

The villages of Sam Ho Lei and Spur-On were mere waterholes compared to the ocean that was Canton. And Ah-Yuen was a little frog at the bottom. He did not want to go home, he really did not. The more he learned, the more he wanted to go on learning. But he could not get out of this nighttime trip to Sam Ho Lei because the League had given him a task to perform.

The gates to Ah-Yuen's school were shut for the night and he did not want to wake the old gatekeeper, so he climbed over the wall into the schoolyard. He went to Kam Sau's room and knocked gently on the window. "Open up…!" A light came on before he had finished speaking;

with her husband away, Kam Sau slept so lightly that the smallest sound wakened her.

She opened the door. At the sight of his heavily bandaged head, her knees almost buckled under her. "What ... what...?" she gasped, her lips trembling in terror.

"It's nothing!" Ah-Yuen was quick to reassure her. "I got hit by a stone." He went straight to their rattan trunk, opened the lid, and began to turn out its contents.

"Have we got any red material?" he asked.

"What do you want red material for at this time of night?"

"To make a flag. For the New China. Canton's been liberated."

"So quickly?" Kam Sau's eyes were like saucers, astonishment and joy mingling on her face.

Then she went on: "You won't find any in here. There's some at the *diulau*. We used it when we got married, and Mum put it away afterwards."

"There's no time. By eight in the morning, we've got to raise the flag along with all the other schools."

Kam Sau sat down on the bed, and considered waking the other teachers to ask for red cloth. Ah-Yuen looked at the quilt which Kam Sau had hurriedly thrown aside. "Get some scissors!" he said. "The quilt cover will do. It's red. There's a bit of red embroidery on it but no one will notice."

As they tore up the quilt cover and made the flag, Kam Sau said: "We've had a letter from Kam Shan. The papers in Gold Mountain are full of news about riots and massacres here. He asked if we want to sneak out to Hong Kong. Then we could go from there to Canada. The Canadian government is allowing Chinese in now."

"Huh!" said Ah-Yuen scornfully. "Imperialist propaganda. Tell your brother not to believe a word of it."

They finally had the quilt cover opened out flat on the table. It made a big red square which gave the room a warm glow. Stuck in his waistband, Ah-Yuen had a copy of the *Chinese Business News* which some members of the Teachers' League had brought in from Hong Kong last month. He took a look at the Chinese flag on the front page. They did not have any yellow fabric but they had some yellow paper left over from the craft class. They followed the design in the newspaper, one cutting, the other pasting, and by the time the first cock crowed the flag was ready.

At five minutes to eight, Ah-Yuen pulled a whistle out of his pocket and blew three sharp blasts to assemble the student body. The sports grounds was already crowded with teachers, pupils and some of the local country folk. Ah-Yuen and Kam Sau released the rope binding the flag and the wind snatched at the material with a savage snap. The rays of the rising sun burnished the fields, the school, the flag and the people in a glow of crimson.

Ah-Yuen mounted the mud-brick platform and began to shout: "Boys and girls...." His voice suddenly cracked and the words would not come out. "The good times are finally here!" was all he could say.

There was a crackle of applause from all around the sports grounds. Ah-Yuen turned to look at Kam Sau, but she was not applauding. She had buried her face in her hands and her shoulders shook.

"Oh, Dad, I wish you had lived to see this day!" She sobbed for the father she had never seen.

The next day was Sunday and Kam Sau and Ah-Yuen set off for the village with their daughter, Wai Heung. The girl was attending the upper primary class at the School for All now, but Six Fingers missed her so much that she insisted that Wai Heung spend Sundays with her. She offered to go and fetch her granddaughter herself but Kam Sau was anxious to spare her mother the journey. Six Fingers was getting on, and it was a long way for her to walk.

When they arrived, Six Fingers and Mak Dau were horrified at the sight of Ah-Yuen's head wound. Ah-Yuen succeeded in reassuring them with a sketchy account of what had happened, and they sat down to dinner.

Six Fingers cuddled Wai Heung and showered her with endearments. "What did you study at school this week, sweetheart?" "Dancing." "Dancing?! What kind of a lesson is that, dear?" exclaimed her grand-mother. "Should people like us be learning dancing?" "My dad's been teaching us folk dances for the Victory March in Canton." Six Fingers was looking more and more bewildered. "What Victory March?" Kam Sau and Ah-Yuen exchanged smiles. "Haven't you heard, Mum? Canton's been liberated. In a few days there'll be a big ceremony to welcome PLA's official entry into Canton. All the children from our school will be taking part."

"Another new dynasty? So soon!" exclaimed Six Fingers. "Don't talk about it as if it was an Imperial dynasty, Mum," said Kam Sau. "The Communist Party is the people's government. We common folks rule, not an emperor." "That's what the Nationalist government said too. Do you really believe it?" Kam Sau's voice rose angrily. "Mum, no more backward talk like that. The Communist Party is different. Life will get better, you'll see."

"We'll have to wait and see if the Communist Party is better or not. But my little Wai Heung's definitely not joining the march. There'll be far too many people. She might get lost and someone might kidnap her. Then what would we do?"

Wai Heung had been rehearsing the dances for the last two days and went white in the face when she heard that she would not be allowed to go. She tugged at her grandmother's sleeve. "Granny, I'll stick close to Mum and Dad. I promise you I won't get lost."

At the look of disappointment on Wai Heung's face, Mak Dau softened at once. "Let her go," he said to Six Fingers. "It's not as if she's going out alone. She won't get lost." Six Fingers' face tightened with anger. "Doesn't anyone take any notice of what I say any more?"

Ah-Yuen gave his daughter a little kick under the table, as a hint she should keep quiet, but the girl banged down her rice bowl, and ran to her room, slamming the door behind her as she went. Kam Sau went after her but nothing she could say stemmed the flow of tears. Finally she said: "Your dad says when the time comes, you'll be going. Only don't tell your granny." Wai Heung smiled through her tears.

Ah-Yuen and Kam Sau spent the night at the *diulau* but neither could sleep. Suddenly he wanted her very much. Kam Sau had refused to allow her husband even to look at her, let alone touch her, since the assault by the Japanese soldiers left her so badly injured. But tonight, after a few attempts to push him off, she gave in, insisting only that he turn the light off. The room was dark, but it was a darkness broken up by bright moonbeams which filtered in through the lattice windows, casting dancing shadows of the trees outside onto the floor. Ah-Yuen caressed Kam Sau, feeling the jagged, lumpy scar between her legs, and she began to tremble all over. At last, after so long, she felt like a woman again as she grew moist at his touch.

Ah-Yuen held Kam Sau in his arms. "The dawn's coming. There's nothing to be afraid of now."

As they lay awake, Ah-Yuen said: "Write to your brother tomorrow and tell him the shoe's on the other foot and this is where the good times are now. Tell him to come home and live out his days here."

Kam Sau smiled. "The new government has new currency. We can't use the American dollars my brother sends any more." "Of course we can," said Ah-Yuen. "It would make nice green wallpaper. If we stick them up, it'll be a reminder that there are still Chinese living a hard life in Gold Mountain."

1952

Spur-On Village, Hoi Ping County, Guangdong Province

When Kam Sau's meeting in town had finished, she picked up her daughter and they set off for Spur-On Village to see Six Fingers.

They had not been home for three Sundays running, for various reasons. Kam Sau had had a number of meetings to attend because the School for All was merging with a local government school and Ah-Yuen had to stay behind for another meeting. Wai Heung had graduated this summer from upper primary and was at the county middle school. This was even farther from the *diulau* than her parents' school so she could not go home every weekend.

Wai Heung had shot up and, at fifteen, was nearly as tall as her mother. She was still a beanpole, although there were signs that she was developing a young woman's curves. In her neat white blouse and blue trousers, she looked ready to burst into bloom.

Kam Sau was delighted to see her daughter again. "How's your homework?" she asked. "Is it more difficult than in primary?" "The homework's easy," said Wai Heung, "but it's hard to learn our lines. Last week the whole class went with the work team to the villages to promote land reform."

Kam Sau was surprised. "What do you know about land reform?" she asked. "Chairman Mao tells us: Get rid of bandits and tyrants, cancel tenancies and mortgages," her daughter began. Her face was screwed up with effort, and Kam Sau could not help smiling. "Do you really understand it? Or are you just reciting it?" "Of course I understand it. It means 'Down with the exploiting class!'"

They plodded on getting hot and sweaty, then sat down by the roadside and drank from their army-issue water bottles. Wai Heung wiped the sweat from her forehead and asked her mother tentatively: "Mum, is our family in the exploiting class?" "Of course not." "But we have fields, and tenant farmers and farmhands." "That doesn't mean we're the exploiting class. Your grandfather was a labourer in Gold Mountain and so were your uncles, and every inch of our family's fields was bought with their sweat and blood."

Wai Heung seemed reassured by her words, but Kam Sau was puzzled: "Who's been giving you those silly ideas?" she asked. "Auntie Ah-Hsien." "Huh!" said her mother. "I suppose I shouldn't be surprised."

Kam Ho's widow, Ah-Hsien, was no longer the dull, bovine woman she used to be. Nowadays she was much more talkative; she had an opinion on everything.

When Six Fingers told her to put more water in the rice, Ah-Hsien responded that that was only what poor people did in the old days, to eke out the little they had. Now that they were liberated, everyone had more than enough to eat, and there was no need to make the rice go further.

On Tam Kung's birthday, when Six Fingers told her to take the fruit offering to the altar and light incense sticks, Ah-Hsien did as she was told, but only after delivering herself of the opinion that rich people did not need to go to sea, so they did not need to worship Tam Kung. That was for poor people but, since Tam Kung did not take any notice of the prayers of the poor, it made no difference if they worshipped him or not.

Ah-Hsien had begun to dress differently too. She still wore the old-style tunic but added a leather belt which she had begged from Mrs. Wong of the work team as a fashion accessory. Every day when she got up, the first thing she did was to fasten it over her tunic. "What on earth do you think you're wearing?" exclaimed her mother-in-law rudely. "If you want to dress up as a beggar woman, why don't you just tie a straw rope around your waist?" Ah-Hsien said nothing but carried on wearing the belt anyway.

Six Fingers dated the change in her daughter-in-law to a meeting a month or so ago, when the work team sent by the provincial government arrived in Spur-On Village. There were three men and one woman. Once they had settled in, they called a meeting of all the villagers. Six Fingers was not as energetic as she once was and felt it was too much trouble to go so she sent Ah-Hsien and Mak Dau's wife, Ah-Yuet, in her stead. The meeting lasted all evening and did not break up till midnight. When they arrived home, Six Fingers asked Ah-Hsien what the meeting was about. "We're setting up a PPA and a WA." Six Fingers had no idea what they were talking about, and Ah-Hsien explained: "The PPA is the association for poor peasants, and the WA is standing up for oppressed women."

After that, Ah-Hsien was always off to meetings. Every time she came home, she would get into a huddle with Ah-Yuet and they would whisper together for hours. Six Fingers had no idea what they talked about—everything nowadays had a new name. Not only that, but Ah-Hsien switched from Cantonese and adopted standard Chinese, like Mrs. Wong from the work team. The difference was that Mrs. Wong was one of the cadres sent to the South to do revolutionary work, and spoke it very well, while Ah-Hsien laboured over the strange sounds and made such a hash of them she was soon the laughingstock of the village. Ah-Hsien did not think it was funny. She began to baulk at doing work around the house too. She no longer behaved like the docile daughter-in-law she had been and there was nothing Six Fingers could do about it.

Kam Sau and Wai Heung arrived at the entrance to Spur-On Village at noon. From a distance, they could see people milling around the clump of wild banana trees. They went closer, squeezing their way through the crowd, until they reached a huge pile of furniture: carved rosewood side tables and high-backed armchairs, a dressing table complete with mirror, a rosewood double bed, reclining chairs for sitting outside on a summer evening, dining tables and chairs. Everything was jumbled up together, and all of it had been brought out of the *diulau*. (The bed was the one Kam Sau and Ah-Yuen had spent their wedding night in.)

Villagers were still emerging from the *diulau* laden like ants with the Fongs' belongings. The tailor's nephew, Big Head Au, led the procession. Big Head was not his proper name, of course; his teacher had bestowed the name "Shun Fong," meaning "plain sailing," on him when the boy started school. But not even his own mother remembered that, and he was only ever known as Big Head in the village. Just now, Big Head was carrying out the old gramophone which Ah-Fat had brought back from Gold Mountain. The gramophone was top-heavy with the weight of the horn and Big Head swore. "What the fuck use is this, anyway? It's no use as a cooking pot or a bowl and whoever gets it'll have to find room for it!"

Kam Sau saw with astonishment that the person helping Big Head carry the gramophone was none other than her own sister-in-law, Ah-Hsien.

The majority clan in Spur-On Village was the Fongs. The Au clan were outsiders and in the minority. The Fongs had always owned and farmed the central land while the Aus had had to break their backs tilling outlying plots on the fringes. Even though there were tenant farmers in both clans, the Fongs always got the best land nearest the village, and the Aus had to make do with poor, out-of-the-way plots. If the Fong family had to marry one of its daughters to an Au, she was certain to find herself in a position of power and privilege in her new family whereas if an Au girl married a Fong, she would find herself scorned even by the Fongs' cats, dogs and chickens. Just like Ah-Hsien, in fact.

Such had been the case for over a century, but nothing lasts forever. When the work team arrived in the village, the Fongs got their comeuppance. The Aus were classified favourably, as "poor peasants" or "hired labourers." When the PPA was set up, most of its members were Aus, and Big Head Au was elected as its chairman. Nowadays it was Big Head Au who called the shots in the village. Big Head Au, once a tiny scrub struggling to sprout between the fingers of the Fong clan, had now grown into a tall tree that no hand could shake, not even the powerful Fongs.

Kam Sau planted herself in front of Big Head.

"Who gave you permission to seize my family's belongings? Was it the work team leader?"

Big Head Au was stopped in his tracks—not by Kam Sau's words but by what she was wearing. He might have been illiterate but he was nonetheless sharp eyed. As chairman of the PPA, he had gone with the work team to attend meetings in the county town on a few occasions. That double-breasted "Lenin jacket" was what county-level cadres wore.

The villagers waiting behind him were getting impatient. "Why are you letting a woman stand in your way, Big Head?" they shouted. "She's only the daughter of a landlord."

Needled, Big Head Au shoved Kam Sau so hard she almost fell and said: "Your family are big landlords. If we can't redistribute your chattels, whose can we take?"

Kam Sau turned to appeal to Ah-Hsien. "Sister-in-law, you know better than anyone where our family's money came from. You're in the Women's Association. Tell them what kind of a life my dad lived in Gold Mountain and how my brother was given a medal for patriotism!"

Of all the members of the Fong family, it was Kam Sau that Ah-Hsien was most in awe of. She was the one with the most education. Her manner was usually pleasant and amiable, and what she said always made sense. So much so that Ah-Hsien found it impossible to pick holes in her reasoning. Her fear of Six Fingers was skin deep, but she feared Kam Sau in her bones.

Today though, she was emboldened by the people standing behind her. And in her mind, Kam Sau's arguments did not seem so irrefutable after all. "You're not my sister-in-law," she exclaimed. "Your family bought me as a servant. Have you ever talked to me about family matters? When your brother writes home, does he ever ask about me?"

There were shouts of "Don't pay any attention to that landlord's daughter! Tell her to get lost!"

Kam Sau and Wai Heung ran into the house and upstairs. Six Fingers was sitting on a stool in her room, her head tilted upwards. There was a streak of dried blood at the corner of her mouth. Mak Dau was holding a wet towel to her forehead. "Granny!" cried Wai Heung, running to her. Six Fingers had her eyes shut and cold tears ran down her face to her ears. The *diulau* was almost emptied of its possessions; all that was left in the room was the bed, a cracked dressing table and the wooden stool she was sitting on.

"Who hit you, Mum?" asked Kam Sau.

Six Fingers said nothing. Mak Dau answered for her, though he seemed to have great difficulty getting the words out.

"That pig-ignorant wife of mine, Ah-Yuet."

Villagers were coming downstairs waving the rifles that had been kept under the roof. Mak Dau went pale. "Mind the bores! Don't let them go off!" he shouted.

"If they do, it'll be you that gets it in the neck!" they shouted over their shoulders.

Ah-Hsien was the last to leave, carrying a bundle of her own bits and pieces.

Six Fingers called her into the room. "Ah-Hsien, wait! I want to talk to you!" She made Mak Dau shut the door.

Ah-Hsien stood, wavering. She could not meet Six Fingers' gaze.

"Legally, you're still my daughter-in-law," she began, "and no matter how much they seize, none of it will come to you. You'll have gone to all this trouble for nothing."

Ah-Hsien pressed her lips together. The barb had hit home.

"I won't get anything, and you won't have anything either, so we're even."

"Big Head Au's got a wife, and in the new society, he can't take you as a second wife. If you hang around him, you'll end up with nothing."

Ah-Hsien flushed and then grew pale as she listened.

"I know you hate me. I've never treated you well ever since you married into this family, and you've had to put up with being a grass widow for years while Kam Ho was away."

Six Fingers undid her bun and the black cloth which covered it, took from it a couple of heavy gold rings, and gave them to Ah-Hsien.

"Don't tell anyone. Find yourself a decent man to marry, put all this trouble behind you and live out your life in peace with him."

Ah-Hsien took the rings and her eyes reddened. She looked as if she wanted to say something but could not find the words. Finally she nodded without speaking and left the room.

When she had gone, Six Fingers slumped on the stool as if the effort of talking had exhausted her.

"Everything your father amassed over a lifetime, I've lost the lot...."

The sound of her voice echoed in the empty room.

"Your brothers will come home one day, and I won't have left them anything to inherit, apart from a few family letters, and some photos as mementoes."

Kam Sau grew distraught. She could not bear to hear her mother talking about her death. She gripped her hands between her own. "Please don't worry," she begged her. "Ah-Yuen and I have met Liu, the head of the county government, several times at meetings. He's a good man and very friendly. We'll go and see him tomorrow and tell him what's happened. He only has to give the word and I'm sure they'll return everything to us."

Six Fingers shook her head. "The world has changed. No one can stop it. Don't wait till tomorrow. Take Wai Heung straight back there now, in case anything else happens."

Six Fingers had a plan of her own. The gold rings she had given her daughter-in-law were not the last of her possessions. She had more valuables hidden in her shoes, but would not use them until her daughter and grand-daughter had left. She had heard about two women in neighbouring villages who had killed themselves after being classified as landlords. One had thrown herself into a well, and by the time they pulled her body out, her belly had swollen like a woman about to give birth. When they poked her navel, brown water spurted out. The other cut her own throat with a vegetable knife. There was so much blood, the shoes of the people who took her away stuck to the floor. Six Fingers did not want to die such a vile and humiliating death. When she was little and living with her elder sister in Red Hair's house, she had heard her nephew's tutor tell the story of Second Sister Yu in the *Red Chamber Dream* who kills herself by swallowing gold. This was the kind of clean ending that she wanted for herself.

"Yes, go now," urged Mak Dau. "Wai Heung's just a young girl. She'll be terrified if there's more trouble." Thinking that she would see Mr. Liu in the county town first thing tomorrow morning, Kam Sau reassured her mother once more that there was no need to worry, took her daughter by the hand and turned to go.

It was too late. Suddenly there was a hammering on the bedroom door. A timid voice said: "Kam Sau, open the door!" It was Ah-Hsien.

As Kam Sau did so, she found herself swept back inside by furious villagers who crowded past her, pushing Ah-Hsien in front of them.

Big Head Au jabbed Six Fingers' forehead angrily with his finger. "So, Mrs. Kwan, you think you can hide your valuables from us, you evil woman!" "They ... they saw them ... I didn't tell them!" stammered Ah-Hsien, not daring to look her mother-in-law in the face.

Big Head's blow had broken the skin, and a drop of blood rose and spread, congealing between Six Fingers' eyebrows like a big black wart.

"So what else are you hiding?" demanded Big Head.

Six Fingers shook her head. "Those two rings were the only valuables I had left."

There were jeers at this. "You expect us to believe that? Your family has papered your walls with American dollar bills!" "Your family sold fields to buy guns! You must have more than a couple of gold rings left!"

"You search her. I bet you'll find stuff hidden somewhere on her," Big Head said to Ah-Hsien.

Ah-Hsien wavered. Then there was a taunt from the back of the crowd: "When push comes to shove, she can't face the class struggle, can she?"

"I'll give you a shove!" retorted Ah-Hsien. She went to Six Fingers and began to undo her top buttons, whispering as she did so: "If there's anything else, better give it up. They won't go away till they've got it."

After a moment's thought, Six Fingers took off her shoes.

The cloth shoes were cut up with a pair of scissors. Finally, the villagers found four gold bands and two pairs of shiny gold earrings secreted between layers of the shoe uppers. There were roars of delight.

"What else have you got? If you don't tell us, we'll carry on searching you!" shouted Big Head.

"Just this *diulau*. If you want to chop it up and divide it between you, go ahead," said Six Fingers through gritted teeth.

"Right, if that's all you can say, I'll have you all searched, starting with the youngest," said Big Head, pointing Ah-Hsien towards Wai Heung.

"She's just a school kid!" protested Ah-Hsien. "Besides she doesn't live here. What's she going to know?"

Big Head pushed Ah-Hsien out of the way. "If you won't search her, I will. And I'll find it even if it's hidden up her cunt."

"She's just a child, you bastard!" cried Ah-Hsien. Big Head paid no attention, and started to undo Wai Heung's blouse.

Wai Heung wanted to scream, but no sound came out. She was trembling like a leaf. Then she struck out as hard as she could. Two bloody scratches appeared on Big Head's face. Furious, he abandoned the buttons and tore at her clothes. With a ripping sound, the top half of her blouse came away in his hands, leaving her skinny shoulders bare.

"Let her go! I've got the gold," Mak Dau shouted, incandescent with rage.

The villagers were cowed for an instant, and then began to swarm round Mak Dau. "I have to do this. But I'll make it up to you in the next life," he muttered to Six Fingers, as he felt in his trouser waistband.

He pulled out his revolver. He aimed it at Big Head and gently pulled the trigger. A red flower blossomed on the man's head. The onlookers sprang back in horror, though not quickly enough to avoid being spattered.

Mak Dau pulled the trembling Wai Heung to him. "Close your eyes, child. It'll be better soon." And he shot her through the heart. Wai Heung twitched in his arms, and then relaxed.

The third bullet was for Kam Sau.

The fourth was for Six Fingers.

The fifth and last was for himself but he had not calculated on the revolver jamming before he could use it.

He threw it down, and pushing the villagers aside, made a dash for the stairs.

After a moment's shock, they ran after him. Mak Dau was getting on in years, and there was no way he could outrun them. They were almost upon him when Mak Dau turned and aimed a kick at the closest one. Then he threw himself from the window.

For many years after that, no one, whether they were Fong or Au, would speak of the terrible events of that day in 1952. The Spur-On villagers, so peaceable that they would have prayed remorsefully to Buddha for days afterwards if they so much as hurt a fly, had witnessed five people killed in one day, and two others driven mad: Ah-Hsien and Ah-Yuet.

The corpses were hurriedly buried and from that day on no one dared set foot in the *diulau*. It was said that in stormy weather someone could be heard weeping inside. And sometimes at dead of night, lights were seen inside the building.

"The Haunted House" was the name the villagers gave it.

Not only did no one dare go into the haunted house, they were also too frightened to till the land around it. As the years passed, it gradually reverted to a scrubby wasteland.

1961
Vancouver, British Columbia

Amy sat in the back seat of the blue Ford as it roared through the streets to Uncle Bill's house with her mother at the wheel.

The car was so old, it had lost its suspension and Amy's bottom had pins and needles from the juddering and shaking.

Someone had given her mother the car, perhaps Uncle Bill, or perhaps it was Uncle Shaun, the one before Uncle Bill, or Uncle Joseph who was around at the same time as Uncle Shaun. There had been a succession of uncles around her mother, too many for Amy to remember them all.

Amy was five years old. She had brown eyes in deep-set sockets, chestnut-coloured hair and a prominent nose. Her skin was so pale she might have been anemic. Unless you looked carefully, there was no trace of her Chinese parentage. And that was just how her mother, Yin Ling, wanted it. Sometimes Yin Ling would look her daughter in the eyes, and say deliberately: "Don't ever ... ever ... change." When that happened, Amy would feel her mother's eyes jabbing her all over, and she would feel like crying. But then Yin Ling would smile and say: "Don't get upset. Mummy likes you just how you are."

Yin Ling never told a soul where she had been in the dozen or so years she was away. She had come back three years ago and since then she had had a succession of jobs. For the last few months, she had been working as a waitress in a restaurant. When she was on the day shift, she left Amy with a neighbour. When she was on night shift, she would leave Amy with one uncle or another, and pick her up the next morning. Amy spent the night in many uncles' houses. Sometimes when she woke in the morning, she would call: "Uncle Shaun!" and Uncle Bill would appear. Sometimes she knew quite well that it was Uncle Joseph who was making her breakfast, but would find herself saying "Thank you, Uncle Luke." But of all the uncles, it was Uncle Bill who had lasted the longest.

The pins and needles felt like ants crawling over Amy's bottom as the car juddered and shook. While her mother applied her lipstick in the mirror, Amy quietly put her hand down her skirt to give the ants a good scratch. Once. Twice. Three times. At the third, her mother spotted what she was doing.

"Amy Smith!"

When her mother called her by her full name, Amy knew she was really angry. Sure enough, Yin Ling threw the lipstick cover at her, scoring an accurate hit on the back of Amy's hand.

"How many times have I told you that well-brought-up girls don't do things like that?"

Her mother's English went to pieces under stress. Of course, it would be some years before Amy understood that her mother had an accent. And several more years passed before she realized that that accent had something to do with a childhood that Yin Ling wanted to put behind her forever.

"Lots ... Lots of times," stammered Amy.

"Then you tell me what I've taught you!" shouted her mother.

"I must not pick my nose, scratch myself, or fart, in front of other people. I must cover my mouth with my hand when I sneeze."

"If you know it, then why do you still do it?"

"But it wasn't ... it wasn't in front of—"

"Shut up!" Yin Ling brusquely interrupted Amy. "Bad habits start behind people's backs!"

Amy shut up. She did not dare ask her mother what a well-brought-up girl was supposed to do when she had an itch, though she wanted to. She knew her mother was in a very bad mood today and anything Amy said might make the storm break over her head.

It had something to do with Uncle Bill.

Uncle Bill had told her mother he would take her to Ottawa on Victoria Day to see the tulips flown in from Holland. But the day before they were due to go, he had gone back on his word. And for the last three days, he had not called her mother either.

"Uncle Bill must be ill," said Yin Ling. "Last time we saw him, didn't he keep sneezing?"

Yin Ling kept on and on asking the same question. The first time, Amy answered that, no, he hadn't been sneezing. Her mother got so angry, she would not speak to her for the rest of the day. So the next time her mother raised the subject of Uncle Bill, she knew what she had to say: "Yes, Uncle Bill must surely have a bad cold." Her mother beamed with joy at that. Amy was puzzled. Why did Uncle Bill having a cold make her mother so happy?

Today was Uncle Bill's birthday, and her mother had a present for him—a lighter in the shape of an eagle. If you gave its legs a little snap, flame spurted from its beak. Uncle Bill smoked Cuban cigars which filled the room with a haze of smoke so dense that Amy felt as if she was choking. Yin Ling put the lighter in a silver-plated box and carefully wrapped it in gold paper.

"We won't tell Uncle Bill we're coming. It'll be a surprise," she said to Amy.

But Amy could see that her mother did not look like someone who was going to spring a nice surprise on a friend. She wore a worried expression.

"All right, all right! Don't give me that long face just because I'm talking to you!" she said shortly from the front seat. "You'll be seeing Uncle Bill soon. Do you remember what you're going to say to him?"

"Happy birthday," said Amy, swallowing the lump in her throat.

"What else?"

"We … miss you very much."

"What else?"

"You look very smart today."

Her mother fell silent, and pulled in at the curb. She took a cigarette from her bag. Her hand was trembling so much, it took her some time to light it.

She finally finished the cigarette, and spent several more minutes clipping her fingernails. Snip. Snip. Snip. The clippings flew about the car like grasshoppers. As Yin Ling propped herself on the steering wheel, she looked very skinny, her bony shoulder blades sticking out like sharp knives under the thin material of her summer dress.

"Amy, would you like Uncle Bill to be your dad?" asked her mother.

The question caught Amy completely unprepared. She guessed her mother wanted her to say yes, but that "Yes" stuck in her throat and would not come out. Luckily, her mother started up the engine without waiting for an answer, and the old Ford rattled off down the street again.

When she stopped again and got out of the car, pulling Amy with her, her hands were still trembling. She pushed Amy toward Uncle Bill's front door, and stood leaning against the car door. She lit another cigarette and, with the first drag, began coughing—very loudly. She sounded like a woodpecker rapping on a tree trunk.

Mum forgot to cover her mouth, thought Amy.

Amy climbed the house steps and knocked on the door. She had to knock for quite a while before someone opened the door. But it was not Uncle Bill.

It was a young, blue-eyed blond woman in a silk dressing gown. Her hair was dripping wet, as if she had just got out of the shower.

"Honey! It's for you!" the woman called casually over her shoulder.

But her mother did not wait for Uncle Bill to appear. She dragged Amy back to the car and backed, revving furiously, out of Uncle Bill's driveway. Out of the back window, Amy saw Uncle Bill rushing out in a pair of undershorts. He waved and shouted something but the wind snatched the sound away before they could hear what it was.

"You look...." Before Amy had finished reciting her lines, something flew past the car window and thudded against Uncle Bill's mailbox. It was the gold-wrapped box with the lighter inside.

"Shit! Shit! Shit!" her mother swore, punching the steering wheel, her hair almost standing on end in fury.

The car zigzagged dangerously as it sped down the street, pursued by the tooting of angry horns.

"I knew it! I knew it! All he wanted was a white girl!"

Amy wanted to say something comforting, but she had no idea what to say. Finally she leaned against the back of her mother's seat and said in a little voice:

"Mum, maybe we don't need a dad...."

Her mother was quiet for a moment, then gave a high-pitched laugh. It gave Amy goose pimples. Then she realized her mother was crying. She kept wiping the snot from her nose with her hand and flicking it at the car window until the glass was covered with trails of slime.

Mum's forgotten how to be a well-brought-up woman, Amy thought.

Finally the weeping stopped and calm descended. They drove on for about fifteen minutes, and arrived at a shabby old street. This was where Amy's grandfather lived. Every time she lost an uncle, or when her mother was between uncles, this was where Amy was left.

They stopped outside her grandfather's house.

The day was hot and the crickets were chirping noisily. From a distance, Amy could see him sitting in the porch dressed in a T-shirt and shorts, one leg propped up on the other, cooling himself down with the aid of a large rush fan.

"For the love of God, put your leg down!" shouted Yin Ling.

She quickly let Amy out of the car, as if she was anxious to be rid of her.

"I'll pick her up tomorrow morning."

And she drove off to the casino, without even stopping to step inside the house. Amy knew she did not need to go to work so early but wanted to avoid her grandfather's endless questions.

"Amy, good girl, what you like your granddad cook you dinner tonight?"

Her grandfather's English was even worse than her mother's. When Amy first met him, she could not understand a word he was saying. But she was used to the way he spoke now, and mostly she could guess if she did not understand.

"Fried chicken," Amy said.

She knew that if she did not make up her mind quickly, her grandfather would be sure to make her pickled egg porridge. She could not understand why he kept eating eggs that looked as if they had turned black from being buried in the earth for a thousand years. The first time she saw him putting one in his mouth, she expected him to fall down dead. But he did not. He even bared his stained teeth and grinned at her.

"OK, Granddad, cut up the chicken," and he went indoors.

She had been secretly hoping he would go away quickly, because she often found coins which had dropped out of his pockets in the chair he sat in.

But today she was out of luck. She only found two cents, which she put carefully away in an inside pocket.

Bright sunlight glared down, bleaching the trees white. She heard the ice-cream van's jingle but it did not stop at her street. It was hours till bedtime, too many to count properly. What was she going to do while they dragged by? Why could she not have a sister, or even a brother? Even a little brother would do in a pinch. Together they could have made the boring hours pass, made things a bit more fun. And why could she not live in one place, like other people did, so she could get to know the neighbours' children and spend the long afternoons cycling up and down the street, skipping and running around?

"Amy, good girl, come and eat *char siu* dumplings," her grandfather called.

Char siu dumplings again. He served them up every time she came. The sticky lumps of red meat always threatened to come back up the minute she had swallowed them down. She had asked her mother once: "Why does Granddad eat such funny food?" "Because he's Chinese" was the answer. "Then if he's Chinese, are we Chinese too?" To her surprise, her mother seemed stumped at that simple question. Finally she just said: "You're not Chinese." Amy wanted to ask if her mother was, but she did not dare because Yin Ling had an ugly look on her face.

Amy went indoors. Her grandfather was chopping the chicken up. *Bang, bang* went the cleaver, until the chopping board squealed in protest. Something wet spattered on Amy's cheek. She wiped it off—it was a bloody bone fragment. Her grandfather wiped his hands on his T-shirt and pulled a *char siu* dumpling in two, giving half to Amy.

"To keep you going till the chicken's ready," he said.

Amy felt like she was going to gag. "I'm not hungry," she said. He did not force the dumpling on her, just shovelled both halves into his own mouth and waved her away. "Go play," he said. "I call you when it's ready."

Play? What with? Where? Amy looked outside at the blazing sunshine, and her heart sank.

Teddy.

Amy suddenly thought of her teddy bear. It was her only toy, given her one Christmas by one of the uncles. She had left it at her grandfather's last time. She would go and search for it.

She searched every nook and cranny downstairs, without success. She went upstairs. The two lodgers had gone to work and their doors were padlocked. Only her grandfather's room was open. She went in and searched in the bed and under the pillow. No teddy. Then she saw that in the corner of the room there were some steps. They led up to the attic, she knew. Maybe her grandfather had found her teddy and put it up there.

She climbed up.

There was a skylight in the attic and the sunlight shone through, making a square shape on the floor. It was all much brighter than she had imagined. Amy thought no one had been up here for a long time. It smelled musty and she sneezed loudly, forgetting to put her hands over her nose and mouth. Good thing her mother was not here. She pushed her way into the room through layer after layer of cobwebs.

There was not much in there. In one corner beneath the skylight there was a roll of paper and, next to it, a cloth bag. She opened the bag, releasing a cloud of dust, the motes sparkling golden in the sunlight. The bag held a stack of photographs. They were old and faded to a muddy sepia. Some were stuck together. Amy tried to pull them apart gently, and found she had left half of someone's face behind.

The photograph on top of the pile had been taken indoors. It was of a middle-aged couple, the woman wearing an embroidered tunic, buttoned slantwise, and the man in a gown that looked a bit like a woman's dress, holding a hat in his left hand and a cane in his right hand. The second picture was of two boys on old-fashioned bicycles. The third was of a young woman with a small baby in her arms, standing on the bank of a river against a thick clump of trees. The sun shone brightly, bleaching the woman's face white. All that was visible was her brilliant smile.

Amy had never seen people, clothes or scenery like that before. She pored over all the photographs, and soon forgot about her teddy bear.

Halfway through the pile, she finally found some faces she recognized: her grandfather and her mother.

Her grandfather had to call her a few times before she came down. She was covered in dust. Her grandfather was startled. "Where you been, naughty girl?" he asked as he wiped her face and served her dinner. Amy bit off a piece of the chicken leg, then stopped chewing and looked abstracted. "Who are those people?" she asked. "What people?" He looked blank. "The pictures. The pictures in the attic." The old man smiled. "So you been messing round up there? That's your great-grandfather, great-grandmother, grandmother and great-aunt and great-uncles."

"What's a great-grandfather?" "That's your grandfather's father." "And a great-uncle?" "Your grandfather's little brother."

Amy was still looking puzzled. Her grandfather fetched a piece of paper, and drew a tree on it. At the foot of the tree, he wrote Guangdong, China. Pointing to the tree trunk, he said: "That's your grandfather's mum and dad." Then he drew three branches on the tree. "That's me," he said pointing to one branch, "and that's my younger brother, your great-uncle, and my little sister, your great-aunt." He drew a smaller branch coming off the first branch: "That's my daughter, your mother." Amy took the pen and drew an even smaller branch joined to her mother's branch. "That's me, Amy!" she said. Her grandfather's face was suddenly wreathed in smiles. "What a clever girl, our little Amy!"

Encouraged, Amy started to ask more questions. "Where are they, these branches?"

"Some are dead," said her grandfather, "and some live in China. We've lost touch." "Where's China?" "Very far away, on the other side of a big ocean." "Could the *Queen Victoria* go there?" The *Queen Victoria* was a paddle steamer that went to Vancouver Island, and Amy and her mother had been on it once. Her grandfather roared with laughter. "No! You couldn't get there even with ten *Queen Victorias!*"

Amy looked disappointed. Finally she started chewing the piece of chicken again. But before she had finished, she thought of a new question.

"Granddad, why are you Chinese and I'm not?"

"Who says you're not? You're at least half Chinese." "Then why do you say I am and Mum says I'm not? And why only half? What about the other half?"

Before her grandfather had time to answer, the door burst open and her mother came in carrying two bags of shopping.

"They've sent all the staff home. There's a power outage," she said to her grandfather.

He found her a clean bowl and chopsticks and served her some chicken soup. "Sit down and eat with Amy. She's hardly eaten anything."

As she ate, her mother caught sight of the piece of paper and pulled it towards her. When she saw what was drawn on it, her face looked thunderous and she slammed her bowl down, spattering rice all over the table.

"How many times have I told you, Dad, not to go filling Amy's head with that nonsense?"

Her grandfather banged down his bowl too. "How long are you going to keep lying to her? Sooner or later she's got to know who her family is. Don't bother ever asking for your ancestors' blessing if you go on refusing to acknowledge them!"

Yin Ling seized Amy by the hand. She dragged her outside, pushed her into the car and banged the door shut on her.

"Blessing from them? Fat chance! Being Chinese brought me nothing but misery. I'm not going to let Amy suffer the same way I did!" she shouted furiously out of the car window as she drove off.

1971

Vancouver, British Columbia

"Rain, what a mess this rain makes...."

Kam Shan sat at the window looking moodily out at the rain. It was the second spell of wet weather they had had this spring. As the rain met the ground, there was a gentle hissing sound. It emanated not from the rain or the earth but from the rampant growth of lush grass. Rain had shrouded the city in a sort of wet haze all week. The grass absorbed the moisture and sprang up, in no time at all reaching waist high. The dandelions, not to be outdone, were even taller, their long stems twisting up through the grass, ending in yellow flowers and fluffy white heads.

Let it grow, Kam Shan thought to himself.

He had stopped weeding and cutting the lawn long ago. He had not touched it at all last year, and the vegetation had grown so tall it almost covered the window. In the end, it was reported to the city council and one day a heavy-duty grass-cutter roared up to his front door. Of course, a hefty bill followed in the wake of the cutter.

For a lawn to thrive it needed young people to play upon it. He and his two lodgers were far too old. Children had not chased and tumbled on the lawn for a very long time. Yin Ling had sent Amy away to a Catholic girls' boarding school, and nowadays he only saw her at Easter, Thanksgiving and Christmas holidays. Yin Ling was a more frequent visitor than her daughter though that depended on how hard he worked to get her there.

"I've made too much chicken soup and there's some left over, Yin Ling. Come over and take it away."

"There's a sale on at the Hudson's Bay department store, Yin Ling, and I bought you a coat. Come and try it on."

"I've got money left over this month, Yin Ling, you can have it."

He sometimes felt it was demeaning to be bribing his daughter like this. Time after time, he said to himself fiercely that he would give nothing more, and then he'd see if she came. But he never found out, because he always dialed her phone number first.

Rat-a-tat-tat.

Someone was at the door.

Surely it could not be the postman. He had not been by for ages. Since China turned Red he had lost touch with his family over there. There were rumours, of course, and the Overseas Chinese press published hair-raising stories every day. The stories went by a succession of different names: first it was Land Reform, then Suppression of Counter-Revolutionaries, then the Anti-Rightist Campaign. The latest was the Cultural Revolution. The names kept changing but the substance of the stories stayed the same: it was always about who was in power and who had been booted out. Of those who were booted out, some lived, others died. Living all boiled down to the same thing, hardship. But there were many ways of dying. Some years ago, people from Hoi Ping had got word to him that his mother and sister and the rest of the family had all died horribly. He did not believe it, he refused to believe it, in fact. Unless and until he got a letter from his brother-in-law, Ah-Yuen, he still had a family, and could cherish his memories of them.

Rat-a-tat-tat.

The person was still there.

It must be the postman.

He shuffled over to the door and opened it. It was not the postman, it was a woman wearing a yellow plastic raincoat.

She greeted him with an exclamation: "Is it really you, Fong? You look so old! And you've got a limp!"

Kam Shan looked blank, then stammered: "You know me?"

The woman pushed her way past him. As she took off her coat, she said: "Making me stand out in the rain is not the way you Chinese usually greet your guests."

Under her outer coat, the woman wore a threadbare old black house-coat, its buttonholes gaping and revealing eyelets of bare flesh. She was old, and her hair was grey and her face wrinkled as a walnut. Still, she carried herself erect and her feet were planted firmly on the floor.

Kam Shan shrugged, and asked again: "Do you know me?"

The woman gave a short laugh: "Heavens! Don't you recognize me? I'm Sundance!"

As Kam Shan looked at her, something seemed to shatter within him: the picture he had cherished all those years, of a young girl chasing butter-flies among the bulrushes, the rays of the sun gilding her hair and skin. He had engraved the image on his heart and was sure it would last forever— but with just a few words, this woman had shattered it into small pieces. Even if he picked them all up, he could never put that picture back together again.

As he shook hands with her, he felt her skin rasping his palm painfully.

"Sundance, I spent years looking for you! Why did you wait till I'm on my last legs to come looking for me?"

"Well, at least it's better than waiting till you're in hell," she said. "Why are you so sure I'll be going to hell?" asked Kam Shan. She burst out laughing: "If we could go to hell together, that would be heaven!"

Still the same old laugh ... Kam Shan thought secretly that even if his eyes had not recognized her, his ears would have told him.

Sundance looked at the photos on the mantelpiece. "Is that your daughter?" she asked. "That's right. I just had one child." "Your grand-daughter?" She pointed. Kam Shan nodded. "Just the one. What about you?" "I've got three sons and two daughters, eight grandchildren and one great-grandchild." "You certainly know how to make a big family," Kam Shan said. Sundance pulled a photo out of her bag. "This is my eldest son, Paul, and his grandson, Ian."

The child was about five years old, and had dark eyes, black hair and flat features. Kam Shan smiled: "Why does he look so Chinese?" "Because he *is* Chinese! His mother's Chinese. She's called Mei."

"Why are there no pictures of your wife?" asked Sundance. "She's been dead for years. What about your husband?" Sundance pulled out a newspaper cutting and pointed to a brief death notice. "He died just last month." "So sorry...." Kam Shan began, but Sundance smiled. "It was a good thing. He'd been ill for years." Kam Shan wanted to ask if that was the reason she had not looked him up, but did not.

Suddenly there was nothing else to say.

Under the easy small talk yawned an abyss of more than half a century. Their words floated briefly on the surface then vanished into its impene-trable darkness. Sundance got up. "I'm off to collect my great-grandson from school," she said. "Where do you live?" asked Kam Shan. Sundance mentioned the name of a street not fifteen minutes' walk away from his house. There must have been thousands of chances over all that time that they would bump into each other—yet they never had.

That's destiny, he thought to himself.

He opened the door for her. "Goodbye," she said, with a glimmer of hope in her eyes. He knew what she was hoping for, but he could not give her any reason to hope. He had spent many years longing to see her again, but when it happened, he wished it had not.

He shut the door behind her and went back to the living room. Then he saw that Sundance had left the photo behind. He turned it over. On the back was written:

Paul's fifty-seventh birthday, with Ian, 22 March 1970

Kam Shan began counting on his fingers. If Paul was fifty-seven last year, he must have been born in 1913. He had left Sundance's tribe in the autumn of the previous year, and Paul had been born the following spring.

In a flash, Kam Shan understood. He ran to the door. "Sundance!" he shouted. Her car had pulled away from the curb but she must have seen him frantically pursuing her in the rearview mirror. She braked and wound down the window. "So you're finally going to make a date with me, are you?"

He held the photo up in front of her.

"Whose child is Paul?" he asked.

Sundance was taken aback. Her smile froze on her face.

The answer was a long time in coming.

"Mine."

Kam Shan had a fall that evening in the bathroom. Just like in a Hollywood film, everything happened in slow motion. He got out of the bathtub, very slowly got dressed, sat down to put on his slippers, and then slipped slowly from the chair to the floor.

He had not had an acute attack of any kind.

It was possible that, after working so hard all his life, he had just died of old age and exhaustion.

At least, that was the diagnosis the doctor gave to Yin Ling after a cursory examination of Kam Shan's body.

Yin Ling did not dare look the doctor in the eye.

If hard work could be measured in pounds and ounces, she hated to think how much extra weight she had added during her father's lifetime.

She had been working that night at the restaurant. She was now the manager. When the hospital called first, she was eating her dinner and refused to take the call. The old man would do anything to get her to the house, she thought. It was only when they called for the third time that she realized something was seriously wrong. She drove like the wind but when she arrived at his bedside, her father's heartbeat was very feeble.

"Amy's on her way, Dad. Wait, please wait," Yin Ling begged him.

His lips trembled, and there was a spike in the heart monitor. She pressed her ear close to his mouth, but his voice was very faint.

She heard just a couple of words: "…kapok flowers…"

He was thinking of the red kapok blossom of his home village.

The doctor filled in the death certificate.

Time of death: 11:27 p.m., 1 February 1971.

Yin Ling watched as the nurse pulled the sheet over her father's face. She tried very, very hard to call up the tears, but they seemed to have abandoned her. A desert, that was what she was, a waterless desert.

She balled up her hand in a fist. Crumpled inside was a news cutting which she had brought to show her father.

It read as follows:

Today was a red-letter day for the Canadian Pacific Railway company, as a nine-person delegation from Red China rode first class in one of its carriages from Montreal to Ottawa. Sub-zero temperatures outside could not dampen the spirits of the delegates as they broke the ice of a twenty-year-long Cold War. The delegation was setting out in search of a site on which to build the new Chinese Embassy. This breakthrough is due to the persistence of Prime Minister Trudeau and his cabinet in the face of criticism of his policy to establish diplomatic relations with China. The Communist Chinese have always harboured friendly feelings towards Canada thanks to the heroic work of Dr. Norman Bethune in wartime China. This time around, as Ottawans will soon realize, the Chinese are here to stay and will soon establish themselves as part of the scenery.

Afterword

2004
Hoi Ping, Guangdong Province

A sheet of plastic. A basket of fruit. A trowel. A bunch of incense sticks.

"Shall we dig the hole?" Mr. Auyung asked Amy.

"Wait a moment. I can't talk to the spirit of my great-grandmother through this."

Amy removed the plastic sheet and knelt on the ground. It was still dewy, and the dampness seeped through her trousers to her knees.

Amy bowed low.

The tombstone had only been erected yesterday. It was of plain white stone with the following names carved on it:

Fong Tak Fat (1863–1945)
Kwan Suk Yin (1877–1952)
Fong Kam Sau (1913–1952)
Fong Yiu Kei (1930–1939)
Tse Wai Kwok (1934–1941)
Tse Wai Heung (1937–1952)

Erected in loving memory by their Canadian descendants, 2004

The burial ground was on top of a hill and the narrow road wound up to it through dense clumps of bamboo. The wind had scattered white flowers under their feet, probably from graves which had been swept and tidied at the Festival of Qing Ming only a month ago. The site was a hillock on which clusters of graves jostled higgledy-piggledy for space. "Are all these Gold Mountain families?" Amy asked. "All the families in these villages have relatives overseas," Mr. Auyung said, "so I suppose you could say they're all Gold Mountain families."

Mr. Auyung had helped Amy choose the gravestone and the inscription. In a red cloth bag, she had the remains of Fong Tak Fat: some nail clippings wrapped in silk. Kam Shan had cut them from Ah-Fat's hand when his body lay in its coffin before burial. Kam Shan had passed the silk wrapping and its contents to Yin Ling and she had taken it with her to each of the houses where she lived. Just before Amy left for China, Yin Ling gave it to her daughter.

Amy took the trowel and dug a small hole at the foot of the tombstone. The soil was a strange colour, it seemed to Amy, and a little shiver ran over her. She put the cloth bag into the hole, covered it with earth and firmed it down. With the bag she was burying a lifetime of secrets, now to be swallowed up by the silent earth.

Mr. Auyung sighed: "A Gold Mountain promise that in the end could not be kept. What a pity."

"I don't see it like that. There are some promises which are never kept but still mean more than kept ones. They're more...."

She struggled to find the right adjective in Chinese, and finally gave up and said: "...profound."

She used the English word, but Mr. Auyung understood anyway.

"There's still a big gap in the Fong family history which I need to fill. You're the only descendant of the fourth generation and I still know very little about your adult life. Can you fill me in on that?" Mr. Auyung asked.

"Ever the investigator!" said Amy with a smile. "Actually, Fong family history has become less colourful with every generation, and when it comes to mine, it is disgustingly conventional. It's simply the story of the daughter of a Chinese single mother who was always looked down on by white people, but whose one desire was to drag her daughter out of the mud and give her a head start in the world. That mother worked in menial jobs for her whole life and spent every last cent of her earnings trying to turn her daughter into an upper-class white girl. She had lessons in piano, art and ballet, everything an upper-class child was supposed to learn. Then she was sent to a private Catholic school. Her mother wanted her to become a doctor or a lawyer or an accountant. She never imagined her daughter would sneak off and study sociology at Berkeley, using the school fees her mother had sweated blood to save up, because she had absolutely no interest in anything else.

"The path that girl took through life was the precise opposite of what her mother expected. Instead of studying hard, she joined every political movement going and was present at every single demonstration. Instead of finding herself a nice man to marry—he had to be white, of course—she got involved with one useless lover after another. In an odd twist of fate, instead of leaving every vestige of her Chinese inheritance behind her, she ended up studying Chinese at university. And to cap it all, a Chinese man has just inveigled her into acknowledging to the whole world that she is half Chinese."

Mr. Auyung could not help smiling. "I've only tapped into an innate positive feeling that you already had."

"Oh, my story isn't finished yet," said Amy, and went on: "At least in one respect, this girl—or rather, this woman—has finally fulfilled her mother's ambitions by becoming a famous professor at a famous college."

"Thank you," said Mr. Auyung. "Now the Fong family story is finally complete."

"Huh! Your story may be complete, but mine isn't. Who are you anyway? Why do you know more about my family than I do?"

"I knew this question would come up sooner or later. It's simple, really. My great-grandfather and my grandfather happened to teach your great-grandfather and great-uncle and great-aunt. But that's not really the reason why I got interested. Thirty years ago, a young man called Auyung Wan On read the diary left by his grandfather, the revolutionary martyr Auyung Yuk Shan. As he did so, he came across stories of your great-grandfather,

Fong Tak Fat's family. In the mid-seventies there was a power vacuum in local politics and, on the pretext of researching a distant relative from Spur-On Village, he broke into the *diulau* when no one was looking, and began to pry into its secrets. He might have been doing what fashionable scholars would later call sociological research, but at the time, of course, he was just an ignorant youth and this was one of many crazy things he did to satisfy his curiosity.

"Of course, the tracks he left behind him just confirmed the villagers in their belief that the *diulau* was haunted."

Mr. Auyung gave Amy a brown envelope and said: "Burn this in their honour." Amy took out a stack of "spirit money" and, borrowing Mr. Auyung's lighter, set it ablaze. She watched the paper burn down to a little heap and then turn into a few black charred scraps which scattered in the wind. There were more sheets of paper in the envelope which, instead of denominations, had scribbled titles such as: "Mustard Seed Garden Manual of Painting," "A Copybook of Regular Calligraphy," "300 Poems from the Tang Dynasty," and "Conservatory of Music."

"Your great-grandmother was a literate woman. She kept her brain working all her life," said Mr. Auyung.

Bit by bit, Amy consigned everything in the envelope to the flames. The last thing she took out was a paper boat, folded completely flat. When she pulled it open, it was bigger than she expected. It had been made with great care, complete with decks, sails and rigging, and a lively dragon's eye painted on the prow.

"That was the sort of boat the emigrants to Gold Mountain sailed in. The locals called them Big-Eyed Roosters."

Amy held the boat in the palm of her hand and examined it closely before placing it on the fire at the foot of the tombstone. It was made of cardboard and burned slowly. The sails had been coated with layers of glue and made a crackling noise when the flames licked them. The boat burned to ash and only the sails were left, winking in the embers.

"Now you can board the boat for Gold Mountain at last, Great-grandmother, and go and see Great-grandfather," Amy murmured.

Something tickled her face. She brushed it away with the back of her hand and discovered it was a tear.

They went down the hill and Mr. Auyung told the driver to take Amy back to the hotel so she could get ready before the farewell dinner. Amy's cell phone bleeped. It was a text message. She read it and suppressed a smile. Then she looked serious. "I'm afraid I can't attend the banquet," she said. Mr. Auyung was startled. "But it's all been arranged!" he protested. "Number one," she continued, "I'm not leaving tomorrow, so you don't need to say goodbye. Number two, if I go to the banquet, I'll have to sign over the *diulau*, as you told me yourself. I've changed my mind. I'm not signing it over for the moment."

Mr. Auyung stared blankly at Amy. "What on earth...." he stammered.

"It puts you in a predicament, doesn't it?" said Amy. "You'll have some explaining to do to your bosses. All that time and energy wasted on me.... So I'll tell you straight up why: I'm not signing right now because I want to use the *diulau* for a wedding, while it still belongs to the Fong family."

"Whose?" asked Mr. Auyung in surprise.

"Mine," said Amy. "There's only one thing I want to ask of you. Will you be my witness?" Amy continued.

"Er ... when?" Mr. Auyung was finding it hard to absorb all this new information.

"Mark's plane has taken off. He'll be here tomorrow about midday."

"Good heavens! You haven't given me much time to get things ready!"

Amy burst out laughing.

"That's your problem. I'm leaving all that to you."

519

LIST OF RESEARCH MATERIALS

❦

Jennifer S.H. Brown, *Strangers in Blood: Fur Trade Company Families in Indian Country*. Vancouver: University of British Columbia, 1980.

Anthony B. Chan, *Gold Mountain: The Chinese in the New World*. Vancouver: New Star Books, 1983.

Denise Chong, *The Concubine's Children: Portrait of a Family Divided*. New York: Viking, 1994.

Harry Con et al, *From China to Canada: A History of Chinese Communities in Canada*. Toronto: McClelland & Stewart, 1982.

Robin Fisher, *Contact and Conflict: Indian-European Relations in British Columbia, 1774–1890*. Vancouver: UBC Press, 1992.

Evelyn Huang, *Chinese Canadians: Voices from a Community*. Toronto: Douglas & McIntyre, 1996.

David Chuenyan Lai, *Chinatowns: Towns Within Cities in Canada*. Vancouver: UBC Press, 1988.

David Chuenyan Lai, *The Chinese Cemetery in Victoria. B.C. Studies* 75, Autumn 1987.

David Chuenyan Lai, *A 'Prison' for Chinese Immigrants. The Asiandian* 2: 4, Spring 1980.

Peter S. Li, *The Chinese in Canada.* Toronto: Oxford University Press, 1988.

Huping Ling, *Surviving on the Gold Mountain.* Albany: SUNY Press, 1998.

Dennis McLaughlin and Leslie McLaughlin, *Fighting for Canada: Chinese and Japanese Canadians in Military Service.* Minister of National Defence of Canada, 2003.

Geoffrey Molyneux, *British Columbia: An Illustrated History.* Vancouver: Raincoast Books, 2002.

Faith Moonsang, *First Son: Portraits by C.D. Hoy.* Vancouver: Arsenal Pulp Press, 1999.

James Morton, *In the Sea of Sterile Mountains.* Vancouver: J.J. Douglas Ltd., 1974.

Stan Steiner, *Fusang: The Chinese Who Built America.* New York: Harper & Row Publishers, 1979.

Christine Welldon, *Canadian Pacific Railway: Pon Git Cheng* (Heritage Series). Laval: Grolier Limited, 1991.

Brandy Lien Worrall (editor), *Finding Memories, Tracing Routes: Chinese Canadian Family Stories.* Chinese Canadian Historical Society of British Columbia, 2006.

Paul Yee, *Ghost Train.* Toronto: Groundwood, 1996.

Liping Zhu, *A Chinaman's Chance: The Chinese on the Rocky Mountain Mining Frontier.* Boulder: University Press of Colorado, 1997.

Videos

Eunhee Cha, *A Tribe of One.* National Film Board of Canada, 2003.

Karen Cho, *In the Shadow of Gold Mountain.* National Film Board of Canada, 2004.

Jari Osborne and Karen King, *Unwanted Soldiers.* National Film Board of Canada, 1999.

OKANAGAN REGIONAL LIBRARY
3 3132 03215 4934